SINFUL MATES

JESSICA HALL

Cover by MCDamon Design

Format design by CED

Edited by Gabrielle Gerbus @incubix

Art work by Athira on insta

BLURB

Imogen is a woman on the brink. Due to her mother's medical condition, she's been forced to live out of her car, in her workplace's car garage, no less. She can barely make ends meet, and her only focus is how to survive just one more day.

Tobias and Theo are her bosses, and it doesn't take them long to discover her secret, but unbeknownst to her, they have a secret of their own, one that could change everything. She's their mate, and they'll do anything they have to in order to keep her for themselves, even if that means breaking her first.

Imogen knows she will never be free of them, and being human against a Lycan and a vampire, she might as well give up.

Only now, she isn't only fighting to escape her mates who kidnapped her, but fighting for her humanity. Forced into a world she never knew existed, one thing becomes evident: no humans allowed! Imogen soon discovers the safest place for her may actually be with her mates, but at what cost?

Will Imogen really just let them take whatever they want, or will she fight back? There's more on the line than just her heart. If Imogen doesn't watch it, she'll lose her life to her Sinful Mates and become a creature of the night herself.

AUTHOR'S NOTE

Warning!! Warning !! Warning!!

Dark Paranormal Romance. It is also a Reverse Harem. If you don't know what Dark Romance is, I suggest you look it up! This book contains triggers, which some might find distressing.

Book Contains:

Stockholm Syndrome

DubCon

Violence

MXM

MFM

BDSM

This is Book 1 of the Savage Series.

Sinful Mates (Book 1)

Sadistic Mates (Book 2)

Sinister Mates (Book 3)

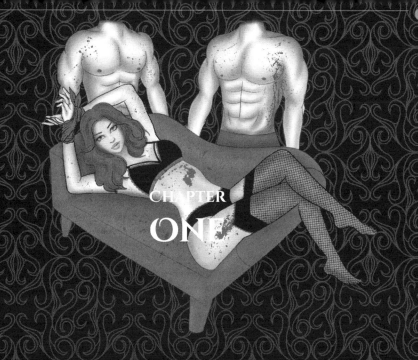

I mogen
The sun is barely breaking through the windshield of my beat-up Honda Civic as I groggily wake up. My body aches as I stretch, trying to get into a comfortable position. I have been living in my car for nearly three months, and my body is protesting my living predicament.

Sitting up, I shield my eyes with my hand from the brutal sun and tug my blanket around myself, trying to warm my freezing cold skin. An empty vodka bottle rolls off the seat and onto the passenger side floorboard. Now, I know what you probably think - I'm an alcoholic. I'm not, nor do I ever, drink and drive.

The first night I had to sleep in my car, it was minus three degrees. I was in danger of freezing. Luckily for me, my mother's drinks had helped save the day. My trunk was half full of spirits. I wasn't lying when I said she liked a drink.

I was going to dispose of it but was glad I hadn't that horrendous night—her bestie, vodka, seconded by her equally harsh friend, tequila. I've never been much of a drinker; watching her was enough to deter me from taking that path. But on that freezing night, I decided, why not? I grabbed a bottle, hoping to help myself sleep and forget that I was now homeless and living in my car. My life was already at a pretty crappy crossroads, so what would one more vice hurt?

That night I learned that alcohol could get you through the bitterest wintry nights. You don't feel the sting of the air when you're intoxicated. In fact, you feel little of anything. My alcohol tolerance has become rather impressive. I don't drink myself to oblivion, but on nights like the first night I spent in this cramped car, I knocked a few back to help chase away the cold like last night.

Exhaling, I watch the sun slowly rise over the horizon, bringing its warm rays to chase the chills away, the heat filtering through the windshield. There is one plus side to living in your car. I am always on time for work; it helps that I live in the workplace parking garage, making me never late. No one knows that little secret except the janitor, Tom. A sixty-year-old man, balding on top, with kind eyes, a cuddly figure, and a grandfatherly nature.

He stumbled upon me sleeping in my car one night. I told him it was only temporary, so he kept my secret. My bosses just think I am an eager and enthusiastic worker. I'm always the first to work besides Tom, who opens the parking garage and the building, and I am always the last to leave. I'm not about to correct them. They can assume whatever they want. I need this job.

Reaching for the ignition, I turn my car on; my phone instantly lights up and charges through the lighter socket while my engine growls in complaint. It is 7 AM. Getting up, I lean over into the back and grab my outfit for the day that is hanging from the roof by the back door.

Sliding my seat all the way back, I shimmy my track pants off and grab a fresh set of panties. Pulling them up my legs, then putting my black slacks on and buttoning them up. Peeking around to make sure no one is within eyeshot, I grab my bra and duck down behind the steering wheel. I don't want to give Tom a heart attack. After ripping my shirt off, I put my white button-up blouse on.

I've just finished slipping my heels on when I notice Tom walking up the driveway to the top level of the parking garage. I toss my sleeping pants on the bottles to hide them and smile at him. Swinging my door open.

"Hey, Tom," I greet, waving at him quickly, then reach in and grab my handbag from the passenger seat. Tom walks over, holding two paper cups. My favorite part of the morning, it has become our morning ritual. Every morning Tom walks all the way to the top level of the parking garage, brings me a coffee, and we both walk back down to the entry together.

"Hi, love. How was your night?" Tom asks, concern evident in his voice.

"It was fine, a bit chilly, but nothing I'm not used to by now," I tell him, grabbing the styrofoam cup from his hand. Wrapping my fingers around the cup, I let the heat warm my palms, almost hesitant to drink the beverage and lose my source of warmth. It is silly; I'd be plenty warm inside the office.

"You know you can always stay...."

Shaking my head, I cut him off before he can continue.

"Tom, I know, but really, I'm fine. This is only temporary." I give him the same smile he gets every time he suggests I come to stay with him. The mask that everything is okay in my world and this is just a minor bump in the road. This small lie slips over me effortlessly like a well-practiced rehearsal. I repeat it daily to him; I sometimes wonder if I'm accepting this as my new normal.

He shakes his head. Every morning for the last few months, he's heard the same excuse. He knows there is no use arguing with me. I'm too stubborn and am not one for accepting help, even if it would help prevent frostbite.

Tom continues to the door before punching in the security code to let us into the building.

He's offered for me to stay with him and his wife more than a dozen times by now. But I don't want to intrude; it isn't so bad here. It is a lot safer than the park I was initially parked at. I shudder at those hazy memories of what could have happened to me. No, being at the top of a parking garage, safe in my car, is far better.

Tom lets me in early every morning. I usually go straight upstairs to my desk, which is conveniently directly in front of the air conditioner.

Catching the elevator to the top floor, I step into the foyer and walk to my desk, my heels clicking on the marble floors. Grabbing the AC remote, I turn the heater up full blast and stand directly under it, warming myself up while I sip my coffee.

Once warmed up, I sit at my desk, start my laptop, and look over the day's schedule and any notes I have left for myself. I have been working at Kane and Madden industries for around twelve months. I'm the secretary for Theo Madden and Tobias Kane. They own the tech company, and I am about 98 percent sure they are a couple.

Not that I have seen them officially together or anything at any of the company parties, or even shared a glance with each other outside these doors. They have separate offices, but they have this way of communicating. They always seem so in sync with each other, and I have caught them staring weirdly at each other. I have also walked in on Theo kissing and sucking on Tobias's neck. So that is a pretty big indicator that they are a little more than business partners.

I must admit it was hot, and it kind of turned me on, until Tobias noticed me gawking which made Theo freeze, and then it got awkward and tense really fast. I ran from the room. They never mentioned it, so I assumed I was let off the hook. I've since added that memory to the "it never happened" file of my brain.

It's a shame they are both gay. They are the hottest gay couple I've ever seen. Or whatever their dynamic is.

Tobias is the more imposing one. His intense gaze sends shivers down my spine and chilling vibes that rival my car; even before I'd walked in on him. If he weren't gay, I'd think I am prey with the way he stares. Sometimes, when he speaks to me, he gets this faraway expression, like he is looking straight through me instead of at me. It isn't the only awkward encounter I've had with Tobias; I swear I heard him growl once. People don't growl, not like predators do. I put it down to the 18-hour shift I'd worked that day.

Tobias Kane is tall, dark-haired, muscular, has a 5 o'clock shadow, possesses a strong jaw, and is gifted with sharp, piercing blue eyes.

Theo Madden, on the other hand, has softer features. He is just as tall as Tobias but has a very casual, laid-back attitude and fluffy brown hair that is short on the sides and a little longer on the top. He has green eyes that sparkle when he talks to me and high cheek-bones. Both are breathtakingly handsome. Even after all the time working there, I still get stunned by their godlike appearances.

I'm astonished that I haven't been fired. I have been caught way too many times daydreaming, staring off into space, and having very inappropriate thoughts about my bosses. But I also know I'm extremely good at my job. No one has lasted this long as their secre-tary, and no one is willing to do the sometimes-grueling hours I have endured in my position.

Once I finish checking my laptop, I check the time. It is 8:30 AM. I still have half an hour before my bosses arrive. Slipping out of my seat, I rush to the bathroom with my handbag. Setting my makeup on the counter, I quickly pull my hairbrush out and brush my unruly waist-length blonde hair.

After deciding to pull it into a high ponytail, I grab my tooth-brush and toothpaste and quickly brush my teeth. I apply some mascara to my already long, thick eyelashes and some eyeliner to brighten my dark green eyes before putting on some red lipstick. It contrasts nicely with my fair skin.

I'm so glad this floor has no cameras because it would be embar-rassing if my bosses found out about my morning routine. Plus, they would see me in all my morning bedhead (or car head) glory. Tom doesn't count. He doesn't care what I look like, and I'm always comfortable around him. But if anyone else had seen me, it might have gotten a bit awkward.

Once I finish, I quickly duck into the small kitchenette and prepare their coffees for their arrival. I hear the elevator ding just as I finish making them. I place them on a tray and hurry back to my desk, tray in hand. It's the perfect routine, and it has never failed me once.

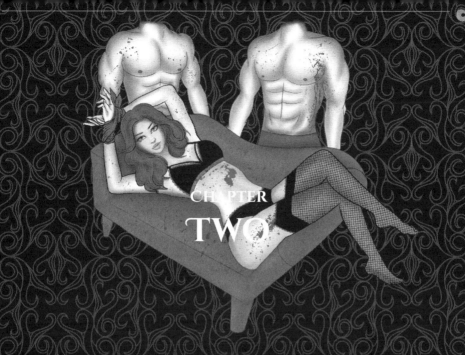

obias is the first to step out of the elevator. He is sporting his black suit today, accompanied by a white shirt and silver tie. His head is bowed, staring at his phone. He grabs his coffee off the tray without even glancing up at me and walks directly into his office.

Theo, on the other hand, has a gray suit on, and the top three buttons on his white shirt are undone, exposing part of his chest. I have yet to see him ever as polished as Tobias, or in a tie, for that matter. Theo stops, grabs his mug, and takes a sip. "Good morning, Imogen," he says with a wink before walking into his office across from Tobias.

Tobias shuts his door, pulling me from my stupor, and I can't help the blush that creeps across my face, making my entire body heat up. I quickly place the tray back in the kitchen and grab the tablet off my desk. Hesitantly, I stand at the door to Tobias's office, giving myself a mental pep talk while hoping he is in a good mood today and doesn't have anything heavy close by to throw at me.

Just before I knock, his voice sings out. "Are you going to enter or stand out there all day?" His husky, deep voice makes me jump, and I quickly open the door enough to slip inside.

Tobias sits at his desk, fingers typing away at his laptop. He still hasn't looked up. I stand there, moving from foot to foot awkwardly. Mr. Kane, I've always found him very intimidating. He's always so formal, so serious.

When I don't speak, he looks up, eyes pinning me where I stand, and I swallow nervously. My hands tremble slightly at his intense gaze. He tilts his head to the side, waiting for me to speak and snapping me to my senses. Clutching the tablet in my hands like a shield, I step closer while checking his schedule.

"You have a meeting at 12 with Mr. Jacobs. I have also forwarded the proposals, ready for your meeting, and I'm sending through now the emails received in reply to the conference meeting you held last Thursday." I'm proud that my voice is still professional and clear, even if my fingers tremble.

"Is that all?" He raises a brow, waiting for more.

"No sir, I need you to sign off on the charity fundraiser for the hospital," I reply, looking for the said paperwork. Have I left it behind? Shit!

"So, where is the document?"

Imogen, you fool, the one piece of paperwork required, and I left it on my desk. I internally facepalm myself.

Cringing at my stupidity, I hold my finger up. Tobias rolls his eyes at me, clearly frustrated by my mistake, with his hand open, waiting for the document. "Ah, one minute, sir."

He sighs, annoyed at me, no doubt. I duck out, retrieve the document, and race back, my heels clicking loudly as I try not to slip on the tiled floor. Skidding to a stop in front of his desk, I wobble on my feet and quickly slide it onto the desk in front of him. He signs it without glancing at it, then passes it back to me.

His attention is once more fully on his laptop. I don't exist in his world, so I take a moment to study him. Stolen moments when I can observe my bosses are rare, and I always take advantage of them.

Gawking like some creep, I can't help but notice that he looks tired. Dark circles hang under his usually vibrant blue eyes, and his skin is paler than his normal sunkissed tan. I stare off into space, forgetting what I'm supposed to be doing, too busy admiring my boss and having another one of those completely inappropriate daydreams. Mr. Kane clears his throat, dragging me from my thoughts. He raises his eyebrow at me, catching me checking him out. That doesn't usually happen. Did I make some sort of noise?

"Oh, sorry, sir." I stumble over the words and duck my head to hide my red cheeks. He shakes his head at me, but I hear a small chuckle as I run from the room and close the door. Both men always make me flustered.

I've always felt cloudy in their presence; I have even forgotten to breathe. The last time it happened, I passed out. To be fair, I hadn't eaten, so my brain was already mush. I awoke to Theo's concerned face leaning over me, all while Tobias just stared at me like I was mentally challenged.

Seriously, who forgets to breathe? It is meant to be a primary bodily function. Instinct! And I couldn't even get that right.

That was the day I figured out why no one wanted this job. It is tough to focus on work around them, on the verge of impossible. They could become a distraction without meaning to.

I've since discovered that Mr. Kane can be quite horrible. I don't think he realizes the nasty things he says when angry.

Luckily for him, I have tough skin and desperately need this job. I also ensure I have my tablet in my hand whenever I go into his office in case he throws something.

Once, I watched him hit the tech guy with a drink bottle when he was in a rage. Seriously, the man has anger issues and needs therapy or something. Everyone walks on eggshells around him, well, except for Theo. The tech guy hasn't been back since, not that I can blame him.

Sitting at my desk, I chuckle at the memory before returning to my computer. My job is surprisingly easy, plus it pays well. Not much physical activity is required unless you count answering phones and carrying files. The only demanding thing is the hours. I'm literally on call 24/7. Not just as their secretary but also as a personal assistant, not that they get me to do much unless it is work-related. The hours can sometimes be ghastly, like working until the early morning hours before big deadlines. But at least on those days, I don't have to worry about the cold.

Hitting the print button, I walk into the printer room that sits off the side of the kitchenette. I'm waiting for my printed document when the printer makes a beep, and an error code pops up. The paper tray is empty. Bending down, I open up the door on the printer and remove the tray before going to the drawer to get some paper.

The cupboard is empty. Walking out, I head over to the store-room. Opening the door, I flick on the light and peer around at the shelves. I sigh when I see where it has been placed. And yet, I'm not surprised; this is the second time some moron has decided to stack it on the top shelf in one giant pile.

Pulling the step ladder out from behind the door, I sit on it, take my heels off, and climb up. I have to stand on my tippy toes to reach the box. I grip it with the tips of my fingers and pull it toward the edge, sending the stack of papers wobbling.

"Need a hand?" Theo asks from directly behind me. I gasp and jump in fright; I teeter as I lose my balance. Quickly gripping the shelf with my fingertips, I right myself and regain my footing. My heart hammers in my chest over the close call. Once my heart rate calms down, I become quickly aware of the hand grasping my ass.

Slowly, I look down at my boss; Theo's hand is holding me steady by grabbing me by the ass. His large hand is firmly pressed on my butt through my pants; I can feel his palm, his thumb nestled between my legs, pressing where my core is. Thank god I have pants on today and not a skirt.

"Um, boss," I say, peering down at his hand. He finally notices where he has grabbed me. A slight smirk creeps its way onto his face. The feel of his large hand on me makes my skin burn and my insides melt. An unfamiliar feeling washes over me. What's wrong? I have to fight the urge to shut my thighs to stop the sudden ache between my legs.

Instead of letting go like a normal person, he runs his hand over the curve of my ass and down the inside of my thigh, pausing to grasp at my ankle. Only then does he pull it away from me. My skin flushes with embarrassment at my crush on my gay boss. Theo pauses and tilts his head up to look at me; a sly smile spreads across his face at my embarrassment.

He then reaches over and grabs the stupid box I was painstakingly trying to retrieve, shoving the rest of the paper to the side as he retrieves the stupid thing as if it were easy.

I quickly step down the ladder, put my heels back on, and grab the box from him while I avoid looking at his face.

"Were you looking for something?" I ask as I walk from the storeroom back to the printer. He follows me with that same little smirk plastered on his lips.

"Yeah, I tried to print something when I realized the printer was out of paper," Theo replies, leaning on the counter next to the printer.

I quickly load the paper onto the tray before inserting it into the printer. Clearing the error, I hit print. The machine prints out the documents, and I grab mine to get them out of his way. Stapling the papers together, I place them on the counter.

When no more come out, I turn to Theo. "Are you sure you hit print?" I ask, raising an eyebrow.

Theo seems to think before speaking. "I think so."

I roll my eyes at him and walk into his office. He follows behind me and stands in the doorway to his office, leaning against the door frame, watching me with those piercing eyes.

CHAPTER
THREE

"The merger document?" I ask, peering at his computer screen. He nods, and I hit print before walking back to the printer. His document prints out. I staple it together and then hand it to him.

Theo watches my every move. His intense gaze makes me feel uncomfortable, but I can't look away. After a few tense seconds, he turns and walks out without a word. I inhale a greedy breath of air, not realizing I was holding it. I make my way back to my desk. Theo has been acting weird since last week. I've caught him staring at me more times than I could count.

Tobias has even been on edge lately. I heard them arguing over something the other day. I tried to tune it out as best I could, their relationship is none of my business. But it makes it a little awkward and tense around the office, and Theo's bizarre stare-offs aren't helping.

Tobias remains in his office most of the day in one of his moods. The only time I hear from him is when I have transferred calls to his phone line. Before I know it, it is 5:30 PM. Where has my day gone? Mr. Kane and Mr. Madden leave at 5:00. I finish shutting everything down before switching the lights off and heading to the parking lot. Once there, I grab my phone charger and some warm clothes to change into and pile everything into my handbag.

I have to be back to my car before Tom locks up. Tom works a few hours in the morning and then returns at night to empty the trash and scrub the floors before locking up the garage and rolling down the doors at 9:00 PM. It gives me plenty of time to visit my mother before heading back.

Walking through the empty parking garage, I come out on the ground floor level, on the park side. Cutting through the park, I head towards the big blue neon sign that sits atop the hospital across from Kane and Madden Industries. Mater Hospital. Every day, I walk over to check on her. Making my way to the second floor, I head to the wards: room eighteen, bed five. I'm lucky the hospital is so close to my job; I can't imagine trying to fight traffic, taking away the precious time I have with her.

My mother has been here for just over four months. I take a seat in the sterile room. I hate hospitals. They always smell of hand sanitizer, and this particular ward reeks of death. No, my mother doesn't have some debilitating chronic illness. I actually wish that were the case. No, my mother, Lila Riley, is in a coma.

She'd been driving home from a local bar she worked at, and a drunk driver ran a red light, smashing into her. Her car was a total loss; they had to use the jaws of life to get her from the vehicle. She has been in a coma ever since. The doctors told me she is brain-dead and that the only thing keeping her alive are the machines she is hooked up to.

The hospital said they couldn't keep her in this state forever and tried to have her life support shut off last month. After appealing their decision to turn off her life support, I'd pushed it to nearly five months. I'm still waiting to hear from the Medical Ethics Association. I know it is a battle I will lose. But for now, it has granted me extra days with her.

It's only a matter of time before they pull the plug on her and tell me I have to say goodbye—also the reason why I live in my car. Mom's medical bills are expensive, and even when the time comes to switch her off, I will have to live in my car for at least another two years to finish paying the debt off. My medical insurance covers a dependent child or spouse, so it is no use. My mother doesn't even have medical insurance. She worked cash in hand and struggled to keep a job for long.

I know most people think it's wishful thinking that she will wake up, but I can't give up on her. She taught me to walk, talk, use a spoon, and how to ride a bike. From the beginning, she has been by my side. She was my first friend. In fact, she is my only friend. She raised me as a single mom from the time I was born. My father walked out when he found out she was expecting. I never met the man; frankly, I don't care to meet him.

I lost our house after three weeks of not being able to pay the mortgage. It turned out we were already months behind when the accident happened, and my mother had kept it from me. I had to choose to keep mom alive or keep the house. So, I chose her.

I know she would have done the same for me. I know I'm delaying the inevitable, but how do you kill your mom? Kill the one person who spent your entire life loving and supporting you? When the time comes, I need to know I have tried everything, or I know I won't be able to live with the guilt.

I look down at my mother; she appears to be sleeping, besides the tube hanging out of her mouth that forces her to breathe and is keeping her alive. She has numerous tubes hanging out of her skinny arms.

My mother used to be strong, lively, and happy. She looked younger than her age. With her blonde hair that was just below her shoulder blades, she had excellent skin, no wrinkles, full pink lips, and a tan complexion. She looked great for a 45-year-old.

But now, her skin has turned gray from the lack of sunlight, and her hair has become oily and flat as she has lost the ability to care for it daily. She has lost all her weight and muscle mass and is now skin and bone. She is wasting away in this hospital bed, a living corpse. Sitting in the blue chair, I scoot closer to the bed and grab her hand.

"Hey Momma, I miss you." I brush her hair off her forehead, which is stuck to her skin. I listen to the beep of her heart monitor, hearing it beep regularly and the sound of the ventilator forcing her to breathe. It is the same set of sounds every day. I used to come and sit with her for hours and tell her about my day or read to her. But after a couple of months, I just tell her I love her. I have run out of things to say.

I miss her soft voice telling me everything is going to be okay. I miss the way she made everything look effortless. Lila Riley may not have been a perfect mother, but she'd been perfect to me. Yeah, she had a drinking problem, but other than that, I know she did the best she could with the hand life had dealt her.

There was never a lack of love, and no matter how badly I fucked up, she was always there to help me pick up the pieces and rebuild.

When I watch her, I think of all the things she will miss and all the memories she won't get to be a part of.

After sitting with her for a while, I quickly duck into the small bathroom. The nurse Sally is on night shift tonight and always lets me shower here. It's the only time I get to shower with warm water. Not hot, but like lukewarm bath water as the showers are temperature regulated. Still, I don't complain. Warm water is far better than cold. The other people in this room need assistance and are bedridden like my mother, so I don't have to worry about anyone opening the door, but I always lock it just in case a cleaner or nurse decides to stop in.

Showering quickly, I wash my hair and my body, scrubbing extra good while I have the power of warm water. When I'm done, I hop out, dry myself off and slip into my track pants so I don't have to change in the cramped car. I also slide my feet into some socks before putting on a pair of flats. I then jam everything back into my oversized handbag while making my way back to my mother's side to say goodbye.

Sitting on the table next to my charging phone are some club sandwiches. Sally must have come in while I was in the shower. She knows my situation and that I have little left over after I pay the hospital, so every shift she is on, I always find sandwiches or any leftover food from the cafeteria on the table waiting for me.

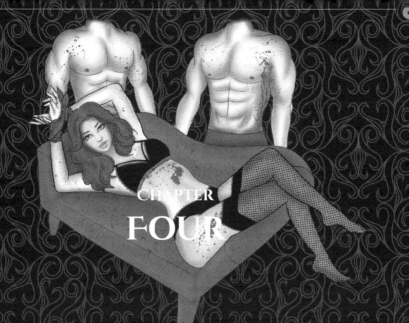

FOUR

Tonight's gourmet dinner comprises thick cheese and sliced tomato sandwiches. I'm starving, having not eaten anything but some dry crackers the entire day. I devour the two sandwiches just before Sally returns with a plastic bag in hand. Sally is the same age as me, 23. She has dark hair cut into a pixie cut, dark brown eyes, and she is about 5'6 tall with a slim build. She's an attractive woman and has a kind heart. Sally is my favorite nurse here; always happy to explain anything I don't understand and has terrific bedside manner.

Every shift, she makes time to see me. When she walks in, I stand up, and she wraps me in a warm hug, rubbing my back softly. Handing the bag over to me, I find some bottles of water and a small orange juice, which I quickly grab out to wash the sandwiches down. Sally's also been to the vending machine and grabbed a few protein bars and some chips. I also find, to my delight, a few pieces of fruit.

"I was hoping you were still in the shower. I know you don't like accepting help, but you really need to start taking care of yourself. When was the last time you ate a proper meal? You look so skinny." I give her a small smile. It's hard keeping my emotions in check around her. Sally has seen me at my most vulnerable. She tugs on my shirt and track pants, trying to emphasize how much weight I've lost. I'm not blind. I know I have lost a lot of weight. My clothes don't fit as they should. I even have to roll some of my pants just to get them to stay on my hips.

"I know, I've been trying. It is just so hard with how chaotic my life is at the moment."

Sally sighs and grips my shoulder. "I have to get back to work, but don't forget to eat. I'm on shift again on Wednesday. So, I will bring a few things for you." She jams the plastic bag into my handbag and zips it up to make sure I take it when I leave, before she walks out to tend to her other patients.

Sitting back down, I wait for my phone to charge a bit more before unplugging it. It's now 8:30 PM. I have to be back before nine to make sure I don't get locked out. Leaning down, I place a kiss on my mother's head before walking out and heading back to my car.

The walk back is quick. Tonight isn't too cold, thank goodness. I open my trunk, grab my duvet and pillow, and quickly climb into the front seat, reclining the seat all the way back. I snuggle underneath my blanket and close my eyes, praying that sleep will come easy.

The next morning, I wake up nice and warm, wrapped up like a human burrito in my duvet. My alarm blares loudly and vibrates on my dash. Groaning, I reach up and switch the damn thing off before the noise gives me a raging headache. Stretching, my body is aching from being in the same position all night. I miss my bed; I miss stretching out and being able to roll around without worrying about getting a seat belt clicker jammed into my backside.

Opening the driver's door and spilling out, I stand up and bend over, touching my toes, then stretch my back and shoulders. Once I stretch like a cat, I open the door to the rear passenger side. I always have a few outfits hanging up in the back on the days I don't set them up the night before. Snatching up some dressy dark blue skinny-leg jeans, a black zip-up blouse, and my blazer. I pull my bra under my shirt and slip my arms inside to maneuver it until I get it in position.

Sitting in the driver's seat, I quickly rip off my pants and replace them with my jeans. Standing up, I realize they are practically falling off me. Damn, these are my favorites. Popping the trunk, I rummage around until I find a serviceable belt, but even that isn't enough. With a sigh, I use my car keys to punch an extra hole in the belt to get it to the size I need to hold my damn pants up. Once done, I peel my shirt off and shrug my blouse on, pulling the zipper up just in time to hear the roller doors to the parking garage open.

Bending down, I check myself in the car window. I look decent enough. This is one of my favorite tops. It was a little too small before the change in my living situation, but now it fits like a second skin, making my large bust stand out more and leaving ample cleavage. I rarely like showing off my assets, but this top? They look fucking fantastic, even if I do say so myself. Quickly grabbing my black heels, I slip them on and bend over to do the straps.

Once I'm finished, I walk down the ramp to meet Tom. His face instantly lights up. "There is my girl. How was your night?"

"Good, wasn't cold last night and was rather quiet. How's the wife?" Tom walks up and hands me a cappuccino in a paper cup. I thank him, then warm my hands on it while taking a sip.

"She is good. I have a surprise for you. Mary made meatballs last night, and there were plenty of leftovers, so I brought them in a Chinese dish for you." I lean into Tom and give him a side hug. He reminds me of my grandfather. Tom hugs me back, wrapping his arm around my shoulders.

We quickly go back to my car. I grab my handbag and the few things I need to finish getting ready, then lock my car and follow him to the entrance.

Getting to my desk, I flick everything on and power up my computer. While waiting for everything to load, I finish my cappuccino and head into the bathroom to do my hair and makeup. Just as I finish making my bosses their coffees, they step out of the elevator like clockwork. They've never been late. They are always on time.

However, I stop what I'm doing when I hear them arguing as soon as they set foot outside the elevator. That's unusual. I stay in the small kitchen, not wanting to be present for their heated argument, but I can't help but overhear part of their discussion. Theo is rarely angry, and I find it odd that he's raising his voice at Tobias, who, I can tell from his clipped tones, is getting angrier by the second. Their voices don't change in volume, so I still imagine them to be in the foyer. Usually, when they have their lover's quarrel, it's in one of their offices, not where anyone can overhear.

"You can't keep ignoring the bond and hiding in your office. You will snap, and that will scare her even more." Theo's voice seems to get higher as he gets angrier. I freeze, listening intently. Who is this mystery woman?

"Stay out of it. I have control of my urges. It is yours I'm more worried about," spits Tobias, the words rolling off his tongue, are dripping with venom.

"Well, at least I am not denying them like you," Theo retorts.

"She's human, weak, and she doesn't belong in our world. I'm sick of having this same argument. This isn't just about us, this would put her in danger. Is that what you want, Theo?" Tobias's voice rises, anger coloring every word.

My mind reels. Humans? Aren't we all human? I must have heard wrong, and who is in danger? I can feel my heart rate pick up, pounding in my ears. Goosebumps spread up my arms; my hand remains frozen in place, clutching white-knuckled onto the kettle. Why are my mind and body paralyzed with fear?

"Boo!" I jump at the voice next to my ear. "You know what they say about eavesdropping," Theo whispers, his breath sweeping across my neck. He steps closer, chest pressing against my back. My hands tremble slightly as I place the jug back on the counter.

"You okay, Imogen?" He sounds concerned. Plastering a fake smile on my face, I spin around to face him, but he is standing by the door. Did I just imagine the entire scenario in my head? There's no way he could have moved that fast and not be heard. I really am going nuts, maybe even having a mental breakdown. Their conversation replays in my head but becomes muddled to the point I can't even remember what they were arguing about. Tobias steps in behind Theo, popping his head around the corner of the door and staring at me. An uneasy feeling rolls over me, and I can't get my thoughts straight. My mind feels foggy, and have Theo's eyes always been so bright? For some reason, I can't pull my gaze from his as unease rolls through me and tension builds. What's going on here?

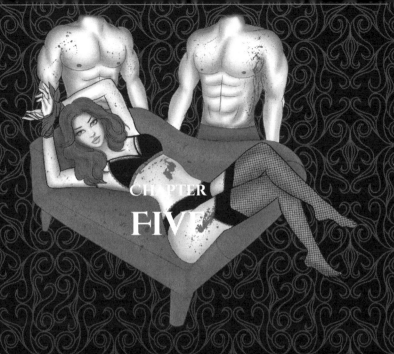

CHAPTER
FIVE

They both stare at me, concern in their eyes. Have I done something alarming? Were they just arguing, or had I imagined that too? What were they arguing about, and why can't I remember anymore? They look like their normal selves. I stand there, just as confused as they are, when Tobias breaks the awkward silence that has fallen over us. His voice forcing me out of my head and into the present moment.

"Imogen... Imogen, what's wrong? Are you hurt?" He seems to sniff the air lightly for a second. I tilt my head, observing them. They glance between themselves, doing their silent communication only they can understand. The room warps and spins, growing darker as the seconds pass by. I see Tobias shove past Theo, his fingers reaching for me. The world falls around me. My muscles turn to weights. No, wait, I'm the one that is falling. Oh no, I remember this feeling. I'm having a panic attack. Shit. I try to breathe, but my body gives up functioning, and I can't catch my breath as the room grows darker; my vision tunnels, and I try to remember the most basic bodily function, one that should be instinct, but I fail. Then the darkness takes my sight away completely.

I don't know how much time passes before I wake up. Groaning, I groggily lift myself onto my elbow, my other hand clutching my head. Within moments I am forced down by Theo's heavy hand on my shoulder. "Woah there, lay back down for a bit." I stare, confused. I'm lying on the brown leather couch in Tobias's office. Tobias is sitting on the edge of his desk, arms folded across his chest, making him appear even more intimidating than usual.

However, concern is etched on his face as he stares back at me. That's new. Theo sits beside me with my legs over his lap, rubbing them of all things. Shit, I did something embarrassing; I know it.

"What happened?" I ask, confused. I try to think of the last thing I remember. But I only remember eavesdropping on a conversation between Tobias and Theo about... Funny, I can't remember a single detail. All I can recall is the vibe that something was off, then the not being able to breathe thing, Theo's enchanting gaze, and, oh yeah, my old friend, the darkness.

"You fainted. Just lay down for a bit and drink this," orders Tobias, walking back over with a glass of water in his hand. I sit up, pull my legs from Theo, and lean against the armrest. Reaching out, I grip the ice-cold glass of water. My fingertips brush Tobias's. He rips his hand away as if I had burned him, before moving back to his desk.

A knock on the door a few minutes later interrupts our awkward tension. Tobias tells them to enter, and a leggy blonde woman steps into the office with a few styrofoam food cartons in her hand. My nose twitches as the smell wafts from it. My mouth waters at the smell of Chinese food. The blonde woman peers around the room, unsure of what to do. Her light blue eyes dart to each of us frantically until she sees Theo, and she freezes in place like a deer in headlights.

She's incredibly attractive; she has white suit pants on and a blazer with a black cami.

"Just leave it on the desk, Merida," Theo speaks quietly. Merida jumps slightly but obeys before quickly darting back out of the room, which has grown incredibly tense. What did I just witness? Why did she seem so scared? And more importantly, how long have I been out? Looking at the clock that hangs above the door, I notice the time. 3:15 PM ... my eyes bulge out of my head. I have been out for hours. Jumping to my feet, I quickly make my way to the door. Shit, I'm supposed to have the Merger files ready by 4 PM. Just as I open the door, a hand shoves it shut above me, the lock clicking into place. Burning heat seeps up my back. I instinctively freeze at the abrupt harshness of the door being slammed in my face.

"Sit back down, Imogen." Tobias's voice is demanding. A cold shiver runs up my spine, his hot breath tickling my neck.

"I have to get the Merger documents for your meeting," I try to argue back. My voice comes out shaky; I can hear the fear in it. But why am I suddenly scared of my boss?

Leaning into me, his front presses into my back, body molding to mine. Lowering his head to my ear, he whispers, "I said sit back down." He emphasizes each word, giving me no choice. I turn towards him only to be met with Tobias' harsh gaze staring back at me. No help there. I shrink under his glare and take a step back, hitting the door with my back, feeling extremely small beside him. Who am I kidding? I'm small beside him regardless, but right now, I feel tiny and weak and hunted.

His eyes soften when they meet my fearful ones. "Sorry, I didn't mean to scare you." He speaks gently, a trace of my former boss in his eyes. Scratch that. My former boss wasn't usually this gentle. Theo, sure, but not Tobias. Reaching down, he places a loose hair back behind my ear before stepping away, motioning for me to sit back next to Theo. I quickly obey as my mind swims with the implications of what the hell is going on.

Once beside him, Theo grips my knee softly. His touch is warm and at least some comfort, but again, my bosses don't touch me. Besides, they're gay, right? "Don't worry about him; he's a bit tense. We canceled the meeting. It's not till tomorrow morning." Theo reassures me, still rubbing my knee. I nod in understanding, but all I want is to get out of this room. I can't believe I slept all day on my boss's couch. How embarrassing. God, I hope I didn't talk in my sleep or fart. Oh my god, what if I did? I suddenly wish the floor could open up and swallow me.

"Here," says Tobias, dropping the styrofoam food carton in front of me before placing another in front of Theo.

I want to tell them I'm fine but am cut off by Tobias' deadly glare. Besides, how long has it been since I gorged on takeout? It's way out of my budget. The food tempts me, threatening to break every ounce of willpower I have.

"It wasn't a choice, Imogen. Eat!" Each word is full of authority, but it also sounds like he's daring me to disobey him. A part of me is tempted to know what might happen if I did. I'm pretty surprised Tobias hadn't just left me on the floor and continued his day. Has he ever said this much to me beyond work stuff?

I do as told. I swear, I see Tobias smirk at me, obeying his demands like a child. Can this be any more awkward and embarrassing? But the food is good, and I'm starving. Maybe that's why I fainted; between being busted eavesdropping and not eating properly for months, maybe I overwhelmed myself.

When I finish eating the fried rice and satay chicken, I sit quietly, waiting to be dismissed from his office, but it never comes. Instead, Theo picks up the empty food containers and disposes of them instead of ordering me to. Tobias walks over to the cabinet next to the window and pulls out three glasses, pouring a brown liquid that kind of resembles whiskey. Turning around, he hands me one. Theo walks over and picks up his own, downing it in one mouthful. I watch Theo leave the room quietly, leaving me alone with Tobias. I suddenly want him to come back. I turn, staring at the door. My palms become sweaty.

Tobias feels less intimidating with Theo in the room. I adjust my position on the couch, trying to avoid direct eye contact. What does he want with me? Is it just concern for my health, or is there something darker here? I notice Tobias watching me over the rim of his glass. I fiddle with the cup between my fingers. I dared not take a drink yet. Bringing his drink to his lips, Tobias downs every drop in one go. I sniff my drink before scrunching my nose. Whatever he has given me, it's sweeter than vodka's scent—nothing as harsh as the vodka and tequila I'd been using for inner warmth. Bringing the glass to my lips, I down it in one mouthful, following his lead. It's sweet and smooth. It burns a bit on the way down, but not like some of the bottles of liquor I have stored in my trunk, especially the cheaper bottles mom liked to drink. Some of those made me think I was drinking gasoline.

I set the glass down, intending to get up and leave this uncomfortable silence. Tobias tips his bottle, refilling my glass back to the rim and tips his own off as well. He continues to stare at me, watching me with those dark eyes of his. I raise my brow at him, but I accept the glass. Theo returns, the door lock clicking softly behind him.

He clutches various boxes of paperwork stacked four boxes high in his hands. "We are being audited, so we need all these files sorted and all contracts arranged by dates. Get comfortable; it is going to be a long night." Tobias speaks clearly. I stare at the boxes Theo carried in, knowing it isn't even half. Downing the glass of whiskey, I get up from the couch, take a seat on the floor and pull files from the boxes. It doesn't take me long to get a system set up as I sort them into neat piles.

I don't know how much time passed. From my position, the moon is high in the sky when more takeout arrives. I guess that they ordered more food and coffee for us as we toiled. I never saw them pick up a phone to order as we work in silence beside each other.

But I'm glad. I'm exhausted, and I've stared at so many words my eyes are crossing. When it comes time to close the building up at 9 PM, Tobias glances at the security guard who has stepped into the office to let us know he's about to lock up.

Considering I'm not going to have my usual bed, I'm going to have to make do here somehow. "You guys go. There isn't much left, and I will get it done." Tobias and Theo look unsure but eventually agree to leave. They give me a set of keys to get out of the building as well as the security code to set the alarms on my way out.

When I finish the last box, I stack them neatly on top of each other before checking the time; it's 2 am. I only have three files remaining. The floor is killing me. I get up, stretch and plop the files down on the table, and sit on the couch. The soft leather pampers me, and I cuddle up against it as I focus on my work. Getting comfy on the couch, I drag them in front of me. My eyes hurt, but I'll finish this.

That has all been my plan, but the couch is too comfortable, and I pass out on the first soft thing I've gotten to sleep on for months.

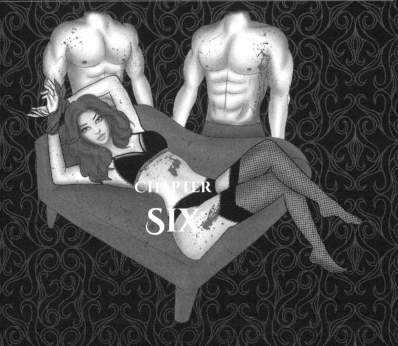

CHAPTER
SIX

I'm jostled awake by warm hands, and files fall off my lap onto the floor in a disorganized mess. Shit, I fell asleep. I scramble to my feet in a panic. Tobias watches me; dark eyes widening at my disheveled appearance. Tobias pinches the bridge of his nose, shaking his head. I fight the urge to yawn and stretch like a cat. Woken up or not, that had been a great nap. No seat belt digging into my hip, no hard seat beneath me, just pure comfort. I feel like a new woman after one night.

"You were supposed to head home, have you been working all night?"

"Shit." My hands fly to my mouth at the language I use in front of my boss. "I must have dozed off. Just give me a minute and I will get cleaned up for the meeting."

Theo steps into the office, looking gorgeous as ever, in his gray suit. He takes in my appearance. My shirt is wrinkled, and my hair is a mess, god knows what my face looks like, but I know it can't be pretty. I've seen the drool a good sleep left plastered to my face, and I probably look like a raccoon from my eye makeup. He raises an eyebrow at Tobias.

"She fell asleep working," Tobias states, clearly not happy that I was asleep yet again at work.

If only they knew I slept here every night, just not in the office. I smile to myself at the thought. If they thought this is crazy, they would completely freak out if they knew the car garage is my current residence.

Moving towards me, Theo grips my blouse. I squeak at his closeness and lean back. Theo reaches for me again and grips the bottom of my blouse, his fingers brushing my stomach as he pulls my blouse off over my head. I quickly cover up my purple lace bra, trying to hide from his lingering gaze on my chest. I have great tits, but that doesn't mean I want to show them off to my boss!

Tobias doesn't even blink. He moves away from me, opening a door that appears to be a closet of sorts. No matter the amount of time I have spent in this office, I never knew there was a closet in the wall. Inside a couple of men's shirts hang, their crisp lines as perfect as the men who wear them. How have I never seen that the wall has a cupboard in it? Are there other hidden compartments? What else is hiding in here, and is Theo's office the same way?

Grabbing a white shirt off the hanger, Tobias walks over to me and stands in front. Theo moves to my side and watches. Tobias reaches to pry my hands away from my chest, but I pull back and scoot out of reach, refusing to uncover myself. Tobias' eyes grow darker under the lighting, making me squirm under his intense gaze.

"We have a meeting in five minutes, and you can't go in there like that." He reaches for my wrist again.

"I can dress myself," I hiss, reaching for the shirt with one hand, the other still firmly across my chest. Instead of giving me the shirt, he shoves my arm through the arm hole and pulls the other half around me, working around the confines of the couch I continue to sit on. I give up and let him finish dressing me. I'm not their type. It isn't like they would be gawking at my breasts.

"Suppose it isn't like it matters with you both being gay," I mutter to myself. I'm being childish about being half naked in front of them. I need to focus on the meeting, it's my fault for falling asleep.

Tobias' hands freeze at my cleavage where he's doing up the buttons. His brows knit. Theo comes over and starts rolling up my sleeves leisurely with a silly grin on his face. I can tell he's trying not to laugh. I watch silently, they seem to be amused by something. I raise an eyebrow at Tobias, who still has his fingers on the button right between my breasts. He hasn't moved, just stares at it as if it's the most interesting button in the world and can tell him life's secrets.

Theo snorts, trying to hold in his laugh, almost choking on it.

"What?" I ask, annoyed that I'm not being let in on this inside joke of theirs. I stare from one to the other trying to decipher the mood change.

"We aren't gay," Tobias replies with a faint smirk on his lips. I meet his gaze, and his attention drops back to that button. My entire body heats up, the blood rushes to my face and probably makes me look splotchy as hell. I have worked here all this time thinking they are gay. How have I read that wrong? I saw them kissing... didn't I?

"You're not gay?" I ask slowly. Maybe they are tricking me? My eyebrows disappear into my hairline.

"Definitely not gay. We both like women," Theo replies, rolling the sleeves of my shirt up. His eyes linger on my exposed chest, a hungry glint just beneath their surface.

I have just gotten semi naked in front of my bosses. What are they thinking? That's a lawsuit waiting to happen. Not that I would sue them, I needed my job, but this entire scenario is mortifying.

"But I saw you kissing his neck," I blurt.

Tobias raises an eyebrow at me. "Not everything you see is what it appears to be."

Can he get away from my chest? I don't have that many buttons! But I can't bring myself to pull away, it's all I can do to just manage to stay upright.

"Well, I'm pretty sure I didn't imagine it, and you both live together." I point to the two of them as if forcing myself to remember their connection.

"We share a home, but that's not all we like to share," Theo's voice whispers beside me. I jump at his closeness, his breath is cold on my neck and makes me shiver. There's that haunted feeling again.

"We aren't gay, we like women too," Tobias emphasizes the last word, licking his lips. Are my bosses hitting on me, or am I blowing this all out of proportion in my head?

I scramble to my feet, doing the last of my buttons and scurrying out of the office. I can swear they laugh at my escape. I rush into the bathroom and do as much damage control as possible. I still have a meeting to get through.

When I walk in, a few people's heads turn at my shirt choice, but no one says anything. Even if they want to, I doubt they would have dared with Tobias and Theo walking in directly behind me. Whenever they are around, people seem to disappear or walk in the opposite direction. No one likes crossing their path for fear of losing their jobs, being yelled at, or having something thrown at them.

The fact that every other secretary quit under them shows how demanding they can be. Once the meeting is over, after endless hours of going through the files I've sorted, I hastily leave the room, going back to my desk, when my phone rings. It's the hospital calling. I don't hesitate to answer. I prepare myself. "Hello."

"Imogen, it's me Sally." Her voice comes out in a rush. My heart skips a beat. I have been waiting for this call, I just wasn't expecting it to be today. "The Medical Ethics Board ruled against you. They have decided to turn your mother's life support off, saying it is no longer medically viable to have her remain on it." Her words make sense, but after her first sentence I find it impossible to focus.

My lungs constrict painfully, the pressure almost unbearable. I thought I was prepared for this phone call. I've wasted a night I could have seen her, one more day holding her hand, telling her I love her. My throat gets tight, it's hard to breathe, and I start hyperventilating. My eyes blur with unshed tears. I can't afford to pass out.

Not when my mother needs me. My heart plummets into my stomach. I fight the tears from spilling over. Sally's still talking, I need to focus on her. Grasping the phone, my knuckles feel like they are going to split through my skin. My voice shakes, I can barely get the words out, I'm surprised Sally can understand me at all. I can't even recognize the simple word that just comes out of my mouth. "When?"

"Tonight, Imogen. I'm so sorry." Sally doesn't sound like she's doing so good herself. But I have nothing in me to care about others. I hang up the phone in a daze and grab my keys and purse. I'm on full autopilot. My hands shake as I try to think of what I should be doing at this moment. Gathering the last few things I need, I make my way to the elevator. My vision has gotten dark, all I can see is straight ahead. I jab the button to go down and the doors slide open, revealing my two bosses in all of their glory. But yet, none of that matters to me. I have to get out, get to the hospital and get there now.

They're talking but stop immediately as I shuffle into the elevator, moving between them. They turn around, both staring at me. Theo speaks but I can't hear a word he's saying, my ears pound with my heartbeat. The only word I hear is tonight, they're taking her off tonight. Theo reaches for me, but I put my hands up, warding off their advances as my body shakes.

"Don't touch me, I... I need to go," I stammer out, before slamming the button repeatedly to go down to the ground floor. They quickly step out of the elevator, concern etched on both their faces before the closed doors erase them from my sight.

I know they're concerned, but right now I don't care to explain my current situation. Not that it involves them, or that they would care. I just need to get to her. Get to my mom and say goodbye before it's all over.

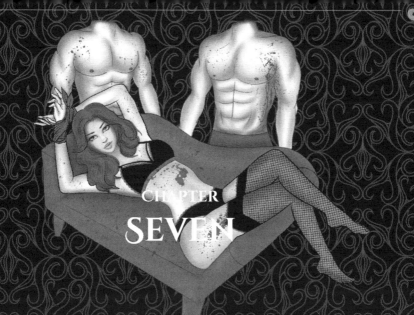

CHAPTER
SEVEN

I watch the buttons light up for each floor I go down, time slows as I watch the numbers tick down. I'm nervous, impatient, and try to hold all my pieces together. Sally's voice echoes through my mind, repeating the words that I feel will stop my heart from beating. Only, it's still thumping painfully in my chest.

When the elevator doors ping on the bottom floor, I take off running, my shoulder smashes into the elevator door having not had enough time to open completely. I can't feel anything but the dread building inside of me. The hospital isn't far, and I make it there in under five minutes. My heels slide on the floor outside my mother's ward door as I grip the door handle, take a breath, and walk in.

The ward is full of doctors moving other patients out. Sally stands amongst them, her green scrubs stand out amongst the doctors in their white coats. She glances at the clock, probably wondering if I'll get here in time. Seeing me, she comes rushing over and wraps her arms around me. "I'm so sorry, Imogen."

I nod, watching as another patient is wheeled out and transferred to another room, leaving only my mother, a doctor, Sally, and myself.

The doctor is an older woman in her fifties. She has graying hair that reaches her shoulders, pulled back with a clip, kind, soft brown eyes, and a pale complexion. She's wearing a doctor's coat and white scrubs. Her name tag reads Laurel.

"Hi, you must be Imogen?" she says, reaching out and grasping my hand softly between hers.

"The Medical Ethics Board has decided to remove your mother from life support. In doing so I will just prepare you for what will happen next." I stare at her, my face completely blank. I think I'm in shock, but at the same time I understand everything she says, even nod a few times.

When she's done, she asks If I want some time with my mother. I nod my head and they both walk out, leaving me alone with her. I walk slowly over to her bed and hold onto her hand. Looking down at her, she looks like she's just sleeping, her face is slack with the tube hanging out of it, keeping her breathing. I stroke her hair gently.

"Momma, it's me, your Immy. They have decided to turn your life support off." I stare at her, hoping for some miracle. But there's none. I can hear Sally and the doctor talking softly outside the door. None of this feels real. "If you can hear me, mom, please know I'm sorry. I tried, I really did. I love you Momma, but I have to let you go." My eyes burn with the need to shed tears but I hold them back.

The time has come. I'm supposed to be prepared for this but why don't I feel like I'm prepared at all? I don't know what to do. I don't know what to say to her now that this is goodbye. So instead, I just hold her hand, rubbing circles into her soft thin skin.

The doctor walks in with Sally. I look up when they enter, Sally looks heartbroken for me and I turn away from her. I can't handle seeing the sadness in her eyes.

I know once I let myself cry, I will never stop. So instead, I take a deep breath and close my eyes, telling myself I can do this, hardening my resolve. The doctor asks me to step out so she can remove the tubes and switch everything off. I shake my head at her. I want to be here for every last moment, no matter how hard. I owe mom this since I haven't been able to stop it.

When she pulls the tube out of her throat, my mother makes a gurgling noise and gasps, but the doctor reassures me it's the body's normal reaction. I squeeze my mother's hand tighter, trying to ignore the noises her body makes. The machines erupt into a scream of beeps, screaming to the world that the patient isn't doing well. One by one, the doctor shuts them off, leaving us in silence with my gasping mother.

When she's done, she squeezes my shoulder tightly before walking over to the side. The doctor says my mother can last a few hours or go quickly. Mom leaves quickly. Her breathing slows, her lips turn blue, and her body convulses, making me jump to my feet. I wrap my arms around her neck, pressing my head to hers.

"It's alright, Momma. I'm right here, I'm right here," I tell her. After a few seconds, it stops and so does her breathing. Her chest no longer rises up and down. The room falls silent, the only noise is my own heavy breathing. I lift my head from hers, Mom's skin is dull and lifeless, and her hand loses its warmth. I know she's gone. The doctor walks over and places a stethoscope on her chest and listens before nodding, confirming her heart is no longer beating and making a note of the time.

I stare at my mother's dead body lying on the gurney - she's gone. I'll never hear her voice again, never hold her again. I can't handle it anymore. Getting up, I pull the blanket up, tucking her in as if she's asleep and I'm saying good night instead of goodbye. I lean down and kiss her head. My lips quiver and my eyes burn with tears that want to fall. Tears I've lost the will to fight.

I just stare down at her. Now what? Do I just leave and never come back? Turning around, I walk out in a daze, almost robotic. When I step into the blue corridor, Sally tries to grab my hand, but I pull away from her touch. I don't want to be touched. I know I'll break. I'm nearly to the end of the corridor when Tobias steps into my view. I don't know what he sees on my face, but he reaches for me. I quickly step out of his reach. What is it with everyone and trying to touch me? I won't break. None of these people will see me break. Tears are a weakness. I'm not weak. My mother didn't raise a weakling.

I keep walking down the long hall, I can hear people talking to me, I can hear Sally calling after me, but I just ignore them and keep on walking. I walk out of the hospital doors. My phone vibrates in my bag that is over my shoulder. I ignore it.

I drag myself to the park across the road.

I collapse on the park bench. The darkness surprises me, but I welcome its ability to hide me from the world. The stars shine brightly down on me, the trees sway in the wind. The night is cold and silent, the only noise I can hear is the beating of my own heart, which I'm sure is broken beyond repair.

I'm completely numb, and I pray I stay that way. I don't want to know what this pain will feel like. The wind whips through my hair, fat drops of rain hit my skin as a sheet of rain passes over me. I can't feel coldness, I can't feel the sting of the wind or the bite of the rain on my skin. For the first time in my life, I don't know what my next move is. There is no plan. I realize I was in denial this entire time because I never planned to get to this point. I knew this time would come but I don't think I believed she would ever actually be gone.

So instead, I let the rain fall drench me where I sit. I don't care if I get sick. I don't care what happens to me. I somehow made myself believe that she would pull through, even though my mind knows she isn't coming back.

At some point I drudge back to my car. Tom has left the parking garage door up slightly. He must have realized I wasn't in my car. I walk up to my car and pop the trunk, grabbing a bottle. I pop the cap and gulp the vodka down. I just want to sleep and forget about this day, or maybe wake up to find this is all a nightmare, one I'm just having trouble waking from. Only I know it isn't, it hurts too much, and you don't feel pain in dreams.

I jerk my car's door open and plop down, bringing my bottle with me. I twist around in my seat, grab my duvet off the back seat and wrap it around myself, seeking comfort in its warmth. My teeth chatter but I can't be bothered taking my wet clothes off. Right now it's too much effort. After a while and a few more mouthfuls of my bottle of jet fuel, I slip into the darkness of sleep huddled into my little ball of grief.

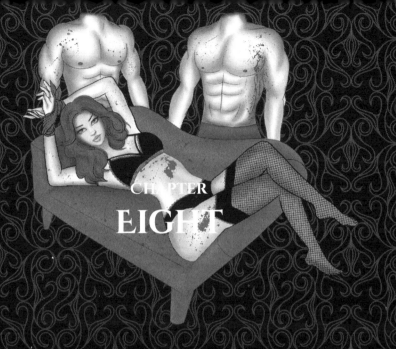

CHAPTER
EIGHT

The next morning, I wake up in my cramped car, my neck is twisted in an awkward position against the center console. Rotating my neck and stretching the sore muscles, I rub the aching spot before sitting up to the sound of monotonous tapping on my driver's side window. Squinting I can just make out Tom standing outside with a coffee in hand and concern etched on his face.

Jumping up quickly I grab my phone. Shit, I slept through my alarm. Tom motions his hand to the hood where he balances my coffee. "I will meet you at the ramp, kiddo."

My head pounds, reminding me that drinking on an empty stomach was a seriously bad idea.

I nod to Tom, hiding my wince as I do. Getting up, I hobble to the trunk and rummage through, trying to find something decent to wear. I stink heavily of vodka. I just want to sleep last night off and god knows how much longer until I pass out completely.

Why did I drink so much, anyway? I know better. The memories of my mother hit me, threatening to make me fall to my knees. Instead, I shove them aside, refusing to think of the shitstorm that has become my life. Finding a passable blouse, I smooth it out the best I can and toss my blazer over the top. I rip the hairbrush through my tangled hair, relishing the pain. Anything that keeps my mind off yesterday I welcome. I stuff my foot into my still damp shoe while I hop on one foot and try to walk to the hood of my car at the same time.

I grab the coffee and try jogging down the ramp towards Tom, who's waiting patiently for me next to the entrance doors. Unfortunately, my actions last night make jogging near impossible. I settle for a quick power walk instead. A quick glance at my phone informs me I have a scant ten minutes before my bosses will arrive.

"Rough night, darl? That's the first time I've ever seen you sleep in." Tom's kindness and warmth threatens to break me.

"Yeah, it was pretty rough, thanks for waking me," I mumble, sipping my coffee and avoiding those sweet eyes. Tom escorts me to the elevator before going about his own duties. Once the doors ping open, I power hobble to the bathroom and do a quick rush job of my make up. My face is puffy, and I look like shit. No, I look hungover with my bloodshot eyes and pale complexion. A slow ache makes its way up to my eyes, sitting directly at my temple. I knew the aftermath of drinking that much would have consequences, but I was prepared.

Once finished, I quickly go to my bag and retrieve 3 ibuprofen and three Advil. I down them with a glass of water. Mom's secret remedy for hangovers besides greasy food. I smile at the memory before my smile crumples to a frown. I'll never see her smile again, let alone hear her endless advice, even silly advice like how to avoid a morning hangover. I'm shoved out of my sadness by the ping of the elevator doors.

Tobias and Theo step out. Their normal business persona shatters as their eyes widen upon seeing me. I still haven't made the morning coffee. I apologize realizing my mistake before racing to the kitchenette and making it. Theo pops his head into the small kitchen door, studying me as if I'm a wounded animal.

"Sorry I was a bit rushed for time this morning. I'm making them now," I sputter, concentrating on the task at hand. When I don't hear a response, I turn to see if he's still there.

He is, but now shadowed by Tobias. I gulp, my mouth suddenly feels like a desert. Tobias's concerned eyes spark a memory. He'd been at the hospital, he'd tried to reach for me. I was rude and ignored him.

Can't I catch a break? Seriously, I don't feel like being scolded. Ignoring them, I finish making the coffees before spinning around and handing mugs to each. I'm late but not so much that our entire day has to be ruined. Theo stares at the offered cup before taking it while Tobias' face is unreadable. Pity maybe? I'm sure.

"You don't have to be here. You can go home if you like." Tobias' voice is unusually gentle. I sigh, relieved I don't have to come up with some excuse as to why I ignored him and ran from him last night. I wonder why he was at the hospital anyway.

"Why would I do that?" I question. Don't they want me here? Have I ruined their schedule after all with my lateness?

"We don't expect you to work the day after your mother passes. If you need time off, we understand. We can manage on our own, Imogen." Tobias continues with his soft manner. If I didn't know any better, I'd think he wants to hug me the way he keeps staring.

Why is he of all people interfering in my life? It's not like we are friends and catch up for drinks after work. I barely know them. I never chat or talk to them outside business hours, I never pry into their lives, and they don't ask about mine. All of sudden they think they can have some input? I don't need their pity. I just need to be left alone.

Theo sniffs the air before cocking his head to the side, studying me from head to toe. I'm well aware I smell like I've been dipped in vodka. Walking past them, I grab my perfume from my handbag and spray myself, completely ignoring them. Like seriously where will I go? Hang out in the garage all day? To the park again? Maybe the storage shed? Yeah, having time off is the last thing I need.

Theo places a cup on the edge of my desk, it's his coffee. "Drink this, I will make another."

I try to get up and stop him, seeing as it technically is my job to be the coffee bitch, but one look from Tobias makes me shrink back down in my seat. Tobias sits on the edge of my desk. He reaches to grab my hand, but I pull away. Hurt shines in his eyes but he quickly masks it. Why would he feel hurt? His reaction seems a little out of place, considering I'm his secretary, not his friend. I must have imagined it.

"Are you okay?" He questions me, that warmth still in tone. It's so uncharacteristic of him. I expect that from Theo, not Tobias.

I would be if people stopped trying to touch me. Knowing I can't say that, I simply nod while turning the phones over to take them off voicemail. We sit in silence with me pointedly ignoring him. I refuse to engage in any sort of discussion with him. He can't just treat me differently because I lost my mother. After a time Tobias gets up and walks to his own office. I breathe a sigh of relief and throw myself into my work.

The day flies by and neither one of them asks me to do anything all day. I remain at my desk, answering calls. I want the distraction, a task, anything instead of being left to my own thoughts. I wish the work day will never end.

Theo pokes his head in the door, his arms filled with files and I grin at the pile, eager for it. He looks relieved at my smile and plops them on the side beside me. I thank him, then get to work.

By the time I have all the paperwork sorted into their allocated files, it's already late again. My time to be distracted with work is drawing to a close. Theo and Tobias have left without preamble, a fact I'm grateful for. I don't need them hovering over me afraid I'd crack. I need more clothes, it's time to take the walk to my storage shed. I don't want to drive, not while in this state.

I need to be back by 9:00PM or I'll be locked out. It's 7:30 now, so I still have an hour and a half, plenty of time to get there and back. Ducking out to my car, I snatch the storage locker key from the glove compartment, along with the empty vodka and tequila bottles. I plan to discard them on the way. I won't be able to keep hiding the bottles from Tom if they keep building up.

Making my way down to the bottom floor, I pause. The hairs on the back of my neck rise in warning and I can't shake the sensation of a pair of eyes on me. I glance around but I can't see anyone else. The garage is just as deserted as always. I shiver, trying to push away the feeling and walk faster. I make my way outside walking up the "in" ramp. As soon as I'm outside, I toss the bag of empty bottles into the trash for the garbage man to collect tomorrow.

The skyrise I work at is on the outskirts of the city, which is convenient for me. Everything is at my fingertips so to speak. My storage locker is two blocks from where I am now. Next to the skyrise is a park that leads into a small wooded area. I like to walk through it. The park is a shortcut to my storage locker. It's also where a lot of people have picnics and hang around.

Cutting through the trees, I can't shake the feeling I'm being watched. It's dark out already. I usually don't come through here at night, but I don't have time to walk the long way. Not if I don't want to be locked out. Shaking off the feeling yet again, I continue walking, faster this time. The moon is my only light, the shadows in the trees stretch over the pathway. Is there someone behind me? I whirl to check but there's nothing there. Just the shadows playing tricks on my eyes. Something dashes through the trees, and it has to be big for me to hear the rustle and breaking of twigs. Swallowing, I pick up my pace. I follow the path that leads towards the industrial area. After about five minutes, I'm deep amongst the trees when I hear a deep growl coming from behind me.

CHAPTER
NINE

Spinning around, I trip, landing on my ass and come face to face with a huge beast. Its black eyes stare directly at me. Shaking my head, I close my eyes. I must be seeing things.

My eyes snap open when its growl resonates through the air. Staring at me is a huge dog or maybe a wolf, but it's massive, like the size of a small bear. It's easily over half my size, its fur is jet black, paws bigger than my head, and its claws look like they can rip me to shreds. More like a tiger's claws than a dog's. I'm going to die.

I've never seen something so magnificent and terrifying at the same time. I hold my breath as it stalks towards me. I try to scoot back, but it growls at my movement. I'm forced to stay still. My heart hammers in my chest. It's going to attack me. I'm going to be mauled to death by the huge beast of an animal. I suppose I had a good run. I'm sure there are worse ways to go than being eaten alive, right? But surely the universe is out to get me. First my mother and now this. Have I run over a black cat? Broken a mirror? My luck can't be this terrible.

"Well, if you're going to maul me, can you hurry up and get it over with?" I snap. The beast stops growling and cocks its head to the side like it understands what I said. I raise an eyebrow at it.

I get to my feet, prepared for it to attack, only it doesn't. I stand there unsure if I should turn my back on it. Time keeps ticking by. If I don't get to my storage shed and back, I'll be locked out. Will this creature follow me the entire way or will he rip into me the instant I expose my back to him? The shiny black fur shines strangely in the moonlight. Its fur has blue undertones. The color shows whenever it moves, catching the moon's light, almost entrancing me with its beauty.

Maybe it's somebody's pet? It seems a little too smart and tame. It walks over to me, sniffing at me. Its fur brushes against my leg. I can't resist, I reach out and run my fingers through it. It's thick, soft and long. The animal nudges at my hand. I guess it likes being rubbed.

"Aw, you're not that bad. You do look scary though."

Great, I'm talking to an oversized dog. I'm really losing my marbles. Shaking my head I turn my back on it and keep walking. The dog trots at my side. I try to tell it to shoo, but it doesn't so much as twitch an ear at me. I even pick up a stick and throw it high overhead, hoping it will give chase, but it doesn't work. Instead it seems annoyed at me and whines loudly, scolding me for daring to try to get away. I don't have time for this. Giving up, I let him follow me.

When I come to the mesh fence surrounding the storage sheds that hold the lockers, I walk along the fence line until I find the spot where the mesh has been broken, creating an opening.

Climbing through, my hip catches on a piece of wire snagging the side of my blouse. I hiss as the wire cuts across my hip, the sting reminds me of my failed efforts to be careful. My white blouse gradually turns red as the cut bleeds. The huge dog whimpers at the noise I make. Spinning around, I stare at it. He seems intelligent for a dog. When I speak to it, I get a feeling like it actually understands what I say.

"Go on, you can't be here. Don't you have a home to go back to?"

He makes a noise and nudges my hip with his nose, moving my hand out of the way. He sniffs at my injury and whines again, trying to lick it through my blouse.

I push him to the side. "Fine, but don't pee on anything." I give the dog a pointed look. It opens its mouth in a mockery of a smile at what I say like he's amused. I really am going bonkers. I need to lay off the horror books.

Walking up the rows of storage sheds, I find the one I'm looking for: number 423. Bending down, I undo the padlock and lift the heavy door. I grunt from the pain of my injury. Boxes and furniture line the entire place. There's a narrow walkway through the middle that I left purposefully so it makes it easier to find things. I take said path and find my closet. The dog follows after me and sits next to my feet, observing what I'm doing. I open the closet and grab an outfit wrapped in plastic. It's a black skirt with a navy-blue blouse and black jacket. One more outfit to add to my rotation in any case.

Grabbing it, I put it aside before moving farther into the locker. I find a box that says kitchen on it. Rummaging through it, I find a small first aid kit. Opening it, I grab some alcohol wipes, gauze and medical tape. I shrug off my blouse, sticky with my blood. The cut is deeper than I thought. Instead of just grazing me, the wire has punctured me deep. My blouse sticks to the wound, and blood runs down into the waistband of my skirt.

Carefully peeling it off my cut, I grab the alcohol wipes and dab it clean. Every swab is like the time mom poured alcohol on my cut knee when I was little. The pain makes my eyes water, but this is necessary. The wound is slightly jagged, like my skin has been opened with a can opener. Cleaning it up the best I can, I place a heap of gauze over the top before securing it with tape. I place the blouse in my handbag before finding a camisole in my closet and tossing my blazer back over the top.

Exiting the storage locker, I place my outfit down then close the roller door. The dog looks around curiously and watches as I padlock the door. Picking up my belongings, I start to hobble back towards work. Despite being cared for, I'm not about to be power walking back with this cut making my body ache.

The park is eerily quiet, usually at night you can hear insects and the hoots of owls, but it's completely silent tonight. It makes me shiver, the giant dog follows quietly. I have become used to his presence behind me. He resembles a wolf more than a dog. There's something familiar about him. I just can't think why I feel that way. Despite earlier, he gives me a sense of peace and protection.

Once back at Kane and Madden Industries, I walk through the car garage and find my car. I made it in time.

"You really shouldn't be in here," I say, staring at the wolf-dog. He seems to return a bored look, sniffing at my vehicle.

"Well, technically I shouldn't be here either," I tell him. Opening the door, I hang tomorrow's outfit up on the hand rest in the back and grab my toiletries bag. Tom gave me a key to the bathroom on the bottom floor of the car garage. It has a shower, a toilet, and a small sink. Tom said it's for the janitors to shower before they leave and slipped me the key during my stupor this morning.

Grabbing my stuff, I make my way to the small bathroom cubicle. The dog trots after me, curious when I open the door. He walks in and lays on the cold cement floor. I shrug at its strangeness and strip my clothes off. That odd sensation of being watched returns and I glance over at the animal to see its dark eyes focused on me. I pause in unhooking my bra and turn around. Why am I blushing over an animal? I rush into the shower. Unfortunately, the water is cold only and I gasp at the assault. I hurry through, not wanting to turn into a popsicle.

By the time I get out, my teeth chatter. I dry myself quickly and chuck my track pants on with a huge wooly sweater and some thick socks. It helps warm me up on the outside. Opening the door to the car garage, the huge dog trots ahead of me towards the upper levels, heading back towards my car.

I pop the trunk, grabbing a half full bottle of Smirnoff Vodka. I also find a leftover bottle of water from yesterday. The wolf climbs up, his paws sitting on the opening of the trunk while he peers inside, then turns to give me a dark questioning look.

"I'm not an alcoholic, it was my moms, but it helps chase away the cold at night," I tell him. "And I have no idea why I am telling you this. It's not like you understand what I'm saying." I shake my head.

I close the trunk and sit down on the ground, leaning against the tire. The dog is too big to fit inside my car and I can't find it in myself to just abandon him, so I stay until he decides to get bored of me and go back home. In a way I kind of hope he won't leave. I don't feel as lonely with him here. Cracking open the water bottle, I hold it near his nose and pour a bit out. He licks the water running out, obviously thirsty. I'm not an animal person but this one is rubbing off on me. I chuckle, ruffling the spot between his ears. I love the feel of his fur.

Swigging from the vodka, I cough before chugging more down. The dog whines at me before stretching out and placing its head in my lap. I stroke his head. "You are very warm. You would make a nice blanket." I giggle at my own joke. The dog lifts its gaze to my face before closing its eyes again, making itself comfortable. I rest my eyes, but after a few more mouthfuls of the burning liquid, I give into sleep, snuggled up with some random stray dog.

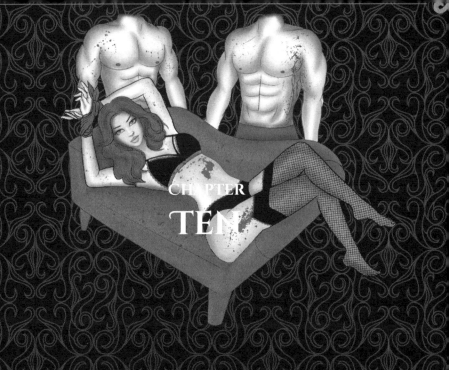

CHAPTER
TEN

The next morning, I wake up inside my car. I don't remember climbing back into the car or the stray even leaving. Maybe I was more intoxicated than I thought. The morning light burns my eyes, forcing me to squint while they adjust to the brightness.

Reaching for my phone, I peer at the screen. The battery is on three percent. The time is 7:30 am, I forgot to set my alarm. Luckily, my body clock didn't fail me this morning. Getting out of the car, I breathe in the clear crisp morning air.

Closing my eyes, the last few day's events come back to me like a bad dream. Only this time more painfully. I can still hear her last gasp, feel the life leave her body as her body turned cold in my grasp.

Pushing the memory aside, I shake my head trying to remove it completely. I don't want that imprinted in my mind. Nothing about it feels real, like it has happened to someone else. Only I can feel the pain of her loss, so I know it's definitely my life that fell into tatters. Now I'm motherless as well as homeless and hopeless.

Two more years and I can have a normal life again, I can do this. Instead of dwelling on my shitty life, I get dressed. Tom doesn't need to see me like this. He already feels sorry for me, so I don't want him to feel worse for me. The last straw will be seeing the pity in his eyes, and I don't want to break down. I'm already a failure at this thing they call life. I don't want to see my failures confirmed in someone else's eyes. Especially someone I care about.

Getting undressed, I forget about the cut from the wire fence. I rip my camisole off, and along with it is the bloody gauze and the skin underneath I gasp at the sharp pain, resisting the urge to double over. I have bled through my rushed aid job and all over the lacy camisole. I must have bumped it in my drunken stupor scrambling into the car.

Reaching inside my vehicle, I grab more gauze and the bottle of vodka. Dousing the cloth in the liquid, I bite my lip before placing it over the wound. The profanities that leave my lips when the cloth brushes my skin would have made a sailor disgusted. This time, I clean it effectively. I don't want to deal with an infection on top of everything else, because I won't take off work to deal with it. I nearly make myself throw up or pass out from the intense burn. Maybe it is a mixture of both. But if I had a choice I would rather pass out.

Once the burning subsides, I redress the wound and slip on my navy skirt and blazer outfit I retrieved from the storage locker. The skirt nearly falls to my knees as soon as I button it up. Surely, I haven't lost that much weight. I know I hardly eat but this is starting to get out of hand.

Reaching in, I grab my belt from yesterday and do it up, holding my skirt in place before shrugging into my blouse, with care this time, and pull my blazer over the top. Luckily, it covers the belt that doesn't match my outfit at all. I decide I look decent enough, but I won't be able to remove my jacket today. Slipping my heels on, I quickly flip the visor down and do my make up. I look terrible and I'm not about to even risk just doing it in the bathroom today. My face is gray and drained of life. My eyes are exhausted, puffy, and have no light left in them, just dull orbs. By the time I'm done, Tom is walking up the ramp towards me, coffee in hand.

49

"Hey Tom," I greet with a wave.

Tom smiles upon seeing me. "Ready early dear, hair and all." He nods at my appearance. At least he thinks I'm doing better. I don't want him worrying about me.

I just nod. Yes, it's a rarity that Tom doesn't see me with my car head glory. He walks me to the elevator like every morning. It's good listening to him tell me what Mary and himself got up to the night before. It makes me forget about everything. When it comes time to part ways, I'm actually sad to see him turn and leave because I know I'm going to be left with my own torturous mind. I've been distracted so far, but once I'm left alone I'm afraid of the darkness that will seep in.

Once I make it to the office, I turn everything on and get to work. Just before 9 am, I make the coffees for Theo and Tobias and have them waiting at my desk for when they enter. I busy myself with sending and replying to emails. When they step out of the elevator, they both stop and stare. For a second, I wonder if I forgot something or that maybe something is on my face, until they continue walking towards me.

"Good morning," I chirp with a broad smile. They both raise an eyebrow at me, looking like twins. I nearly laugh. They clearly don't think there's anything to be cheery about this morning. Truthfully, there's nothing joyful in my life at the moment. But hey, fake it till ya make it, right?

"Are you sure you should be here? We don't expect you to work, Imogen." Theo's voice is soft as he studies me with concern. I notice Tobias glance away, guilt stamped on his face. It kind of pisses me off. I don't want their pity and sad, worried looks. It isn't his business to tell what he has seen, even if he has only told Theo. It's bad enough that I listened to this yesterday.

"Nope I'm good," I say. My face goes blank. I don't want to talk about my mother, I want them both to drop it. Just treat me like they do every day. I need this job to survive until all the bills are handled.

"No, really Imogen, if you need some time off to organize funeral arrangements. We can manage on our own," Theo tells me, repeating exactly what Tobias said yesterday.

"No, everything is fine. Funeral arrangements have already been organized," I say, turning back to my computer. There won't be a funeral; I can't afford one. Instead, the hospital will have her cremated and notify me when I can pick the remains up. Of course, they will add it to the already never-ending hospital bill. Besides, where will I even go with time off? Go stare at all my junk in the storage locker? That won't make me feel any better, I'll only be lost in memories.

No, I need the distraction of work. Need something to do. But most of all, I need to be left alone about the matter. One thing I'm good at is hiding my emotions. I make sure never to rely on anyone, that way when they don't come through or step up when I need them, I can't be disappointed. I'm already disappointed in myself. I don't need the added disappointment of others.

"I have your schedules here and coffees," I tell them, passing them everything they need before putting my head back down and ignoring them. They must have got the message because after a few tense seconds of feeling their eyes lingering, they both walk away into their offices. I sigh, relieved to be left to go about my work with hopefully no more mention of death and funerals. I shove my problems to the back of my mind. I throw myself into the tasks in front of me, focusing only on them.

When lunch time comes around, I know that means seeing Theo and Tobias, so instead of staying at my desk like I do most of the time, I duck down to my car. Sitting in my passenger seat, I recline my chair all the way. The sun feels nice and warm on my skin. There's a slight breeze but not too chilly. My lunch break is an hour long.

Rummaging through the bag Sally gave me, I pull out the last protein bar. I quickly unwrap it and take a tiny bite. If I hadn't been so damn hungry, I would have spat it out. The taste is terrible, like cookie dough but chewy and sugarless. The bar has nuts in it that are rock hard, and I'm surprised I don't break a tooth. Swallowing the last mouthful down, I try to rid the taste from my mouth by licking the back of my hand. Even that doesn't help.

My teeth ache from constantly chewing, I have never eaten a protein bar that resembles nutty chewing gum. When I try and fail to remove the taste, I look at the bottle sitting on the floorboard of my car. Smirnoff Vodka, it's one of the better tasting ones. Will it be inappropriate to have a mouthful while at work? It's definitely inappropriate, I know that, but the taste is foul, and I also need the liquid courage to go back up there and pretend everything's peachy.

Reaching over, I grab the bottle and twist the cap off. Bringing the bottle to my lips, I take two big mouthfuls and swallow them down, suddenly feeling the burn all the way to my stomach. Placing the cap back on, I sit back, only to find the watchful eyes of my new stray friend staring at me. He's sitting directly in front of my car, looking through the windshield. Maybe it's my imagination, but I swear he looks like he's scolding me with that glare of his.

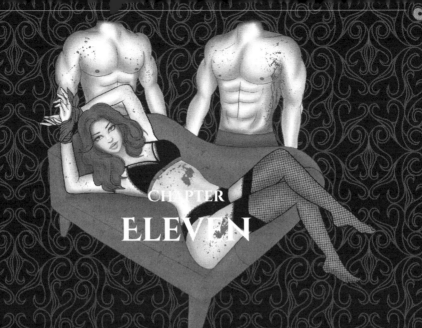

CHAPTER
ELEVEN

For some reason seeing him sends a shiver up my spine. He looks more like a predator now that I can see him in the light. He's huge. Even sitting down, his head can easily peer through the windows. I wonder what mutated breed he is. I assume it's a he, I'm not game enough to go check.

And that was the last area I paid attention to last night. I know I wouldn't want anyone checking between my legs to see what I am, if I were a dog. Cracking my car door open, he walks over to me. I pat his big head and sigh. He's just as soft as last night. He presses his nose onto my side where the gash is. I hiss a little from the direct pressure on it. I don't know how but since he touched it, I'm fully aware of the zig zagged cut across my side.

Deciding I should recheck it and be on the lookout for an infection, I lift my shirt. The dog watches, turning his head from side to side like he's studying it too. I pull the gauze back. It holds together well and isn't pouring out blood at least. Examining it in the light, I'm pretty confident that across my hip bone, that juts out under my skin, the puncture might have gone down to the bone. I try to pry it open with my fingers a little so I can see layers of tissue outside my skin instead of under it. I have thankfully stopped bleeding, but I need stitches or it will either get infected or leave a terrible scar. That's the last thing I need.

Placing the gauze back over it, I reach for the bottle of vodka. The stray tilts his head watching me. His eyes look so human-like as he stares at me. Is he still judging me? I turn away from his watchful gaze and take another mouthful. The dog sticks around for a few more minutes before he trots off back down the ramp, leading to the lower levels of the car park. I have only five minutes left of break so I decide to lock my car up and go back inside.

When I reach the office, Theo is perched on the end of my desk like he's waiting for someone. That someone is me.

"Where did you go?" He asks and sniffs the air for a second. It's such a strange thing to do. I have caught him doing it multiple times over the last few months, maybe it's like an involuntary tick or something. But it's definitely strange. I have even seen his eyes go dark a few times after doing it, like right now when he glances at my face before quickly looking away.

"I had to go get something from my car." I tell him. He eyes me suspiciously like he doesn't believe me. I know I don't smell of vodka. Not with only a couple of mouthfuls and there aren't any cameras on the top level of the garage, so he couldn't have seen me either. If there had been, everyone would have been witness to my house by this point.

The way he stares at me gives me goosebumps. His eyes dart down to my injured hip, staring as if he can see through my blazer and peer at it. I shiver but he stands up and walks away without so much as a glance back in my direction. Shaking my head, I walk into the kitchenette. I place the kettle on, needing a caffeine hit.

I make myself, Tobias, and Theo coffee before walking back out to the foyer. I place my cup down on my desk before knocking lightly on Tobias's door. No answer. I crack it open, searching, he isn't in there. The curtains are closed, and the only light comes from his computer screen. I walk over and place the cup on his desk. I turn around and I bump directly into him. I jerk back at his closeness, my hand goes to my chest as my heart hammers away. "Sorry you startled me," I whisper. He stares down at me. I feel tiny next to him, my face is level with his chest. I have to crane my neck to look up at him, his eyes glued to me.

I try to step to the side but he moves closer, effectively trapping me between him and his desk.

I gulp and take another step back, my ass comes in contact with the edge of his desk. I dare a look up at him, and he stares down at me with eyes that for some reason feel familiar and not because I see him every day at work. I can't place why I feel that way. He reaches his hand up. It lingers in the air for a second when the door opens. His hand drops to his side and I peer around him and notice Theo stepping into the office. Using the distraction, I scoot away and practically run from the office. Theo's eyes widen when he sees me, having not noticed me when he stepped in. He moves out of my way as I bolt from the room.

Closing the door behind me, I return to my desk and melt into my seat where my coffee waits, my heart pounds in my chest. I can't figure out what just happened, but I know one thing: the way he moved and silently stood there staring at me, made a knot form in my stomach.

Something happened under his gaze. I'm not sure what it is, but it's definitely new, it sent thrills through me and fear at the same time. Something dangerous is behind the way he looks at me. That thought alone scares me.

The day passes by slowly. I resist the urge to jump whenever Theo comes and goes. I'm not comfortable with either of them, not after that strange encounter. But Theo is actively avoiding me for some reason. He barely even looks in the direction of my desk, just darts past and never lingers like he usually does. When it hits 4:30 Tobias walks out of his office and places a document on my desk. "I need you to copy this and email it off to all employees, and this is your copy for future reference," he says. I nod and he turns and walks away.

Glancing at the paper I notice it says changes to Medical Insurance Policy. Scanning over the page, I stop when I notice one of the clauses is amended effective immediately. I read it and nearly cry. This would have helped me and my mother so much, if only it was changed before the accident.

I'm glad though; this has the potential to help so many people. Tobias has changed the Medical Insurance Policy so if you don't have dependents or are single you can nominate one family member of your choosing to be on the policy with you. A lump forms in my throat as I get up.

I force back the tears that brim. I walk over to the printer and scan the documents in and walk back to my desk. I email every employee the document, letting them know of the changes to their Medical Insurance Policy. I receive a few emails back straight away from people who aren't exactly in my position but have family that could really benefit with this sort of help. Mark especially, his message coming back instantly excited about the changes. Mark is single like me but has a sibling with ongoing medical issues. Mark works in the lobby downstairs and is one of the first people I met when I started here. I have seen him a few times at the hospital with his sister. We have spoken a couple of times, saying how we wished our medical policies could cover our family members. I was expecting a reply from him. I knew he would be just as excited as I am for him.

Unfortunately for me it's too late. Mark though will at least get some help to support his sister. His message hits my email, and I quickly read it. "Is this real? Have they really changed the policy?"

I reply, "Yes, Tobias just gave it to me. The changes are effective immediately." I hit send before closing my email down. I know I will be bombarded with questions but figure I will deal with them tomorrow.

Tobias walks back out and nods his head at me before leaving for the day. I can't form words right now, so I just nod back. I don't trust my voice not to break at his thoughtfulness. Maybe he isn't as heartless as everyone thinks. Theo however, I don't see him leave. He must have snuck out when I was sending off emails.

I turn everything off, making sure to turn off all the lights and check to make sure I switched the phones over to voicemail. I then step into the elevator. Thanks to this one change, I'm truly proud to work for my employers and want to do the best job I can for them. I hope my stray is around, I want to hug him and tell him the great news.

TWELVE

Making my way down to the now empty garage, I open my door and rip the blazer off, jumping into some loose-fitting leggings. It's the weekend. I'll have two whole days of trying to fill the time. Just as I get comfortable, Tom walks up the ramp, a container in his hand. Tom opens my door and passes the container to me. "Hey, I forgot to give this to you. I heated it up on my way down. Mary made lasagna last night."

"Thanks Tom," I say, grabbing the hot container from his hand. The cheese, spices and meat scent fills my car, my mouth waters.

Tom leans against my car. "Eat, I have something to tell you."

Opening the container, I dig in. Tom even provides a fork and butter knife, my empty stomach welcomes the lasagna. Mary is a great cook. I can see why Tom is always so excited to get home to see what she made. Tom waits for me to have my mouth full before he speaks. Probably to stop me from cutting him off, forcing me to listen to him.

"Theo and Tobias know you're staying in the garage." I nearly choke on my food. My eyes widen. How? I'd been so careful! "I swear I didn't say anything," he says, holding his hands up in surrender. I don't know what to say. I have to move on but how? Where?

"How then if you didn't tell them?" I question, biting my lip. The hot food is too good for me to stop eating but my brain swims.

"I'm not sure. Tobias came and saw me today. I'm not sure how they found out, but he asked security to check the lower-level cameras, then came to see me when he realized every day I walk up to the top level and come back with you."

"What did you tell him?" I ask, horrified. They will fire me, I know it. I never should have stayed here, and now Tom is probably going to get into trouble because of me. I'll survive somehow, but I can't handle it if they fire Tom just for helping me.

"I told them the truth. You shouldn't have to struggle like this, Imogen." I nod my head in understanding. Tobias has done his homework and really got up in my business.

Is that why he changed the Medical Insurance Policies?

"I'll move on, I suppose I won't have a job on Monday. I really hope you didn't get in too much trouble, Tom. I never should have put you in that position," I apologize.

Tom holds up his hand, stopping me from continuing. "They aren't firing you. I think he wanted to help. He sounded genuinely concerned, which is odd, I know. That man is definitely terrifying, but he seems to have a soft spot for you."

I raise an eyebrow at the last part, Tobias possesses a soft spot? I find that impossible. I think back to all the times he has scolded or yelled at me. The way he ignores my presence half the time. Something has changed the last couple of weeks though, he has become more intense and watches me when he thinks I won't notice. Then I think about what happened today in his office. Soft isn't the way I'd describe that. I think back to the meeting when he dressed me like a child.

My face burns up at the memory, making me feel self-conscious and embarrassed. "I don't need their help. I manage just fine on my own," I mutter.

Tom shakes his head. "Please, Imogen, if they want to help let them."

"They have helped plenty. My job is enough help, that is if they don't fire me. I'll move on somewhere else, so he doesn't harass you, and you don't get in any further trouble, Tom. Really, I'm fine. It is only temporary." I force a bright smile at him. I want him to relax, let me deal with this news on my own.

"Always the same excuse. You are too stubborn for your own good. You know that?" Tom shakes his head at me, concern still shining in his kind eyes.

I just nod and eat the lasagna. Tom waits for me to finish and takes the container for me. I decide to wait for him to head back inside before I pack the car up. Turning the car on, I check the fuel. The fuel light is on. My next best option is the storage locker. The compound is pretty large, and I might just ask the locker company if I can store my car there. I know it will cost an extra forty dollars a week, but what choice do I have? That will leave me twenty-seven dollars a week to live off. It will be tight, but I can survive on that.

I remind myself this is only temporary, that I can do this for the next couple years. Pulling out of the garage, I drive the couple blocks to the storage locker parking just inside the compound behind the gates. Getting out, I make my way to my locker.

Maneuvering and restacking half the storage locker, I make enough room that I can use my blankets to make a makeshift sleeping quarters. At least this won't be as cramped as the car. My only concern is being crushed to death by falling boxes and furniture. Grabbing my washing bucket, I make my way out to my car, grabbing my dirty laundry. I fill the bucket and go to a nearby tap and fill the bucket with cold water. I found my shampoo at least. I'm out of laundry powder, but it's easier to wash clothes in the shampoo anyway. At least I don't have to scrub so hard to make the crystals dissolve.

I go back to my storage locker, pull the door down behind me, and hand scrub my clothes before hanging them on coat hangers along the wall where the fire sprinklers hang in case there's fire, using it as a makeshift clothesline. Unfortunately, there's no saving the camisole. The bloody garment won't return to white no matter how hard I scrub, the blood has set.

I take the bucket back out and empty it on the grass. Sensing eyes on me, I glance up and come eye to eye with the stray. I can't help the gasp and the involuntary jump back. Rolling my eyes at my foolish reaction, I call him over. "How did you find me?" I ask. Of course, he doesn't answer. I pet his head before standing up. "Come on then," I say, patting my leg trying to get him to follow. He tilts his head to the side and his ears perk up before he follows after.

The weekend passes by in a blur. I remain for the most part inside my storage locker, only leaving occasionally to stretch my legs. The stray came and went but would always come back at night, which I was always happy to see. Although he took up most of my makeshift bed, he acted like a hot water bottle. His temperature was always hot like he had a fever. I just put it down to the fact he's an oversized dog and all the fur makes him warmer than usual.

When Monday morning comes I get dressed and lift the roller door. The stray runs off. I assume he needs to pee, only he doesn't return before I have to leave. Walking through the woods that back the park, I make my way to the entrance of Kane and Madden Industries. Tom waits outside for me this time, instead of in the garage. I smile when I see him waiting patiently. "Hey Tom." I wave while walking up to him. "How was your weekend?" I ask.

"Great. I went and played golf, probably one of the few things I'm actually good at." He beams. "And yours?" he asks.

"Fine, I have a new friend. Well not the human kind. More the four-legged furry kind that likes to growl and whine. He just keeps coming back." Tom looks a little confused. "It's a dog, Tom, what did you think I meant?"

Tom shakes his head. "Oh, nothing dear, I was just a little shocked. I thought you meant a person not a pet."

"I don't know if you could really call him a pet. He comes and goes as he pleases and takes up my bed, but he keeps me warm." I laugh.

Tom seems lost in thought for a moment, before nodding. "That's great, shall we head inside?" I nod and follow Tom in. When I reach the elevator, just as the door is about to close, a hand stops it. Theo steps in. I look out expecting Tobias to be behind him but can't see him. This never happens, they always come up together.

"You are early today. Where is Tobias?" I ask.

Theo watches me for a few seconds. He looks nice and very casual today, wearing jeans and a buttoned up shirt. Vanilla and sandalwood drifts from his body. I resist the urge to close my eyes and sway towards him. It's an amazing smell, and also how Tobias always smells. I move farther away, my heart hammers in my chest, and my stomach tightens. I have never had this reaction to him before. He moves as far away from me as the tight space allows, but I can tell from the darkening of his eyes whatever this tension is between us, he feels it too. What might have happened if Tom weren't there? I shiver at the thought.

CHAPTER
THIRTEEN

"Tobias is busy, he will be in a little later," he tells me. I just nod and look away. As soon as the door opens Theo walks out and straight to his office. Thank God I have done my hair and make-up in the car. That was the most awkward exchange we have ever had. It's like he couldn't get away from me fast enough.

Going to my desk, I switch the computer on and turn the phones over when I bump my hip on the edge of the table. I hiss at the jolt of pain, my eyes almost cross at the sudden flare. I have been cleaning it regularly and changing the dressing, but it's taking a long time to heal, and I'm reminded of my infection worry. Checking Theo is still in his office, I sneak over to the small bathroom. I haven't checked it since yesterday.

Pulling my blouse up, I peel back the bandage. The edge is stuck and I can feel the fabric pulling at the edge of the wound. It starts bleeding. Grabbing a tissue, I dab at it. It's definitely infected. I should have just tried to sew it myself.

My skin is red and angry with traces of pus oozing from the center, and the edges just won't close together. The slightest bump makes it reopen. The door bursts open, I drop my shirt, covering myself, but it's too late. Theo sees my battle wound in the mirror above the sink. His face contorts before he drops his gaze to the ground. His jaw clenches and I can see the vein in his head near his temple pulse. I'm positive I locked the door. How did he get in?

I lift my head up and he meets my gaze. His eye is twitching and that vein is pulsing. What is he angry about? He's the one that walked in on me! Ignoring my stunned expression, he walks over and lifts the corner of my blouse, exposing my wound. "How did you do that?" He demands, staring into my eyes.

My ears have to be playing tricks on me, because I swear I hear him say something else but his lips barely move. "I knew I smelled blood." I look back wondering if I heard what I think I did, but he's inspecting the slash across my hip. "I asked how did you do this?" He snaps at me.

What a weird turn of events, the mean one has turned gentle and the nice one is growling like an animal at me.

"On a piece of wire," I reply, glancing away from his eyes.

"When?" He stresses. I try to pull my shirt down, to hide the wound. I'm taking care of it, I don't need him. He pushes my hand aside, "This is infected, come with me," he says, grabbing my hand and tugging me towards his office. He makes a phone call, talking so fast into the phone I don't catch a word of what he says. "Sit," he orders. I sit down, not knowing what else to do. I don't want to get in any more trouble than I know I'm already in. I'd be grateful if they don't fire me after learning I have been trespassing for months in the garage, on their company property.

I don't know how long we wait. Him staring at me, and me trying to do everything but meet his eyes. After an eternity, a man walks in, he has a white doctor's coat on and scrubs underneath. He carries a huge box that I assume is a medical kit. Theo motions towards me and I stand up before the doctor pushes me towards the couch. "Lay down, Imogen," Theo orders, I wince at his tone. He's furious, but what have I done?

I quickly obey and the doctor lifts my shirt. He doesn't say a word to me. He pulls the side of my pants down, exposing my hip. He prods the area with his fingertips, eyes focused on my reaction. I manage to only swallow instead of whimper like I want to. He doesn't exactly have a gentle bedside manner. Nodding to himself, he gathers some supplies from his bag and gets to work. He cleans the wound, a lot more aggressively than I have prior to this. The alcohol burns and I clench my eyes shut to keep from breaking down. He pulls out a needle next. I jump up, but Theo forces me back, his hands on my shoulders pushing me back down. "Don't make me hold you down," he challenges. I relax my shoulders and muster up what courage I have. He can't fire me after all this torture at least.

"This may hurt," the doctor warns me. I nod and focus on his face while he goes to work stitching me up. The doctor is maybe thirty years old at most, not that old at all for a doctor. He has dark hair and brown eyes the same color as mud. He tries to be gentle, but it doesn't stop the hurt and sting, my hands begin to sweat, he stops a few times when I wriggle too much. One look from Theo though makes me freeze.

When he finishes, he places waterproof gauze over the top and stands up. Rummaging through his bag, he hands me a bottle of pills. "Take these three times a day, they will help clear up the infection. You'll probably want some pain pills as well, you let it get pretty bad. Take what you need to fight the fever and drink plenty of water." I grab the small bottle and read it, Cephalexin, an antibiotic. I nod and look up to say thanks, but he's already gone.

Theo however watches me. "Why didn't you get that looked at earlier? You could have avoided all this," he motions with his hand. He sounds angry and I drop my eyes to the floor. Wait, this is what he's angry at me about? The wound?

"Because I hate hospitals," I answer in a soft voice, almost a whisper. Theo steps closer, his hand guiding my chin forcing me to look at him. His eyes search mine for any deception. I don't know what he sees but he lets go and walks out, leaving me standing in his office.

Left alone, I make my way back to my desk and sit down. I answer emails and phones. Theo strolls back about three hours later and places a glass of water on the desk. "Your antibiotics, take them then eat this. Come and see me when you are done, I need to speak to you. Tobias will be back soon," I nod.

He shoves the glass in my hand and waits for me to swallow the tablets down, before shoving a sandwich in my hand, it's a BLT. He slides a container of steam towards me as well. I open it to inspect and he walks away. The sandwich is great, but I'm not expecting chicken noodle soup. The fragrant broth and the giant chunks of chicken make me drool.

Regardless, I eat quickly, not wanting to make him wait. I just want to get the scolding over with and hopefully still have a job after. Nerves kick in as I walk towards his office. I go to knock when he opens the door and motions for me to sit down across from him at his desk. Taking my seat, I go to apologize and beg for him not to fire me. "Just wait, Tobias will be here in a second."

No sooner has a second passed and in walks Tobias. He walks over to us and places his hands on either side of the chair I'm sitting in, towering over me. I look up and swallow. Losing my train of thought, I'm completely stunned by his mesmerizing eyes. He has on a black suit but for the first time, no tie. His shirt buttons are undone, revealing his chest. I can tell he has a tattoo but can't tell what it is.

"We need to talk," he says, his voice like velvet. I have to remember to breathe. When I look straight ahead towards Theo, he has moved. He sits on the edge of the desk between my legs. I gulp, my fear consuming me. Usually, Theo is more laid back, but even he right now is towering over me, making me feel even smaller. Tobias's heat seeps into my skin through my back. His breath paints my neck, he's that close.

Tobias' hands slip from the seat to grip my shoulders. His hands travel down, gliding down my arms. Everywhere he touches goosebumps rise on my exposed skin. He stops just above my elbows. I shiver involuntarily, Theo notices my reaction and smirks. His eyes darken a little, and I find my eyes locked on his. I struggle to look away, only managing to break my gaze when Tobias' hands travel back up to my shoulders. His warm fingers brush my hair off my shoulder. Looking up, his face is barely an inch from mine. He looks like he's in a trance, his eyes glazed over as his fingers brush the sides of my neck, gliding lightly over the skin there.

Something swells within me, coming alive. Sparks move along my skin and my lips part. A moan escapes, shocking not only me but Tobias. I quickly cover my mouth with my hands, stunned by my reaction to his warm hands sliding across my skin. It makes me wonder if the rest of him feels that way as well. I'm back to having inappropriate thoughts about them again, both of them, and their touch just makes the wheels of fantasy turn faster.

I go to escape, and Tobias pulls himself together and walks over to Theo who stays perched on the end of his desk. He just watches the entire thing and hasn't tried to stop it.

Tobias takes a seat beside him. They both stare for a second at me before Theo speaks. "We know you have been staying in the garage, don't try to deny it. We have spoken to Tom who verified." I want to apologize and beg for my job. Yeah, pathetic I know but my job is the only thing I have left, I can't afford to lose that too when they keep going. "Where are you staying now?" Theo demands.

I try to come up with a believable lie. I suck at lying. I'd never be a good poker player. How the hell am I going to lie to them and not give myself away?

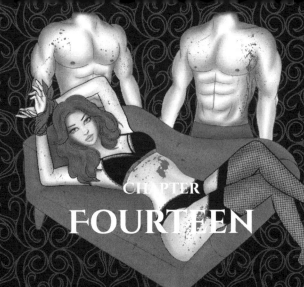

CHAPTER
FOURTEEN

Tobias beats me to it by answering first, "She's staying at the storage lockers a block from here." He turned me in! Tobias' eyes dare me to try and lie, I know better than to try.

How does he know though? I've been so careful. No one knows, not even the manager as it was a weekend, and I hadn't even had a chance to tell him that my car needs to be stored there.

My hands turn clammy, and a bead of sweat runs down the back of my neck. Has someone turned on the heater? I'm panicking, my heart rate rises, and I hear the pounding inside my head. I'm about to be fired. I'll lose the last piece of normalcy left in my life. Then what? I don't know what I will do. File bankruptcy maybe? Try and get a job at Costco. Every answer isn't enough. I can never pay my debt back at another job.

"I'm sorry, please don't fire me. I need this job." My words sound pathetic and desperate. But I don't have a choice, they are.

If I lose my job, I'll have nothing. Maybe they should fire me. I just wish they would speak instead of staring at me. They make my anxiety go through the roof. I know what is coming, just get it over with already. Rip that band-aid off quickly.

"We aren't firing you, Imogen. We are just disappointed you didn't say anything earlier. We could have helped sooner." Theo scolds me.

I drop my head in my hands, and relief floods through me, making me giddy. I'm not going to lose my job! But how can they help? I got myself in this situation, I can get myself out of it. I don't want help. They need to let me be, I can handle this.

"I promise I won't trespass again." I do my best to take back my professional persona. They both stare at me like they think what I'm saying is absurd. I suppose it kind of is, who lives where they work? Not a normal person, but hey I never claimed to be normal.

"No, you won't. I spoke to Tom who said you would refuse any help, so I took it upon myself to not give you a choice," Tobias informs me. He too has returned to his business self. I stare blankly at him, trying to understand.

"I don't understand," I blurt. Okay, I lost the whole professional thing but this is really weird! I'm getting seriously weird vibes from both men and I don't know how to handle it.

"You won't be staying at the storage locker either. Actually, there is no longer a storage locker. I have told him to not let you back, and I took the liberty to move all your belongings to your apartment," Tobias continues.

"I don't have an apartment?" I tell him, confused. Where has he taken my stuff?

"I have moved you into our apartment building. You will be staying on the floor below us. This is nonnegotiable and if you don't accept our help, I will fire you," he replies. He folds his hands over his knee like the matter is solved.

Why would Tom say that to them? They are dangling my job above my head like a carrot on a string.

I cross my arms across my chest, defiant. This is absurd. I have barely had any contact with them outside the workplace, and now they are telling me I have to accept their offer of help to keep my job. Why the sudden interest in my life? Did Tobias follow me after work on Friday? I just can't wrap my head around how he knows where I moved to.

I don't have a choice at the moment. "Fine," I say through gritted teeth. This is so degrading and embarrassing. I have never accepted a handout, and it's killing me inside that I'm being forced to.

Tobias nods, accepting my answer. "Theo will take you home and help you unpack. I will see you in the morning." He chuckles for some unknown reason. I raise an eyebrow at him. Theo motions for me to follow and I do. Walking into the foyer, Theo grabs my handbag that I keep under my desk and helps himself into it, fishing out my keys.

"We will go get your car from the storage locker, then head to your new apartment." I roll my eyes at him but follow anyway. What else can I do? The elevator trip down to the ground floor is silent, I don't want to speak to him. When the doors open, Theo grabs my hand and pulls me towards the exit. I must admit I like his big hand holding mine. Weird, it is a little chilly. I would have imagined it to be hot. He keeps rubbing circles into the back of my hand while he tugs me along.

He walks through the park cutting through the woods taking my short cut towards the storage facility. Has he been this way before? I can't really picture Theo in his suit just marching through here, and what possible reason would he have to walk through the woods to a storage facility in the first place? It is literally the only thing there on the other side of the small forest.

He moves too fast for me, I jog to keep up with his long strides. When we come to the mesh fence, he stops. He sniffs the air for a second. I observe him closely, it is such a strange thing to do, but if it's a tick, I don't want to embarrass him. I open my mouth to tell him where the entry is, when he spins around and strides towards the broken bit of fence. He pauses and runs his fingers over a piece of wire that sticks out. The same wire that slashed me open. I'm filled with the desire to find a pair of wire clippers and kill the thing for causing me all this trouble. It doesn't make sense but I have nowhere else to vent my rage.

"I take it this is where you received that cut?" Theo questions, pulling me from my violent wire-ripping daydreams. I nod to his question, but stop, how did he know that? I can barely see any blood on it. Shaking my thoughts out of my head, he pulls the mesh aside and I step through the opening. He pauses, grabbing that bit of wire and snapping it off from the fence like it is a stick. Huh, maybe my blood weakened the wire or something? Not wanting to be left behind, I hurry to catch up again.

I walk over to my car, which is still sitting in the garage inside. I turn to retrieve my keys, knowing I'll have to use my last twenty dollars in my account to put fuel in my beast. I'll just have to survive on water until payday. What other choice do I have? I turn around with my hand out, and wait.

Theo cocks his head to the side, examining my car. "This is what you drive? It has more dents than a golf ball." I roll my eyes at him and snatch my keys from his hand. Unlocking my car, I walk around to the passenger side. Theo follows and watches as I frantically try to clean the passenger floorboard.

I toss clothes and empty bottles of liquor over the seat and into the back. When I finish, I stand back and motion for him to get in. I'm tempted to bow like he's some prince, but my side hurts too much for that kind of childish behavior.

"What?" I snap when he just stands there staring. He's probably never taken a ride in a vehicle like this. So what, it's his fault about this entire situation. Him and Tobias both are determined to ruin my life and I can't do anything about it since they hold my job captive.

He shakes his head and climbs in. The seat is scooted all the way forward and his knees are nearly pressed to his chest. He pulls the lever to slide the chair back but grabs the wrong one and is thrown backwards with enough force for his head to bounce off the headrest and he's stuck in a reclining position. I snort, laughing at his unamused face.

He looks funny enough crammed into my tiny car. But this? This is comedy gold. I'm loving every minute of it. He cocks his eyebrow, not finding the funny side. I slam the door and walk over to the driver's side and hop in. Theo adjusts the chair and finally manages to get the seat to slide back, giving him enough room to put his legs down. Regardless, he looks squished in my Civic and everytime I glance over, I chuckle to myself.

Putting the key in the ignition, I turn it over. My car starts and the fuel light turns on. Pulling out, I drive to the closest gas station. Theo glances around my car, studying the loads of crap I have stored in it. He opens the glovebox, well, that's rude. I try to warn him, but it's too late. Paperwork that I'd stuffed in there shoots out like a confetti all over him, his lap, and the floor. I snort while laughing again and he slowly turns towards me. Theo holds up the glove compartment door in his hand that's no longer attached to the car.

I stop laughing and rub my dash. "You have to be gentle with her. Stop going through everything." I want to add he's being nosy but keep it to myself. He's still my boss and I'm probably in enough trouble for openly laughing at him twice now.

"Gentle? There is nothing gentle about this car. What did you do to it? It's falling apart at the seams. I'm surprised it even runs." He clicks his tongue and shakes his head.

How dare he! My baby has got me through too much to be talked about like that. "Leave my car alone. Hey, I said stop going through my stuff!" I growl as he rummages through the back. Turning back to the front, he holds out a pair of my panties and an empty bottle of vodka. I see red.

"Looks like someone was having fun back there," he chuckles, swinging them around on his finger. I snatch my panties out of his hand. I seriously consider taking the empty bottle and bashing it over his head. What right does he have to go through my things? My panties! Thank God he didn't grab a used pair. I can only imagine what Mr. Sniffer would do with that. How could I ever fantasize about this asshole? I jerk the wheel and turn, making my car squeal from the mistreatment but at least I get to see Theo be crushed against the window, his eyes wide at the suddenness of it all. Serves him right! I park by a pump and pop the cap as I scramble out and away from him.

I fill it up, trying to calm myself down, completely ignoring Theo. He can rust inside the car as far as I care. At this point I don't even care if he wants to fire me. He pushed me too far. The tank clicks, letting me know it's full and I set everything back, prepared to go spend the last of my funds to feed the beast. Hopefully, this apartment of theirs won't be too far that I spend all my income on gas. I can survive on water for one week, but more than that and I'll be the one in the hospital.

Just as I reach the station doors, out steps Theo. "Come on, I paid already. Let's see if that death trap will start again." He says, ignoring me and walking past me towards my car. I watch him open the driver side door and slide in and my eye twitches. Maybe I should be grateful he paid for the gas, but his smugness is just too much to deal with after the day I had.

"You don't know where we are going, hand the keys over." I look down at my keys clutched in my hand. "I'll be gentle, I promise," he says, emphasizing the word gentle and rubbing my car's dash. I throw my keys at his chest, which he easily catches and scramble into the passenger side. The drive to the apartment block isn't long, only about ten-minutes. So the gas will be able to last a while at least. When we pull up to the front of the apartment block, I gasp.

The place looks like some fancy hotel. All white with beautiful hedges and gardens full of roses. It also has a roundabout driveway with a valet out front.

Theo pulls up next to the man. The guy's lip curls when Theo tosses him the keys. I feel more embarrassed knowing a stranger is going to see the state of my car. Shit, the panties! I wrench around in my seat and grab the damned things, cramming them into my pocket. I can't find my bag for some reason.

Theo walks over to my side of the car, my handbag slung over his shoulder like he owns it. Reaching towards me, he grabs my hand and pulls me toward the entrance. There's no other choice but to follow him and see what else awaits me on this horrible day.

FIFTEEN

O nce inside, Theo pulls me towards a desk sitting in the large foyer. Is this how it's going to be from now on, Theo just pulling me wherever he wants me like I'm some damned pet? Off the side of the desk are some elevators, I can see my own reflection in the stainless-steel doors. Suffice to say, I have something else to be embarrassed about. I look down feeling very out of place. Theo is talking to the receptionist. The place is indeed like a hotel with its red and gold décor and thick black carpets.

Turning around, Theo thanks the woman, who's eyeing me with the fakest smile plastered on her face. "Come, the movers left every-thing in the apartment." I follow after him. I'm on the bottom floor, which I'm relieved about, as I always thought apartment buildings were fire traps.

Stopping in front of a black door, Theo pops the key in and opens the door. He strides in and turns the lights on. Stepping inside, the room is spacious, the carpets are a dark smoky gray color with lighter gray walls and white trim. A bookshelf sits on the wall in the living room. The place is open plan, and I can see the marble counters in the kitchen at the back of the apartment from the living room.

There are three doors that Theo walks over to, opening them one after the other like he's some stage magician. One is a huge bathroom with large black tiles on the floor and gray tiles on the walls. The bathroom has a large shower that can easily fit a few people and a garden bathtub off to the side. I'm not looking forward to having to scrub those tiles. It may be pretty to look at but it's going to be a real bitch to clean.

Door number two is a laundry room complete with a washer and dryer. The last room is a bedroom which has a huge king-sized bed in the middle and a smaller bathroom off to the side. Walking in, I look around, there's also a walk-in closet and double doors that lead to a small courtyard, complete with outside table and chairs.

Come to think of it, I don't recognize any of the furniture but did recognize my messy handwriting on the boxes that are stacked in the living room, kitchen, and bedroom.

"What did you do with my mother's furniture?" I ask, bile rises in my throat at the thought of it being thrown away. I don't care about the furniture really, only one particular piece, the dining table which my grandfather had made. My mother's father was a carpenter before he died and had made a huge dining table that my mother had adored and had hand-carved an intricate floral design into the top and on the legs.

Theo, seeing my panicked expression, quickly answers. "It's in our shed at a property we own just outside the city. Why? Something you need? I can go retrieve it for you." I shake my head, relief floods me that it hasn't just been discarded like trash.

"No, but the dining table was my mother's. Her father made it for her."

"I promise it is safe, now what do you think? Do you like it?"

I do like it, and that's what burns me up, I don't want to like it. I don't want to admit I'd sleep better and be far safer than I have been in the parking garage. Grudgingly, I give in as he waits for an answer. "I do like it, although I think it's a bit much. But thank you," I tell him. The place is beautiful, but it isn't like home. I will miss the storage locker, the garage, and my car. It has been home for so long now, I'm uncomfortable with so much space. But one thing I don't miss is not having a toilet within a few steps, or hot water. And I definitely won't miss freezing my ass off in the underground garage shower or having to run through the dark underground garage just to pee.

Theo opens boxes and pulls stuff out. He has unpacked the entire kitchen by the time I have unpacked one box. I get too busy looking over old photos of me and my mom.

God, I miss her. Putting some of her personal belongings into my new room, I try on one of her jackets. It still has her perfume on it. I remember the last time I saw her wear it. I'm getting choked up. Memories are threatening to overwhelm me. I take it off before sniffling and rubbing at my eyes, stopping any tears from falling that are starting to brim.

Walking back out, I hear a knock on the door before the handle twists and in steps Tobias. "I thought I would stop in and see how you're doing with unpacking." I walk towards Theo, who has just opened a box of books. How can he move through everything so fast?

"Theo has mostly done it. I have been too busy looking through photos." I admit.

Tobias nods and walks over toward Theo and kisses his cheek. I blinked at the display. "I thought you said you weren't gay."

"We aren't gay." Tobias replies. His eyes are twinkling in the lights. "But we never said we didn't like each other," he chuckles at me.

I smile back. It's so different seeing them acting like normal people instead of just my bosses. Though in Theo's case, I kind of miss my normal boss. It will take a while to get over how he treated my baby. "Why? Does it bother you?" Asks Tobias.

Theo's head jerks up to study me. He holds some books that need sorting in his hand, but pauses to hear my answer.

"No, the opposite, actually. Doesn't bother me at all," I state. I won't admit seeing them together kind of turns me on in a weird way. Theo reads the back of one of the books he has in his hand, while Tobias pulls books out and stacks them on the bookshelf.

"You like fantasy novels?" Theo questions.

"I wouldn't own them if I didn't." I'm proud of my little bookshelf. Some of my favorite authors are up here.

They insist on sorting the entire thing while I sit on the black leather couch and watch them. Theo sits in an armchair opposite me, a book still clutched in his hand. "You can borrow it if you want," I tell him. "It might not be your cup of tea though." I hide my smile by turning my attention to the windows. My lips twitch.

"Why do you say that?" He asks, flicking through the pages. My face heats up, suddenly feeling a little embarrassed as he gets closer to the end.

"Because it's a spicy reverse harem book." I point out. At their blank stare I sigh, "You know, erotic romance?"

"You read erotica books?" Tobias questions. He doesn't laugh at me, that's interesting.

"I read anything that piques my interest, but yes, I like erotica novels and mainly fantasy, horror, and romance novels. Why? Does that bother you?" I throw Tobias' own words at him. His lips turn up into a smile before he looks over at Theo who's also smiling. "No, just an interesting thing to read, I was curious."

"If you do borrow it, I expect you to return it in one piece. That's a signed copy of Moonlight Muse, she's one of my favorites."

Tobias chuckles. "Her Forbidden Alpha." He reads the title to Theo who shrugs.

"I'll still borrow it. Coffee?" Asks Theo, changing the topic. I go to get up, but Tobias pulls me back down beside him on the couch.

"You're not a secretary here, Imogen." He says the words softly but his eyes are dark. Without Theo around, it's hard to breathe again.

Theo rummages through the kitchen cupboards, which apparently, they have filled. How strange would it be to have hot food whenever I want it? To be able to just poke around the fridge and not have to force myself to eat something questionable before it goes bad? I'm honestly excited about it.

"So, do you believe in all that supernatural stuff you read about?" Theo calls from the kitchen.

That's a bit of a weird question. He's more interested in the supernatural element than one woman being drilled several different ways by multiple men? "I don't know. Some, yes. I believe some things, others not so much. I believe there has to be some truth to some of it. People surely couldn't have imagined it all," I tell him.

"What about werewolves?" Tobias questions from beside me.

My eyebrows furrow, confused at the sudden interest in mythical creatures. "Do I believe in people turning into dogs?" I ask, trying not to laugh. "Is this some sort of psych evaluation? I can assure you I am not off with the pixies, and for the most part I'm sane."

Tobias goes to say something else but stops. Theo brings coffees over, placing them on the glass coffee table in front of us. We drink our coffees in silence. After a while, Tobias stands up and so does Theo. "Well, we will leave you to it. We will be upstairs if you need us," Theo says after the silence starts to become a little awkward.

I walk them to the door, and Theo drops the apartment keys into my hand and winks. As they are leaving, I ask, "Where did the man take my car? I need to get something from the trunk." Tobias freezes before turning to look at me. He crosses his arms across his chest.

"In the underground garage. Just take the elevator down," Theo says. Tobias eyes me, like he knows what it is I want from the trunk and is disapproving. I step back, his glare makes fear bubble up and give me goosebumps. His sudden mood change makes me want to run, anything to get away from his piercing blue eyes, which are burning with simmering rage. Theo nudges him questionably. Tobias shakes himself, obviously not realizing the effect he's having on me, he turns and walks away, leaving me staring after them confused at why he's angry.

Shutting the door, I walk around the place and started flickering lights off, only leaving the kitchen and living room one on. Grabbing my keys, I step out of the apartment and make my way to the elevator. Hopping inside, I hit the button for the underground garage.

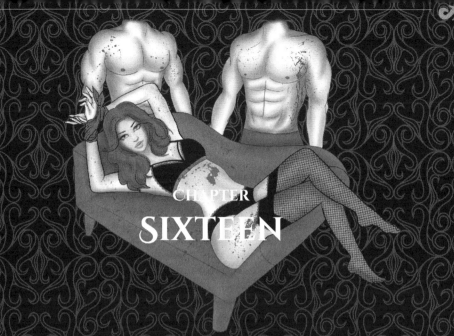

CHAPTER
SIXTEEN

Going down in the elevator, the doors open into a dark underground garage. I walk the aisles of cars, trying to find my little beast. The entire time I walk, I can't escape the weird sensation of someone watching me. You'd think I'd be used to this sensation by now, but it still gives me the creeps.

I pick up my pace, finally finding my car right at the back in a more deserted part of the garage. Reaching my car, I pop the key in the trunk and unlock it. Pushing it open, all the hairs on the back of my neck rise, the feeling of being watched won't leave and sends goosebumps all over my body.

How many times have I looked before, only to be greeted with nothing? There's no way I'm wasting time over this paranoia. Reaching into the trunk, I grab the liquor, careful to hold the bottom of the worn box so the bottles don't fall through to the ground. I don't relish the idea of chasing them everywhere. Closing the trunk with my elbow, I place the box on the back of the vehicle before unlocking the driver's door. I need to get my hair straightener and dirty laundry out from the bag on the back seat where it has lived for too long.

Wind races past my legs that stick out of the door while I lean into the cab. I'm not being paranoid this time, something is down here with me. I turn slowly, not trying to entice whatever it is into attacking me. But once more, nothing is there.

My heart pumps hard, my adrenaline floods through me preparing me to either fight or run for my life. I reach into the box of liquor and grab a bottle, it isn't much of a weapon, but I can swing at anyone who tries anything. Whoever is here, won't find me easy prey. I snatch everything I need, scurry back to the trunk and throw the bag inside the box and seal it again. I grab it and turn to head back up to the apartment.

Before I can even finish my turn, a gust of wind tickles the back of my neck. I yelp, swinging my box around prepared to do battle. Theo watches me, an indecipherable expression on his face, he catches my box in his arms. Okay, maybe that isn't the best weapon I could have thought of.

Damn it, Theo! "For god's sake, don't sneak up on people. You nearly gave me a heart attack," I scold. I hold a hand to my still wildly fluctuating heart.

"Sorry, I didn't mean to scare you, I just saw you and thought I would see if you needed a hand."

"What are you doing down here?" I ask. Just saw me? He knew I was going down here. Why is he following me like this?

"Nothing, I was getting something from my car." He replies so calmly, like it's common knowledge or something. I doubt his explanation, I've seen his car on the floor above this level. Why would he come all the way down a level, let alone be able to see me at my car? I step forward, and grab my box back from him. I pull away not wanting him to see what's in it, suddenly feeling like he won't approve. Not that I need his approval, I'm well above the legal drinking age. When I don't pass him back the box, he frowns faintly at me.

"Pass it back, it's too heavy for you," he says, moving closer. He makes me uncomfortable. I back up, back towards the elevator, box snugly against my chest. When I reach the elevator, I maneuver the box enough to twist my hand to jab the button. The elevator dings and opens, giving me a chance to escape this ominous pressure. Theo strolls in first, standing in the small space, waiting for me to enter. Squeezing in, I press the button to the first floor. My back is to Theo, the box in my arms forces me closer to him to allow the doors to shut. His breath tickles the back of my neck, only his breath is cold, too cold. I shiver involuntarily.

"So, what's in the box that you don't want me to see?" His voice is by my ear. I jump and glance his way, his face is only a few centimeters off mine. His mesmerizing eyes capture me. I try to pull away, but I am frozen. I can't think straight, all I can focus on is his velvet voice. My body relaxes, and I can't tear my eyes away from his. Is this what it feels like to be hypnotized? Will he ask me to do something and I won't be able to resist?

Theo moves closer, his lips are so close. All I have to do is lean forward and they'd meet mine. I have the urge to give in, I want to kiss him and see where it takes us. I stare at his lips, licking my own.

Theo doesn't give me the chance to make the decision. He moves first, leaning in and softly his lips barely brush mine. A teasing smile creeps its way onto his face and his eyes sparkle at me.

I open my mouth to answer him, to ask why when the elevator doors ding, signaling our arrival back to the first floor. Theo pulls back, a mischievous smile on his face, and I shake my head trying to understand what just happened. Did I imagine it? I could have got lost in his hypnotic eyes for hours and not noticed the time pass by. Shaking my head, I step out of the elevator.

"Goodnight Imogen." Theo's words snap me from my daze.

"Night," I whisper, my brain foggy. Theo's arrival, the offer of help, the kiss, it's just too much to process. I feel like I'm a cartoon character - I have smoke pouring from my ears.

I stumble back to the apartment, the box held close to me. The receptionist glares at me as I pass by. No more fake welcoming smiles now that I don't have Theo or Tobias around. Juggling the heavy box on my hip, I slip the key into the door and open it. I plop my loot down on a bench and fish the bag of dirty laundry out. I toss it in the washing machine, which even comes with its own detergent, before unpacking my hair straightener and my make up bag in the bathroom. Walking back out, I grab the first bottle I lay my hands on and pop the cap. Pouring a large glass, I mosey back over to the couch and get comfortable. I turn the TV on, flipping through the channels till I find the local news station.

I sit there for hours, sipping my drink and gradually chipping away at the bottle until it's half empty. I reach to pour another glass and notice the heft is off on the bottle of tequila. Oops, I'd probably had enough at this point. I get up to put the alcohol away when the room spins around me, making me feel like I stumbled off a tea cup ride. I abandon the bottle and grab onto the counter, trying to hold myself steady. I kick the glass coffee table while righting myself and I wince at the dull throbbing pain.

Hobbling my way into the bedroom, I collapse backwards onto the king-sized bed. I enjoy the sensation of the bounce I get when my body hits the mattress. I want to throw my hands out and laugh, but I also don't want to risk getting really sick. I yawn hard, staring up at the ceiling, they live up there. I wince at my stench, I really need a shower, but this is just too comfortable. I'll take one in a few minutes.

Sunlight pours into my eyes and I wince, reaching for my cover to throw over my head. The stupid windshield seems to reflect that crap right at me in the mornings, and my alarm hasn't gone off so I know it's early. Wait, something's off, I blink hard and stretch my non sore body. I'm not in my car, or the storage unit.

I sit up and reach for my head as it throbs, a punishment from overdoing it last night. My whole night rushes back to me and I groan, dropping my face into my hands. I really need that shower now. I stretch, and hobble out of bed. My alarm hasn't gone off, but here I am up again just in time for 7. I'm a human alarm clock by this point.

Forcing myself up, I jump into the shower. I sigh and relax under the hot stream of water, my skin turning pink from the heat. This is heaven. Finally, hot water that isn't restricted I can get as close to burning as I want and just let it pound into my tight muscles. I haven't had a shower this hot in months. The memories of the showers at the hospital and the parking garage fade away. I stretch my back in the shower, moaning at just how good it feels, this is better than sex. Granted, it has been more than a while since my last sexual encounter, but still. Unless it's Theo and Tobias in here with me all soaped up in the middle, I don't see how anything could be more perfect in this solitary moment of bliss.

Spending far more time than necessary in the shower, I reluctantly get out and notice the time. No! I'm going to be late at this rate! I race around, trying to find something decent to wear for work, settling on some black slacks and a white button up blouse. It's strange, having my clothes all hung up, waiting for me to pick them.

Everything looks so crisp, and I'm pretty sure there are clothes in there I've never owned before. I finish getting dressed and work on my makeup, without having to worry about using a small mirror or worrying about jabbing my eye out because someone comes up behind me.

I finish straightening my hair, slip on my tan heels and retrieve my purse and car keys. My hand is on the doorknob when I hear two sharp knocks. No one knows I live here, who could it be? I open the door and stare at the two gorgeous men outside of it. Theo has the same sly smirk from last night that I just want to smack off of him. My cheeks burn at just the memory of the whole incident. I duck my head so they can't see the blush stealing across my features. "Morning?" I say.

Tobias's eyes are hard, glaring down at me, making me take a step back into the apartment. "Morning," his voice is colder than usual. I can tell he's angry about something, I'm just not sure what has him in such a mood so early in the day. Have I forgotten something when getting ready?

"Come on, let's get to work," Theo says. He throws his arm over my shoulder like we are best buddies. Tobias' jaw clenches and unclenches out of the corner of my eye. How have I managed to make him even more upset? "I thought you could come to work with us. I don't trust that car of yours," Theo tells me.

I roll my eyes. "There is nothing wrong with my car, you are just a snob," I scold. This man will never understand what it's like to live by a certain means. He pulls me in closer, squeezing my shoulder before letting me go completely and letting me walk by myself. I follow them out to their car, the sleek blue BMW M340 which is waiting out the front. The valet tosses the keys and Tobias catches them in the air before walking around to the driver's side.

My hand is on the rear handle when Tobias speaks. "No, in front, with me." I looked back but Theo had already hopped in the back-seat. Can this be any worse of a start to my day? I take a seat beside Tobias and do my best to not make him anymore upset with me.

Tobias is a demon, of the speed demon variety. The man doesn't pull away as we drive out. No, he stomps his foot on the pedal and the car screams as we race through the city. He plays a game with weaving between the cars. Honks, screams, and curses meet my ears and I slump a little in my seat. Is this because he's mad at me, or is he always like this? Theo doesn't seem the least bit disturbed. Tobias swerves the car into a parking spot and stomps on the brakes. My head thumps against the headrest and I whimper at the whiplash. If either of them hear my complaint, they ignore it. Once safely stopped, I scramble out of the car, knees shaking. I've never been so grateful to get out of a vehicle before. There's no way I'm driving with him behind the wheel again. I'll walk home first, or try to summon my missing stray and ride him. Anything has to be better than this experience.

Tobias exits on his side and slams the door behind him, stalking off. I shiver at the palpable rage.

Theo chuckles, eyes on me, "He is just jealous at how well we get along." I can hear the mocking in his tone, I roll my eyes before following after.

My heels click on the ground as Theo and I race to keep up with the angry Tobias. Stepping in the elevator, I stand between Tobias and Theo. What is it with elevators? The smell of both their colognes fills the tight space. On one hand, Theo's scent brings back the memory of that kiss, and that other elevator ride. But on the other, Tobias's aroma makes my mouth water. I want that softer Tobias that stood behind me. I lean closer, inhaling Tobias' thick masculine scent. Tobias moves closer to me, snapping me out of my trance. I glance up at him to see if he notices, but his eyes are closed. Still, he's leaning in to me, almost giving me a better chance to indulge in his unique aroma. I lick my lips and take a timid step back. My thighs are wet at this point, I have to reel it in.

I bump into Theo and Tobias' eyes snap open. They flicker between dark and light, this has to be a trick of the light, right? I grip his forearm and shake him, "You okay, Tobias?" As soon as my hand touches the warm skin of his arm, I gasp and a tingling sensation runs up my arm. Moving my hand, I run it up his arm to the crook of his elbow completely enthralled by the sensation of his skin under my hands. The door dings signaling our arrival at the office and breaking me out of this new trance. I want to touch him more, explore if all of him gives me that little zap. What am I thinking? These are my bosses! But, I can't deny there's something there, something dangerous that is pulling me closer and closer to my boundaries every time I'm alone with them. I don't know how much longer I can hold back before I snap and cross that line.

CHAPTER
SEVENTEEN

"**S**orry," I mumble. What the hell is wrong with me? I can't believe I just touched my boss like that, and that I would have gone farther if the trip had been longer.

Stepping out of the elevator, I rush to my desk, trying to keep my distance from both of them. I'm clearly not in the right headspace. Something in me keeps craving them, making me react in ways I normally wouldn't. They both walk into their own offices, not even sparing me a glance. Maybe I imagined it? Can it really be all in my head?

The minutes tick by, keeping me in agony. It doesn't help that my head throbs from the overindulgence of last night. I want the day to be finished so I can curl up in my fluffy bed and get some much needed sleep, but it isn't even lunch time yet. At least I have enough money to actually get a decent lunch today. I won't be surviving on crackers or scraps. I don't even have to worry about gas because of the forced carpooling so it's best to just indulge for once. I grab my purse and head downstairs.

The day is a nice one, perfect for a scenic walk. I'm not about to ask either of my bosses to drive me anywhere. Alone with either of them in the state I'd been in lately, is just asking for trouble. I make it to the ATM by the cutest cafe and fish out my card. I pull out a simple twenty. It'll be more than enough to take care of me.

The machine spits out my receipt and I reach for it, preparing to just toss it aside. I never have spare money since I'm indebted for the next few years, but something is off, there are too many digits on it. I stare at it, trying to comprehend. What has happened? My entire pay is on here, the hospital's fees hadn't been taken out. I gulp, rip out my cell phone and call the hospital. A late fee will cripple me. I won't be able to afford lunch for who knows how long.

The ringtone mocks me as whoever is on the other end refuses to answer until the fifth ring. "Mater Hospital," answers a cheery woman on the other end. "How may I direct your call?"

I tell her everything. Who I am, about my bill, and that I can't possibly afford a late fee. I don't understand what has happened but I need her help to get it all fixed.

"One moment please," she blurts out. Her rapid keystrokes fill my ears, "Ma'am?" She questions, her tone off. Oh no, has something else happened? I close my eyes, fearing the worst and make an affirmative grunt for her to continue. "Your account has been paid in full, that's why nothing was taken out. There's nothing left to be paid."

I pull the phone away from my ear, studying the number. I dialed it too many times to get it wrong. So that part isn't wrong, but can this really be the truth? That makes no sense. I don't make enough to cover the hospital bill in one go. "Please, check again?" I whisper as I clutch my phone tight.

She pauses on the other end, sighing at me. "You are Imogen Riley, correct? Please, give me your date of birth again and I will double check for you."

"August 15th, 1995," I recite. She types my information in again and I wait.

"Ms. Riley, your account has been paid in full and is completely closed."

"Who paid it?" I blurt. I have a vague idea at this point, but that doesn't make sense. Why would anyone take on a debt like that?

"Kane and Madden Industries," she replies with that chirpy voice of hers.

"That son of a bitch," I growl into the phone. I don't know which one of them I'm going to strangle for getting in my business but I'm not some fucking damsel in distress for them to save.

"Excuse me?" The woman on the other end doesn't sound so happy anymore. Oops.

"No, not you. Thanks for your help." I hang up the phone with one well-timed jab. What the fuck do they think they are doing? Those are my finances, my bills! The only thing either of those assholes need to know is how much I'm paid a week. Beyond that? It's all my business, not theirs.

I don't even bother eating lunch. Rage is my food for the day and its fiery grip is enough to fuel me as I march straight back to work. I nearly break a nail when I jam my finger into the up button. They are lucky I'm wearing heels, otherwise I'd just run up the stairs. I have that much fire in my stomach, desperate to leap out and burn them for this stunt. Tears of rage shimmer to life in my eyes, my hands tremble as I clench and unclench them, imagining myself strangling two business executives that don't know how to pay attention to their own lives.

The sound of the bell is like the start of a fight. Before the doors are completely open I march, my heels echo my aggressive pace on the marble floors. Tobias's office is my first target. If he isn't the one responsible, I'll ream out Theo next. I grab the handle and throw the door open, letting it slam into the wall.

"How dare you?" I demand. Theo and Tobias are both in the office. I appreciate that I don't have to run around yelling at them both. They jump at my growl.

No, that isn't nearly strong enough for what I need to get across to them. "How fucking dare you? You have no right to go snooping into my business. I can't believe you would do that." Most people might have been relieved by this timely rescue, but not me. My mom had raised me to be independent. Is life hard? Sure, but I have it under control, I know what I'm doing. This is just straight up an invasion of privacy. I visibly shake, tears still threatening to spill.

"Imogen?" Theo has his hands on his chair, he looks torn between staying in his seat and coming to my side. He glances between me and Tobias, his brows furrow. "What are you talking about? What happened?"

"Both of you, that's what's wrong," I mock him while pointing at both of them. Because even if Tobias is this particular fault, they both keep getting in my way, determined to be my own personal prince charmings somehow. "You, both in my business. You have no fucking right to do that! I'm not some fucking charity case or some damsel in distress you need to rescue!" I pant from all the screaming. Every fiber of my being vibrates. I grab my hair in fistfuls, clutching hard and rip them as I laugh maniacally. I won't cry, it doesn't hurt, but I'll laugh my ass off seeing the shock in their eyes. "You caused this!" I sneer at them both, throwing my hair at them. Dramatic? Maybe, but I've never entered a realm of rage like this before. I can't even get over the death of my mother without these two interfering. I open my mouth and scream wordlessly at them both.

My screams are cut off when Tobias gets up from his chair, crosses the floor in two strides and pulls me to his chest. Theo continues to stare at us.

Someone else might have relaxed against Tobias' chest and been gentled, but not me. I jab my finger into his chest, poking him. He's the one responsible, so he's the one in the doghouse for this. Theo is an asshole, but not the one ruining my life at the moment. "It was you, wasn't it?" I growl at him.

He doesn't answer, just stares down at me with those dark eyes of his. Does he think that will stop me? That I'll magically just fall into his arms and be a good girl?

"Fix it right now or I'm done. I'll fucking quit." I toss the receipt at him, but since there isn't much heft to it, the stupid thing lands in front of him instead of against his face where I aimed.

He catches it before it hits the ground and uncrumples it. His eyes scan the numbers and something like realization sparks in his eyes. The pity that has been present before dies out. Good! His chest heaves and his lips lift from his teeth. "No, you needed the damn help. If I had known about your mother when she was first admitted, I would have changed the policies right then. But you never let anyone in your life."

What? He has no right to be mad at me! He's the one at fault! I take a step away from him, not letting him get close enough to touch me again. "Fuck you, Tobias. I didn't ask for you to come rescue me, I don't need your fucking help, and I don't need you. I'm not some broken person you need to fix." The tears I held back before stream down my cheeks. Hopefully mom will forgive this moment of weakness. I let someone else see me cry, I failed her. It only serves to make me cry harder.

Theo reaches out to me again, fingertips brushing against my back. "Imogen."

I glare at him, moving out of his way too. "Don't you fucking touch me either, Theo. I'm done with you, done with both of you."

"Imogen," Tobias snaps my name. Where Theo's cry of it has been soft, Tobias' is harsh like he's disciplining a dog. "I never said you are broken. But, you are fucking broke. I won't have my fucking MATE living in her car and rotting away because you're too damn stubborn to ask for fucking help," he snarls every word at me.

The red in my eyes fades away. I focus on this word, this thing that he stresses so hard. What the hell? "Excuse me? Mate? I'm not even fucking dating you. I don't know what you thought I'd agreed to by taking that apartment, but you're going to cut this shit out now. You're going to stay out of my business. You're my boss, nothing more, act like one. You'll never be my mate, Tobias."

Those dark eyes widen, I have the sensation of punching him with my words. The color drains from his face and he staggers back, hand curling around the chair and swaying. "Get out," he whispers softly, body trembling. He gets the strength to look me in his eyes, rage and pain etched on his features. "Get the fuck out of here! Take the rest of the day off, I can't even look at you." The last words are soft, but he punctuates them with a punch to his desk. A large dent forms underneath his hand and the metal holding the desk up creaks as it physically bends underneath the pressure.

I open my mouth to tell him I quit when Theo jumps from his seat. He pushes me out of the room and shuts the door behind us. I don't wait to hear what he has to say. Flipping my hair behind my shoulder, I march back to the elevator, smacking the button with my palm. While I wait for the damn thing to show up, I can feel Theo's gaze on my back. Why is this taking so long?

I whirl around and Theo takes a step backward, still staring, but not engaging with me. Fine, let him be a coward. I slip my heels off and sling them from my fingers as I head to the stairwell. I kick the door open and jog down the stairs as fast as I can.

I must have been halfway by the time I work the rage from my body. Am I being a bitch here? Any other boss would have fired me once I slammed the door open. I slow down, muscles aching from the extra pressure I put on them. My feet ache from doing this stupid childish stunt. Why won't I be an adult and not let my emotions get hold of me like that? It takes a while, but I finally get to the bottom. Instead of kicking the door open, I weakly push it and hobble over to a bench by the elevator.

I slip my shoes back on my now sore feet and cradle my head in my hands. How has life gotten this bad? When did I become some cosmic joke? What I wouldn't give to have my stray here, I want to hug him. Did he even know I'm okay? Is he still at that storage garage? Maybe I'll see him again. Lunch isn't happening for me, but maybe I can get something for him. I head to the cafe and buy him some quality dog food. It's even good for dogs with long fur. Not that he needs much work on his beautiful hair but I want to keep it in good condition.

With nothing else taking my time, I head to the park and to the place I met him before. "Here puppy, puppy," I call out. I hope he recognizes my voice. But no matter where I look, he doesn't appear. Maybe he's mad about the puppy thing. He's the size of a small bear. I need to get him a proper name the next time I find him, if I find him again.

My brain turns to the dark and I force it away from the negatives. I'm sure the dog is fine, probably just with his real owners. I need to get back to the apartments and it's a fairly long walk. I hope I can remember how to get there. But isn't this what I wanted to do at the start of my day? Ironic, I'm being forced into it now. My phone buzzes and I glance at the screen. What does Theo want? I try to ignore it but after the fourth ring I give up. It's not like things can get that much worse for me. "What do you want?" I demand.

CHAPTER
EIGHTEEN

N o, that isn't what I need to say, even I know that. I take a deep breath, I'll retry this. "Look I'm sorry, I know what I said was wrong. I was just angry." Weird, I thought apologizing would be harder. Maybe because it's Theo?

I expect Theo to be upset with me snapping at him, but his voice is warm, concerned even, "Where are you?"

"In the park," I reply with a deep sigh. "I thought I could find something here, but no luck."

"You can come back if you want, he has calmed down. He's not going to run you out again. We are your ride home."

I shake my head. I'm not ready to give up yet. "No, I think I will stay here for a bit longer. I'm looking for something."

"Looking for what? Did you lose something? Is that what you meant when you said no luck?"

I try to talk nonchalantly but it comes out in a nervous cackle. I'm about to admit my only friend is a stray dog, "I'm looking for a dog."

"A dog?" Theo echoes my words, a hint of amusement in his

voice. I guess not much gets to him if he's in good spirits so quickly after my blow up. "Why?" he questions.

"Because he used to sometimes stay with me when I lived in my car and the storage garage. I just miss him." I think this has to be a personal record for the length of time Theo and I could have a civil conversation. Or at least not make me want to strangle him.

"Really? I will keep a lookout for your furry friend. If I see him, we can bring him back to the apartment." When did Theo learn to be so nice? "By the way, turn around." I follow his instructions and Theo walks across the grass towards me. I can't help it, I smile at him. While I probably look like a splotchy raccoon, there's no hint of anger in the man. He grabs my hand and puts his balled up one on top, transferring some bit of metal to me. I glance at it and stare at the BMW keys. I look from them to him, questioning him.

"After you left like that I kinda realized you came with us this morning. You don't have another way home, so drive. Tobias has calmed down, but there's no need for you to wait until we're ready. Just go and get some rest. It might really help."

My body warms at his words, I could get used to this Theo. Maybe I should complain about being pampered, but I really am exhausted. I need to get back and unwind. But wait, "If I take the car, how will you two get home?"

"It's called a taxi. Oh, and please don't destroy my car. If I get back and it looks like your train-wreck of a car, I will be pissed," he says. But even with all this, he keeps smiling at me, even nudging my arm playfully. I rub my eyes with my fleshy palms. I look like a mess. "Here," Theo offers me a handkerchief and uses it to rub at my face, removing some of the black smudges. I really look like a raccoon.

"Thank you, Theo."

"It's nothing. Come on, I've got to get back to work, but I'll walk you the rest of the way, if that's okay." He raises a brow, waiting for my response.

"Sure," I reply. I follow him back to work, parting ways at the elevator. I head in and he gives me a little wave. He waits for me to go down to the parking lot, and heads right back to the offices. I touch my lips, thinking of the last time with Theo. At least now I can look at it fondly without all the anger and rage.

I make it to the car without issues and drive it back to the apartment. The valet glares at me, ready to accuse me of stealing I bet, but he bites his tongue and just takes the keys from me. He isn't willing to anger my bosses. I'm just glad I got the damn thing back in one piece. I hadn't been so confident getting home. I was terrified of scratching or denting the car.

Even I will admit, I'm not the best driver. I'm shocked I even passed my driver test. I managed to parallel park once for the test, and since then didn't even attempt it. Hence all the dents on my car. I'm one of the worst parkers and have hit many stationary objects mainly trying to reverse, not that I'll admit that to Theo. He can believe all of that is from a previous owner.

I get back to my apartment, sit down, and glory in the absolute silence. I have free time! I don't have to worry about running out my battery on my phone for once. I open up one of my reading apps and pick out a good story. I need a drink to fully appreciate it. I pour myself a large glass of vodka and drizzle it with raspberry syrup from the pantry.

I take a seat on the couch, stretching my body out and diving straight into my current favorite book on the platform. I flip through page after page, unable to set it down. I barely even drink my drink, I'm on edge the entire time. I wish I could give the author a tip!

A loud knock interrupts my reading and I glance over at it, scowling. I'm on the last chapter, I don't want to stop. "It's open," I call. I don't even bother leaving my seat, this is too good.

Theo walks in, closing the door behind him and takes a seat across from me. What is he doing here? I want to look to see the time but considering I managed to get to the last chapter I don't want to stop.

"What are you reading?" Theo questions after I ignore him. I hold a finger up motioning for him to wait a minute. Thankfully, he actually listens.

"A book on Patreon called Dark Desires by a woman named Jane Knight."

"What's it about?" Theo questions, shifting closer to me.

My lip twitches, should I really tell him everything? It's hard to sit there with my thighs clamped together as my heart beat pounds through my body. Jane is a master at heat and I can easily imagine the two male leads in the reverse harem as my bosses. "There's a waitress that works at this diner. She's having these heated dreams and then this guy shows up that's from the dreams. He ends up being one of her mates and is trying to protect her from this crazy killer beast."

Theo's eyes widen a bit. "One of?"

I nod. "Yeah, I told you, I like reverse harems. One woman, lots of men. Though a few of these men are perfectly fine with keeping each other entertained while they're waiting for their lady," I chuckle at him, but he doesn't turn red. If anything, he looks genuinely interested.

"Hmm interesting, I will have to check it out. What did you say the author's name was again?" Theo asks, pulling his phone out of his pocket.

"Jane Knight, but it's on Patreon."

Theo nods to my words. "Yes, and I signed up for it to help support her. If you like her, then I'm sure she's great at her craft." He turns his phone around to show me he's signed up for her highest tier, show off.

"So, what has brought you here?" I ask, keeping the snap from my voice.

He chuckles at me, eyes twinkling. "You've got my keys."

My cheeks burn, I forgot all about it. "Sorry."

"And, I got you a present." He announces with a smug smile. "And before you get worried or yell at me, no, I didn't spend any money on it."

"Present?" He said he hasn't spent any money, so that means I can possibly accept whatever he has done. But he doesn't have anything in his hands.

"Go open the door to the courtyard," his words are soft, but excited. He wants to see my expression over this present of his.

I set my phone down and make my way to the courtyard door. I pull the curtain away from the windows. Out in the dark, a blob of black is pressed against the door, waiting for me. I squeal, thrusting the door to the side as I race out and throw my arms around his big neck, I thought I lost him! "Where did you find him?" I gasp.

Pesky tears are brimming again. I've been so emotional today and I've read instead of taking that needed nap.

Theo pretends not to see me on the verge of breaking down. He rises up another several notches on my rankings. I wipe my eyes off on the dog. "He was at your old storage shed, sulking and lonely and crying over a belt you left there. Bit of a crybaby if you ask me. He was a bit bigger than you let me believe, I barely got him into the taxi, and do you know how upset the driver was?"

I shake my head, burying my head in his fur and resting my face against his furry one. He licks me, clearing away all traces of my tears. Am I allowed to be this happy?

"What are you going to name him?" Theo questions, eyeing us both.

Name? I have just treated him like a stray all this time. I've never dreamed that I could keep him. "Are dogs allowed here?"

Theo chuckles. "Yes, but there is a strict policy on cats. No cat, not even therapy ones."

I shrug. "I have no idea yet. Maybe he'll help me think of one." I tap my leg and the dog bounds over to me. He jumps onto the couch and stretches himself out, getting comfortable right next to my reading spot. What a smart pet.

Theo takes a seat beside him, roughly petting his head. I wince for my new friend. "He's just getting comfortable wherever he wants, huh?" Theo questions.

"Yeah," I agree with a grin. "I'm glad. I was worried he wouldn't adapt to apartment life but I think we're going to be great." Oh! I get to my feet. "Hey boy, I've got a surprise for you." I go to the kitchen and grab the can and a can opener. "Where's Tobias anyway? Waiting for me to grovel and apologize?" That'll never happen. I could apologize to Theo, but Tobias has gone over the line.

"I think he's still sulking over your last argument. I'm sure he'll turn up once he realizes how much of an ass he was to just do things without telling you. I bet it was a shock getting that receipt."

The can opener pierces the metal and I aggressively turn the wheel a few times. I wish that Theo hadn't reminded me of all that. I cut the top off the can and throw it away. Grabbing a bowl, I pour the dog food into it. Huh, considering how much I spent this doesn't exactly look gourmet, and it smells even worse.

"Imogen? What are you doing there?" Theo calls with a cough. "Something smells hideous."

I want to be a smartass, but I agree with him. This dog food stinks badly.

"I got him some dog food," I answer, Theo snorts from the couch. "What?" I demand, I don't know why but my brow is wrinkled. Why is he laughing? Shrugging, I grab the bowl and set it on the ground. I crouch beside it and pat my legs. "Come here boy, I've got some din din."

The stray walks over and spots the bowl. He stops and stares at it like it's some vicious enemy. He growls, edging closer, nose working overtime.

I look between the dog and the food. "What's going on here? It says beef. Dogs like beef, don't they?"

Theo joins me in the kitchen and crouches by the dog. It looks at him and sniffs, "They love it," he reassures me. He grabs the dog by its muscular shoulders and pushes forward. "Come on big boy, eat your dinner. Imogen worked so hard to provide that for you. Doesn't it look wonderful?"

The dog snaps and snarls, baring his teeth and growling at Theo.

I have to agree with him, the food is far from wonderful. The dog sits down, digging his claws into my floor and I wince. I hope he doesn't leave gouges behind. How will I explain that away?

"I don't think he wants it. I will see if I can make him something else." I offer. The dog snaps at Theo's hand as Theo picks the bowl up and puts it beneath his nose. Walking over, I smack him softly on the snout. "Bad dog, don't bite," I scold him. The dog stares at me like I've grown another head. He drops his head to his paws and whimpers like I beat him.

"Aww come here, big fella," Theo tells him and rubs his face, pulling on his furry cheeks. The stray growls in his face.

I wince, prepared to break up a fight. "Maybe you should leave him alone. He looks like he is getting cranky," I warn Theo. Theo's teasing smile makes my insides warm. Maybe my friendship circle has grown by one, maybe.

"You know who he reminds me of? Tobias. Look, he even scowls like him. You should name him Tobias," he turns to grin at me in expectation. I laugh at the twinkle in his eyes, "Their temperament is similar."

"Somehow, I don't think the boss will like it if I name a dog after him." I chuckle. Besides, it will be weird having my pet named after someone I've fantasized about.

My nameless pet stares at Theo, and my boss gets to his feet, stretching. "It's been a long day. I'm going to get back before Tobias returns. If I don't have dinner prepared by the time he gets home he'll get cranky. I'll leave you two to enjoy your night."

I wait until after he leaves before I retreat to the kitchen. I get a steak out of the freezer I found the night before and toss it in the microwave on defrost. It isn't the best cooking method, but I'm pretty sure my companion will be happy with anything as long as it isn't the slop from the can.

Once the microwave finishes I pull out a skillet and turn on the stove. I put the pan on it and let it heat up before I throw the steak in there and cook it to medium rare. After a few minutes it's done. I cut it in half and place it on two plates.

I take the plates back to the living room and place one on the ground beside me. Maybe I should chop the steak up, what if it's too big? I reach for it to fix my error when the dog grabs it and tears a chunk out of it. We finish our steaks in silence and I let the events of the day filter through me.

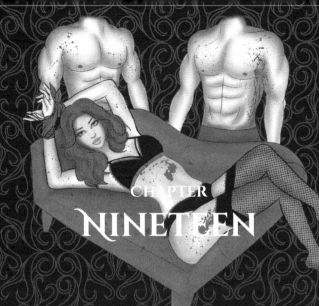

CHAPTER
NINETEEN

When we finish eating, I dump the plates in the sink and rinse them off. I grab my clothes and something out of my bedroom and return to the bathroom. The dog watches me as I come and go. His head tilts to the side, but he doesn't bother following me. "Stay," I order before wandering into the bathroom.

Jumping in the shower I am in there all of five minutes when I hear a low whining coming from outside the bathroom door. Reaching out the shower, I open the bathroom door before turning back to rinse the shampoo that is now burning my eyes. Opening my stinging eyes, the dog is watching me through the shower door.

"You know it is rude to stare," I tell him. He cocks his big head to the side, not fazed by my comment. Feeling his eyes on me, I rush to get out. I don't know why but sometimes his gaze makes me feel a little uneasy, it's almost human-like. Wrapping the towel around me, I get out and dig through the drawers finding an old shirt and a pair of panties. Slipping them on, I walk back out and find the bottle of tequila I was drinking the night before.

I don't have a problem, I need it to help me sleep lately, that's all.

The nightmares are terrible, reliving the night my mother passed over and over again. Alcohol helps make sleep easier. I reach for the bottle to pour it in a glass and pause. I only have a quarter left, why not just drink straight from the bottle? One less dish to worry about.

I tip the bottle to my lips, the stray walks over, his fur brushing against my side. He sits on my feet staring up at me. I take a swig from the bottle, coughing from the intense burn it leaves in my throat. The cough will go away after another mouthful. A few more and it will be like drinking water. Come to think of it, I need to find another way to sleep. If I keep doing this, I may just become an alcoholic like my mother. The dog whines when I take another big mouthful.

I enjoy the sting in my throat for a moment before pulling the bottle away and addressing him. "What? Don't look at me with those judging eyes. You really do remind me of Tobias when you glare at me like that. You don't know my life, you aren't allowed to judge me." Great, only a couple of swallows in and I'm arguing with the dog like he understands me.

The dog pulls the bottom of my shirt with his mouth, tugging me out of the kitchen. Grabbing the bottle and wrapping my arms around it, I follow and grab a blanket out of the linen cupboard. I open the doors leading outside in case the dog needs to pee during the night. Curling up on the couch, the dog jumps up beside me.

I don't even remember what I choose to watch on TV, and it doesn't matter. I just need my brain to die. I take another deep swig and smile, my eyelids are heavy. Sleep is blissfully close, but I can't sleep in the bed, I'm used to my cramped car so I know I won't be comfortable in such a huge bed.

Instead, I stay on the couch, cuddling with my furry hot water bottle. His head rests on my hip, and eventually I fall into a dreamless sleep.

The next morning, I wake up, and the dog is gone. I look in every room but can't find him. He must have left to go outside. I hope he'll show up while I'm getting ready for work, but I don't see any sign of him. My head pounds, and my eyesight is blurry. A migraine builds up, the pressure against my cheeks makes me wince. If I don't take something soon I'll regret it later. I look for some Tylenol when Tobias walks in, followed by Theo. What is this? I don't even get a knock anymore? Sure, come on in, make my morning even better.

"Good morning, Imogen. I hope you're decent," Theo's voice rings out in a sing-song. I'm glad I've suffered to make sure I got dressed before searching for medicines. I'll have to put my clothes out the night before to make sure they never catch me unprepared.

Digging through my oversized purse, I try to find a bottle of Tylenol, or anything else at this point, to get rid of this damn headache. After a few minutes, Tobias must have got tired of waiting because he burst through my bedroom door. I yelp and resist the urge to throw my bag at his head.

"How much longer?" He asks, tone cold. Another morning, another pissed off Tobias. Maybe he just isn't a morning person?

"Just a sec, I need to find some medicine. I stayed up too late reading." I resume my search.

Tobias walks past me to the dresser and pulls a bottle of pills from the top drawer. "If you weren't so fucking hung over you'd know where you put your damn things," he snarls. I wince, how did he find out about my hangover? I thought I was covering it up well.

"Come on, Imogen, next time hide the bottle. You left it on your couch, leaking all over it, mind you. Do you know how expensive that thing is?" He shakes his head and turns away from me, slamming the door behind him.

I scramble to get ready in record time, throwing my hair in a bun. Once ready for work, I join them and Theo gives me a weak smile before handing me my apartment keys and a bottle of water. Great, he probably heard our conversation too. I take the bottle and down the pills that Tobias found for me.

Walking out, the valet tosses Tobias the keys. I pause at his car. I don't want another ride like yesterday, especially with Tobias in this kind of mood, yet again. His attitude is bad enough but I don't want to lose my precious pills if I get sick from his driving and being flung around in the car like some helpless pinball.

When I don't get in, Tobias stares at me over the roof of the car. "Get in the car."

I look to Theo for help, but he's already in the backseat. "I think I'll drive myself today."

"It wasn't a choice, Imogen, get in the car," he repeats, this time daring me to tell him no.

I stare into his dark eyes, I don't feel like bowing to him. "No," I respond calmly. "I'm good." I turn away, walking to the garage.

"Don't make me come get you, Imogen. You won't like the consequences if I do." I stop, frozen in my tracks. Consequences? What, is he going to do, smack my ass like a child? Scold me, put me in the naughty corner? "Don't make me repeat myself." His words are harsh. I can hear the anger behind them.

Turning back around, I gulp and his eyes blaze. I take a step toward the car, he doesn't drop his intense gaze. I open the door and slip in, something about him today makes it impossible to say no and mean it.

"Good girl," he praises before getting in himself.

I freeze and glance over at him, I should be pissed. I should want to throw something at his head, but instead I find myself doing as he asked.

I buckle my seat belt and Tobias starts the car. I grip the oh-shit bar white knuckled the entire way. Theo laughs a few times when I clench my eyes as Tobias screams around a corner. My stomach plummets to somewhere deep inside me as I wait for us to hit something.

Only we never do. When the car stops, I open the door and jump straight out. My stomach rumbles, threatening to make me lose my water and pills. I stand with my hands on my knees, bent over, taking deep breaths, trying to stop myself from puking in the parking lot.

Tobias gets out of the car and stands behind me, inspecting me as I struggle to breathe. I hear the crack before I feel the sting on my ass. He slaps me with the palm of his hand. "Don't drink and you won't get sick," he scolds before walking away and into the building.

Standing up, I flip him the bird behind his back. Theo chuckles at me before he chases after Tobias, leaving me in the car garage by myself. Walking in, I see Tom, he comes over and gives me a warm hug. "God, I miss seeing your face every morning," I tell him. Hopefully, he won't watch the embarrassment of me on the cameras with the whole flipping off Tobias thing.

"I miss our morning coffee dates too," replies Tom. He turns and watches Theo and Tobias leave. Once they are out of sight, he turns back to me. "So where did they put you?" He asks.

I roll my eyes. I should feel angry at Tom, but I know his heart is in the right place. "At their apartment building."

"Really? That's interesting. Just be careful, Imogen. It's not the best neighborhood for someone like us to be in." I stare, confused. Someone like us? I wonder what he means by that. It's an odd thing to say considering how ritzy the place is.

"I'm fairly sure it is one of the safest areas around here," I reply. Will he explain more?

He pauses, considering his words. "I suppose you're right dear. Don't mind me. I just worry about you." I can tell he wants to say something else, but Tobias pops his head back around the corner.

"Imogen, hurry up," he snaps at me.

Why is he in such a bad mood all the time? What have I done to him? I think about it for a moment, lips twitching. The correct question would be what have I done to him today? "Shit, got to go, Tom," I sing, scrambling to catch up with Tobias.

The elevator ride is tense the whole way to the office. Once free from my metal confines, I race around, turning everything on. Theo lingers behind, following me around like a lost puppy. Not even he's game enough to piss Tobias off today, more than he usually is anyway. Today will be another long day, Tobias' mood swings have been getting worse. We are constantly walking on eggshells at work, and outside of it things keep going downhill with him.

At lunch time, I escape into the small kitchenette, needing another caffeine hit. While I'm busy pouring the hot water, I feel a presence behind me. I know instantly who it is. "What do you need, Theo?" I ask with my back turned to him.

He steps closer. His chest moves against my back, soft breathing against the back of my neck. Putting the jug down on the counter, I turn around, only to be entranced by his hypnotic eyes. They burn brightly and I swallow, almost forgetting to breathe. Fog takes over my brain. I hold onto the counter with my hands, the only thing grounding me before I'm lost in his gaze.

He presses his lean body into mine, his leg sliding between mine and lodging there. My breasts are squashed against his hard-toned body. I can even make out the muscles on his abdomen. Theo's hand leisurely moves up and brushes a piece of hair back that has escaped my bun behind my ear.

"What are you doing, Theo?" I whisper, trying to keep my voice low so Tobias won't overhear and come yell at me more today.

"Getting a reaction," he whispers back against my lips. I don't get a chance to ask more before his lips smash into mine, cold yet demanding. His tongue brushes my bottom lip and I gasp from the chill, my lips parting. Theo's tongue plunges into my mouth, capturing mine and toying with it. While I'm distracted by the coldness of him, he reaches up with one hand and grabs my breast though my dress. He squeezes it hard and I am unable to stop the embarrassing moan that escapes my lips.

He chuckles against me and my senses return. I'm kissing my boss! And not only that, he's my other boss's partner.

I place my hands against his chest to shove him back. His lips leave mine and he nips at my jawline. My eyes flutter and the hands meant to place him away, hold on instead. I can't fight this, it feels so damn good. His hands curl around my hips and he sets me on top of the counter, pushing against me so his hard erection brushes against me.

His lips move down, kissing and sucking on the skin of my neck, his cold tongue tracing a pathway. My hands bury themselves into his hair. Theo's mouth devours my skin, sending goosebumps everywhere his lips touch. I moan in encouragement, lost to his every touch. The contrast of my now burning skin to his cold lips makes me shiver. When he gets to my collarbone, he pulls the top three buttons of my dress open kissing the top of my breasts. My thoughts are lost to the teeth nipping at my sensitive skin.

It hurts when he bites my breast. I squirm, but even then I can't push him away. His tongue glides over the bite mark and the chill of it takes away the sting. My head falls back against the wall. Theo tugs my dress down lower, my breasts threatening to spill out. My eyes flutter, and the fog fades in a blink. There, just over Theo's shoulder and watching us, is Tobias. He stands in the middle of the doorway, calm enough, but his dark eyes burn. His arms are crossed over his chest, not interrupting us, but just watching.

I gulp, looking away and tugging my dress back into place. Theo looks up, following where I'm staring and his eyes lock onto Tobias. He helps me adjust my clothes back and stands up, releasing me from whatever spell that gripped me.

"About time you came looking for us," Theo winks at me with a cocky smile on his face. I'm breathless and confused, looking between the two of them. Is this the reaction he wanted? A pissed off Tobias catching us being inappropriate in the kitchen? Theo strides out of the room like nothing notable happened, like he hadn't just been caught making out with their secretary.

Tobias just calmly stands there for a second before turning around and walking out, his fists clenched tightly. I know Tobias's silence is deadly, like a ticking time bomb.

I quickly fix my dress and try to get my bearings. What the fuck just happened? I had no intention of doing anything. I know it's wrong, yet my body reacted like I was possessed. Theo overwhelmed my senses completely, overriding my common sense. Jumping down from the counter, I quickly grab my coffee and go back to my desk. After this, I can't let myself slip back into fantasizing about them, either of them. That has to be why I can't resist Theo. I've been lost in another one of my own imaginings.

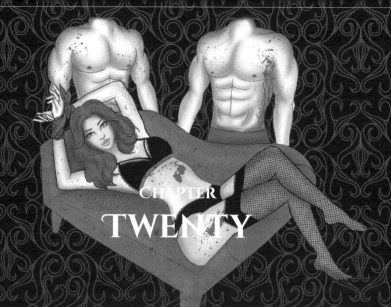

When work is just about finished, I receive a call from the lobby downstairs. A package has arrived. Seeing it as an opportunity to escape from the tension hovering over the office space, I hurry downstairs and retrieve the box. I take it back upstairs, grab a pair of scissors and get to work. I slide the blade down and to the sides to tear the tape. Once the excess tape is removed, I open the box.

Whatever joy has been left in me dies. I stare at the dark plastic urn nestled in the box's confines. I forgot all about my mother's remains. I was supposed to get a call to pick them up, not have them mailed to me. The hospital is directly across from us. Why didn't they ring me instead of shipping them over?

My bottom lip trembles. I pull the urn out, hugging it to my chest. I bite myself, trying to stop the shaking. This is all that is left of the most important person in my life. The woman that was so strong willed and full of life, reduced to handfuls of ash. I slip the urn back into the box. What is the whole point of living if we are just going to die anyway? I remember when I was a child and a close friend of mine died, I asked my grandmother at the time that exact question.

My grandmother's reply was simple, "It's the memories in between that of life and death that matter." I didn't understand what she meant back then. In a way, I do now.

It's the memories we leave behind, both the good and the bad. The memories others hold of us that get to live on. Now that's all I have left of her - memories. Memories are what I will have to hold closest to my heart because they will be the only thing to remember her by. I will never get to hear her voice again, never get to feel the warmth of her hugs. Everything I'd forced to the back of my mind rushes forward because of this small plastic urn, the only thing left of the amazing woman she was.

I pack the urn back into the box, secure the lid and stare down at it, lost in my thoughts. I stare off blankly into space, I don't notice Tobias until he speaks. "What's in the box?" He asks, moving the lid, ready to peer inside.

I close the box before he can see. "Nothing," I say, picking it up. It's already time to leave for the day. I follow Tobias, Theo walks out of his office and heads to the elevator seeing that we are ready to leave.

I step into the elevator and move to the back behind them, the box clenched tightly in my hands. I'm back on autopilot, going through the motions but not really experiencing any of it. When we get to the car, I retreat to the backseat, the box still cradled in my arms. I ignore Tobias trying to tell me to get in front. I don't want to be next to either of them after today's earlier incident. Guilt eats at me over Theo kissing me, did I lead him on in any way? Tobias hasn't mentioned it. But by the way he refused to talk to me most of the day, I can tell he's pissed off.

The other back door opens and Tobias slides into the seat next to me. Theo hops into the driver's seat and gives me a confident grin from the rearview mirror. At least I won't have to worry about mom's ashes getting knocked around due to Tobias's awful driving.

Tobias moves closer, his leg brushing up against my bare one. I sigh, letting my head fall back against the soft cushion and let my gaze float to the window. The drive back is slow with a lot of stops and pauses. Maybe there is an accident somewhere, I move the box to the floor of the car.

Tobias glances at me out of the corner of his eye, "What are you doing this afternoon?" He asks while we are stopped at yet another intersection. Theo pulls off the highway, deciding to go another way and the car moves in and out of traffic once more.

"Nothing, as always," I answer softly, still staring out the window.

"Good, that means you will be happy to have visitors then." I flop my head to the side to inspect him. Tobias is such a hard person to figure out. He'd been pissed at me this morning when I hadn't done anything to him. And yet, after what happened today, when I'd expect him to be upset, he's warm again. I try to think of how I can word the fact that I don't want visitors. I just want to get home, snuggle my stray dog, if he's around, and sleep.

"Who?" I question.

"Myself, and maybe Theo later, if he behaves."

I gulp. How am I supposed to behave towards Tobias outside the office? He's always so domineering to be around, let alone be stuck alone with him in the apartment. Every time I have been around Tobias, usually Theo is there, so it isn't too awkward. Why does Tobias want to come over after everything that happened? Or maybe that is why, maybe he'll concoct some sort of punishment for kissing his boyfriend.

"Why?" I demand.

"To make sure you don't find the bottom of that bottle that was left on the floor this morning." Tobias replies dryly, "Or find your way to another one."

I roll my eyes, "You make it seem like I have a drinking problem."

"Do you?" He questions, moving closer to me, I glare at him. The car stops again, this time at the lights down the street from the apartment building. Unclicking my seatbelt, I prepare to hop out at the traffic lights. I'm not going to sit here and be told what I can and can't do with my body. If I want to drink, that's none of their business. It's not like I'm hurting anyone.

When I open the door, Tobias' hand comes down on my knee grabbing it. "What are you doing?"

Cold Tobias is back, big surprise. "Here I was thinking it was pretty self-explanatory. I'm getting out," I say, snatching my purse and my mother's urn before stepping out in the middle of the backed-up traffic. I walk to the curb only to hear Tobias open his door too. He follows me down the street, he even jogs over to catch up to me. I ignore him and walk faster, the box cradled to my chest. He falls in line with me, keeping pace. Why won't he just leave me alone? "Will you just leave me alone? I'm not in the mood to deal with you right now."

"I am not done speaking to you. Until I am, you will listen to what I have to say." Tobias replies.

I ignore him and walk straight up the stairs of the apartment building. Theo waits in line with the build-up of cars that line the street. Tobias however is right on my tail, refusing to let me escape him.

Walking through the lobby, the young woman at the front desk calls out, "Boss, I have some letters for you." She grabs something from behind the desk and runs over to him. Tobias stops and huffs in annoyance, eyes burning a hole through me.

Boss? Let me guess, he owns this place too. Wouldn't surprise me. Escaping while he's distracted, I make my way to my apartment, jamming the key in. I unlock the door, quickly step in and close the door and lock the deadbolt.

The stray is gone again, but I have no doubt he will be back later tonight. He always seems to go walk about during the day. Going over to the courtyard door, I quickly close it so Tobias can't get in to go on one of his rampages. When I return to the living room, Tobias is leaning on the counter. I jump and shriek at him just appearing out of thin air. "How did you get in?"

"I have a key," he tells me, holding them up and showing me.

"Please, Tobias, can we argue another day? I'm sorry I kissed Theo, I know it was wrong. I get that, but please can we do this tomorrow?"

He doesn't say anything, just turns around and rummages through the cupboards. He pulls bottle after bottle out of the box I have stored mom's spirits in. Walking over, I grab them, trying to place them back in. He ignores me and pulls them out again.

"What are you doing, Tobias?" I demand. I'm close to my limit, how much harder is he going to push me today?

"You have a problem, and I am removing the problem." He answers so calmly like I asked about the weather.

"I don't have a problem," I snarl the words. Why does he have to make me feel like a caged animal all the time? I wish my stray was here to chomp on his fingers. I won't even scold him for it, I'll praise him.

"Well, this says otherwise and the fact that you are constantly hungover at work." I jump up and sit on the counter, watching him as he continues to butt into yet another aspect of my life. But this time I can't fight him, at least not yet. After everything today, I'm drained. I settle for glaring at him as he goes through my personal things yet again.

CHAPTER
TWENTY-ONE

I watch as he pulls every bottle out and then starts opening them. He sniffs one and wrinkles his nose before pouring it down the sink. "Hey, don't do that!" I reach out to stop him, that was my mom's!

"Don't start, Imogen. Either help me or shut up," he answers me coldly, like I'm a fucking child! I snatch a bottle off the counter beside me and open it. I quickly steal a mouthful from it and Tobias glares at me. "Really, you can't drink them all," He shakes his head at me.

I scowl, I'm not trying to drink them all! He just doesn't understand. I pass him the bottle and he pours it down the drain. "I don't plan on drinking them all. I don't have a problem, I just did it to piss you off," I reply with a sneer.

Tobias raises his eyebrow at me, he isn't exactly buying it. I pass him another bottle and watch him pour the contents down the ravenous drain. When he's halfway through, he pauses, side-eyeing me. "Why do you have so many anyway? I'm sure one bottle would have sufficed."

"They aren't mine, they were my mother's. She used to work at a bar and would bring them home." I close my eyes. The memories threaten to drag me under and I will NOT break under Tobias' gaze. Never.

"Your mother was an alcoholic?" He asks, while he continues pouring out all of my sleep aids.

I stare at him. "Yes, but not a bad one. She was a happy drunk," I defend. I can't believe he just came right out and said that about her. He didn't know her! He'd never been there when she'd send me off to sleep with gentle head pats and her warm hand on my back.

When he's done, he places the empty bottles back in the box beside me on the counter. We kind of stand there awkwardly for a second. I'm lost in my thoughts, and who knows what this man is thinking, God knows I never do. He opens his mouth to say something and then stops.

He hands me some tea bags and the sugar container. Strange, I have never seen him drink tea before. I reach for a cup and put the kettle on to prepare it when he puts a hand over my hand. "What"" I snap, harsher than I intend.

"Too much caffeine will keep you up at night. This kind of tea will help you naturally prepare for rest." His hands gently run up and down my sides before getting to my hips. He growls, his eyes grow ever darker. I stare up at him, I haven't heard that, right?

I turn around, trying to ignore the strangeness. But his hands don't leave my body. They travel back up my sides, curving around my breasts. He shudders and my breath hitches. My hands shake with the cup still in them. Is this another punishment?

"Tobias," his name is thick in my throat. His grip tightens and I can't help the moan that slips past my lips. "About Theo," I don't get a chance to finish my thoughts. Tobias' hands brush my hair away from my shoulders. His lips caress my neck and my eyes flutter at his warmth.

His hand slips up from my breast, to my lips as he pushes his finger into my mouth, the tip brushing over my teeth. I open my mouth to ask him what he's doing when he nips at my skin, blunt teeth dragging over my pulse. His finger softly thrusts in and out of my mouth and a familiar ache throbs between my legs.

Tobias pushes me into the counter, my hips dig into it painfully. "Tobias, stop. Theo..." I try to speak again to stop this before it spirals out of control.

Tobias cuts me off, he slips his hand free from my lips and spins me around, settling me on top of the counter. "Stop talking about Theo," he growls, "Right now you're just mine. Besides, I know he doesn't mind." He doesn't give me a chance to soak in any of this. He kisses me hard, devouring every inch of my mouth with a fire that contrasts greatly with Theo's cold chill. There's nothing gentle about Tobias, instead of our tongues dancing, he forces me to submit. His hands move from my hips to beneath my dress, cupping my breasts and squeezing them hard.

I can't pinpoint when the break happens, but I'm tired. If my bosses want to throw themselves at me to fulfill my fantasies, what's the point of stopping them? I bury my hands in his hair, pulling him closer to me, his teeth, tongue and lips praise me. His hot lips trail to my chin and then down to my neck.

This is wrong on so many levels. This is my boss, he has a boyfriend, and here I am willing to mess it all up. But this is my fantasy come to life, it'd be nuts to hold back. They both started this, and they are giving me a glimpse of pleasure that is beyond my fantasies.

Tobias's hands trail down my legs before he finds the hem of my dress and pushes it back up. Pushes is too gentle of a term - he jerks it up my hips and a gasp escapes me. I wrap my legs around his waist, pulling him all the way against me. He's rock-hard, his erection threatens to split his pants to get at me. He lifts me off the counter, his hands cradling my ass. I kiss his neck, biting and sucking on it. He groans beneath my touch and fire blazes through me.

He slams me against the bedroom door, a reminder of who's in charge. His hips grind against me while his lips assault mine again, swallowing every moan and groan that escapes me. He adjusts so just one hand holds me upright, and with the other he rips my dress from the top to the bottom. His lips descend to my breasts, nipping and biting as the skin is exposed. He licks at the mark Theo left, gentle on that spot, but his teeth graze everywhere else. I'm on the edge, worried he'll bite me but also excited.

I reach behind us, fumbling for the handle. It takes a few moments before my clumsy efforts pay off and it swings open. Tobias slips his other hand beneath me for support again so I don't fall. But he only holds me close for one more soul-burning kiss before he tosses me onto the bed.

I sit up, my hair spills over my shoulders, panting at him. This man doesn't resemble my cold boss at all, he's a predator, and I'm his prey. He's so beautiful it makes me ache, but the danger in him sets my senses on fire. Everything inside shouts for me to run, almost everything.

He undoes his belt and a knot forms in my stomach, my eyes glued to his body. His pants fall to the floor. I want to wince at how many wrinkles will be caused, but I can't focus. His black boxer shorts do little to hide him from me. His erection presses against the tight fabric, threatening to rip it apart. I never would have imagined Tobias is so huge. I wince, will this really work out? I don't know if I want it anywhere near me.

Tobias' gaze dips down to where I stare and he smirks. He climbs onto the bed, between my legs. He wraps his hand around the back of my neck, lifting me up for another soul-devouring kiss. He grinds his dick against my wetness, making me forget everything but him. Without letting me go, he slips his hand between us, caressing my pussy over the drenched fabric. He tugs at it, making it crawl even more into my body. I moan into his kiss, I'm lost to this man.

"Good girl," he praises, pulling away from the kiss. He grips my panties, ripping them, the burn of them tearing stings my skin and he tosses them over his shoulder. He pushes a finger inside me as his thumb circles my clit. He watches my reaction as he pumps his finger in and out, using my own juices as lubricant. His eyes shift from mine to watching my greedy body swallow him. With another smirk, he pushes another finger inside. I lose all ability to do anything but lose myself. A building moan escapes me, and my head falls back against the pillows, my hips naturally rising and falling to meet his thrusts.

"Look at me, Imogen," he snaps, voice like a whip. My eyes pop open at the command. His thumb circles faster, applying just the right amount of delicious pressure. I bite my lip, I'm on the edge of my orgasm.

He pulls away from me before I can be pushed over that edge. I gasp at the emptiness and glare at him, prepared to join fight club if he leaves me like this. He chuckles, eyes dark like a storm. He bends over me on the bed, lips bruise mine as he kisses me so hard it hurts. He grabs both my hands in one of his, holding my arms above my head.

He reaches over the side of the bed, grabbing the belt from his pants and wraps it around my wrists, pulling it tight until I whimper. I can't move, no matter how I wriggle. I gulp, shivering as I stare up at him. He slips the loop over the post on the headboard and tugs it hard, making sure I can't escape.

It hurts, I squirm, trying to get away. My bones grate against each other. I don't like being confined. My breaths come faster and I bite my lip, the lust in me dying away. My heart races, "Tobias," I plead.

He answers me with another painful kiss. His tongue dominates me, leaving me breathless and unable to think. His dark eyes stare down into mine. "Relax," he scolds. "I won't hurt you if you're a good girl. Let me indulge in you." He reaches over, grabbing my scarf from my dresser drawer and pushing it into my mouth. "All I want to hear from you are moans."

He pushes it too far in my mouth for me to spit it out. I watch with wide eyes, his hands run down to my strapless bra. His fingers circle around my back, unclipping it. He whips the fabric away and tosses it to the side to join his poor pants. My breasts spill out, on full display for him.

His eyes glisten in the light, shining from the window above the bed.

His fingers pinch my nipple, rolling it between his fingers. My eyes roll completely back. His touch isn't gentle, it's rough and painful, and damn, I'm in love with it. He twists and pulls on it, watching to see how much I can take. Leaning down, he sucks my nipple into his mouth, grazing it with his teeth. I arch my back, his hot tongue flicking over my hardened nipples, spiraling around it and pushing me close to that edge again.

Moving his attention to the other one, I gasp when he bites down hard, making me hiss out in pain around my gag, before his tongue swipes over his bite soothingly. The fucker draws blood, the whole spot stings. Moving down my body, he kisses the side of my ribs going lower with each kiss, sucking and nibbling on my flesh, making me squirm as his stubble tickles. He kisses my hip bone where my stitches were before he pauses. He stares up at me, the eyes that I witness don't look like a human at all. He's a beast and he's ready to devour me.

He shoves my thighs apart before placing my legs over his shoulders. He keeps his eyes locked on me, tongue dragging over my soaking wet pussy. His tongue swirls around my clit, sucking hard on it. I try to shut my legs and force him out, but his grip on my thighs keeps me exposed to him. His mouth continues its slow and steady assault, forcing me to writhe like a brainless doll.

I moan and pull on my restraints, I want to touch him or pull him away. I don't know what I want, all I can focus on is his tongue as he pushes it in inside of my dripping entrance, fucking me with his tongue and devouring my juices that I can feel spilling out and coating my thighs. I flush as an overwhelming heat burns through my skin, my stomach tightens, and my legs tremble. Waves of pleasure ripple through me as I come, I sag against the restraints.

But I don't expect Tobias to continue on. He isn't even slowing down, determined to torment me. His tongue moves faster and faster, not giving me a moment to regain my bearings. I squeal against the gag, trying to break free but he's relentless. He pushes harder on my thighs, forcing them wide, his fingers dig into my skin, his tongue all over me, sucking and licking every drop of moisture away.

I can't take it anymore, I break being shoved over the edge once more. I sob, going slack once more. My heart thuds and I struggle to calm it, but Tobias isn't done with me. Instead of just fucking me like a normal person, he's determined to drain out every drop of moisture from my body. His tongue fucks me again, slurping at my wet pussy, dragging over my too sensitive clit. I squeal, trying hard to get away, but nothing I can do stops him. I can't take another! My stomach tightens low, reminding me that yes I can. I'm forced into another orgasm, this one hitting me so hard gold flecks take over my vision.

I plead against my gag, screaming. Tobias places soft kisses on my thighs, kissing his way back up my body. He removes the thin scarf and tosses it to the side. Leaning down, his lips capture mine, his tongue twins with mine and shares my own juices with me. I'm too exhausted to care, I'm ready to sleep and submit to the darkness. My eyes flutter shut, not even able to stay awake for the kiss.

He shifts, his lips tickle my ear. His deep, demanding voice sends a chill through me. "Not yet. You have to stay awake, Imogen."

I do my best to focus on him. My eyes are lidded, my head rolls from lack of support. His lips move to my neck again, lavishing me with his tongue and sweet gentle kisses. Huh, who knew he could be gentle when he put his mind to it? The sweet kiss pauses. Something sharp pierces me and I wince, trying to wriggle away.

Tobias reaches over, bopping my nose, "Bad girl," he growls against my skin. Before I can ask him anything else, his teeth sink into my flesh. I scream, pushing against him. Fire floods through me, the pain is unbearable. And then, like my world is turned upside down, I spasm, pleasure has me in its grip again and I become a slave to the pleasure. Did he drug me? Whatever it is, it's fucking great, I can die like this.

When I open my eyes, Tobias wipes blood from his mouth. I remember wondering why he's bleeding, when my eyes flutter closed and I give into sweet, blessed exhaustion. Huh, Tobias is right, maybe I don't need the alcohol to sleep.

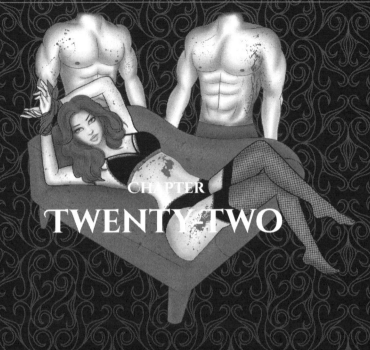

CHAPTER
TWENTY-TWO

Waking up the next morning, I am alone in my bed, my hands are no longer tied but faint bruises remain. If it wasn't for them, I would believe I just had another intense fantasy.

I struggle to slide off the side of my bed as my muscles quiver like jelly. I am sore and unable to even hold myself up, I need to rehydrate, desperately. I stumble my way to the bathroom and quickly pee. Standing up and flushing the toilet, I make my way to the shower and freeze. There, in the corner, the garden tub is filled to the brim with a bubbling fragrant concoction of steaming water.

Hopping in, I flinch at the hot water stinging my skin. I wash quickly, my tense muscles relax in the soothing water. When I run my loofah over my neck, it stings, and I rip my hand back. My loofah is stained with dark blood, I push it to the side, determined to finish my bath first.

Tobias has to be the one that set this all up and though I am pissed at him, I appreciate it as much as I can before I start my hell of a day.

Once cleaned and relaxed I hobble over to the fogged-up mirror above the sink. Using my hand, I swipe it across the mirror. I can't stop the gasp from escaping my lips, a giant bite marks my skin. This is no fucking hickey, this is like a fucking vampire went at me. I didn't know Tobias is that kinky.

It has a scab on it, thankfully my bathing hasn't washed it away, but it isn't pretty. It is red, angry, with ugly bruising around the edges. I pat it and the sting makes me bite my lip. "Argh, I'm going to fucking kill him," I scream to the void.

I storm out of the bathroom and look for some clothes, not giving a single fuck about how much I hurt. Thank god today is Friday, I'll get a chance to be away from those assholes for two whole days. Hopefully, this thing will disappear by Monday. And if I'm really lucky, no one will notice it today.

Grabbing my makeup bag, I walk back into the bathroom and start applying my makeup, trying to conceal the bite mark Tobias left. At least I know I didn't imagine it, the bite mark proves that he has indeed been here. Shit, what if Theo finds out? Will he be pissed off that I got hot and heavy with Tobias? We didn't fuck, though my body feels like it has been, thoroughly. I didn't even know you could come that many times without losing the ability to think.

I toy with my hair, trying to hide the mark that's impossible to cover completely. I wear my hair down, it's my best chance to escape notice. Finding my clothes, I put on a high waisted black skirt and a white blouse, tucking my blouse into my skirt before grabbing my perfume and quickly spraying my wrists and the side of my neck that isn't a bloody mess. I slip my heels on and grab my purse. I don't even get to the door before I hear them knocking. "I'm coming, jeez," I complain. How am I supposed to face Tobias after last night?

The door opens, giving me no time to prepare. Theo gives me a little wave before leaning against the door frame, a smug smile tugging his lips. "Good morning, Imogen." He whistles, "Damn, Tobias really gave you a good one."

My head hangs. Even with all that prepping I still can't hide it? "Where is Tobias anyway? I need him to answer for this."

Theo chuckles at my anger. I thought he would at least be jealous that his boyfriend has gotten all hot and bothered with me. Instead this guy sounds like he's cheering us on, "Tobias and I don't have secrets." I huff, annoyed he thinks there is nothing wrong with any of this.

This is all wrong, they are my bosses there's nothing right about any of this. I stare at Theo, he's way too amused at all of this. But I don't want to get too close to him. I remember too well what happened in the kitchenette.

"Calm down, you're always so angry. What did you think? I'm gonna fight you for my man?" He bounces up and down, shadow boxing. I can't hold back, I laugh, this is why I like Theo. Yet I also know he has a darker side, I have only seen it a few times, but Tobias is always there, sending me home, or in my case, back to my car.

Unlike Tobias, I have only seen Theo angry twice in the time I have worked for them. Once when we were in a meeting, everyone seemed to scatter, and I was sent home. The second time when he and Tobias had a huge argument, I can't remember what it was about though, actually I can't remember what it was that set him off at any time. Theo stops jumping and wraps his arm around my shoulders, pulling me towards the foyer. "You don't want to be late, do you?" he chirps.

Tobias isn't anywhere to be seen. I get the one thing I wished for so vehemently, a safe ride to work. I can't believe it when we get into the garage safe and sound and I haven't had concern for my life even once!

I even have time to scan my newsfeed on Facebook. When we arrive, Theo opens my door and escorts me inside.

I see Tom in the lobby. He waves but puts his hand down fast when he sees Theo walking beside me. He turns his back, going back to mopping the already clean floor. I think it's strange that Tom changes around both of them. I'll have to remember to ask him about it.

Getting in the elevator, we get upstairs but Tobias is still nowhere to be seen. And here I was, thinking he would come early and torment me. It's very unlike Tobias to not show up at work at all. I open his office door and peer inside, but the lights are off and the room is dark.

"Looking for me?" His voice whispers behind me, making me jump. My heart skips a beat. I turn around, he stares down at me before he steps into his office and flicks the light on. My heart is going crazy just seeing him.

I wait by the door, gathering my anger at seeing his smug face. He knows I'm pissed, Theo must have warned him I'm on a warpath and want blood, his in particular. He sits on the edge of his desk and motions for me to step in.

"Let's have it then, I'm ready," he says, rolling the sleeves of his shirt up. Theo steps in behind me. Is he here on my side, or to stop me from running after I finish Tobias off?

"Should I get popcorn?" He offers. He leans his hip against the door, closing off any escape. "What was it you said this morning?" He asks me, the picture of complete innocence. Innocent my ass, I want to kick him. Theo pretends to think, and I roll my eyes. "Oh, that's right, she would like to give you a piece of her mind, and to think, all this over a little love bite," Theo mocks with a shake of his head.

"Love bite? Does this look like a love bite to you?" I demand, pulling my hair off my shoulder. Theo looks and his face splits into a grin as he chokes on his own laugh.

"Why would you do that? You better hope it doesn't scar." Theo laughs again, making me glare at him.

"What the fuck is so funny, Theo? I don't see you walking around with your neck looking like it has been bitten by an animal." Tobias doesn't say anything, but I can tell he thinks it's just as funny as Theo. Am I missing something?

Theo straightens and walks over to me, slowly unbuttoning the top two buttons from his shirt, eyes locked on mine. The smile is still on his lips as he pulls the first one open and then the second. Grabbing the fabric, he slowly, teasingly pulls it away from his neck and cranes it to the side, exposing it to me, and pulls his shirt from his neck and shows me. He has an identical bite mark to mine, only it isn't red and angry. His mark is a few years old at least. Fuck, does that mean I'll have a scar forever too? Body shaking, I ignore the smug Theo, launching all my rage at Tobias.

My eye twitches, the nerve of this man! "You just go around biting people? Branding them like cattle? And you let him?" I jab a finger at Theo but he dances back out of my way, buttoning his shirt back up. He shrugs, I open my mouth, ready to scream like a banshee again.

"Let me remind you, Imogen. You didn't seem to mind." My face burns and I can't even look at Theo, dipping my eyes to the ground. Does he have to bring up anything from last night in front of Theo? Does he have zero care about his boyfriend? When I peek back at Theo there's no rage, just a mocking eager smirk, his eyes drifting from one of us to the other, licking his lips as if it all excites him.

"How could I mind if I didn't even know you had done it? I didn't find out until this morning! You want me to just bite you randomly without telling you I'm leaving a fucking scar on you for life?"

Theo's composure breaks and I turn and glare at him. I can tell, I'm getting nowhere with this argument. "Will you stop laughing, Theo? It isn't funny!"

"You will understand soon enough." Tobias interrupts me. "And I don't go around just biting people, I have only marked you and Theo."

"Understand what? That you're a cannibal?" I hold a hand to my poor neck. "And what the fuck do you mean by marking? This is more than a scratch or some tiny mark. It's like you tried to give me a tattoo with your teeth. You didn't tell me you were into that type of kinky shit."

"Like I said, we will explain this later. I have a meeting, but we will sort this out tonight. You'll be joining us for dinner. I don't have time to scour through your apartment to make sure all of the bottles are gone." Tobias explains everything calmly, a faint smile on his lips.

"Hell no! I'm not going to your apartment! What, so you can bite me again?" I whirl on Theo. "And same with you; you're just as sick in the head as he is. You both need to just stay away from me, I'm sick of this little game you're playing," I whirl, done with talking to these two.

Tobias's hand shoots out like a snake, faster than I can blink. He grips my wrist tight, not letting me break free from him. "I'm sorry." I stop, blinking at him, all the rage inside me vanishes. Did I just hear Tobias apologize? Maybe the world is ending. "I should have asked you," he says softly, his other hand gently brushing the mark. Not enough to hurt but like an artist surveying a masterpiece. "I knew you would say no, and I couldn't let you walk around unmarked for much longer."

Is he mentally challenged? Did I just hear that right? Leave me unmarked what the fuck does that even mean? And this gentleness, this isn't like Tobias at all. "I'm not your toy," I snarl at them, but my voice has lost its bite.

"No one thinks you're a toy, although I do like playing with you," Theo's voice speaks from behind. He sweeps my hair away, exposing my neck. I shiver at the feeling of his fingertips brushing my skin.

"I think she likes being played with," Tobias whispers, making me turn my attention to him. Theo chuckles, and I roll my eyes his way, his hypnotic green eyes glint, burning brighter. I can't escape. My breath catches in my throat when he pushes his body into mine, forcing me to lean back against Tobias. Theo's lips hover a few centimeters off mine, while his hand moves to my hip, his thumb rubbing circles against it, leaning in closer. "Do you like being played with, Imogen?" he whispers, his voice husky.

I can't think, I can't breathe. His hand moves languidly up my side to cup my breast, thumb lazily rolling over my nipple. The thin fabric of my bra isn't enough to stop my shudder. Tobias' hands wrap around my waist while his lips suck on the bite mark he gave me. It stings for a moment before that familiar pleasure from the night before dances through me. I moan as the bliss follows the path of this tongue.

Theo's lips brush mine, "I think you like being our toy." He whispers against my lips, he smiles before kissing me. My lips naturally part and his cold tongue brushes mine before a hand goes to my cheek, deepening the kiss. Tobias grabs my hips, pulling me into him. His erection rubs against my ass, sliding between my legs, promising me so much more than what we enjoyed the night before.

My mind clouds, this is so wrong, but yet I can't pull away. I hate to admit it, but I want them both. I like Theo's cold skin against mine and Tobias unnaturally warm hands on my body. One hot, one cold, but both feel so right. Natural even, although there's nothing normal about any of this and I find myself drowning in this sensation. A knock at the door makes me jump away from the two. The fog lifts as our little bubble of lust bursts.

I was ready to have sex with both of them, right here and now. When did I become such a woman? That thought scares me. Tobias growls from behind me, it's primal and predatory, like a tiger about to rip its prey limb from limb. It vibrates up my spine making me tremble. I look at Tobias over my shoulder. His eyes aren't his normal piercing blue, they are pitch black. Even the whites of his eyes are stained. I stumble into Theo, trying to get away from him, this isn't real. He looks like a creature from a horror movie! My hands tremble with fear taking over, Theo lets me go and I step back, studying them both. Every hair on my body rises, fight and flight kicking in, adrenaline and fear pulsating through every cell in my body. Tobias' eyes go back to their normal color, but I know what I saw. Whatever my boss is, he isn't human. People's eyes don't change like that, and they certainly don't growl.

They are twin statues, watching my every movement but not coming for me. I think if either did, I would race out of the room like a scared bunny. Like this, they are too beautiful for me to tear my eyes away. The knock resumes, unaware it has changed the fate of my day.

Without the interruption I would be writhing between the two of them, urging them to make me theirs as I lose myself in the sweet bliss they bring with their touches.

I don't belong to them in any sense, but I was willing to give all of myself before the truth came out. Something has always been off with these two, but not human? I dare not speak my thoughts, I'll be nothing but labeled insane and threatened to be thrown into a mental asylum. The knock happens again, a sharp impatient rap at the door.

Theo moves first. He unfolds himself from his position on the edge of the desk and walks forward, arms outstretched, eyes gentle. "Imogen," he whispers.

I don't give him a chance. I whirl, bolt for the door, throw it open and run straight into a woman I don't recognize. She has long black hair and emerald green eyes just as hypnotic as Theo's. She's visibly shocked to see me running from the office.

"Sorry," I mutter, bolting past her.

Theo tries to come for me but freezes when the woman steps in his way, blocking him from exiting. I run to the stairs, not wanting to wait for the elevator. Slipping my feet out of my heels, I run down the stairs, skipping some in my haste.

Coming to the bottom, I open the lobby door and he stands there with his arms crossed over his chest, blocking my exit. How the fuck did he get here so fast? Even if he took the other fire escape, it's on the other side of the building!

I take a step back, prepared to run all the way back up, but Theo stands on the stairs behind me. I'm trapped. Both watch me, like two snakes observing their prey before they decide if they are hungry enough to devour it. Tobias steps into the stairwell, closing the door behind him and pushing his weight against it, cutting off any escape I could manage.

"Oh, my. This is so very interesting. Tobias, your father is going to be quite disappointed, you took a human for a mate," she says the words to him, but her cold calculating gaze remains on me. She's just behind Theo, elbow propped on the railing. She studies me with a bored and unphased expression.

I am cornered, no escape. My heart pounds so hard I can hear it. I'm lightheaded, dizzy, ready to collapse into a pile of goo and give up, just let these monsters do whatever they want. How can I fight them? I shake and pitch forward, falling to the ground and the endless black that awaits me, but at least it's an escape. Maybe it'll be better if I never return from it.

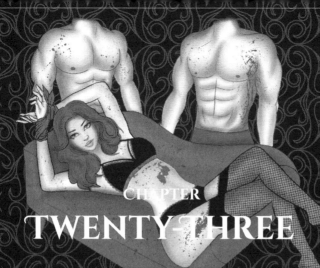

CHAPTER
TWENTY-THREE

T he buzzing of whispers wakes me. I crack my eyes open, unsure if I should sit up. I'm on a soft bed, but the ceiling doesn't look like anything I've seen before.

I rise up on my elbows, glancing around. Heavy red patterned drapes hang from the windows, blocking any light. A soft breeze wafts in, sweeping over my skin. The ceiling is too high for anyone to reach without a ladder. What a bastard it would be to change the lightbulbs on the light fixture hanging from the ceiling. A nonsensical thought, but I need something to focus on instead of the growing worry that I have no idea where I am.

I glance down at my body. I am covered with a gray duvet tucked tightly around me. It makes me feel claustrophobic, I wiggle my arms out. It's like someone made the bed not realizing I'm under the blankets. I sit up the rest of the way, inspecting the rest of the room. It's huge, and makes me feel like a doll in a dollhouse.

The bed is a four-poster with a canopy on top that matches the thick curtains. A huge bear skin rug is spread on the floor of the room. And a fireplace larger than me blazes in the corner, a brown curved couch sits in front of it. The stone walls fit perfectly with the mahogany and red cedar furniture. The room is something more fitting of a castle than a house. The buzzing whispers that woke me come from the cracked door.

I strain my ears, struggling to catch on but the soft feminine voice is too hard to make out. From what I can remember, she sounds similar to the woman from the stairwell. Similar except for a soft fury in her, and she argues with another voice I've never heard. It sends a chill through me. Have I been kidnaped? I slip out of bed, moving just a little closer until I can make out their words.

"I'll give you a month, Tobias, and you too, Theo. Fix it, or I will. Whatever it is you have going on with that girl needs to end. Why you would even think of doing this is beyond me," the unfamiliar voice sends a chill through me. Fix it? What are they planning to do to me?

"She is our mate, what did you expect us to do? Ignore her?" Tobias whisper-growls back, his voice rising. I'm torn between cheering for Tobias or just wanting to get out of all this. But the other man's coldness makes me think he wants to kill me, being Tobais's prisoner is a better alternative to that at least.

"Precisely, you should've left her alone to go about her life and you should've forgotten about her. You know the consequences for bringing a human into our world. You have condemned that girl to a fate she has no idea about." The woman from before continues to scold him. A fate I have no idea about?

"If you really love her like your mate, you wouldn't let this happen. I thought you would've known better than to put her life at risk, Tobias." I can hear the anger in the strange man's voice.

"One month like your father said. One month either you convince her, or we'll have no choice but to kill her. We can't risk being exposed. The council will have your heads if they find out you broke the most sacred law we have." My heart skips a beat. They really are talking about killing me. And the strange man is Tobias's father? I have to find a way out of here, but I want to hear the rest of the conversation. What is this mysterious fate they have in store for me?

"And if she says no?" Demands Theo. There's an icy softness to his voice.

"She dies. We can't have a human running around knowing all our secrets. It's too risky." The woman's voice sounds tired and drained. "You know the rules."

"No, I won't allow it!" Tobias snarl-shouts like a wild animal pushed to its limits. His voice is breaking, hurting my ears.

"Either she chooses, or you choose for her, Tobias. I won't risk our family. If you don't fix this, I will kill her myself." Tobias' father's words sound so final, like the matter is settled. He pauses. "Shh, she is waking." His voice grows softer, and more alarming, closer.

I rush back to the bed as quietly as I can, slip back under the covers and pull them tight around me before pretending to be asleep. The door creaks open, a shadow fills the room. I stay still, not willing to risk their wrath. The door closes again, and I look up. I need to get the fuck out of here. As quietly as possible, I walk to the open window and peer outside. I'm three floors up but there are vines wrapped around the stonework of the house and another roof of an outbuilding just below. It would be risky, and isn't without its dangers. But if I can get out there, I'm pretty sure I can scale my way down from this prison and find a way to escape. I won't wait here to be killed off.

Opening the window wider and as quietly as I can, I slip my top half through the window, grabbing onto the thick vines before climbing out completely. I swallow, my mouth dry. My arms wrap around the thick vines. Now that I'm out here, staring down, it doesn't look as easy to scale as I thought. I try to climb down the vine, but the skirt I have on makes it extremely difficult. I try to get a better grip and slip, falling a couple of feet onto the rooftop below with a loud crash, the tiles breaking beneath my weight, sliding me closer to the edge.

I scramble to my feet. Someone has to have heard that. I push my back against the wall, praying that I can hide. I tear the sides of my skirt. I need to be able to run. A woman sticks her head out, leaning out of the window and spotting me. My pathetic attempts at being one with the wall have failed. I squeak like a caught rat, look around for an escape, and seeing none I edge closer to a totally unsafe jumping point. But what choice do I have?

My perfect escape is going as badly as it could. I've already been discovered less than five minutes into the plan.

"Let her try; she won't get far. Let her tire herself out." I can hear the challenge in her voice. Not waiting to see who she's talking to, l jump, my ankle rolls on impact and shooting pain runs up my legs. I stand on shaky legs and run, but I have no idea where I am.

The entire property is surrounded by trees. I glance back at the house, trying to figure out which way to run, and how many people are after me by this point. The house is a huge stone farmhouse. It has three stories and a huge veranda wrapping around the entire house. I don't see anyone spilling out of it after me yet, but who knows how long I have. I don't wait, I sprint towards the treeline. The sun is starting to go down. If I don't make it to the other side of those trees, I'll be stuck in the middle of nowhere with no safety.

The tall grass comes up to my thighs, the sharp edges dig into my skin, punishing me for running. Trickles of blood appear all over my skin. I run through the yard as it turns into a paddock, domesticated beasts turn big eyes on me as I streak by - straight for safety, only to come to a wire fence. Lifting the taunt strings, I ignore their bite into my flesh and squeeze through their grasp. Once through, I race away, hobbling, but still able to move.

My ankle screams for me to stop. When I finally make it to the line of trees, I keep running, refusing to slow my pace no matter how much my body hates me for it. Pain is way better than being killed. The branches and twigs dig into my feet, making me hiss in agony. Tears stream down my cheeks, the monsters' words echo in my head. They want me dead or in a state of suffering they won't even put details to. I don't stand a chance out here in the woods by myself. I don't understand what I'm dealing with exactly, but I know they are sinister and dark. Everything inside me screams to keep moving, to escape or I'll never survive.

The sun finishes its path, dipping below the horizon and casting me into the darkness. There's no moon tonight, it's just me and my imagination. Every rustle of wind amongst the trees makes my body shake and more tears well. But no matter how far I run, I haven't spotted a single animal, not even a bird. The place is eerily silent, the only noise is my feet breaking twigs while I run and my own heavy breathing.

It takes all my willpower to keep going. I want to curl up into a ball and wake up from this nightmare, I must have slipped into from drinking too much. None of this can be real. I stagger forward, hands stretched in front of me. The trees thin out, I head toward them, the twigs slide over my cuts, trying to push me back to this side of the tree line.

I burst through, to a long road, barely visible without the moon around. A twig snaps behind me and I whirl to stare into the inky black. My heart pounds, but I can't see anything. But I can hear the heavy breath right beside me. A breath that isn't my own.

I turn on my heel, heart threatening to force itself out of my body. "You don't need to be scared, Imogen," Theo's voice is soft, soothing. He is treating me like a wild animal again. No, maybe more like a pet will be accurate. Is that what I am to these monsters? A pet?

I take a step backwards, back towards the woods, letting the bushes grab my skin again. I can't outrun Theo, I know that but my brain is being really stupid. Theo doesn't take any steps towards me so I whirl and run forward, straight into a brick-like chest. Tobias's arm circles around my back, stopping me from falling. His chest is bare, my fingers slide over his muscles. He only wears a pair of red draw-string shorts. I grab a piece of the brush, wielding a butter knife-sized stick and push away from them both.

"Put the stick down, Imogen," Tobias' voice cuts through the silence.

"No, stay back," I warn them, holding it out. It won't do much if they get serious with me, but I won't let them just kill me or hurt me. I'll fight until the end.

"Come back with us. We won't hurt you, I promise," Theo holds his hands out to me again. His green eyes practically glow in the dark. "Come, you will catch a cold out here. It's freezing." I haven't noticed the cold, adrenaline is keeping me warm. They step close, too close. I swing the simple weapon and they step out of the way. Theo frowns at me, eyes reproachful and hurt. Why does he look hurt? I'm the one about to be tortured.

"Imogen put the fucking stick down. You will only hurt yourself," Tobias voice snaps, a vicious growl overtakes his voice.

I grip it tighter. He's one of the ones I need to fend off, doesn't he understand? Tobias' eyes change back to deep black orbs, which is even more nerve wracking in this darkness. He's a demon, possessed and very ticked off.

"What are you? Stay away from me!" I scream. My hands tremble, holding the stick out in front trying to ward them off.

Tobias sighs, head dropping, "I'm a werewolf, Imogen." The light returns to his eyes bit by bit.

I laugh, a long drawn out cackle. I thought demon that wants to suck out my soul, or even damn vampires considering his fucking bite. But werewolves? People that can turn into dogs? "You expect me to believe you both turn into furry dogs?"

Tobias huffs, clearly insulted by my words. "He does, not me," Theo's voice rings out like twinkling bells. I forgot he was standing there, my attention mainly on Tobias as he is closer, but now Theo is close again, his eyes focused on mine, a self-confident smirk on his lips. I turn and swing the stick at him, he moves quickly avoiding being hit.

"Then what are you? We have fluffy over there, what furry creature do you turn into?" I spit sarcastically. I can hear Tobias growling from behind me, making my skin crawl and a shiver runs up my spine. My body breaks out in goosebumps, his feral growl echoes off the trees. But it's replaced all too soon with something worse, the cracks of bones snapping, changing, becoming something different. I cringe, dropping the stick to cover my ears. I can't escape the noise. I turn to look at Tobias, it isn't him but the stray stalking towards me, teeth bared and dangerously sharp.

Then, Theo's voice is in my ear. "I'm something much worse," his whispers send chills down my spine. I scream at the soft touch of his hands on my wrists. The whole escape plan has failed. I've fallen to monsters.

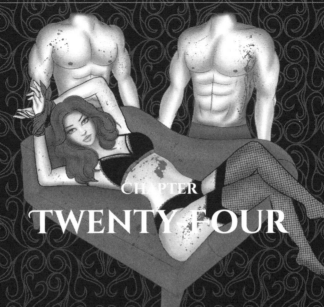

CHAPTER
TWENTY-FOUR

T heo moves faster than I can predict. He slides behind me, pulling me into his arms and scooping me up, a hand under my ass to hold me steady. He forces my legs around his hips and he runs back into the forest. My scream is stolen by the wind's speed whipping past us. Everything blurs, no human can move this fast. Bile rises and pools in my mouth, burning its way up my throat.

I clench my eyes shut. I can't even tell if we are going to hit a tree but how can we go this fast safely? It's like being stuck in Tobias' car with the windows down. I curl against Theo's chest, the only place of safety, and my stomach lurches. Why can't this monster stop or slow down? I'm going to fall apart at this rate. I bury my head in his neck, protecting myself from the biting wind stinging my skin. He moves in and out of the trees like a professional and soon my surroundings return bit by bit. The long grass from the paddocks snaps my bare feet, a final painful reminder of the futility of my escape attempt.

In the time it has taken me to get an hour's worth away from this place, I'm returned in mere minutes. Theo skids to a stop at the doors, the stone house looming above us. I shiver in his arms like a scared little animal. His hand strokes my back in reassuring pats. His other hand stays firmly beneath my ass, but now that we have stopped, his middle finger rubs my panties against me, making me wet from just his touch.

"You alright, Imogen?" His eyes hold mine, the thick fog clouds my mind again. Why does his presence always make me feel like all I can focus on is him? "You're safe with us, understand?" The calming sensation rolls over my body in waves, fear leaves me while his words blaze in my mind. I'm safe with them, how silly it is to run. If anyone can help me, won't it be them? They won't hurt me, only bring me immeasurable pleasure as long as I let them.

Theo smiles at me, his lips press softly against mine. Cold but demanding, I moan when his tongue brushes mine. His middle finger slides into the crotch of my panties, directly rubbing my clit. His eyes are hooded.

I'm lost, trapped in the feel of his icy tongue playing with mine. Everything else fades away. All that matters is that tongue, and that cold finger sliding inside of me, promising me all the things he wants to do to me. I loop my arms around his neck, pulling him closer. His fingers work faster, until I moan into his mouth. I've forgotten my own name by this point. I want this man, want him with every fiber of my being.

Behind us, Tobias clears his throat, no longer in his other form. Theo slips his finger out of me, placing me on the ground with one hand wrapped around my shoulders, while he sucks on the dripping digit. "About time you caught up, I wanted a taste of what you got to enjoy earlier." He casually pushes me closer to Tobias. Once his skin leaves mine, the fog from before lifts, my memory snapping back into place like a rubber band returning to its original form. These men are dangerous, lethal monsters. What the fuck am I doing getting aroused by one of them? I back up away from them. My instincts scream for me to run, but that obviously is a bad idea. It didn't work last time. Will they kill me slowly? Is that why they didn't slaughter me out on the road?

"You are safe, Imogen," I can still hear Theo's words. His cat-like eyes focus on me again. He leisurely sucks the tip of his finger. "No one will hurt you."

Lies. I remember the conversation. I know everything they are trying to hide from me. I stumble onto a side of them that has taken away every impression I've ever had.

"Calm down, Imogen. I can hear your heart pounding, practically see your thoughts running through that head of yours," Tobias says, trying to move closer, his hand reaching for me. I contemplate taking it, which monster will I survive with? Will they both devour me? Leave nothing left but maybe Tom's memories of me?

"Nothing has changed, Imogen. We are still the same people." Theo wraps his arms around Tobias shoulders, his eyes swirling with lust. There's no doubt in my mind that this creature still wants me.

"You're monsters!" I snarl at them. "You shouldn't exist." My voice is soft by the end of my words. I have to think of a way out of this fucked up situation. Pleading is a longshot, but what else do I have? "I want to go home, please take me home. I won't tell, I promise. Everything will be the exact same at work."

Theo's eyes soften, the predatory grin fades from his lips. "Imogen," he whispers. "Our poor girl."

"We can't let you go home, Imogen," Tobias replies to me, voice cold. And if I can't go home, that means they will be my executors. My heart races and my throat closes up, making it difficult to breathe. I take sharp shallow breaths, I'm hyperventilating, I realize. They really are going to kill me. My legs give out from under me as I slip into darkness, fighting for air as I choke on my own inability to control my emotions. I don't want to pass out. I will myself to stay conscious, but it's inevitable, my body collapses in on itself as darkness takes over.

The last thing I hear is Theo's voice. "And she is out again, I told you she would not pay up."

Waking up, I roll over. My body brushes something cold and I sit upright, blinking, trying to once more get my bearings. A light flickers on in my brain, registering the fact I passed out because my stupid body was having a meltdown. Maybe my brain is fried, and I imagined everything. But such hopes are dashed when I look to see what the cold thing is. Theo smiles over at me, turning the page of a book, his arm brushes against me again.

"How are you feeling?" he asks, his eyes not leaving his book. I don't speak, I just watch him fascinated by how fast his eyes scan the page before he flicks to the next one. He hardly seems dangerous, he looks like a normal man, only I know that he isn't. He's dark and sinister yet looking at him, he hasn't changed. He's still his flirty bubbly self. I pause, studying the book. Wait.

"You're reading Dark Desires?" I blurt.

Theo smiles, "You suggested it, remember?"

Theo puts the book down and rolls to his side, laying down so he's eye level with me.

"You're doing better, not as scared. Your heart isn't pounding, and I can't smell your fear," he whispers while brushing stray hair behind my ear. He inhales deeply. His cool fingers brush against my cheek softly. The calming fog rolls in again. He's the one that causes all this.

"Please don't," I whisper, turning away from his touch.

He blinks at me as his hand hovers in the air. "Don't what?" His husky whisper washes over my body, relaxing every muscle.

"Whatever it is you're doing to me, making everything foggy." I wave my hand in front of my head, trying to fight the sensation. He nods and the fog lifts, my body is my own again. "Are you going to kill me?" I question, in the same soft tone he used on me.

"We will never hurt you, Imogen, I promise. Well, not hurt in that sense," he says, a sly smile creeping onto his face as he bites his bottom lip.

I believe him, "Where is Tobias?"

"Asleep, behind you," He leans up to glance over my shoulder. Gulping, I turn, my eyes following Theo's to see Tobias fast asleep and lightly snoring. I half roll onto my back and the heat of his body seeps into me as I lean on him, chasing his warmth. "Don't worry about him. He looks scary but he's a big softie, you'll see. Besides, you're the only person ever to try to feed him dog food and he let you live." Theo laughs, making the bed vibrate.

I laugh too, remembering feeding the stray, then it clicks. "That was Tobias?" I laugh, only just realizing I tried to feed my boss dog food and I smacked him on the nose. No wonder that asshole had bopped me on the nose! He got revenge. Theo laughs again, nodding his head. The movement makes Tobias roll over and he throws his arm over me, pulling me in. I freeze before realizing he's still asleep and then relax. "What does mate mean? Obviously it doesn't mean friend."

"No, it doesn't. Just think of it as soulmates. Be easier to wrap your head around." Theo offers.

"So, you're saying I'm Tobias's soulmate?" I whisper. How can any of that be true? And how can they tell? Tobias has been cold to me for so long.

"Yes, but not just his, you're mine too." Theo adds, his eyes lock on me again. My eyebrows furrow, trying to understand. How can someone know who their soulmate is, and how can someone have two? Looking back at Theo, he watches me carefully. "You still don't understand," It isn't a question.

"She will soon enough," Tobias' voice is a sleepy rumble. He presses his lips to my shoulder. I look over my shoulder at him, his blue eyes stare back at me. My heart rate increases. He's a monster, all teeth and claws. He pulls me tighter against his body. I crane to get a peek at Theo, but he just watches; that green glitter in his glaze. Tobias's mouth moves to the mark on my neck, worshiping it softly with light kisses before sucking on it. My eyes roll into the back of my head, a moan escapes my lips, my body melts back against him. Pleasure floods my senses, my panties become soaked, even more than Theo's teasing. I love the hot tongue playing with my flesh. I can do nothing but moan again, lips parting, legs spreading. I'll worry about survival later, I want what they are offering, all of it.

144

Theo's face moves closer, his lips pressing softly to mine, before deepening the kiss and swallowing my moans. His hand slides under the blanket and unbuttons my blouse.

They work in tandem. Theo's fingers leave my blouse, burying themselves in my hair. His tongue tangos with mine, his teeth nibble at my bottom lip, sucking it into his mouth and lapping at it with his tongue. Tobias pulls the blouse apart, snapping the rest of the buttons and throwing the fabric to the side. He unclips my bra and kisses my shoulder before he slides the straps down my arms and drops it to the floor.

Tobias pulls me down with him, his lips on my flesh, tongue circling my bite mark. Theo tears my skirt, ripping it completely from my body so I'm now pressed between them with only my soaked panties on. Tobias's erection presses against my back while he fondles my breasts, rolling my nipples between his fingers. I whimper, lost in pleasure, it thrums through my body.

Theo rolls off the bed, standing up and pulling his shirt off over his head, revealing his bare chest and tight abs. His jeans hang low on his hips, showing his deep V-line disappearing into his pants, I lick my lips.

Tobias sits up, pulling me between his legs, making me lean back into him. Theo slinks towards the end of the bed, my heart skips a beat. He leans over, not taking his eyes from mine, and pulls my panties down and off my legs before crawling up the bed towards me. I press my knees together, closing my legs, feeling very exposed under the dim lighting.

"Relax, we won't hurt you," Tobias whispers in my ear before sucking on my neck, hitting that sweet spot where he bit me. My body instantly relaxes, bliss ripples through me. Tobias hooks his legs beneath mine, pulling my legs apart so they are draped over his, and I'm left exposed to Theo's hungry gaze. My eyes snap back open and Theo's face is between my legs. I try to shut them but Tobias keeps forcing them apart, farther and farther until Theo has complete access. He nibbles on the lobe of my ear. "Be a good girl, let us take care of you. You're going to love this."

Theo kisses my inner thigh, soft, cold kisses traveling higher. He pauses, sucking a piece of skin into his lips and his teeth teasing me when they graze against my flesh. My head rolls back on Tobias' shoulder, I become a limp doll, my eyes flutter close. Theo breathes on my clit, a chill makes me shiver but I spread my legs, eager to find out what this monster will do next.

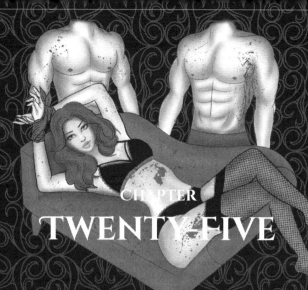

CHAPTER
TWENTY-FIVE

His icy breath paints my entire pussy, the lips, my insides, my clit. Everything tingles. His tongue parts my pussy lips, licking a straight line from my drenched opening to my throbbing clit, he sucks the bundle of nerves into his mouth and I see stars. The coldness from his tongue makes me shiver and my head rolls back and forth on Tobias' shoulder as Theo swirls his tongue around my clit, his tongue moving faster and faster in a circular motion around it. My juice trickles down my thighs.

The only soundtrack in the room is Theo's soft slurps, and my endless moans lost to their touches.

Tobias growls softly at me, grabbing me by the neck and squeezing slightly before forcing me to face him. His hot mouth devours my lips, making Theo's ministrations even more vibrant. His tongue plays with mine, fighting for dominance, while Theo's unrelentless licking and sucking make my toes curl and my stomach tighten. My body gets hot, and the flames erupt from just behind my belly button, spiraling through me as Theo gets me closer and closer. Tobias twists my nipple again, plucking at it at the same time Theo sucks my clit into his mouth and gently nibbles. I scream into

Tobias's mouth, losing myself while my body spasms between them. Theo keeps my trembling legs open, his tongue not pausing in the slightest.

My back arches off of Tobias' chest, that delicious slow build-up gaining strength. I want to push Theo away because it tickles, but it's also too damn good. I moan into Tobias' kiss. I'm on the edge, just waiting to be shoved over again. Theo slips a finger inside my entrance, gently at first, but as his tongue picks up steam so does his finger. Then he pushes in another, curling them upwards. His tongue never slows its assault. Tobias squeezes harder on my neck, at the same time plucking and twisting my nipple to the point of pain. But fuck, I don't care about the pain, not when the pleasure is this intense. My orgasm hits me like an ocean wave.

My walls clamp onto Theo's fingers and my body sags in exhaustion. My eyes flutter closed, my body wants to retreat to sleep. Theo moves up, and Tobias withdraws from kissing me. Theo kisses me hard, tongue toying with mine. The mixture of his cold tongue and my juices is too strange. Completely different from the heat of Tobias.

Theo pulls away and his fingers trace the lines of my face. "See what being good does for you?" he whispers. The bed creaks as he rolls off of it. He walks out of the room, but I'm not aware enough to figure out where. Tobias brushes my hair from my face, giving me a small smile.

Tobias cleans the sweat and remnants of tears from my face, the warm rag gentle on my skin. I gasp, another warm rag is placed beneath my legs and when I peek, Theo's calm gaze meets mine. He cleans the outside of me first, then gently rubs my insides with the softest of touches. They are cleaning me, I'd never imagine that.

Tobias moves back against the bed, bringing me with him. My back is warmed while he nuzzles my neck. Theo curls up with me from the front, his cold body giving me a chill. "Your skin is so cold," my voice barely audible to my own ears, but clearly, they both hear as Theo's chest rumbles from his laugh. I rest my head on his chest, enjoying the coldness. Tobias rubs circles on my lower back, working on each muscle until it loses its tension. I don't last long between their tender care, I drift off to sleep once more, feeling more secure than I ever had before.

I wake to warm fingers teasing my pussy. They don't enter me, but circle around my entrance and follow my sensitive skin. I push back into them, I want that warmth inside of me. I rested enough, my arousal is a wildfire raging out of control. The finger dips to the edges of my entrance, gliding across from my growing wetness. Not enough to satisfy me, just to tease and torment and make me want it. I wiggle my ass back into Tobias's erection. Tobias lifts my leg and settles it over Theo, spreading my legs for better access for him to tease. Theo sleeps on, oblivious for the moment. I try to roll to face Tobias but he keeps me faced away. He slides two fingers inside of me, curving them and rubbing my g spot inside at a torturously slow pace.

I moan at the stroking inside me and push myself back onto his fingers, trying to get more friction. But he keeps himself at the same slow pace. His thumb pressed against the tight muscles of my ass, tight little circles while his fingers fuck me slowly.

"Didn't you tell me it doesn't matter how fucking horny we are, she needed rest?" Theo scolds. He rolls over, pulling my leg up higher on his hip. His hand floats over my thigh, making me shiver from the contrast of hot and cold. Theo's face moves to my neck, kissing and sucking on my skin, Tobias's fingers slip in and out faster as my excitement coats his fingers, his thumb pressing harder against my ass. He slips it inside me, slowly and teasingly. "Good job," Theo praises. "Let yourself feel it all, Imogen."

Theo's fangs graze my neck while he devours my flesh, nibbling and sucking. Wait, fangs? I sit up and Tobias' fingers slip out of me. I stare at Theo, heart pounding and jaw-dropping.

Theo's lust fades and he cocks his head, giving me that familiar smile. "I won't bite you, I promise. Not yet anyway." His voice sounds calm like this is a perfectly normal thing. I twist back to peer at Tobias. His hands slip around my waist, pulling me completely against him again. He nods his head towards Theo. Theo's face becomes distorted in front of me. I reach out, finger's brushing against his cheek. He snuggles into my palm, a smile tugging at his lips.

"You're a vampire?" I whisper. Theo nods, watching my reaction, his fangs protrude. They aren't what you would see in a movie with the two pointy fangs. He actually has three on each side, and they run side by side. I watch his eyes darken, turning to the darkest shade of red, similar to blood. Veins stick out under his eyes, moving and wriggling under my thumb as I brush it over them slowly. Theo doesn't move, just waits for me to finish observing him.

Moving my hands back down his face, I brush my thumb over the point of one of his fangs. I wince the sharpness nicking my skin like razor-sharp needle points. Blood runs down my thumb and Theo stiffens, licks his lips, and closes his eyes. He tries to wait for me to pull away, but I don't. Instead, I brush my bleeding thumb across his lips, painting them crimson. Theo groans, licking his lip, body shuddering as he tastes my blood. I push my thumb onto his bottom lip until he parts it and brush it against his tongue. His eyes snap open, darkening before his lips close and he sucks on it, his tongue gently twirling around it. His eyes glow brighter, never leaving mine. When he lets go, I find my thumb is completely fine. I stare at it before looking back at Theo. He leans forward, kissing me gently on the lips.

I'm more surprised at my own reaction. I don't feel any fear towards them, but they still make me a little on edge, like when you're lining up for a crazy thrill ride and the butterflies are loose inside, but they don't scare me.

Theo smiles slowly at me, head tilting to the side, "You're over your fear." I stare back into his mesmerizing eyes, watching him. Tobias pulls me back against him, nuzzling my neck, his hot breath tickling me, his stubble brushing my shoulder near his mark. Pleasure ripples through me.

"Why does it do that?" My voice comes out in a moan rather than a whisper.

"Why what?" Whispers Tobias, but his eyes glitter. He kisses the mark again, making my eyes flutter. He has to know exactly what he is doing to me. But he wants me to say it out loud.

"Your bite mark." I moan again, louder, he sucks softly on it, tongue teasing the center. "Why does it make me feel so good?" I pant, riding high from his soft touch. Can I come from just this?

He chuckles, dragging his tongue over it. "It's a claiming mark, shows everyone you're mine. Only Theo and I will be able to give you this reaction, make you feel this way," he nibbles on the spot while I'm lost in the ecstasy of pleasure. I know what he is saying should alarm me, but it doesn't. It somehow feels right.

"Once Theo marks you, it will be even better. It'll be so intense you'll come for me no matter what else is going on," he whispers, kissing just below my ear, licking the shell of it.

I shift away, reaching one hand up to brush my throat. "Marks me?" Does that mean he is going to bite me too? I sit up, fighting to slow my heartbeat. Theo's eyes move to mine, an intensity glittering in them that takes my breath. The fog creeps around me.

"I won't hurt you, Imogen, and I won't mark you until you say I can." I stare wide-eyed before quickly nodding my head. The thought of being bitten scares me, being owned like some sort of property scares me.

"I shouldn't have marked you without permission, that's not usually how it's done," Tobias comments, voice laced with guilt. He gets up and walks into the bathroom adjacent to the bedroom, "You want a shower?"

I nod before climbing off the bed and following. I'm still naked, but my nudity doesn't phase me anymore. They both have examined my intimate bits extremely thoroughly, so nothing really left to be shy about. "Where is the man and lady from yesterday?" I ask, or is it the day before? I passed out so many times lately I have no idea what day of the week it is anymore. But being lost in a haze-filled lust kind of makes nothing else matter.

"They went home, this is mine and Tobias' place. Our parents don't live with us," Theo comments, walking up behind me and nuzzling the back of my neck. Wait, did he say their parents as if they are brothers? I stop. "You're brothers?" I whip around, smacking Theo's eyes with my hair.

They look nothing alike, and they aren't even the same species or creature. I don't know what to classify them without sounding rude.

"Not in the biological sense. We aren't inbred; we'll explain later. For now, I want to get you all wet," he whispers in my ear again, giving my lower back a push toward the showers.

TWENTY-SIX

T he bathroom is huge, with soft gray tile and black countertops with gold finishes. Tobias is already in the shower which could easily fit another three people and has multiple shower heads. Reaching out, Tobias grabs my wrist and pulls me under the stream of water. I chuckle when I smack into his chest, nearly slipping on the soap suds on the floor. Tobias holds me upright, steadying me. Theo steps in behind me and reaches for a loofah and shower gel that's sitting on a shower niche behind Tobias.

I move over to the second shower head and start wetting my hair before shampooing it, trying to untangle the knots that have formed. While rinsing it out, I feel hands touch my breasts. I know who it is because even under the hot water his hands are colder than mine and definitely colder than Tobias' hot skin, though the stream of water has warmed them some. I try to quickly rinse the shampoo out that's stinging my eyes when I feel Tobias' chest press against my back, his hands grip my hips as he pulls me flush against him.

"Not fair, I can't see," I whine. He pushes me back under the stream and I manage to get the shampoo out and open my eyes to

Theo, whose darkened eyes are watching me. I step back into Tobias, his hands go back to my hips.

Theo's fangs elongate. "You said you wouldn't," I gasp, stumbling over my words. The way he looks at me is like a predator watching its prey.

"I won't, your scent is just stronger from the steam. You don't need to worry," he says, reaching for me. I step closer, his hands taking the place of Tobias's as I'm lifted and forced to grab a hold of his shoulders to stop from falling backward. As I wrap my legs around his waist, Theo's lips crash into mine, making me moan out before I feel Tobias at my back, pressing into me, hot and cold. Tobias kisses my shoulder, letting go with one arm. I reach back and grab his hair, pulling softly.

I hear him groan. His mouth nips at my skin while his hands run over my ass cheeks and down my thighs that are secured around Theo's waist. I can feel Theo's erection standing tall. I wriggle down, trying to get enough friction or get him to enter. Theo, realizing what I want, loosens his grip so I slide down slightly. I feel his cock part my lips but not enter, which makes me groan into his shoulder.

"You want this?" he asks, thrusting upwards, but still not entering. I feel Tobias push his warm body against my back and I lean back into him, my head rolling onto his shoulder as one arm goes around his neck. Tobias hands go to my nipples as he pinches and twists them between his fingers. Theo's lips go to my neck as he thrusts inside me with one hard push.

My walls instantly clamp down at the sudden pain of having to try and stretch around him. He holds still for a few seconds, letting my body adjust and accommodate his size. Tobias starts sucking on my mark, my body instantly relaxes under his touch as pleasure builds inside me. Theo pulls out before slamming back into me.

I moan out and grip his shoulders with both hands, letting go of Tobias when Theo repeats the motion, moving faster. His hard cock slams into me, making me moan out and my legs squeeze tighter around his hips. My stomach tightens, and I can feel my orgasm building. Theo's face moves closer, and I feel him nipping at my chin and the side of my lips before he kisses me hard, sucking my bottom lip into his mouth, his teeth grazing it. I can taste my own blood, but it is soon gone when his tongue plunges into my mouth. He groans against my lips. I feel Tobias hand move along my ass before his fingers slide between my ass cheeks, pressing on the tight muscles of my ass. I moan at the pressure, my head falls into the crook of Theo's neck as he continues to pound inside me.

"You like what Tobias is doing, Imogen?" I moan as his finger pushes inside me, all while Theo continues to thrust harder. Tobias pulls his finger out before adding another. Then, he pulls them in and out slowly. Tobias lips move to my shoulder as his fingers play with my ass, moving faster. I push back into him.

"Not yet, you're not ready for that yet," Tobias says, his lips moving to my mark as he continues his movements. My walls clench onto Theo's cock, and he slows, groaning, before shoving his cock in harder and I'm shoved off the edge.

My orgasm makes my walls clamp down on him, and I feel him twitch inside me as pleasure ripples throughout my entire body. I feel Theo come inside me as his movements slow and I ride out my orgasm. Soon, Tobias pulls his fingers from me.

My head slumps on Theo's shoulder as my arms drape lazily around his neck. My breathing is ragged, and my eyes start to close. I feel Theo's flaccid cock pull out of me.

Tobias starts washing me. Eventually, I unlatch my legs from Theo's waist and slide to my feet. We quickly shower, both of them help me wash before I step out and grab a green towel off the towel rack, wrapping it around my body tightly.

Walking into the bedroom, I sit on the bed. Theo destroyed what was left of my skirt the other day, and I can't see my blouse anywhere. I sit on the edge of the bed, not having anything to put on. Theo walks into the closet and comes out with a pair of shorts on and a shirt in his hand. He walks over to me and pulls the shirt over my head, so I quickly slip my arms in and remove the towel. I hang the towel up in the bathroom and follow them out of the bedroom.

Tobias walks down some stairs, and I find myself marveling at the house. It's huge, its stone walls and exposed wooden beams on the roof gives it a rustic feel. Walking down the staircase, I can see onto the floor below which has slate floors. I feel Theo's hand on my shoulder, steering me in the right direction as we step into a living room with a huge fireplace. Bookshelves line the walls from floor to ceiling, on either side of the fireplace. There is a fluffy gray rug and cushions sitting in front of the fireplace, which is crackling and casting shadows throughout the room. It looks very cozy, considering the size. Walking past the couches, which are a soft brown fabric, I run my hand along the top of it, liking the feel of its fabric under my hand.

Theo steers me through another door, which turns out to be a galley style kitchen. It has brown cupboards, black marble countertops, and top of the line appliances. I sit on a stool at the island in the center of the kitchen. Tobias is rummaging in the stainless steel fridge. I rest my head on the cool countertop, "Don't fall asleep, Imogen, you need to eat." Tobias says while walking over and brushing my hair that has fallen over my face. He leans down and kisses my cheek, chuckling to himself before going back to whatever task he's doing. I hear Theo pulling pots from the cupboard and look up.

"Want any help?" I ask.

"Nope, we're good," Theo says, turning around and winking at me. I rest my head on my hand and yawn.

"When are we going back?" I ask. Neither of them acknowledges my question, which I find strange. So, I ask again. "Hello, when are we going back to civilization?"

Tobias looks up from cutting tomatoes. "You're not, Imogen. You'll remain here," he says, dropping his gaze. Theo looks over his shoulder at me before turning back to the stove.

My eyebrows furrow in confusion; they can't expect me to stay here. "What do you mean? I can't stay here forever. What about work?"

"We don't have to be at work till Wednesday, and only Theo or I will go."

"And why is that?" I ask, suddenly getting irritated. I can tell they are hiding something. Theo looks to Tobias and shakes his head as if not to tell whatever it is.

"You're not going back Imogen; we can't allow you to leave here," he simply says.

I stare at him. "I'm not staying here like some prisoner, Tobias; you can't do that," I scream, my fists clenching. Tobias looks up, his eyes flash and his jaw clenches.

"You will be staying, Imogen. It isn't a choice. You won't be leaving this property unless we say so." I look to Theo for help, but he just pretends he doesn't hear our exchange of words.

I shake my head, tears filling my eyes as anger starts bubbling up inside me. How dare they bring me here and then tell me I can't leave? How dare they believe they can control me like this and keep me prisoner?

"No, I'm not fucking staying here, Tobias. If that is what you think, just fucking kill me. I refuse to rot here for the rest of my life," I scream.

Tobias is in front of me in seconds, his grip on my arms hurts. I can feel his grip will leave bruises, but I don't care. "I'm not staying here," I yell again, refusing to back down. His eyes darken, turning to pitch black orbs. And one of his hands grips my throat, not hard enough to hurt me but more to show I can't escape even If I try.

"It's not a choice," he whispers next to my ear, the anger in his words makes me shiver. Theo comes over and places his hand on Tobias's shoulder, snapping him back. He lets go and steps back. I storm out of the kitchen and back to the bedroom, slamming the door behind me.

CHAPTER
TWENTY-SEVEN

How they think they can keep me here and expect me to be okay with it is beyond me. Maybe if they would give me a reason, and it would need to be a damn good one for me to be okay with having to toss my life away to rot here, I would be okay with their demands and rules.

Hopefully, Tobias will leave on Wednesday. I feel like I will have a better chance of getting through to Theo than Tobias. But if they think I'm going to sit and wait patiently for them to decide my life, they are sadly mistaken.

The knock on the door pulls me from my musings. I ignore it, but then Theo's voice reaches out to me through the door. "Imogen, open the door please." Always so polite, but I still choose to ignore him. "You know, I can just break the door, but I would rather not. It's antique. Be a shame to ruin it," he states.

I roll my eyes and look at the door, it does look old. Probably as old as the house with its strange hinges and thick wood. I hear him twist the handle, hear it straining under the pressure.

I jump up, it really would be a shame if the door would be destroyed because of my stubbornness. I always appreciated the craftsmanship that went into old buildings and furniture. "Wait, I will open it," I sing out before he breaks the brass handle.

Opening the door, I walk back to the bed. Theo leans on the doorframe, arms crossed over his bare chest. "He's being unreasonable. I will talk to him later, okay? Just come down and eat. Then, I want to take you somewhere," he says, holding his hand out to me.

"Off the property?" I ask, hopeful, thinking I might be able to give them the slip. I have no intention of spending the rest of my days out here. There isn't even cell service or internet reception.

"No, but you will like it. I promise." I roll my eyes but stand up anyway and walk past him, ignoring his hand. As I walk past, Theo slaps my bare ass. I jump at the sting from his hand. He ignores me and grabs my hand, leading me downstairs and back to the kitchen.

"Done sulking?" Tobias asks as I walk in, his back turned to the kitchen sink. I flip him the bird behind his back. "I can see your reflection in the glass, Imogen. I saw what you just did, I wouldn't recommend doing it again." His voice sounds like he's challenging me. I roll my eyes at him, at least he isn't in a homicidal mood anymore.

Tobias walks over and places a plate in front of me, "Now be a good girl and eat." I go to flip him off again, but suddenly Theo's arms wrap around my shoulders, his hand grabs mine, the one I intend to give Tobias the bird with.

He leans down so his lips next are to my ear. "You want him to punish you? Play nice," he whispers, kissing my cheek and letting me go before sitting next to me. Tobias places Theo's plate in front of him before sitting across from us.

"So, if you're a vampire, how come you eat real food?"

"I still eat, I just require blood as well."

"So, you drink from blood bags?" I ask.

"No, cold blood is disgusting. Remember when you said you saw me kissing Tobias's neck? Well, I wasn't."

"So, you drink from Tobias?" Tobias nods, like it isn't a big deal. "And you both have the same parents?"

Tobias looks at Theo before speaking. "Yes, but in case you forget we have different last names, we aren't biological siblings. I was raised by Theo's family."

"So, your parents are like you?" I ask, turning to Theo. He nods his head, but I can tell this conversation is making him uncomfortable. "So, when did you start living with Theo's family? How old were you?" I ask, looking at Tobias.

"I was six and Theo was four, that was what? Early 1746?" He asks, turning to Theo. Theo nods his head but doesn't say anything.

"Wait, how old are you?"

"280 years old. Theo is 278 years old." Tobias responds.

I feel my eyes go wide, horrified by the thought of having to live that long. "280," I whisper, not realizing I say it out loud.

"Enough worrying about our age Imogen, eat."

"I didn't mean it as a bad thing. I was expecting you to say 30, not 280 years old," I say, completely shocked.

"I stopped aging when I was 32. Theo is stuck at the age of 29, when he was turned," Tobias states.

"Turned? What about your parents?" I ask, trying to make sense of any of this.

"That's a conversation for later. For now eat please, you haven't touched your food," Theo starts tapping my plate with his fork. I roll my eyes, they're always so secretive, and I can tell Theo wants the topic changed, but why? I pick up a piece of tomato and pop it in my mouth, not realizing how hungry I actually am, until I taste its juicy goodness. My stomach instantly growls. I devour my food in a very unladylike manner, barely even tasting it. I finish mine before either of them finishes half of theirs.

"Did you even chew or just inhale your food?" Asks Theo, chuckling at my empty plate.

I get up, walk to the sink and wash my plate. I feel full and return to sit back at the table, suddenly wanting to go back to bed, seeing as I have had continuous broken sleep. I'm well and truly over tired now. I rest my head on the cool countertop and close my eyes. When

I hear them get up, I open my eyes, and rest my chin on my hands as I watch as they clean up after themselves. They are both so in sync with each other, they never seem to get in each other's way and pass things to each other without even looking or knowing if the other is going to catch it. When they turn around, I blush and look away. Knowing I'm caught red-handed, gawking at them like some pervert.

"Come on, let's find you some clothes," Theo says, walking out of the kitchen, heading towards the stairs. I follow after him, back into the bedroom. Theo rummages through his drawers and pulls out some shorts with a drawstring, tossing them to me. I slip them on before tying them as tight as they will go. Even now, they are still threatening to fall down.

"I need to at least go back and get my clothes; I can't keep wearing yours. I might as well walk around naked."

"I wouldn't mind. One of us will go grab some stuff from your apartment on Wednesday for you," Tobias says, walking into the room and grabbing a shirt from the hanger.

"Or, I could go with you," I plead.

"No Imogen, my word is final," he says.

"No Imogen, my word is final," I mock back with my best impersonation of Tobias's deep voice. I'm so not in the mood today. I hear Theo chuckle beside me and catch him shaking his head out of the corner of my eye.

"Stop encouraging her, Theo. She is in enough trouble when we get back."

"Yeah, and what is the big bad wolf gonna do? Stop me from leaving? Oh that's right I'm already a prisoner here," I reply dryly. I hear Tobias growl a throaty growl, coming from the back of his throat, vibrating through his chest.

"That's the third time now, Imogen. That attitude of yours is going to get you in trouble." I roll my eyes, so over hearing about being punished.

"And I'm starting to think your bark is worse than your bite," I retort. I see Theo's lips turn up slightly, repressing a smile. I watch as he walks out and starts walking down the stairs. I start to follow him out when I'm suddenly picked up from behind and walked over to the railing, Tobias lifts me over. I hear Tobias' throaty laugh before I'm suddenly dangling over the railing of the second floor. Tobias, not even breaking a sweat, as he holds me with one hand like I weigh nothing. I look down at the ground below and gulp.

"Not so sassy now, huh?"

I look down and see my feet dangling in the air, I hate heights. "I swear to god, Tobias, if you drop me..."

"You'll what?" He says tauntingly, letting go of my arm only to grab my hand before I plummet to the ground. I scream and look back down at the slate floor below me. "Fine, fine," he says, lifting me back to the railing. I put my foot on the side when Tobias grabs me and pulls me closer. He kisses me hard, then shoves me backwards. I fall towards the floor, closing my eyes. A scream escapes my lips, my hands go to my face as my heart drops into my stomach. Next thing, I find myself in Theo's arms, he pulls me into his chest. My hands are shaking as I grip his black shirt.

"I warned you not to test him," Theo whispers, I hear the smile and laugh he is trying to hold back.

"You damn asshole, you could have killed me," I scream up at Tobias, who is proudly standing next to the railing looking down at us, a smug smile on his face, like he finds this all very amusing.

"I knew Theo would catch you. Stop being a baby, you were never in any danger."

"Fuck you, Tobias" I say, letting go of Theo as he places my feet back on the ground. I turn my back on them and walk to the front door.

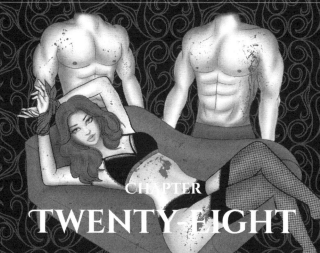

CHAPTER
TWENTY-EIGHT

G oing outside, I sit on the wooden chair next to the stairs. After a few minutes, Theo and Tobias walk out. Theo has a bag on his back, he sits on the steps and puts on a pair of hiking boots, Tobias does the same.

"So where are we going?" I ask. I really hope not hiking. Me and hiking don't mix, and I don't even have shoes, only heels which I'm not wearing.

"You will see when we get there, come here," Tobias says, holding his hand out to me.

"No, you just dropped me off the second floor, I'm not going near you." I cross my arms defiantly.

"I can take her," Theo says, trying to break up our standoff.

"No, she can come with me," he says. Theo shrugs and Tobias holds out his hand expectantly. "Now, Imogen," I hate when he says my name like that, sounds like he is scolding a child.

I shuffle closer but refuse to take his hand. Tobias grabs me around the waist, forcing my legs around his hips. "You're going to want to hang on," he says and starts running. I hear him laugh when my arms quickly wrap around his neck. Tobias' skin is warm and stops the chill from the wind. I close my eyes, so I don't get dizzy, but the motion of him running doesn't help as my stomach does backflips.

After a few minutes, we stop, but Tobias doesn't put me down. I look around and see that we are beside some river edge, Tobias walks along the river before stopping. I turn to look and see that we are on the edge of the small cliff; I look down and see a waterfall next to us and a lagoon looking area below. Looking ahead, all I see are trees for miles, they almost look like they never end. "Ready?" Asks Tobias, I stare at him, confused.

"Ready for what?" Instead of answering, he jumps. I squeal and clutch tighter to Tobias. I can hear him laughing before I feel water rushing past me as we are plunged into the water.

Tobias lets go as soon as we go under, and I frantically swim upwards to the surface. Once I catch my breath, I look around. The drop wasn't as big as it looks from up the top. Tobias surfaces next to me, wrapping his arms around me and pulling me to him. I don't argue and let him.

"Where is Theo?" Tobias points to the top and I watch Theo drop the bag off the edge over the cliff, it lands on the dirt just outside of the water. Theo then dives off the top, landing in the water. I look around for him, but he doesn't surface. Then, I'm tugged under water by my feet, slipping out of Tobias arms as I'm dragged underneath the water. I make my way back to the surface to see Theo, smiling at me.

I dunk his head back under the water before swimming away. "You like it?" Theo calls out when he resurfaces.

"It's beautiful here," I call back before floating on my back. I focus on looking up at the sky, which can only just be seen through all the trees that make a sort of canopy above the lagoon. Tobias and Theo swim over to where I'm floating.

"It's peaceful here," Tobias says.

"Of course, it is, we are in the middle of nowhere," I tell him.

"Not true, we are only half an hour out of the city."

I stand up and look at him. "You're lying. I trekked through this forest for hours the other day and never found a road."

"Well, it would help if you were going in the right direction. You were moving further out, not closer," Tobias says. I ponder for a second, well in that case, maybe I will be able to leave. I don't let that slip though; they have given me a little too much information on our whereabouts.

"How come there is no cell service out here then, if we aren't that far out?"

"The mountains," Theo says, before dunking me under water.

I come up coughing and spluttering, having had my mouth open when he dunked me. I splash him before darting back under the water and swimming away, towards a giant rock on the water edge. Climbing up, I sit on the rock, my feet dangle in the water. I can hear the insects in the trees chirping loudly. But yet, I still notice no animals around or birds. I find it strange.

Tobias and Theo follow but remain in the water near my legs. Lifting my legs, I put them on Tobias shoulders and shove him back under the water. He grips my ankles and yanks me back in the water, pressing me against the rock.

I wrap my legs around his waist; I can feel his erection through his shorts pressing on my core. Tobias kisses me and grinds his erection against me. I moan into his mouth at the sudden friction. I feel his hands go to my shorts as he undoes the drawstring. I unwrap my legs and pull them off before wrapping them back around him.

"Hmm someone is eager," Tobias says against my lips, his hands gripping my ass as he rubs my crotch on his rock-hard cock. I kiss him and feel him chuckle against my lips. I use his shoulders to lift myself up, trying to get him to slide in my now throbbing core, but he holds my hips in place.

"You want this," he says, rubbing himself against me. I groan at the feel of his cock rubbing against my clit. "Hmm," My lips go to his neck. "Words, Imogen." I grind myself against him before he moves me off the rock and I feel Theo slip behind me. I feel Theo's cool lips on my shoulder.

"You want Tobias to fuck you, Imogen?" He says against my shoulder.

"Yes," my voice comes out in more of a gasp, as I feel Theo's hand go under my shirt to my nipples that have pebbled from the cool water. My head rolls back onto Theo's chest as Tobias shoves inside me. His lips on my collarbone, his teeth grazing and teasing my skin. I push against him, meeting his thrusts, loving the feel of his hard cock stretching and pushing against my walls, his cock hitting my G-spot, making me clench around him. Theo moves away and retrieves the bag before coming back and retaking his position behind me, his hands rubbing my ass cheeks under the water. Tobias hands wrap tightly around my waist, his lips go to my breast before he sucks my nipple into his mouth. He bites down on it hard, and I gasp before his tongue soothes the sting. He moves to my other nipple, just as he bites down, I feel something hard push between my ass cheeks and inside me, I flinch at the sudden burning pain, when Tobias stills for a second.

"Breathe Imogen, it's only a vibrator, not Theo." Theo's hand moves between us and I feel him step closer behind me, his fingers go to my clit and rub in a circular motion. My body starts to relax, and I find myself lost in the feeling of his fingers. I start grinding against his fingers and riding Tobias cock at the same time.

"That's our girl," says Tobias as he thrusts into me, his hands on my hips, guiding my movements. Theo's fingers play with my clit, his lips against my neck, sucking on Tobias's mark, sending thrills all through me. His other hand pushes the vibrator in and out of me. I feel my stomach tighten, my body feels overly full and sensitive to everything. Everything feels overstimulated and almost too much.

My head goes forward, landing on Tobias' shoulder as my body spasms. As my body suffers the most mind-blowing orgasm, my walls clench tightly around Tobias. I feel him thrust in harder before stilling, as I ride out my orgasm that just keeps going in waves, my legs tremble as I feel Theo slide the vibrator out of me and Tobias finds his own release. My body goes completely limp as I slump against Tobias shoulder, my eyes flutter closed and I'm completely out of breath. I feel the water get lower and know Tobias is getting us out of the water.

"You can sleep, Imogen," Theo says as he wraps a towel around me before taking me from Tobias. I relax into his hold, absolutely exhausted. I can't sleep even if I want to, the winds are chilly and Theo's cold skin keeps me awake and alert. My body is continuously shivering, goosebumps spreading all over. When we stop, Theo puts me down, "Sorry I forgot you feel the cold worse than us. I should have let Tobias bring you back," he says.

Tobias walks over and throws an arm over my shoulder, pulling me into him. I instantly put my hands on his chest as that seems to be the hottest part of him. He flinches a little at my cold hands before pulling me tighter against him. "Come on, let's have a hot shower." Theo races ahead of us and I hear the water already running as we walk up the stairs.

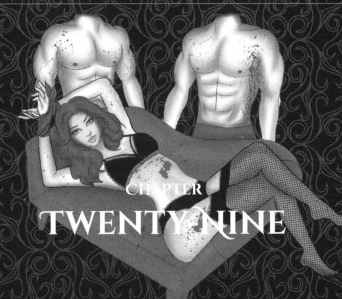

TWENTY-NINE

After showering, I have just slipped on one of Tobias's shirts when I hear a phone ring. He walks over to where it is laying on charge next to the bed, picks it and answers; it looks like a sat phone. "What?" His voice is angry. Theo walks out, clearly listening to whoever is speaking on the other end. Tobias abruptly hangs the phone up, not even saying goodbye.

"I can go," Theo says. I stare, confused. Tobias shakes his head, the phone call clearly angered him.

"No, I will. You watch Imogen," he says, going into the walk-in in a robe and coming out with a suit.

"Where are you going?" I ask, although I already think I know he has been called into work.

"Work. Now, stay with Theo and behave."

I shake my head. "I'm not a child, Tobias, don't speak to me like that," I argue. He raises an eyebrow at me, clearly angered by my attitude. "Can we come please; I just want to grab a few things," I try again.

"No, you don't leave here, Imogen." He shakes his head.

"Why? You make no sense. I can't just rot here, Tobias," I argue back. Tobias' hands clench and unclench, the veins in his arms bulge. He ignores me, putting his shirt on. I move towards him and he grips my hands, before letting them go. I start buttoning up his shirt. "Please, I will stay with Theo, I promise."

"No! I am sick of this argument. You're not leaving, Imogen, so stop asking." He grits out.

Theo moves closer behind me, placing his hands on my shoulders. "I will watch her. She will be fine, Tobias, then I will bring her back here," Theo said calmly.

Tobias shoves him, knocking me to the ground. Theo's eyes blaze red with anger as he shoves Tobias back. I see Tobias skin start to ripple; I know he is about to shift. Tobias grabs Theo's shirt, yanking him forward, his eyes completely black. I jump to my feet, frightened. I don't want him to hurt Theo, so I grab Tobias hand, which is clutching Theo. He lets go of Theo, throwing him to the ground, before turning on me and grabbing my neck. I clutch at his hand, but he squeezes tighter, his anger completely engulfes him.

I claw at his hands, my nails scratch his skin. I can feel my face changing color, then, something snaps in him and he realizes he has grabbed me just as Theo tackles him. His grip is gone from my neck as I fall to the floor and start coughing, choking for air.

Theo and Tobias are on the ground, fighting. I crawl onto my hands and knees. Trying to breathe, my windpipe feels like it has been crushed in a vice. I can still feel where his fingers gripped me. Tobias, coming to his senses, gasps, making me look at him. His horrified expression at seeing me on the floor turns to panic. He moves to me in an instant, but I swat his hands away. Theo looks relieved as he comes closer, standing behind Tobias, who is on the floor next to me. Tobias moves his hand to my cheek.

"I didn't mean to; you can't touch me when I'm like that." I feel his fingers brush my neck and I see his eyes change, going darker and an indecipherable look appears in his eyes. "I'm sorry," he says before getting up and walking out, slamming the door behind him. I stare at the door. Theo steps closer, offering me his hand. I take it, and he pulls me to my feet.

"He wouldn't have hurt me. Don't ever do that again, Imogen," he says. "You need to remember we aren't human. We aren't breakable like you."

His words anger me, I let go of his hand and walk into the closet to find some pants. Theo follows closely behind me and passes me a pair when I can't find any. "Don't be upset, he feels guilty enough. He is just on edge because I haven't marked you yet. He will settle down once I have." I stare at him, my anger clearly on display as I slip the pants up to my waist.

"Why is marking so important? You men are infuriating. Why couldn't I have been gay?" Theo chuckles before pulling me into him.

"Because Tobias has only marked you. The mark isn't complete, and you can still leave."

"Leave?" I ask, confused.

"Yes, once I have marked you, you will be bound to us for eternity, Imogen. The bond will never allow you to leave, and you won't want to anyway. The bond gets stronger, you will be able to feel what we feel, and us, you." He explains.

"Just from you marking me?" I raise an eyebrow at him.

"Yes, after a few days and your mark is healed, you won't want to leave us. Before then though, you can reject us still. That's what scares Tobias."

"But he has already marked me. How can I leave?" I keep pressing for more answers.

"Because Tobias and I are fated mates, just the same as you're ours, so his mark is like half, mine is the other half. It won't be complete until I mark you. If you leave, it will destroy him, and after a few years, you will forget about us."

Do I want to forget about them? I'm not sure what I want, I just know I want to go back to the apartment, where my mother is still sitting in her box. That thought upsets me, I haven't even had a chance to release her. I sigh and walk out, Theo follows behind me as I walk down the stairs and into the living room.

I sit on the couch. Theo sits beside me, and I lay down, putting my head in his lap. "Would it hurt? You, marking me?" I ask, suddenly scared but if it is the only way I can leave, I might not have a choice.

"Yes, but Tobias will help." Theo whispers.

"What do you mean?" I ask, confused.

"He will distract you from the pain. It will only hurt initially, then will be pleasurable, but you being my mate and human complicates it a little. I'm a vampire, so I'll want to feed on you. Tobias will make sure I stay in control; he won't let me hurt you, Imogen." I nod my head not feeling any better about being bitten again when I can't remember being bitten by Tobias.

"Do you want to watch a movie?" He asks, distracting me from my thoughts.

"On what? There is no TV." I chuckle.

Theo reaches over to the coffee table and grabs a remote control out of the drawer. He presses a button and the painting above the fireplace opens up. Only it's not a painting, it's a cupboard hiding the TV inside. Really, this could have saved so much boredom. Not that I have actually been bored, but still, I didn't even notice it. Theo selects a movie and presses play.

"How do you have service when I can't even get cell service?"

"There is a hard drive in the back. We don't have service, we never needed it. We rarely stay here." I nod in understanding before turning on my side. Halfway through the movie, Theo starts a fire in the fireplace, comes back and slides in behind me, wrapping his arm around me.

Before the movie is over, I fall asleep, only waking up when I feel warm hands lift me up. I snuggle into Tobias, his manly smell fills my nose. He dips his head into the crook of my neck, inhaling my scent. I reach my hand up and put it on his cheek. He lifts his head and kisses my fingertips before moving his lips to mine, sucking my bottom lip into his mouth and deepening the kiss, his tongue playing with mine. I moan into his mouth, arousal floods me, and my legs squeeze tighter to stop the ache. Tobias pulls back and sniffs the air, I blush, embarrassed. My sex drive is so out of whack it is becoming ridiculous. Tobias smirks before kissing my forehead but doesn't put me down.

"Where is Theo?" I ask when I realize he is no longer on the couch.

"Cooking dinner," Tobias says, walking us into the kitchen.

Theo is busy cooking some pasta dish. My stomach growls at the delicious smell, and Tobias places me on a stool before going to help Theo. I watch Tobias take his suit jacket off, placing it on the back of a chair before rolling his shirt sleeves to his elbows. I watch them both, amazed at the fact they are both mine. It somehow doesn't feel real.

"Mmm, someone smells nice." I look at Theo, confused, then realize he is talking about me. I press my legs together and I can feel the dampness of my panties from kissing Tobias. Theo walks over, his hand grabs my breast through my shirt and pinches my nipple as he kisses my cheek. "Keep smelling like that and the only thing I will be eating is you," he whispers before pulling my hair, forcing me to look up at him.

His cold lips crash down on mine hungrily, sucking my tongue into his mouth before biting down on my lip. My stomach tightens, and I can feel my juices spill onto my thighs, arousal coursing through my entire body.

"Theo, leave her be. After dinner you can play," Tobias says, placing three plates on the table. I'm no longer hungry, I want something else, and it isn't food. I pout when Theo moves away, sitting opposite me. Tobias sits next to me; he squeezes my thigh. "Eat." I roll my eyes at him for ruining our fun. Tobias grips my chin, making me look at him. "I think it's about time you drop that attitude you have." I swallow, and he notices, his lips turn up slightly. He kisses me softly before biting my lip hard. "Now, eat without the attitude."

He lets my chin go and I fight the urge to say something snarky back, but I can tell he knows I'm holding my tongue. Theo smirks and I glare at him.

After dinner, I wash the dishes and follow them back out to the living room, Tobias leaves for a few minutes and comes back with wood for the fire. He stacks the timber and stokes it. I drop onto the couch and flick through the movies. Not long after, I chose one movie - the conjuring.

"You want to watch a horror movie?" Asks Theo, incredulous.

"Hey, I like horrors, just don't like going to bed afterwards," Theo shakes his head before holding his arms out for me. I nestle into his arms; Tobias sits next to both our heads.

I jump a few times during the movie, making Tobias and Theo both laugh as my heart hammers in my chest. Tobias even waits for the movie to build up suspense and takes great pleasure in grabbing me, scaring the living daylights out of me. Halfway through, I need to pee, I look at the stairs a few times. This old house becomes as intimidating as the one in the movie, with its dark shadows. I wriggle a bit, trying to hold my bladder. "What's wrong? Stop wriggling," Theo says.

"I need to pee," Tobias looks down at me.

"Then go pee," he says, raising an eyebrow at me, I stand up and walk to the stairs. All the lights are off, and I can't see the top of the stairs, only shadows. Tobias and Theo watch me, frozen, with one foot on the step, clutching the railing. I hear one of them laugh.

"What's wrong, Imogen? You're not scared, are you?" Theo says, trying not to laugh.

"No," I say defiantly, but my heart rate gives me away. I move up a step and freeze again and look over the railing at them. "Can one of you come with me please?"

Tobias gets up laughing, "I thought you said you weren't scared."

"I'm not, it's just dark up there," I say, walking up the steps, stopping halfway when I don't feel him behind me. He's standing on the bottom step, arms folded, an amused expression on his face.

"Tobias," I squeak.

"You're in a house with a vampire and a werewolf and that doesn't scare you, but a movie does," he states, walking up the steps behind me.

"Yeah, but you're not scary," I state, walking up the steps.

When I reach the landing, Theo jumps out of the shadows. "Boo!" I scream and run before realizing it's Theo.

"You asshole, you just scared the hell out of me. How did you get past us?" I say, slapping his arm and walking past him into the bathroom, flicking the light on.

"There are stairs at the other end of the house leading up here," he tells me. I shut the door and quickly pee, I wash my hands and open the door. Both of them lean on the door frame, waiting for me.

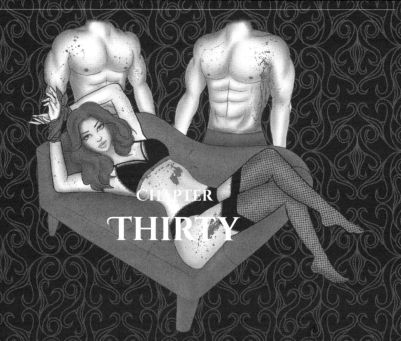

THIRTY

"We need to head to bed soon, I have work in the morning," Tobias states. I yawn, suddenly feeling tired, it must be late. I go to say something but then stop, not wanting a repeat of earlier. I follow them into the room and climb into bed. Tobias takes his shirt off and climbs in next to me.

Theo turns a small lamp on and grabs a book before lying beside me. My eyebrows furrow confused. "You're not tired?" I ask.

"Vampires don't sleep, Imogen," he chuckles.

"But I saw you sleep," I point out, confused.

"No, we don't sleep, but we do get stuck in a trance which resembles sleep," he tells me. Tobias yawns next to me and pulls me against him.

Although I am tired, I still want to know more, so I keep questioning him. "What do you mean?"

"Well, it's kind of like being stuck in your own thoughts, becoming trapped in a way. You don't realize time is passing," he explains.

I would hate to be stuck in my own mind; it's my biggest critic. I seriously can't imagine being trapped in it. "How long does it last?"

Theo seems to think for a second before answering. "My longest would be a month before Tobias pulled me out of it."

"A month?" How lonely must have he felt during that time? I reach out and drape my arm across his lap. It doesn't take long before I fall asleep.

I'm awoken in what must have been only a few hours by Theo, suddenly climbing back into bed with yet another book. I yawn and wriggle out of Tobias's grip, moving closer to Theo. I put my head on his lap; his hand playing with my hair. "What are you reading?" I mumble, fighting the urge to yawn again.

"Nothing important, you should go back to sleep." I shake my head, I always struggle to go back to sleep after waking, and if I do manage to actually go back to sleep, I will feel ten times worse when I get up again.

Instead, I get up and walk over to my phone. I pick it up and the screen lights up, revealing that it's 4:30 am. I place the phone back down and walk into the bathroom. I quickly pee before stripping the shirt off and turning the shower on and hopping in. I wet my hair, letting the water wake me up completely. Grabbing the soap, I start washing myself, and Theo walks in.

He drops his shorts, opens the shower door and I move over to allow him to join me. Theo turns the other shower head on and faces me, watching as I wash myself. I turn my back on him feeling self-conscious under his gaze.

When I turn around, he is still staring. "Stop staring, pervert." I mumble but he just smirks.

"I can look, you belong to me." My heart skips a beat and Theo moves closer, placing his hand on my hip and pulling me flush against him. I let him and continue to wash the shampoo out of my hair as his fingers move up my side, stopping at the side of my breast.

His thumb rubs over my nipple, making it harden. I rinse the shampoo out and open my eyes. As soon as I do, Theo kisses me, sucking my bottom lip into his mouth. My body is shoved into the shower wall. His tongue plays with mine, searching and tasting every inch of my mouth. He pulls back, letting me catch my breath, only to lift me up, his hands on my ass, my arms grabbing his neck to stop from falling.

Theo pushes me into the wall, and I can feel his erection resting on the inside of my thigh. Theo's hand reaches into my hair, pulling my head to the side, his fangs grazing my neck as he hungrily kisses and nibbles on my skin. I freeze when I feel his fangs break my skin slightly. I hiss at the pain, and Tobias walks in.

"You know how hard it is to sleep when I can hear you two fooling around in here?" He grumbles.

Both Theo and I stop, Theo kisses my lips, a sly smile on his face at us being caught. The next moment, Tobias steps in the shower, "Well, don't stop on my account."

I feel Theo chuckle and shrug before his lips move back to mine. Tobias washes himself while Theo continues his assault on my neck before moving lower to suck my nipple into his mouth. I throw my head back, forgetting the tiled wall behind me. My skull makes a loud thud as it connects with the wall.

"See, it's karma for fooling around without me," Tobias says, rubbing the spot I just smacked into the wall. Theo places my feet back on the floor, and I step between the pair of them before opening the door. "Where are you going?"

"To get dressed," I tell them, grabbing a towel.

"What about this?" Theo laughs and points to his huge erection. I look down, it does look tempting, but If I leave, they will have to fuck each other. I smile at my new idea.

"Tobias will have to help you with that," I retort, smirking and wrapping my towel around me and walking out. I hear Theo curse and call Tobias a cockblocker. I chuckle to myself, amused.

As soon as I find the blouse from the first day here, I lay it on the bed and walk into the walk-in closet. It takes a bit, but I manage to find some track pants and a shirt.

Tobias and Theo walk out of the bathroom, towels wrapped

around their waists. "What are you doing?" Tobias asks when he sees I'm dressed, not in my clothes, but still covered and not just wearing my usual shirt and socks combination.

"Going to work, but first I need to go home to get clothes," I state.

I hear him growl behind me but ignore him. "I have told you, Imogen, you won't be leaving the house."

"I'm so sick of hearing you dictate my life, Tobias. Either I can go to work with you or neither of you will be getting laid unless you fuck each other," I say, folding my arms across my chest defiantly. I raise an eyebrow at him, "So, what will it be?"

Tobias chuckles and shakes his head. "Fine, I will play your little game, Imogen. It won't work. You will be begging for us to take you," Tobias says.

I pout and Theo chuckles. "Is it because Theo hasn't marked me?" I ask, turning to Tobias.

"Yes, among other reasons. That is the main one though."

This is ridiculous. "I'm not leaving you, Tobias; I won't take off I promise." I try to reason with him, even though it feels like he's the most brick-headed man I've ever met.

"You're right, you won't take off because you're not leaving this property." I look to Theo for help but he doesn't seem to want to go against Tobias this time, so I storm out of the room.

I make my way down to the kitchen and put the kettle on. It's about time I get some coffee in my system.

As soon as it's ready, I take my cup and sit outside on the wooden bench seat. Tobias walks out, my handbag in his hands, he drops it on my lap.

"I have your keys; you just want your clothes?" I ignore him, looking in the other direction. "Imogen, what do you want from your apartment?"

"Fuck you, Tobias," I tell him. He pinches the bridge of his nose and lets out an annoyed breath.

Theo walks out, and I ignore him too. "I will send you a list of what she wants later, okay," he says, kissing Tobias on the cheek.

When I get up and walk inside, I hear Tobias speed off. I walk up the stairs and back to my prison. Once the door is closed behind me, I lock it and lay back in bed.

T en Days later

I have been stuck here for ten days. I haven't spoken to either of them; I barely come out of the room. The first few days they tried without luck, in every way possible, to get me to talk or react to them.

I know it is starting to get to them, Tobias has been a moody asshole. He left three days ago and has been staying in the city, saying my silence is driving him crazy. This house is driving me crazy, so I guess he knows how it feels now. Theo, on the other hand, is always hovering. I feel his presence everywhere I go, always watching. Always trying to get me to speak to him.

I'm lying in bed when he walks in, "Breakfast, Imogen," he sings out from the doorway. I ignore him and roll over, turning my back on the door. "It's been two days and you haven't left this room, Imogen. If you don't eat today, I will be forced to tell Tobias you haven't eaten."

Pfft, two days is that all it's been. I'm starving but I know I can last a lot longer. I refuse to give in. Either I get to go back to my normal predictable life, or I'm not talking or eating. Even despite the fact that the food does smell nice.

When he doesn't leave, I sit up and walk to the bathroom and hop in the shower. This place is a mansion, but it is starting to make me feel claustrophobic. Despite its size and how beautiful the place is, it's still my prison. I have walked the property and the house so much I'm surprised I haven't actually walked tracks around the place.

I thought about running but Theo is always right behind me wherever I go. The first day, I tried to convince him to just take me home, but he wouldn't go against Tobias. This place with its no neighbors, no passing cars, no people is lonely. I like the hustle and bustle of the city, but mainly I like the people, watching as they go about their lives. I miss seeing Tom, but mostly now that I haven't spoken in over a week, I have been left to my own thoughts, and my mind always drifts to the one person I loved most in life. My mother. My life suddenly feels lonely and small without her in it and having no one to vent my problems to.

Getting out of the shower, I open the door and Theo is leaning against it. I roll my eyes and shove past him. "Tobias is on his way home," I freeze.

I like that he hasn't been here. I struggle the most around him. He is so hot headed and so am I. It always turns into a screaming match, or in my case, at the moment, me just glaring at him. I chuck my clothes on just in time to hear him pull up. Theo leaves to see him, I quickly walk over and lock the door, hoping he won't want to break it, the same as Theo and leave me alone. No such luck, I hear him walk up the stairs, his feet moving quick. He doesn't even knock, just kicks the door in.

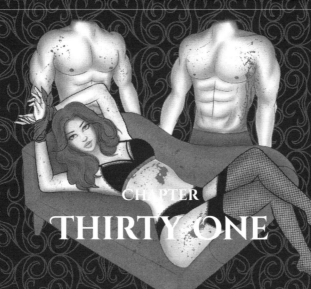

I jump to my feet; Tobias walks over to me and grabs my arm. "Why aren't you eating?"

"I want to go home," I tell him, ignoring his question and trying to yank my arm free. His grip is too strong and his arm doesn't even move. It's like pulling on a brick wall.

"That's not an option, you know this already," Tobias growls, visibly angry. His eyes flick between their usual blue to black onyx. Tobias pulls me towards the door, intending to take me down the stairs.

"Tobias, let go, you are hurting me." He lets go and instead, throws me over his shoulder caveman style. I smack his back once and only manage to hurt my own hand. Tobias slaps my bare ass and I jump; the sting is intense and makes my eyes water.

"You didn't need to smack her that hard, Tobias," Theo scolds him. I can feel every finger welting on my skin.

"She has to learn," Tobias simply says.

"I'm not a fucking child; you don't just go smacking people like that. It fucking hurt, dickhead."

Tobias walks into the kitchen and places me on the stool in front of the breakfast Theo made, which is now cold. "Eat now or I will force feed you."

"Like hell you will. I'm not doing anything you want, Tobias." I snap at him.

Tobias punches the island counter, making me jump. I refuse to back down and stand up, walking back out. I know he won't hurt me, at least not intentionally. I sit on the couch and flick the TV on. I can hear Theo and Tobias arguing in the kitchen but tune them out. Not being able to find something I want to watch, I give up and head back to the bedroom.

Theo comes up with Tobias and I sit up. "Just leave me alone, please."

"If I let you go back, do you promise to grab your things and come back here?" Tobias asks.

"Yes," I lie.

Tobias must have heard my heart rate pick up because he is standing over me in a second. "You're lying," He looks down at me. I really am a terrible liar, now even worse with their super hearing picking up my heart rate.

"I don't want to be here, okay? I want to go back to work; I don't want to stay out here till I drop dead, Tobias." Tobias and Theo exchange glances. Tobias is about to walk out, clearly not going to let me leave, but Theo stands in the doorway. That, however, doesn't stop him as Tobias barges past Theo.

"I will let Theo mark me," I say softly.

I give up. That's exactly what Tobias wants. If it means going back to normal, I will do it. It's clear he heard me when he freezes, turns around and walks back into the room.

Tobias grabs my chin with his fingers, forcing me to look up at him and meet his eyes. "Say it again."

"I will let Theo mark me. There, I said it. Can I please go back?"

Tobias thinks for a second as his eyes focus on mine, probably to ensure I'm not lying again. After a moment of tense silence, he speaks up again. "I have to go back to work, so he can't now."

I sigh. What's another day, I suppose.

"I will drop you off with Theo. You don't leave his side until I come get you, understood?" I nod, eager to go back, even if it is for only for a few hours. I can at least get my mother out of that darn box. The guilt of knowing she is still sitting in it has been eating at me.

Theo grabs me some pants and chucks them to me. I quickly slip them on and follow them back downstairs. Tobias walks outside and hops in the car, I go to get in the back, but he winds the window down and I already know he wants me in front. I open the passenger door and hop in.

Theo comes out and gets in the back, he passes me a muffin. "Eat it. He is letting you go back. Now eat." Tobias waits for me to take a bite and my stomach growls from being empty for two days, Tobias growls and starts the car. With traffic it takes us forty-five minutes to get to the apartment building. Getting out, the valet looks at me with a strange expression, probably because of my clothing choice. It isn't really a choice, I'm still wearing their clothes. Tobias walks us to my apartment door, unlocks it and lets us in. He gives Theo a kiss before grabbing me and shoving his tongue down my throat.

He pulls away and smirks. "Behave or this will be the last time I let you back here, Imogen." I nod, and he walks out, closing the door. I walk straight into my bedroom and Theo walks in behind me, carrying a suitcase.

"Pack what you need. We won't be coming back for a while." He mutters.

I turn to him, not quite understanding what he means. "But I said you could mark me; how long will I have to stay out there for?"

"Probably a week till the bond kicks in. Then, he will let you come back to work." Theo looks away nervously. I have never seen him look nervous before, but I feel like he's lying to me. Why do I have a feeling I won't be coming back here at all? Knowing I can't run, I decide to pack. I chuck my clothes in the suitcase as Theo walks in, holding my photo album and places it in the suitcase.

"He isn't letting me come back, is he?" Theo looks away at my question. It's all the answer I need to feel more frustrated than ever, so I leave him in the bedroom and walk into the living room.

"He fucking lied to me and you went along with it." Theo doesn't say anything, and I know I'm right. They plan on keeping me locked away. "Why?" My voice makes him look back at me. I'm furious. "I'm done, so fucking done with everything."

"We have our reasons, Imogen," Theo says.

"Explain then, make me understand," I beg, tears brimming in my eyes. I can't keep doing this. If this is what my life will be like with them, I want no part of it. I walk over and grab my make up bag, hairbrush and dump it in the bag.

"Once I have marked you, and the bond has kicked in, we will explain everything. You just need to be patient." Theo mutters.

"Patient? I have been patient for two fucking weeks. I'm done Theo. I don't want to be a part of whatever the fuck this is." I raise my voice.

Theo looks hurt but walks out into the kitchen, giving me space to calm down. I continue to pack, knowing I don't have a choice. If I run, they will just drag me back. Finally, having my own clothes, I slip on a pair of black leggings and an oversized sweatshirt.

When Tobias arrives to pick us up, I grab mom off the counter and walk out to the car. Theo and Tobias put my things in the car, and I climb in the back. I ignore Tobias when he asks me to get in front. Instead, I turn to look out the window. The ride back to my prison is silent and tense. Nobody speaks and when the car pulls up, I open the door and get out before he stops completely. I open the front door, which they left unlocked and walk upstairs. I don't bother closing the door, seeing as it is now broken.

I place the box on the side table and open it, grabbing the plastic urn out. I stare at it, wondering what I can do with her. I don't want her trapped in the urn forever like I am in this house. I also don't want to let her go either; I know that will be the last step before I'm forced to move on without her. I know mom wanted to be set free, she mentioned it a few times in passing whenever loved ones died. Mom would always say she didn't want to be buried in a coffin with worms and critters, that she wanted to be set free somewhere nice. I know I need to honor her wishes; I'm just not sure I'm ready yet.

Tobias walks up and places my bag in the walk-in robe. "What's that?" he says, pointing to the urn in my hands. To be fair it doesn't even look like an urn, it's literally a blue plastic container.

"My mother," I say, my voice empty, emotionless. Tobias hesitates before sitting next to me, he doesn't say anything, just sits there. His company is nice, but I'm still furious with him for lying to me, and what he is doing. After about ten minutes of sitting in silence, he speaks.

"I never knew my parents. I know they were both werewolves, obviously. I was placed up for adoption when I was born. I was adopted when I was five and I turned. My adoptive parents freaked out, said I was cursed and a demon from hell." He chuckles, like he thinks it's funny. Honestly, I think it's harsh, especially for a five-year-old; to just chuck him away like garbage, not once but twice.

"I lived on the streets until I met Theo's mother. She found me sleeping behind a dumpster, out front of their house, and then, they raised me."

"That woman that came here was Theo's mother, wasn't it?" I ask.

"Yes, her name is Caroline. The man that was here is Josiah, Theo's father."

"And they didn't care that you were a werewolf?" I ask. They must be nice people if they would take in a random child, one that wasn't human.

"No, for years they pretended not to notice, even covered up for me when I would accidently kill livestock on neighboring farms, but no they didn't care. People feared what they didn't understand, they still do. Caroline just saw me as a child, not a monster." Tobias explains, seemingly lost in some memories.

I think about his words for a second, trying to imagine what it would have been like so long ago. Getting up, I place her back in the box. I don't want to put her in it, but I also don't want to leave her here, where I sleep with two supernatural beings. That doesn't seem appropriate. Tobias grabs the box from my hands, realizing I'm trying to think of somewhere to put her.

"Come on, she can sit on the mantle till you figure out what you want to do." I nod and follow him down. He reaches up and puts her on the mantle below the TV. Theo comes out and wraps his arms across my shoulders, his lips going to my neck and I shiver under his touch.

"Want to have a shower with us?" He asks, pressing himself into my back so I can feel the bulge in his pants. I don't even get to answer before I'm whisked off back upstairs and into the bathroom. Tobias and Theo seem to be racing each other to see who can rip my clothes off first.

In no time, I'm stripped completely bare. Tobias picks me up and places me on the sink, standing in between my legs. I wrap them around his waist, completely forgetting I'm angry at him, just loving the feel of his hands on my body, softly caressing my thighs and sides. I put my arms around his neck and lean forward, kissing him. I run my tongue along his bottom lip, wanting entry. When I feel his lips part, I brush my tongue on his. He pushes into me, taking control and kissing me deeper. I moan into his mouth as his hand moves up squeezing my breast. I hear Theo step in the shower and look over Tobias' shoulder, he shakes his head smiling and I can't help but chuckle.

I push on Tobias' chest, so he steps back, and I hop off the counter, getting in the shower. Tobias walks in directly behind me, his hands go to my breasts as he pulls me back towards him, my back pressed against his warm chest. Theo moves closer and I can feel his erection pressing into my stomach as he leans in to kiss me. One of his hands moving between my legs, his fingers parting my lips before he shoves a finger inside me.

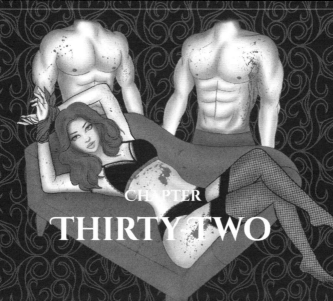

CHAPTER
THIRTY-TWO

I lean back into Tobias, his hands on my breasts, teasing my nipples. They instantly harden under his touch, Theo pulls his finger from me. I can feel the slickness of my juices on them as he slides another inside me, curling his fingers upwards and rubbing on my G-spot.

I moan loudly and I hear Theo chuckle at my reaction. I feel my skin heating up, and it has nothing to do with the water temperature. Tobias grabs the soap and loofa while I continue to lean on him, and he starts washing me. I shiver as he pulls my hair over one shoulder, his fingers softly caressing the skin of my neck, as he runs the loofa over my skin. Theo's fingers move faster, making me grip his hand, trying to slow his rhythm as it becomes too much. He doesn't stop though; instead, he leans in. His lips move on mine as I shatter, my walls grip his fingers. I can feel my vagina pulsating and quivering as my orgasm runs through me.

I can't help but moan, my legs tremble and my grip loosens on his hand. Theo slides his fingers out before moving closer to me, pressing his body into mine that is leaning on Tobias. My face feels hot, and I can still feel his fingers inside me. We quickly shower, knowing if we don't, we won't leave. Everywhere I touch, my skin feels sensitive and alive to every sensation.

Getting out, I wrap myself in my towel and start drying myself. I have barely dropped the towel when I feel Tobias grab me, spinning me around so I'm facing him. He kisses me hard and demandingly, as he backs me towards the bed until I fall backwards. Tobias lands on top of me, his weight held up by his arms.

Tobias' arm goes around my waist as he lifts and moves us to the top of the bed. He pins my hands above my head, pushing them into the mattress. His lips move to my neck as he licks and sucks my skin. I feel cold hands grab mine and the bed dips slightly. Tobias releases my hands as Theo puts my wrists in leather handcuffs. I look up, wondering what he is doing, my heartbeat picking up. I pull on my restraints and Theo pulls my hands back before pulling a rope between the cuffs and securing it to the headboard.

Panic surges through me, fear of being left exposed and vulnerable takes over. It scares me, being left completely at someone else's mercy, completely defenseless and giving them full control.

Theo moves towards my legs and places a leather cuff on my ankle, I pull my leg away, completely forgetting about Tobias, who is still teasing my skin under his relentless kisses and sucking. Theo stops and watches me for a second. "Stop Tobias, she is freaking out," I tug on my cuffed hands frantically.

Tobias stops, "Your heart is racing. Calm down, we won't hurt you," he says softly. But his words don't have the effect he's hoping for, as I continue to panic. Tobias hops off me and Theo moves closer, each of his arms on either side of my face while he looks down at me.

"I won't cuff your feet. Do you want me to uncuff your hands, or I can make your fear go away? We won't do anything to cause you harm." I try to think for a second, but my heart rate slows as his words sink in. They won't hurt me; I tell myself. I can trust them. Theo hears my heart slow, and I stop fighting against the restraints. He leans in and kisses me.

I warily answer his kiss, his tongue running along my bottom lip.

I feel Tobias remove the cuffs from my ankles. My body instantly relaxes, knowing I won't be fully restrained. I can always kick them if they piss me off.

I wrap my legs around Theo's waist and pull him to me. He chuckles before leaning in closer, his erection pressing between my pussy lips. I moan into his mouth at the feel of his hard length, wanting him inside me, my body craving their touch.

Tobias moves to my side, lying next to me, completely naked. I go to move my hands, wanting to touch his flawlessly sculpted body. I want to run my fingers over the lines on his stomach. But my hands don't leave the position they are trapped in. Theo moves lower, sucking my nipple into his mouth, his cold tongue making my nipple harden again.

Tobias brings his face to mine, his tongue slipping into my mouth as he tugs my wet hair, forcing my head in an upward position as he takes control of the kiss, his tongue tasting every inch of my mouth until I'm left breathless. He pulls back, untying my restraints, so I'm left with only my hands cuffed. Theo moves off the bed and walks to the cupboard, but I don't have enough time to wonder what it is he is doing, or retrieving, as I'm suddenly pulled on top of Tobias, my legs straddling his waist as he moves up the bed. His back rests on the headboard. He grabs the rope, securing my hands again just above his shoulders, my fingers brush his neck. I like this position better; I can at least touch him.

I lower my head to his shoulder before sucking on the skin of his neck. Tobias thrusts upwards and I feel his hard cock rub between the wet folds of my vagina. I moan and rub my pussy along his shaft, I feel his hands go to my hips as he positions himself at my entrance. I sit down on him, feeling my walls stretch to accommodate his large size. I feel the bed dip behind me before I see only darkness, soft fabric of a blindfold being tied to my face, my vision is cut off. Tobias thrusts up, making me bounce on his cock. I moan at the sudden connection before moving my hips, his hands guiding and making me move my hips faster.

The blindfold that cuts off my vision makes his thrusts and my movements more intense. I get lost in the feeling of his cock, pounding into me, stretching and rubbing my walls. His cock becomes coated in my juices as I ride him. I moan out when I feel his teeth bite down on my nipple, loving the sting before he soothes it with his tongue.

Everything feels heightened and more sensitive without my sight, and I love every movement. The sensations make my walls tighten around him with each thrust. Theo's hands brush my sides, making me shiver before I feel something cold and wet press against the muscles of my ass. His fingers penetrate my tight muscles, and I ride Tobias cock. Theo's fingers slide in and out of me. I feel full, but only become wetter and wetter at the different sensations.

"I'm not hurting you, am I?" Theo whispers below my ear as he slides another finger in my ass. My voice is airy, completely enthralled in the feeling of them both, my body gets hotter and hotter.

"No, I want..." I moan as he shoves a third finger in me, stretching me.

"What do you want, Imogen?" His voice is soft, but I can tell by his tone that he knows what I crave.

"I want you both. I want to feel both of you," I moan out as his fingers move faster and Tobias thrusts harder. I'm completely at their mercy. I'm willing to surrender to both of them as long as they don't stop. I would have done anything, addicted to the feel of them.

Theo removes his fingers and Tobias' hand moves to my clit. I move my hips faster, his fingers rubbing faster against my clit. I'm overwhelmed with the feeling of them, only able to focus on how they make me feel. Theo positions himself behind me, his hands go to my hips, slowing me slightly before I feel his cock press to the tight muscles of my ass, pushing inside me.

He stills once he is inside me, letting me stretch around his hard length. Tobias' fingers move faster as my body relaxes, and I start to move my hips again, riding both their cocks. Tobias' other hand goes to my nipple as he rolls it between his fingers. I moan out, my head falls back on Theo. He kisses my cheek, then rams inside me, making me moan louder. My orgasm sits on the edge, waiting for me to be shoved over. I move faster, their cocks slip and move inside me at the same time, both meeting each other's thrusts. Tobias' fingers are still rubbing my clit. My body surrenders, taking what they give as everything becomes over sensitive. I feel drunk on them, I don't want it to stop. Ever.

Tobias' voice breaks up the sounds of our sex, as I try to focus on what it is he says.

"Focus on the feeling of our bodies, Imogen, focus on my fingers." I do as he says, wondering how I can possibly think of anything other than feeling of their bodies connected to mine. My body is high on the ecstasy they are giving me. Then I know what he means when I feel Theo's fangs break the skin of my neck.

"Arghhh." I flinch, my flesh feels like it is being opened with a jagged tin can. His bite burns hot, threatening to set my entire body on fire. Tears well up in my eyes, slipping down my cheeks to my chin. Tobias thrusts in harder, and I drop the feeling of pain, instead, focusing on him. Theo moves faster in rhythm with Tobias as they both pound into me. I feel myself tighten and a fog slips over me, which I know is Theo trying to lessen the pain, as I feel his venom slip through my veins.

I moan at the intense friction they are causing. My pussy is throbbing as I can only think of the feeling of both their cocks inside me. Theo lets go of my neck, and I feel my blood run down my shoulder and over my breast, warm and wet, just as my orgasm explodes and I'm shoved over the edge violently. My body tenses as I ride out the most intense orgasm. My body is only held upright from the restraints on my wrists.

"We aren't done yet, Imogen." All I can do is nod as they pound into me relentlessly, making me writhe and moan out in pure ecstasy. Pleasure ripples through every part of me, my toes curl as I'm shoved over the edge again, my body clenching down on their cocks and I feel them both spill their hot cum into me. I slump forward, out of breath and exhausted beyond belief. I feel Theo kiss my shoulder and Tobias moves my hair from my face as I lean my face into his warm hand. Theo pulls out of me and walks over untying my hands, I collapse on top of Tobias.

"Good girl, sleep Imogen," are the last words I hear as my body gives into exhaustion.

CHAPTER

THIRTY-THREE

I wake up to the feeling of Tobias getting out of bed. I roll to his side and stretch my arms out. Tobias sees me waking, so he leans over and kisses me softly. "Go back to sleep, it's early."

"Where are you going?" I ask, yawning and sitting up.

"I have to go to work, go back to sleep."

My eyebrows furrow in annoyance. "You said I could leave once Theo marked me. I did what you wanted, let me come to work. It's boring here."

I hear him sigh before getting up. "No Imogen, just wait a bit longer. You're safer here." Safer? What does he mean by that, what could be unsafe by going to work?

"No, please, Tobias," I plead, grabbing his hand and pulling him back to the bed.

He sits on the edge, his eyes focused on me as he brushes my hair back behind my ear. "It's not safe out there for you, not yet." Tobias mutters.

"What do you mean? What's unsafe?"

"It doesn't matter right now. We still have two weeks, just let the bond kick in, then we will talk," he says, kissing my forehead and standing up. I throw the covers off, ignoring him and walk in to retrieve my bag. I bring it out and start rummaging through it, pulling clothes out. Tobias grabs my bag, but I grip the handle. He tugs it and I smack into his chest.

"I said no, what part of that don't you understand?" He says, his voice getting louder.

"The no part! Now, give me my fucking bag. I'm not staying here bored all day when I can be working." He growls lowly, and I step back, placing my hands on my hips, glaring back at him.

I hear Theo racing up the steps before running into the room. I completely forget I'm still naked until Theo's eyes roam over my body. A blush creeps up onto my face before it vanishes when Tobias speaks again. "You don't make the decisions around here, we do."

I shake my head. "We had a deal, I could leave if I let Theo mark me. Stick by your word, Tobias, or I won't stick by mine."

"What's that supposed to mean, Imogen?" Tobias glares at me.

"Means I will fucking leave the pair of you," I retort, my voice steady for once.

He growls loudly, but I stand strong, folding my arms across my bare chest, refusing to back down.

"What's the problem?" Asks Theo.

"Ask growly over there. He's the one with the problem," I say, motioning to Tobias, who is shooting daggers at me.

Theo looks at Tobias, but his eyes never leave mine. He steps toward me and I don't move, refusing to be intimidated by him. He grabs my arms in a vice like grip, but I keep my eyes steady, refusing to lose this stand-off.

"See, he has a major stick up his ass and clearly it's sideways," I tell Theo.

Tobias throws me and I land on my back on the bed, my legs spread in a not so ladylike manner. Before I have a chance to get up, Tobias is on top of me, pinning me down. His face barely an inch off mine. "I'm growing very tired of your constant attitude, love. Watch your tongue," he snaps.

"You want me to remove the stick or should Theo?" I snap back sarcastically.

Tobias grabs my hair, pulling my head to the side, his lips teasing the skin on my neck as he sucks on my mark. Tingles spread through my body. Well, that's new. My toes curl and my back arches off the bed. How is it possible he has this effect on me, my body reacting like it's been deprived of sex and he is the remedy it needs? The need for him to touch me is almost painful. He pulls back a smirk on his face.

My face falls at the loss of contact. "I have control, not you. So, stop testing my patience or you will find the end of my tether. You won't like what you find." I shiver at the venom in his words.

He climbs off me, I watch the tight muscles of his back ripple as he moves away to the walk-in. He's sculpted of pure muscle and looks like sex on legs. What the fuck is wrong with me? Annoyed at my own daydreaming, I forget his warning and grab a pillow before sliding off the bed and chucking it right at him. It hits him with a soft thud, and I hear Theo gasp.

"Fuck you, Tobias." He turns on me in a second. He moves so fast I have no time to react, as I'm thrown over his knee. I struggle to push myself up, but his hand on my back shoves me back down. I pull at the sheets of the bed he is sitting on, trying to claw away from him as I kick my legs. Tobias jams his fingers between my legs before violently shoving them inside my core. I squirm at the intrusion before he slides his fingers out and rams them back in, only this time it doesn't hurt, it actually feels good from this angle. Well, if this is his punishment, I can live with that. I can feel my juices coating his fingers, making them slide in and out effortlessly.

Then, he pulls them out, I huff at the loss before I hear the slap of flesh. A stinging burning pain on my left ass cheek makes me squirm and cry out. Oh god that fucking hurt, I'm going to murder him when I get up. I buck trying to get off his lap. "I warned you," he says, as his hand comes down again. I squirm, trying to get away from his large hands branding my ass. Tears well in my eyes at the humiliation and the searing pain. I can feel every finger imprinted on my ass.

"Stop, it hurts," I plead. His hand comes down again. I flinch on impact, but his hand rubs over the mark, soothing the sting a little but not much. "Please Tobias stop," I cry, trying to roll over or get up, anything to stop the burn and get away from him. But it is no use, his hand comes down, biting into my flesh. I know my ass is red raw.

"Tobias that's enough," Theo says, making me look up at him, tears running down my cheeks. I feel Tobias shake his head, as his hand comes down again. It hurts but isn't as hard as the last one. I wince before his fingers slide inside me, he moves them around.

I'm wet, soaking wet. How the fuck is that even possible after that torture? He slides them in deeper, fucking me with his fingers, I try to hold back but can't as my moans escape my lips.

It feels so good, but damn is my ass sore. "Who has control, Imogen?" he asks. I don't answer, lost in the feeling of his fingers as he twists them inside me, making me breathless. When I take too long to answer he stops moving. I almost whimper at the loss of his fingers, I'm so close.

"Who has control, Imogen?" He says again, sliding his fingers back in, teasing before pulling them out again.

"You, you do," I say, needing the feeling of his fingers inside me.

"Good girl," he says, shoving them inside me again, making me moan out. He keeps moving them in and out of me. I can feel my walls start to clench around his fingers when he pulls them from me just as I'm about to come.

I whine loudly frustrated, I need release. He sits me up and places me next to him on the bed before getting up. "I find out you give in to her, I will punish her again, understood?" Theo nods and looks away from me. Tobias walks into the walk in and grabs his suit, quickly putting it on. He stops at the door, looking back at me where I'm still on the bed, my pussy throbbing in need.

"You will learn not to disobey me, Imogen. If I were you, I would learn fast," he says before walking out leaving me sexually frustrated and needy.

Theo quickly walks out after him. I get off the bed and walk into the bathroom, hoping a shower will help dull the ache between my legs. It doesn't help, I get out feeling no different. I walk into the closet and grab a pair of leggings and an off-shoulder top, the fabric feels soft on my skin and super comfy. I walk down to the kitchen and Theo is cooking breakfast. I admire the way he moves around in the kitchen. Is it just me or does everything feel different? Just looking at them makes my panties dampen, the need comes back to the front of my mind.

I walk over to the island counter and jump up, sitting next to where Theo is cutting up tomatoes and onions.

I take the knife from his hand before pulling him between my legs. I can feel he wants me just by the bulge in his shorts pressing into me. "You smell divine," his husky voice next to my ear makes me wetter. I know he can smell my arousal, but right now I don't care enough to be embarrassed by it. I kiss him and he groans, "I can't babe," he says, pulling away.

"Please," I beg. Great now I'm begging, but I can't stand the ache, it will drive me insane. He groans loudly when I use my legs to pull him closer.

"I'm starting to wonder who he is punishing, me or you," he says as he grinds his hips into me.

I pull on the waistband of his pants before reaching in and grabbing his smooth, hard cock. It twitches in my hand and he thrusts into it. Then, he pulls away and starts chopping up vegetables again.

I jump off the counter and stomp away annoyed. I go and sit on the couch and flick the TV on, putting the first movie on the list. About ten minutes later, Theo walks out and puts a plate on my lap, he made an omelet. We eat in silence until he clears our plates and comes back. I turn to him, "What did Tobias mean by saying it's dangerous for me to leave here?"

Theo thinks for a minute, I can tell he doesn't want to tell me. "He means it's not safe for you now that we have marked you." I look at him confused, trying to figure out how that could put me in danger.

"What do you mean, I don't understand." I raise an eyebrow.

"You're human, Imogen. It's forbidden to take a human as a mate." Theo explains. If it's forbidden, why mark me then? They're not making any sense. I go to ask that question when he cuts me off. "That's all I'm telling you. I don't want to anger Tobias, not at the moment. I want to tell you, I do. But I agree with Tobias, now is not the time, let the bond kick in first."

Always back to this imaginary bond. I feel the same. Well, kind of, I do feel more sensitive around them. I wonder if that's what they mean, just looking at them overwhelms me and makes me flustered. I hope that it doesn't get worse; I won't be able to think coherently if it gets worse than it is.

We watch movies all day. Theo refuses to touch me, and the need for his touch gets worse with every second, but I do my best to ignore it. When Tobias walks in, I ignore him, I'm still angry at him. I don't see why I can't go to work, and I can't believe he forbade Theo from touching me, leaving me aching all day.

"How was your day?" He says, leaning over the couch and kissing my head. I ignore him, my eyes not leaving the TV. I know I will crumble and beg him to fuck me if I look at him. He leans over, grabbing Theo's face and kissing him hard. Arousal floods me and I press my thighs together. I love watching them, it turns me on in a weird way and also makes me a little jealous, wanting to be touched. I avert my eyes and pretend I don't notice. "Not talking to me, love?" I answer him with my silence.

"I brought dinner," he says walking into the kitchen. I can smell that it's Chinese. My stomach instantly growls.

Theo pulls me to my feet, "Come on, you can punish him later."

Oh I am going to punish him, alright. I know he wants me just as much as I want him, this will be interesting. Maybe, I will make him beg. Yes, it is definitely time for him to beg.

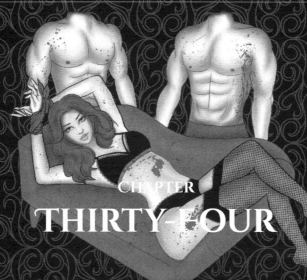

CHAPTER
THIRTY-FOUR

After dinner, I walk up to the bed and climb in. I hear them come in some time later, but I just roll over, refusing to acknowledge their presence. I feel the bed dip on both sides, feel both of them reaching for me, trying to get any reaction out of me.

I feel Theo's erection pressing into my back, so I roll onto my stomach. "Punish him not me," Theo says, his cold hands rubbing my ass. I know whatever we do, Tobias will feel through their bond. Not wanting to give him the satisfaction, I fight my own desires, choosing to ignore the feeling stirring in my stomach. I actually have trouble telling if they are my own feelings; they feel a little foreign to me. Then, I realized what they meant about the bond and feeling what each other felt.

"Babe," Theo whines, tugging on my hip, trying to get me to roll over. I feel terrible, knowing he has been wanting to touch me all day. But I don't want to give Tobias the satisfaction of this victory over me.

"Nope, you have both turned me off men for life. Not interested." Tobias moves his hand, rubbing my lower back, but I don't give in, holding strong, although I want to crumble and beg them to be inside me. I toss and turn all night, fighting their desires that are pushing on me and fighting my own. My sleep is broken and restless.

Waking up the next morning, I feel exhausted. I roll over and Tobias and Theo both have suits on. I sit up hopeful.

Tobias destroys the feeling almost instantly, "Nope, don't even ask."

"So what? I'm supposed to wait here all day for you both to return? Sorry to tell you but I'm not housewife material." Theo smirks.

"Clearly your cooking is terrible." Tobias throws back at me. I cross my arms across my chest. I feel tears burning my eyes at not being allowed to leave. I just want to feel like a normal person, why is that so wrong?

Theo leans over and whispers in my ear. "Go, get dressed." I jump off the bed and Tobias turns on Theo.

"What the fuck, Theo, you know she can't leave."

"It's just work, Tobias. She has been stuck here for weeks, and you know we need the help there." Theo explains, finally standing up for me.

Tobias mutters something too low for me to hear.

He isn't happy and follows me into the walk-in wardrobe. I instantly think that he is going to stop me, but instead, he reaches in and grabs my black dress off the hanger and passes it to me. I look at him, excited. "Hurry up before I change my mind."

I happily grab my make-up bag and rush into the bathroom. I quickly throw on my mascara and eyeliner as well as some red lipstick. I brush my hair and straighten it, feeling somewhat girly today. I grab the dress and put it on. It's a black mid length dress with lace on the back. I walk out and Theo walks over and quickly zips the back of my dress up. Tobias grabs a pair of my black heels, and I put my hand on his shoulder as he slides my foot into each one before buckling them up.

Theo retrieves my bag and hands it to me. I throw it over my shoulder before grabbing my phone off charge. We make our way downstairs but are running late because they had to wait for me, so we go straight to the car. I hop in the front before Tobias tells me to. He grabs my knee when he gets in, squeezing it softly. Ten minutes pass and my phone starts ringing like crazy, coming into reception. Multiple emails coming through, and text messages. One is from Mark, I start replying.

Tobias looks over and sees I'm texting. "Who are you messaging?" he asks. I feel Tobias lean over, trying to read over my shoulder.

"Mark, from work," I say simply.

"And what does Mark want?" I sigh when I look up and see Tobias' white knuckles from his death grip on the steering wheel.

"He was wondering if you fired me because he hasn't seen me at work." I also notice missed calls from Tom. My phone dings again, a reply from Mark. Theo leans over and reads my message asking if I want to have lunch with him.

I hear Theo growl, so I turn to him, raising an eyebrow. "What's got into you? Jealousy doesn't suit you, Theo."

"Tell him no," Theo growls out. I roll my eyes and reply telling him I'm too busy today.

"Tell who no? This Mark? What did he ask?" Tobias asks angrily.

"He only asked to have lunch with me. Geez, calm down, we are just friends!"

"You're ours," they both say at the same time. I roll my eyes, It's pretty obvious already by the fact that they are holding me prisoner. I know Mark likes me, but he also knows he is in the friendzone, not the bed zone.

When we get to the office, Tom sees me and walks up, giving me a side hug. I hug him back, but he steps back when he sees Tobias and Theo walk up the stairs and through the doors. I know something is up with them, so I mouth, "I will find you later." Tom nods.

Tobias puts his hand on my back and escorts me to the elevator with Theo. We catch the elevator upstairs, and I go straight to the kitchen and pop the kettle on, desperately wanting coffee. I then walk out and turn the phones over and start up my computer. I groan when I see the amount of emails.

I then walk back to make our coffees and walk into Tobias's office, where they are both looking over documents. I place the coffee on the coffee table. I go to walk out and to my computer to get onto the horrid task of answering everyone, but Theo grabs my wrist and walks me over to the desk and bends me over it. His hands run over the fabric of my dress.

"What are you doing? I have work to do." I ask.

"I have always wanted to bend you over this desk and fuck you," he replies.

"Another day, I'm busy." His hand runs under my skirt, hoisting it up. I smile when he realizes I don't have any panties under the tight fabric.

I hear Tobias growl, noticing my bare ass in the air. I stand up and fix my skirt. "Where are your panties, Imogen?" Tobias asks. I know he doesn't like the idea of me walking around with nothing under my dress, in a building full of men. I ignore him and walk out.

I go to my desk and start working, the day passes quickly. I have so much filing and Theo and Tobias are in meetings all day. When I get to my desk with my seventh coffee for the day, my phone vibrates. I receive a text message from Theo, who I know is in a meeting with Tobias. I open it.

Theo: Meet me in my office 😊

Me: No can do, busy.

Theo: ☹ So yay or nay?

Me: Definitely feeling Mysexual.

Theo: Mysexual?

Me: Yep Mysexual, #Mefucksmyself

Theo: Ha, Mysexual I like it, kind of like self-coupled.

Me: Why not? They have bisexual and homosexual, yadda yadda. Might start a petition to find other Mysexuals, get it classed as a sexuality under fucking my hand. It's better than cock.

Theo: Can I watch you fuck your yourself?

Me: No, wouldn't want you to get jealous, that my hand lasts longer. 😊

Theo: Is that a challenge?

Me: Maybe.

I put my phone down and turn back to my computer. I'm typing away when I feel hands run over my shoulders and stop on my breasts. His mouth, below my ear. His cold breath tickles me, making me shiver. "Challenge accepted." I almost moan just at the sound of his voice. Theo spins my chair around before pulling me to my feet. I giggle when he starts pulling me toward his office.

"Theo, we're at work. Where is Tobias?" He closes the door behind him, locking it.

"In the meeting, still," he says as he grabs me. I wrap my legs around his waist as he puts me on top of his desk. His mouth devours the skin on my neck. I feel his hands run up my thighs, pulling the dress up. I grab his belt, yanking him to me, undoing his belt.

"We are going to be in so much trouble," I whisper against his lips, but continue to undo his pants until his cock springs free. I wiggle myself to the edge of the desk, eager to feel his large cock moving inside me. Theo rams in and I moan out loudly, Theo's hand covers my mouth, muffling the noise. The walls are only thin in the meeting room. I chuckle, knowing Tobias would definitely know what we are doing here. Theo rams his cock into me repeatedly, my moans fill the room despite his hand covering my mouth, my walls flutter around his cock as my juices coat him.

Theo pulls me over onto my stomach, bringing my ass into the air, he slaps it but not like Tobias did. My stomach tightens, arousal floods me, moisture pools between my thighs as he rams into me from behind, my hips digging into the desk as he pounds away. I feel my orgasm building, hear the moist sounds our bodies make as they collide together. Theo grabs my hair, pulling my head back, his lips smashing into mine, sending me over the edge. I come screaming his name as my legs tremble and my walls tighten around his large thick length. Theo slams into me harder, finding his own release. He pulls my skirt down as he kisses my shoulder. I stand up, trying to catch my breath. Theo passes me a G-string; I recognize it instantly as one of mine.

I raise an eyebrow at him. "You think I didn't know you had no panties on, Imogen?"

"How?" I ask. I got dressed in the bathroom away from them.

"I noticed when I zipped you up, this morning. Naughty girl. Tobias will spank that ass for walking around bare like that," he says, kissing my forehead.

My stomach tightens and excitement rushes through me.

"Although I think you want to be spanked, don't you?" I wrap my arms around his neck, his wrapping around my waist. I lean in and kiss him softly before pulling away. I then quickly slip on my panties before fixing my dress.

We walk out of the office just as Tobias and a group of men walk out of the meeting, heading towards the elevator. I stop, Theo walking into my back. Tobias glares at us and I know we will be copping an earful. He bids them farewell, then storms toward us. I turn to Theo and see his office door click shut. "Chicken," I sing out to him.

Tobias folds his arms across his chest. I look down and see the huge bulge in his pants. Yep, he definitely felt what we were doing. I reach my hand down and grab his cock through his pants. He groans and I rub my hand along his shaft, through his pants and his eyes shut. I lean closer, kissing his cheek down to his chin before I let go and walk off. I chuckle to myself, I know he will punish me for it later. I hear him groan before walking into his office and slamming the door.

CHAPTER
THIRTY-FIVE

Looking at the time, it's nearly time to finish up, I'm exhausted and for once actually excited to go home to my prison. I need sleep. I'm mentally and physically exhausted, and my brain feels like mush from constantly looking at screens all day. When it is nearly time to clock off, I switch everything off and decide to go down to the lobby and see if I can find Tom.

I grab my bag and head for the elevator. Once on the ground floor, I walk over to the counter at the front. Merida, the lady that brought us dinner the night we stayed back late, is at the counter on the phone, arguing with someone who wants to organize a meeting. After a few minutes of me waiting, she becomes annoyed and slams the phone down, hanging up on the person. She runs her fingers through her blonde hair and lets out a breath.

"Hi, Imogen," she greets. Her voice sounds tired.

"What happened to the other lady that was working here? I thought you worked on the tech floor?" I try to start a casual conversation to distract her from the call.

"I normally do, but the bitch quit and now, I'm stuck here till

205

they find a replacement." She sighs, clearly annoyed and tired. "So, what brings you down here Imogen? Where are Tobias and Theo?" She glances around nervously, looking for them.

"Why does everyone do that? Look around nervously at the mention of them?" I ask her, curious. Am I the only one not terrified by them?

"You for real? The vibes they give off." She shakes her head. "I don't know how you work all day up there with them. I do not envy you, having to work under them. I still remember the last time when Theo went postal and nearly strangled Max for interrupting him during a meeting. The poor guy quit, and I transferred to the tech floor. I was originally one of their secretaries, I couldn't handle the hours or tension of working up there. They are way too intense, I don't know how you do it, girl." She rambles.

"Max?" I raise an eyebrow at her.

"Oh, he was here just before you started, apparently he works for a rival company now, they used to be friends but after that not so much."

Jealousy courses through me, knowing she worked for them. Although I can tell she fears them, I can't help but wonder if they were attracted to her and treated her like they treat me. I shake the thought away, wondering where my sudden jealousy surged from. I don't want to think of them with another woman, though she doesn't seem like she was involved with them sexually.

"So, what brought you down here? I know it wasn't for a friendly chat," she asks, looking up at me from her seated position. I completely forgot my original intentions of coming down here.

"I was actually looking for Tom, have you seen him?"

"He is probably in the back office," she waves off the statement.

Alright, this is interesting. Tom is a cleaner, why would he be in the back office? Do they get offices now too?

"The cleaner's office?" I ask, a little skeptical.

"Huh, what are you talking about? Tom works in publicity, little OCD if you ask me. I sometimes see him cleaning up around here, and I caught him mopping the floors the other day. I actually thought he was demoted." She chuckles. Now that is weird, Tom told me he was a janitor. What the hell is going on around here?

"Just follow that corridor down and you should see his office on the left," she tells me, pointing to the corridor next to the stairs.

I turn and start walking towards it, but stop at someone calling my name. "Imogen, wait up."

Oh for god's sake, I groan. I was really hoping I don't run into him today, I really need to speak to Tom. I stop and turn around to face him. I watch Mark jog over to me from wherever he has come from. I like Mark but sometimes he can be a flirt, though I know he is harmless and just overly friendly. I don't want Theo and Tobias getting mad if they see me speaking to him after this morning's incident.

Mark stops in front me, his brown eyes light up and he smiles, running a hand through his black hair. He is a good-looking man with a strong build, but I don't find him attractive like Theo or Tobias. He embraces me in a hug, and I step back, looking around nervously.

"I haven't seen you at the hospital in a while. How is your mom?" he asks.

I swallow. No one other than a handful of people know my mother was even in hospital, and I haven't really spoken to Mark or seen him to let him know what happened. "Um, the hospital pulled the plug; she passed away." I look away, trying not to show how much her death has hurt me.

"Oh, Imogen I'm sorry to hear that, if you need someone to talk to you have my number," he says, grabbing my hand. I pull my hand away before speaking.

"And your sister, how is she doing?" I ask, changing the topic from my life.

"She is doing better, still a long way to go but they have started her on a trial drug now, hoping the results come back good."

"That's great Mark, well I have to go see someone." I say, turning away when his hand grabs my elbow gently. I stop and turn back to him.

"I have been wondering if you would, like," he suddenly stops, looking behind me. Just as I'm about to turn and see what he's looking at, strong warm arms wrap around my waist, tugging me toward them, I flinch. I know instantly it is Tobias, he sweeps my hair over my shoulder, then leans his head down, kissing my neck softly. Mark watches and takes a step back. I look at him apologetically.

"I was wondering where you went," Tobias says. I can hear the anger in his words and Mark pales a little.

"Well, I will catch up with you next time Imogen," Mark says, eyeing Tobias before he all but runs away.

I sigh and turn in Tobias's arms. "Did you have to do that? Seriously, Tobias, sometimes you can be a bit much." Tobias lets go of me and glares down at me.

"I don't want you talking to him again, is this why you left without letting us know? To come see Mark?" Really, he thinks I'm trying to run off with Mark? I roll my eyes and Tobias grabs my chin, forcing me to look up at him. "You are ours, nobody else's." His words make my stomach tighten from the dominance and control behind his words. I like the sound of being theirs even though I know I shouldn't.

"Why were you down here without us?" Theo walks over to stand next to him, clearly having heard our conversation. My eyes glance toward him and Tobias lets go of chin.

"I was looking for Tom, geez. Nothing sordid going on." I'm well aware of Merida's eyes on us and probably other workers watching. I want to run, just to avoid their speculative gazes.

Tobias and Theo both watch me, seeing if I'm telling the truth. I wouldn't lie, they would know instantly. Besides, I am a terrible liar.

"Come on time to go home," Tobias says, grabbing my hand.

"I just want to see Tom really quickly, I will only be a second." I say, moving away and toward where Merida said his office is. Theo's hand catches my other hand and they pull me back.

"You aren't to go wandering without us Imogen, you can see Tom another time, when we are present, understood." Theo tells me.

Anger rises in me. I try to pull away, but give up when they start tugging me toward the exit. I know if I cause a scene Tobias will lose it. So instead, I let them pull me to the car that is waiting out the front.

Tobias opens the passenger door and waits for me to get in before shutting the door behind me. He hops in the driver's side and starts the car. I wait until he pulls out and starts driving through the traffic. I turn to look at him, now deciding I will confront him over humiliating me, since we are no longer at work and have no witnesses. "Was that necessary? Seriously, Tobias, why would you do that and why can't I see Tom?"

He ignores my question, "Put your seatbelt on Imogen." Tobias growls out.

I cross my arms across my chest. "Why did you have to go and scare Mark off like that? He is a good man, you just humiliated him and me." My voice is getting higher.

"I don't want you talking to someone, who is clearly interested in being more than your friend Imogen, you will do as I say. Now, put your fucking belt on!"

Like hell I will, they can't control me like that. Tobias jerks the car to the side and Theo grabs the back of my seat from the sudden movement to steady himself. Tobias turns and glares at me, before reaching across me and grabbing my seatbelt and plugging it in before taking off again.

"Why do you always have to get under his skin, Imogen?" I look over at Theo, who is picking up documents that fell in the footwell from Tobias's erratic driving.

Great, just fucking great, now they are both ganging up on me.

"You weren't there, you didn't see what he did, Theo, so butt out." I hear him growl behind me.

"I saw the entire thing, Imogen, and you may think Mark is being friendly, but he wants more than just to hang out with you. Don't just assume because you can't see us that we aren't watching." I roll my eyes and cross my arms before closing my eyes and sitting back in my chair.

When we get back home, Theo opens my door, Tobias has already stormed into the house.

"Look. I'm sorry for snapping at you. Tobias is just on edge and so am I. Seeing him with you just became too much." I look at him, before taking his hand letting him pull me to my feet. He pulls me into a hug and kisses my head. "We can make it up to you, Tobias has a surprise for you anyway, it should have been delivered while we were at work."

"Is it an Internet connection?" I ask, hopeful.

Theo chuckles, pulling me towards the house. "No, but I will have someone come out and fix that, if it is such an issue for you."

I nod excitedly, "Oh my god, yes this place is boring."

He pulls me into him when we reach the door, leaning in, his lips going to my neck, sucking on it before breathing in my scent. "I can think of a few ways to keep you entertained," he whispers, nipping at my neck. I lean into him and squeeze my legs together, trying to stop the sudden ache. Tobias walks out, wondering what's taking so long.

"If I can't have her neither can you," he says, leaning on the door frame, watching us. I reach out and grab his hand, pulling him towards me. His warm body presses into my back as he pulls my head to the side, kissing me deeply. His tongue tastes every inch of my mouth, making me moan and my panties dampen.

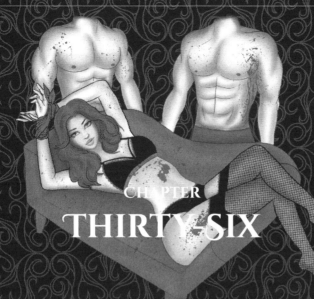

CHAPTER
THIRTY-SIX

I feel Tobias pull the zip down on the back of my dress, I kick my heels off while his lips devour the skin on my neck. Theo grabs my waist, pulling me into him and I reach down, rubbing my hand over the front of his pants to find he's already rock hard. He groans before I'm suddenly spun around, Tobias lifts my skirt up before grabbing me. I wrap my legs around his waist, my hands go around his neck, and he starts walking inside and up the steps. I heard Theo close the door before following us.

Once in our room, Tobias places me on my feet and pulls my dress over my head. I feel cold hands unclip my bra, so I know Theo is behind me, his hands going to my breasts.

"Don't think I forgot you didn't wear panties to work, love," Tobias' husky voice sounds next to my ear, "Or what you and Theo got up to in his office." I open my eyes and Tobias is staring down at me. Desire is clear in his eyes, they darken as they roam over my body. The G-string that Theo stole from my drawer is the only article of clothing left on me.

Theo hooks his fingers underneath it, pulling them down, leaving me completely bare standing in front of them. Tobias steps closer till his chest is nearly touching mine, his body heat seeps into me, making me shiver and my core throb at the intense look he's giving me. I slide his jacket off his shoulder and down his arms, letting it fall to the floor. I then start undoing his shirt buttons.

He watches, allowing me to undress him. When I reach for his belt buckle, he pushes me towards the bed, so I'm seated on the edge. I see Theo walk over to the chair next to the bed. I look up at Tobias and he raises an eyebrow at me, I smile back at him, undoing the buckle. Tugging his pants down, his cock springs free, nearly hitting me in the face. I grab it in my hands, he's large and thick, but his cock is smooth. I like the feeling of it in my hand.

He thrusts into my hand once, before waiting to see what I will do. I kiss the tip, feeling his cock twitch. I bring my lips to it before sucking on the knob, swirling my tongue around the edge of it.

Tobias groans and I look up to see him close his eyes. I move my hand up and down his shaft, as I take more of him in my mouth. Moaning, arousal floods me as I suck on his hard cock. I move my head, finding my own rhythm. Moving faster and faster, while my hand moves up and down the part of his shaft that I can't fit in my mouth. He groans, as I feel his hands grab my hair while he thrusts into my mouth, making me choke on his hard length. He does it again, but I'm more prepared, relaxing my throat as he continues to thrust into my mouth.

I feel the bed dip behind me, Theo's naked legs drape either side of mine, his hands go to my breasts. He rolls both my nipples between his fingers, and I moan at the feel of his cold hands, my nipples hardening under his touch. I can feel his erection pushing into my back, as Tobias fucks my mouth. My juices spill onto my thighs as I become soaked in my own arousal.

Theo lifts me slightly before placing me on top of his lap, his legs moving between mine, pushing mine apart. I move my hips, hearing him groan before his lips tease the skin on my shoulder as he drags his teeth across it. I flinch as he bites into my neck. I can feel my warm blood running down my shoulder and over my breasts. I wiggle my hips, and Theo's hands slide down my sides, lifting me before he positions me over his cock.

I sit down, a moan escaping my lips, the vibration makes Tobias still for a second before he thrusts back into my mouth. Theo, using his legs, thrusts into me, his hands on my hips moving them in sync with his rhythm, my walls clamp down on him. I'm so wet I can feel his dick slide in and out, slick with my fluids. They both speed up their movements as I writhe and moan around Tobias's cock. I'm so close.

Suddenly, Tobias pulls his cock from my lips before dropping to his knees in front of me, his face between my legs, as he sucks my clit into his mouth, sucking hard. My eyes roll into the back of my head and I throw my head back onto Theo's cold shoulder. Theo stops moving under me and Tobias' hands push my legs up until they are resting on top of the bed, his mouth not stopping the delicious torture of licking and sucking, my hips move on their own, loving the pleasurable torture I'm under.

Tobias moves his hands down to my ankles before reaching for something on the corner bed post. He stops, lifting his head and placing a cuff on my ankle. He tightens it before pulling on another chain, forcing my legs open further in the same position. He does the same on the other side, watching to see my reaction and if I will freak out.

I don't have time to think about anything before Theo's hand brushes over my stomach, making me shiver, before going between my legs rubbing my clit in circular motions. My hips move instinctively against his fingers as his cock remains buried deep inside me. Tobias stands, reaching above my head, he tugs on something, and two chains with leather handcuffs fall from above me. He grabs my hand, holding it above my head before securing it. He does the same on the other side, my hands being forced above my head. I tug on them, but they don't budge. The material is soft on my skin, but tight. Tobias stands, watching me writhe and move my hips on Theo against his fingers, my legs spread wide as he watches Theo's cock move in and out of me.

I can feel Theo's cool breath on my neck making me shiver. Theo lifts me slightly, his cock slipping from my body as he places me on his lap. Tobias moves closer, positioning himself at my entrance before ramming in all the way. Theo's hand starts moving faster between me and Tobias as he rolls my clit between his fingers. It hurts but feels good, and I can feel myself getting wetter as Tobias thrusts into me.

Tobias grips my hips, lifting me slightly off Theo's lap. All my weight pulls down on the chains, digging into my wrists, when I feel Theo position his dick against the tight muscles of my ass. "Breathe, Imogen," Tobias speaks in that husky voice next to my ear, as he bends down to me.

I feel fog wash over me, forcing me to relax. I know it's Theo's doing, Tobias brings my hips down and I feel Theo slide into my body. I let out a breath and they wait for me to get used to the feeling of them both, fully inside me. Tobias brings his lips down to mine, my shoulders relaxing when I feel his tongue brush my bottom lip before sucking it into his mouth. He bites down on it, breaking the skin, sucking on it before letting go. He looks down at me, beneath hooded eyes, "I'm going to fuck you now."

Before I can say anything, he pulls out and slams back into me. I'm surprised when he continues to thrust into me with so much force, my pussy clenches and pulsates around him. I'm a screaming mess as his cock is repeatedly slammed into me, making me bounce on Theo's hard length that's deeply seated in my ass. I can feel my orgasm building, completely consumed in the feeling of their cocks slipping in and out my body as they fuck me. I can barely handle it when he pushes my knees to either side of my chest while Theo holds them there, his grip strong as Tobias continues to fuck me relentlessly, his thrusts getting harder and faster.

My body is exhausted, I can't do anything but moan, going completely limp as the chains bear all my weight, keeping me in the position I've been put in. I feel my orgasm build until I'm thrown violently over the edge. Panting as I ride it out, pleasure washes over me in waves. I feel Theo's grip on my knees tighten, my head rests on his shoulder. My lips brush his neck, I feel him still before his dick twitches inside me as he cums.

Tobias' movements become jerky above me as he finds his own release. His hands on either side of me fist the sheets as he cums, I feel his warm cum coating my insides. I'm exhausted and can't move. Theo lets go of my legs, which feel like putty as they drop back onto the mattress on either side of Tobias's hips. He pulls out of me and I know I will be sore from the pounding I just received.

He kisses my knee as he undoes the first ankle cuff, my foot slides off the bed heavily before he undoes the other side. I feel Theo reach up and undo one of my wrists' cuffs, my arms fall heavily into my lap. Tobias rubs my wrist, which has the imprint of the cuff on it. My other hand falls beside me as it is released from the cuff, I can't feel my fingers. Tobias rubs both wrists with his thumb, trying to bring back circulation to them, while I just rest against Theo.

I try to get up, but my body feels heavy, and I'm on the verge of passing out. Theo, realizing this, lifts my hips, his cock slides out of me before he turns me so I'm across his lap. I rest my head on his shoulder, my eyes closing, enjoying the feeling of his cold skin against my burning skin. My entire body feels hot and clammy.

Tobias walks into the bathroom, I hear water running. After a few minutes, Theo lifts me, carrying me into the bathroom. I feel him step into the bath before sitting down with me still on his lap. The water is warm, and I shiver from the contrast of hot and cold. I feel a hand move between my legs and I flinch, my eyes fly open. I'm much too tender for them to do anything right now.

"Tobias is just cleaning you," Theo speaks into my hair.

I look up and can see Tobias, leaning over the tub. He looks down at me, before kissing my forehead. I let Tobias clean me, eyes closing as I can feel sleep trying to take over. Water runs down my hair and the sides of my face, I shift, trying to open my eyes that feel heavy.

Fingers run through my hair before massaging what smells like strawberry shampoo through it. Tobias' skilled fingers massage my scalp, I relax under his touch before falling asleep against Theo.

I can hear them talking as I'm lifted out of the tub; my eyes open. Tobias walks out and Theo follows, as I move my face to Theo's neck kissing it. I move my sleepy legs and Theo lets go as I place my feet on the floor standing on unsteady legs. Tobias wasn't lying when he said he was going to fuck me, my body feels like it just ran a marathon, every part of me hurts. Tobias starts drying my hair, and Theo reaches over grabbing another towel off the bed and he helps me dry my body. When I'm dry, Theo leans over to kiss my lips.

"I'm going to start dinner," he says, leaving me with Tobias. I walk over, dropping onto the bed, when Tobias walks over pulling one of his shirts over my head and I automatically push my arms through it. He lifts my chin with his fingers, his eyes searching mine. "You okay?" I nod, before his hand cups my cheek. I lean into his hand, it's so big and warm, and I love the smell of his skin.

"Rest, I will wake you when dinner is done. Then we need to talk." I nod and climb up the bed to the center, before crashing onto the mattress, completely exhausted.

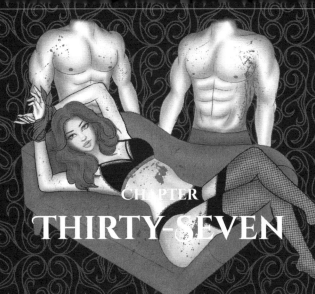

THIRTY-SEVEN

Gentle, cold hands wake me up, I shiver at his cold touch. "Dinner, babe, you should eat." I roll over, completely exhausted before snuggling back under the covers. Tobias places his hand on my head before turning it over and feeling it with the back of his hand.

"Does she feel like she is burning up to you?" Theo touches my back and I flinch from the coldness before he too places his hand on my forehead. "I'm not sure her skin always feels hot to me," he says.

"I'm fine I just need sleep," I grumble, rolling onto my stomach, trying to dive back into my slumber.

Stupid men, always trying to force feed me and keep me awake. Tobias flicks the light on, the light shining through the backs of my eyelids. I squeeze my eyes tighter before pulling my pillow over my head. "Yep, she is fine, just being a brat," Tobias says as he kneels on the bed beside me. In one swift movement, he rolls me and picks me up.

"Hey, what are you doing, I was trying to sleep." I groan. He tosses me over his shoulder. "Why do you have to be such a dick? I was enjoying my sleep before you ruined it." He slaps my bare ass before walking out the door. I stretch my sore limbs, stretching out like a stiff board on his shoulder, before relaxing and slumping over it again. I can feel his whiskers on my hip before he turns his face as he is walking down the stairs and bites the side of my butt.

I hiss and turn, smacking him on the head as he descends down the stairs. Well, I'm awake now. I brace my elbows, digging them into his shoulder and propping my chin up, I know they won't feel comfortable to him. Theo is walking behind me, and I reach my arm to him, he grips my fingers with his.

"Theo would have let me sleep, that's why he's my favorite." I state, sticking my tongue out at Theo. He winks at me, following behind us.

"Well, I'm not Theo and I have something to show you. Besides, who goes to bed when it isn't even 8 o'clock yet?"

Tobias dumps me off the side of his shoulder, I squeal before landing on the couch, the wind being knocked out of me. I land with a soft thud, grabbing the gray cushion and lob it at him. I hear him chuckle before walking into the kitchen followed by Theo.

"You coming?" Tobias sings out.

"Nope, I'm good here."

"Imogen." I roll my eyes before climbing off the couch. I follow them into the kitchen which is empty, I can see dinner plated up on the counter but no Theo or Tobias. I feel a cool breeze brush over my skin before I see the curtains above the sink move. The door leading out to the back deck is ajar. I walk over to it and stick my head outside.

On the deck is a rose bush. I step out and see Theo and Tobias walking down the steps onto the footpath. "Grab the rose bush." I look at the pot that has a white rose tree in it. They don't honestly expect me to carry that do they? I won't even be able to get my arms around the pot it sits in, let alone carry it with all its dirt.

"Yeah, sure thing, nothing like some night-time gardening," I mock as I walk over to the ceramic pot.

The thorns look sharp, but it has about thirty huge white roses on it. I try to drag it toward the stairs. Once to the top step, I look down the five steps. trying to figure out how the hell I'm actually going to get down the stairs without either breaking the pot or getting pricked by its thorns. "You're kidding right?" I say before turning and finding Theo directly behind me, watching me. "What are you doing? Help!"

"I think I would rather enjoy the view of your panty-less ass trying to drag that over to us."

I stand, putting my hands on my hips. "Help or I'm going inside." I bend down dragging it closer to the step so it's hanging over the edge slightly so I can get a good grip on it. Suddenly, it's gone. Theo picks it up like it weighs nothing and walks along the concrete path over to Tobias, who is busy digging a hole between two red rose bushes in the huge garden. I stomp across the grass, towards them.

"Get off the grass. You know how long it took me to get it like that?" Tobias yells out to me, looking up from the hole he's digging.

"Didn't picture you to be a green thumb," I tell him, still treading on his precious grass. I stand next to him.

"That's because you barely know us, besides our secret," he states.

I think for a second. He's right, I don't know much about them personally. I know a little about Theo, his love for reading and his family, which I suppose is also Tobias's family. But other than that, not much really.

I look for Theo, but he's gone again. "So, what are we doing out here?"

"We are letting your mother go. We know you're having trouble letting go, which is understandable, but we thought maybe you would like something in her memory, so she is released but still here with you." Says Theo, coming up behind me, in his hands is my mother's urn. I reach for it and he places her in my hands.

I don't speak, just nod, my throat suddenly feeling clogged. I don't know what I want to do with her, I know she can't stay in the plastic container, but I hate the thought of letting her go. This idea of theirs, I do like, though. Tobias finishes digging and steps back.

I clutch my mother's urn to my chest. "If you don't want to, we can figure out something else." I look at Tobias, he almost seems normal, not so intimidating. I shake my head.

"No, this is good. Thank you." He nods before placing his hand on my shoulder and squeezing it. I undo the lid, my hands shaking slightly. Bending down, I pour her ashes into the hole; I feel my tears trying to brim but I shake my head and clear my throat before stepping back.

That is all that is left of her. My amazing mother is now just dust, and a memory I never want to forget. I hope I don't forget her smile, her warm welcoming eyes, the feel of her hands. I never want to forget those parts of her. Theo places the rose bush in the hole and Tobias fills in the dirt.

Now, she is a rose, it's fitting. She was strong and durable like a rose and just as beautiful as one. When they are done, they walk inside, leaving me with the now planted rose bush. I look up at the clear sky, the breeze caresses my skin. The moon is shining brightly down on us, "I miss you mom." I whisper.

I can feel my tears running down my cheeks, quickly wiping them away before closing my eyes forcing them to stop. Crying won't help me, and it certainly won't bring her back. I look at the rose bush, touching the giant rose in front of me, gently, making sure I don't break its petals. I turn to see Theo and Tobias watching me from the deck. I walk towards them and back into the kitchen, like I didn't just let go of my hold on her.

I sit at the table, Theo and Tobias have made homemade pizzas. "Want me to heat it back up?" I shake my head, picking up a piece before biting a chunk off. I chew it before swallowing it down. It tastes good even when it's cold.

"Nope, I'm good." I tell them.

"Are you okay?" Theo asks.

"Peachy." I grab another slice before walking out. I'm good at masking my emotions, I hate showing them in front of anyone. I hate the thought of them seeing me as someone weak. So, I put my walls up, add a few extra bricks, and bury those feelings like a normal person. Well, at least I think it is normal. Going to the living room, I flick the TV on and put Underworld on. They come out and sit beside me. Only speaking when they realize what movie I picked.

"Seriously? You live with a vampire and a werewolf and you want to watch this garbage?" Tobias asks.

"It's a good movie." I shrug.

"It's unrealistic."

"You can't think it's that bad if you own it," I retort, biting into my pizza slice.

Once I finish eating, I curl up on the couch. I think I'm only a quarter of the way through when I feel myself dozing off back to sleep.

The next morning, as I wake up in the bed, Theo, and Tobias are both gone. They left for work without me, and I know they deliberately did it to keep me stuck here. Getting downstairs, I sing out to both of them. No answer. Walking outside, I stroll over to mom's rose bush. It's even prettier in the day, with its giant blooming buds. When I'm walking back, I notice the garage on the other side of the house. It's the only place I haven't explored since coming here.

Walking over, I push up the roller door. My heart skips a beat with excitement, as I see Theo's Black BMW. I wonder where the keys are. I walk over and pull on the handle and it opens. I search all through it, looking for the keys. I can't find them anywhere, so I give up and close the roller door and walk back inside. Deciding I'm going to make some breakfast, I walk into the kitchen. I'm making toast when out of the corner of my eye, I notice the car keys sitting in the fruit bowl. I grab them, forgetting about my toast, I race up stairs and grab my suit, getting dressed in record time and throwing my hair in a high ponytail. I chuck on some lipstick and grab my heels from the cupboard before quickly going back out to the car.

They are going to be so pissed when I rock up to work. They can't blame me though, it's their fault they left the keys where they can be found. So surely, they don't expect me to wait all day here. I turn on the ignition and speed out and down the driveway.

The entire drive, I'm constantly jamming on the brake, not used to the speed this car has compared to my little beast. Theo is definitely going to need new brake pads; on the plus side, I'm only going to be twenty minutes late. Once I arrive, I walk into the lobby. Tom is talking to Tobias and to say he's surprised to see me is an understatement. Tobias and Tom look like they are having a heated conversation when I step in. The conversation abruptly stops when Tobias lays eyes on me. He walks towards me and Tom scurries off, toward a corridor by the stairs. I definitely have to try and see him today, to find out what the hell is going on.

Tobias walks over to me, the way he walks makes me feel like he's about to slap me. But he just stops in front of me and grabs my arm. "What the fuck are you doing here?"

"Thought it was pretty obvious, considering I showed up to work." His grip on my arm tightens and he starts pulling me toward the elevator.

"How did you get here?" I hold up Theo's car keys and he raises an eyebrow before snatching them out of my hand.

"I don't see what the problem is, Tobias. I only want to work." The elevator doors open, and he pushes me in before pushing the button and the doors close. Once upstairs, Tobias walks me to my desk. Theo, hearing us come in, walks out, shock on his face at seeing me.

"What are you doing here?"

"She found your keys, next time put them up," Tobias says, chucking them at him. He catches them and folds his arms, annoyed.

"You better not have wrecked my car, Imogen."

"Or what, you buy another one? Not like you can't afford it. You will probably need new brake pads though, I wore those out pretty well on the way here." I say, my face lighting up as he glares at me before walking off.

"You don't leave the office, not today. You stay here till one of us can take you home."

"Yes sir." I salute him and he storms off, slamming his office door.

I have no intention of being confined to the office. I plan on seeing Tom today, whether they like it or not. I spend most of the day sending emails and printing off various documents and filing them. Theo and Tobias both keep coming out at different intervals, checking I'm still on this floor but don't say much. I can tell they are going to give me hell when we get home.

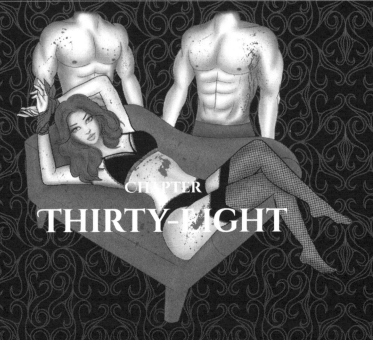

I walk back to my desk from making a coffee and sit down. From the corner of my eye, I see my phone buzz and light up. I check it and it's a message from Tom, telling me to meet him in the parking garage, where I used to park. I quickly reply and tell him I'll be out soon. Honestly, I think it's a little strange that he wants to meet me where there are no cameras. I know Theo and Tobias are hiding something and I'm determined to find out what exactly that is.

Looking up toward both their offices, the doors are still shut. Surely, I can zip out really quickly without getting noticed, though I still have doubts. Their hearing is extremely good, and I know if I use the elevator, the dinging noise it makes will alert them to me leaving.

Getting up, I slip my heels off so they won't hear them on the marble floors. Clutching them in my hand, I all but run on my tippy toes to the fire escape, closing the door as gently as possible behind me. I wait to check if I can hear any movement or their office doors opening.

When I'm sure I'm in the clear, I run down the flights of stairs to the lobby. Before opening the door, I sit on the bottom step and put my shoes on, walking into the lobby and toward the doors that lead to the parking garage. I open them and start running up the ramps, towards my usual parking space.

When I get to the top of the parking garage, Tom is standing against the barrier that stops people from driving off the roof. He waves when he sees me and glances around. It's odd that he's so paranoid.

"Where are they?" He asks, looking down the ramp.

"Still in their offices. What's going on, Tom? Why the sneaking around?"

He looks nervous and loosens the collar of his shirt. I have never seen Tom so worried and awkward before.

"How well do you know Tobias and Theo?" He asks.

That's a strange question to ask. I'm fairly sure I know their darkest secret, not that I can voice that to Tom. But the way he's looking at me, I have a feeling he knows.

"I know them well enough Tom, what is this about? You told me to let them help me and now you're freaking out."

"That was before I knew you were their mate." That word again, and Tom obviously knows what they are. I take a step back, this conversation... I know I'm not going to like it.

"What are you getting at, Tom?" I nervously glance down the ramp, now paranoid myself they are going to jump out at us.

"Tobias is a werewolf, Imogen, and Theo."

I cut him off. "I know what they are, Tom," I say simply. Tom's eyebrows raise, a look of confusion on his face.

"They told you and you aren't running for the hills?" He looks at me like I'm mad.

"Well, it doesn't change who they are, Tom. They are still good people." I answer.

"Good people, Imogen? They aren't even human," he all but yells.

"Shh keep it down, stop freaking out." I try to silence him.

"Do you have any idea the danger you are in when they try to mark you? Do you have any idea of the sacrifice you will have to make?"

Now, I'm confused. Sacrifice? What sacrifice?

Tom, seeing the look on my face looks like he's about to pass out or throw up. I'm not sure, but all the color drains from his face. He suddenly steps forward and sweeps my hair to the side.

"Shit, I'm too late; I can't believe you let them mark you. You need to get out of here, Imogen, before the bond kicks in completely." Tom speaks in panic.

I push his hand away. "How do you know so much? What you're saying isn't making any sense. Why would I run?"

Tom runs a hand over his balding head and loosens his shirt collar more, sweat is starting to bead on his brow. He looks panicked, "My family has worked for them for generations. Don't you think it's weird that no one knows who owns this company? No one has any photos of them. No matter how big this company has grown and become recognized, it's because my family covers up for them, and have done it for generations. My father did, his father and so on. We are bound to them from some old treaty. As far as the public knows, the owners want to remain anonymous. But if you check the filing and all social media accounts, you never see photos of them. People would ask questions, people would find out what they are. So, every generation, and even my future generations will keep them covered. They move the company every few decades and come in as the grandson or sons to run it and my family follows and makes sure they go unnoticed to the public. That's how I know what they are." Tom explains, sounding more frantic with each word that passes his lips.

I furrow my brows, still rather lost. "But what's that got to do with me? I haven't got anything to do with it."

"I know, but soon you won't have a choice, Imogen. Soon, my family will have to cover up for you too. They have marked you, you belong to them now."

"Don't be ridiculous, Tom. I'm my own person. Nobody owns me," I say, rolling my eyes annoyed with this conversation.

"Yeah, right now they don't, not till that bond kicks in." He grabs my shoulders and looks me dead in the face. "You need to run. Get away from here while you can. Your relationship in the supernatural world is forbidden. No humans allowed."

"I know this, but nobody knows except their parents that I even exist. Just spit it out, Tom. I don't have all day. What aren't you telling me?"

"Think about it. Imogen, you're the Forbidden Mate. There are only two options for you. They either kill you or..." He stops, hesitating and looking down the ramp nervously. I do the same, thinking I hear something, before turning back to Tom again.

"Or what, Tom?"

"They change you, Imogen. They have to change you, make you like them."

I gasp and take a step back, "They wouldn't do that." But suddenly, I'm not so sure. Them, hiding me away and telling me to wait for the bond to kick in. Theo's words come back to me.

"You won't want to leave when the bond kicks in." I shudder, now understanding what he meant, meaning I will choose to be changed. I don't want to become like them, trapped, forced to live forever. And how would they do that, change me?

I stumble backward, the gravity of what he just told me pushing down on me. Fear consumes me, I don't want to be a monster. I don't want to live like that, always hiding in the shadows. Yeah, in stories it sounds good, but real life? No, I don't want that. I'm content with being me, I don't want to change. I sure as hell won't allow them to decide that for me.

"You need to leave, Imogen, before they either kill you or, well, kill you. The only way for you to become like them is to die or for Tobias to change you into what he is, which I heard is extremely painful."

I step back, nodding. I don't want this. I never asked for this, I sure as hell don't want to turn into some furry oversized dog. Do they get fleas? My mind is rambling, not being able to cope with the information I just heard.

The noise Tom makes pulls me from my rambling, frantic mind. We are no longer alone, Theo comes out of nowhere and grabs Tom by the throat. I scream at seeing my friend being choked, his face changing color, his hands clawing at Theo's to get him to let go. My scream makes him turn and look at me, I step back. The look on his face is demonic, his eyes are burning blood red, his fangs protruding, even his nails are now deadly points as they dig into Tom's neck. "Let him go, Theo, please," I beg, taking another step back. I need to run, but I can't, knowing Tom is going to die if I do.

"Please Theo, let him go," I cry, tears falling down my face. I start sobbing hysterically. He's a monster, the thing of nightmares. The thing that goes bump in the night. The promise of death and right now, he is going to kill Tom. I can't watch this; I can't bear to watch his death.

"Run, Imogen," Tom chokes out, his voice barely audible.

I turn and run. "Imogen!" Theo snarls as I take off.

"I should fucking kill you for what you have done," I hear him say behind me. I look over my shoulder and Theo drops him. He falls on his knees, choking. I turn and keep running down the ramps. I feel an arm go around my waist and I'm pulled back against a warm chest. I kick my legs and hit wherever I can, trying to escape his vice like grip on me.

"Settle down, Imogen," Tobias's voice is angry. I don't listen, just keep thrashing. I hear him growl before throwing me over his shoulder.

"Fucking kill him," he growls out. I look up and see Theo, walking back up the ramp towards Tom.

"No, no, please don't hurt him." Theo stops and looks back, "Please," I beg. I stop thrashing against Tobias, hoping Theo will walk back toward us. Theo keeps walking up the ramp after a second. I start punching Tobias and hit him wherever I can. "No, please, no!" I thrash wildly, wanting to go to Tom.

"Imogen, enough!" Tobias growls out, I flinch at the venom in his words, it makes my blood run cold. "You kill him, and I will never forgive you." Tobias doesn't say anything at first. He starts walking and I start thrashing again, trying to escape.

"Please, Tobias, don't be so cruel. He is my friend, he didn't do anything wrong," I cry.

He kept walking till we reached his car. He opened the back door and tossed me in.

"It's too late, Imogen." I don't understand what he means at first. Until he walks around to the trunk and opens it, Theo walks down the ramp, Tom's limp body in his arms. I scream and open the door and run, only for Tobias to grab me again. He throws me on the backseat, and I start kicking him and reaching for the other door handle. "Enough, Imogen, or I will put you in the trunk with him."

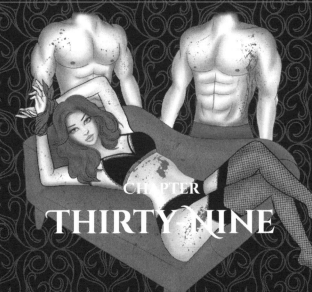

CHAPTER
THIRTY NINE

Anxiety kicks in and adrenaline pumps through my veins. My head is spinning, how can this all happen, an hour ago everything was fine and normal. Now Tom is dead. He's gone, another person dying on me, and this time it's all my fault.

The back door opens, and I slide as far away as the seat will allow, my back hitting the door. Tobias gets in next to me. Theo jumps in the driver's seat and tears out of the car park, the car bottoms out on the driveway. Tobias reaches for me and I kick him in the shoulder. He grunts and grabs my legs, pinning them to the seat.

"You killed him, you fucking killed him! Get away from me! You fucking monster!" I scream.

Theo slams on the brakes, and I'm thrown into the footwell. Tobias reaches down and grabs the front of my blouse and rips me back up and onto the seat. We are in heavy traffic. He reaches over and tries to clip my belt in, but I scratch his face, trying to get away from him.

"Fucking stop, Imogen." He pins my back on the seat. Tobias leans over me and I start screaming, hoping that since we are stopped in traffic someone could hear me. Tobias growls and puts his hand over my mouth. I bite him hard enough to draw blood. He rips his hand away and I can see it bleeding.

"Do something, Theo. I'm about to fucking lose it with her." He isn't lying when he says he's losing control. Fur is growing on his arms, and his claws extend, digging into my arms. His canines protrude right in front of me, his teeth look sharp next to my face.

"Swap places with me," Theo says, letting go of the wheel and putting the handbrake on before jumping in the back. Tobias jumps over into the front seat. Cars are honking their horns behind us because traffic is moving and the car is stopped. I try to sit up but am shoved back down by Theo. He leans in, trying to calm me with the fog, but I lash out and slap him across the face and kick him back with my feet. Theo snarls before pouncing on me, pinning me with all his weight, his face barely an inch off mine. "Stop fighting."

"You killed him. I fucking hate you!" His eyes blaze blood red, burning brightly.

"He isn't dead yet, now stop or I will make you watch when I do kill him." His voice is cold as ice and a shiver runs up my spine. My heart rate picks up as panic kicks in again and I start trembling.

Hot tears form in my eyes and run down my cheeks. Theo's eyes soften before he loosens his grip slightly. I feel the fog washing over me, calming every muscle in my body. I don't fight it, I relax into the feeling. I can't cope right now; I just want it to go away.

Tobias continues driving, and when we hit the dirt road, I know we are out of the city. Theo allows me to sit up and I scoot over, pressing myself against the door to stay as far away from him as possible. When I see the bend leading onto the side road before our turn off, I grip the door handle, waiting for the car to slow down enough. Just as the car slows down, I throw the door open and throw myself out.

Theo screams, I notice him trying to grab me, but he isn't expecting me to throw myself out and is too slow. I fall from the car, skidding and rolling across the dirt. The idea seemed good at the time, until I feel like I'm being skinned alive. I feel the air leave my lungs on impact. Feel the palms of my hands being ripped to shreds, and my wrist snaps, making a sickening noise on impact.

The car screeches to a stop, dirt and dust flying everywhere. I pull myself up onto my hands and knees, screaming at the pressure on my wrist that's sending shooting pain up my arm. Coughing on dirt and trying to get air in my lungs, I hear the door open, adrenaline shoots through me and I manage to stand, stumbling forward before finding my feet.

I take off running straight for the tree line, only I don't make it. I collapse onto my hands and knees, and before I know it, feet appear in my line of vision.

I clutch onto his pants legs, trying to pull myself up. What a stupid idea that was. Fear makes me do some stupid shit sometimes, but this definitely takes the cake. I should have realized I can't outrun them. I'm now paying dearly for that stupid decision.

Tobias leans down and picks me up from under my arms and places me on his hip.

"That was the most irrational thing I have ever seen you do," he growls out. I nod, resting my head on his shoulder. My entire body aches, my face feels like it has a gravel rash on it, and my skin burns. Tobias places his hands under my ass to support and hold my legs around him before walking back to the car.

He places me on the passenger seat before buckling in my seat belt. When he climbs in, he locks the doors before taking off again. I groan in pain.

"Why would you do that? You could have died, Imogen," Theo spits out with a growl. My whole body is trembling in shock. Five minutes later, we pull up out the front of the house and Tobias unlocks the doors. Theo gets out, slamming the door so hard the windows shake. I see in the mirror him walking around to the trunk.

I realize Tom is still in the trunk. Now that we stopped, I can hear him banging around, very much still alive. I push the door open, forcing my legs out of the car. I use the door to help me stand, my legs feel like play dough. I lean on the car, walking to the back end when Tobias grabs me around the waist. I see Theo help Tom out of the trunk, Theo grabs him by the front of his shirt, and I start screaming, trying to get out of Tobias' grip. Theo throws him on the ground and Tom lands on his back. Turning my head, I bite Tobias' bicep, his grip loosens immediately, and I run to Tom, throwing my body over his.

"It's ok, Imogen, I'm fine," Tom whispers under me. I don't know if he's trying to reassure himself or me, maybe both. Tobias grips my waist, trying to pull me off him, but I hold onto his clothes, refusing to let go and ignoring the pain in my wrist.

"Don't hurt him please, please." Hot tears stream down my face. I hear Theo growl before he pries my fingers off Tom's shirt. I start kicking and screaming as Tobias lifts me up, pulling me against his chest. I manage to kick Theo as Tobias pulls me away, which only angers him more.

Theo grabs my shoulders and shakes me. "Enough, Imogen, that's enough. Fucking stop," he screams, clutching my face. His grip squishes my face in his hands. I can feel his hands shaking before Tobias shoves him away from me with one hand.

I look up at Tobias, tears spill from my eyes as I start sobbing uncontrollably. "Please, Tobias, tell him to stop." Tobias' eyes soften slightly before he looks over to Theo. Theo pulls Tom to his feet, holding him by one arm.

"Stop Theo, we kill him, we are only hurting her."

Theo's head snaps in my direction; the look he gives me sends chills down my spine. I push myself closer to Tobias, frightened. Theo's eyes look demonic, and I can tell he wants to kill Tom. I can also tell if he does, he will enjoy killing him, like he craves it. This isn't my happy go lucky Theo, this is the monster he kept at bay and hidden from me.

Theo walks towards me, pulling Tom with him by one arm as he approaches. I flinch, not liking his red-hot anger directed at me. He stops, realizing he is indeed scaring me. I can feel my heart rate thump loudly in my chest. Hear it my ears, my entire head pounding to the same beat as a migraine starts to form.

"Mom will pitch a fit if we kill him. Think Theo, we don't have to do this." I watch him think for a second, practically see the wheels turning in his head as he thinks long and hard about what it is he wants to do. I know he wants to kill Tom, I can feel the rage that consumes him, I fear it. What if he loses his temper like that with me? Will he kill me too?

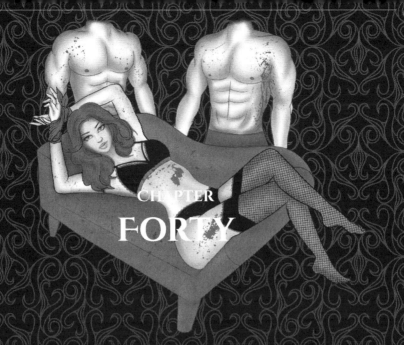

CHAPTER
FORTY

"I f I let him live, you don't leave this property," he says through gritted teeth. I quickly nod, looking toward Tom. He visibly relaxes when Theo lets go of him, shoving him towards the car.

"How do I know you won't kill him when you take him back?" I ask, scared that if Theo takes him home, he will snap on the way and murder my friend.

"I will take him home; you stay here with Theo." I shake my head, not wanting to be left alone with Theo, not when he's like this. I never thought I'd see the day where I actually feared him.

"Either Tobias takes him, Imogen, or I kill him. Pick," he says, moving toward me. I look up at Tobias who is watching me.

"You're scaring her, Theo. You will be fine, Imogen. Theo won't hurt you. I promise." I have my doubts after seeing him like this, but I nod anyway.

"Get in, I will take you home." Tom moves to the passenger seat. Tobias lets go of me and Theo immediately grabs me, his cold hands make me shiver. I watch as Tobias gets in the car and leaves. I turn around when Theo tugs my arm, pulling me toward the house. My entire body shakes in fear and pain, I groan, trying to walk up the veranda stairs, my legs feel like every muscle is put through a meat grinder.

Theo, seeing it's taking so long for me to walk up the stairs, becomes annoyed and scoops me up in his arms, forcing me to grab onto his shoulder. He walks inside and up the stairs to the bathroom, placing me back on my feet.

He starts the shower before turning to grab my shirt. I move away from him, taking a step back. He grips the front of my shirt and yanks me towards him, and I smack into his chest.

"I have more control than you think, Imogen. Don't doubt me, I won't hurt you." His voice sounds angry but at least he doesn't sound homicidal anymore. He rips my shirt open, seeing as it is already torn and barely hanging onto my body anyway. I lean on his shoulder as he bends down removing my pants, he removes my underwear before standing up and removing my bra. I stand freezing and shaking in front of him.

He strips his clothes off before getting in the shower, pulling me with him. As soon as the water touches my bleeding and grazed skin, I flinch, pushing myself out of the water and to the wall, clutching my broken wrist to my chest. I hiss at the pain and my tears burn the grazes on my face. Theo pulls my hand from my chest to examine it. I gasp, holding in my scream when he prods it with his fingers.

"I can heal you if you want." I shake my head.

Theo stares at me. "You're in pain. I can fix it, let me." I don't know what to say, I know they won't take me to a hospital. They will see it as another way for me to escape, and I don't think I will be able to get past them in this condition. I nod my head. Theo pulls me to his chest, my back flush against him. He wraps an arm around my waist before I see him reach his hand above my head, biting into the side of his palm. Blood starts running out. He presses it to my lips, I shake my head, trying to get away from his bleeding hand. No fucking way, I'm not drinking his blood.

"Imogen, drink it or I will force you." I shake my head again, the thought repulses me. I feel him press his wrist harder against my lips and feel his blood running down my chin.

"One." Really, he is counting like I'm a child? Not wanting to find out what happens at three, I open my mouth. His blood floods into my mouth. At first, it tastes disgusting as it runs over my tongue. After a few seconds pass though, I feel something else. I grab his wrist and moan. I can't get enough, his blood is addictive, like being high, giving me a floating feeling. Better than I ever thought possible. I feel his hand brush my hair back before I hear him press his head back onto the shower door.

"Good girl," I hear him mutter. After a few minutes, he pulls his hand away. I miss it almost immediately before realizing I'm actually drinking someone's blood.

I gasp when I have no pain, none at all, if it weren't for the blood staining my skin, I wouldn't believe I was injured. I move my wrist, waiting for the sharp pain, but it doesn't come.

I look up at Theo, and he winks at me before kissing the top of my head and pulling me against him. I let him, leaning into him more. My body feels amazing and tingly. I feel like I can run a marathon, no more aches or pains even the migraine that was starting to form disappears. Theo reaches for the soap and pushes me back under the water.

Blood and dirt run down my legs, I'm filthy. He washes me quickly before turning me around to wash my hair. His fingers massage my scalp so good that I almost fall asleep standing upright. When he's done, he rinses me off before washing himself and turning the taps off.

I step out of the shower just as Tobias walks in with two towels. He wraps one around me before pulling me into the bedroom.

"Tom?" I ask. Theo growls from behind me, stepping closer. I flinch and move closer to Tobias.

"He is at home with his wife. I promise he is okay." I nod.

I dry myself, and Theo walks out of the walk-in dressed and

passes me my pajamas. I turn to walk into the bathroom to put them on when Tobias grabs my wrist.

"No, get dressed here; you don't go anywhere by yourself from now on." I look at Theo, who is watching, his face expressionless.

I look back to Tobias, the look on his face is daring me to disobey him. I drop my towel right in front of him. My eyes don't leave his as I slip my pajamas on. I don't care that they see me naked, they obviously have more times now then I can count. What I do care about though is not being given any privacy.

I fold my arms over my chest defiantly. Tobias clicks his tongue, annoyed at me glaring at him. He stands up, his chest pressing against mine. "You ever pull something like that again..." I look down at the ground to get away from his gaze. He grips my chin, forcing my head back to look at him. "I will let Theo go back and kill not only Tom, but his entire family. Understood?" I can feel tears brimming. "Understood?" I don't say anything which angers him slightly, his grip on my chin getting tighter. "Understood?" His eyes burn into mine. I feel Theo press up against my back. I swallow quickly, trying to get moisture back in my mouth that has turned dry as a desert.

"Yes, understood," I whisper. He turns my head slightly before looking up at Theo and nodding. He lets go and pulls me to him. Wrapping his arms around my waist, he puts his head in my neck, running his nose from the crook of my neck to my chin, inhaling my scent before gently pressing his lips to mine.

I feel his tongue brush my bottom lip, but I don't react. He becomes more forceful, and I give in parting my lips, I kiss him back. Theo steps closer to me, running his nose along my shoulder to behind my ear. I shiver at the contrast of hot and cold, Theo's husky voice in my ear. "You won't run again, will you, Imogen?"

My stomach tightens, arousal flooding me. "No," I moan into Tobias's mouth, right now I will tell them anything they want to hear, loving the feel of them touching my skin. The voice in my head tells me this is wrong, that I shouldn't allow this after everything that happened, but I feel an even greater pull towards them, my body acting on its own.

Eventually, my mind submits to the feeling of their hands caressing and touching my skin. I lean back into Theo and I feel Tobias hands move to my face, his lips hungrily devouring mine. Theo's hands go underneath my shirt and run across my stomach before moving to my breasts. Then, I'm suddenly hit with a need that I know isn't mine but that of Theo's. His fangs graze my neck sharp on my soft skin.

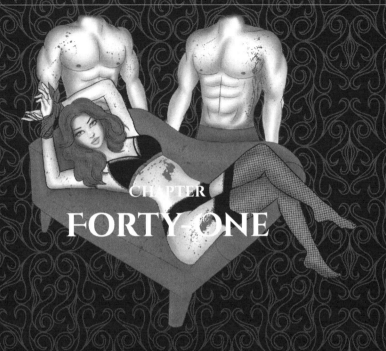

CHAPTER
FORTY-ONE

Theo's teeth press harder and harder against my skin as he hungrily sucks on my soft flesh, I flinch when his fangs pierce my skin, before relaxing into him. I can feel his tongue lapping and sucking at the bite mark as he drinks my blood. I thought it's supposed to hurt, they said his bite is painful, but I feel euphoric, tingling spreads throughout my body. I can feel my temperature rising, despite the coldness of his body pressing into mine.

Tobias steps back, watching, waiting for him to stop. Theo pulls his mouth away, some of my blood running down my shoulder. Tobias wipes it with the towel on the floor. I lean back into Theo, suddenly feeling a little queasy. It doesn't feel like he drank from me long but why the aftereffects? Theo wipes his lips with his thumb before sucking it into his mouth. I look up at him, his grip on my waist holding me tight against his body.

"I thought you said it would hurt when he bites me?" I ask Tobias.

"Must be the mate bond, it hurt for years when he fed on me

until I marked him, I just assumed since you're human it would be painful." I nod.

"It's probably the mate bond kicking in. I must say you taste way better than Tobias," he says with a chuckle.

Tobias crosses his arms. "Well then, you can feed off her, if I taste so bad." He pouts, I roll my eyes at their bickering.

"I never said you tasted bad, but you try eating the same thing for years, it gets a little boring after a while." Tobias doesn't seem pleased with his answer.

"Come, you should eat," Tobias says, grabbing my hand and pulling me out of the room.

We end up having grilled cheese and tomato on toast for dinner. We eat silently before watching TV, I'm not really watching though. I feel a little off, I feel like I'm heating up like I'm put in an oven. I start sweating profusely and excuse myself to go have a shower. Tobias, refusing to let me be on my own, follows and sits on the sink watching me, after a few minutes of watching, he strips and hops in.

He jumps as soon as the freezing cold water touches him. "Geez, Imogen, that's freezing, turn the heat up," I ignore him. Instead, I slide down the shower wall to a sitting position. No matter how cold the water is I feel like I'm overheating; my skin feels like it's on fire. Tobias glances down at me and turns the heat up slightly. "You okay love? You smell different."

I shake my head, I feel out of breath, hot and on the verge of passing out. Tobias pulls me up to a standing position, pulling me against his chest. "Shit, you are burning up. Theo, get in here." Within seconds Theo is in the room with a panicked expression on his face. Theo pulls me out of the shower and Tobias turns the water off before stepping out himself. I can see my reflection in the mirror above the sink. My face is flushed, my cheeks a bright crimson color.

"She definitely has a fever," Theo tells Tobias.

"Heat?" Tobias asks, Theo gives me a weird look. "I don't know, can humans go into heat?"

"Your guess is as good as mine, she smells different though." Tobias announces.

"Yeah, she does, it's the only thing that makes sense," replies Theo. I stare between the pair of them confused.

"What is heat?"

"Means the bond is kicking in, will make you more sensitive to us. You will want to mate, and if your scent gets any stronger, we won't be able to help ourselves. We will mate you." Tobias explains.

"What, like a dog? I'm not a dog, I'm not bleeding either. I don't want to be a dog," I say, appalled at the thought. This is fucking ridiculous because of them I'm turning into a dog.

Tobias growls lowly. "I'm not a dog; will you stop saying I am? There is a clear difference between a dog and a werewolf."

I lean into Theo, liking the coldness of his skin. "Well, you turn into a furry dog and look like one." I mutter, Theo laughs behind me, clearly finding our arguing amusing.

"No, I am different. What dog do you know that is the size of a bear, Imogen? And is immortal, for that matter." Tobias keeps arguing even though I don't think he can change my mind anymore.

"Great Danes are pretty big, and you bark or growl or whatever that thing is you do."

"I do not bark; I also don't cock my leg on trees to mark my territory either, if you must know. I am not a dog, I'm a fucking werewolf and it is insulting that you keep saying it." He has a point: they are vastly different, but still, they do have some similarities. Like the tail and all the fur.

"Fine you're not a dog, chill, settle down Fido." He growls, and I turn my back on him, ignoring him.

I walk over to the bed, I need to lie down. I dry myself with Theo's help before laying down. Theo places the blanket over me, and I immediately kick it off.

Theo says he's leaving to go get Tylenol to try and bring my temperature down. I sometimes forget they aren't human and have no need for such things. I don't know what time he comes back but

I'm woken listening to the pair of them trying to figure how much of it to give me.

"Just give them, here," I say, sitting up and holding my hand out for the box. They pass me the box and I tear three out of the foil wrapping as they hand me a glass of water.

"Just so you know, it tells you on the back of the box the dosages." Typical men, not bothering to read the instructions. Theo glances at the box while I swallow them down.

"It says two, not three," he states, worried.

"They are weak, they aren't morphine, I will survive. Clearly, you haven't taken pain medication for a while."

Getting up, my legs feel unsteady, but I decide to go find something stronger to kill the cramping in my stomach. I walk downstairs and into the kitchen. They both follow, wondering what I'm doing as I search through the kitchen cupboards before walking into the pantry. I manage to find some whiskey.

Unscrewing the cap, I start chugging it down. Coughing on the sudden burn, I walk out and sit at the counter on a stool. Tobias walks over and grabs the bottle, "You're not drinking." I snatch it back out of his hand. "Imogen," he says angrily.

"Leave her, she is in pain. Just let her go, she might sleep better." Theo argues for me. Tobias isn't happy but doesn't try to take the bottle from me again.

"When will it stop?" I ask, hoping that it will be over by morning.

"I'm not sure, you're human. Your scent is getting stronger though," replies Tobias.

He shifts uncomfortably, adjusting his pants. I look down and can see his erection, pressing against the fabric. Looking at Theo he looks just as uncomfortable. I swipe the bottle off the counter and head back to the room. I chug a good amount of the bottle before Theo walks in and hops on the bed. I lay next to him, his cold skin soothes my overheating body. I move closer, resting my head on his chest enjoying the coolness.

"Sit up." I quickly do, and he takes off his shirt before pulling me onto him, my whole body cooling slightly. I close my eyes and before I know it, I drift off to sleep.

I gasp, my eyes snap open. I'm still on top of Theo, he looks down at me before putting his phone down that he was reading off of. I turn my head and can see Tobias moving around in his sleep like he's extremely uncomfortable. Everywhere Theo's skin is touching me feels electrified, like static electricity, I run my hand up his side, he shivers from the heat of my hands.

My whole body aches to be touched, my core is pulsating with need. I move my legs to either side of Theo's hips, I can feel his erection pressing between my legs, I rub myself against it, needing the friction.

He doesn't say anything or try to stop me, but I can tell by the look on his face, he's a little concerned for some unknown reason. I kiss him, forcing his lips to part, my tongue hungrily diving into his mouth. I feel possessed and out of control, needing their hands on me. Theo rolls me onto my back, so he's between my legs and thrust his hips into me.

I moan at the sudden movement, reaching my arm out to Tobias, I tug on his arm. He rolls instantly before waking. His face looks similar to how I feel - hungry and needy. His eyes, not their usual, hypnotic blue, now black orbs staring back at me. Theo unbuttons my shirt and I pull Tobias to me, his lips pressing to mine softly before I deepen the kiss, moaning into his mouth as my hand goes to his hair, pulling him closer.

He groans against my lips and Theo moves to the waistband of my pants before peeling them down. The cool air on my burning skin makes me shudder.

I sit up, removing my shirt before rolling onto Tobias's naked body. I run my hands over the tight lines of muscle on his abdomen, loving the feeling of each bump under my fingers. Consumed by the feeling of his skin against mine, Tobias grabs my hips, rubbing his erection into me, his cock running between my wet folds straight to my clit. Theo's hands wrap around me, going to my breasts. I lean my head back onto him while Tobias fingers move between us, rubbing my clit before he slid a finger inside me. I sit up slightly, so I'm on my knees, Tobias' fingers slip in and out of me before he adds another.

"She's so wet," Tobias speaks, but the words come out more of a growl. He holds his fingers up, they glisten with my juices before popping them in his mouth and sucking on them. I watch, arousal flooding me as he sucks his fingers clean. Theo rolls my nipples between his fingers, sucking on my neck. Everywhere they touch, I can feel sparks lighting up my skin. Tobias' fingers move back inside me as he thrusts them in and out, my hips move against his fingers, and then I feel my walls tighten. My skin heats up and I feel pleasure wash over me. My walls clamp down on his fingers, as I ride out my orgasm. Tobias moves his fingers slowly, in and out of me, waiting to see what I want.

"Better?" he asks, I shake my head. My body needs more, as soon as I come down from the high of my orgasm, waves of heat wash over me, my arousal gets worse to the point it's almost painful. "I... I..." Tobias moves his fingers faster and I move my hips in the same rhythm.

"What do you need, Imogen?" Theo whispers below my ear before sucking on my neck.

"I need more, I need more." My voice is airy and light, as I pant, trying to word what I need from them.

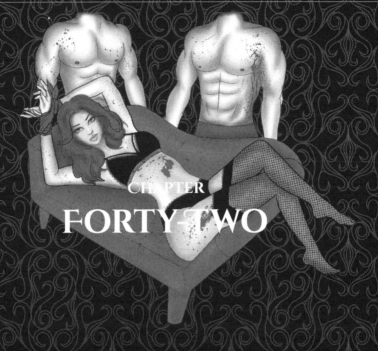

FORTY-TWO

Tobias' other hand moves to my breast, squeezing it hard. I can feel his fingers digging painfully into my skin. I enjoy the pain, a distraction from the burning of my skin. His fingers never let up as they slide in and out of me. Theo's cold hands run over my skin soothingly as they caress my overheated skin.

Pushing my hair over my shoulder, his cool lips move to my neck, light as a feather, moving down and across my shoulder making me shiver. I reach back and run my fingers through his hair. Tobias shifts below me, pulling his fingers from me before positioning himself at my entrance and slamming my hips down onto him. His hard, thick length slips between my wet folds before sinking into me deeply. I moan at the feeling of him filling me, my tight walls stretching around his large size. His hands grab my hips as he guides my movements to the rhythm of his thrusts, my body feels instant relief with him, buried deep in me. I roll my hips above him before he lets go, letting me set the pace. My hands run up his chest, moving to his broad shoulders. I move my hips faster and faster against him, loving the feeling of his hard length slipping in and out of me. My stomach tightens, my heart rate quickens, and my breathing becomes airy as I relish the feeling burning inside me, my eyes fluttering closed.

Every nerve and cell in my body buzzes and comes alive with every movement, every touch. I'm sitting on the edge, teetering dangerously, almost high as waves of pleasure consume every part of me. I can feel Theo's hands run up over my hips and up my sides before going to my hair.

He grabs a handful, pulling my head back and to the side, his lips crash into mine, his tongue demanding as it tastes every inch of my mouth. Tobias grabs my hips, using his legs, he thrusts into me harder, his cock hitting against my cervix.

Theo's harsh grip on my hair only excites me more, my fluids coat Tobias cock as it slips in and out. I feel Theo move closer, completely lost in the euphoria when I feel him slide into me, his hips slamming into me with a hard slap. Theo shoves me forward and Tobias seizes my lips, sucking my bottom lip into his mouth. His tongue fighting for dominance when I kiss him back. Theo's grip tightens on the handful of my hair as he slams into me repeatedly, making me bounce on top of Tobias.

My head snaps back under his grip before I feel Tobias shift slightly so he's sitting half upright, both of their mouths on my neck, one on each side. Their teeth tease my flesh before I feel them both sink their teeth into the soft skin on my neck, sending me flying over the edge, my walls clamping down on Tobias and I feel him still underneath me, his seed spilling into me. Soon, Theo's movements slow as he finds his own release.

My head is spinning, and my body feels light and no longer burning as I feel the heat coursing through my body die down. I collapse on top of Tobias as I come down hard. The only noise in the room is our heavy breathing. The lingering smell of sex, enticing my senses. I feel Theo slide out of me before I feel him brush my hair from my face where I'm laying on Tobias's chest.

"Better?" He asks, breathless.

"Much," my voice a soft murmur. My body is spent but no longer pained. I finally feel relieved.

I lay on top of Tobias, not able to move my limbs. I feel heavy, my entire body starts to tingle. Tobias' warm fingers run up my spine, making me shiver.

I wonder if I would always feel this way with them, wonder if they would eventually get bored with me. I don't know if it is my own feelings or that of the bond making me doubt whether or not I'm good enough for them.

"What's wrong?" Asks Tobias.

I look up at him, propping my chin on the center of his chest. "Nothing is wrong."

"I know something is wrong. I can feel your emotions have shifted." I look at him quizzically. "The bond has kicked in already for me and Theo. We could feel everything from the moment we marked you."

"Will I be able to feel both of you?" I ask, curious. Now, I need to try to get better control of my emotions. I don't want them to be able to read me like an open book.

"I'm not sure how long it will take. For shifters and vampires it's instant, but you're human so the bond may take a bit to kick in. You will notice when it does, you will feel drawn to us, and be able to feel what we feel."

Theo walks back in the room and lays on the bed next to Tobias. His hand moves to my cheek before resting his hand on Tobias's chest. I like the way they are with each other; I don't find it weird or strange. To me, it is normal and makes my heart swell with happiness.

"What are you talking about?"

"Just the mate bond."

"Ah." Theo searches my face for a second. It's a bit strange to watch his eyes glaze over like this. It's as if he's looking straight through me.

"Don't think like that."

248

I try to make sense of what he says until I realize what the words mean. "You can read my thoughts." The thought horrifies me, it's an invasion of privacy.

"Don't be mad, he only wanted to know what was bothering you," Tobias says.

"So, you can do it too?" I gasp.

"No, just Theo. Vampire trick. I can feel what you feel but can't read your thoughts. Theo can do both." Tobias shrugs, as if it's no big deal.

I look towards Theo. "It bothers you that much?" He asks.

"I like to keep my thoughts private."

"I will try not to do it." I don't believe him, but let it go. I wonder what else he has overheard in my mind. Tobias rolls me to the side between them before standing and grabbing some shorts, Theo looks up as well, towards the window and Tobias quickly runs down the stairs leaving us.

"Where is he going?" I ask, looking towards the window. I'm not sure what they can hear or see but I can only see the darkness of the night before I hear tires on the dirt driveway.

"We have visitors, get dressed." Theo whispers, quickly pecking my cheek.

"Who?" I ask. Who would stop by so late at night?

"My parents."

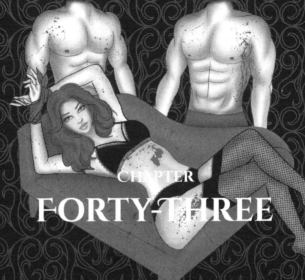

CHAPTER
FORTY-THREE

y heart skips a beat, nervousness kicks in. It wasn't so long ago that I did a runner from these very people. What a great fucking first impression that was, they probably think I am unhinged. Maybe I am, now that I think of it, what normal person would be involved in their world? One thing I do know is his parents don't accept me, that much is clear from what I overheard the last time.

I quickly grab the first thing I lay my hands on. A pair of leggings and an oversized sweater. My nervousness is making me sweat already. Theo runs downstairs to Tobias to greet them. I don't realize how badly my hands are shaking until I grab the banister. My hand is trembling, and my palms are sweaty, sticking to the lacquered wood as I descend. I stop halfway when I hear angry voices talking in the living room. I hear glass break and Theo's father's voice rise, I stop and listen.

"I won't give you any more time, the month is nearly up. If anyone finds out about her, we will have the council breathing down our neck, especially after the little stunt you pulled with Tom."

I hear Theo growl lowly at the mention of Tom's name.

"Don't you start, boy. I warned you both to keep her here until she decided. You think what you did went unnoticed? For fuck's sake, I can't believe the pair of you. I thought you had more brains than to take a weak human as a mate. Not only is it forbidden but no one will accept her how she is."

"Who we choose as our mate shouldn't even be anyone's business but ours," Tobias yells.

"Anyone but a human, Tobias. You're giving our family a bad name. She is fucking human. Either fix it or I will, and you won't like the consequences if I have to."

I hear furniture crashing. I race down the stairs in panic, worried about Theo and Tobias. Theo has his father by the throat, pressed against the fireplace, the couch lying on its side, which Theo must have pushed out of the way when he grabbed him. His fangs bared at his throat.

"Nobody fucking touches her. I don't give a fuck if you're family. Threaten her again and I will fucking end you," he spits at his father.

"Please, Theo, settle down. Let's be rational here." His mother tries to calm him, her hand on his arm.

No one notices me standing there, watching the entire thing play out, but one thing I won't be seen as by this stubborn man is weak. I square my shoulders and walk further into the room. Theo lets go of his father as soon as he sees me, his father straightening out his suit jacket before turning and glaring at me. Like seriously, who wears a suit this late at night, or is it early morning, time has escaped me.

Caroline walks past her husband, giving him a glare on her way past, before extending her hand to me. "I'm Caroline, it's nice to finally meet you properly, Imogen."

I shake her hand, she squeezes softly, her eyes glinting oddly under the light. I let her hand go before looking towards his father, Josiah, who is killing me with his eyes. I hold my chin up, refusing to be intimidated by him.

I extend my hand. "Hello Josiah, I'm Imogen the weak human," I say, my voice coming out strong, showing none of the fear I feel inside.

He holds my gaze for a second and I refuse to look away. I raise an eyebrow, waiting, before I see his lips tug slightly upward and he grabs my hand, shaking it. "Nice to meet you, Imogen. I suppose my boys have told you about me then?"

I nod before he lets go, "Yes, your names, but not much other than that. Coffee?" I ask. I'm impressed with how calm I sound. I turn my back on him and start walking to the kitchen, not even waiting for an answer.

I see Tobias trying to hide his smile as I walk past. I'm not going to be intimidated by one old vampire when I live with two mythical creatures. I may look weak, but I won't be talked about and treated like trash, I don't care how big and scary he is supposed to be. To me, he just looks like an ordinary man, the resemblance between Josiah and Theo though is uncanny.

They both share the same light brown hair and green eyes. He is shorter than Theo, but has a stocky build and looks like a man, used to getting his way.

I turn the kettle on before leaning against the counter as everyone fills into the room and Theo comes over kissing my cheek before leaning against the counter next to me and crossing his arms. Tobias gets some mugs and hands them to me.

"Sugar?" I ask, looking at Caroline and Josiah.

She nods before answering. "Yes, two with cream," she says with a smile.

I glance at Josiah, but I have a feeling he is a black coffee, no sugar type of man. "Black no sugar," he says. So my guess is correct, I busy myself, making coffee.

I hand them their coffees before leaning on the island counter with my coffee in my hands. Caroline goes to say something but is cut off by her husband.

"So, all this trouble for you. Although, I'm surprised you even came downstairs, most humans would run."

"Well, I suppose I'm not like most humans then," I state. My words make me question my own sanity. Maybe there is something really wrong with me. I do seem to be questioning everything at the moment, especially my sanity. "So, you don't have a problem with your sons being bisexual, but have a problem with me being human, correct?" I raise an eyebrow.

"Correct, it is against the rules we have lived by for centuries. I have nothing against you personally, Imogen. How could I? I barely know you. But you don't understand the risk my sons are taking by keeping you." The way he speaks is like I'm their pet, not a person.

I nod. I do understand their reasons but that doesn't mean I'm going to throw my life away for the sake of a few broken rules. If no one knows I exist, why is it a problem? Caroline clears her throat awkwardly, obviously fearing this is going to become another argument that she would be stuck in between.

"I'm not changing. I don't want to be like Tobias or Theo, I like my humanity," I say, not taking my eyes off him.

"You won't be given the choice if that's the case, Imogen. There are only two options for you: death or change. You need to hurry up and embrace one." I hear Tobias growl behind me. The sound is low and deep in his chest, it gives me goosebumps.

"I never asked for any of this. My choice has already been taken from me. I have been held prisoner here for weeks, and now you're saying I don't have a choice, yet I'm still alive. If you're going to kill me, get it over with then," I challenge.

His lips tug up into a sly smile. "I like her, she has sass. But you boys are aware it's going to get her killed," he says, looking at both of them behind me. I know they won't allow their father to hurt me. While they stand behind me, I feel safe enough to say what I need to say. This choice they are trying to make isn't theirs to decide but mine, and I'm fine with being the way I am. Either they all accept that or I leave, one way or another. I don't want this man deciding my fate.

I look at the grandfather clock, it is a little after 4AM. Noticing the time makes me yawn. I quickly swallow my coffee down, hoping to give myself some energy. Josiah keeps his eyes on me the entire time. I'm very aware of his gaze. It reminds me of a snake about to strike.

We sit and stand in awkward silence for a few seconds, everyone drinking their coffee. "If you refuse to be changed, what sort of future do you see yourself having with my sons? You will grow old and then die. I'm not sure if they told you this but a mate bond..."

Tobias cuts him off. "She doesn't need to know anything else father, I won't have her decision swayed because you're speaking nonsense."

"She has a right to know, not that it will matter when she is dead, which by the sounds of it will be sooner rather than later, son."

Tobias goes to say something, but I stop him speaking first. "I want to know, finish what you were going to say."

His father grins triumphantly, like he won. "Like I was saying, a mate bond doesn't just stop or go away after you die. If something were to happen to you, they would never be able to take another woman again. Mates are for life, not like you humans with this whole death do us part nonsense. Something happens to you, they will forever be left with each other, and that's only if your death doesn't send them crazy. Losing a mate, I have heard, is equivalent to losing part of your soul."

His words make my heart skip a beat. They know even if I say no that me leaving could destroy them, yet they marked me anyway. Did they just assume I would bow down to their needs? The thought scares me; I don't want to be the reason for their destruction. I also never asked for any of this. Yet, if I chose wrong either way I'll die or be killed, the options aren't all that appealing. I also worry that eventually, aging I'll look beyond their immortal age. I will be older than them if I do stay human. Will they still want me when I'm old and wrinkly like a worn-out leather handbag?

I look toward them, Theo and Tobias are watching me. "You knew marking me could destroy you, yet you still did it?"

"You will understand once the mate bond kicks in, Imogen. Don't think too much of it right now, please. Ignore my father, he is just rambling," Theo says. The mate bond, everything comes down to this invisible bond we are supposed to have. I find myself more needy of them, but do I feel the same way as they do about me, I'm not so sure.

"Something to think about, Imogen," Josiah says. I nod but don't answer, too busy stuck in my own head, which is trying to grasp what the hell Tobias was thinking when he marked me.

"We will head off; I will give you as much time as I can boys, but either convince her or..." He glances in my direction, he doesn't finish the sentence, instead stands up, his wife following after him. I follow them to the door and his mother kisses my cheek softly before getting in their red convertible.

I turn and walk inside, with Tobias and Theo chasing after me.

"I'm sorry, Imogen. I didn't know they would show up before the month ended," Tobias says when I shut the door.

"How long do I have?" I whisper.

"Pardon?" Tobias asks.

I can hear the fear in his voice, like he thinks I have already chosen death. To be honest, I was planning on remaining human, but after what his father said, can I really go ahead with my decision, knowing how badly it will affect Tobias and Theo?

"How long do I have before I have to decide?" I ask louder.

"Till the end of the month," Theo speaks up, moving next to me. So, we have nine days, that is it.

"What are you thinking?" Asks Tobias, his gaze softening from his usual penetrating gaze.

"I don't know what to think, but it's clear I never had choice in anything, you took that choice, and one thing I can't fucking stand Tobias is not being able to control my own life. You made sure of that when you marked me, knowing full well what the repercussions were going to be." I say, pointing at him.

I'm so mad at him right now. Not only is he forcing my hand in this, but he has also put Theo at risk. What he did is selfish, if he hadn't marked me, our lives would never have changed and none of this would have happened, I would still be clueless about what they are.

"It's not that simple, Imogen. You don't know what it's like when you find your mate because you are human. We would have marked you eventually anyway, we wouldn't have been able to help it. The bond doesn't give us a choice."

I giggle, they probably think I've lost the plot because I'm laughing about this entire situation. I'm so over, hearing about this stupid mate bond.

"Fuck you, Tobias, and you can shove this whole mate bond up your ass. I'm done." I turn to walk toward the stairs, only to spin around and smack into Theo who is glaring at me. I roll my eyes and push past him, only for him to grab my arm. I turn to look at him, but the look on his face makes me take a step back. I glance at Tobias, his face also holds the same deadly stare.

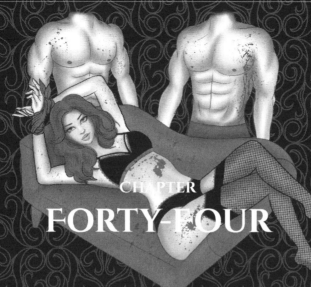

CHAPTER
FORTY-FOUR

"L et go of me, Theo," I demand, trying to shake my arm from his grip.

"Why do you do that? As soon as you don't like the topic of conversation you want to run off. You have every right to be mad at Tobias, but this would have eventually happened anyway. No matter what you think, you were always ours, this was always going to happen."

"So, what now? Do you expect me to be okay with turning into a blood sucking monster or a furry monster that howls at the moon?" I raise my voice. I hear Tobias huff behind me. "Now, let go of me, Theo."

"Not until you listen, if you don't choose willingly, I will choose for you, Imogen. I won't risk your life. We won't let you go." His grip on my arm tightens.

"So, what then, I either become like one of you or I never leave the property? Newsflash, asshole, I have been stuck here already for weeks." I spit at him.

"Watch your mouth, Imogen. I won't have you disrespect Theo." Tobias growls.

"Or what, Tobias, seriously? Things can't get any more fucked up than they already are. What exactly are you going to do about it?" He growls but doesn't say anything. "Like I thought, now fucking move out of my way!" Theo crosses his arms over his chest, refusing to move.

"You are really testing my patience Imogen, just hear us out, fucking listen for once." Theo snaps at me.

"I have done nothing but listen to your mate bond bullshit! I feel exactly the same as when I first got here. Nothing is going to change that, not even some stupid imaginary bond."

"Really, you feel exactly the same?" He asks, incredulous, his eyebrows raising.

He moves so fast I don't have time to react, I find myself suddenly shoved up against the door. His lips at my neck, I can feel his fangs brushing the skin of my throat. I shiver and my stomach tightens. I swallow, my mouth suddenly feeling dry. All I can focus on is the feeling of his body pressed against mine, his legs pressing between mine, separating my legs. He sucks on my mark and sparks move across my skin, a moan escapes my lips as they parted. I can feel him sucking and nibbling on my skin, arousal flooding me. Then, I feel the fog and I try to shake it off. I know I feel more for them, oddly connected to them, but knowing he is doing his mind control mumbo jumbo pisses me off, overriding the feeling that's making me want to give in to anything he wants.

He pulls back, his lips leaving my skin his voice below my ear. "You can't tell me that feels the same, Imogen. I can smell your arousal, I know how much you want us."

I shake my head, trying to clear the fog that's creepy in, getting stronger. Managing to clear my thoughts, I push him, releasing the hold he has over me.

"That's because of your mind control thing, not the bond."

"It's not that and you know it, Imogen. Why do you keep denying it?" Asks Tobias, who is casually standing and watching us.

"I want to go to bed, just let me leave please, it's still dark

258

outside." Theo moves to the side, letting me pass only to wrap his arms around my waist. The familiar fog moves over me again. I turn around and face him before slapping him, annoyed that he is using his vampire tricks on me. My slap sounds like it echoes through the house, the sound of flesh on flesh.

I'm actually surprised at the amount of force I use. I can tell I don't hurt him even the slightest, but the look of pure rage on his face shows just how angry he is.

"Imogen, apologize to him now," Tobias demands.

I do feel guilty. I can't believe I actually hit him, but I'm sick of him using the fog to get what he wants out of me. "Tell him to stop doing his vampire voodoo then," I spit back at Tobias.

Theo grabs me and I gasp at how strong his grip is as he yanks me towards him. I see Tobias move closer out of the corner of my eye, a worried look on his face.

Theo's lips are so close I forget how to breathe, fear consuming me as I watch his eyes turn red. He leans in closer, his voice holding the anger he feels towards me. "The fog works both ways, Imogen. Now you're going to learn that the hard way." I see Tobias go to grab him, but Theo is faster.

I'm suddenly ripped completely against him, his fangs sink into my neck. I scream at the shock, then scream at the pain. I feel like my neck has just been ripped open with a can opener. He bites straight onto the side of my neck and shoulder, tearing through my flesh. I can feel my blood running down my shoulder before Theo is suddenly ripped off me by Tobias. I fall to the floor, landing on my butt, my hand clutching my neck.

Theo shoves Tobias away before noticing what he has done, his eyes go back to their normal, hypnotic green. I pull my hand back and my blood coats my palm. I look towards Theo, he looks panicked and goes to move toward me, arms outstretched, but I stand up and run up the stairs.

"Imogen, wait I..."

"Just let her cool off, you should do the same," I hear Tobias tell him.

I slam the bedroom door. I can't believe he just bit me like that, I don't realize I'm crying until I have to wipe my face. My neck feels like it's on fire. His bite never hurt before, even when they thought it would. This time Theo wanted to hurt me and that's exactly what he did.

I walk into the bathroom to clean my face and check the damage he caused. Looking in the mirror, my face is blotchy and tear stained. My sweater is soaked in my blood. Even my blonde hair is stained red, but it doesn't appear to be bleeding anymore. The bite mark is red and angry looking, the skin raised where his fangs sunk in. I wash my face and my neck before realizing I need a shower to get it out of my hair, which is now sticking to my skin. I strip off before turning the shower on.

I get in before changing the water temperature, the hot stream burns my skin. I suddenly feel guilty. He never would have done it if I didn't slap him. Hell, he might not have done it if I had just apologized like Tobias asked me to. I know it still didn't give him the right to do what he did.

I know he's already wound up from his father. I also know they aren't human and feel things differently to normal people, at the end of the day. I shouldn't have done what I did. I just finish washing the conditioner from my hair when Tobias walks in.

He strips his pants off and opens the shower door. Seeing him, I feel a lump form in my throat. He steps closer before opening his arms. I move toward him, letting him hug me. I rest my head on his chest and turn so water isn't in my face, trying to drown me.

He kisses the top of my head. "You okay?"

"I didn't mean to piss him off, he just got under my skin," I murmur. If it were anyone else, they probably wouldn't have heard me, but he answers so I know he heard what I said.

"I think sometimes you forget we aren't human; you have no idea how hard it is for him to deny his true nature around you. He shouldn't have done what he did, but I know he wouldn't have done it if he had control of his instincts." I nod against his chest.

"Just remember next time Imogen, there is a reason vampires and werewolves are portrayed as evil in books and movies. We are technically what you would call monsters and run off strong emotion and natural instincts. We feel things differently, everything heightened, anger is the strongest to try and control." I wrap my arms around his waist, loving the feel of his warm skin. I find it comforting, being in their arms, it feels like home, where I belong but it doesn't make me feel any less scared of the choices that need to be made.

"How would Theo or you change me?" I ask.

It's one question that bothers me, exactly how do they become the way they are.

"Werewolves are born, we can make a human into a werewolf though the same as a vampire, well, like most supernatural creatures."

"So, there are more supernatural beings than vampires and werewolves?" I ask.

"Yes, most myths and legends hold the truth, Imogen."

"Like what though?" I furrow my eyebrows.

"Fae, witches, mermaids, demons are a few but there are more. We live in the shadows, though. This world is too dangerous for our kind, if people found out, they would want to experiment and find ways to recreate it. Humans are good at one thing and that's making species extinct and that is why we have rules," he states.

I look up at him, he is right, humans in a way are bigger monsters than they are. He kisses my nose.

"So how would you change me then?"

"We would give you our blood." I'm confused, I have already drank Theo's blood and I'm still human so if that is it, then how come I haven't changed already?

"I have drank Theo's blood and I'm still the same," I voice my thoughts out loud.

"That's not all there is to it, Imogen." He looks uncomfortable like he doesn't want to say what the next part is.

I tilt my head. "Then what happens?"

He looks away; his voice barely audible. I'm not sure I hear him correctly. "You die."

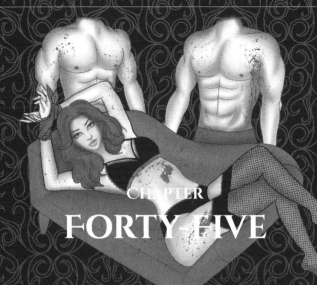

CHAPTER
FORTY-FIVE

"I die?" My voice is barely a whisper. I'm horrified, so in order for them to make me like them they have to kill me first.

"We will make it quick." Tobias tries to reassure me.

Make it quick, who the fuck is he kidding? I'm not willing to make that sacrifice. What if it doesn't work, then I'm just dead? Who, in their right mind, would agree to dying to be with someone?

"No." I say, shoving him back and getting out.

"No? That's your answer?" Tobias asks, stepping out of the shower behind me and grabbing a towel.

"Exactly what I said. No."

I can't believe how fucked up this is, either way I die. I don't change, I die; I change, I die. I can't believe they expect me to be okay with any of this. I don't want to die, especially at their hands.

"Either way the options are death, just choose the one where you get to come back, Imogen be reasonable."

Be reasonable, is this fucker for real? There is nothing reasonable about dying. Once you're dead, you're dead, there isn't meant to be a way back from the dead. If there is, my mother would still be here.

I walk out of the bathroom, and into the bedroom before pulling on some clothes. The sun is starting to break through outside, the bedroom not even needing the light on to see anymore. Looks like no sleep for me now. I pull on a sweater dress before walking downstairs. I can hear Tobias following me around silently. Going to the kitchen, I flick the kettle on before grabbing some mugs.

I grab three out before Tobias speaks. "Don't bother making Theo one, I'm not sure when he will be back."

I wonder where he went, to think he told me not to run from confrontation, yet he has left the place completely - hypocrite. I make my coffee before walking out the back. The sun has turned the sky orange and red as the light moves between the mountains, surrounding the place.

"You want to talk about it?"

"Nope, I have given my answer, Tobias. We don't need to talk about anything." I state before walking over to mom's rose bush.

I see Tobias walk back inside before I sit down on the concrete path. What would mom think about all this? I wonder, as I stare at the blooming bush. I know she would have told them to get fucked, probably even smack them one. I smile just thinking about it. She was a tough woman; she never would have allowed me to get into this mess I have found myself in. Would she be ashamed of the life I live now? I know she wouldn't be, but I still question myself. I lay down on the concrete, looking up at the sky.

It's beautiful out here, quiet but I can also feel the loneliness of being here. Sometimes, quiet can be too much, deafening even. Being left to your own thoughts constantly can do some serious damage, if you don't have the right mindset.

My mindset. The one that makes you question everything, including yourself. Every decision you make, everything you have ever said, everything you have done. Yes, the mind can be a dangerous place to be trapped in. Is that why mom didn't wake up? Was she just trapped in her own mind, lost, not able to find her way back or was she gone already?

These are some of the thoughts that have been playing through my mind since the accident. That I wasn't enough for her to come back, for her to stay.

I sniffle, hot tears run down into my hairline, so I close my eyes.

"Tears won't bring her back, tears won't fix anything, they are weak, don't let anyone see you're weak." I mentally scold myself. My tears dry up as I become angered by my own weakness.

I stare up at the sky blankly, clearing my mind of everything, just focusing on my own breathing. The air is crisp, I can smell the flowers, the roses. The air is that clear out here, no pollution. No hustle and bustle, just tranquility. I know that tranquility will eventually send me crazy, I've never been one for quiet and calm. My thoughts out here are already becoming as destructive as my life. They are both going to send me insane.

I sit up, I need to get out of here. I need to find a way to get away from them. But can I really leave them? Can I walk away and not look back? What are my options, besides death, or death. I have to try.

Getting up, I walk inside. Tobias is in a blue suit, "Work?" He nods his head. I walk over and do up his tie, maybe this is my chance. "What about Theo?"

"He is already there." I don't bother to ask how he knows that information. But I'm glad he won't be coming back anytime soon.

"Can I come?" If I don't ask, he will know something is up.

I know the answer before I ask it. "No, Imogen, not today. Let Theo calm down, we will talk when we get home."

I nod, watching as he grabs his keys and kisses the top of my head. "Get some sleep." Then, he walks out the door before stopping. I walk up stairs, pretending to go to bed. He turns and calls out to me. "What are you thinking about right now?"

"Going to bed. Why?"

"Nothing, your emotions are all over the place. I can stay, if you like."

"No, I am just going to bed, go to work. I will be fine, promise."

He stares for a few seconds before walking out the door. As soon as I can no longer see his car out the bedroom window, I start chucking my things in a bag. I know if I follow the driveway, it will lead me to the dirt road heading towards the city. I just need to get to my car, then, I can leave the city, hopefully before they get home. They said we are only half an hour away from the city, so hopefully that means an hour or a little more on foot.

I throw only what I need in, everything else I can replace eventually. Ducking downstairs, I grab my photo album off the bookshelf and cram it into the blue backpack I found. Grabbing my tennis shoes, I slip them on before grabbing my phone and wallet from the kitchen. Rustling through my handbag, I find the keys to my beast.

Walking outside, I start walking towards the driveway, stopping to glance in the direction of my mother's plant. I can't take it, and the idea of leaving her is eating at me, but I know she will understand.

The driveway is so long, it takes me nearly ten minutes to walk down it. I'm dreading the walk but, hopefully, I see a car and can hitchhike into the city. When I get to the end of the driveway, I turn left and follow it all the way to the bitumen road. I look at the time and it is a little after 8:30. I still have plenty of time, but I'm also still miles away from the city. I see no cars, just proving how deserted this area is. After another hour of walking, my phone starts dinging, messages coming through.

Then, an idea hits me. I scroll through my contacts and find Mark's number before dialing it. He answers after a few seconds. "Imogen?"

"Hey Mark, are you at work?" I ask.

"I'm on my way, I'm running a little late. What do you need?"

I tell him I'm stuck out of town and within ten minutes of walking toward the City. He pulls up in his blue Mazda and I can't describe the relief I feel upon seeing him. I'm finally doing this, escaping. Getting my life back.

Mark rolls down the window. "Need a lift?" He jokes.

"You're a lifesaver, thank you."

"So, work?" He asks.

"Um." Can I trust him not to tell Tobias and Theo? I decide I can because I don't really have a choice and I also know he wouldn't willingly seek them out after the other day. "Can you drop me to my apartment by any chance?"

"Everything okay?" Mark asks, seemingly worried.

"Yep, everything is fine. I just need to pick up my car."

"Oh, okay, tell me where to go then." He turns the car around and heads towards the city, listening to my directions.

He looks like he is dressed for an interview in his black slacks and white button up top. I really hope they didn't fire him. Why can't Tobias and Theo be normal like Mark? Not that Mark isn't attractive or anything, but he definitely isn't my type. He's nice and friendly, but there's no chemistry, which is a shame. Being with him would be easy, normal. Not this shit storm I'm living in.

"So, what were you doing all the way out there anyway?"

"I was visiting a friend, but they left before I woke up." I say, not wanting to tell him that Tobias and Theo have a house out there. When we pull up at my apartment, I tell him I will meet him at work. He waves goodbye and I take off running for the parking garage.

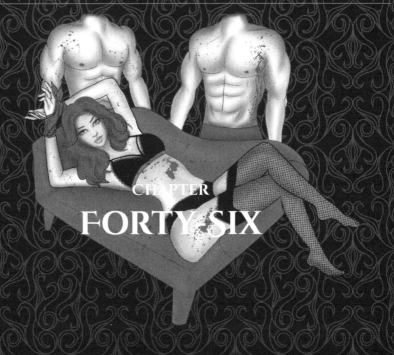

FORTY-SIX

Racing through the parking garage, I find my car on the bottom level. I unlock it before throwing my bag over the seat and into the back. I put my key in the ignition and turn it, but nothing. I check the dash - no lights come on, so I try again, holding the ignition on, it whines loudly. "Come on, not now!" I say, smacking my dash and my car finally starts.

"She may be ugly, but she is reliable when I need her." I shut my door before reversing out the side of my car, scraping the bollard. Whoops, I didn't lie when I said I am a terrible driver.

I tear out of the parking garage and head for the highway only to realize I need gas, so I decide to pull over to the first gas station I see. I fill the tank; my poor car gets the shock of a lifetime having a full tank in it for once. I grab my wallet and quickly pay for my fuel.

After I pull onto the highway heading out of town, I only get excited when I see the sign stating I'm leaving the city limits. I relax and smile, seeing the city in my rearview mirror. I'm finally out of here, I turn the radio up and keep driving. I have no idea where I'm going, but hopefully, I can make it to the next city which is over eight hours drive from here.

After about three or four hours of driving, I feel this sudden rush of fear hit me, sending goosebumps all over me. I look around nervously, my anxiety kicking in. Pulling over, I think I will stretch my legs and have a break from driving. I have about four hours of daylight left and really need to find somewhere to stay for the night. Getting out, I stretch my legs before raising my arms above my head to stretch my back. My heart is pounding in my chest, and my eyes move over my surroundings frantically, but I'm in the middle of nowhere. All I can see is fields and trees, not a house in sight.

I can't shake the feeling of dread consuming me, deciding it's best to keep moving. I hop back in and start driving again. I have to stop in a small town for fuel again, refilling my car, then jumping back on the highway that seems to be never ending. Just as the darkness slowly settles on the horizon, the feeling gets worse only this time, I'm forced to pull over when I feel like I'm burning from the inside out, boiling alive. No, not again. It's the heat washing over me, doesn't this shit ever stop? I lay my chair back, tucking my legs to my chest. Wave after wave of burning pain sears through every part of my body, the pain increases to magnitude levels. It's already starting to get dark outside, and I'm stopped on the edge of the road, surrounded by nothing but trees. I reach over, digging through my handbag for anything to take the edge off. Finding one lousy Tylenol, I pop the pill in my mouth before grabbing the water that I got at the last gas station. Sculling half the bottle before tipping the rest over my head, trying to cool myself down.

Getting out of the car, the cool air does nothing to soothe my burning skin. I stumble to the trunk, clutching onto the side of the car. I guess I'm sleeping here tonight. I'm not going to be able to drive like this. Popping open the trunk, I try to find something, anything, the Tylenol isn't helping. I find a small throw down bottle of tequila and drink it in one mouthful. I can't find anything else, nothing, my trunk completely empty.

To make matters worse, the fear I feel I'm fairly sure isn't mine. I have nothing to fear out here, yet my anxiety is high. I almost feel manic, completely beside myself and on top of it all, in pure agony. I manage to climb back into the car, laying across the backseat, trying to find a comfortable position, but nothing works. I can't find any sort of comfort for what I feel right now. When it's completely dark, I close my eyes trying to dive into some form of sleep. Then, I hear howls, forcing me to sit up. Is this a bad area for wild dogs because all I can hear are howls ringing through the darkness. My heart rate skips a beat as I look out the windows, only to be met with darkness, the trees casting shadows under the moon.

Then, I see them, yellow eyes in the forest, lots of them. I move back on the seat, pressing against the door. Reaching over, I lock the doors. It's okay, I'm okay they will leave, they are just wild dogs. That's what I try to tell myself. Only I have this gnawing feeling they aren't just dogs, I watch as they slowly come out of the shadows of the forest, revealing about fifteen to twenty huge wolves. I know they aren't no friendly pooches. They circle around the car, I can't take my eyes off them. They are huge, white sharp teeth gleaming under the moonlight.

I move to the center of the seat. What the fuck do I do? The biggest question though is why the hell are they lurking around my car, I am a nobody. I don't know them, yet here they are, trapping me. I hear one growl, moving towards the car, I move away only for another to move closer, my head spins back and forth, trying to keep watch on all of them. I quickly glance around the car for anything to defend myself. I think about jumping in the driver's seat and trying to take off but as soon as I move, one of them charges, hitting the driver's side door, the entire car shaking at the impact. I jump back.

I only manage to find an empty bottle; I can see it on the passenger side footwell in the front. I just need to reach it. I watch as one shifts. His bones rearrange before he stands up, his fur turning to skin, he cracks his neck. There's an evil glint in his eyes that makes me forget the pain I'm in, I know they are up to no good. He stands completely naked, his entire manly body on display. I gulp, he walks over, and I decide it's now or never. I scramble over the seat, grabbing the bottle just in time to hear the window smash, glass hitting me and spraying over the backseat. I scream and shield my face, clutching the bottle tightly in my hand.

He reaches his arm in and unlocks the door. I scramble to the other side only to jump when I hear another one tap on the window behind me, making me jump. I turn to see another dark-haired man, standing on the other side of the door, completely naked.

My heart is hammering in my chest so hard I can hear it, adrenaline kicks in. When I hear the door open my eyes fly in the direction of the noise. The man leans in and I smash the bottle on his head, glass breaking leaving the neck of the bottle in my hand. He shakes his head as if he's just been hit by a small child, not a glass bottle.

"You're going to regret that sweetheart," He says, his voice sending shivers up my spine. He tries to grab me, and I start kicking before he grips my ankle and rips me out of the car.

My head smashes on the bottom of the door on the way out, making my head spin as shooting pain spreads across the back of my skull. I scream as I hit the ground violently. My entire body aches as the rocks dig into my palms and my knees, as I try to get to my feet, only to be kicked in my side, making me clutch my stomach, winded. The man rolls me over onto my back before flicking hair over my shoulder.

"Where is your mate, little one? He should know better than to let you out in this state," he taunts.

"Doesn't she smell divine, boys?" Another voice says. I try to swat his hands away, as he tries to push the hem of my dress up my legs. I can hear the rest of them hollering and laughing. I kick my legs, making him let go. As I try to crawl away, my entire body burns up, my vision is blurring. I feel a foot press onto my back and then, I hear him speak again. "We're going to have some fun with you," he chuckles next to my face.

He stands up and kicks me again. I gasp as I feel the air expel from my lungs. His foot goes back between my shoulder blades, holding me still. I feel someone grab my hair, ripping my head backwards to see the dark-haired man's face only inches off mine. I spit in his face, "Get the fuck away from me!"

He wipes his face with his other hand and smiles before licking his fingers clean. "She is a feisty one," he calls to his friends. I feel the pressure on my back lift before I feel hands on my hips, flipping me over. I struggle, kicking my legs and arms, trying to hit anywhere I can. I start screaming, panic sets in as I feel my underwear get ripped away.

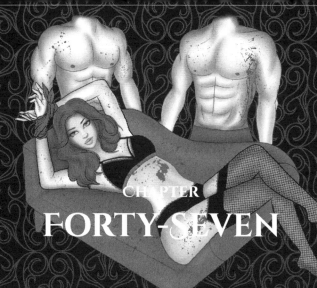

CHAPTER
FORTY-SEVEN

I feel someone grab my arms, pinning them above my head on the ground. I struggle to get away, kicking my legs, trying to keep him from getting nearer.

I feel his hands force my legs apart. I scream and start hysterically crying when I feel his weight press onto me. I can feel his dick brush my thigh, making me struggle more. The man holding my arms is laughing. I know what they want, I just don't know why me. The man on top of me licks the side of my face; I cringe, moving my head away from his revolting tongue, and shaking my head. Hot tears run down my face as I struggle, moving my lower body trying to get away from him. I bite down on his lip when tries to jam his filthy tongue in my mouth. I can taste his blood in my mouth. He groans and sits up, his hand comes in contact with my cheek as he slaps me across the face, my head whipping to the side with the force, making my ears ring.

Suddenly, his weight is gone. I hear a strangled scream and feel the air blow straight over the top of me. The man releases my arms and I scramble into a sitting position when I feel the hands holding my arms leave my flesh. I look around and all the men are looking around for their two friends. I hear another scream. Then, the sound of flesh being ripped apart. The person moves so quickly all I see is a blur, moving too fast for my eyes to see, especially in the dark. Soon after, a man's head falls next to me, his shocked eyes looking back at me.

I scream and push it away with my foot. I hear the rest of them start shifting, I move backward on my hands, trying to get away as they turn into werewolves, teeth bared. My back comes into contact with the car's rear wheel. I see the blur again and watch wolf after wolf drop to the ground. Then, I hear another wolf attack the person.

My scream resonates through the air as I see the person stop, as a wolf bites into his arm and flings him away from the other wolf he has by the throat. Theo hits the ground and rolls before jumping to his feet and lunging at the wolf, his arms wrapping around its neck and head, tackling it to the ground. Another wolf turns toward me, teeth bared, and I look around frantically before grabbing a rock.

Just as it starts to stalk towards me, I feel fur brush my face and see dark fur, the black wolf which I recognize as Tobias growls loudly. It's a menacing sound, my blood runs cold at the power behind it. He shields me, blocking it when the wolf launches itself at us. Tobias bites into his neck, blood splatters all over my face when more wolves jump into the fight, ripping it apart till there is nothing left. Tobias, doesn't leave my side, standing over the top of me like a shield.

It's over in a few minutes. I feel Tobias lick the side of my face, and I run my shaking hands through his fur, pressing my head against his furry one. I stand, using the car to help pull myself up. My entire body feels like it's vibrating with the amount of fear and adrenaline running through me.

When I stand completely upright, I gasp at the sight before me. Body parts and dead bodies are everywhere. Blood turns the dirt to mud around us. And three wolves, a sandy colored one with yellow eyes and two light gray ones with black eyes. They are huge, but not as big as Tobias. I feel him brush against my leg before I see Theo walk out of the trees, completely drenched in blood, wiping blood from his arms.

It literally looks like he has bathed in blood. There isn't a clean piece on him, blood is dripping from him onto the ground. He walks towards me and I take a step back. The sight of him alone terrifies me. His face is all distorted, his fangs having not retracted. He looks like a demon from hell. He wipes his face, flicking blood onto the ground. His eyes turn to their normal, hypnotizing green.

Theo stops and stares, I feel relief rush over me, only it isn't mine. I know the bond has kicked in. I can even tell who it is I'm feeling, I know it's Theo. He hesitantly takes a step towards me, stopping, unsure of whether or not to approach me.

I can feel he just wants to check I'm not hurt. I hear the sickening sound of bones snapping as the Sandy-colored wolf shakes itself out before standing upright, only to reveal Merida. Completely naked, her perky round breasts on display. Her blonde hair is drenched in blood. But the smile she wears on her face shows how happy she is to see me. And boy, am I happy to see her. A little weirded out that she is a werewolf, but happy. My head is spinning at what just happened and starts to throb where I hit it on the car's door.

"Hey, Imogen," she greets.

Theo takes off his shirt and hands it to her. Not once did he even look at her body, his eyes not leaving my stunned ones. I don't know how he doesn't look, she's gorgeous, even naked; I'm having a hard time taking my eyes off her.

She pulls his shirt over her head. "Eww, so gross," she cringes at the blood on the shirt that's sticking to her like a second skin and goes to her thighs.

"What are you doing here?"

"Alpha called, said his mate needed to be found. You owe me fifty bucks, Derek," she says, nudging the wolf beside her with her knee.

My eyebrows furrow and I hear Tobias shifting behind me. His arms wrap around my waist, his face going to my neck as he inhales my scent. I take comfort in his touch, sparks moving over my skin. I look at Merida, puzzled. She's clearly comfortable with nudity as she doesn't even glance at Tobias, standing naked next to me.

"Oh, we had a bet. I knew you were their mate; this idiot is my brother, Derek. He bet you weren't," she explains, shrugging her shoulders.

"That one is Floyd, my Beta," Tobias says, pointing to the other gray wolf. Beta? What is a Beta? As confused as I am, I'm glad they showed up. But how did they find me?

"Beta?"

"I will explain later." My entire body starts to calm down with his closeness. The heat even dies down under his touch.

Merida walks over to my car and opens the door. "Man, this car has had a rough life," she says, getting in the driver's seat. I chuckle, yes it has had it rough. I wonder why she hates working under them if she's a werewolf too. Or is it just Theo who scares her?

Merida grabs my bag out and tosses it to me. I try to catch it, when suddenly, Theo's hand catches it before I can grab it; I freeze. His hand moves toward my face and he cups my cheek. As soon as he touches my skin, I relax into his hand, leaning my head onto it.

Merida walks over and pops the trunk. I glance at her before I see her walk over and pick up the head off the ground, chucking it in the trunk like it's a ball.

"You head back, we will clean this mess, boss," says another man, coming up behind us. He has long blonde hair that sits on his shoulders and man is he hung like a horse. I can't take my eyes off his body. I feel my face heat up before cold hands go over my eyes. Is it just me or are all werewolves just born to look like gods?

"Pervert," Theo whispers next to me, before removing his hands. The man is now standing with one of my shirts covering his manhood. I raise an eyebrow.

He holds the piece of fabric with one hand before holding out his other for me to shake, I quickly shake it. "I'm Floyd."

"Imogen," I say.

"Oh, I know who you are," he says with a wink.

"How did you find me?" I ask, turning to Theo.

He steps closer, his chest pressing against mine. Leaning in, his lips brush my neck before pressing softly to my mark. I shiver. "Your mark. We will always find you while you bear our mark," he whispers against my skin. For the first time I'm actually happy they did mark me.

"Kind of like a homing beacon, just doesn't give us an exact location, more a feeling of direction," confirms Tobias.

Well, I'm glad it's correct then. I watch as Merida and Floyd dump body parts in the trunk of my car.

"Who are they?"

"Rogues, you can't leave when you're in heat, Imogen. It's too dangerous," Tobias says behind me.

"Yeah, I could smell you from miles away before we found you," Merida speaks up while picking up a bloodied leg and tossing it in the trunk.

"So, all werewolves can smell me?"

"No, mainly just males and me because I'm your mate," answers Theo.

"How come Merida could smell me then?"

I hear her chuckle, Theo growls softly, and she stops, taking a step back. "What, worried I'm going to steal your mate, Theo?" I raise an eyebrow before it clicks.

"I'm lesbian, Imogen, that's why I can smell you." Well then, that definitely explains it then. Merida walks over and hugs me, Theo's bloodied shirt staining my already dirty dress.

"Take her home. I will stop by and see you tomorrow Imogen," she says with a wink. I smile, but then wonder how I'm actually going to get home, if they are using my car for body disposal.

Theo moves toward me and I know instantly he's going to run

with me. I gag when he grabs me, his skin sticky with blood, but his cool skin is soothing. I feel his hands go into my hair before he tucks my face into the side of his neck. "Ready?" He asks.

"No." I hear him chuckle before I feel air brushing past me, whipping my skin.

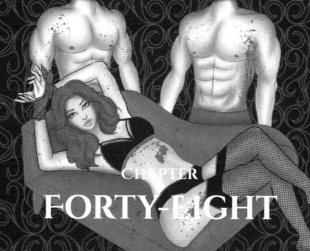

CHAPTER
FORTY-EIGHT

CHAPTER 48

My body relaxes against his skin. I can hear Tobias behind us, hear the noise of his paws on the ground. Surprisingly, he can keep up.

I knew Theo was a lot faster than Tobias, but this time Tobias is able to keep pace. I feel like he's running for hours, when we suddenly stop at the end of the driveway. I lift my head and see Tobias shake out his fur before rising completely naked. Theo lets me go and I slide down his body onto my feet.

I can just make out the house lights from where we stand. Tobias walks over to me and grabs my hand. I'm actually glad that this place is so secluded, we definitely would have raised some eyebrows if someone drove past; walking hand-in-hand with one naked man and another soaked in blood, I'm sure it definitely would have raised some questions.

We walk for about five minutes before one of them speaks up. "Did you leave because of me?" Asks Theo.

I don't answer, leaving was definitely the wrong choice. I can feel that Theo honestly believes he's the cause of all this. Truthfully, he is, and the way they need to keep me hidden away. When we make it to the house, I stop, looking up at it. This place actually feels like home or maybe it is their feeling toward it. But it doesn't change the fact it is also my prison. When I stop, they do too.

"What is it?" Tobias asks, looking at me.

"I don't want to be trapped here again. I also don't want to be forced to change." I hear Theo sigh. I can tell he doesn't agree, I can feel it, the same as Tobias, but they never voice that out loud. "Are you going to keep me here?" I watch as they look at each other.

"Please, Imogen, can we just go inside? We can talk about it later, I promise," Theo says. He sounds tired despite the fact he never sleeps.

"Not until you answer. I'm not going in there if I can't live like a normal person, Theo." I say, letting go of both their hands. I'm surprised when I feel Tobias get angry. I expect it from Theo after the other day, but he seems calm, almost resigned to the fact I won't be held prisoner anymore. Like he accepts it, but Tobias on the other hand, I feel burning anger ripple through me, making me angry, feeding off his emotion.

"Please don't make me force you inside, Imogen. Not tonight, I don't want to argue about this." Before I can answer, Theo shoots him a look and then turns to me.

"If we let you go back to work, will you stay?" He asks.

I nod; I just didn't want to remain cooped up in this house twenty-four seven. Tobias growls at Theo but holds his tongue and doesn't argue back. I can tell that later this is going to turn into another argument between them.

After a few seconds of them glaring at each other, I walk between them and up the veranda stairs. I turn the handle, walk inside and collapse on the couch. I'm not there long before I'm scooped up and taken to the downstairs bathroom. The bathroom is similar to the one upstairs, only difference is the floor tiles are black, not gray and it doesn't have a bath, just one giant shower, which is actually bigger than the one upstairs.

Theo starts the shower, and I strip my clothes off and step in. I notice Tobias doesn't come in and can feel he is still angry.

"Don't worry about him, he will calm down," Theo says, pulling me under the stream of water.

The entire shower floor is red with blood, some even congealed in his hair and he has to wash his hair three times to get it all out. The steam in the bathroom makes the entire room smell of blood and mud, making me gag. Theo reaches up above his head and opens the window since the exhaust fan isn't doing much to rid the room of the pungent smell. Once he washes what he can see off, I grab the soap.

"Turn around," he does, and I run the soap and loofah over his back, washing until he is no longer bloody. When I'm done, I start washing myself, hissing every time the soap burns the grazes on my skin.

When I wash my hair, I nearly jump completely onto Theo. "What is it?"

"I smacked my head on the door, when they ripped me out of the car." I tell him. My head is burning, I touch it and there is a huge lump. Theo pushes my hands away and examines it.

"Yeah, ouch, that looks painful. Got a nice egg on your head and a cut."

"No shit, Sherlock," I say, sarcastically.

Tobias suddenly walks in, a towel around his waist. He must have had a shower upstairs. "What's wrong? Are you hurt?" He demands.

"No, I'm fine," I say before getting out and wrapping a towel around me tightly.

"Imogen, I know you're hurt, I can feel it."

"Seriously Tobias, I am fine. Promise." He eyes me for a few seconds but lets me pass. I climb the stairs, heading up to the bedroom. After finding out they only have to kill me to make me like them after I drink their blood, I'm not willing to take the risk of them forcefully changing me and using a bump on the head as an excuse.

When I'm putting my pajamas on, I hear them walk in.

"Is that really what you think that we are trying to trick you into drinking our blood just so we can change you?" Theo asks, pulling some pants off the shelf above my head in the walk-in.

"Stay out of my head, Theo." It annoys me slightly that he feels the need to invade my personal thoughts.

"I wouldn't do that, Imogen. I know you would hate me for it. I will let you make your own decisions. It's not worth losing you, not after tonight." Theo tells me. I feel no deceit from him coming through the bond.

Tobias, however. "Speak for yourself because I would. It needs to be done." Exactly my point. I may have let them bring me back, but I still don't trust them, especially with how strong Tobias's feelings are coming through the bond. I can tell he is growing impatient with me not deciding.

"I won't let him, I promise. Not tonight anyway," Theo says, giving Tobias a pointed look. Tobias growls lowly in his chest but says nothing. I can tell he wants to yell at Theo and disagree.

"I won't," Tobias confirms.

"You won't, what? Kill me tonight?" I ask.

I see him cringe at my words, but nod his head. I'm about to climb in the bed when I feel Theo's arm snake around my waist, pulling me against him. Sparks fly all over my body. I wonder if it will always feel like that or if I will eventually become desensitized to them after a while. Theo bites into his wrist and brings it to my lips. I watch Tobias and he's watching me, waiting to see what I'll do.

I hesitate until I feel Theo's lips next to my ear. "I promised, didn't I? I meant it, love. I won't let him change you, not tonight." His husky voice makes my stomach tighten before I open my mouth, waiting for the initial gross taste of his blood. Only it never comes. His blood fills my mouth and I moan loudly before swallowing. I can already feel the bump on my head leave, my grazes heal and once I have no pain I suddenly stop. Tobias adjusts his pants, and I can tell he has a hard on.

I nearly run when I see him start to move towards me. But Theo's grip just tightens on my waist. Tobias hand goes to my face and I tremble slightly, a shudder running through me. Will he do it now? Is he going to kill me?

I cringe back from his touch when he places his hand on my cheek, his thumb brushing my lip softly. And I relax when I feel through the bond that he just wants to touch me. I reach my arms out, wrapping them around his neck. Theo lets go and Tobias pulls me to him before picking me up. I wrap my legs around his waist tightly.

I giggle when I feel his stubble brush my neck as he dips his head to inhale my scent. His stubble tickles my skin again when he realizes that he's tickling me. He does it deliberately, rubbing his chin on the side of my neck, my body cringing away from it, my face rubbing on his, trying to get his face away from my neck.

"Someone's ticklish," I hear him say.

"We better get to bed. I have work in the morning," he states. I'm about to ask if I'm allowed to go, but he speaks before I can utter another word. "Just wait till your heat is gone, I don't want a repeat of today, please."

I nod instantly, remembering the feeling of that disgusting man's tongue on my face. I shiver remembering, it makes me feel dirty, despite the fact I just showered, like I can still feel him touching me.

I hear Theo growl behind me, making me look back at him. I can tell he is in my mind again, snooping. Tobias places me on the bed before climbing in himself. Sleep comes fast, I'm completely exhausted. But the dreams of golden eyes haunt my dreams, the memories of the night before creep in, even though I know they are all dead, I just can't shake the feeling of their hands on me. The feeling of their hands on my skin, even their repulsive smell.

I wake up startled, sweating profusely. My hair sticks to my face, my heart hammers in my chest. I sit upright and flick the lamp on;

I'm in bed alone. I look toward the window - it's still dark outside, maybe I wasn't asleep for as long as I thought. Confused, I get up, intending to get a drink to soothe my suddenly dry throat. I wonder where they went but figure they will be back. Maybe they went to work early. As I walk past my phone, I press the power button, letting the screen light up which shows it's too early for work. It's only three am.

Opening the door, I can just make out the sound of arguing. Angry whispers. I silently walk to the stairs and creep down them.

"If we don't let her decide, she won't forgive us, Tobias. Think about it, please. We can speak to the council to get her more time. Let her come to this decision on her own. I can't lose her, and neither can you." Theo pleads for me.

I can tell Tobias isn't happy, I can hear a low growl coming from him. Before I hear Theo get up, I creep down the stairs a little further and look over the banister. I sit down on the step. Theo walks over to Tobias, placing his hands on the side of his face. "Just give her more time."

"Fine, but you can deal with your parents then," Tobias says, not happy but agreeing.

I relax, knowing they are giving me more time. I'm about to get up and tell them I'm there, but stop when I see Theo lean his face closer and kiss Tobias. Tobias doesn't react at first, still angry, but then, a new sensation rolls over me - arousal as Tobias kisses him back forcefully. I hear Theo groan when Tobias deepens the kiss. Theo's hand goes between them and he grabs Tobias's cock through his pants, making Tobias moan into his mouth as he almost frantically starts pulling off Theo's shirt.

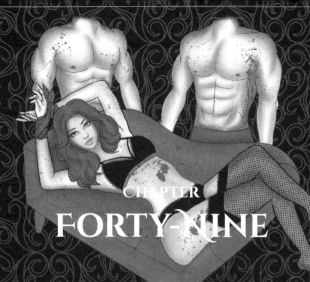

CHAPTER
FORTY-NINE

I think about giving them some privacy, but at the same time I can't pull my gaze away from the scene playing out in front of me. They are both pulling each other's clothes off, I can feel nothing but desire and an almost desperate need for contact.

I can also feel how much they love each other. I don't know how I never realized before how strongly they feel for each other, yet they are happy to share each other with me, like pieces of a puzzle that fit together.

My arousal watching them together is growing. I didn't think I would get so turned on watching two men together, or maybe it is because they are both mine and that's why I love watching them. Theo shoves Tobias back, making him lean on the back of the leather couch. His hands grip the top of the couch as Theo kisses and sucks on his neck. Tobias' eyes are closed, just enjoying the feeling of Theo touching him. Theo's hands run down Tobias' bare chest, over the tight muscles of his stomach before slipping inside the waistband of his pants. I can feel my arousal spilling onto my thighs just from watching such an intimate moment between the pair of them.

I squeeze my thighs together, trying to stop the sudden ache of desire rushing over me. I can feel my skin become flushed as it heats up when Theo grabs Tobias's cock in his hand. Tobias groans, kissing him fiercely. Theo uses his other hand to push his pants down his legs, Tobias' hard cock springing free before Theo grabs his balls and tugs on them softly. Theo's other hand squeezes the shaft of his cock, making Tobias groan and thrust into his hand.

I moan out loud. Realizing what I have done, I quickly cover my mouth, embarrassed that I'm watching them. I'm worried that they will be angry. But it's too late, they hear me, and their eyes turn in my direction. They smile devilishly, and I blush.

Theo motions for me to come to them with his finger. I sit frozen like a deer in headlights. I even think about taking off and running up the stairs as I stand up, looking in the direction of the stairs before I hear Tobias speak. His voice is rough, making my insides clench at the demand behind his words.

"Don't even think about running up the stairs."

I look at him, still thinking I can make a run for it but decide against it before taking the steps down to them. I walk over hesitantly, worried I'm in trouble for watching like some creepy peeping Tom. When I'm close enough to them, Theo reaches over, grabbing my hand, pulling me between them. My back presses against Tobias' chest as he leans on the couch. I can feel the heat of his skin seeping into me, warming me up. Feel his erection pressing against my back.

I feel like I'm intruding, I feel Tobias breath on my neck before I feel his lips kiss my mark teasingly. Theo moves closer and I can feel his erection press into my stomach through his boxer shorts. The contrast of hot and cold makes me shiver.

Theo inhales my scent, and I blush, knowing full well he can smell how turned on I am. Leaning in, his hypnotic green eyes hold mine.

"Do you like watching me with Tobias?" He asks, his lips barely an inch off mine.

I nod guiltily. I hear Tobias chuckle behind me before I feel him pull Theo's face up by his chin with two fingers, pulling him closer and kissing him. I look up, turning my head to the side as I watch Tobias tongue run over Theo's lip before biting down on it.

I moan, my thighs becoming wet with arousal. Theo inhales and then groans into Tobias's mouth at the smell of my arousal. I'm sandwiched between the pair of them. Tobias chuckles, letting Theo go before Theo's lips suddenly move to mine. My nipples harden when I feel his tongue brushing mine, making me moan into his mouth. My hands reach up and brush through his hair, tugging him to me.

I feel Tobias' hand run under my shirt, brushing my stomach. Sparks move everywhere, his touch makes my skin tingle. I pull Theo to me, sudden desire, and longing to be touched being amplified by their own emotion, spewing into me through the bond. Tobias kisses my neck as I run my hands down Theo's chest, loving the feeling of his cool skin under my hands.

Hearing Tobias' husky voice just below my ear makes me moan, "I want to watch Theo fuck you." I nod my head, wanting nothing more than to have them inside me. Hearing him wanting to watch us together turns me on even more, I feel like I'm about to erupt, and we have barely done anything besides touching.

"Do you want Theo to fuck you, Imogen?" I nod, my lips going to Theo's neck, sucking on his skin. He groans and thrusts his hips into me.

"Words, Imogen." Tobias growls.

"Yes." I don't even recognize my own voice, I sound breathless and needy.

Theo grips my hips before lifting me, my legs wrapping around his waist. I can feel his hard cock against my core. I move my hips, seeking friction, wanting him inside me. I feel him move and next thing I'm back in our room. Theo drops me on the bed, and I bounce slightly. I watch Tobias walk into the room and sit on the chair at the end of the bed.

Theo pulls my pants down, his cold fingers brushing lightly

against my thighs making me shiver. He leans over the bed and tugs the hem of my shirt and I lift my arms, letting him pull it off. I'm completely naked, laying on the bed. Theo kneels on the bed, pushing my thighs apart, Tobias has a full view of my swollen wet lips. I try to close them but Theo forces them back open again.

"Let him see you Imogen, you have nothing to be ashamed of. You're ours," he says, kissing my lips, softly, before giving me a devilish grin. I sit up on my elbows as he walks into the walk-in wardrobe.

I'm about to close my legs and sit up, but his voice stops me. "Don't even think about closing those legs and hiding yourself away from me Imogen," Tobias says. I quickly open them.

"Touch yourself," he says, cocking his head to the side and licking his lips.

I hesitate before moving my hand between my legs, my finger sliding between the wet lips of my vagina. My head drops back at the feeling churning inside me, which I know is Tobias's desire from watching me touch myself. I slip a finger inside myself, moaning at the feeling, my finger wet with my own juices. Sliding my finger out I slide two in. Tobias' eyes darken watching me, I have never touched myself in front of anyone, yet I'm doing it in front of Tobias, his eyes watching me do things to my body I never would have expected, making my walls clench around my fingers. I move my fingers faster, sliding them in and out.

When I feel the bed dip, my eyes snap to Theo's. I pull my fingers from myself, Theo grabs my hand and sucks on the fingers I had inside myself. He moans before letting them go and kisses me. I can taste myself on his tongue.

Theo brushes my hair out of my face. "Trust me?" He asks.

I nod, but his words make me a little uneasy. When he places a blindfold over my eyes cutting off my vision, my fingers instinctively move to the blindfold. I try to push it up, but his voice is next to my ear, I can feel his erection against my thigh long and hard. "I won't hurt you, my love. You can trust me."

"I trust you." I nod before feeling his lips move to mine, he sucks my bottom lip in his mouth. I moan when he bites down, he pulls back, his hands running down my sides moving south down my thighs to my ankles, making me shiver. I'm suddenly tugged to the end of the bed.

FIFTY

Since my eyesight is cut off, I can't see, only feel what he is doing and hear what is going on around me. I hear the sound of the rope dropping on the bed next to me. I turn my head to where it falls beside my face. Then, the sound of Velcro. He pulls me to my feet and spins me around. "I want you to put your hands behind your back," he whispers while nibbling on my neck. I do as he asks and clasp them behind me. I feel a strap go across my wrist before I hear the Velcro securing it to my wrists, so they are stuck together. I try to wriggle my wrists but they stay behind my back.

"Spread your legs," he says, sliding his leg in between mine. He then pushes me forward so the top half of my body is on the bed, but my feet are on the floor and my ass is in the air.

I feel his hand go between my legs, running up my thigh, to my core, then between my ass cheeks. I shiver at his cool hands running softly over my skin. I don't even have a chance to feel self-conscious at the position I'm in, all my parts on display before I feel his fingers ram inside me. My walls clench down on his fingers at the sudden intrusion. I gasp as he slides them out.

"So wet," he murmurs, which only makes more juices expel.

He slides two fingers back inside me, my body instantly responds as arousal floods me. I moan loudly and move my hips against his fingers when he suddenly slaps my ass. I can feel his handprint burning my ass cheek. I enjoy the sudden pain. Does that make me fucked in the head? Probably, but I like the sudden burn.

"Don't move," he says, pushing his fingers back inside me. I try to not push myself back onto his fingers, but it's impossible, my body has a mind of its own.

As soon as I move, I feel his hand come down on my ass again, which only excites me more. When I move a third time, he reaches between my legs and pinches my clit. I hiss at the sudden pain, which is soon forgotten when his fingers dive back into my wet core again, making me moan out.

He keeps this slow torture up for what feels like hours, but is only minutes. Theo pulls his fingers out of me before I feel both his hands push my thighs further apart and I feel his cool breath on my core. His tongue moves through my wet lips to my clit, making me wriggle. His grip on my legs tightens, holding me in place and I know I will have bruises on them in the morning.

I can feel Tobias' arousal washing over me through the bond at watching Theo eat me out. I feel his tongue move between my wet folds, licking a line straight to my ass.

I wriggle, trying to get away from him as his tongue continues to lick and suck me relentlessly, making me writhe in pleasure, his hands hold my thighs apart and upright, it's the only reason I'm still standing. My hips grind against his face as I feel myself come, he licks up all my juices before standing and slamming himself inside me.

He waits for my body to adjust his hard length. I moan loudly as I wiggle my hips. His cock is so deep inside me. I can feel him hitting my cervix, I feel so full.

"I'm going to fuck you now." His words make my walls tighten around his cock. I hear him groan before slowly pulling out and slamming back in, my body bouncing on the bed at his harsh movements.

I feel his hands grip my hair, pulling my head back before I feel his tongue in my mouth, tasting every part of it. I'm a screaming mess as I'm shoved over the edge repeatedly, to the point I think I can't handle coming anymore.

When I feel him slow, I wonder what he's doing before I feel him slide out of me and pull me to a standing position. I stumble before I feel Tobias' warm hands grab my arms, pulling me, so I'm sitting on the chair with him.

Theo pushes my knees up into my chest, my arms stuck awkwardly behind me. I can't see, only feel, I can feel Tobias' warm naked body beneath mine, feel his cock against my fingers. When Theo slams back inside me without warning, making me cry out, my walls clench around him, my hand grips Tobias cock without realizing.

"Squeeze it again and I will put it in your ass," he whispers before kissing the side of my neck. I squeeze it again and he groans.

Theo slows his pace. "Tobias is a lot thicker than I am, Imogen. You sure you know what you're asking for?"

I nod; I know Tobias is thicker than Theo, but they are roughly the same length. I don't care. I know I'm wet enough to take him, and I know my body can handle him. I wiggle my ass on his lap and feel his dick jerk. Theo pulls out of me before Tobias lifts me slightly, my feet still on his knees. I feel Theo's tongue brush my clit before he sucks it in his mouth.

"You will tell me to stop if I'm hurting you," whispers Tobias.

I nod before I feel his cock at my back entrance. Theo's tongue moves faster, it burns badly but then eases a bit when I feel Theo's tongue brush along Tobias shaft before moving back to my clit. I relax and Tobias lets my hips go as he slides completely inside me. My hips move against Theo's face as he continues to fuck me with his tongue. I moan loudly, grinding myself on his face. Tobias doesn't move, he just waits, letting me move and get used to the feeling of his hard thick length inside me. I feel my skin heat up and my breath comes in pants as I'm thrown over the edge, coming completely apart. Everything feels more intense with no vision, but I hate not being able to touch them.

I feel Theo stand before pushing my knees to my chest where I feel Tobias pull my legs further apart, holding them in place before Theo slides back inside me. He kisses me, his tongue running along my bottom lip, seeking entrance which I grant. I feel Tobias move my hips, so his length slips in and out me at the same time Theo does. My orgasm is building up again. Theo's lips never leave mine as he pounds into me. When I feel him slow, I know he's close and by the sound of Tobias breathing behind me, so is he.

His teeth graze my shoulder before I feel him bite down, making me come instantly at the pleasure and pain that washes over me. I feel Theo's movement become jerky and deeper along with Tobias as they come, spilling their seeds into me and stilling completely.

I'm out of breath and my muscles ache, I feel Tobias kiss my shoulder where he bit me. Feel Theo slide out of me. I slump against Tobias, my legs falling from his knees heavily. My legs feel like they have been weighed down with concrete, they are that heavy from the position I'm in.

I feel cold hands brush a piece of my hair away from my mouth, before the blind fold is removed. My eyes squint at the light, as they readjust to the brightened room.

"Lean forward, I will undo your hands." I do as he asks, and he quickly undoes them.

I'm surprised to find Tobias still hard inside me. My legs are killing, and I'm not sure if I can stand. "You need to climb off, I might hurt you if I pull out too fast." I nod, not sure exactly how I'm going to find the strength to get up. Placing my hands on his knees, I push up slightly and feel the burning pain. Now that my body has come down from its high, I'm painfully aware of how big Tobias actually is.

"Nope, I'm good. You're just gonna have to remain part of me now; we are just going to be connected forever." I hiss out in pain as I hear him chuckle.

Theo walks over to me with a wet cloth. "I did try to warn you." He presses the cold cloth between my legs.

I slump against Tobias. "I'm pretty content with remaining seated."

"That's because you're too scared to move." Theo chuckles. He holds out his hand and I take it, he helps me to stand, Tobias sliding out of my body, making my eyes water.

"If I ever say I will do that again, promise to say no." I hear Tobias chuckle, before walking into the bathroom and turning the shower on.

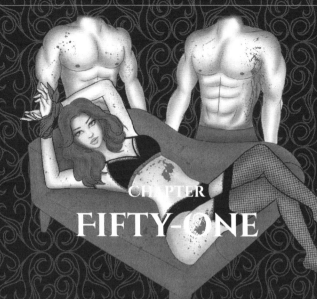

FIFTY-ONE

The next morning, Theo heads to work, leaving me with Tobias. I told them I don't need a babysitter, but they ignore me. I can tell they don't trust me. I have no intentions of running again after what happened the last time. While I sit on the couch, Tobias comes over handing me a hot cup of coffee.

"What's the plan today then?" I ask, hoping he will have some idea of what we can do that doesn't revolve around the TV. This place is boring sometimes, especially with its lack of internet and there aren't many books left on the shelf I haven't read, and I have no intentions of reading the dictionaries or geography books that remain on the shelf.

"I don't know, what do you want to do?" He asks, rubbing my leg.

"Well, that's why I asked you; if I knew I would be doing it. What do you and Theo usually do out here?"

He shrugs his shoulders. "Nothing. Work, have sex, that's about it."

"And I thought my life was boring." I roll my eyes.

Maybe living in my car wasn't so bad after all. At least I could walk down to the beach or to the park or something. There's nothing to do here unless I wander around the bush which I won't be doing.

"Hey, we aren't boring; we did stuff just things you can't do." Tobias defends himself and Theo.

"Like what?" I instantly regret asking. I can feel what he means through the bond.

"Bianca," he says.

Bianca? Who the fuck is this Bianca and why is she out here? "Who's Bianca?" I ask.

He stares at me, blinking a couple of times. "What did you just say?"

"Only the name you just told me, so who is she? Who's Bianca?"

"Imogen, I didn't say her name out loud." I'm mystified, I swear I heard him say the name Bianca. But if he didn't say this woman's name, why does it sound like he knows who I'm talking about?

"Who's Bianca?" I ask again, hoping this time for an answer.

"No one you need to worry about, Imogen." Tobias tries to wave me off.

"So, you did say it and you know who I am talking about?"

"I didn't say it, you must have picked it up through the bond. I thought it, didn't say it, Imogen," he mumbles before walking out of the room.

Who is this woman for him to have such a strong reaction to her name? I get up and follow him up the stairs. Just as I get to the top step, he shuts the door, locking me out. I bang on it. "What the fuck Tobias, who is she?"

"Leave it be, she isn't an issue now go away."

I feel nausea build up in my stomach. Why is he acting like this? Does he love her? Who is she to him, to them? And why does he instantly think of her when I asked what they got up to?

I'm not the only one, and that realization makes my blood run cold. I'm not naïve, I know they probably have been with other women before me. But why so defensive over this woman? I feel tears build up and I have to swallow down the lump that forms in my throat.

I turn around, suddenly wanting to get away from him. I know without a doubt this woman means something, and more than he is willing to tell me. I walk down the stairs while I have a million questions running through my head. If I don't find out who she is, I know it will eat away at me.

Opening the front door, I walk out toward the garden. There's no point in leaving, they will track me down. Sitting next to my mother's plant, I cry, I can't hold it in any longer. Everything is moving too fast, my life moves out of my control and now they are keeping secrets from me. I don't know how long I'm out there for, when suddenly, Theo sits beside me. I wipe my eyes, embarrassed to be seen crying. He places his hand on my shoulder before pulling me to him and wrapping his arm around my shoulders. I feel him kiss my head.

"Why are you here?" I ask.

"Tobias." He simply states.

I shake my head and stand up. "I want to go back to the apartment; I won't put up with you keeping secrets."

"Secrets?" He asks, his eyes brows furrowing like he doesn't understand. "Who's keeping secrets?"

"You and Tobias." Theo looks up toward the top floor of the house. Standing at the window is Tobias, watching us and listening in.

I roll my eyes; he hasn't got the balls to tell me so instead sends for Theo, the damn coward.

"Take me back to the city," I say sternly.

"Imogen, you know we can't do that." I shove past him, walking back towards the house, deciding to head to the shed I detoured the house. I can feel him following me, but I can also feel his confusion. Well, I'm not explaining shit he can speak to his other mate. I open the garage door, only to find both cars not here. I slam the roller door down. How am I going to leave with no car?

"I want to leave, let me leave."

"Imogen you're being unreasonable, what happened?"

"I was talking to Tobias and he got angry because I mentioned her name. That's it, now if he won't tell me who she is I want to leave."

"Mentioned who's name?"

"Bianca." I watch his reaction.

Theo takes a step back, so he knows who I'm talking about as well. "Where did you hear that name, Imogen?"

"I thought Tobias said it, but he thinks he only thought it, which makes no sense because I can't read people's minds like you can."

While we are arguing I hear a car pull up, I walk to the front of the house, praying for it to be anyone but their parents, someone who could give me a lift in town.

I feel Theo grab my arm, stopping me, pulling me back. "No, you're not leaving,"

"Get your fucking hands off me, Theo, I'm leaving unless I get fucking answers."

I see Merida walk around the corner, she must have heard us yelling. She stops, looking unsure for a second. I wave to her. I completely forgot she was coming over today, I honestly didn't think she would show, but man am I happy to see her.

"Hey Imogen, what's going on?" She asks, nervously.

I can tell she is wary of Theo, keeping a good distance away from him and not really approaching us, so I turn and walked toward her.

"Stay out of it, Merida." Theo spits.

Merida puts her hands up and goes to leave. "Don't talk to her like that! Wait up, Merida!" I call out to her before jogging after her.

Suddenly, Theo is in front of me, his easy-going attitude completely gone, in its place the version of him that scares me. I stop dead in my tracks. I cross my arms across my chest, refusing to be intimidated by him. Merida stops and watches; I can tell she looks panicked. Like she thinks he's going to harm me. I stand my ground, refusing to back down.

"Merida, leave now!" Theo screams in a rage.

Oh, hell no I am not putting up with this shit. "No, Merida. Stay. I'm coming with you."

She hesitates, unsure of what to do, but I can tell she's scared of Theo, she looks between us and the direction of her car. I know any minute she's going to leave me behind. I move and Theo copies me, side stepping and moving in front of me again.

"Unless you're going to tell me who she is, move." My voice is ice cold.

"No, you're staying here and that's final."

I shove past him, his hands snaking around my waist and lifting me off my feet from behind, he uses his other arm to trap my arms across my chest holding tightly as he walks toward the house. When we approach the house, Tobias has finally come out from hiding in the room. Theo walks up the steps while I continue to struggle.

"Either you tell me who this woman is to you or I leave," I say to Tobias.

Merida walks up the steps behind us, she keeps her distance, but I'm glad she didn't tuck her tail and run. Theo tries to take me up the steps, but I throw my head back, my head connecting with his nose. I hear the crunch of it breaking, and man does my head throb. I think I do more damage to myself, but it's effective. He lets me go and clutches his nose.

He's livid, his fangs protruded. He grabs me, shaking me by my arms. Tobias places his hand on his arm. "Let her go now." Theo stops shaking me but doesn't let go, instead he pulls me closer, his nose nearly touching mine. His eyes staring into my fearful ones.

"You want to know who she is?" He screams; his cool breath makes me shiver.

"Theo, don't you fucking dare!" Tobias tells him, gripping his arm tighter. I can see Merida behind him, her eyes wide and fearful. His eyes gleam, he wants to upset me but what he says next doesn't upset me, it destroys me.

"She's our fucking wife!" I feel like I have been punched in the gut, completely winded. I blink back the tears that are threatening to fall. My mouth suddenly loses all moisture. She's their wife.

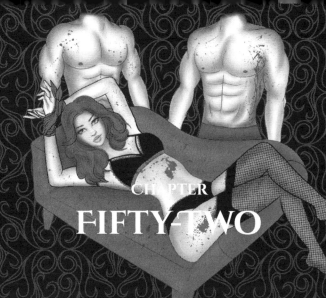

CHAPTER
FIFTY-TWO

"What? You're fucking married?"

Tobias looks panicked. Theo finally realizes what he said, lets go of my arms, and staggers back. Merida looks on the verge of running and is visibly shaking.

"Let us explain. Please."

"No, I want to leave now," I scream, tears running down my face. Merida is about to bail, turning toward the front door, but I call out to her. "Merida wait." I run up the stairs and grab my handbag.

I can hear Theo and Tobias yelling at each other. I don't care, I'm not going to be someone's mistress. Grabbing my phone off charge, I walk back down the stairs, ignoring them both fighting in the living room. I can hear things getting broken.

Merida stands frozen, not moving, her eyes watching the fight that has broken out in the living room. I touch her arm and she jumps; "Let's go." I say, she nods but as soon as we turn to the door, Theo is standing in front of it.

"Leave, Merida. or I will make you." His voice is ice cold. Merida pales and goes to walk around him, his eyes never leaving her. I push Theo to the side to follow after her. "Not you, you're staying."

301

"Like fuck I am. I won't be the other woman, Theo, now fucking move. What did you think you could be married and we would all live like one happy family? Fuck off." I snap.

Merida opens the door and walks outside, heading toward the car, she looks back at me fleetingly.

"Tobias, tell him to move or so help me god I will fucking reject the pair of you right now."

Tobias moves to my side, his lip is bleeding and his shirt ripped. "Let her go Theo, we need time to cool off. She will be safe with Merida." Tobias says, his chest pushing into my back.

I have to fight the urge to lean into him. This stupid mate bond is going to be the death of me. Theo glares at Tobias, refusing to move. My face is drenched in tears, my hands shaking. How can they do this to her, how can they do this to me?

"Move please," I beg. I just need to get away from them, clear this constant fog taking over my brain, that's them.

"She's dead, Imogen. You don't have to worry about her." Theo's eyes search my face, waiting for a reaction, but I don't care that she's dead.

The fact is they are or were married and didn't say anything, yet she was on Tobias's mind. How do you compete with that? "Move please," I repeat, as I look at Tobias. He nods at Theo and Theo steps out of the way.

"She can't get far, Theo, just let her go." Theo growls lowly.

I dart past; Merida looks relieved when I walk out heading towards her white Subaru Liberty. I open the passenger side sliding into the seat. Only when I try to plug my seatbelt in do I realize how badly my hands are shaking. Merida, seeing me struggle with the belt, leans over and clips it in for me.

"Thanks." She nods and quickly starts the car, doing a U-turn. She turns the car around and starts heading down the driveway. I lean back on the seat, closing my eyes.

When we are out of the driveway, Merida finally speaks. "What do you want to do now that you have escaped?" She asks.

SINFUL MATES

"I have no idea, I just wanted to get away from them, I could really use a damn drink though." She nods her head, a smile playing on her lips.

"We could have a girl's night at mine, maybe later go out?" I smile, that sounds nice.

It's actually nice to be in another female's company. "That sounds awesome, but I don't have anything to wear out."

"You're my size, you can borrow something. Let's head back to mine."

We drive to the City before heading toward the apartment block. It's the same apartment block where my apartment is.

"You live here too?" She nods before turning the car off, we get out and she tosses the keys at the valet, who catches them.

"Yep, this is actually the packhouse."

"Packhouse? I lived in an apartment building full of werewolves?"

No wonder they have a strict policy on no cats. I chuckle, remembering Theo telling me before getting angry for even thinking of the jerk.

Her lips turn up slightly. "Yep, come on I will see if any of the girls want to head out with us tonight." As we enter the lobby the girl behind the desk calls out to Merida.

"Alicia hey, want to go out tonight with me and Imogen?" Merinda asks her.

The girl stands up, she has curly red hair and green eyes, and a smattering of freckles on her nose. She's quite pretty but in a delicate kind of way, she looks innocent. But the grin that lights up her face, I can tell she is anything but innocent. Oh, this is going to be fun I can tell already as a devious smile lights up her face.

"Martin's?" Alicia asks.

I have heard of it but have never been. It's on the other side of the city and a huge nightclub.

Merida looks at me questionably, letting me decide. "I have heard of it, so I'm down."

303

Alicia yips and claps her hands excitedly. "Let me get someone to cover the lobby. I will be up in a minute, it's time to party!" She says, shaking her ass.

Merida and I laugh at her enthusiasm before walking over to the elevator. We get in and Merida takes me to the second floor. When the elevator door opens I see Floyd, nearly walking into him as we step out.

Floyd smiles before doing a double take, realizing who I am. "What is she doing here Merida? Does Tobias know?" He asks, looking worriedly at her.

"Yes, he knows and we're going out."

"Tobias won't like that, Merida," he replies, looking down at me.

"I don't care what Tobias or Theo like, we are going out."

Man are all werewolf men this overbearing and this god damn sexy? I watch as he pinches the bridge of his nose, his eyebrows furrowing.

"Where are you taking her?"

"Martins," Merida tells him, unfazed by his line of questioning. He opens his mouth, gaping like a fish. We ignore him and turn, heading in the direction Merida is leading me.

"Wait!" We both stop and look back at him. "If you're taking her, I'm coming. Tobias will fucking kill us if anything happens to her."

"Fine, be ready by nine, Beta," she says Beta sarcastically. Why do I have a feeling Floyd might be the killer of fun?

When we get to the apartment, Merida opens the door and I step inside. Her apartment is the same as mine, yet has a hippie feel to it, nothing I expected from the proper and prim lady I see at the office. She even has tie dyed curtains, beaded curtains on all the doorways. Huge round rugs in all different colors on all the floors and giant bean bags instead of couches.

"Make yourself at home," she says, and I do, feeling relaxed for the first time.

"What does Beta mean? I have read plenty of werewolf fantasy books, yet never heard the term before." I ask her since she seems to be the only one who always answers me truthfully.

"Basically, it means second in charge. But don't worry about Floyd though the man is strict, he won't be too annoying tonight, well not once we get him drunk anyway." She giggles.

I chuckle.

"Drink?" She asks, holding up a bottle of red wine. I look at the time, well technically it's evening already, lunchtime isn't too early to start drinking. I nod and she walks over handing me a glass as I watch her fill it. And I mean fill it, the glass is huge. I stare stunned, if we keep drinking like this there is no way I'm actually going to be awake to leave tonight.

I sip it and Merida laughs, "Come on, let's find something for you to wear."

We walk in her bedroom which is also decorated similarly to the rest of the house. She rummages through her closet, pulling different dresses out that are extremely revealing. Tobias will throw a fit if I wear one of them.

"Which one?" Damn they are short; I won't even be able to bend over without flashing something.

I point to the black bodycon dress, and she holds it up. "Yes, that will fit you nicely." She states, holding the dress against me, it barely reaches mid-thigh. It certainly doesn't leave much to the imagination. Just as I go to try it on, there's a knock on the door.

"That will be Alicia." she says, walking out of the room. I follow after her, Merida opens the door and Alicia steps in with three other women around our ages. All are strikingly gorgeous. One has brown hair cut into a pixie cut with big brown doe eyes, thick lashes and pouty lips. The other two are both blonde and have blue eyes. They look like sisters, the resemblance between them is uncanny.

The dark-haired woman introduces everyone."You must be Imogen. I'm Tammy, this is Maya and Cara." She points at herself and her friends.

"Hi," I say nervously. I've never been one for hanging out with other girls, to be honest I'm not all that girly, more nerdy than girly. I feel awkward, out of place beside them.

"Come on, let's get lit." Tammy says, tugging on my hand and pulling me back towards the bedroom, on the way past she grabs the bottle of wine that is sitting on the counter.

Why do I have a funny feeling these girls are trouble, but in a good kind of way? They do my hair and make-up before I slide into the tight dress. Maya walks over and zips me up. By the time everyone is ready, we still have an hour before we have to leave.

Merida wears an off shoulder blue bodycon dress, and the other three might as well be naked with the little dresses they are wearing that show off more skin than I thought possible.

Grabbing another bottle of wine, we sit on the bean bags, which, with the amount of alcohol I already consumed, I know I'm going to need help getting up. I look up when my phone starts ringing in the kitchen, dreading having to try and stand in these heels from the position I'm sitting on the bean bag.

Merida looks at the screen. "It's Theo," she says.

All eyes focus on her before Maya holds out her hand for the phone.

"Don't answer it, just ignore it," I say, worried. She doesn't listen, instead answering it and putting it on loudspeaker. Fuck my life, I know this isn't going to end well.

"Imogen's phone," Maya says in her best secretarial voice. I have to muffle my laugh.

"Who is this? Where is Imogen?"

"Oh, Imogen can't come to the phone right now. She is currently in the middle of a wild orgy," Maya says, giving me a wink. I shake my head at her.

"You better put Imogen on the phone right now!" I hear him yell.

"Jesus chill, Theo, it's Maya. I will put her on," she says, handing the phone to me.

I rolled my eyes. "What Theo?"

"Where are you, and why do I feel like you're drunk right now?" He immediately attacks me with questions.

"I'm not drunk. Tipsy, but not drunk, and I'm at Merida's." I hear him growl. Instead of listening to him for any longer, I hang up on him. Theo's voice is the last thing I want to hear now.

I know I will cop it later for hanging up on him. My phone instantly starts ringing and I reject the call.

"What did they do that made you so pissed off?" Cara asks, sipping her wine.

"Bianca." States Merida for me. They all scrunch up their faces in disgust, making me confused.

"Oh, the bitch of a wife," says Tammy, and I just nod.

So, they all know of this woman and by the sounds of it don't like her.

"Don't let her worry you Imogen, you are way better. Besides, she is dead. They killed her."

"Cara!" Merinda snaps, giving her a stern look.

"What did I say?" Cara asks.

Merida shakes her head. I'm about to ask what they mean about them killing her but I'm cut off by Merida. "Enough depressing talk, let's finish getting ready before Floyd gets here."

Cara makes a gagging noise. "Why is that buzzkill coming?" She whines, and I smile at her pouting.

"Because he doesn't trust us to look after Immy over there," says Alicia.

I smirk at the nickname. I barely know these girls, but I can tell we are going to become good friends. At the mention of his name, another knock sounds on the door. "And that would be the fun police." States Cara, getting up and walking toward the door to open it.

"Ladies," Floyd greets us, walking in.

The girls don't look impressed, and I have to stop myself from laughing at the looks on their faces. Floyd walks over, holding his hand out. I grab his hand and let him pull me up. I stumble slightly in the heels, but he steadies me. "How much did she already drink?" He asks, eyeing the girls.

They look away guiltily before Merida points towards the counter. I hadn't realized we went through so much wine. On the counter are six empty wine bottles. I know I haven't drank that much compared to them, but I never realized how much we have already drank between the six of us.

He shakes his head. "Ready to go?"

"Yep, let's do this." The girls holler. I walk over to Merida and she hooks her arm through mine, leading me out of the apartment.

FIFTY-THREE

W e get downstairs and two yellow cabs are lined up. I hop in with Merida and Floyd, while the other three girls get in the other one. I slide across the seat; the fresh air outside hits me as soon as I walk out the doors. We make our way across the city toward our destination. Getting out, Floyd pays the cab driver and hooks his arm through mine.

"You stay within my sights at all times, understood?" I nod, not feeling like getting into an argument with anyone.

I just want to have fun and do things people my own age do. Walking up the steps, we are greeted by the bouncer. Floyd nods to him, the bouncer recognizes him and lets us straight in, ignoring the crowd that is lined up and booing loudly. Merida tugs my arm, pulling me forward and dragging me toward the bar.

She orders drinks while I look around, there is a huge dance floor in the center and tables and chairs sit randomly around the room, which is dark. The only light coming from the disco-style lights flickering on and off. Music is blaring and we have to yell to hear each other. I have never been in a nightclub before, the few times I have been out had only been to small bars with not so many people. This place is very lively, and I can tell it is a huge attraction in the city.

The dance floor is just a sea of people jumping and moving in rhythm to the music. Merida passes me a pink cocktail. I'm not sure what it is, but it smells like regret. I sip it and I can taste guava, it is sweet.

When we finish our drinks, Merida and the girls pull me onto the dance floor while Floyd chats to another man, who I have no doubt is another werewolf. I'm now starting to be able to tell the difference between humans and supernaturals, there is something with the way they carry themselves, the look in their eyes, and also the way their eyes dart around, watching nothing in particular, yet watching everything.

I shiver when they both look in my direction; quickly look away. The biggest give away is the fact that most werewolves are all brawn, muscle and otherworldly gorgeous.

After dancing for a while, I decide to sit down. Tammy brings me over another drink as well as two shots, thrusting them in my hand, she grabs two of her own. One in each hand. Holding them up, Tammy is the sort of woman you could tell lives on the wild side and knows how to have fun. I envy her and her carefree ways.

"One, two THREE!" She screams, I can't help but laugh at her face. Her excitement is contagious. I swallow the first one, then the second.

I'm at that point of intoxication where it just tastes like drinking water. I sip the purple drink she got me. I look around and Merida waves for me to come back to the dance floor. I shake my head, no longer trusting my ability to walk now that I have sat down. I watch as she pouts before turning and dancing with the girls.

I look around and people watch, Floyd is talking happily with his friend, then I look over and turn back quickly when I realize who is walking toward me. God, I hoped he didn't see me. This can't be fucking happening. Mark is here.

He walks over, placing his hands on my shoulders from behind me. "Hey, what are you doing here?" he asks.

I can tell he is drunk as his words slur slightly. He's wearing jeans and a button up shirt, quite different to his usual business attire. "Come, dance with me," he says, tugging on my hand softly.

I shake my head, "No, I'm good, I just sat back down." I tell him, trying to yell over the top of the music.

Mark leans in closer, trying to hear me over the music. I'm very aware of all the eyes on me, watching me. Floyd leans across the table, grabbing Mark's attention. Mark smiles before holding his hand out to him. "I'm Mark," he says.

Floyd has a sly smile on his face but shakes his hand anyway. "Floyd," he says with a nod.

Mark turns back to me. "Are you here with anyone besides him?" Just as he asks, Merida walks over and sits on my lap, throwing her arms around my neck.

Mark looks stunned for a second. "Oh, you're with Merida?" He looks even more confused now that words escape him. Obviously, Mark knows Merida is gay.

Maybe I'm the only one that didn't realize. I don't know if it is because she's drunk or what, but I'm just as shocked when she kisses me, her tongue brushing mine.

Floyd almost chokes on his drink behind us. Merida's lips are soft, I can taste her lip balm and the strawberry taste of the last drink she drank, vastly different from kissing Theo and Tobias. I'm surprised to find it actually turns me on. She's gentle, her tongue brushing mine softly before she pulls away and winks at me.

"Yep, Imogen is with me," she says to Mark while he stands there awkwardly.

"Maybe I will see you later, Imogen." Mark mutters before walking off, clearly unaware of what to think.

Merida bursts out laughing. "Did you see his face?" She snorts while laughing, and I can't help but laugh with her. Well, at least he's gone.

"You might regret that though Merida," Floyd says, nodding his head up to the VIP lounge upstairs.

Standing above us, looking directly at us, are Tobias and Theo. I groan, really this shit can't be happening. They don't look impressed and are eyeing Merida with disapproval.

"It was harmless, come on Merida." I say, pulling her onto the dance floor, hoping to blend into the rest of the people dancing. "Why are they here?" I screamed over the music.

"They own the place, Tobias brought it, so shifters have a safe place to go where we are all in one place. Man, I am going to be in so much shit for kissing you." She giggles, pulling me closer as we dance.

"Well, if we are gonna get in trouble, might as well make it worth it," I grab her and kiss her, her tongue tangling in mine. I feel her smile against my lips before kissing me back. Our bodies grind against each other as we dance.

When we pull apart, we are both laughing and make our way through the crowd toward the bar. I order more drinks and we sit on the stools at the bar. I don't bother to see if they are still watching and quite frankly, don't give a shit after a few more drinks and god knows how many shots, I'm completely wasted.

My surroundings spin as we walk out of the club. The crisp air is refreshing, making me realize how stuffy the club actually was. I'm not even sure how we are still upright as we all cling to each other, trying to walk toward the taxi stand.

When we arrive, all six of us girls slump on the seat. There isn't enough room, so I sit across from them. We are completely wasted and a giggling mess. When a car pulls up, I look up, thinking it's the taxi only it isn't. I groan loudly.

"Imogen, Merida and Alicia in, Theo will drop the rest of you back. He will be here in a minute." Merida gets up, pulling me with her. I climb in the front, Alicia and Merida get in the back. Floyd comes over and speaks to Tobias through the window.

"Traitor!" I call out giggling. I know it is him that told them where we are.

"Night, Imogen," he says, a cheeky grin on his face.

Tobias winds the window up and pulls away from the curb, the car ride is silent from Tobias who barely utters a word. The girls are chatting happily in the back. I lean over the seat, joining in the conversation, until Tobias slaps my ass and tells me to sit properly.

When we arrive, the girls get out. I try to get out when Tobias grabs my hand. "Nope, you're coming home with us." I pout, folding my arms across my chest, but I'm much too drunk to really be mad. And honestly, I'm exhausted.

Theo pulls up behind us and chucks the keys to the valet before hopping in the car with us.

"What the hell are you wearing, Imogen?" He scolds.

"Clothes, I can take them off if they bother you so much, Theo."

He shakes his head, annoyed. "You might as well be wearing nothing with how tight and short that dress is," he replies.

I roll my eyes and rest my head on the window. I'm half asleep by the time we get home. Theo opens the car door I'm leaning on, only just managing to catch me in time as I fall out of the car. He scoops me up and walks inside, taking me upstairs and placing me on the bed.

I feel them tug my clothes off, and shoes.

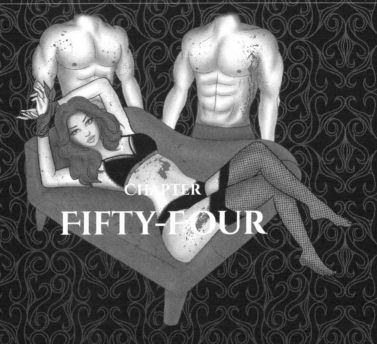

CHAPTER
FIFTY-FOUR

Waking up, I roll on my side, my hand comes in contact with a warm, bare chest. I sit up, my heart skipping a beat for a second before I realize it's only Tobias and not some random dude from the club. I instantly relax, my head is cloudy and throbbing, I can hardly remember what we got up to last night. The last thing I remember is kissing Merida.

I rub my head, which is pounding against my skull. Tobias is watching me with a strange look on his face. I go to get out of bed when he pulls me on top of him. I slump heavily against him, I have the worst hangover and feel so dehydrated. Theo walks in, carrying a glass of water and some Tylenol.

I sit up, my legs straddling Tobias's waist. He passes them to me. I quickly swallow the pills down and chug the drink, the coolness of the water soothing the dryness of my throat. Theo places the glass on the bedside table.

I decide to crawl out of the bed, the sudden urge to pee taking over. I climb to the edge of the bed, stopping when Theo grabs my chin, making me look up at him.

I roll my eyes, annoyed. "Don't roll your eyes, it's disrespectful."

I'm in no mood to put up with their orders. Plus, I really need to pee. "You know what's disrespectful? Lying about the fact that you're married," I spit back at him.

I try to climb off the bed again only for his grip on my chin to get tighter, forcing my eyes to meet his. "Don't ever let me see you kiss another person again, understood?" I hear Tobias growl behind me, obviously remembering mine and Merida's display of affection.

I laugh and slap his hand away before shoving past him. This fucker lied about being married and he thinks he can tell me what to do.

"Imogen!" I ignore Tobias calling out to me and walk into the bathroom, quickly peeing, and washing my hands before walking back and climbing under the covers.

I just want to go back to sleep. No such luck, I feel the bed dip as Theo gets under the blanket next to me. Tobias rolls over closer, and I snuggle into his warmth. I'm still angry, but his warm skin is nice against mine and it's cold this morning. I feel Tobias fingertips gently rubbing my hip.

I can hear them talking softly but tune them out before going back to sleep. They let me sleep and I eventually wake up a few hours later. Tobias is lying next to me. I can hear him snoring softly, but Theo is gone. I can smell bacon, making my belly rumble loudly.

Climbing out of bed, I pull on one of their shirts and put on some socks. My hair looks like a bird has made a nest in it as I walk past the glass on either side of the front door, making me laugh at my own reflection. I look as bad as I feel.

I make my way into the kitchen and turn the kettle on. "Sit, I will make it, here eat this," he says, passing me a plate of bacon and eggs with French toast.

I dig in, nothing like greasy food when hungover. Theo hands me a coffee; I sip, its hot, caffeinated goodness awakening my soul. Sometimes, coffee is better than sex, well right now it is anyway.

Tobias walks downstairs, running his hand through his hair, the muscles on his abdomen flexing as he moves. It's so hard to remember how angry I am at them when they keep walking around half naked, looking like god damn gods. Stupid mate bond, making me fucking horny all the time. I turn back to face the kitchen, and Theo is watching me with a silly smirk on his face, like he knows what I'm thinking. And I wouldn't be surprised if he did snoop in my thoughts.

Tobias sits next to me, putting his hand on my knee, I push it off.

"Really, Imogen, she is dead. Are you really going to be jealous over a dead woman?"

"I'm not jealous of a dead woman. I'm pissed off because you didn't tell me you were married, and I'm not stupid, I can tell you're hiding something else."

Tobias sighs. "What do you want to know then?" He asks.

Now, he wants to talk, really this wouldn't even have become a thing, if he had just told me yesterday instead of running from me and hiding in the room like a coward.

"Did you kill her?" Theo and Tobias look at each other, clearly wondering where I got that information. "Well, did you?" I ask again before they can ask where I had heard that information.

"Tobias did," Theo answers.

"Why?"

"Because she lied, we thought she loved us and we were going to mark her, then we found out she was with another vampire and she was just using us, so one of us would change her and give her immortality." Says Tobias.

I can hear the anger in his voice. Feel it through the bond; this is a topic he doesn't like speaking about.

"So, Tobias lost control and snapped her neck, she was human. This was also over a hundred years ago, Imogen, not recent and certainly not an issue you need to worry about." Theo states.

They killed her, and I don't know how I felt about that...

"How long were you married for and why didn't her boyfriend just change her?"

"Because he was part of the council and he couldn't, his parents wouldn't allow it, this is also one of the reasons the rules around humans are enforced. Bianca was going to out us if we didn't change her. So instead we killed her, we were together for about six years," answers Tobias.

Six years? They killed her after being with her for six years. I feel nauseous, knowing they could kill her like she meant nothing, after loving her for six years. I barely know them; will it be easy for them to kill me? "So that's why the council is against humans, because of her?"

"Not just her, but if we went around changing anyone we wanted the world would be overrun with vampires and shifters, and that would not be a particularly good world to live in. We prefer to stay in the shadows. One thing humans are good at is making species become extinct, experimenting on things they can't understand, or trying to replicate it. It is safer for everyone, if humans don't know of our existence."

I nod, understanding what he means. There would be people like Bianca, coming out of the woodwork tempted by immortality. "I don't understand. You said Theo was changed, and yet you were born, but you can make me like you?"

"Yes, vampires are made. They can't procreate once they change because their bodies don't change, males can technically impregnate a human, but no vampire woman would be able to bear children, their bodies no longer compatible to give birth. Werewolves can procreate, meaning males and females can have children together and a male vampire can impregnate a werewolf creating a hybrid. Which is frowned upon so rarely happens. Werewolves' bodies can change because we can shift, so all she-wolves are still fertile. I can still change you though because our blood is like a venom. If you have enough in your system it will alter your DNA making you like me." Tobias explains.

"Me on the other hand, you only need a drop of my blood for me to change you," adds Theo.

This is a lot of information at once. I don't know if I actually prefer to be in the dark about it. Seems too unreal to make sense.

"And If I don't want to change?"

"You know that's not an option, you will be forced eventually, the council already found out about you."

I stare, stunned and also a little scared of this human hating council.

"Our parents are going to speak to the council to buy more time, just means we might have to take you before the council and ask for permission to hold off on changing you. If they agree, and we can find a way to convince them, things don't have to change for now, but they will change Imogen. You will change." Tobias words leave no room for argument; he isn't going to let me die, at least not of old age.

"I have another question then." They both nod, waiting for me to ask but something with this whole Bianca situation still rubs me the wrong way.

"If your wife is dead, why did you instantly think of her when I asked what you and Theo got up to out here?" They both look at each other nervously.

Theo answers for him. "She lived here with us. We only moved back here when we found out you were our mate. We hadn't been back here since she was killed."

I don't know what to think of his answer, it creeps me out slightly. Am I destined for her path, to end up dead, like her?

"That won't happen, Imogen. You're different, don't compare yourself to her," Theo tells me after invading my personal thoughts.

"Stay out of my head, Theo. You have no right to know what I am thinking."

He doesn't look happy but keeps his mouth shut. I eat the rest of my breakfast before getting up. I leave and sit on the couch and flick the TV on before remembering they don't have service out here and I have already watched the majority of the movies.

Tobias walks out, sitting on the couch next to me. Annoyed, I get up and he grabs my hand. "Please don't run off."

"You still lied." I say, spinning around and shaking my hand out of his grip, only to run into Theo who is standing silently behind me.

He moves closer, his hands tugging on his shirt I'm wearing. He leans in closer, his lips so close to mine, I lose my train of thoughts for a second.

"You can be mad and still want us," he says before kissing me, his tongue playing with mine. His hand slides under my shirt, at my back before sliding into my panties and grabbing my ass.

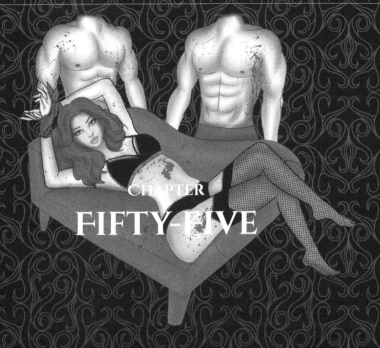

Theo pulls me against him so my body is flush with his. Sparks erupt all over my skin, giving me goosebumps under his touch. My body reacts even though my mind has other ideas. I put my hand on his chest, about to push him away, except he deepens the kiss, making me forget entirely that I'm angry with them. How I hate the mate bond, it overrides everything or maybe I'm just too weak to go against it.

Tobias gets up from the couch, his hands grabbing my hips tightly, so tight I know it will leave bruises, his lips going to my neck as he softly sucks and nips at my skin. His teeth make me shiver against him as they brush my mark. His hands move underneath the shirt and up my stomach to my breasts, my nipples hardening from the feel of his rough hands caressing them.

I moan into Theo's mouth, my hands wrap around his neck, pulling him closer. Oh, how I love the feeling of both of them touching me, setting off every nerve ending in my body as arousal floods me, taking over all rational thought.

I feel Theo grab my thighs lifting me, so I have no choice but to grab his shoulders to stop from falling backwards and into Tobias.

My legs lock securely around his waist and I can feel his erection pressing against my clit, when suddenly, I hear Tobias growl. His growl makes everyone freeze. Theo stops, pulling back slightly, I suck in a breath of much needed air.

I feel Tobias step back and Theo places me on the ground, my feet softly landing on the cold floorboards before listening intently.

I watch as they both look at each other, hearing something only they can hear. After a few seconds I too, can hear the sound of tires on the dirt road coming toward the house at great speed.

"Go get dressed, my parents are here," Theo says, before pulling me closer and kissing me.

His tongue licks my bottom lip before I feel him suck it into his mouth and bite down slightly. He steps back and motions for the stairs. I make my way back upstairs and into our room.

I wonder why his parents decided to show up, the thought makes me nervous. I can hear Tobias walking into the room as I rummage through the walk-in, trying to find something decent to wear, settling on some leggings and a tank top. Tobias reaches in and pulls a shirt from the hanger and he grabs a pair of jeans, quickly slipping them on before coming over and wrapping his strong arms around me and kissing my head. I pull back and out of his reach.

I quickly walk into the bathroom and wash my face and brush my hair, so I don't look like I have just awoken, trying to make myself look somewhat functional. After washing up, I slip on my bra, gray leggings along with a black tank top. Tobias is no longer in the room and I can hear soft talking coming from downstairs. Along with Tobias' angry whispers, which aren't really whispers with how high his voice booms towards the end.

Walking down the stairs, I'm greeted by Caroline. She is in black suit pants and a blouse, looking very formal, like she just stepped out of an important meeting.

"Imogen, lovely to see you again." I nod, making my way down the rest of the steps and onto the landing below.

Caroline quickly walks over to me and hugs me, which I think is slightly strange. She has never been this welcoming before. I freeze as her arms wrap around me tightly before placing my hand on her back and hugging her back. When she lets go, she holds me at arm's length.

"Come, we have much to discuss," she says, motioning for me to sit on the couch.

When I turn toward the couch, I nearly freeze. Josiah is sitting there, staring off into space like he is deep in thought. I shiver slightly at the intense look on his face before sitting as far away from him as the couch will allow. When he looks toward me, he softly smiles, his lips tugging up slightly. His eyes sparkle under the lighting emitting from the fireplace.

"So, what's this about?" I ask nervously. I almost prefer the over-bearing, intimidating version of Josiah that I'm accustomed to, not this man, who's looking back at me as if he is exhausted and mentally drained. I notice Theo sitting on the armchair next to the fireplace with a strange look on his face. Theo almost looks like he's in a trance.

When no one answers, I ask another question just as Tobias walks back into the room with four cups of coffee on a tray. "What's wrong with Theo?" I ask, staring at him, but he doesn't even glance in my direction at the mention of his name.

He hasn't moved at all, he's just staring oddly at the space in front of him, like he can see something I can't see. His eyes seeing but not really seeing, it gives off an eerie feeling like he's looking through whatever it is he is looking at.

Tobias sits the tray down and Caroline instantly reaches for her coffee cup and passes me mine. I accept the coffee and thank them.

"Theo is stuck in his own mind," Tobias says, worriedly glancing at him.

I remember Theo telling me about how they don't sleep, yet could go into the depths of their own minds and become stuck. I can't feel anything but worry through the bond as he stares off vacantly.

"Why did he go like that?" I ask, looking at Caroline.

"We have some news, and it must have shocked him into this state. Don't worry, dear, Tobias will eventually pull him out of it." She says. Tobias walks over to him and waves a hand in front of his face, but it is as if he doesn't see.

"So, what was the news?" I ask, turning back to Caroline again.

"The council wants to meet you, sooner rather than later. That's not why we are here though. The council needs your birth documents, as you know humans aren't usually mated to werewolves or vampires. The council wants to look up your lineage; they aren't convinced you are a hundred percent human. If you are, you would be the first human ever mated to someone like them." Josiah says, motioning toward Theo and Tobias.

"Okay, so that's what shocked Theo?" I ask, looking towards his frozen posture sitting in the armchair.

Tobias growls. Josiah stands up, placing his hand on Tobias arm and squeezing it before letting him go. "That's enough son, we can't change the past, but your mother and I have sorted it. The documents will come soon in the mail, they said they would post them to this address."

Tobias stares at me intently for a few seconds, I can feel worry and something else coming through the bond. I don't have a chance to ask what documents they are talking about when Josiah turns to look at me.

"Imogen, do you still have your original birth certificate? I will also need a vial of your blood for the council." I nod my head, knowing it is amongst the boxes that are in the office in the shed, along with the rest of my belongings that Theo has stored here.

"I think it is in a box in the shed," I tell him, suddenly feeling nervous. I know it holds nothing about my so-called lineage. My mother's name is the only one on the birth certificate. I never knew my father, don't really want to either after he abandoned her to raise a child on her own.

"We will have to find it, but first finish your coffee, I need to speak to Tobias in private." Tobias gets up and walks toward the kitchen, Josiah following behind him silently.

Something has Tobias on edge, and I glance back at Theo, who is still looking off, his eyes glazed over like he is there, but nobody is home. His eyes are burning bright red and hollow looking.

"Well, hopefully we find something that will help your case." Caroline says.

I look at her. How will it help my case? "And if we don't find anything?" I ask but I have a feeling I already know the answer.

"If there is nothing to be found, the council will probably give Tobias and Theo a time limit on when to change you, Imogen. I know you don't want this, Tobias has made that very clear. Unfortunately, Tobias, taking that choice from you was very selfish and wrong of him to do so. He shouldn't have marked you, but I also know my sons would never willingly put you in danger, the mate bond is that strong it would have happened eventually, he just should have spoken to the council first." She tells me, glancing at Theo nervously. I watch as she stands up and walks over to him.

CHAPTER
FIFTY-SIX

I watch how she brushes his hair back like a mother would a child and at that moment, I can tell she truly does love her sons. It looks innocent like a doting mother would do. It suddenly makes me wish my mother would still be here. I feel saddened by the fact my mother would never again look at me the way Caroline gazes at Theo. But it does no good, he doesn't even bat an eyelid.

I hear her sigh. "This is one of the things I hate about being a vampire, the rest is okay but once we become stuck like this, it's always hard to come out of it. Consumed by one's thoughts can sometimes be the worst sort of torture." I hear her murmur, as her thumb brushes his cheek soothingly.

"May I ask how you became like this?" It's something that I have wondered about because Theo doesn't like talking about it.

"Did Theo tell you he is a twin?" She asks. I shake my head. This is the first time I have heard any mention of it. She nods, understandingly. "I had two sons Theodore and Benjamin," she says, looking down at Theo. "They were identical twins, when the plague hit Benjamin didn't survive. I couldn't risk losing Theo or Tobias, so I spoke to who I thought was a doctor who reckoned he had a miracle cure for illness. I was scared for my other sons; I would have done anything for them. We weren't aware that Tobias could change us back then, we didn't realize because, him being a werewolf, was shocking enough and we were still learning about what it is he was." She stares off absentmindedly like she has been thrown back to the time she is talking about.

"So, I met this man. He claimed to be some form of witch doctor. He was strikingly handsome and a little mad, very eccentric. But he said he could help. If I had known back then what he would do, I never would have agreed. So, I brought Theo and Josiah to him, he gave us some wine and we gave him a hefty sum of cash, literally everything we had. Tobias didn't agree, he said something smelt off about him. It all happened so fast, Tobias was in shock and didn't have time to react. Vampires are a lot quicker than werewolves, which I am sure you know already."

Her gaze settles on me and I nod. I've witnessed it myself, Theo always gets to me faster.

"So, we accepted the wine, which at the time we didn't know was actually laced with his blood. The next thing we saw was darkness. Tobias said he snapped our necks and started laughing like a madman. We woke up, not even realizing what it was we were. Well, that is until the hunger took over. Tobias dragged some drunk man in, and we couldn't help ourselves - we killed him, draining him of his blood. We became monsters and for a long time Tobias had to cover up for us. Until we found the watchers, that is, and they introduced us to the council. We made an agreement with the watcher after saving one of their family members' lives. He is one of Tom's ancestors. In exchange for helping us, they get to live long lives, free of illness. In exchange they help cover our tracks when needed, which is rare with the council nowadays."

"So, Tom's family helped you back then, and because you saved a family member made the treaty that you still have today?"

"Yes, exactly. Tom's family are called watchers. They originally worked under the council, but after Tom's ancestor became ill and we found our blood had healing properties, we saved her and Richard. Tom's ancestor asked to be permanently assigned our family, which was granted and in return, if someone falls ill, we help ensure they only die from old age and not before their time. With medical technology advancing over the years, we aren't being required much, but the treaty still stands."

"So, what happened to the vampire that changed you?" I ask.

"We never saw him again. Tobias tried to catch him, but he thought the madman killed us and panicked. When we woke up, Tobias was beside himself and we didn't understand until Tobias explained what he did. It wasn't long after we killed the drunk man and Theo was no longer human, that Tobias felt suddenly drawn to Theo like a moth to flame. Theo was the same. Back then, it was frowned upon for a man to love another man. They fought their own desires for years, until Tobias accidently lost control and marked Theo, making their bond stronger till they no longer cared what others thought."

I look at Theo before getting up and walking over to him. "So, Tobias didn't feel the bond until after Theo had been changed?" I ask.

"Correct, that's why the council is wondering if there is more to you than meets the eye. No werewolf has ever had a bond with a human, they have fooled around with humans, even got a few pregnant, but never established a bond. It is unheard of. Did you know your father, Imogen?"

I shake my head. I know nothing of the man, don't even know what he looks like, and from what I gathered, he isn't worth knowing. I know my grandfather hated him because, I assume, of abandoning my mother. Mom never really spoke of him and if she did it was when she was extremely drunk. I know they knew each other for a while before she fell pregnant but that is it.

"Not to worry, I am sure we will find the answers somehow," she says, I believe more to herself than to me.

"So, werewolves that mate with humans. They can fall pregnant, so it creates a half human half werewolf, correct?"

"Sort of, they won't be able to shift, but they do get some of the benefits, like longer life span, most will have short temper and are stronger. For a werewolf child to be born only two werewolves can bring a full werewolf into the world. Same with vampires they can create a hybrid with a werewolf but with a human the child comes out more or less human. We aren't sure why that is. I think it's a safety mechanism human bodies have to stop the world becoming overrun with supernatural creatures. Though, their DNA is slightly different, and what humans consider rare blood types. Whereas a vampire and werewolf or hybrid child will crave blood and be able to shift. It is all very confusing, I will try and explain more later but for now, we really need to see what we can find amongst your things." She says, standing up. Tobias and Josiah walk back out, heading towards the front door.

I grab my tennis shoes that are near the front door and slip my feet into them, Tobias waits while Josiah and Caroline walk towards the shed. Tobias moves closer and grabs my hand before kissing my fingertips.

I brush my thumb over his lip, and he relaxes slightly before keeping a strong grip on my hand and pulling me with him towards the shed. Caroline lifts the roller door, just as I get there, and we all make our way to the back of the shed, which has an office behind the glass door. I noticed it the few times I have been in here, yet never actually went in. I didn't need the reminder that my mother isn't here any longer. That, I'm already painfully aware of. But I must admit that after talking to Caroline, I'm a little curious to see if there is actually anything hidden amongst my mother's things.

As soon as I step in, the first thing I can smell is the old table my Grandfather made for my mother. I love the smell of lacquered wood, always have. I run my hand along the top of it, the wood feels smooth and familiar under my hand. My family spent many Christmas's around this table, and it holds a lot of memories. It was my mother's favorite possession and now mine, knowing what it always meant to her. Tobias starts opening boxes and Caroline waits along with Josiah, obviously feeling awkward about going through my things.

"You can start opening boxes, I don't mind. It will be faster if we are all looking" I tell them.

They look relieved, but I can tell they don't want to overstep. I grab the first box I lay my hands on, pulling it off the shelf and placing it on the table. Caroline does the same, coming to stand next to me and we start rummaging through the boxes.

I continue opening boxes, until we find every document stored in the room, my birth certificate and even an old phone, and address book of my mothers. When we finish stacking the boxes and putting them away, we stand around the old table, flicking through the various documents. Like I thought, my birth certificate holds no answer, just my mother's name.

Josiah is turning page after page of a small hardcover notebook. It has a floral design on the front. Josiah suddenly drops the book and gasps, it lands on the table facedown. I pick it up and a photo falls from between the pages.

"What?" I ask, grabbing the photo and looking down at it. I don't see anything wrong with the photo at all, it is just a photo of my mother with me, and some man whom I don't recognize. I must admit, the resemblance between him, and me is uncanny, with his blonde hair and blue eyes we even have the same nose and lips.

Josiah shakes his head, "Do you know this man?" He asks, pointing at the photo.

I shake my head and Tobias walks over, peering over my shoulder and looking at the photo. I hear him growl and I look over my shoulder at him. His eyes are narrowed and have turned to pitch-black orbs. Caroline walks over and takes the photo from my hand, wanting to see what they are so bothered by.

She drops the photo, her hands go to her mouth. "It can't be him," she whispers.

I'm completely baffled, obviously they recognize the man in the photo. But I have no recollection of this photo even being taken and I'm around ten-years-old in it. I know if I had seen this man before, I would have recognized him.

"Can't be who? Who is he?" I ask.

They don't answer, just stare, Josiah picks up the photo and puts it in his pocket. Tobias ushers me out of the shed, his father has my birth certificate, not that it is going to do any good with the lack of my father's name. He also takes the floral notebook.

"Who is the man, Tobias?" I ask, annoyed no one is answering my question. Tobias moves closer, putting his arm over my shoulder before turning to his parents, ignoring my question.

His mother, Caroline, looks nervous, and Josiah pats Tobias on the back before walking towards their car. He grabs Caroline's hand, and tugs her along with him. Tobias walks me up the front veranda and we climb the stairs. As soon as his parents are out of view, I turn to him.

"What the fuck is going on Tobias, who is he?"

Tobias growls at my tone of voice, but I'm sick of no one telling me what is going on. "He is a member of the council. He is also the same man that turned Theo and his parents."

"But Caroline said she has never seen the crazy vampire doctor again." I protest. Did she lie or is there more to this story then she told me?

"Look, that's all you need to know right now, my mother didn't lie, we haven't seen him since. He left the council before we even knew about it. We only found out he is a council member upon visiting the council for the first time. His photo is hung in their gallery. He went missing the year he changed them. We thought he had been killed by hunter's because no one, including the council, has seen him since. But that photo proves he is still alive."

"If he is alive, why is he in a photo with me and my mother then? And why don't I remember meeting him?" This is all becoming too much and so god damn confusing.

"I'm not sure who he is to you, but my parents will find out. Shit, they forgot to take your blood." Tobias walks inside and goes to the wine rack, he presses down on the wooden top and it springs open, the lid opening up to reveal a hidden compartment.

He grabs something out, it is a bulky phone. He turns the screen on and dials a number. I stare, dumbfounded. I thought they didn't have a way of contacting anyone out here. Clearly, I'm wrong.

Someone must have answered because Tobias starts talking. "You forgot to take a blood sample." I can't hear the other half of the conversation, but I know he is talking to his parents. "Okay, I will bring her over on Thursday." He says and hangs up the phone.

"You have cell service out here?" I ask, annoyed.

"It's a satellite phone, on Thursday you are coming to meet the council, so they can run some tests."

I suddenly feel nauseous. I don't want to go to the council to meet the same people that will decide my fate.

Tobias, seeing how nervous I become, places the phone back in the cupboard before closing the lid and wrapping his arms around me, pulling me to his chest. I relax against him and he rests his chin on top of my head. "Don't be scared, I won't let them hurt you, Imogen."

"No, you will just let them kill me." I say, stepping back and away from him.

I hear him sigh as I turn and walk off towards the living room. Theo is still in the exact same position on the armchair by the fireplace. A perfect statue.

"How long will he remain like that?" I ask, worried. Tobias walks over and places a hand on Theo's shoulder. Theo doesn't even blink, just stares off vacantly.

"I'm not sure, hopefully not long," he says.

I turn the TV on and put a movie on. I'm suddenly feeling mentally drained. I try to watch the movie, but it is hard, seeing Theo out of the corner of my eye sitting so still. It is starting to give me the creeps. Tobias, obviously used to Theo going into this state, just watches the movie, his big, warm hand resting on my thigh.

I roll onto my back. "When we go to the council, will they decide then, how much time I have left?" Tobias turns, looking at me before climbing between my legs, his arms resting on either side of my head as he holds the weight of his body off mine.

"I'm not sure, but Theo and I will be with you, so will my parents, so don't be worried. You may think they don't like you, but they do. They just aren't used to dealing with humans. They won't let anyone hurt you either Imogen, not even my father," he says, kissing my forehead.

When he pulls back, I kiss him. I feel him smile against my lips before he thrusts his hips into me. He is already hard underneath his pants. I moan, his lips move to my neck as he sucks on the skin. Then, I catch sight of Theo over his shoulder, still staring off blankly. I shiver, not really comfortable with him staring, even though I know he isn't watching.

"What is it?" Tobias asks when he feels me shiver.

"Nothing. Theo, is creeping me out staring off like that."

Tobias looks over his shoulder before sitting up. "I can try and wake him."

"How did you wake him last time?" I ask, raising an eyebrow at him.

He has a silly smirk on his face. "By touching him," he says, his lips turning up slightly, obviously remembering the last time he was in this state.

I laugh, of course he will wake up. I stand up and Tobias watches me. "What are you going to do?" He asks.

I know it is childish but right now, I'm bored. "You got a sharpie?" I ask, a silly smile on my face, lighting up at my idea. Tobias eyebrows furrow, wondering what I want a sharpie for.

He stands up and walks off before coming back with a permanent marker. "What do you want that for?"

"Well, the pair of you still aren't forgiven, so while he is like that I plan on giving him a make-over." I walk over to Theo, suddenly excited about doodling on his face. I take the lid off, standing in front of him. He is the perfect canvas, still as a statue.

"Imogen, will he kill you," Tobias snorts, but doesn't stop me.

I have to stop myself from laughing, not that he can hear or see me, but that doesn't make it any less funny.

Tobias walks out before coming back with another marker. "You ever do this to me, and I will spank you so hard, you won't be able to walk for a week," he says, a silly smile on his face as bends down in front of him.

I color in his eyebrows before joining them together. I'm impressed at Tobias drawing skills as he draws a huge cock on Theo's face that goes from the bottom of his ear to Theo's mouth. It is unbelievably detailed and veiny. I also draw a huge, curly mustache. By the time we are done, we both stand back and admire our artwork.

"Done now? You had your fun?" Tobias asks.

"Don't act like you didn't enjoy doing that Tobias, I can feel you through the bond." I say, nudging him with my elbow.

He chuckles slightly. "Maybe a little, but he is going to be so pissed off when he wakes up."

I chuckle and Tobias wraps his arms around my waist, tugging me to him. I turn in his arms, wrapping my own around his neck.

Tobias's lips move to mine as he kisses the side of my lips, to my chin. I lift my legs, wrapping them around his waist, his hands going to my ass, holding me against him. I run my fingers through his hair at the back of his neck.

"Not here. Not with Picasso over there," Tobias chuckles and turns, carrying me up the stairs while I suck on his neck.

He groans, liking the feeling of me, kissing and sucking on him. I hear him open the bedroom door before depositing me on the bed. Tobias leans over the top of me, and I tug his shirt up. He removes it when he realizes I want it off. I run my hands up his chest, loving the feeling of each muscle moving under my fingertips. Tobias moves his face closer, kissing me softly, his hand going under my shirt as he grabs my breast, squeezing it. I wrap my legs around his waist, trying to pull him closer.

His lips move to my neck as he pushes my shirt up higher before removing it. He kisses the top of my breast, before biting down. I hiss at the pain before his tongue soothes it. I can feel his erection through his pants. Reaching down, I tug on his belt, trying to loosen it. Seeing I want his pants off, he quickly stands and removes them, while I pull my leggings down, removing them and tossing them at him. They hit him in the face, and he smiles before climbing on the bed between my legs. I can feel his erection on the inside of my thigh.

Reaching between us, I wrap my hand around his shaft, squeezing slightly. Tobias groans and thrusts into my hand. I stroke his shaft up and down, his teeth now grazing my collarbone as he nips at my skin. I can feel my thighs slick with my juices. Tobias moves closer, forcing me to let go of his cock as he positions himself and pushes inside me. His lips move to mine as he sucks on my bottom lip. It feels strange without Theo being with us but Tobias, for once, is almost gentle. His cock fills me, and I move my hips, taking him in deeper, loving the way his cock stretches me to accommodate his large size.

Tobias moves his hips, gently pulling in and out. I wrap my legs around his hips, my hands go to his hips as I tug him to me, needing him to go faster.

"So impatient," he whispers against my lips. He thrusts in hard and deep, and I moan out, my walls clamping down on his cock. I hear him groan before picking up his pace and ramming his cock into me continuously, faster, and harder each time giving me no rest.

I move my hips to meet his thrusts, my moans, and our heavy breathing, the only noises in the house. I'm sitting right on the edge of my orgasm and a few more thrusts shove me completely over. I feel my walls tighten around Tobias, he groans, finding his own release before stilling inside me. He kisses my lips and then, we hear someone clear their throat.

We both look over Tobias' shoulder and Theo is standing in the doorway with a silly smirk on his face, which only makes him look more ridiculous. The dick on his face is wrinkled as his lips move upward into a lazy smile. Both Tobias and I burst out laughing.

Theo laughs till he realizes we are laughing at him, not at the fact he caught us. "What?" He asks, confused.

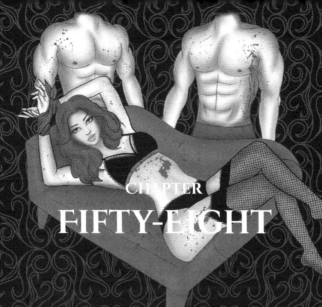

CHAPTER
FIFTY-EIGHT

The next few days pass in a blur. It is now Wednesday, and Tobias and Theo have been stressed about some document that was supposed to arrive at the house and never did. Sitting up in bed, I stretch out, only to find Theo and Tobias are no longer in bed. I can hear the shower running and feel arousal through the bond, making my heart rate quicken.

Getting up, I swing my legs over the side of the bed and stand up. I start walking toward the bathroom door, where I can hear Tobias groaning. A lazy smile turns my lips up, I know what they are doing. Reaching for the handle, I turn it slowly, opening the door as quietly as I can, which must have worked because neither of them hear, or look in my direction, as I lean on the door frame, watching them.

Tobias has his back pressed against the tiled wall in the shower, his eyes closed and lips parted slightly, his hand in Theo's hair. Theo is on his knees in front of Tobias. The water runs down his back as one of his hands grip Tobias's hip and the other braces on the wall beside him.

I watch Tobias' grip get tighter on Theo's hair, earning a growl from Theo that vibrates through me, making me cross my legs as arousal floods into me from the bond. I watch as Tobias thrusts into Theo's mouth before stilling and I know he has just finished. Theo rises from the floor, pressing himself into Tobias, kissing him, while Tobias' hand goes to his hip pulling him closer.

I clear my throat, both of them turn to look at me where I'm leaning on the door frame with my arms folded across my chest. Tobias has a huge grin on his face and Theo turns and opens the shower door.

"We knew you were there, could smell your arousal the moment you opened the door," he says, reaching out and grabbing the front of his shirt I'm wearing, pulling me into the shower.

I shriek at how cold the water is, it is barely lukewarm. My shirt becomes drenched as he pulls me under the stream of water, the shirt sticking to me. Tobias adjusts the temperature and I relax under the hot stream. Theo peels the shirt off that is now acting as a second skin.

He tosses the shirt over the shower door before gripping my hips and lifting me. My arms wrap around his neck as he presses me against the shower wall, which is fucking freezing. Another yelp leaves me as my back comes in contact with the cold tiles. I hear them both chuckle, Theo moves before pressing me against Tobias chest which is always unnaturally warm. Tobias grunts at the impact of Theo pushing me against him.

"Better?" Tobias whispers into the crook of my neck.

I lean my head back on his shoulder and kiss the bottom of his jaw. "Much better."

Theo's lips move to my collar bone, nipping at the skin as he slowly makes his way up to my throat, then to my chin, moving slightly. I lift my head off Tobias's shoulder and kiss Theo. He growls as he bites down on my bottom lip, hard enough that I can taste the metallic taste of my own blood in my mouth, his tongue soothing his bite. I moan against his lips and my legs tighten around his waist. Tobias' hands grip my hips when I suddenly feel a different urge through the bond, one that definitely isn't mine. The need for blood, an overwhelming urge to feed.

I feel Tobias tense slightly, his arms go between Theo and me, and wrap around my stomach.

"Theo, careful," I hear Tobias growl out.

Theo freezes as I feel his fangs graze my shoulder, making me shiver and desire runs through me. Desire that isn't completely mine, I know the arousal is, but the desire to feed is definitely all Theo. Theo stops and looks up, his eyes are no longer their beautiful green but a demonic red. I watch him shake his head slightly, trying to get his bearings and control back. I move my hand, running it under the black veins under eyes that are twitching and rippling beneath his skin. His lips part, and I can see just how sharp his fangs are, my legs tighten around his waist. I can't even remember the last time I saw Theo have blood. I'm pretty certain it is when he hurt me. The memory sends a shiver up my spine, remembering how painful it was.

I know he was trying to hurt me then, but the other times it never hurt. Theo watches me for a few seconds, his eyes still crimson, but I can tell he looks uncertain. I move my hair that has fallen over my shoulder and offer him my neck. He hesitates and looks up at Tobias.

"You don't have to," Tobias says behind me, his grip around my stomach becoming tighter.

"I want to," I tell Theo.

He looks uncertain still and doesn't move, his hands running up my thighs before stepping closer. I feel his breath on my neck, which makes me shiver and he stops and kisses my jaw instead, before pulling my face to his. I can feel his erection underneath me, but also his fear of hurting me comes through the bond.

I wiggle my hips and he pushes up, his cock burying itself in me, making me moan out. I feel Tobias lips go to my shoulder and I move my hips as Theo pulls out before ramming back in. I turn my head, offering my neck again to Theo, this time he doesn't hesitate, and I feel sharp pain as his fangs break my skin before he thrusts in harder, making me relax. I moan, and his initial bite no longer hurts, instead it turns to euphoria as he drinks from me.

I can feel his tongue lapping against my skin while he sucks on it. He bites down again, harder, making my blood rush into his mouth, I feel a trickle run down my shoulder and over my breast, making my nipples harden.

The high of his bite makes me flood with arousal as I move my hips against him. Theo grips my hips, moving them faster against him as I feel my orgasm build before I'm shoved over the edge, my walls clenching around his hard length that is buried deeply inside me.

I feel him go still as I ride out my orgasm, obviously finding his own. I slump against Tobias and feel him kiss the side of my face. Theo pulls his mouth away from neck, his fangs slowly retracting. I smile lazily at him and he kisses my lips softly. I can taste my own blood on his lips when he pulls away, his cock slipping from my body, but he doesn't let go of my hips, instead pulling me against him, so my head is resting on his shoulder, my arms draped heavily over his. I feel Tobias move behind me and open the door, hopping out of the shower. I see him grab a towel and wrap it around his hips.

Theo lets me slide down his body, but he keeps a good grip on me as I'm hit with vertigo. His hand around my waist is the only thing keeping me upright, as I lean my head on his chest. I feel him start washing me, rubbing the loofa softly over my skin.

"It will settle. I think I fed longer than I should have," he says softly.

I can feel his worry through the bond. The room is already starting to right itself as the dizziness subsides. My legs no longer feel like jelly. "I'm okay, it's fine, Theo," I whisper, looking up and running my fingers through his chest hair and his hypnotic eyes stare down at me.

He kisses my nose. "I will feel better once you eat. Come on, let's hop out," he says, pulling me out of the shower. Theo grabs a towel and wraps it around me before grabbing his own. He puts his hands on my shoulders to make sure I'm still steady as I step into the bedroom. Tobias is putting his suit on and I know they have to go back to work today.

"She looks a little pale Theo," Tobias says angrily.

"I'm fine I promise."

"I will go make her something to eat," he says, storming out of the room.

"Really, I'm fine." I tell Theo. I walk over and sit on the bed. Tobias has pulled one of my blouses out and black slacks. I look at them before looking at Theo. "I can come to work?" Theo nods before bending down and kissing my lips softly.

"Yes, Tobias and I were talking last night. We are giving you your freedom back. Just please don't run off or go too far away from us." I nod. I don't care as long as I can leave the house.

"Tobias has also organized someone to come out today to put in a landline and internet. Should be on when we get home." Theo adds.

Finally, the internet. God only knows how much I miss my reading platforms. I quickly get dressed and then walk into the bathroom. Theo is still lingering, making sure I'm not about to drop dead on them. I quickly do my make-up and am surprised when Theo picks up my hair straightener that is plugged in next to me. He clicks the tongs together while I'm doing my eyeliner, I raise an eyebrow at him.

I'm about to take it from him, but Theo stops me. "Let me try," he says, pulling it away from me.

I stand straight while he picks up the brush and uses it to pick up some of my hair before clamping the hair straightener on it. "Don't burn my hair off," I warn him as I hear him snicker behind before I feel him do the next piece.

When I realize he isn't going to set my hair on fire, I start doing the rest of my make up. Theo has finished doing my hair and is inspecting his handy work. I nod at him in approval, and I see him kiss my shoulder in the mirror.

Walking downstairs, I can smell the delicious aroma of freshly brewed coffee. I sit at the counter and Tobias places a plate of pancakes in front of me, covered in different sorts of berries and syrup. My stomach rumbles just from the sight of it. I dig in, suddenly feeling ravenous.

When we finish eating, Tobias grabs my purse and phone from upstairs and we walk toward the garage. I hop in the passenger side and Theo hops in the back. We drive to work and pull up in the parking garage. I notice Tom, waiting for us as we get out of the car next to the elevator. He waves upon seeing me, a grin lighting up his face. I'm so relieved to see him, and that Tobias kept his word and hadn't killed him.

I walk up and wrap my arms around him, giving him a hug. Tom is wearing a suit instead of cleaning scrubs and looks quite professional. I hear Theo and Tobias walk up behind us and Tom nods to both of them.

"Did any documents get dropped off while we were off?" Asks Theo.

"No, are you talking about the..." Theo cuts him off with a growl.

It's a strange reaction, but whatever Tom was about to say dies on his lips at the warning growl. "No documents have been dropped off," he says, looking at Theo.

My eyebrows furrow and I wonder what the documents are that Tobias and Theo clearly don't want me to know about. "What documents? Maybe they have been emailed? I can check when we get upstairs" I ask.

"No, these would have to be personally dropped off," Tobias says, tugging me towards the entrance. Theo shoots Tom a look.

"I might go check the emails just in case," Theo says, taking off up the stairs next to the elevator.

"I could have checked when we got upstairs, what's so important about these documents anyway?" I ask Tobias.

"Nothing that concerns you, but they were supposed to have been dropped to the house by now." I wonder what the documents are, but mentioning them does remind me that tomorrow I'm supposed to go to the council and have some tests run, and meet the people that are going to decide my future.

I suddenly feel nervous. Tobias presses the button in the elevator to our floor before looking down at me. "What's wrong, love?" He asks, staring at me while I chew on my nail. It is a terrible nervous habit, Tobias pulls my thumb away from my lips. "What's wrong?" He asks again.

"Nothing, I just realized I have to meet the council tomorrow."

He pulls me against him, wrapping his arms around my shoulder. "You will be fine, no one will hurt you. I promise."

When we step out the elevator, I'm shocked to see Theo's mother, Caroline waiting in the foyer talking to Theo.

"What are you doing here, ma?" Tobias asks, as he steps out of the elevator.

"Good morning, Imogen, son. We have a slight problem, the council want to meet today. We need to leave after lunch."

"Where's dad?" Tobias asks, looking around. Josiah isn't here, only Caroline.

"He is sorting out your other issues, they are being quite difficult."

I hear both Theo and Tobias growl lowly, Theo's eyes darken. "When do we leave?" Tobias asks.

"We have to meet them at two." Tobias nods, while I stand there shaking, fear consumes me and something else. I'm not sure what it is, but I feel like something is slightly amiss. I just have a feeling something is going to happen, and I'm not going to like it.

CHAPTER
FIFTY-NINE

aroline waits at the office, constantly on edge pacing back and forth. I can't understand her nervousness, she isn't the one about to march into this so-called mythical council and beg for her life.

She keeps checking her phone constantly. When I ask what is wrong, she just says she is waiting for her husband to come back. I wonder what her husband is doing that has her so on edge. When Josiah finally does show up, she all but runs to the elevator, watching the numbers above the stainless-steel doors till it dings on our floor.

Josiah steps out of the elevator, an annoyed look on his face like he brought bad news. I feel my stomach drop instantly, thinking it is the council as he speaks to his wife in a hushed voice before realizing I'm standing, watching them.

"Tobias isn't going to like this; I can't believe that evil wretch." I hear his mother say.

Tobias walks out and motions for his parents to step into his office. "Did you get it?" He asks.

His father shakes his head. "Not yet, they want to meet you in person. Tomorrow," he says as he steps through the door, closing it behind him.

Theo comes out of his office, looking at the door before looking towards me. I hear him growl lowly before walking over, obviously listening in on the conversation behind the closed door that I can't hear.

"What's going on? Why is everyone being so secretive?"

"It's nothing that you need to worry about, just having issues with a client from the council," he tells me.

I can feel through the bond he isn't lying, that whomever it is they need these documents from is from the council, yet I can feel something else, like he isn't telling me the whole truth.

Stepping out from behind my desk, I walk over to the bathroom, wanting to wash my face and freshen up before we have to leave in an hour. It is nearly 11:30 am and apparently, the drive takes an hour, and we will have to leave no later than 12:30.

Grabbing my handbag, I walk into the bathroom and rummage through my bag, looking for my lipstick and eyeliner that I always carry. Digging through the oversized handbag, I become annoyed before tipping the contents into the sink and start rummaging. I find my lip balm but not my lipstick. I sigh, picking it up thinking it will have to do before digging in the sink, looking for the rest of my things. I pick up my phone and start dumping stuff back inside my bag. I really need to clean my bag out one day, I have so much junk in it I can barely find anything. Picking up the handkerchief I hear a foil packet drop out of it and into the sink. My heart skips a beat when I realize what it is.

I pick up the foil package - it is my birth control, unused. I completely forgot all about taking it, in fact I haven't taken it in months, not really needing to. Although I should have. However, with everything going on with my mother, and Tobias and Theo keeping me hostage, it hasn't been exactly the first thing on my mind.

Picking it up, my hands are shaking. I try to remember the last time I had my period, but no matter the amount of times I recount in my head, it comes back to the same thing - before my mother died.

I am late. Grabbing my phone out, I check the app on my phone that usually sends me an alert to tell me when they are due. My heart is bumping frantically in my chest when I realize it never alerted me because of the lack of cell service at the property. I check the last date and nearly pass out from holding my breath. I'm a month and seventeen days late.

Grabbing everything and tossing it back in my bag, I wet the back of my neck, trying to cool down, suddenly feeling extremely hot. This can't be happening, right? I was in heat not long ago so I can't be pregnant, werewolves only fall pregnant when in heat. Then, the sarcastic voice in my head starts taunting me that I'm not a werewolf, so it doesn't work that way for me. No, I'm human, so vampire and werewolf shit doesn't affect me. Looking at the clock, I still have time. I can duck down to the convenience store and grab a test, but will they let me leave? I have to try. Dumping everything back in my bag, I regain my bearings and walk out. Theo is leaning against my desk, a worried look on his face as I come out.

"You okay, hun?"

"Yep, never better. Can I go to the shop down on the corner? I'm starving" I lie. My appetite is completely gone with worry. I hate that I have to ask permission but if I just leave, they will panic and send out a search party.

Theo thinks for a second. "I will come with you."

"No, I won't be long. Promise." My voice comes out as nearly a squeak.

He seems taken aback before he moves closer. I can feel him looking through the bond, wondering why I suddenly want to leave. I make sure to clear my head and start rambling about seeing Tom, so he won't catch on to what is actually on my mind. He cocks his head to the side. "You're only going to the shop to see Tom?" He asks.

"Yep, that's all, I will come back," I say, my voice is off even I can tell but he must have given me the benefit of the doubt, because he pulls out his wallet and hands me his card.

"Here, Tobias took your cards when you did a runner. Remind me when we get home to put them back in your wallet for you," he says, passing me his and giving me the pin number, which funnily enough is the month and day of my birthday, 0815.

I grab the card and walk to the elevator. I step in and I can see Theo watching me like he is deciding whether or not he actually did the right thing by letting me go. I hit the button to the lobby. As soon as the doors close, I let out the breath I have been holding. When I get to the bottom, Merida is at the front counter, calling me over when she sees me.

"You still stuck here?" I ask as soon as I approach her.

"Yes, I think Theo is punishing me over the other night. They have had quite a few apply for the position and he keeps turning them away, forcing me to play secretary. It's driving me nuts, the phone never stops, and the emails just keep coming." She huffs, annoyed.

I chuckled slightly. "I will ask Theo to hire someone so you can go back to your normal position. If he won't, I'll ask Tobias, he will sort it for you."

She nods, looking thankful. "Where are you off to without your bodyguards?" She asks.

"To the shop, want anything?"

"Oh, yes can you grab me a cappuccino." I nod.

"Sure, I will be back in a minute." I tell her before walking out and towards the convenient store. On the way past, I stop at the Starbucks and order everyone a cappuccino, remembering to get Josiah a black coffee, like his soul. I don't actually mind their parents, they aren't so bad, we all just started off on the wrong foot because of Tobias. I chuckle slightly before paying and heading next door.

I walk down the aisle towards the feminine products. As I stand in the aisle, a young girl comes over to me. Her hair is in dreadlocks and a friendly smile is plastered on her face.

"Can I help you?" She asks when she sees me staring at the pregnancy test section for too long, trying to decide which one is the better one.

"Um, yes actually, which one is better? The most accurate?"

She picks up a box and hands it to me. "This one can be done from the date of your missed cycle and it tells you in the window roughly how far along. It seems to be the most popular choice," she says, handing me the box.

I nod and thank her before following her to the counter. Realizing I'm meant to be buying food, I also grab a muffin and pay before walking out.

I walk to the coffee shop and wait for my name to be called. While I wait, I jam the test into a secret hidden hole in the side of my bag and zip it up. As long as no one goes into my bag, they shouldn't notice, but the box is pretty bulky.

When my name is called, I grab the two little trays before walking back to the office. When I walk in, I give Merida hers and she takes a sip before moaning loudly.

"I can feel it in my soul." She says, making me chuckle.

I head toward the elevator and press the button to the top floor. Waiting, I start to become anxious. Then, I feel it's not me, it is actually Tobias and Theo. I feel Tobias getting angry, then the elevator doors open. Everyone is standing next to my desk, staring at me like I just grew two heads.

"See, I told you she would be back," says Theo to Tobias, pointing at me.

I step out with coffees and my muffin. "Everything okay?" I ask.

"Yes, Tobias is being a dick, thinking I let you run away," Theo says, walking over and kissing my temple before picking up a coffee.

He takes a sip and nearly spits it out when he realizes he grabbed mine, which has more sugar than he likes. I place the cardboard trays on the desk and grab my coffee off him before handing him his and shake my head. I give Josiah his, "Black, like your soul," I tell him. His lips turn up slightly and he thanks me while I give everyone their coffees.

"We will be leaving soon, so make sure you are ready, dear," Caroline tells me. I nod suddenly feeling nervous.

"Nothing will happen, not today anyway. Josiah is just taking you to meet them, and the council has ordered some tests, you may also have to meet the oracle."

"Oracle?"

"Just a fancy word for, I suppose... a fortune teller, nothing to worry about. She will just look into your past and maybe your future, it's just precautionary to make sure you won't speak of what you see when we arrive."

I nod my head and take a bite of my muffin.

"Well, your father and I are going to head off, we will meet you there," she says softly to Theo, before touching my shoulder and rubbing her thumb over my cheek. "Nothing to worry about dear, I promise," she says, before walking to the elevator with Josiah.

CHAPTER
SIXTY

I'm sitting at my desk when Theo walks out of his office and Tobias steps out of his a second later. I stand up, knowing it is time to leave.

"Ready?" Tobias asks.

"As ready as I'll ever be," I say, grabbing my handbag from under my desk and throwing it over my shoulder.

We make our way to Tobias' car. As soon as the car starts, I know there will be no turning back, the seatbelt suddenly feels more like a restraint as we leave the city to meet the people that will decide when I die.

The drive takes about forty-five minutes. Tobias pulls the car over on what appears to be an abandoned school in literally the most deserted place, hidden amongst the trees. We get out of the car and I look around. It is an old school building, with trees going through it, the roof has caved in and the place looks desolate. Like it hadn't been a functioning school in hundreds of years. No signage, no nothing.

"Are we at the right place?" I ask, looking around confused.

There are broken swings in the distance and the gate out front is rusted. Tobias and Theo nod before walking through the gate and suddenly, vanishing into thin air. I stop, shocked. Where did they go? Then, suddenly Theo's hand comes out, waving at me on my side of the gate, his body invisible. I take a step back; I must be tripping what the hell was in that coffee?

Suddenly, Theo steps back into view, my heart skips a beat as he materializes in front of me.

"Come on," he says, holding out his hand.

I nervously take it and he pulls me through the gate. I can hear a high pitched whistling, and have to fight the urge to block my ears then suddenly, a feeling like I'm being sucked through a vacuum, before finally feeling air again. I suck in a deep breath. What I'm not expecting when I look around is the sight of the huge mansion in front of me, that can't be the school I just saw.

I turn around and look back at the gate, I just walked through which is no longer there. I can see the car and the dirt road, but the abandoned school is gone. I take a step back and bump into Tobias.

I look up at him and he smiles. "Cool huh?" I nod, not really knowing what to say. I look around, the place is huge as we walk up the grand steps towards the huge archway in place of a door.

"How?" I ask, not understanding how this place is so hidden from the world.

"Witches put wards up, to humans and anyone else it just appears as an abandoned building, anyone who walks past the gates just feel uncomfortable and don't understand why. It's for protection, to stop anyone from discovering this place. There are many around the city as well." Tobias explains.

Theo walks over to the door and bangs on it. A man or should I say strange looking goblin/elf thing walks out, a snarl on his face. He looks at me then at Theo, his face lighting up excitedly.

"Theo, I heard you were coming to visit today, did you bring them?" He asks, his voice sounds really squeaky, kind of like listening to a mouse. He kind of reminds me of Golem from the Lord of the Rings, except he is dressed like a butler.

"Yep, sure did. Did mom and dad already head to the chambers?" He says, pulling a paper bag out of his pocket.

The elf looks inside before pulling out some stringy, red liquorice. The very moment, he grabs one and bites a piece off with his sharp looking teeth. "Yep, they are inside already, this must be your mate. Nice to meet you, Imogen, I am Percy," he says, holding his hand out which is the size of a small child's but with long sharp looking nails.

I shake his hand, wondering how he knows my name.

"Josiah told me about you, you're much prettier than I thought," he says with a wink, answering the question I'm thinking.

I smile, I like him already. He shoves the doors open. It opens up to a huge square room before we walk directly across to another set of doors. Theo opens them before placing his hand on my lower back. "Don't freak out and whatever you do, don't stare, it will be awkward," he says.

I wonder what he means. I don't have to wait long to find out though, stepping through the door, we are in some sort of quadrangle. The place is bustling with people and creatures I have only read about in fairy tales. Shops and buildings along every side, the place is like a little town. I can't help but stare when a centaur walks past me. A fucking centaur.

"You're staring," says Theo, whispering in my ear.

"How the hell does he hide in the human world?" I ask, not being able to believe my own eyes.

"He doesn't, his name is Bruno and he lives permanently here at court. He is the last of his kind." Theo answers.

Maybe there really was something in that coffee, or maybe my mind conjured up this delusion, or I'm dreaming. None of this makes sense; first, an elf creature, now a centaur. Is every mythical creature real?

"Not all, just some, where do you think the stories come from? Humans aren't that imaginative to come up with that stuff on their own. There is always a little truth to legend," Theo says, answering my thoughts.

I drag my eyes away from the half donkey looking man. Theo's hand on my lower back pushes me along, seeing as my feet just aren't cooperating. When we are halfway through the quad, I start really looking around. I feel Tobias grab my hand before bending slightly blocking my view. "What are you looking for?" He asks, an amused look on his face as I stare at all the people, and half peoples roaming around.

"I figured since all these exist that I should make sure jebus isn't here too. I might need to ask for forgiveness since every other mythical creature exists, I am assuming he does too and need to make sure I cover all my bases if I'm gonna die." I say, looking past him and searching the faces of the many people passing by.

I hear Theo chuckle. "Ask forgiveness for what? And just so you know, Jesus or jebus as you like to call him is human, not a supernatural creature."

"What, so he does exist?" I question. Shit, I'm going to hell for being an adulterer.

I hear Theo chuckle, obviously reading my thoughts. "Human, not supernatural, Imogen, and he is just some man someone wrote a story about, doesn't mean what they wrote is real or not real, people just needed to believe in something bigger than themselves to help them sleep better at night."

Tobias and Theo both find my shock at this place amusing. We walk for a few minutes, finally coming to the biggest building in the quad. It kind of resembles a sandstone courthouse. It is a huge imposing building with guards out the front that I can tell are vampires by their red eyes and godly looks. We march up the steps and walk inside. Caroline and Josiah are inside, waiting patiently on some red velvet seats.

Caroline stands up and walks over, giving me a hug. "We have registered that we are here, so we shouldn't have to wait long," she says.

I sit next to her; this room is some kind of waiting area, lined with seats and pictures on the wall of scary looking men and women, who definitely aren't human. The huge paintings and photos lead up a huge corridor with doors running off each side.

I sit nervously twiddling my thumbs when Tobias places his hand over mine, covering my shaking hands. I instantly calm down, the heat of his skin is soothing.

Suddenly, a tall woman in a black dress that reaches the floor walks out, her red eyes indicate she is another vampire, her eyes roam over all of us, before settling on Tobias and Theo.

"Alaric will see you three now," she says, brushing her long, black hair over her shoulder and turning her back on us. Tobias pulls me up from my seat and suddenly, my mouth goes dry. We walk up the long corridor to the last door, he opens it and steps aside allowing us to enter.

I walk in after Tobias and Theo, a man is sitting behind a huge desk, wearing a suit. He looks up as we enter. "Tobias, Theo," he says, standing up and walking around his desk. He shakes their hands before turning to me.

"You must be the human woman, Imogen," he says. I can hear the distaste in his mouth as he looks at me before escorting us over to some chairs and a table on the other side of the room. The room is full of bookshelves and old looking scrolls dumped on different surfaces, the walls covered in old painted portraits. A portrait of the man from the photograph Josiah found is hanging above the fireplace. Only he doesn't look like the same man from the photo, he looks demonic, with his red eyes he looks slightly crazed, the perfect predator, the sort of man you wouldn't want to bump into on a night down a dark alley. I swallow and freeze, staring up at the picture.

CHAPTER
SIXTY-ONE

Theo suddenly pulls me down on the soft gray armchair that is behind me.

The man, Alaric, looks over his shoulder at the painting I'm so engrossed in before he growls, snapping my attention back to him. "Sorry," I whisper.

He cocks his head to the side, his beady red eyes boring into me as his lips pull back slightly, revealing his fangs.

"Alaric," Theo growls when he realizes the man is scaring me.

"Apologies, miss. I find it hard being around your kind when you smell as delightful as you do." I nod, not liking the way he is staring at my neck.

"Well let's get down to business, then. The courts have ordered some tests to check for anything in her bloodline. Tarina will escort her down soon to have her blood taken. I'm still waiting to hear back on when it will be decided what will happen with your mate, but seeing as you have marked her already and your family's reputation, we have decided we won't condemn her death and you won't be punished for taking her as your mate. However, we can't allow her to remain human. I honestly don't know what you see in this human, but luckily for you, your father has said he will leave the council if anything happens to her that would jeopardize his sons. You're lucky your father has stepped in on your behalf and that Maxwell has a soft spot for your father, because if it were my choice, she would already be dead," he says, looking over at me with disgust on his face.

I suddenly feel exceedingly small, I can tell humans are nothing but blood bags to this man. The way he keeps glancing at me makes my skin crawl.

"Don't talk of my mate like that, Alaric. You may be in a position of power now, just remember who got you where you are today, disrespect my mate again and we will have problems," Tobias growls.

Alaric smiles challengingly at him but doesn't glance in my direction again. The door opens and the woman from the lobby steps in, making me glance in the direction of the door.

"Go with Tarina, she will take you next door to have some blood taken," Theo says, not taking his eyes off Alaric.

I can tell he wants nothing but to kill the man, I feel his hatred strongly through the bond. Walking over to the woman, she smiles down at me before I follow her into the room next door, which is like a small infirmary, with different creatures on the wall and their anatomy. I sit on the stool next to the steel table.

"I really don't understand his hate for humans. We were all human at one stage, after many centuries as a vampire, I think he often forgets that" she says softly.

I relax a little, realizing she doesn't share the same view he has. She puts a strap on my arm before pulling a needle out of the drawer under the table and a vial. She attaches the vial to the needle and holds my arm.

"You won't pass out on me, will you?" I shake my head.

She is vastly different to the man next door; she is actually nice, and she kind of reminds me of Sally. I flinch when she jams the needle in my vein. I can tell she is holding her breath, as she holds my arm steady, letting the small vial fill with my blood. She then withdraws the needle and places a cotton bud on it.

"I was a nurse before I was changed, back in the 1800's" she says.

That explains why she looks like she knows what she is doing. She holds the vial up to the light, obviously able to see something in the red liquid that runs through my body.

"Most peculiar indeed," she whispers so low I don't think I'm meant to hear. She then places the vial in a small box before placing it in the fridge under the desk.

"Come on, I should take you back."

I suddenly don't want to go back there. "Is there a bathroom around here?" I ask, wanting to stall for time, I don't want to go back to that room where I know that man is waiting and looking for any reason to kill me.

Tarina nods, her hypnotic blood red eyes searching my face. "Yes, down the hall, the last door next to the waiting area on your left." I follow her instructions and walk to the bathroom. Just as I open the door, I notice Caroline and Josiah are no longer in the waiting room; I wonder where they have gone. I step into the bathroom, it has a few stalls, three sinks and a huge mirror. The white tiles gleam under the bright fluorescent lights.

I quickly wash my hands and wet the back of my neck. I already want to leave. Looking in the mirror, I will myself to go back in the room and face the man. When I turn around, though, I'm not alone.

I didn't hear the woman that stands in front of me come in. She is gorgeous with her blonde hair and green eyes, she has soft facial features, and I can tell she has a lovely figure under her tight floor length gown.

Her eyes narrow when I look at her face, her lips pressing into a tight line. "You must be Tobias and Theo's new plaything," she says, looking at me not even hiding her disgust. "I just had to see which pathetic thing they decided to take as a mate, although you are prettier than I thought you would be. So, where are they?"

"Excuse me?" I ask, wondering who this stunning, yet nasty woman is standing in front of me.

"Your mates, you pathetic human, where are they?" She says, leaning on the door frame.

I roll my eyes and go to walk past her; she is really getting on my last nerve. She places her arm in my way blocking the exit. "Move," I say, glaring up at her.

"Well, aren't you a feisty one, not even intimidated when I could snap you like a twig. I figured you must have a backbone to take something that doesn't belong to you."

"I don't know what you're talking about, now move!"

She leans in closer with a smile playing on her lips that indicates she is up to no good. Suddenly, the door bursts open and she straightens up as Caroline walks in, a shocked look on her face, before it turns to anger.

"Imogen come here," she says, not taking her eyes off the woman, who I can tell she hates for some unknown reason. The woman moves her arm and steps slightly aside, allowing me to pass.

"What are you doing here?" Caroline spits at the woman.

"I'm here to drop off the documents and to see for myself if the rumors are true."

Caroline glares at the woman. "Go back to my son's, Imogen," she says, not taking her eyes off the woman.

"I'll be seeing you real soon, Imogen," the woman adds, throwing a smile that shows her fangs to me as I walk out.

I make my way up to the last door again and step into the room. Alaric's eyes snap to me and he smirks when I walk in. I stand awkwardly, not wanting to get any closer. And again, the door is thrown open and in walks the woman from the bathroom. Alaric smiles at her before holding out his hand, which she takes.

"I don't believe you have met," he says, a cruel smile on his face.

"And they won't." Says Theo, moving between me and the woman and cutting him off.

The woman steps forward and hits Theo in the chest with a

white envelope. He growls at her. "Next time you want to divorce someone, do it in person, don't send your parents." She spits at him.

I look at Tobias confused, and Theo tries to pull me from the room. I pull my hand from his before walking over to the woman and standing in front of her. "Who are you?"

"Bianca, their wife," she says, her voice so cold I fight the urge to shiver.

My stomach drops somewhere deep, I can feel the blood leave my face. They lied to me. I can tell she is enjoying the reaction I have to her name.

"I'm also the one who gets to decide your fate." She smiles cruelly.

Tobias looks at Alaric, shock and anger on his face. "What is she talking about?" He spits, taking a step towards him.

"She is a member of the council, and since you decided to take a mate before divorcing your wife, we thought it is only fair she could have a say in it. Decide when your new mate will be forced to choose, death or the change," he says.

I look at the woman, she has a sly smile on her face. One I don't like, she is taking great pleasure in my discomfort and I know instantly I'm not going to like the next words that come from her pouty lips.

"You have three days, Imogen. Enjoy them; I will take great comfort in watching them snap that pretty little neck."

I feel tears build up, before they can fall, I rip my hand from Theo's and run from the room. I can hear yelling behind me as an argument breaks out, but I don't care. I just want to get as far away from here as possible, Josiah and Caroline jump to their feet as I run past. "Imogen!" I hear Caroline call out to me, but I just keep running.

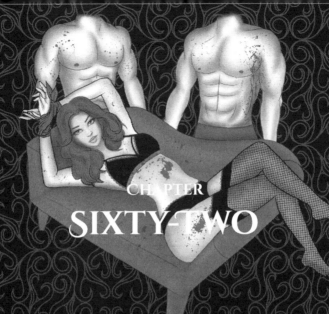

CHAPTER
SIXTY-TWO

I keep running, bumping into people in my haste to get away from the nightmare that is becoming my life, only stopping when I run into Percy at the doors leading into this place.

Percy looks up at me with a red licorice strap hanging from his lips as he chews on it with his pointy teeth. He pulled the strap from his mouth, startled. "Imogen, what's wrong?"

"I need to leave. Let me out, please." He looks around me, noticing Theo and Tobias aren't with me, he scratches his bald head nervously.

"I don't think I should. Where are your mates?" He asks.

"Either open it or I will."

"That's not possible. Only supernaturals can open this door once inside, I'm sorry, Imogen, I can't let you leave without your mates."

I can tell he genuinely feels bad for not being able to let me out, to escape this suffocating place. Panic seizes every atom in my body, my heart hammers in my chest so hard, I'm afraid it is going to bounce right out of my chest. I clutch my chest, trying to calm myself. I haven't had a panic attack in ages. I suck in a breath, trying to get much-needed air. I close my eyes, trying to ground myself as the adrenaline starts pumping through my veins, the familiar fight or flight kicking in.

Percy touches my shoulder. "Are you okay, love?" He asks worriedly. "Your mates should be here soon. I'm sure they wouldn't leave you for too long. That I'm certain of." He speaks softly.

"My mates are the fucking problem I want to escape from!" I scream, anger taking over. I'm so done with the lies, done with them getting their way. I shove past Percy and walk to the doors. "Open it now!" I demand.

Percy takes a step back. I do feel guilty for yelling at him, but I just need to get out of this place, need to get away from them. Percy shakes his head. "I'm sorry Imogen; I can't do that," he says, looking back towards the door nervously that leads to the quadrangle. I look up and people have stopped, looking in at me. Their curious faces watch me argue with the elf. I turn my back on them before hitting the door with my fist.

"Imogen, I wouldn't do that, you could hurt yourself, there are wards all around the place, you are human it could have a negative impact on you," he tries to warn me.

I don't care, just wanting out, I push on the doors with both hands and to my shock, and the shock of everyone else watching, the doors fly open, banging loudly on the sandstone of the building. I look at my hands, shocked with how hard I must have been pushing them for them to fly open like that.

"How, I don't understand, how did you do that?"

"Beats me, but I'm out of here," I say, walking out the doors and heading towards the car I can see on the other side of the shiny veil. How didn't I notice it before? I can see it glimmering slightly.

"Imogen, you must wait," I hear Percy call out to me.

I ignore the strange elf and walk through, feeling the weird suction sensation and the loud ringing in my ears, as I'm sucked out through the strange portal into the real world. My world. I walk to the edge of the road, looking in both directions. I have no idea how to get home, I didn't even pay attention on the drive here. I'm unfamiliar with the area. I only know the direction in which we pulled up. I walk over to the car, pulling on the handle, I'm shocked to find it unlocked.

I jump in the driver's seat and smile when I see the keys dangling from the ignition. I start Tobias' car. I put the car in reverse before stomping on the gas, reversing out and hitting the tree next to the gate, not used to the speed. I fall forward only just catching myself before my face smacks on the steering wheel. I quickly clip my seat belt in. My heart is hammering in my chest, then I laugh. Tobias and Theo both love their cars. Whoops, my bad.

I turn the car around and pull out, hitting the gas, and the car jerks forward at speeds that would normally petrify me, going over a dip in the road, the car bottoming out, as I head for what I hope is the city. I can't help the sadistic laugh when I hear the front bar of the car come off from the force of the front hitting the cattle grid I run over, leaving the bumper and ripping the grill off. They are going to kill me, and I put my foot down just as soon as the thought hits me. After driving for a few minutes, I see a sign saying the city is twenty miles away. I slow for the bend before jamming the brakes on as Theo stands in the middle of the road, an enraged look on his face.

I'm not fast enough, and I plow into him. I close my eyes, so I don't watch as the car is about to run over the top of him, both my feet on the break, trying to get the car to stop in time. I jerk forward, smacking into the steering wheel; my hands instantly go to my head. I can feel blood trickling down the side of my face. Touching my head, I pull my fingers back, I have cut my forehead open on the steering wheel.

Looking up, I see Theo with both hands on the hood, leaving a full impression of his hands. He stopped the car. By the look on his face, I can tell he is furious.

I start pulling at my seat belt, trying to get it off, managing to get out and climb halfway over to the back seat just as the driver side door is ripped completely off by Tobias. He grabs my ankle, pulling me back into the driver's seat. I kick and slap at his hands. Tobias rips me from the car, my feet dangling in the air. He slams me back into the rear driver's side. I flinch at the impact of being roughly slammed into the door, my back aching from the force, knocking the air out my lungs leaving me winded.

"What the fuck are you doing?" He screams.

I do the only thing I can think of, seeing as my arms are pinned in his hands against the car. I throw my head forward, head-butting him, though I'm fairly sure it hurts me more than him.

He drops me and I fall on my knees, clutching my head. Man, he has a hard head. I can feel a lump already forming above my eyebrow. Looking up, Tobias breaks his nose back in place before growling lowly, making my hairs stand on end. I crawl to the back tire, pulling myself to my feet. My surroundings spin as I stand up.

I scream when cold hands grab me, pulling me against them. I know it is Theo, he puts me on the trunk of the car, holding me in place with one arm while I struggle and kick him.

"Stop!" He screams, punching the trunk right next to my head, leaving a huge dent.

I freeze, fear consumes me as his eyes turn red. He leans in closer, and I fear he is going to attack me. His arm around my waist is getting tighter, his hand on my shoulder forces me down. I slap him, the sound echoing and my hand stinging from the force. He growls lowly before ripping me off the trunk and yanking me forward, when suddenly, I hear her voice.

"Let her go now, Theo. I will not watch you treat your mate that way!" Caroline screams, furious at her son.

He lets go and I stumble back, leaning against the trunk. Tobias grabs my handbag out of the car. He is livid and his shirt has blood on it from his already healed nose. He glares at me before shoving my bag back in my hands. I flinch under the look he gives me. I feel their anger running through me from the bond.

"That's enough, both of you. Can't you tell you're scaring her. Come here, Imogen," she says.

I look towards her and can see Josiah waiting in the car a little up the road, shaking his head clearly, annoyed. I run toward Caroline, preferring to be in her presence than her sons.

"Clean this mess up, I'm taking her home," she says before pulling me toward her car. I can hear Theo and Tobias growl, but they don't argue back at her. I honestly think they are too scared to. Caroline, I can tell, is the sort of mother who would give them a dose of their own medicine if they defied her. She squeezes my shoulder softly.

"I'm sorry about them, Imogen. They shouldn't have carried on like that. I'm not defending their behavior, but they became quite panicked when they realized you managed to get past the wards," she says.

"Did Percy let you out?" she asks, curious. I shake my head. "Well, that is interesting," she adds, thoughtfully. She opens the rear car door and I climb in.

Josiah looks in the rear-view mirror at me, his eyes crinkled slightly, and I can tell he is smiling. "Remind me to never let you borrow my car," he says with a wink.

I can't help but chuckle. Their car is totaled now; especially after Theo destroyed the front end. Josiah pulls away, driving around the wrecked car. I can see Tobias is on the phone and see Theo arguing with him, both throwing their hands in the air, obviously arguing with each other. Theo steps closer, indicating for Josiah to roll down the window.

"Drop her off at home we won't be long," he says, sending a glare my way in the back.

I cringe back, pushing myself into the seat.

"I won't be leaving if I feel you are a threat to the girl in anyway, Theo. You made this mess, you clean it," she says, leaning over her husband and glaring at her son.

He stands up straight before giving his mother a nod and turning away from the car.

"Hungry dear? We will grab dinner on the way home," she says.

I nod, feeling a little awkward. Why is she being so nice? And even Josiah? We stop by a Chinese place on the way home. When we pull up Theo and Tobias are sitting on the step out the front. I can feel their guilt through the bond, but I ignore it, they don't deserve forgiveness after that.

They told me she is dead, let me believe she isn't an issue and now, she just decided my fate. As if finding out they lied isn't enough, she got the last laugh. I never did anything to her, yet she can choose my death. I wipe a stray tear as it falls running down my cheek. Opening the car door, I grab my bag and walk past them into the house, ignoring their pleas to let them explain.

CHAPTER
SIXTY-THREE

N o amount of pleading will make me forgive them this time; I want the truth. But even then, will it be the truth coming from them or just another lie, another excuse? We all sit awkwardly at the dining table, eating.

Tobias and Theo's eyes never leave me. When Caroline announces that they will be leaving, my heart skips a beat. I don't want to be left alone with them. I don't want to be around them.

Seeing my panic, Caroline stands up, placing a hand on my shoulder. "I will be back tomorrow," she says.

"We have work tomorrow, you will have to come to the office," Tobias says, his eyes never leaving my face.

"I'm not going, you can go by yourself." I spit at him, not even bothering to look at him. I hear him growl but one look from his mother makes him shut up.

"I will come over first thing in the morning, okay?" She says, looking down at me.

I can feel through the bond Theo and Tobias don't want me anywhere they aren't. Well, they are going to have to suck it up. I have no intention of spending more time than necessary with them.

Caroline and Josiah eventually leave, leaving me alone with my mates. When I can't handle their stares anymore or the awkward silence, I get up and walk upstairs.

I grab my pajamas and head for the shower, I don't care for their excuses. While showering, Tobias and Theo walk in. I'm currently finishing my hair. I turn my back to them when I hear the door open. "Let us explain Imogen," Theo speaks first.

"Save it. I don't trust you and how am I supposed to know it isn't more lies? Seems to be the only thing you know how to do."

I hear the door lock click and turn to see that Tobias has locked the bathroom door. I glare at him before turning around.

"You will listen." I roll my eyes at his tone.

"Let's hear it then, get it over with so I can leave." I'm annoyed, I'm not stepping one foot out of this shower. I know they want to touch me and if they do, I will turn to putty in their hands because of a stupid mate bond I have no control over.

"I never lied when I said I killed her. We caught her in bed with Alaric, he bolted when we found out. I grabbed her in anger when we realized she had played us all along. What I didn't know was that Theo had given her blood the night before and it was still her system. I thought I killed her, and Theo was too slow to react to stop me. Only after I snapped her neck and her body fell limp on the floor, did Theo realize what I had done. A few minutes later she woke up and started laughing before walking out. She knew we couldn't touch her now without the council's permission, that was her plan all along. She wanted us to kill her so she could be with him. Alaric couldn't change her; his parents would never allow him to be with a non-supernatural. So, he had us do it."

"Did you love her?" I ask.

"We thought we did. We refused to find another female until we saw you. I felt an instant pull to you. I ignored it, but Theo couldn't. We agreed not to act on it. We didn't want to be involved with another human. But the mate bond just got stronger, the pull to you got stronger, to the point I couldn't ignore it anymore." Tobias explains.

I shake my head. They only want me because some invisible bond makes them.

"That's not true, Imogen. We love you and not just because of the bond. Don't think that," Theo says with a growl.

I turn around to face them, my face devoid of emotion. I honestly don't care for their reasons anymore; you can only lie and treat someone like that for so long before they have had enough. Before they find the end of their rope and snap.

"Stay out of my head, Theo. I heard your excuse, it doesn't change anything. Now, unlock the door," I say, reaching out, I grab a towel and wrap it around myself. Theo tries to grab my hand, but I pull back. "Don't touch me, your excuses don't change anything, not anymore." My voice is level which even I'm impressed by the lack of emotion behind my words.

Theo doesn't listen though, still trying to reach for me even after I walk towards the door, where Tobias is leaning on the door frame.

"You can't ignore us forever, you know this, Imogen. You can't ignore a mate bond, we tried already; it will be no different for you," Tobias says, his face moving to mine as he blocks my exit. His breath fans my face and his lips are so close, it nearly makes me forget everything. His close proximity and the heat radiating off his body overwhelm me. I shake my head, trying to shake off the feeling. I hear him chuckle slightly knowing he is winning and that only angers me.

"Move, Tobias, now," I say, putting my hand on his chest, trying to get him away. I ignore the sparks that are moving up my arm, threatening to take over all my rational thoughts. He steps to the side, letting me pass. I grab my purse and clothes before walking towards the door.

"Where do you think you're going, Imogen?"

"Away from you, I'm sleeping in the guest room," I say, throwing the door open and walking out.

I quickly get changed before climbing in the bed. I'm exhausted but the bed feels cold and lonely without them and way too big. I'm so used to Tobias' warmth, that I didn't realize I would actually miss it, miss the feeling of our legs getting tangled and the weight of their arms draped over me. I wiggle around a lot, but I'm not giving in. That's what they want and after a few hours of rolling around trying to get comfortable, I finally manage to get some sleep.

I'm awoken after what feels like only a couple hours by the cold hands running down my arms, making me shiver, before I feel his cool lips on my cheek. I open my eyes to find Theo, staring down at me while sitting next to me on the bed. I roll over, trying to go back to sleep.

"You can't be mad at us forever, hun, so I don't know why you're even trying."

I ignore him and close my eyes.

"We have to go to work," he says. I can tell he is hoping I want to go with them.

"Then go," I say, not even trying to hide the anger I feel towards them. I hear him sigh and the bed moves as he gets up. A few minutes later, I hear the front door open, and the sound of Theo's car being backed out of the garage before speeding along the dirt road. Sitting up, I wander downstairs and turn the kettle on, needing my caffeine fix.

I have just finished making my coffee when I remember the test in my bag; my heart skips a beat. Quickly chugging the coffee, I run upstairs to retrieve my bag. I sit it on the island counter, reading over the instructions. Seems simple enough, I just have to pee on the stick and wait. When it comes time to do it, though, I suddenly feel nervous. I pick the box up and stare at it before putting it down again. It's just a test, Imogen, doesn't mean it will be positive; you're late because of stress. I keep telling myself even though I have this nagging feeling I'm lying to myself. Glaring at the box, I snatch it up, removing the stick from the wrapper I walk into the bathroom. I quickly pee then wash my hands, leaving the pregnancy test on a hand towel.

I walk out and finish my coffee. My heart is hammering in my chest during the three-minute wait. I keep looking at the clock and back towards the bathroom. Please be negative, please be negative. This will be a disaster if I'm pregnant, I only have two more days of living left.

When the time comes, I walk over and pick up the test and nearly faint. I feel bile rise up in my throat and run for the toilet before being violently sick. My hands become clammy and sweat runs down my neck. I can't stop the tears from coming as sobs rack my body. I don't know what to do, as I look down at the test window which has two lines confirming, I am indeed pregnant. And if the estimation is correct, I'm five weeks along.

I suddenly hear the front door open, Caroline's singsong voice coming to me. "Imogen?" She calls. I quickly grab everything, dumping it back in the box and throwing it in the trash just as she comes around the corner. I walk out of the bathroom.

"You okay dear? You look a little pale," she asks, looking at me. I nod, not trusting my voice.

"Tea?" I ask nervously. She nods and I see her eyes dart behind me. Before she looks up at me questionably. I try to close the door when she stops me.

"What's that?" She says, pointing to the sink. I'm positive, I threw everything out in my haste. She walks past me and picks up the pregnancy test that is resting on the counter. I was so busy trying to get rid of the box, I forgot about the test.

She picks it up and I hold my breath. "You're pregnant." She gasps, looking at me.

Her hands are slightly shaking as she examines the test. I don't know what to say. She has the proof she needed in her hand, I can't exactly deny it now.

Her next words shock me and make my blood run cold. "You can't tell them, Imogen." She says, her voice sounds sad as she grabs the trash can and starts walking out, dumping the test in. "I will get rid of this," she says and for a second, I think she means the baby.

"What do you mean?" I ask, suddenly feeling scared.

"They won't care that you're pregnant, Imogen. They won't risk losing you."

"You're not making sense, Caroline. I can't hide it from them," I tell her.

"Imogen, you have two days before they change you, this won't stop them," she says, coming to a stop and turning around to face me.

I let her words sink in. "They would still change me even if I'm pregnant with their child?" I ask.

She nods her head. I never wanted to get pregnant, but I also don't want to kill an innocent baby. "You need to run; we need to get you out of here. I have lost enough to this life, so have you. I won't lose a chance at having a grandchild," she says, her voice thick with emotion.

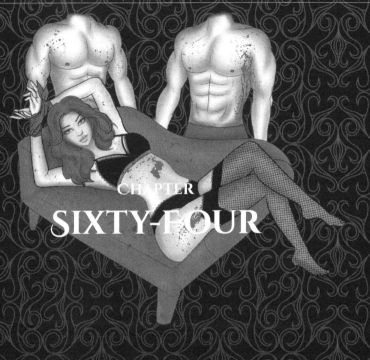

CHAPTER
SIXTY-FOUR

I look back at Caroline, fear consuming every cell in my body, paralyzing me as she gazes back with tears in her eyes. "They must never know, Imogen. Not until your baby is due. If they find out, they won't hesitate to change you."

"Don't they want kids, though? It would be one of their kids. I don't understand why they wouldn't be happy about this," my voice comes out just above a whisper. I'm confused. If they love me as they claim to, why would they hurt me in such a way?

Caroline seems to hesitate for a minute, unsure if she should answer.

"You're hiding something. What aren't you telling me, this is a good thing, I don't see how they would think it is bad."

"You have been given a deadline, Imogen. Three days. I may be able to push it out to four but that's delaying the inevitable, this is the only way." I have a feeling she isn't telling me something, I know it can't just be that. After spending so long trying to hide in the shadows, hoping for a human life, how could they turn down the thought of having a child?

"That's not it, you're hiding something. Either tell me the truth,

Caroline, or I will call them. I can't believe you would try to lie to me. I know we haven't known each other for long, but you know how I can't stand the lies and the secrets they keep. So please, just be honest with me," I tell her, feeling suddenly emotionally exhausted, everything would be easier if everyone would just speak the truth instead of this back-and-forth yoyo effect they are trying to cover up their lies. It is really starting to bug me that every supernatural creature I have met has outright lied to me, time and time again, then they scratch their heads and wonder why I have trust issues.

Caroline sighs. "I worry you may change your mind," she says, thoughtfully.

"If this is my only chance to have a child before my life ends believe me, I will take it," I tell her, truthfully.

She nods and sits down on the stool at the island counter. I sit across from her, waiting for her to answer.

"You're human, Imogen. We don't know which of my sons fathered this child."

I'm confused, what's that got to do with anything? We are all mates. I don't think they will care who the father is biologically. "Your point?" I ask, trying to figure out what she is trying to tell me. She looks away, not meeting my gaze before she sighs.

"If the baby is a werewolf, it will kill you, they won't take that chance," she says, her voice coming out shaky before she turns her eyes back to me.

"I don't understand? You said werewolf and human babies come out for the most part human, with only a few advanced abilities but not enough to distinguish between them."

"Yes, that is true. But no human has ever survived giving birth to a werewolf baby. They may not be able to shift or anything, but in the uterus the baby will literally tear itself out of you."

"How, when they can't shift? You said it yourself that werewolf babies born to human mothers can't shift and don't carry on the traits of a werewolf."

"Yes, because after the child is born and the child grows the DNA that makes them a half breed slowly loses its essence if you like, in the uterus they are half Lycan DNA. It's not until the child hits about four when they lose the majority of the Lycan DNA or venom, if you will."

"And if it's a vampire baby?" I ask, now hoping this child is actually Theo's and not Tobias's.

"Nothing, you will crave blood during your pregnancy, but the child would be born like any other human baby and they will be human. Sure, it would weaken you because the baby will be feeding off you more than a normal child but won't kill you." She states.

This whole procreation shit is giving me a headache. Everything is so confusing.

"They won't take that chance with you, Imogen. If they find out you're pregnant, they will change you without even considering what you want. I know my sons, they won't risk losing you."

I nod in agreement and Caroline suddenly stands up.

"I will come back tomorrow; I can't risk staying now. Your emotions have been heightened and they will be able to feel your distress. I actually wouldn't be surprised if they are on their way here already."

"But what do I do?" I ask, suddenly frightened.

"Don't give them any reason to expect anything we have discussed, I will bring a friend tomorrow and we will come up with a plan. No one must know, Imogen. I can't even trust Josiah with this secret. Be careful with what you think around them. Theo will snoop if he becomes concerned, just keep them distracted until tomorrow and then, you and I are leaving."

"How do I keep them from reading my mind?" I ask incredulously.

I suck at lying. How am I going to keep them distracted till tomorrow?

"You're their mate, Imogen. I don't think I need to tell you what will distract them." I know what she is talking about. My face heats up with embarrassment.

She chuckles lightly at my embarrassment before grabbing the trash bag and leaving. I hear the door click shut softly and I walk over to the window and watch her drive down the driveway towards the front gates.

It is only around twenty minutes later when the front door opens again. I'm sitting on the couch, watching Netflix, thankful that they finally have the internet fixed here.

Tobias and Theo place their keys and wallets in the bowl on top of the mantel piece. I ignore them coming in, trying to think of only the show, suddenly feeling nervous around them and the secret I'm trying to keep from them. Tobias walks over with Theo and both stare down at me.

"You're back early" I state when they don't say anything.

"Did my mother come see you today?" Theo asks, sniffing the air lightly.

I can tell he can smell her scent. I nod my answer to them. They both walk off when they realize that is the only answer they are going to get from me. I sigh, feeling relieved.

Theo comes over a few minutes later and sits next to me on the couch. He pulls me over to him and places me on his lap, wrapping his arms around my waist. I let him, not wanting to give him any reason to invade my thoughts.

"What did my mother want?" he asks, speaking into the crook of my neck.

"Nothing, she came over for coffee, she will be back tomorrow. She had to do something," I tell him. I can't risk lying. They will pick up straight away through the bond if I try. I just avoid telling them everything instead. Theo nods.

"I have a surprise for you," he says.

"If it's that you have another wife, I don't want to hear about it," I tell him, not evening trying to hide my anger from him.

He sighs and shakes his head. "No, something else," he says, standing up and placing me on my feet just as Tobias walks out. I watch Tobias grab a set of keys off the mantel and walk towards the door.

"Come on," he says, tugging my hand. I follow and walk outside. I notice two cars out the front. Theo's car and the exact same model of Tobias' I destroyed yesterday only in silver.

Tobias tosses me the keys and I catch them. "It's yours," he said.

I'm a little annoyed. I can't be bought, and I know they are hoping for a different reaction from me.

"You don't like it?" Theo asks, squeezing my fingers softly.

"No, it's nice." I hesitate. "But I can't be bought. This doesn't make up for anything, your actions do," I say before walking back inside.

I hear them walk in behind me, slightly disappointed. "We know, but you need another car. Your car is a death trap, and I'm sure you don't want a car that carries bodies in it." Tobias says behind me.

I shiver at the mention of that night. Tobias moves closer, touching my cheek when he sees I visibly tense at the memory. I lean into his touch, letting it relax me before pulling back.

"I'm hungry," I announce before walking off toward the kitchen. I rummage in the pantry and grab a bag of chips and sit on the stool.

Tobias walks in with Theo and I feel lips on my neck, sparks move over my skin. I clench my thighs together as the mate bond starts doing its thing and makes me aroused. I feel Theo chuckle slightly, feel his erection press into my back.

"Can you stop? It's so hard to concentrate on being mad when you do that, I'm not sleeping with you." I whine, annoyed that they think they can just touch me and get what they want.

"Who said you would be sleeping?" Theo whispers, his voice like velvet below my ear. I huff, annoyed.

Tobias chuckles slightly on the other side of the counter before Theo moves away, giving me back my space. He walks over and starts making coffee. I watch the pair of them before witnessing Tobias reach down and grab Theo's ass, squeezing it. I clench my thighs together before getting off my stool and walking out.

I can feel through the bond that their coffees are long forgotten. I try to ignore them as best I can, but I know the entire living room is starting to fill with the scent of my arousal and that they know what effect they are having on me. I watch them walk out and up the stairs. Tobias stops halfway up and leans over the bannister. "We are having a shower if you want to join us," he says. I roll my eyes, knowing exactly what they are trying to do.

CHAPTER
SIXTY-FIVE

I sit on the couch for what feels like forever, when it is probably only a few minutes. The ache between my legs becomes stronger, my core throbs in anticipation as I feel their emotions fishing over me through the bond.

Feeling their arousal makes my thighs slick with need. I close my eyes, hoping I can sleep the feelings off. They are invading my every thought, wondering what exactly they are doing in there. My imagination runs wild with ideas. My eyes squeeze shut tightly, making the feeling of my own arousal impossible to ignore. They are doing it deliberately, trying to make me beg them to be inside me.

Refusing to give them that satisfaction I slide my hand inside my shorts, my panties saturated as my fingers brush over the wet fabric. My fingertips rub my slit through my panties before moving higher and slipping beneath the thin fabric. I moan as my finger slips between my swollen lips to my clit, electricity shoots directly where my fingers brush as pleasure tightens the muscles in my stomach. Opening my legs wider, I slide a finger into my tight pussy, which is pulsating with desire. My walls instantly clamp down on my finger at the intrusion. I slide my finger out before adding another my back arching as I try to find that sweet spot. Lost in the feeling of my own fingers curling inside me, I don't hear them walk down the stairs until one of them clears their throat.

My eyes snap open to find them both staring down at me from the back of the couch, my hand jerks out of my pants as my face heats up at being caught.

I can tell they are both still naked. See the water dripping from Theo's hair as he leans over the couch and his hand moves over my exposed stomach from where my shirt rode up, his fingers slipping under the waistband of my shorts and cupping my pussy.

I moan at the touch as it sends sparks over my skin, making me push my hips up into his hand as I feel him run his finger through my wet lips before sliding them inside me. Tobias reaches down, grabbing my hand, making me look at him before he sucks on my wet fingers. He groans and his eyes darken. He lets my hand go and leans over kissing me, forcing his tongue in my mouth tasting every inch of it. I can taste my own arousal on his tongue as it brushes mine, making me moan against his lips.

Theo moves around the couch before ripping me toward where he takes a seat on the floor. He rips my pants off, literally tearing them down the seams. I feel the burn as the fabric burns my hips at the force he uses. Before I have a chance to complain about him destroying my favorite pants, my legs are thrown over his shoulders and his tongue brushes my slit, and I surrender to the feeling. His tongue moves between my folds before he sucks my clit in his mouth. I grab his hair, trying to jerk him away as I feel his tongue circle my clit so fast it's almost too much stimulation.

He shoves my thighs apart, holding them open as they slide over his arms. I shiver from his cold skin and mine. Tobias leans over the couch and grabs my breasts, squeezing them before rolling my nipples between his fingers. He leans over, kissing me, forcing my face up, to look up at him.

Theo suddenly moves before pulling me against him, my legs wrapping around his waist as he stands upright. His hands grip my ass so tight it's almost painful as he squeezes my ass in his strong grip while nipping at my neck.

I grab a handful of his hair, pulling his head back and kissing him, my tongue brushing his bottom lip before sucking it into my mouth. I bite down on it and Theo slaps my ass hard. I hear him chuckle before I'm suddenly thrown on the bed. I bounce on the bed, both of them standing at the end, watching me.

Sitting up on my elbows, I open my legs invitingly. They both smile seductively before Tobias's eyes turn to pitch black orbs. My heart skips a beat. He looks dangerous, but it only turns me on more as he crawls up my body between my legs. I feel his erection on the inside of my thigh, and I arch my hips, wanting nothing more than for him to bury his cock deep inside me.

"You like it when my beast wants to play," he asks, his voice velvety smooth next to my ear.

He suddenly lifts my legs, putting them over his shoulders before ramming into me. He doesn't give me time to adjust to his hard length before he starts slamming into me. I try to catch my breath as I feel every muscle in my body tighten at his brutal fucking, my fluids coating his cock as it slides in and out me. When I'm sure I'm about to explode either in pain or pleasure, I'm not sure it is a mixture of both, he stops and rolls on to his back, pulling me on top of him, so I am straddling him. His fingers dig into my hips painfully as he moves them to his own rhythm. The pain of him moving my hips and his cock hitting my cervix is almost too much.

I feel the bed dip as Theo moves beside Tobias. I moan as I watch him bend down and kiss Tobias hungrily, making Tobias let go of my hips, giving me a chance to readjust my position. His hand goes to Theo's hair, holding him close. I feel his dick twitch inside me. I move my hips slowly, watching them, feeling relieved that Tobias is distracted enough to let me set the pace, instead of his large cock brutally destroying my insides. When Theo pulls away, I see Tobias eyes are back to their normal blue, showing he has full control back now. Theo kneels on the bed before kissing me. His hand goes between my legs as he rubs my clit in circular motions. I feel my walls tighten around Tobias cock as his hands go back to my hips. I flinch as his fingers dig into me, where I know they bruised my hips.

I moan against his lips and Tobias speeds up his movements. Theo climbs off the bed before walking behind me and climbing back on the bed. I lean into him, liking the coolness of his skin. His hand reaches around, squeezing my throat in a strong grip. Opening my eyes, I see Tobias watching me as I lean back into Theo. His grip on my throat is getting tighter and I feel my airways becoming restricted.

Tobias thumb brushes over my clit, playing with it, making me move faster, trying to build up the friction, when suddenly, Theo thrusts inside me. His grip getting so strong on my neck, I can feel my face changing color. They both start moving, thrusting into me, I start to feel dizzy as my orgasm rushes over me and I feel my body start to go limp. Theo lets go, pulling me against him as I catch my breath. I feel Theo's fangs break my skin as he sinks his teeth into me, making me gasp at the sudden pain before I moan, which sounds strangled from being so breathless.

I can still feel the lingering feeling of his hands around my throat. When I finally feel them both still and Theo pulls his face from neck, I slump forward onto Tobias, my hair sticking to my face, as I try to suck in much needed air.

I feel Theo pull himself from my body and Tobias rolls until he is resting between my legs, watching me. My eyes feel heavy, and my head is spinning with the lack of air and sudden blood loss. Tobias looks concerned before looking in Theo's direction. Theo walks over, looking down at me.

"Her blood tastes different, I thought it did last time too. Thought I was just imagining it. But it's definitely different, almost..." He tries to think of the word he is looking for.

"Almost, what?" Tobias asks. Theo shakes his head, he looks unsure if what he is going to say is correct.

"Almost like yours," he says, making me become fully alert to what he is saying. I taste different because I'm pregnant. I shiver slightly, hoping they don't dig too deeply into why I would taste different.

CHAPTER
SIXTY SIX

They both seem to ponder for a few seconds, both their eyes train on me while I think of anything but what the real reason is. After a few minutes of them staring, I grow uncomfortable and impatient. Jumping off the bed, I head for the shower. A few tense minutes later, they both come in and start showering alongside me. I quickly wash before hopping out and getting dressed. I race downstairs and start making a sandwich. I'm starving after that work out session and the blood loss. I'm thankful when I feel through the bond that their thoughts have turned elsewhere.

When it is time for bed, I'm exhausted and fall asleep as soon as my head hits the pillow. Tobias and Theo beside me. I'm glad when the darkness of sleep consumes me, knowing the only thoughts they can pick up on are those of my dreams as I sleep peacefully.

When I wake up, I'm shocked to find that it is still dark outside. I roll and Theo is reading beside me; I stretch and sit upright before leaning on him. Tobias is still fast asleep.

"Try and go back to sleep, we still have a few hours before work," Theo says, putting his book down and pulling me against his chest.

I'm wide awake which is a little unusual. I check the time on my phone beside Theo. It is four am.

"I think I will stay home today," I whisper, trying not to wake up Tobias. Theo pulls his face away; I can tell he wants to know why. Every other time I would normally pitch a fit about not being able to go.

"My mother can meet you at work, is this because you're nervous about tomorrow?" He asks.

I shake my head. "No, I just don't feel like going," I mumble between yawning.

"Want one of us to stay with you?" He asks.

My heart skips a beat, knowing that it isn't an option. "No, I will be fine," I tell him, not wanting him to read too much into my decision to stay home. I feel him nod before pulling me closer and inhaling my scent.

"Well, if you don't want to sleep, what do you want to do?" He asks. I look up at him and he has a silly smirk on his face as he wiggles his eyebrows. I chuckle softly before climbing on top of him, my hips straddling his waist as I lean down and brush his lips softly with mine.

Theo's hand grabs my hair as he pulls me closer and deepens the kiss. I can already feel his erection underneath me. Like seriously, do they both just walk around with erections ready to go? I snicker at the thought and I feel him smile against my lips, obviously invading my thoughts to see what I think is so funny.

He bucks his hips into me, grinding his erection against me. I reach between us and grab him through his boxer shorts before he wastes no time getting rid of them. My hand wraps around the base of his shaft which is smooth and rock hard.

I feel his fingers tugging the waistband of my pants down before fisting them in his hand and I know he is about to rip them off. I quickly stand, not wanting him to destroy them.

"What?" He asks when I stand up before sliding my pants down my legs.

"I don't want you to ruin them, they're comfy. Besides, I'm starting to run out of clothes because you keep tearing them," I say before climbing back on top of him.

"You look better without them." He chuckles softly before running his hands up my sides and pulling my shirt off over my head.

He sits up slightly with his back against the headboard, his lips moving to my neck then, to my breasts, biting down on my nipple. I gasp at the slight sting before I feel his tongue run along his bite, soothing it. I position him at my entrance before sitting down, letting him fill me completely. His head leans back, hitting the headboard with a thud as he groans at the feel of my walls squeezing him tightly. I giggle as he rubs his head. I move my hips, and he places his hands on my sides. Finding my own rhythm, I move slowly, still sore from last night.

My walls clench him in a vice-like grip when I feel my orgasm building, his cock slides in and out me smoothly, slick with my desire. When I feel my orgasm build and am about to tip over, I reach back, grabbing his balls and tugging on them. I feel Theo's grip on my hips tighten before he moves my hips faster, sending me over the edge, my orgasm washing over me as my pussy pulsates around him, making him find his own release. I press my head to his, both of us panting, having come down from our high, I feel the bed shift slightly. Theo's lips tug up as he realizes Tobias is awake.

"As entertaining as that is to watch, it's my turn," I hear Tobias say, his voice thick with desire before I feel his hands grip my waist and rip me off the top of Theo. I giggle as I feel my body being maneuvered before I suddenly find myself underneath Tobias. His lips go instantly to my neck and his cock slides into me, making him groan against me as I slide my hands through his hair, tugging him towards me and bringing my lips to his.

. . .

A few hours later, Tobias and Theo leave for work. I'm relieved because now I can prepare for when Caroline comes over today, bringing her mysterious friend. After packing a suitcase with clothes, I decide to go out to where my stuff is stored in the shed, hoping to retrieve a few pieces that I hold dear from my mother, seeing as I don't know how long I will be gone for.

I'm rummaging through boxes when I hear a car pull up. Thinking it is Caroline, I continue to dig through the box, looking for my mother's bracelet. I used to wear it when I was a kid. My mother actually did tell me once that it is a gift from my father that he had given her.

Finding the bracelet, I quickly put it in my pocket and walk towards the door when she steps in front of me. Shocked, I take a step back. What the hell is she doing here?

She is dressed very casually today, in her jeans and black tank top she has ankle boots on, and her long hair pulled into a high ponytail. I freeze as she steps into the small office space in the back of the shed. The room is already cramped with my mother's furniture everywhere. I take another step back until my ass comes in contact with my grandfather's table. I watch as she looks around before flicking her blonde hair over shoulder, turning her nose up in disgust.

"What are you doing here, Bianca?" I ask through gritted teeth. Isn't it bad enough she condemned me? Now, she is here to rub it in my face.

Her eyes snap to me. "I just wanted to make sure you hadn't decided to run," she says, her lips turning up in a cruel smile. I watch as she walks around the room, looking at all my belongings. I refuse to take my eyes off her, this woman is a snake, and I will never take the chance by turning my back on her.

"You need to leave, now," I say. I'm shocked at the amount of anger behind my words.

She looks up at me, holding a photo album in her hands. "I see you have your mother's temper," she says while flicking to the next page, my blood running cold before I turn confused. What did she mean? I watch as she turns the pages of the album, inspecting every picture closely before dropping the album on the table with a loud thud.

"Get out, you have no right being here, Bianca." I say, standing firmly.

"No right?" She says, raising an eyebrow. "This was my home first before you took it from me, exactly like your mother you are. Always taking things that don't belong to you. Let's hope you don't meet the same end she did." Her eyes sparkle with mischief, the venom of the words rolling off her tongue, daring me to ask what she is talking about.

"I didn't steal them, you cheated on them. You did this to yourself. Now get out." I say, grabbing the closest thing to me, which turns out to be a lamp. Great move, Imogen. You can burn her retinas with its light. I know it's silly, but still clutch the lamp tightly. I hear her chuckle before walking toward me, stopping just a few centimeters away.

"Did they ever find who ran your mother off the road?" She asks, a triumphant grin on her face.

I pushed her back. "What are you playing at, Bianca?"

"Who says I'm playing? I just wanted to give you a little insight, the closure you never had." She pouts.

"I knew your mother. In fact, I watched her for months while she worked. She never once recognized me; she would tell me all about her wonderful daughter. At first, I was curious about her, then it turned to hate. Your mother is the reason mine is dead. So, I thought it is only fitting that I let you know the same pain."

"What are you talking about? I don't even know you." I tell her.

"Of course, you don't, how could you? But when you started working under Tobias and Theo, I could tell straight away you were their mate, I couldn't take it. It infuriated me, watching them, watching you. And you were completely unaware of the effect you had on them. Your family, once again, taking from mine. What's the saying? Like mother, like daughter. So, I decided I would take something from you."

I don't like where this conversation is going, my brain tries to come up with anything to make sense of her words.

"So, when I saw your mother leaving work that day, I followed her. She was singing happily to the horrendous music coming from her stereo when I plowed into her. You should have seen the look on her face when I got out of the car and walked over to her. She honestly thought I was her friend. I went to finish the job, killing her there on the spot when people started coming out while I tried to squeeze the life out of her. So, instead, I broke her neck, but even that didn't kill her. Your mother was a tough bitch, I will give her that."

I take a step forward clutching the lamp.

"I wouldn't do that if I were you, you don't stand a chance. But wow that feels so good to get off my chest, like a weight lifted. Do you feel better, Imogen, knowing the truth? Did it give you closure?" She says, stepping impossibly close.

I want to kill the bitch, want to rip those hairs off her head and skin her alive. Only I know she has the power here and she won. The triumphant smile that breaks out on her face, as my tears start to brim makes me want to smash her face till there is nothing left of it.

"I can't wait to see the heart ache on their faces when they come home and realize their mate killed herself, so weak and pathetic like her mother," she says before she grabs me, her hands going around my throat and squeezing as she lifts my feet off the floor, my legs kicking at air, as I struggle to breathe.

I claw at her hands, trying to loosen her grip. My head is becoming light from the lack of air. Giving up on clawing at her hands, I instead jam my thumbs in her eyes, digging in deep, I can feel the slimy feeling of her eyeballs as my thumbs glide into the sockets. She releases me, dropping me on the floor and clutching at her eyes and screaming.

"You fucking bitch!" She screams, making me look up at her.

She moves toward me, her foot swings back as she goes to kick me where I lay on the floor, I even brace myself for it when her strangled scream breaks out in the room, everything happens so fast I'm sure I imagine it. One second, she is aiming her kick, the next she is thrown backwards. I sag in relief when I realize it is Caroline. She grabs Bianca by her hair, ripping her upright before dragging her towards the door.

"You can't kill me," Bianca laughs.

"No, I can't but that doesn't mean I can't teach you some respect," she says, before throwing her through the door and into the shed. I can hear Bianca screaming and begging as Caroline does god knows what to the woman. I stand up just as she walks into the room again, dusting off her clothes.

"Are you okay, Imogen?" She asks. I nod but I'm not alright, that bitch killed my mother, took the only person I had left away from me, for reasons I don't know. How could anyone be alright after learning that information? I feel tears start to brim before flowing over.

Caroline's arms wrap around me, pulling me close. "There, there, child she can't hurt you anymore. I'm here now," she whispers soothingly.

"She killed my mom," I whisper between sobbing.

I feel Caroline freeze before pushing me at arm's length. "What did you just say?"

"She killed my mom, said it is to pay back for my mother killing hers." Caroline looks just as confused as I feel about Bianca's reasoning. My mother would never take anything from anyone, she was a good woman and a great mom to me.

Caroline pulls me back towards her, hugging me tighter. "We need to leave; we can figure out everything else later. But for now, we have to go before they come home," she tells me. I nod and let her drag me to the car. When I get in the silver Audi, I notice a woman sitting in the passenger seat. Caroline ducks inside to grab my suitcase.

The woman has an eerie feeling about her, she isn't that old, she looks around my age but there is something off about her. Her energy is off, I can't explain it. She doesn't scare me, but it is like I can literally feel the power rolling off of her. She turns in her seat, flicking her auburn hair over her shoulder and peers back at me. Her pale blue eyes flick to mine before she smiles softly.

"You must be Imogen, I am Claire," she says, reaching over the seat to shake my hand.

CHAPTER
SIXTY-SEVEN

A s soon as I place my hand in hers, she gasps, gripping my
hand tightly, her eyes turn white, she has this faraway
look. Like she is seeing through me at something I can't
see. I rip my hand from her grasp, alarmed, watching as her eyes
seem to come back into focus and the color comes back. Claire smiles
softly, but she can't hide the worry in them. The driver's side door
opens, and Caroline hops in the car, looking between us, as Claire
just remains calmly staring like she is trying to figure something out.

"What happened?" Asks Caroline, looking as confused as I feel.

"I don't know?" I answer honestly. Claire remains silent but
turns around in her seat, looking out toward the front.

"We need to leave, now," she says, looking toward Caroline.

Caroline hastily jams the keys in the ignition before taking off at
a fast speed down the dirt driveway, making dust and dirt spray
everywhere. Claire leans forward, grabbing something from between
her legs, it is a black leather backpack. Sitting in the middle seat, I
watch as she rummages around in her bag before pulling out a necklace. The necklace seems familiar; it takes a few seconds for me to

figure out where I have seen the intricate design before. Sitting forward slightly, I pull the bracelet from my pocket.

It has the same design as the necklace Claire holds in her hand, the same silver vines and leaves wrap around the bracelet to the pendant which has a lotus hanging from it, that is caged in by the vines.

"What's that?" I ask her.

"It is a witch's talisman," she says, her eyes darting to the bracelet I hold in my hand to show her.

"Turn back around," Claire says when she sees the bracelet hanging from my fingertips.

"What, you just said we had to go?" Caroline says, I can hear the panic in her voice as she looks at Claire. Caroline spins the car around anyway, heading back toward the house.

"What's going on?" I ask, suddenly worried. Claire grabs the bracelet before dropping it and hissing in pain.

"That's why I couldn't read you, why it looked like you had no future. Where did you get that bracelet?" She asks as I grab the bracelet from where she dropped it on the carpet between the seats.

"It is my mother's, I found it in the shed." I tell her.

Claire shakes her head. "The fact that you can hold it proves that it is not your mother's. A witch can't hold another witch's talisman."

"What?" Nothing makes sense. What she said never makes sense, I'm not a witch. Caroline pulls up out the front of the shed and I jump out when Claire does, followed by Caroline.

"Why are we back here?" Caroline asks, looking around nervously.

"If she has a talisman, I'm willing to bet her family's grimoires will be here as well."

"Grimoires? Like spell books?" I ask.

Claire nods her head, pushing the roller door up and walking inside.

"Look, I have been through that shed so many times, if my mother or father were a witch, I would have found something resembling spell books by now." Claire pays me no attention and keeps walking towards the office in the back of the shed.

When she opens the door, she gasps. "I knew it!" She states.

I looked around, trying to find what it is she thinks she found. Claire walks over to my grandfather's table. "Honestly Caroline, I'm surprised you didn't notice this when you were in here," she says, running her hand along the top of the table.

Caroline looks at the table and I mean really looks at it. Caroline walks over to the table, running her fingers over the design carved in the top, which is five different circles. One on each side before a bigger one is in the middle. The same vine-like structure joins the four outer circles before vines from each connect the middle circle to the other four.

"It's an earth pentagram," Caroline whispers before knocking on the wood.

The wood makes a hollow sound, like it has a compartment below the tabletop. I have never paid attention to the table before, believing the story my mother told me that my grandfather made it.

Claire runs her fingers along the table's edge before she stops, obviously finding whatever it is she is looking for. She bends down to look at what her fingers landed on underneath the table. "Imogen, bring your bracelet here," I walk over to her and hand it to her. She shakes her head. "I'm not touching that thing, burned my fingers damn near off. Place the pendant in the lock," she instructs.

My eyebrows furrow before I bend down to see this so-called imaginary lock only to be surprised when I actually find there is indeed a metal lock below the tabletop. I waste no time in placing the pendant inside, fitting it perfectly. The lotus shaped pendant is actually a key of sorts. The wood groans and sounds like it is cracking before we hear something click. I stand up, thinking for sure the table is going to be split down the middle by the sounds the wood makes. Only it isn't but I can tell the table is different. The five circles glow fluorescent green.

It is like nothing I have ever seen before, Claire pushes on the lid and it springs open, revealing a long compartment inside. There are dried herbs and some candles, along with four books, covered in fabric cloth. I reach in and grab one, pulling the cloth off. Opening it, I find the book has no writing in it, just blank pages.

I turn to Claire to show her. "That must be yours then. The others will be family members of different generations, grimoires. Grab them, we need to leave now." I quickly grab the other three books. For the first time, I'm getting a glimpse of my mother's secret life I never knew about. Caroline quickly shuts the lid on the table, I hear the wood groan before the circles go back to their normal wood grain look.

"How?" I ask, confused.

Claire stops and glances at the table, "Someone spelled it," she says before running out.

I have to jog to keep up with them as they run towards the car. As soon as I shut the door Caroline takes off again, making me fall back into the seat and nearly drop the books. I quickly place them in the footwell and chuck my seat belt on.

"How long?" Caroline asks Claire.

"We have enough time," she answers.

Claire is absent-mindedly playing with her necklace. After a few minutes, she reaches back inside her black bag and pulls two silver bangles. "Put this on," she says, handing one to Caroline and one to me.

I grab the bracelet, not knowing what it is for, but I feel like I can trust Claire. "What's it for?" I ask, curious why we are all getting blinged up.

"To stop your mates from being able to track you through your bond. They won't be able to feel you. You can still feel them, but to Tobias, Theo, and Josiah, they won't feel the pull towards you and be able to find you."

I look at Caroline. I didn't know Vampires have mates; I'm a little tripped out that Josiah and Caroline are mates when they were both human to begin with. Caroline chuckles slightly, noticing my gaze through the revision mirror.

"Vampires have bonds too, not like werewolf bonds, not like what you have with Tobias and Theo. They aren't as strong but once we pick a life partner and spend a long time with them, we pick up on each other, influence each other until eventually a bond is formed." She explains. I nod, still a little confused.

"What you have with Tobias and Theo is a little different. You are all pieces of whole if that makes sense, like puzzle pieces. Without the other ones, the pieces in the picture can't be made; together and joined you become a whole. Does that make sense?" Claire says, trying to explain.

"Yes, but where are we going?"

"I have a cabin out in the woods a few days' drive from here," Claire answers.

"We are going to Claire's until we come up with a plan. At least now, we may be able to find out something about your family, and what you are. The blood tests came back yesterday, and all we found is that your father is a vampire."

"My father is a vampire?" I ask, stunned.

"Yes, we found trace amounts of vampire DNA in your system. It is very weak," Caroline explains.

"Well, we know one other thing, the mother's side were witches," Claire chimes in.

I don't know how to feel about that. If they were witches, how did they hide it from me and why am I not a witch? As if reading my thoughts, Claire answers. "You don't believe me?" She asks before looking at my bracelet around my wrist. "That talisman holds your power or magic, as we like to call it. When we get to my place and are safe, we can try to unlock that talisman and let the magic find its way home."

"But if I'm a witch, why do we have to run?" I ask, confused.

"Because you may not be forced to change from the council, but you are still technically human. Tobias won't allow you to die just to have a child, Imogen. They will still change you, regardless." Caroline explains.

Her words remind me of what Theo said last night. "Theo said my blood changed, that it reminded him of Tobias's." I tell her.

Caroline glances at me in the mirror. "That means you're having a were-baby," Caroline says, confirming my assumptions.

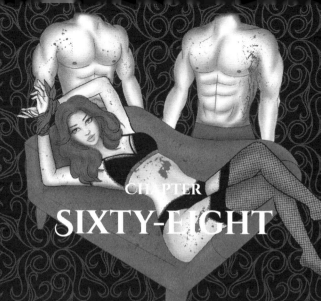

CHAPTER
SIXTY-EIGHT

Theo

The moment she stepped into our building looking for a job, I could smell her innocence. Not in the sense of her virginity, no that was gone long before we got to her. She is experienced in that area and very open-minded. But a purity that is near impossible to explain. It isn't just the way she looks; it's more a sense. Everything about her is pure, her thoughts are pure and no malice, despite her pain, her intentions, the way she carries herself.

She has this aura around her, following her, leaving pieces of herself everywhere she goes. Her heart truly has no limits for ever giving, not asking for anything in return. Imogen is the sort of person who will give until she has nothing left, give herself over completely if she thinks it is in another's best interest. She trusts blindly, yet when betrayed, fights wildly, almost irrationally in her anger, only to continue to forgive and let others take from her even when it is killing her slowly piece by piece.

But I doubt the girl has ever held a grudge in her life longer than five seconds. It isn't in her nature, she can forgive and forget like it is a flick of a switch, always choosing to give another chance, no matter how much we wrong her. I do fear that will be what gets her killed, though.

I know we have taken from her, taken her choice, taken that innocence from her. But what we found after taking everything from her is everything she is capable of. The girl has flair and fire deep within her that she keeps hidden away, never trusting of her own emotions, never letting them show, even when we know she is breaking. She has the ultimate control within herself and what she feels, yet in her thoughts she feels out of control. Sure, we have seen her anger, but with it comes her forgiveness. It is like she isn't satisfied unless she has nothing left. Like she is more comfortable, having nothing; like she thinks she is undeserving.

When I leave that morning, leaving Imogen, something pulls at me. This overwhelming sense of longing, even though she is right in front of me. Walking out of the house, I feel like I'm losing everything I love about her, yet I know by the look in her eyes that she has found an additional reason for life. Her eyes hold hope, even in impending doom.

She no longer fears her death, and I wonder why she suddenly has the light back in her eyes. I almost wonder who else she has to fight for. Same as last night when she woke, I had this immense feeling she was saying goodbye, the way she touched me, the way she said my name was almost like she was afraid it would be the last time she would speak it.

Getting in the car and driving to work with Tobias, I know he feels the shift too, something has changed. I just can't put my finger on it, something deep is nagging, trying to pull me back to her. The pull she has over us has always been there, yet right now, we truly have to fight against her pull just to stop ourselves from turning back and going home again. Neither of us utters a word, both trapped in our own heads. When we pull up to work, we both stand silently, waiting for the elevator, both watching the numbers go down.

"You feel it, right?" Tobias asks, glancing in my direction before looking at the stainless-steel doors, I nod my head. "Something has changed, I can feel it in every part of me. What if we broke her?" He asks.

Worry laces his words; I have never seen Tobias like this, he is always so concealed in the way he feels. Even after centuries being by each other's side he has always kept those walls up, never letting slip how he truly feels, kept himself guarded, not giving anyone the chance to hurt him, not even me.

Yet, Imogen has softened him. It used to bother me, jealousy can be a cruel thing sometimes. We have known her for a year, yet her impact on him had him opening up, letting both Imogen and myself in.

I haven't had that effect on him, and we have been together for centuries. Yet, she broke down that wall the moment he marked her. Tobias has always been the dominant one, the one that needs control and I let him have it, but with her came a sort of possessiveness that both of us weren't prepared for.

I love Tobias, yet if I have to choose, I will choose her and know Tobias would choose the same. We both share the same desires for her that we have for each other, yet she is different and neither of us could live without her. She is light in our darkness. I worry the darkest parts of us are tainting her and will be her undoing. We have already condemned her, took her idea of life away from her selfishly, all because we can't live without her.

"We haven't broken her. I don't know, I could even taste it in her blood. Something is different like something is coming alive in her. Then, there is also something else..."

"Something else?" Tobias asks, pressing the button to our floor.

"She tasted like a werewolf. I could literally taste you in her blood." Tobias glances at me and I can feel his head racing, trying to think of why until I suddenly feel a light click on inside him. "No, can't be. I saw that she was on the pill. I noticed them in her bag." I answer his thoughts.

"I haven't seen her take them though, have you?" I try to think, yet I come to the same conclusion: the only pills I have seen her take are pain meds.

"She can't be, can she?" I ask.

"Call the council and get her blood test results. Surely, they looked for everything," Tobias says. The door rings open, and my eyes instantly dart to her desk even though I know I won't find her there. Walking to my office, I pull my phone from my pocket, deciding to call Tarina. If anyone has seen her blood test result, it is her, and I know she will answer with honesty. The phone rings for a few minutes and I tap my foot impatiently, sighing when I hear her chirpy voice.

"Little unexpected, Theo. What are you calling me for? I know it isn't for a friendly chat," she asks, not even hiding her shock. Besides going to the council, I never speak to her. Yet, I know I can trust her.

"You know me too well, I'm actually calling about Imogen's blood results."

"Oh, your mother picked those up yesterday for you, I can check her file though."

"Yes, please, Tarina." I can hear her typing away on her computer, before I hear her make a weird noise and rapidly typing again. I can hear her fingers moving fast over the keyboard repeatedly.

"Her file has been deleted, completely wiped," she murmurs. "Give me a second, Theo, let me check the other computer." I wait, but the same result. "It's gone, Theo. I think someone has tampered with her files and wiped them clean. Her name doesn't even appear in the database at all." My heart starts hammering when Tobias walks in the room. I hang up the phone, not even saying goodbye.

"What?" Tobias asks, alarmed.

"She said mom took her physical file, yet when she checked her digital file it's gone as well."

"What would your mother want with it?" Tobias asks, his voice not even hiding his anger.

"Call her now," he hisses at me as his eyes change to that of his wolf. I dial her number, and it goes straight to voicemail. Then, suddenly, fear comes through the bond and it isn't either of us. We have nothing to fear yet, the feeling vanishes as quickly as it appears.

"I know you felt that," I state, looking at Tobias.

He nods. "Yes, but maybe, she startled herself? She feels calm again. Or maybe your mother is with her?" Tobias guesses, making me relax slightly.

The morning passes by quickly, I try to call my mother a few times, but I always get the voicemail. Yet, I know if she is with Imogen, she will have no service. So, I let it pass and know I will be able to ask Imogen for her results once we get home. My mother would have told her, yet nothing comes from the bond and after an hour of feeling nothing coming from Imogen, worry sets in. I pull on my teether to our bond, pulling on the link that joins us, but when I feel nothing, I walk into Tobias's office.

"What, Theo?" He asks as I step in the room. It still pisses him off that my mother took her files. I'm almost nervous to ask him. Sensing my nervousness, he looks up, his eyes softening slightly. "I'm sorry, I'm just stressed," he says, running his hands through his hair. I watch him; God, I love this man no matter how infuriating he can be.

"I can help with the stress," I say, my eyes darkening as my dick twitches in my pants.

"Tempting, but first, what's wrong?" I completely forgot the reason I originally came in for, suddenly feeling guilty for distracting myself.

"Can you feel her through the link?" I watch his eyes glaze over, searching for her. The pull we always fight so hard against.

He stands up abruptly, knocking over his chair, his beast enraged, flinging the table into the wall. I step back. I know he won't hurt me, but I know his beast doesn't enjoy coming up empty. The fact he has come forward at all is proof enough at what Tobias found. His entire being shakes with anger, yet there's also panic.

The ringing of the phone that lays on the floor pulls him to his senses, distracting that primal side of him long enough for Tobias to regain control of his emotions. He walks over, trying to pick up the phone, his claws impeding it, as they slash through the carpet. I quickly walk over, picking it up. "Hello?"

My father's worried voice comes through the phone. "Have you spoken to your mother today?" That's when I know something is definitely wrong. Something that includes not only my mother, but our mate. This is no coincidence.

"You there, son? Did you hear me? I can't feel your mother, like she just vanished, leaving no trace, no pull to her." My father is almost frantic.

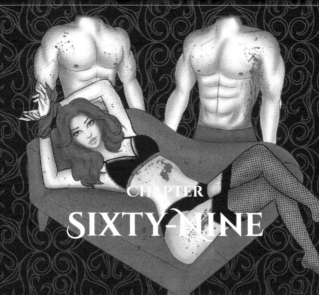

CHAPTER
SIXTY-NINE

Tobias

Three months, three long months without her, without touching her milky skin, without smelling her intoxicating scent, three months of nothing but anger and darkness.

Three months of sleeping in shitty motels while we travel around looking for her, only to come up empty. No word from her, not even to tell us if she is okay. Nothing but deafening silence through the bond. So silent it is chilling, trying to pull anything from it.

Is this some sick punishment from her? Can she not feel us either? Feel our desperation and longing for her?

My father went in the opposite direction to us, searching for his mate just like us. The despair I know he feels must be nearly killing him.

We aren't as hopeless yet, still having Theo by my side is enough to keep my beast and darkest thoughts at bay. This won't last forever though, not without her. The nightmares haunting my sleep put me more on edge, because I have this feeling they aren't mine.

Yet, Theo doesn't sleep, and we feel nothing through the bond to know if they are Imogen's, or just my tormented mind is making me suffer more. When I sleep, Theo still prowls the night, searching for her. We don't even know if we are going in the right direction, not that there are many directions left to run in.

Until we have her back, I will never stop searching. The only thing we have figured out is that she is carrying our child, well mine, but the biology doesn't matter. This child belongs to all of us, just like she belongs to both Theo and me.

I understand why she ran. I never would have allowed her to go through with it. There is only one way this ends for her. I wouldn't have cared if she hated me for it, at least she would have hated me and still been alive.

Now, nothing but fear plagues me. Were-babies don't need as long as human babies to be created and born. So, it's only a matter of time before this child will rip its way through her, killing her in the process.

I just hope my mother had some back-up plan before she took off with our mate. My mother has never kept it hidden how she wishes for a proper family, one with children. I know how she longs for grandchildren, yet with me and Theo it would never be a possibility.

We thought she accepted that, then this happens and now, we have to race against time to find her. Yet, my father is racing to save his mate. He knows if something happens to Imogen, I won't hesitate, even if it kills Theo, I will kill her for letting her die.

Mother must know this, and that's why she must have gone with her. I just pray she isn't too late in changing her. I know I'm bringing my mate home, either dead or alive, I will find her and then, I will kill those that helped her with her suicide.

We have just pulled up at yet another crappy motel in the middle of nowhere. I look at the rundown building and its neon sign. Theo is out of the car already, walking to the small office and checking in. I open my door, letting the cool crisp air run over my heated skin, running my hands through my hair that is damp with sweat from yet another nightmare while I slept and Theo drove.

Theo comes back out, holding a key on a chain. I look up at him as he tosses it to me. We decided this time to bring the car. It is becoming too difficult for me to keep running, my beast is becoming stronger while I grow weaker. I never even put up a fight anymore, trying to control emotions, I let that primal side take over at the slightest emotion.

I know it will be something I will have to reign in when we get her back. I have spent nearly the entire three months in my wolf form. Theo said enough when I nearly killed some locals in the town a few days ago.

Like he's the one to talk; I notice the moment he stepped out of the office with the key in his hand that he has blood on the collar of his shirt. Even though he tries to hide it from me, I know hunger is slowly taking over him.

"I hope you didn't kill this one," I mutter before standing and following Theo inside the shitty motel room. I flick on the light and instantly regret turning it on. The outdated furniture and its floral bedsheets are crawling with bugs, more specifically flies.

"Did something fucking die in here?" I ask as the smell makes me crinkle my nose in disgust.

"This is the only motel or hotel in this town, you're going to have to manage" Theo snaps.

"I prefer to sleep in the car or outside," I whine.

Theo starts ripping the linen off the bed, ignoring my comment. Dust flies everywhere, I can see the little dust particles floating in the air, making me swat at them, not wanting them to land on me. God knows how many dead skin cells are now flying through the air. I walk outside, not being able to handle the uncleanliness. Do they never clean around here? Theo emerges a few minutes later and walks towards the office with the filthy linen before walking to the trunk and pulling out brand new linen and blankets from the trunk.

"When did you have time to get those?" I ask. I can't even remember the last time I stepped into an actual store, only ever going into gas stations. We never have time.

"You forget I don't need sleep. I have plenty of time," he says, kissing the edge of my mouth on his way past. I feel my cock twitch painfully in my pants at the innocent gesture, something I haven't felt since she left, or maybe I'm just denying that part of me.

Arousal hits me as I step into the room and watch him make the bed. The smell is gone, now the old blankets are out, and the only smell is Theo's scent. Feeling my eyes on him, he looks up. His red eyes peer back at me, I miss his green eyes. It has been a while since I saw them. The longer we go without her, the more our darkest parts take over, threatening to undo the control we spent years building, both too exhausted to fight our true selves, giving ourselves over completely to the side we have tried to conceal.

"Sleep, Tobias. I will start searching the forest for any cabins and will keep heading north, pull on the link when you're awake. I will come back," he says, chuckling the comforter on the bed.

I watch him remove his shirt, changing it for a clean one as he walks towards me to leave and keep searching, doing the buttons up on his way towards me. When he brushes past me, I don't even realize what I have done till he stops looking at me. My hand is tightly wrapped around his wrist, preventing him from leaving.

"Don't start something you have no intention of finishing, Tobias." He growls.

We have been so consumed with finding her that I often forget he still needs me, and right now, I need him. Grabbing the front of his shirt, I pull him towards me, my lips hungrily devouring his as I pull him closer. His lips freeze in place until he feels through the bond, searching before realizing I'm not letting him leave. My cock is painfully pressing against my jeans while his teeth bite down on my lip, making me growl as I shove him towards the bed, using my foot to close the door behind me.

I can tell he is hungry for more than just my blood. When I move closer, he starts tugging on my belt, removing my pants as I step out of them, my cock springing free, only for him to grab it. His large hand strokes my shaft. Leaning down, I kiss him softly before pushing his shirt off, my hands running over his strong shoulders and down across his pecs. I groan, only now just realizing how much I missed him, missed his touch.

"Take your pants off." My voice is rough, my breathing hard as I watch him squirm before doing as he is told. As soon as his pants are off, I shove him back, making him fall on his back.

I rarely do this, I always like being in control, and I can tell Theo is wondering what I'm doing. Sure, we fuck, and Theo has no problem with his sexuality. We are both bi, yet I never do half the things he has done for me. Old beliefs are sometimes still hard to get past. Moving between his legs, I grab his shaft, squeezing it before running my hand up its hardened length.

"Tobias, you don't have to."

I ignore him; I want to, I want him. Even if things haven't been the same since she left, it doesn't make my love for him any less. Swirling my tongue around his knob, I hear him moan underneath me, his hand going to my hair, only making me want him even more as I take him completely in my mouth. His cock finally bottoms out in the back of my throat. I move my head, finding my rhythm. I have always wanted to do this, yet could never actually bring myself to take him in my mouth. I know it sounds stupid, yet doing it now, tasting his cold salty skin on my tongue, I just want more. He tastes different to Imogen, she tastes sweet; Theo however, is salty in a good way. Sweet and savory. So different, yet both more intoxicating than any amount of alcohol I have consumed.

I suck his cock hard, my hand rubbing at the parts of him I can't fit in my mouth. His hips move involuntarily, trying to thrust into my mouth, so I move faster, knowing he needs release just as much as I do.

He groans loudly before I feel his seed spill into my mouth, just as intoxicating as he tastes. I swallow him down only to be ripped up to him, his lips slamming into mine hungrily. I pin his arms above his head, loving the feeling of his cool skin against mine. I suck on my mark he wears, loving the way he instantly reacts to my tongue running over it.

Flipping him over, I pull his hips towards me. Grabbing his hair, I pull his head back, and he grabs hold of the headboard. "I'm gonna fuck you now." My voice is ragged, his answer just a breathy groan, making me smirk as I ram into him.

His body stills before he pushes back against me. I haven't felt this satisfied since before she left, and that thought alone makes me drive into him harder than intended, yet he never complains. He knows how I feel, I can feel him through the bond always pulling against me, trying to gauge my emotions, feeling his thoughts swirling around in mine.

When I'm on the verge of exploding, I grip his hair, forcing his head back and ramming my tongue in his mouth. I groan, my seed spilling into him as I still. Both of us breathless, I kiss his shoulder as I pull out and slump on the bed.

Theo hovers above me, a smile lighting up his face for the first time in months. I place my hand on his cheek. His stubble feels scratchy as his face is pushed into my hand. Sitting up on my elbow, I run my hand over his thigh where he sits next to me. The familiar sparks make me feel alive for the first time in ages. What I would do to feel her soft skin.

Theo, knowing how I feel, stands up. "I will keep looking. Get some rest, Tobias," he says.

I yawn but shake my head. "Not until you feed," I tell him.

"I did already," he admits, yet I know he wants mine or Imogen's blood. He is sick of feeding from strangers and his appetite has been huge lately. More than I can actually handle, yet even though I know the man in reception is dead, I know he needs more blood, craves it.

"Not until you feed," I say, turning, baring my neck for him. He moves closer and runs his fingers lightly over the skin of my neck. I grab his hand, pulling him down.

I also need him to feed off of me, need him to need me and not just her, just like he needs me to need him. It is the only way to survive, making sure we are still in one piece for when we get her back.

I feel his fangs sink into my neck; I groan, loving the endorphins running in my bloodstream, loving the feeling of his tongue, lapping at my skin.

He doesn't feed for long, but when he finishes, he doesn't have the same hunger that has been burning in eyes for weeks. He has just finished getting dressed, and I have laid down when the phone rings, making both of us jump.

I answer quickly, not even checking the caller ID, only to be disappointed when my father's voice comes through the speaker. "I'm going to the council. Alaric has information, apparently that bitch ex of yours may know where they are." I jump to my feet, my father going there in his anger is not a good idea. If he snaps and hurts that bitch Alaric, things will end badly.

"Father, wait," Theo says, snatching the phone from my hand.

"It's too late son, I'm already here. I will let you know what I find out. Don't worry about me. We need answers. I intend to make sure we get them. We need our girls back."

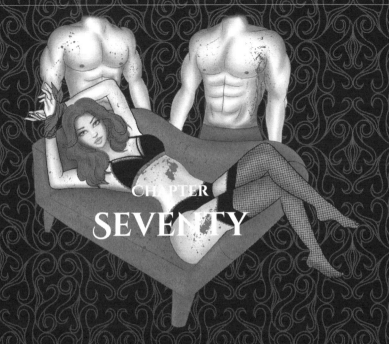

CHAPTER
SEVENTY

I mogen
For months we have been hiding at Claire's cabin in the woods. Months of feeling their pain, though they can't feel mine. Claire assured me that much.

I don't think they will cope if they know how much I want them. I rub my hand over my swollen belly; it is hard and round while I look out the window over the breathtaking scenery. We are high in the mountains, nothing to be seen except the dense forest. It is peaceful here, but lonely. I crave to be back in their arms, crave their touch, crave the smell of them, my entire body yearns to be with them. What makes it worse is being able to feel them. Feel their heartache, feel their anger, feel their need for me. But knowing they are slowly going insane without me pulls at something deep within me. It aches more deeply than I can explain.

Like it is pulling on my soul, yet looking down at my growing belly, I know it is worth it. Caroline thinks I can have the baby any day now. Yet, we never talk about what will happen afterwards. Never talk about whether I will still be alive to see my child. I know she fears the unknown too, fears what Tobias and Theo will do if I die. Claire told me she can't see my future, can't see if I will survive the birth. Said she can only see darkness when she tries.

Claire has been teaching me spells and how to make potions, using the herbs and plants from her gardens. Yet, actually conjuring magic is proving difficult. I can kind of feel it, yet nothing happens. I have scoured over my family's grimoires so much; I now know every spell and enchantment off the top of my head. I can't do anything with the power I apparently possess and can't quite seem to grasp it.

Claire seems to think I need to find my grounding place; I know I won't find it here. I feel more grounded with them, calm. Here, I feel nothing but loneliness.

Looking out at the mountains, I watch them slowly disappear under the clouds. A storm has been brewing all day. I can feel its vibrations and know it's going to be a bad one. Caroline and Claire seem to think it's because I'm feeling my inner power. I'm not so sure, I don't know what to believe anymore.

All I know is I need them, like I need oxygen to breathe. Without them, my life is hollow. I feel like I'm slowly losing myself. Constantly consumed by the chatter in my mind. Getting up from my position, I walk down the stairs to find Caroline and Claire. The cottage is more like a log home or a giant playhouse. I walk down the creaky wooden stairs that spiral to the floor below, an enormous fireplace sits in the center of the house going through both floors. This place has its own aura, its own life about it, with its branches snaking in creating the roof protecting us from the elements outside these walls.

Standing on the slate floor, I feel the vibration through it as thunder crackles outside. The wind picks up and howls loudly. I walk to the front door and peer out. Caroline and Claire are running around, trying to secure everything. Claire is throwing nets over her garden beds, while Caroline moves all the outside furniture. Stepping outside, the wind blows my hair wildly as it picks up in intensity, nearly knocking me off my feet.

Caroline, hearing my gasp as I breathe in the frosty air, looks in my direction. "Imogen get inside, you shouldn't be out in this!" She yells, yet by the time her voice carries over the wind it sounds more like a soft murmur.

Claire staggers over to me, grabbing my arm, pulling me inside and shutting the door. "I will make some tea," she says, trying to distract me from the storm raging and building up outside.

"Will this place hold when it hits?" I ask.

Claire looks around nervously. "It should do. I will have the trees outside reinforce the place and bend them to build a canopy," she says. "Would be handy if my element was wind," she mutters to herself.

I can tell it worries her. There have been plenty of storms while we have been here, but nothing has felt like the one building up outside.

I learned that Claire is an Earth witch like my mother. By the grimoires, I'm certain my grandfather's element was fire. Mine is yet to be seen. There are only five elements: Earth, Fire, Water, Wind, and Spirit. Though Spirit is rare, it has control over all four other elements.

Claire and I have been working on trying to crack my talisman, but she seems to think only strong emotion or a vehement reaction from me will break its bindings. Being here, I feel nothing but hollow and she seems to think that is why I can't break it.

I tug at the bracelet as it itches my wrist, my hands and feet have become so swollen, and my blood pressure so high, that everything swells and itches. I make my way over to the table and sit down. My back aches from the extra weight. Yet, I have been lucky enough not to get stretch marks, not that it will matter once the baby tears itself from me. I often wonder how bad it will hurt.

Claire thinks the baby is a girl, yet I have this feeling it's a boy. In my dreams, I see a little boy with the most beautiful green eyes. He has Tobias's dark hair and rosy cheeks. I have been finding one thing strange; we know this baby is a were-baby. Yet, I have actually been craving blood, and not just human blood, any blood. I haven't had the guts to tell Caroline, not wanting her to worry. But I even crave her blood, which I find weird. Vampires crave human and Lycan blood, not their own species. I don't know what to think of it. So, I try to ignore it as best I can, plus the whole thought of drinking blood grosses me out.

Caroline comes in just as Claire finishes making the tea. She sets a cup down in front of me. I can smell the lavender in it and my mouth waters. I never thought of lavender as edible, yet Claire puts it in everything. Caroline watches me sip my tea, a strange look on her face before grabbing her cup.

She sighs after she takes a sip. "How are you feeling today?" She asks, watching my face.

"The same as always," I murmur.

"It will be over soon." She says but adds nothing else like my death is an unwelcome topic. I go to ask her a question when a pained expression takes over her face.

The cup she is holding drops from her hands, shattering, and her eyes glaze over. I watch as she grips the table, the broken glass cuts into her hands. Caroline tries to ride out the sudden pain. I stand up alarmed, moving away from her as I watch her eyes regain focus turning a crimson shade, her fangs protruding making her features look malevolent.

The pain seems to leave her, yet her breathing remains ragged. Claire is watching her worriedly. "I know," she says to Caroline, touching her shoulder. Caroline looks to me in panic, before pain has her clawing at her back as she screams in agony. Her voice is distorted as she tries to talk through her pain.

"I have to go: I can't let him bear it," she screams. Claire is frantically racing around the kitchen while I stand paralyzed in fear.

"Bear what, Caroline?" I stutter. Her eyes flick to my face, her teeth bared as an animalistic glint flits across her features.

Claire is busy making something before walking over, a green concoction in a cup in her hand. "Drink this, it will help." Caroline clutches the cup, her hands trembling as she tries to hold it to her lips, gulping down the liquid fast. It works instantly, I can tell she is in pain, yet somehow it becomes bearable for her.

"I need to go. Claire, you need to watch over her," she gasps out.

"What's going on?" I ask in panic.

"They're torturing him, something has gone wrong. I can feel my mate being tortured. Josiah, I need to get to him. I'm sorry Imogen, I must go!" She says, trying to stand on shaky legs. I have no idea how she thinks she can run to him in this state, yet I can tell she is determined to try. She walks over to the sink and I nearly throw up as I watch her grab a knife and run it across her wrist, letting the blood run into a cup.

My mouth instantly waters at the smell of it, I swallow loudly, my mouth filled with my saliva. "It will congeal but you're going to have to force it down, Imogen. They will kill me if you die," she says before turning toward Claire.

"Make sure she takes it as soon as she is in pain," Claire nods, before giving Caroline a hug.

Caroline walks on wobbly legs as pain hits her again. She wraps her arms around me before rubbing my swollen belly. "Take care of yourself, I will be back as soon as I can." She says before running out the door. I can hear the wind howling; the storm is going to hit soon. I just hope Caroline clears the mountains and doesn't get stuck outside in it.

"Maybe you should go lay down, Imogen? I will call out when dinner is done."

I nod my head at Claire, I feel like all I do is sleep. Feeling constantly drained and exhausted. My mind goes to Josiah, wondering what could have happened, to cause such panic in Caroline. I can feel Tobias and Theo's anxiety, they also feel almost closer to me; like they aren't far at all. I play with the bangle Claire gave me that blocks the bond, knowing I only have to take it off and they will find me. I can't risk my baby. So, I drop the bangle and it presses back against my wrist. I lay on the bed before slowly drifting off.

My sleep is restless, and I can't find a comfortable position;

tossing and turning constantly. When I finally wake up opening my eyes, it is because the storm is raging outside. The wind sounds like a freight train against the walls. The entire place shakes in its wrath. I throw my legs over the side of the bed and notice there is no light, the cottage is eerily quiet. The only noises are the crackle of the fireplace. I stand up and stretch, taking a deep breath only to see my own breath in the air. I can feel the heat coming from the fireplace, so why is it so cold all of a sudden? My breath makes little clouds in the air.

Opening my bedroom door, I see darkness; the lights are all off. I trudge down the stairs, excited to see the flames in the fireplace casting a little light. I can't hear Claire anywhere or smell her cooking I have become familiar with. I feel a sense of dread wash over me when I feel the first sharp pain stirring deep within my stomach. I clutch my belly, trying to breathe through the pain and stumble down the rest of the stairs. That's when I smell it. Blood and lots of it. My mouth waters at the delectable smell.

I stagger into the kitchen as pain ripples through me again, knowing I have to get the glass of blood from the fridge. But where is Claire? Flicking the light switch, no lights come on, the storm having knocked the power out somehow, even though it runs off solar.

I feel my way into the kitchen at the back of the house, listening for any sounds, but all I can hear is the storm raging outside, and my own footsteps on the slate floor. It's not until my feet step in something warm and wet that I know something is wrong. I bend down, pain searing through my abdomen at the movement and feel the ground, my hands coming in contact with the intoxicating liquid spilt on the floor. I feel around, my hand becoming coated in the gooey liquid before I feel hair, curly hair and I jump up. "Claire" I gasp.

Knowing it's her body, bleeding out on the floor at my feet, I stagger back, panic setting in. That's why she couldn't see the baby being born, why she thought my future was just darkness. She never got to live to see it. I scream in agony as I feel something shift within me. Pain, being the only thing I can focus on.

I hear her laugh before I see her figure standing in the kitchen's corner in its shadows. She steps forward; I step back, toward the living room with the fireplace. I turn and try to run, holding my stomach, but she is in front of me in seconds.

The fire crackling, illuminating her features as I come face to face with the homicidal bitch.

"Miss me?" She taunts just as another wave of pain ripples through me, bringing me to my hands and knees. My scream echoes and dies in the storm raging outside.

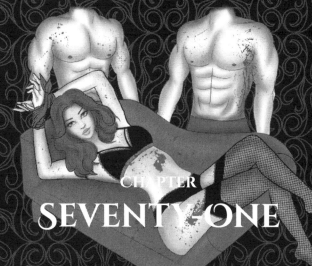

CHAPTER
SEVENTY-ONE

"What, no sisterly hug?" She taunts me, while I try to bear the pain.

As I cough and sputter, my blood spatters on the floor. I clutch the bangle from my wrist and toss it into the fire with the last bit of strength I have left, before collapsing. I look up at her, a devilish grin on her face. "Now why would you do that? I was hoping to enjoy myself but now, I have to make things quick."

"What do you mean?" I choke out, coughing on more of my blood, so I try to turn my head and let the blood drain out of my mouth.

"Well, since you are dying which, is such a shame. I figured the baby will need a mother, and since that can't be you, why not aunt Bianca? Though, mom I feel has a better ring to it," she says, her manicured finger tapping her chin in thought.

My blood runs cold at her words, she wants my baby. And I know there is nothing I can do to stop her. I can't even stand, let alone fight her.

"You're not taking my baby!" I snap back at her, trying to crawl to my feet.

"See, that's where you're wrong. You're dying, Imogen. I can do what I want," she says, shoving me onto my back with her foot, my body rolling onto the cold floor.

"Why are you doing this? Help me, please," I beg her, trying to reach any part of her humanity, she can't be this evil. Something human must remain surely.

"Help you? Your mother killed mine, when she found out she was pregnant with you. My father left us in the wind, completely forgetting the family he started and deciding to start a new one. I'm the last person who is going to help you, Imogen. You destroyed my family, forcing my mother to kill herself. You have no right to ask for my help; don't you think?"

I shake my head, hoping she will understand I have nothing to do with her mother's death. How can I? I never even met her mother, so why put the blame on me? But she just keeps rambling, and I let her, hoping it will distract her from what she is here to do, hoping it will distract her enough for them to get to me in time. Please get here in time, I wish with everything in me.

"Do you have any idea how hard it is to kill yourself when you're immortal? She tried everything only to keep coming back, or for me to stop her just in time. Only to do it all over again. The whole staking thing is bullshit. You not only have to stake yourself, but you also have to remove the head," she giggles at her own rambling.

She's out of her mind; sounds like the ramblings of a madwoman. Pain has me screaming as I feel my insides being torn, like my organs are being cut to pieces as I feel the baby shift within me, my belly feels like it is doing backflips as it moves.

"So, in the end, I couldn't say no, I couldn't keep watching her try anymore so I ended her suffering. Then, I hunted down our father, ending him too. Your mother didn't like that, she became a pathetic alcoholic, assuming he left her. Yet, it didn't kill her the way it killed my mother. She lived for you and that pissed me off, knowing I wasn't enough for my own mother to stick around." I try not to move, hoping she will forget me laying at her feet. I cough up more blood and I can feel myself fading into the darkness.

I watch as she kneels beside me, brushing my hair from my face, grabbing my chin, forcing me to look at her evil eyes. "Such a shame to think if we were born from the same mother, I may have actually liked you. Well, until you stole them from me too," she whispers, more to herself than to me. I feel her lift my shirt up.

I try to swat her hands away, but she clicks her tongue, annoyed. "Now, now, sis, be a good girl and hold still. Don't want to cut your precious bundle now do we?" She laughs.

"This is going to hurt," she snickers.

Then, I feel her hands rip me open. I vaguely hear the sounds of crying and her voice.

"Aw, he is perfect, Imogen. A little boy." I can feel myself fading. Then, I lose myself to the darkness. I feel like I'm floating and falling at the same time; weightless and surrounded by darkness. Her voice echoes around me on repeat, a little boy, a little boy. I have a little boy. I feel tears run out of my eyes; I just want to see him, just once, see his little face. What I would have done to see him, to hold him. Then, I feel nothing at all but the agonizing pain of my death. I slip from this earth into nothingness. Dead and cold.

Tobias POV

My father never should have done what he did, yet I know why he did it and I know he doesn't regret it. He would do anything for my mother, just like I would do anything for Imogen or Theo. We are driving to the council, knowing we can't do much else. My father is to be punished for killing Alaric.

Alaric taunted the wrong man, promising information when he had none. My father lost it, ripping him to pieces before being detained. Theo is driving, and I'm trying to rid my mind of my toxic thoughts.

The phone brings me back to reality as it rings. My hands are shaking as I read the name that pops on the screen. Mom.

"Where is she?" I answer, not even trying to hide the anger I feel towards my mother.

"She is alright. I'm trying to get to your father. What happened?" I growl before the phone is snatched from my hand by Theo. I growl, ready to attack him until I hear my mother's voice come through the phone.

"They are both fine, but your father isn't. Imogen is protected. Now, tell me what happened!" I relax, hearing that she has a plan, and that Imogen is okay for now.

I relax in my chair as Theo tells her of the events that took place. We have been driving for about two hours. We would be there by now if Theo let us run. But he thought it's best to drive instead of letting instinct take over, worried we might tear apart the entire council in a rage and we don't need that.

In the third hour, I feel it, I feel the bond stir to life, only we are driving away from her. Theo slams on the brakes as fear runs through both of us like a freight train, knocking the air from my lungs. Something is wrong. I open the door only to be flooded with every emotion she feels, then searing pain, forcing me to double over. Theo too is clutching the side of the car.

I look over at him. He needs to go, he's faster. That kills me, knowing he will get to her before me, but he has to try.

"Find her!" I growl in pain, and he takes off. I drop to the ground, giving into the warm feeling rushing over me, feeling my bones snap as I shift.

Letting instinct take over as I take off toward her. Using the bond to know what direction to run in. Getting distracted by her emotions as they shift between fear and pain, I howl, agonized at what she's going through. My paws hit the ground at extreme speeds, pushing me faster and faster to get to her.

And then, I feel it; my teether snaps. I feel my soul drop somewhere dark, somewhere cold and unrelenting. I howl before feeling Theo scream through the link. His feelings rush over me, making the unbearable pain I feel worse. It is hard to breathe, my lungs feel like they are constricting. I follow Theo's link until I come across a small cottage. We have been past this place many times, yet never noticed it, never even picked up her scent. I shift back, enjoying the pain of my bones breaking in place, anything to stop the pain in my chest. But that all changes when I walk in the door.

No sounds come from the house, but the noises Theo makes. No heartbeat, no breathing, just dead silence.

My heart breaks, Theo's agonized scream can not only be heard but felt, as he clutches her lifeless body against his chest. Her small frame is completely limp in his arms, drenched in her own blood. Her hair spills over Theo's arm and onto the floor as her head just lolls in his arms. I drop to the floor at the sight, my legs losing function. She is dead, gone. We weren't fast enough. I feel like we cry and scream in agony for hours, our souls being ripped from both of us repeatedly every time we look at her.

"I can't hear crying, can you?" I whisper, my voice breaking.

Theo stands up, Imogen in his arms. Theo isn't willing to let her go. I turn away from her, not able to bear the sight of her dead. My soul is crushed into dust, my heart broken beyond repair, this is my fault. I let this happen by not supporting her. We should have been here; this never would have happened if we were with her.

"Where's our baby Theo?" I say, shoving everything out of my mind, forcing myself to focus on anything but her.

Theo places Imogen in my arms, forcing me to take her lifeless body. I cradle her and breathe in her smell that is faint, nearly gone. Her body is cold in my arms as her head lolls against me. I brush her hair out of her face. Theo disappears inside somewhere, and I can't tear my eyes away from her face. I kiss her cold lips, tears running down my face onto her porcelain skin.

"There is no baby Tobias. Where is our baby?" He asks, panicked.

He looks down at Imogen's angelic face before collapsing beside me. "I need her back, I want her back, please. I will do anything," he whispers and begs. I don't know who he is praying to, but hearing his broken voice breaks me even more.

"We need to find our child, if not for us, for her," I whisper, looking down at her face against my chest. We owe her that much.

CHAPTER
SEVENTY-TWO

Theo

I can't believe it, she is gone, dead. Tobias looks as broken as I feel. Imogen, laying in his arms, drenched in blood. I pull her shirt down, not being able to stare at her belly torn open. The damage to her body is haunting, seeing it makes me remember her pain and fear. I'm sure it will haunt me forever, feeling how much she wanted us and how helpless she felt in that moment. I could literally feel her begging with everything she had for us to get to here. We failed her and I know that will drive me insane with guilt.

"Take her, we need to leave," Tobias says almost angrily.

I know he is hurting, but I hate the way he says it as he dumps her in my arms and tears his eyes away from her. I start walking toward the path we came up, his voice echoing through the wind over to me.

"What are you doing, Theo? We need to find our child!" He growls harshly.

"I'm not leaving her here," I spit back at him, clutching her to me, refusing to let go. I can't leave her. I can't leave her here alone in the cold.

"We don't even know who took the baby. That's our priority now, we can come back for her, we don't even know how far whoever took the baby is. You, carrying her will slow us down," he growls, stepping toward me.

Tobias tries to take her from me, but I shove him away, growling at him threateningly.

"Fine, I will go by myself then." I watch as he shifts, taking the form of his beast. He shakes out his fur, turning away from me and heading back up towards the house, obviously looking for any scent.

I continue to walk down the path, the storm is still raging around us, yet I don't feel its rage. I can't feel anything. I'm numb. Completely empty and dead inside. I keep walking, pulling Imogen closer, trying to shield her from the storm. It makes me feel warmer, having her in my arms. I have been walking for around five minutes when I notice a gold light coming from somewhere. I look around but can't see anything that would cause the light that is on the ground in front of me. Adjusting Imogen, I notice the glowing gold light is coming from her wrist. I pick up her limp hand and realize the light is coming from the strange bracelet that sits on her small wrist. I run my fingers over the pendant that is glowing. I recognize the intricate pattern woven around it, but I can't remember where I have seen it before.

I inspect the bracelet closely before I hear her gasp, jumping forward, coughing like she has been underwater and is taking a breath after holding it for a long time. Her eyes open to reveal a magnificent gold color, the same as her bracelet, glowing before she looks at me.

"Imogen." I gasp, clutching her tighter.

She is rigid in my arms, stiff like a board. She looks around confused, before looking at me, her hands go to my face as if to see if I'm real. Then, her hands clutch onto her belly, her hands clawing at her shirt as she pulls it up. She suddenly starts thrashing in my arms, screaming, forcing me to drop her. She lands on the ground with a thud but springs to her feet faster than I can imagine.

"Where is he?" She says, looking around frantically.

"Tobias?" I ask.

Her eyes dart to mine. I take a step back from her, her eyes are blazing with something I can't decipher. I have never seen eyes like hers before, never seen that expression on her face. I know every one of her expressions, and made mental notes of all of them. Yet, this look I have never seen before.

"My baby, where is he, Theo?" I shake my head, not knowing how to answer when I don't know. She suddenly takes off, up the path back towards the cottage. She runs so fast I can't keep up with her. I make it back to the house to see her barge through the door. I hear Tobias barrel up behind me before digging his claws into the earth and sliding into me.

He looks at me with his black obsidian eyes, with a hopeful look on his face, wondering if he feels it right. The bond is surging alive with Imogen's anger. He shifts, and we both chase after her. We hear doors opening and closing upstairs before she races past us, screaming for the last name we thought we would hear come from her lips.

"Bianca, Bianca!" She comes running back out and stops next to us before looking down.

I watch as she sniffs the air before dropping to the floor, her hands running over all the blood on the floor. She wipes at it with her hands, clawing at the floor, digging through it looking for something.

"Where is he? Where is my baby?" She asks, peering up at us with a look of pure fear and desperation on her face. Tears run down her cheeks.

I look at Tobias, he looks just as shocked as I feel at seeing her.

"We aren't sure, we got here too late" I whisper.

Her face crumples up and my guilt hits me saying it. She starts wailing and screaming loudly at my words, rocking back and forth, her hands becoming drenched in her blood that is congealing on the floor. The bracelet on her wrist glows brighter and brighter, flashing like a beacon.

When she lets out the most heartbreaking guttural scream I have ever heard, the noise seems to burst straight from her chest. Light consumes everything as her bracelet explodes blindingly, and so does she. Her emotions knock me through the bond, before I see darkness as I am thrown backwards.

I hit the ground with a thud, having the air knocked right out of me. I roll to my side, trying to get to my hands and feet.

Tobias groans loudly, making me look in his direction, but all I see is dust and dirt. I jump to my feet and gasp at the sight before me. Imogen is still in the same position, cradling her belly and rocking back and forth, sobbing. But that isn't what shocks me, it is the house; or the lack thereof.

It is gone, blown to smithereens like it never existed. I look around at all the flattened trees, creating an enormous circle like a crater. Nothing is left standing. My mind is jumbled as I try to figure out what she just did and how she did it.

"Did she do that?" Tobias whispers, coming through the dust towards me, his body covered in dust and dirt.

I don't know what to say, I can't explain what I just witnessed. The dense forest literally has a huge part of it blown away, leaving nothing but debris everywhere. I walk over to Imogen, who is on the ground. I touch her back, and she flinches, turning her head to look up at me. What is she?

"She took him, she took him," she repeats.

Her eyes blaze with fury and sadness, and that same strange look I can't decipher. She blinks slowly, like she is understanding what she said. Her face transforms into hatred and darkness as her fangs protrude, making me jump back. She looks like an angel of death. The feelings through the bond are dark and cold, a hatred so cold I would hate for it to be directed at me. I shudder, realizing the darkness she is surrounding herself with. The only thing I can work out is that she is a vampire, but vampires don't possess power like she just showed. She looks crazed and her eyes shine brightly with a hunger I have never seen, in a color that is out of this world and ours.

"Who took him?" Tobias asks, holding his hands out like he is trying to catch a wild animal. Her eyes flick to his. I watch as he too takes a step back from her. I can feel her anger coming through the bond, but this isn't like any anger I have felt. This is burning hot, threatening to boil the blood in my veins, anger that is all consuming and rabid. Looking down at her, I think how she used to be so pure, so innocent. Now, though, she looks lethal and murderous. I don't like this look on her, it scares me, makes me wonder what she has become.

"My sister," she spits.

I can feel her hunger as her anger takes over, the darkest parts of her taking over and she isn't even fighting against it, instead embracing it, letting it wash over her and take control. Stepping towards her, her head cocks to the side, her eyes snap to mine, watching me like a predator. I can feel Tobias' confusion through the bond, matching my own. Imogen is an only child, who is she talking about?

"Bianca," she says, answering both our thoughts. "I'm going to fucking kill her!" She spits so vehemently I flinch at her words, because I know she means them. I stare at her, something is off about her. I would hate to be Bianca when she finds her. And I have no doubt she eventually will, nothing but determination and anger washes through our bond, her emotions overriding everything we feel.

Chapter
SEVENTY-THREE

Imogen

The cold, I remember feeling cold, drowning in freezing temperatures. I never remembered being this cold before; too cold to even shiver. But that's not all I remember. I remember the darkness ebbing and rolling over me as it sucked me in, swallowing me completely.

So dark, it erases the pain that is consuming my soul, the darkness that comes with each breath, shoving me deeper into my mind. I try to push against it, knowing there is someone waiting, something I need to remember. Yet, I can't remember what my mind is trying to fight against. I just know it is bigger than me, more important than me. Something worth fighting for.

I continue to push against the darkness, catching glimmers of images dancing in front of my eyes. Each image warms me slightly, but not enough to take away the cold I'm slowly being plunged into. The darkness threatens to consume me, my mind whispers something to me. I can't understand what it is saying until I recognize one word. "Boy." The word slowly slips into my mind, louder and louder echoing throughout me. Until I understand what the whispers mean.

It isn't them talking, it is her; I recognize the voice, yet can't remember her name. Her voice gets louder and taunts me, pulling at my heart, which feels like it stopped as it twitches in my chest at her words.

"Aw, he is perfect, Imogen. A little boy." The taunting voice grows louder, igniting something within me. Calling to me to keep fighting against the darkness, pushing me out of the numbness that is trying to consume me. Little boy, I have a little boy. My little boy.

Every emotion I have ever felt around that one word floods into me, crashes over me like waves on a beach, tumultuous and unrelenting. Light breaks through the darkness, shining like a beacon above me, showing me just how far I have fallen into the depths of my own mind, trapping me in the darkness.

I feel like I can't breathe, choking on every emotion, choking on my despair, choking on the thought of my son. I try to reach the beacon of light glowing brightly above me, stretching myself. So close, yet I can't quite break free of the binds trapping me within myself, weighing me down. I struggle with everything I have, my fingers outstretched, trying to grasp the light. My fingertips light up as the light finally touches, warming me before I feel like I'm rushing upwards, reliving every pain, every memory flooding into me. Watching the time fly past me, my life flashes like an old movie before my eyes.

Watching my mistakes, watching my triumphs, then, seeing them. My body turns to static, everything electrifies as I see her and what she did, what she took from me.

Something within me wakes, as panic takes over every part of me. I'm thrown forward with so much speed, I try to catch a breath, desperately needing air. I suck back, feeling my body breathe as I'm plunged back into my surroundings jolting me awake. I open my eyes, fearing what I will see, praying it's not the darkness.

Seeing green hypnotic eyes watching me, yet looking straight through me. I look around, the thunder and lightning cracking above us, seeing trees and the smell of damp earth. I breathe deeply relishing the air, it smells different, stronger. I can smell and hear everything, making me snap my head from side to side trying to pick up every little detail. Only to see the green eyes again. I clutch my hands onto him, to make sure he is really there and not a trick of my mind.

His stubble feels rough under my hands, tears prick my eyes when I realize, I'm not dreaming, he is really here. I'm still alive, still breathing. I look down to rub my swollen belly only to feel nothing, ripping at my clothes, trying to find what I know should be there.

"Where is he?" I ask, hoping he will have the answer, hoping they got here in time.

"Tobias?" He asks, watching me closely. I thrash around, trying to get him to release me.

"Where is my baby, Theo?" I yell, my voice breaking and echoing back to me.

He lets go and I fall to the ground. I look around before seeing the house up the path, I take off up the path, running. Please, please be still here. I run through the bottom floor singing out her name, begging her to give him back before running upstairs, throwing every door open and looking inside.

"Bianca, Bianca!" I scream, hoping to hear her taunting voice only to be met with silence.

Running back downstairs, I skid to a stop in front of the fireplace, Theo and Tobias stare at me, when I notice it. My life's essence spilled on the floor. I drop to the ground, running my hands through it, hoping and praying I'm wrong. I died. She killed me. I'm supposed to be dead. She killed me and took him, took my baby. Tore him right out of me. Every detail flows into my mind as I relive the nightmare of my life.

"Where is he? Where is my baby?" I ask, peering up at them, tears run down my cheeks.

"We aren't sure, we got here too late," Theo whispers.

His words cut me deeper than any knife could. She has him, she has him, is all I can think of in his words. She took everything from me. I'm breaking, she broke me. She said she would, and she did. The bracelet on my wrist glows brighter and brighter. How have I not noticed it before? I can't think what it means; I can only think of her with my son. Is he crying for me? Is he hungry? Does he miss me like I miss him? I can't take it anymore.

I scream, not being able to hold on anymore as everything in me breaks and shatters; sharp edges, piercing my soul, taking everything out of me, as I feel nothing but overwhelming sadness, that is all-consuming. Then it lifts, shattering like a burst light bulb as it rushes out of me, bursting from my broken heart.

I don't even recognize the noise that comes out of me, I just feel it break everything, break my world apart. Until it fizzles out, leaving nothing behind but darkness. I let it consume me, enjoying the feeling of power, rage washing over me, igniting a storm within me. So angry, I think I will combust; hatred. I have hated no one more than I hate her. She took everything and now I feel nothing but a burning desire to take it back, and take her to the pits of hell where she shoved me.

Theo touching my back makes me jump before looking up at him. I don't know what he sees in me, but he takes a step back. I almost laugh, feeling crazed as I feel my gums splitting. My anger at everything snaps me back.

"She took him, she took him," I yell. I feel the words leave my lips, leaving a bitter taste on my tongue.

"Who took him?" Tobias asks, holding his hands out like he is trying to catch a wild animal.

My eyes flick to his, I watch as he too takes a step back from me. My anger takes over as they stare at me like they don't know what I'm talking about. Are they hard of fucking hearing? It angers me that they can look so clueless. Do they not know what she took from us? I can feel their fear coming through the bond before I can smell it running in their veins. Sweet and inviting, intoxicating, promising to extinguish the burn that is searing throughout me.

"My sister." I tell them. Theo steps forward, making my eyes dart to him. I can hear their thoughts running rampant as they try to piece everything together. They are wasting my time. I need to find her, not willing to wait for them to catch up, I scream her name at them. "Bianca." I spit the word out. Feeling nothing but the desire to rip her apart, piece by fucking piece, and watch her die. I will take great pleasure in watching her beg for her life like I begged for my child. And she will beg.

"I'm going to fucking kill her!" I laugh at my newfound clarity. I'm going to kill her and enjoy every part of her death.

Tobias tries to reach out to me, holding his hand out. I don't want his hand; I wanted them to get here on time. Where were they when I fucking needed them? Where were they when our fucking son needed them?

I know my anger isn't for them, that they aren't to be blamed. Yet, I can't help it, as it is the only thing keeping me going. I growl lowly, smacking his hand away. I hear his heart rate pick up, then, that's all I can hear, the soft thumping of his heart as it pushes blood through his body. My mouth waters at the intoxicating scent emanating from him and before I can even register what I'm doing, I lunge at him.

Hunger takes over every thought as I wrap my legs around his waist, my arms holding his shoulders, my nails digging in as I sink my fangs into him. His blood rushes into my mouth and makes me moan loudly, I have never tasted anything so sweet. I feel blood spurt on my face as I sink my teeth down into his warm, inviting flesh again. He groans before trying to shove me off. I growl, bloodlust takes over before I feel muscular arms wrap around my waist, yanking me off him.

As I spin around and try to throw the hands off, I realize it's Theo. I watch him as he places his hands out in front of him.

I laugh and it sounds foreign, making me laugh harder before I see him take a step forward. I move quicker, side stepping before jumping on his back and sinking my fangs into his neck. He stops and I can feel his shock running through the bond. But my hunger is insatiable as I drink greedily until I can't drink any more. I slide off him, falling to the ground. He spins around, clutching his neck as I wipe my mouth with my thumb before sucking the blood off.

"Looks like you're not the only predators around here," I chuckle before jumping to my feet, making them step back. I sniff the air and can smell something familiar, something that reminds me of them, yet different.

"Can you smell that?" I ask, my head snapping towards them. They both shake their heads.

"Imogen, I know everything feels different, heightened, but you need to fight it. You're not thinking, you need to take back control." I nearly burst out laughing at Theo pleading with me. My head has never been clearer; they are the ones not seeing clearly.

I know what I am, and it isn't the weak, pathetic girl they knew. No, I have never been clearer, never felt stronger, and most of all never felt the sort of power surging and charging throughout every piece of me.

Yes, things have changed, I like the darkness. The slickness of it rolling over my skin, igniting every cell in my body. Not wasting any more time, I take off running. I can hear them chasing me and figure they will catch up as I go to find her. She couldn't have gone far.

I don't know how long I have been out for, yet I can feel a pull in the direction I'm running. Feel something tugging me in this direction, feel the power running through me, showing me the way. Showing me images flickering in front of my eyes. I can sense him, sense he is still alive with every fiber in me. Which only fuels me more, making me run through the trees at blinding speed. Everything around me slows as I feel the air whip around me. Pushing myself faster, I finally catch a whiff of her scent and the scent of him. He reminds me of Tobias and Theo. They smell the same, yet my son smells purer, innocent.

She is running further into the storm, moving towards the safety it offers as it washes her scent away. Only I don't need her scent with the urge that is pushing me towards them.

I can feel I'm getting closer, I don't know how. It is like a sense ringing loudly through my body, like a tether pulling me in her direction. Breaking out of the dense forest, I come to the edge of a town; the thunderstorm is raging, all I can hear is thunder and the crack of lightning as it rolls over the town.

I sniff the air before catching a glimpse of blonde hair disappearing around the corner at the end of the street. I follow the feeling tugging me toward my son. Getting to the corner, I look down the street that is lined with houses, not a streetlight in sight and no lights come from the houses.

I close my eyes, trying to listen to my instincts, listening to the magic that flows around me, thick and strong like a band protecting me from the storm, showing me the way.

Shadows form and creep along the ground, licking at my bare feet, leaving a tingling sensation in their wake. I know I should fear the shadows, trying to entice me, whispering to the darkest parts of me. But instead, I embrace them, letting them show me the way. I don't care what the cost is on my soul. I can live with them, but I can't live without my son.

I know the price I will pay, yet I don't let it scare me. I know Tobias and Theo will save me from myself when the darkness comes for me. At least, I hope they can. My sanity won't last long with the shadows attaching themselves to me. I read about it in the Grimoires, how with death comes the shadows. Witches stay dead until reborn. I came back unnaturally, and I'm sure it is because of my father's DNA running through my veins.

I know I have never consumed blood, I would have realized with the cravings I had. So, it is the only thing that makes sense. The shadows are the only thing urging me here; without them I would have never found them, so I know I need to let them have what they want. Even if it costs my soul. My son is worth every piece of my soul.

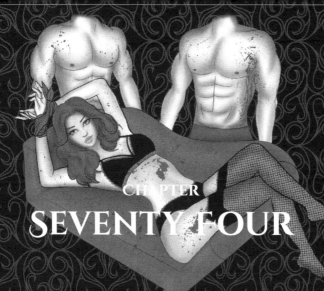

CHAPTER
SEVENTY FOUR

Tobias

    She takes off, leaving us behind to follow something only she can smell. Theo and I stand stunned at what just happened. She fed off both of us, something that I have never seen before. Vampires don't feed off vampires. Not only did she feed off us, but she also marked us in the process. Not that I don't want to be marked by her, I just didn't think it would be under these circumstances.

"That's because she isn't just a vampire, Tobias, haven't you noticed? There is something seriously wrong with her. Did you see her eyes, feel the darkness surrounding her?" Theo asks, wiping his neck. "The worst part though, I think she likes it consuming her, like she is letting it in." He mumbles.

I move toward him, examining his neck which has already healed but left a black mark from where her teeth had sunk in. This is the first time I have seen markings that are tinged with darkness. As I examine mine, it looks the same.

"We need to find her, come on." I say, as I take off running, shifting mid-jump.

I can just faintly catch her scent, Theo tears ahead of me, chasing after her. I hate that I'm not as fast as him. But I doubt he will be faster than her. She is a newborn vampire on a warpath. Her senses in overdrive will fuel her like air to a fire, a raging inferno. I just hope we can get to her before she does something reckless. Killing Bianca won't do anything but cause more trouble. Our laws aren't to be broken lightly. No matter the crimes, everything is meant to go before the courts first.

My father is paying for his wrongdoings now, for killing his own kind, for killing Alaric. Imogen won't survive that torture. My father knew the consequences of doing what he did. Imogen has no idea the torture they will put her through for killing Bianca. I won't let her pay that price. She has been through enough already without being subjected to such barbaric cruelty.

I have been running for what feels like ages when I finally hit the town. Theo is nowhere to be seen, yet I can feel the bond pulling me towards the piers. We have been here before, searched every part of this town already and are quite familiar with it. Shifting back, I walk through the backyard of the property I came out beside, praying that a man lives here and not some old lady. I need clothes or people might become curious about a random man, walking around butt naked.

I cuss when I see the only thing on the clothesline appears to be women's clothes. I quickly grab the floral denim shorts off the line. They seem to look big enough and other than that, there are only a few pieces of children's clothing. I quickly slip them on, my balls being squished in the tight fabric. I try to do the zip up, nearly howling when I zip the sensitive skin of my family jewels. I don't have time to be picky and instead, readjust my large length down my leg and take off running towards the piers.

I look like a fool, but the things you do for those you love, right? Coming to the piers, I see Imogen's glowing figure at the end of the pier, her hands outstretched. I can feel her burning anger through the bond but also something else. Fear. I feel Theo's disbelief through the bond. I run towards them, my feet creaking on the wooden pier, making Imogen and Theo turn tó look back at me.

I never should have run onto that pier, my heart skips when I see Bianca, our child in her arms. Noticing me running towards them, she uses their distraction to her advantage as she acts, hurling the blanketed bundle in the air before diving off the pier. My voice echoes, as I scream to them. Theo reacts just in time and catches our child before falling into the ocean. I hear Imogen's bloodcurdling scream as she looks on frantically into the black water raging below. Bianca is long gone as we wait for Theo to resurface, breathing only when we see him break through the water's surface.

My heart is hammering in my chest so hard I think it is going to burst. The sound of crying is like music to my ears as I watch Imogen collapse on the deck in relief. Theo moves through the water swiftly before climbing the pier, the baby no longer inside the warmth of its blanket as he screams loudly.

I mogen POV
I follow the pull which leads me to sand. I'm on a beach and I can see Bianca running with all her might before she darts onto one of the piers; she knows I'm chasing her. I don't know when she figured it out, but she is now running like her life depends on it and it does. My heart stops as I see her run towards the end. I skid to a stop as she holds her arms outstretched over the water, my baby tucked in the confines of the blanket. I stop in my tracks.

"Give me my baby, Bianca" I tell her. I mean to plead with her, yet my voice comes out as a growl, threatening, not hiding my murderous intent.

"How the fuck are you alive?" She screams angrily.

"Bianca, you don't want to hurt him, you don't want to hurt your nephew." I tell her, hating even calling her any relation to my son. She looks at him and I move closer, making her eyes dart to me as she moves closer to the edge. Theo suddenly appears beside me, stopping when he sees what is in her hands. I refused to look at him, not able to take my eyes off my precious boy, clutched in that vile woman's arms.

"Perfect, he's here," she growls, glaring at Theo.

Theo tries to reason with her while I just want to kill the bitch, but I won't risk endangering my son.

"Isn't this great? Not only did you impregnate your mistress, now you're going to help her kill me, Theo. I bet you're getting a real kick out of this, aye Immy?"

"Don't call me that, I just want my son. You had no right to take him. He is mine!" I scream. She takes a step back, her foot falling off as I get ready to jump in after her, but she steadies herself. My heart rate returns to normal when I see him still tucked in her arm.

"Now that was close." She snickers, enjoying the torture she is putting me through. I growl, taking a step forward. "Ah, ah, ah, not so close." She says, angling him above the water again.

Theo tries to reason with her, but she won't have it. She knows as soon as I get my son, I'm going to kill her. She isn't stupid. The only reason she is alive right now is because she has my baby in her arms, and she knows that.

"Here comes the other one, look at the family reunion," Bianca says sarcastically, making my eyes dart to what she is staring at behind us, Tobias is running toward us.

Then, he suddenly screams. "No!" Theo's eyes flick to mine before both of us look at Bianca, who is gone. Panic rushes through me when I see Theo dart forward, noticing something I haven't. Our child in the air, heading directly into the raging water below. His hand outstretched, gripping the cloth of the blanket he is wrapped tightly in. I scream as I watch them both sink below the surface.

My heart feels like it is going to stop, when I hear Theo gasp and the sweet sounds of my son screaming his lungs out. I drop to the ground, my legs giving out with my sudden relief. He is alive and screaming. I never thought a baby's cry would be the most melodious thing I have ever heard, singing to my soul.

Theo climbs the pier, and I finally see the perfection that is my son. Theo walks over to me and I instantly rip off my shirt to wrap him in it. Theo places him in my arms. He is perfect and exactly what I envisioned in my dreams, dark onyx-colored hair and dazzling emerald green eyes like Theo. He has my nose and lips, though.

"Hi baby," I whisper looking down at him, tears spilling over and running down my cheeks as he continues to cry in my arms from being cold. Looking up, Tobias and Theo are in awe, looking down at him.

I sniff his little head, breathing in his scent, and then, I jerk back, my gums tingling before protruding. I try to shake off the feeling that is threatening to take over before standing up. I try to tell them, but Tobias holds out his arms for the baby and I'm relieved that I don't have to explain. I place the baby in his arms and he instantly stops crying as Tobias's warm skin heats him up, keeping him warm.

"We have a boy," Tobias says, looking down on his cute little face.

"And what a boy," Theo says. I chuckle slightly; men always think the size of the package determines the man. I keep my distance, not really trusting my hunger around him right now. But he looks quite content in Tobias' arms, looking up at both his fathers.

Theo looks down at Tobias' pants, making my eyes dart down too. "What are you wearing?" He asks.

Tobias growls and I raise an eyebrow at his clothing choice. "I don't even want to know how you squeezed in those," I tell him.

"Come on, we should head home," Tobias says, looking at me. I can't help but look out at the water, wondering where my sister went. Fear gnaws at me, I wonder if she will come for him again. I feel my anger resurface as I remember what she did. Theo touching my arm pulls me from my memories.

"We can deal with her later, for now let's get home," he says, kissing the side of my face. I reluctantly follow after them.

The trip home is longer, we can't run for too long with the baby or as fast. Tobias and Theo abandoned their car not far from where I was actually living. So, we drive the rest of the way, well they do. I ask Tobias to pull over halfway back as I can't handle my son's intoxicating scent filling the car. This isn't what I envisioned motherhood to be like. I never thought my son would need protection from me. I run thinking of everything on replay, my thoughts getting darker and darker before finding myself on the familiar porch of our home.

I walk around the back and sit next to my mother's rose, waiting for them to get home. How my life has changed in a day, how I have learned many secrets I wish I never knew. Yet, I can't shake the feeling of the darkness. I know with my death I have to pay the price, I'm unnatural, a witch's hybrid, so what does that make my son? I knew as soon as I smelt him, he isn't just Tobias's son but also Theo's, their DNA creating the perfect predator.

Will he be the same? I hope not, because this darkness trying to swallow me is addictive, and I don't know how I feel about loving the sweet, intoxicating slickness of it calling to me. I don't want this for him, don't want this for myself. Yet, nothing can be done now. I am what I am, I just hope it's good and not evil, like the shadows calling out to me.

If only my mother could see me now. What would she think of what I have become? I don't get to ponder long before I see the headlights coming up the road, turning into the long driveway. Will they still want me when there is nothing left but darkness?

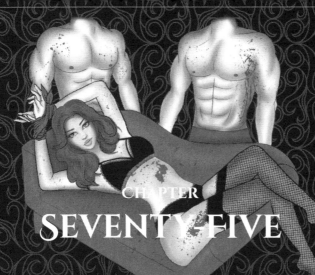

CHAPTER
SEVENTY-FIVE

I mogen

    I walk back around to the front of the house; the car pulls up beside me. Tobias gets out of the car with the baby nestled in his arms, still, fast asleep. Theo then grabs some things from the trunk.

"Why didn't you go inside?" Asks Tobias, walking over to me.

He passes me my son and I hold him close to my chest. "It feels strange being back here." I answer him truthfully, I feel him nod before kissing my cheek.

"We stopped on the way here, we couldn't get much though with nothing being open. But Theo got some formula and diapers. It will have to do until morning, and then we can go get a car seat and some other stuff for him." He explains, pulling me into him.

I breathe in his scent, finding comfort in him, Tobias is always so warm. Theo comes around the car with some bags clutched in his hand. "Come on, let's go inside," Theo says, pecking me on the lips as he walks past.

I follow them inside; walking in, I'm hit with a sense of Déjà vu. I haven't been here for months, but it still feels like home. The place is a mess, though. Everything is covered in dust and smells like it has had no windows opened for a while. Theo walks into the kitchen, I hear him flick the kettle on and place the bags on the counter.

I walked in behind him and he is reading the back of a formula tin like he is about to mix some complicated science experiment. It doesn't take him long before he places a few scoops inside the bottle and adds water to it before shaking it. I watch as he heats the bottle using a bowl and water from the kettle.

Tobias makes us all coffee, and I sit on the stool, watching them. Everything feels different, not in a bad way, just different. I never pictured them being father's or myself a mother. Yet, watching them now, I can see the excitement they are trying to hide. I look down at our baby, his hypnotic green eyes now open and staring back at me, his lips making kissing lips as he sucks them together.

Tobias sits a steaming mug of coffee in front of me before grabbing a bag of diapers and opening it. He pulls one out, examining it and turning it around like he is trying to figure out how it works. I sometimes forget they aren't from this time period or that they haven't had to deal with babies before. I hold my hand out for it and he gives it to me. I lay my son down on the counter, still wrapped in my shirt, his little arms and legs stretching out as he yawns. Tobias watches as I put the diaper on him. When I'm done, I almost laugh when I realize Theo too has stopped and is watching intently, forgetting what it is he is doing.

"Seems easy enough," Tobias says with a nod. We all watch as he sucks his fingers making frustrated noises. Theo hands me the bottle and I pick him back up. He drinks down the formula hungrily and I can hear him gulping it down.

"What are we going to name him?" I ask, realizing we can't just keep calling him baby.

They both seem to think. "I don't know, what do you want to call him?" asks Tobias.

"I don't know, what about Thaddeus?" I suggest.

They both seem to think for a second before nodding. "Yes, Thaddeus has a ring to it," Theo says as Tobias nods in agreement.

"Have either of you rang your mother to let her know?" They both shake their heads and Tobias growls. It's clear he still isn't happy with his mother and I running off, but looking down at Thaddeus it is all worth it, every miserable second of it.

"I will call her tomorrow, she is with dad and I don't think it would be a good idea to call right now. He isn't in a good mindset at the moment," Theo answers.

When Thaddeus finishes drinking down his bottle, Theo holds his arms out and I gently place him in them. Theo rubs his back softly, placing him over his shoulder and kissing the side of his tiny head. I feel Tobias move behind me, wrapping his arms around my waist, his warmth making me yawn, I'm exhausted mentally and physically.

"Why don't we get some sleep? You may me be a vampire but you're still half witch," Tobias says, kissing my neck. I lean back into him, his lips on my skin making me moan softly. "Or we could not sleep," he says, thrusting his hips into me. I can feel his erection pressing into my back, making me realize just how much I have missed being with them.

"I can't, what if she comes back?" I say, my eyes darting to Thaddeus in panic.

"Get some sleep, I will watch him, Imogen. I won't let anyone take our son," Theo says, watching me.

"We already rang the council on the way here. They have sent people out looking for her. We can deal with it tomorrow, for now let's get some sleep." Tobias whispers into my neck. I reluctantly follow him upstairs, Theo follows too, with Thaddeus in his arms. I strip my clothes off, heading for the shower. Turning the taps on I stand under the steady stream, blood that stains my skin slowly washes down the drain. Tobias steps into the shower and I look back in panic, worried.

"He is fine, I promise. Theo won't let any harm come to him,"

Tobias says, grabbing the loofa and soap. I lean against him, resting my face into the crook of his neck. The steam is heating up the room. Tobias washes me, never letting his fingers linger too long as he rubs the loofa over body. His scent fills up the room as I feel my gums tingle.

"Will it always be like this?" I ask him.

"What do you mean?" He asks, kissing my head.

"The hunger, will it go away?"

He grips my chin, forcing my eyes to meet his. "You might have to ask Theo that, he would know more, but it will get easier. I promise."

I nod before I feel his fingers on the back of my neck. He pulls me against him, kissing me almost desperately. His tongue plays with mine as a new sensation rolls over me. Lust.

I grip onto him, moaning into his mouth. I feel him chuckle slightly before gripping my hips and lifting me against the wall. I can feel his erection below me before he slowly buries himself inside me. Stopping only to let me adjust to his size. I push my hips against him, wanting him to move; he doesn't need to be told twice as he slams into me, making him groan loudly as he sucks and nips at my skin. My nails dig into his back as I feel my stomach tighten, my arousal building to an insurmountable level. His lips move to mine as his tongue plunges into my mouth, tasting every inch of it.

I moan loudly, loving the feeling of him so deep inside me. When I'm sitting on the edge of my orgasm, Tobias shifts slightly, offering me his neck. I don't hesitate as I sink my fangs into him. I feel him moan loudly at the feeling of me feeding off him, before my walls clench around him. My orgasm rushes through me, my pussy pulsates as I ride out the high. My fangs leave Tobias as I feel him still inside me, having reached his own release. He kisses me and my arms tighten around his neck; I feel his hands squeeze my ass before he lifts me slightly, letting himself slip out of me.

"God, I missed you." He mumbles against my lips. My head snaps to look at the door when I hear Theo clear his throat. The baby is no longer in his arms. I look at him panicked before he shakes his head.

"He is asleep, I can see him from here. I promise, Imogen, he is safe here." I nod, not really believing he is safe until I know she is dead. Tobias hops out of the shower, wrapping a towel around himself. He kisses Theo's shoulder on his way past, walking back into the bedroom.

Theo leans against the door just watching me. I raise an eyebrow at him, "Well, are you going to get in?"

His face lights up and a smirk forms on his lips. I open the shower door, and he pulls his shirt off over his head. I'm slammed against the shower wall with a thud. My legs wrap around his waist as he crushes his lips against mine. The soft cries of the baby coming to my ears make me freeze.

"He is fine, Imogen, I have him." Tobias sings out, obviously feeling my hesitation through the bond. I relax and feel Theo nipping at my skin, his teeth grazing my flesh, his erection pressing against my clit, making me moan into his mouth.

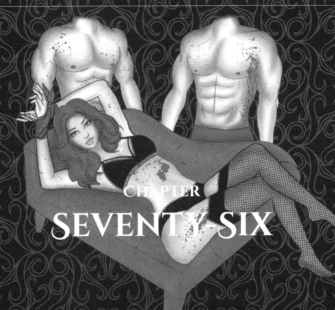

CHAPTER
SEVENTY-SIX

Days pass by and the council still hasn't caught Bianca. I'm beginning to think they aren't even looking for her. I have hardly slept; my mind won't let me. My mind never gives me rest, fear consumes me. Not fear of her, but fear of who she could take from me. Tobias and Theo take turns going to work, swearing to remain by my side until they catch her and until I have my bloodlust under control. I fear it won't ever be under control, the more I feed, the more I want. My hunger is insatiable and my darkness ever consuming.

Moving back to my position at the bedroom window, I watch the night pass, time goes by quickly and sometimes, I find myself trapped in my thoughts only to come around and another day has passed. My days seem to blur into one and I honestly have no idea how many days have passed since I returned here.

When the morning rises, Theo walks in, kissing my cheek, forcing my attention to him. "I need to go to work, Tobias has Thaddeus," he tells me before walking out of the room.

Following him downstairs, I find the house is a mess. For people with nothing but endless time on our hands, we still can't manage to keep the house clean. Tobias is laying on the couch with Thaddeus on his chest, his eyes closed. I walk over, leaning over the couch and kissing Thaddeus' head before kissing Tobias' lips. His eyes snap open, and I realized he dozed off.

"Hey," he whispers, not wanting to wake up the baby.

"I swear this kid waits until daylight to sleep, I'm so tired." He yawns. His hair is sticking up at odd angles and he hasn't shaved in what looks like days, his eyes are also darker as he peers up at me.

I feel like a terrible mother. His words make me feel guilty when I realize Theo and Tobias have been pretty much doing everything while I have a pity party, stuck in my own thoughts and too scared to hold my own son in case my bloodlust kicks in. Walking back upstairs, I find the baby wrap Tobias and Theo have been using. I then look at the contraption I have seen them wear multiple times, yet can't work out how to put it on. As I walk back downstairs, Tobias opens his eyes.

"What are you doing?" He asks, staring at the baby sling in my hands.

"How does it work? I feel like he will fall out of it," I tell him.

"You need to tighten the straps at the back," he says. Standing up, he places Thaddeus in the bassinet next to the couch. "Come here," he tells me, and I walk over. He tightens the straps, and it feels a lot more secure. I go to grab him out of the bassinet when Tobias touches my arm. I can see the concern in his eyes, he glances at Thaddeus, who is sleeping peacefully. "You should feed first, Imogen." I feel like he just punched me in the gut. I can feel his apprehension through the bond. He thinks I will hurt him. It hurts knowing they don't trust me with our own son.

"It's not that okay, just better to be safe. I didn't mean to make you feel like I don't trust you." He blurts when he feels my mood shift.

"Just feed. Then, I will help you get him in the sling." I nod and he sits down on the couch before tapping his lap. I walk over and hesitate, Theo isn't here to pull me off, if I lose control.

Tobias grips my hips, pulling me forward, making me straddle his legs. He kisses my lips before yawning. He looks exhausted, the sleepless nights are taking a toll on him. Tobias shifts and angles his neck towards me, I kiss the side of his neck, my hand rubbing his cheek, his stubble feels rough in my palm. I feel my fangs break through my gums, and I sink my teeth into his neck. Tobias moans loudly from the endorphins in my saliva. I feel his blood flood into my mouth, stopping the burning ache in the back of my throat.

I feel him rub my back, his warm skin making me shiver before I pull myself back. Looking at Tobias, he looks a little buzzed, a lazy smile slipping onto his face. I climb off his lap and eventually, he gets up and helps me put Thaddeus in the sling. He feels heavier, like he has put on some weight as he snuggles into the sling across my chest. I feel Tobias's eyes on me, watching me carefully, as if he is too afraid to leave me alone with him.

"You good? I can stay up; I just need coffee." He mumbles out while yawning.

"No, go to sleep, I will be fine. You will feel it if I'm not," I tell him, and he nods before laying down, his eyes instantly closing.

I look down at Thaddeus, stroking his nose with my finger. "Let's clean house," I whisper. Walking into the kitchen I start stacking dishes and cleaning the counters.

The entire day goes quickly, and I finally haul the last load of washing inside, when I feel Thaddeus stir. Tobias is right, his sleep pattern is way out of whack. He sleeps the entire day. I quickly make him a bottle and change his bum when I hear tires on the dirt road.

"That's daddy," I tell Thaddeus, while I feed him, waiting to hear the door open. Tobias is still asleep on the couch when I hear, not one but two car doors shut, making me get up.

I walk into the living room just in time to see Caroline, helping Josiah walk into the house. I haven't seen or spoken to Caroline since before I had Thaddeus, Josiah I haven't seen in months. He collapses into the armchair with a grunt. Tobias' eyes fly open as he jumps to his feet. He sighs when he realizes it is just his parents before locking eyes with his father. Josiah looks terrible, his suit is filthy, his hair a mess, he looks exhausted, and I notice he has a slight limp as he walked in. He rests his head back on the chair.

Tobias is about to say something when his mother cuts him off. "Give him a second son, let him catch his breath." She tells him, Tobias nods.

"I will go get him a change of clothes," he tells her, before disappearing upstairs.

Caroline notices me standing there and a huge grin breaks out on her face as she walks over, embracing me tightly from the side. She looks down in my arms and rubs the back of Thaddeus' hand. "He is perfect," she says, before ducking down and smelling his little head. Thaddeus stares up at her, wondering who she is.

"You want to hold him?" I ask, and she immediately puts her arms out and I place him in them. She then goes and sits next to Josiah, who immediately sits up a little better to see, while he rubs Thaddeus' tiny feet. Josiah smiles brightly, looking at his grandson.

"I will go put on some coffee," I tell them, walking into the kitchen.

When I come back out, I hear more tires on the road and I notice Josiah wearing a pair of sweatpants and a normal T-shirt. You can tell he isn't impressed with his attire, but he looks comfy. I have only ever seen him in suits, so I find it funny with him looking like an ordinary person. The front door is thrown open and Theo steps inside. He hugs his mother briefly, before his attention goes to his father.

"Oh god you're okay," he whispers.

I knew Theo was worried about his father, but I didn't realize to what extent. I've been so caught up in everything else, I forgot to ask him how he felt about everything. I feel selfish and guilt is gnawing at me.

"We do have some news," his mother announces, and I place the tray with coffee on the table, completely forgetting I was even holding it. Quickly sitting next to Tobias, Caroline hands Thaddeus to Josiah, who is all too happy to hold his grandson as he ignores her, paying all his attention to him.

"They caught Bianca." Caroline says, making my eyes dart to her. I feel excitement bubble up at her words, only for it to be squashed with her next words. "They are holding the trial in a month, but the council feels reluctant to punish her, especially after Alaric was killed. Seems like Bianca has gotten quite cozy with a few of the council members." She tells us. This can't be happening, she can't just get away with what she did.

"What do the other council members think?" I ask.

"They want her punished, of course, but they won't go against Christopher."

"Who is he?" I ask.

"He is an elder, unfortunately he doesn't like Josiah or Theo for that matter." Caroline says.

I feel my anger bubble under my skin. "Why didn't you run for council, Josiah?" I ask. Everyone looks at him, only paying attention when I call his name.

"I was a council member, I stepped down and Tobias and Theo didn't want any part of it," he says. I can tell he isn't happy about neither of them volunteering in his place.

"So, what do you think will happen?"

Josiah seems to think for a second. "I think she won't be punished, Imogen. Unfortunately, with no one challenging Alaric's position we have no say in what the council does, and I can't now because I killed him."

I flop down on the couch, feeling defeated.

"We will find a way, I promise," Theo says, sitting beside me and rubbing my leg.

I lean forward, grabbing my coffee, which has now turned cold. Josiah and Caroline leave after dinner. When they leave, I start doing the dishes. After a bit, I feel Theo's hands slip around my waist, his chin resting on my shoulder.

"What's wrong?" He whispers.

"You know what is wrong," I tell him. He kisses the side of my neck and nods his head.

"We can go to the trial to state our case and see what happens," he tells me.

"And if that doesn't work?" I sigh.

"Well then, we appeal or hope someone steps up for Alaric's position," he tells me.

"Why don't you do it?" I ask.

He seems taken aback for a second. I can feel through the bond it never really crossed his mind and that he is content with how we live, without having to worry about the politics. "The council wouldn't allow it, not while Christopher is in charge," he mutters.

"What's so important about him, that no one will go against him? Aren't everyone vampires?" I ask.

"Well, yes, but he is an elder and a strong one. What are you getting at, Imogen?"

"I just think it might be time for a change in power. You can't tell me you agree with what happened to your father, and that Bianca will just get away with what she has done. We just need to convince the others to agree."

"And if they don't?" Theo asks.

I have been thinking about it all night, everything is off about the council. I don't understand how Bianca isn't being punished. If not for what happened, but for killing my mother and our father. She admitted to both crimes, yet is getting away with everything, and I know she must have something against them, either that or she is sleeping with them. Which I wouldn't put past them.

"If they don't, I make them," I say, my voice level.

"You think you can take down the council?" Theo asks.

I feel anger at his words and feel the darkness slipping over me. It's magic, dark and twisted as it flows through me, fuelling my anger further. I chuckle slightly as I feel its dark tendrils slip over my skin. Wrapping around me protectively, strong and powerful. I have no idea what magic I have, but I know it's not normal elemental magic, it is dark, twisted, sadistic and addictively sweet.

"I know I can," I tell him. I feel my eyes burning and I see Theo step back before a seductive smile spreads onto his lips.

"Let's hope it doesn't come to that," he whispers, feeling the power surging throughout my body from the bond. I know I should fear my magic, but if I have it, why not use it?

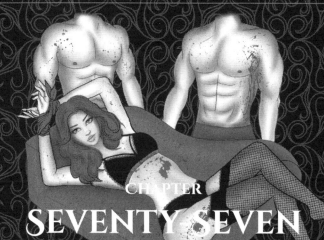

CHAPTER
SEVENTY-SEVEN

Theo

    Getting up this morning I can tell Tobias won't cope with working today. I feel him slip out of bed, sitting upright, his hands run through his hair as he tries waking himself up. One of the plus sides of being a vampire is I don't feel tired and don't require sleep, Tobias, however, does. Even though I do the night feeds and get up with Thaddeus, he still wakes every time he cries. Being a light sleeper is really exhausting for him. Imogen, however, refuses to sleep, forcing herself to stay awake. I hear her at night, walking around the house, always so restless, her mind always racing, and if she isn't walking, she is staring off vacantly.

I wish she would just let herself go to sleep. She may be a vampire, but the witch part of her needs rest. The darkness that I feel through the bond might lessen if she just gets some sleep, but instead, she fights against us on the matter. She is paranoid that someone is going to take him from us. I didn't realize the paranoia that comes with magic, yet watching her is like watching someone slowly lose their grip on reality, slipping ever so slow into madness.

Putting my book down, I turn toward Tobias. "Go back to sleep, I can go in," I tell him.

"You went yesterday," he mumbles and yawns. I know part of the reason he struggles to sleep is that Imogen isn't sandwiched between us anymore. We both find comfort knowing she is within arm's reach. I know that is the primary reason he can't seem to find rest.

"Lay back down, it is fine I don't need sleep," I tell him, watching him flop back down on the bed. He rolls, throwing his arm over my lap, pulling me closer.

I run my fingers through his hair. "We need to do something about Imogen," I whisper, not wanting her to overhear, though I can tell through the bond her mind is preoccupied.

Tobias yawns and I feel him nod. "What do you want to do?" He yawns again, rubbing his eyes, looking up at me.

"I don't know, she needs to sleep; she is getting worse, always pacing and she never stops." I tell him, I can feel his worry through the bond.

"We can put her to sleep," he says, and I hear the thoughts running through his head. Imogen won't like that but if we can distract her enough and we can get her to slip her guard down, it might work.

"The only problem would be Thaddeus. She won't let him remain unwatched while we distract her." I tell him.

"Maybe call mom and see if she will take him for the night? I will convince Imogen to let her. She knows they won't let anything happen to him." Tobias offers.

I nod, it could work. "I will call her today and ask. You can work on Imogen; she doesn't like him away from us." Trying to convince her will be the hardest part. "What if she says no?" I ask, not liking the idea of forcing her.

We might just have to, though. I have noticed the longer she stays awake, the stronger the darkness gets through the bond, cocooning her. I don't like the way she is becoming comfortably familiar with it, almost like she depends on it. Making her feed into it, allowing it to slowly take over her. I don't know everything about witches but I have read enough over the years to know that with it comes a slight craze, especially when it comes to dark magic. I can feel it enveloping her.

"You know we have to do it, even if I have to hold her down. She will forgive us once she feels better," Tobias says, his hard exterior slipping back into place.

One of the many things I love about him. He knows I struggle with being hard on her, yet he is willing to be the bad guy and force her down, so I don't have to. Even if I'm the one that will actually be doing the task of knocking her out, he will be the one to hold her down. He is willing to take the blame for me.

"Just call mom and tell her to come grab Thaddeus after you finish work."

I nod, getting up and heading for the walk-in. It doesn't take long before I walk out, dressed in a suit. Tobias' eyes watch me as I move about the room getting ready. "Tobias, stop, or I will just want to crawl back in bed with you," I tell him, turning to look at him.

He smirks, and I can tell he would prefer that more than me leaving, so I quickly place my shoes on.

"Where is she?" He asks.

"Downstairs, at the kitchen window." I sigh.

Thaddeus stirs in the bassinet and Tobias picks him up. I watch him scrunch his face up before I can smell that he has soiled himself.

"Rock, paper, scissors?" Tobias suggests not wanting to change him. I chuckle at him before putting my hand out, Tobias groans when he chooses paper and I scissors. "I feel like you snoop into my mind every time, surely I can't be this unlucky to lose every time."

"It would help, if you stopped choosing paper." I chuckle, throwing a diaper at him before walking downstairs.

Imogen is standing at the window, staring off vacantly at the scenery. She jumps when I place my hands on her hips, coming up behind her. I kiss her neck and feel her relax into me. I love how her body reacts to us. I just hope tonight, she reacts this way, the idea of forcing her down has me on edge.

"Are you going in today?" She asks, her voice soft.

I nod, running my hands down her body before slipping one underneath the thin fabric of her top, my hands caressing over her stomach before moving to her breasts. I feel her nipples harden and soon, a moan escapes her lips, making my dick twitch in my pants. I can get lost in the feeling of her body under my hands, loving every inch of her. Loving the sounds that spill from her lips.

I hear Tobias step into the room, Thaddeus cooing and eating his little hands, making her attention go to him. She turns in my arms, looking over my shoulder at Tobias who I know is watching us.

"You want to feed him?" He asks, and I feel her nod.

Excitement floods through the bond before it dies slowly as fear sets in. She hasn't fed and newborn vampires require a lot more blood. I can go days, sometimes a week, but Imogen, she needs to feed daily, sometimes twice, depending on her mood. Anger and fear, even arousal, make it hard to control the bloodlust.

Tobias moves awkwardly, shifting his weight from one foot to the other. It makes him nervous when he feels her hesitation and neither of us like handing him over to her. We know it only takes one slip up and she could hurt him, but she is his mother and we can't keep her from him. We aren't that cruel. Turning my head, I kiss her temple before removing my shirt. It is unheard of for vampires to feed off each other; I have never craved my own kind's blood, yet she does and I'm pretty sure it is because it feeds into her magic, strengthening her like a never-ending power source. Undoing the buttons, she watches me, and her eyes glow brighter as uncontrollable hunger takes her over.

She seems to have more control feeding off Tobias, but me, she knows she doesn't have to be so gentle, and I can endure more blood loss than him. Although, it makes me want to feed. I know I can wait till I get to work and retrieve a blood bag. As soon as my shirt is off, her hands run over my chest before she leans in, inhaling my scent.

Her nose runs across my collarbone, making me shiver. Gripping her hips, I lift her, placing her on the edge of the sink so she can reach my neck better. She wraps her legs around my waist, pulling me closer, her hand going to my face and I feel her fangs sink into me.

She moans loudly as my blood rushes into her mouth. I feel her tongue lapping at my skin, making me want her mouth somewhere else, as I feel my pants become a little too tight as I press myself into her. Bloodlust and arousal tend to go hand in hand with us. She bites down again as hunger takes over her, so insatiable and addictive.

When I know she is struggling to pull away, I slip my hand into the waistband of her leggings, my fingers slipping between her folds that are wet with her arousal. She moans, her head falls back, liking the feeling of my fingers inside her and I kiss her. Her fangs scratch my lip. I then pull away from her, she feels annoyed yet doesn't try to stop me.

"When I get home," I tell her, kissing the side of her face. She huffs, annoyed at being riled up only for me to stop. A pout slips onto her face.

Chuckling, I see Tobias step closer, kissing my cheek as he passes Thaddeus to Imogen. Her face lights up at being able to hold him, as she takes the bottle from Tobias's hand.

When I button up my shirt, I walk out to the car. Tobias follows me. "I will call her when I get to work, convince her, Tobias, I really don't want to force her." I tell him, climbing in the car and starting the car. The engine roars to life and I drive down the driveway, heading to work.

CHAPTER
SEVENTY EIGHT

Imogen

While I feed Thaddeus, Tobias walks Theo to the car. I can feel through the bond that Theo and Tobias are discussing something serious, just slightly too far away for me to hear them as they talk in hushed voices. When Tobias walks in, I open up my mind, letting me slip into his mind. Nothing, I know he is deliberately making sure he locks his thoughts up tight where I can't reach them.

"What are you hiding?" I ask when I can't read him.

"Nothing you need to worry about, stay out of my head, Imogen. You don't like when Theo does it to you." He states.

"It doesn't usually bother you," I tell him.

He looks at me, before grabbing a frypan and placing it on the stove. He starts cooking but doesn't say anything else. I can feel they are up to something and it angers me that they are trying to hide it from me.

"Calm yourself, Imogen, remember who is in your arms," he says, eyeing me.

I glance down and readjust him, letting myself focus on feeding him. I play with his hands, letting him calm me. When he finishes his bottle, I place him over my shoulder and start rubbing his back. Every day, I notice slight differences in him, slowly getting bigger and more alert to his surroundings. I feel like I'm going to blink and wake up one day and he will be grown. I don't want him to grow up.

Tobias makes breakfast, placing a plate in front of me. "Please, tell me I didn't just make that for you not to be hungry now?" Tobias says while he eats his own.

I pick up a piece of bacon and bite into it. Food has lost its taste now, I can still taste it, but it doesn't have the same appeal anymore. I force myself to eat, knowing Tobias made it and I can feel him through the bond, worried because I don't eat as much anymore.

By the time I'm done, Thaddeus is asleep again. I sigh, we really need to find a way for him to stay awake during the day so he sleeps at night. Tobias cleans up the dishes before taking him from me.

I try to take him back. "Go shower, your hair is a mess, and you didn't have one last night." He tells me.

"Is that your way of telling me I stink?" I ask him.

His lips turn up into a smile. "No, you could never smell. But it might make you feel better, and you have been wearing the same clothes for two days now," he says, watching me.

Getting up, I walk upstairs, grabbing some clothes as I go. I place them on the bed and walk into the bathroom, turning the shower on. Tobias comes in a few minutes later, placing a towel on the sink before walking out again. I can feel he is nervous about something and I find it getting to me. Washing quickly, I hop out of the shower and find Thaddeus in his bassinet asleep, Tobias sitting on the edge of the bed, waiting for me.

"What is it?" I ask, drying myself. He doesn't say anything, making me suspicious. "I know you have something to say, so say it." I tell him before dropping the towel and putting some jeans on.

"Mom is going to take Thaddeus tonight," he says.

"Are you asking or telling me? Because it sounded like you said she was taking him" I argue.

"I'm telling you she is taking him for the night," he says, his eyes holding mine.

I growl, annoyed by his tone. "No, he stays here." I tell him.

"Imogen, let her take him, it gives us a night off."

"No, I don't want him away from us. What if Bianca-"

Tobias cuts me off. "Bianca is at the council under watch, I know you don't like this but it's happening whether you like it or not. Mom is taking him, Imogen." He states standing up.

I close my eyes, frustrated and pinch the bridge of my nose. I can feel my nails digging into the palm of my other hand.

"Imogen, you will let her. I need sleep, you need sleep."

"He doesn't need to leave though, Tobias. Theo doesn't need sleep and I feel fine," I retort.

"You are not fine, Imogen. It is already organized, Thaddeus is going with mom and dad. They won't let anything happen to him. This isn't up for discussion we already decided." He growls, daring me to go against him.

"So what, Theo wants this as well?"

"Yes, Imogen, one night that's all," he says, moving closer and rubbing my arms.

I feel my anger dissipate as I feel the familiar spark rush over my skin. "Fine, but only one night," I tell him, giving him what he wants.

"Good girl," he mumbles into my hair, as he tugs me to him, holding me in his arms.

I spend the day doing housework before going out and weeding the rose garden. When I come back in, I find Tobias packing a bag for Thaddeus. He looks up when he sees me walk in through the kitchen door. I walk over and wash my hands.

"Theo is coming home early, mom will be here at four to pick him up."

I ignore him, they both know I'm not comfortable with this. Walking out, I walk upstairs and check on Thaddeus. He is asleep, and I jostle him awake as I pick him up. His big green eyes stare back at me.

I remain in the room until I hear the door open downstairs and I know Theo has returned home. I hear footsteps on the stairs before I see him walk into the room, he leans on the door frame watching me and I can feel him rummaging through my thoughts.

"Don't do that!" I snap, shoving him out.

"I was just checking on a scale of one to ten how pissed off you are with me."

"A ten. Now go," I tell him.

"Tobias said you were angry, but it's one night, Imogen. You will survive, I promise," he says, walking in the room toward me. He holds his arms out for Thaddeus and I reluctantly hand him over. "Come say hello to mom," he says, looking down at me. I sigh and get up, walking downstairs. Theo is quick to place Thaddeus in his car seat while I quickly hug Caroline and Josiah.

"I promise he will be fine. I raised three boys. I know what I am doing." She tells me.

I nod but still don't like the idea of him leaving. Caroline and Josiah are quick to leave, probably so I don't change my mind. As soon as the door is closed, Theo and Tobias turn and face me. I roll my eyes, annoyed, turning my back on them and walking upstairs.

Laying on the bed, I feel restless. My mind goes everywhere at once, not able to focus on one thing. My mood gets darker and darker with every minute passing by that he isn't by my side.

"Are you going to just ignore us all night, or are you going to come down?" Tobias's voice says, pulling me from my head. I look out the window and see it is actually dark outside. Grabbing my phone off the nightstand, I look at the time. It's 8:30 pm. Four hours, over four hours, I have been sitting in the same position, time rushing by in what I thought was minutes but is actually hours.

"I'm good here," I tell him, placing the phone down and laying back on the pillow.

Tobias walks over before climbing on the bed. He shifts, placing his legs over me so he is straddling my hips. His hands go to mine before he pulls them above my head.

"We have all night to ourselves and you want to mope," he whispers next to my ear. I feel his breath on my neck before I feel his kiss below my ear, his lips move down my neck, then back up to my chin.

Feeling the bed dip, I turn my head and see Theo lay beside me, propped up, leaning against the headboard.

"What are you two up to?" I ask.

Tobias kisses me hard, his tongue forcing its way in my mouth. I hear him groan before I feel him shift, his knee goes between my legs as he pushes my legs apart and presses his weight down on me. His hands hold mine above my head when I feel something cold touch my wrists. I look up and Theo is placing some metal cuffs around my wrists. I try to pull my hands away when I hear the click of him securing them in place. He yanks my hand higher, attaching the cuffs to the rope on the headboard.

"What are you doing? Untie me, Theo." I want to say more, but cold lips crash on my own, silencing the words that don't leave me. His tongue tastes every inch of mine. I feel Tobias's hands on my waist before I feel him slip my pants off, pulling them down my legs.

CHAPTER
SEVENTY-NINE

obias moves between my legs before pushing them higher and draping them over his broad shoulders, his grip on my thighs pulls my legs apart and I feel his hot breath on my core before he sucks the inside of my thigh, his teeth grazing and I get lost in the sensation, no longer wanting to be set free.

My hips buck when I feel his tongue move between my wet lips, running a line straight to my clit before he sucks it into his mouth. I hear him groan loudly; the vibration makes my legs tremble as his tongue swirls around that sensitive bundle of nerves.

Theo moves, hovering over me, his hands on either side of my face, before leaning closer, a seductive smile playing on his lips, his hypnotic green eyes staring down at me.

"Still want me to untie you?" He whispers, raising an eyebrow.

I shake my head and moan out as Tobias' mouth devours me, making my back arch off the bed. My juices gush out of me as arousal floods me. Theo rips my tank top apart, leaving me only in my strapless bra. He makes fast work of getting rid of it too.

Theo's mouth goes to my nipple as his teeth bite down, my skin heating from the sensation of pain and pleasure. I become a moaning, writhing mess under their hands and lips, my sensations overloaded. Tobias suddenly rams a finger inside me, slides it out and adds another, his tongue still moving and sucking on my clit. I move my hips, riding his face and fingers. I'm so close to the edge, it's almost painful.

He then uses a third finger, slipping it in my ass. My hips buck at the fresh sensation and he uses his other hand to pull my legs further apart. His assault on my pussy becomes too much and I feel my juices spill into his mouth as I come. A long moan escapes my lips before being swallowed by Theo's lips as he kisses me. I feel him chuckle softly against my lips at my reaction to them.

My legs are shaking as Tobias sits up, moving between my legs.

"Uncuff her hands, I want them behind her back," he says to Theo. Theo undoes the cuffs and my arms feel heavy, flopping down on the bed above my head. Tobias picks me up under my arms, placing me on top of him, so my legs are straddling his hips. I feel Theo pull my hands behind my back before securing them with the cuffs. I move my wrists, the cold metal digging in painfully to my wrists.

Theo undoes Tobias's jeans before pulling them down, I feel his erection flop out, hitting my ass cheek. I wiggle my hips, trying to move lower, wanting to sink down on it, but Tobias pulls me forward, his lips capturing mine, and I can taste myself on his tongue as it fights mine for dominance. He groans into my mouth before thrusting his hips upward, his cock pressing between my wet folds but not entering.

I wiggle, trying to move lower when he does it again, making me moan into his mouth.

Tobias pulls away and I feel his lips move on mine as he speaks. "You want this," he says, thrusting upward again, his cock sliding between my folds before hitting my clit.

"Yes, all of it" I moan, kissing him harder. He grips my hips, pushing them down on his cock. I move my hips in a circular motion, loving the feeling of his cock, stretching and filling me.

"Ah, fuck," he says, his grip on my hips getting tighter as I continue to move my hips in the same slow, circular motion. Theo suddenly grabs my hair, pulling my head back. His tongue plunges into mouth as he climbs on the bed behind me. His other hand runs up my side before it squeezes my breast, my nipple hardening under his cold hands. My skin feels like it's boiling and Theo's cold touch makes goosebumps rise over my body and makes me shiver.

He lets go of my hair and I feel him position himself behind me, his icy, cold hand running lower to my abdomen before sliding between my legs. His fingertips rub my clit as I feel him push inside me, making me moan at the overfull sensation. I move my hips, adjusting to the new sensation before I feel Theo grip my hips, and he slams inside me, making me bounce on top of Tobias. I wiggle my hands, wanting to touch them, but they don't budge.

I feel my stomach tighten as they both thrust in harder, and I have trouble staying upright, not being able to use my hands. Theo grabs the handcuffs, pulling me back to him, one hand going back between my legs and rolling my clit between his fingers, while his other hand wraps around my throat. His grip tightens and I feel my orgasm building to an entirely different level with not being able to breathe, my head becoming dizzy. Theo let's go for a second, flicking my hair over one shoulder before it goes back to my neck, squeezing tightly.

Tobias' hands pinch my nipples, making me moan out at the sudden pain as he rolls them between his fingers, my orgasm ripples through me, making my walls clench around them, but they don't let up, thrusting harder and I feel my stomach tighten again. I feel Theo's lips on my neck, then his fangs; I shiver. It runs through my entire body to my toes. Then, I feel his fangs break my skin, it hurts for a second then feels fantastic as the endorphins in his saliva send me over the edge again and I feel both of them still inside me, knowing they both found their own release. Riding out my orgasm, I feel light-headed and weak. I try to move when Theo's grip on me tightens. His arm wrapped securely around my stomach, the other still around my throat.

My eyes dart to Tobias in panic, but he just watches, which has me confused. The dizziness becomes too much, and I struggle against him trying to pull away, but I'm much too weak. I try to breathe, but his grip on my throat only tightens, my lungs burning for air. My body feels heavy, Theo's grip is strong and unrelenting. I can feel his tongue lapping at my skin, hear my heart pounding in my ears before I feel a strange sensation roll over my entire body, a weightlessness I haven't felt since I was plunged into the darkness of my death. I feel my body go slack against Theo, my eyes getting heavy, too heavy for them to remain open as they flutter shut.

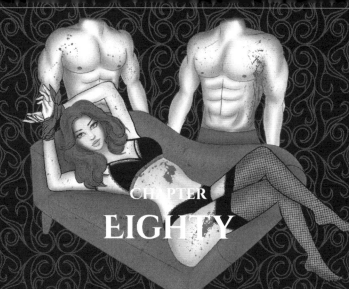

CHAPTER
EIGHTY

Theo

From the moment I sunk my fangs into her neck, I could feel it. Slithering through her bloodstream. Her blood tastes the same as before she changed, which shocks me. The initial taste of it hitting my tongue overwhelms me, so much that I feel my grip on her throat become tighter. Bloodlust takes over completely.

But that's not all I taste. At first, I didn't recognize what it was. Well, until I feel its icy tendrils seep into me. I knew something was wrong when I first sank my fangs into her but couldn't figure out what, until I felt it.

The darkness that has been plaguing her, addictive and sweet. Yet, so cold. I haven't felt the cold since I was changed. But this is like ice cold, and I can't help but shiver as I feel it consumes me. I try to pull away, but I fail; the darkness sinks into me, refusing to let me go, making me crave it like a drug addict. I can literally feel it bleeding into my soul, scarring it as it leaves its mark there forever, tainting the darkest parts of me.

If insanity has a flavor, this is it, sitting on the verge between slipping from light to darkness. I feel Imogen wriggling, trying to loosen my grip on her, but I just hold on tighter, refusing to let go. I know I should have the moment I feel it, yet I can't seem to pry my lips away from her neck. And after a while, I don't want to anymore. My hunger becomes insatiable when I feel the darkness leave her, her blood changes taste to an entirely different level of purity and I can taste her magic. Strong and powerful, flexing like a muscle as it pulses through her.

Imogen goes limp against me. Yet, it still isn't enough. I can feel the darkness leave her and creep over me like a snake wrapping itself around me. Tobias' voice pulls me out of my hunger filled craze.

I feel him grab my hand that is on her waist. "Theo, let her go, she is out." His voice is stern and laced in panic.

When I can't let her go, he suddenly rips her forward, her body pulling from my grip as she slumps onto his chest. I growl, and it sounds foreign even to me. Sadistic and crazed.

"Theo, stop," he growls warningly at me before I feel his claws dig into my arm and I realize I'm trying to take her back from him.

I freeze, realizing I'm being taken over by the darkness that consumes her. I fight against it, shaking the feeling off though it never leaves. I feel it move about my body, wriggling under my skin, trying to find its way back in.

Tobias rolls between my legs, turning and laying Imogen beside him, her hair falls over her face. She is so blue looking, drained of life, and the sight is quite shocking to witness.

Standing up, I move to the window, forcing myself away from her. Tobias glances at me and I can tell he is feeling through the bond, trying to figure out what is wrong. My fangs ache in my gums, almost throbbing; the pain is so great. Hunger is something I usually have a good grip on, but whatever magic she possesses is throwing my control out the window.

"You okay?" He asks, brushing Imogen's hair out of her face.

"Fine," I tell him, but the words are slurred from my fangs still protruding painfully.

"Shit, Theo, she is ice cold," Tobias says, making me walk over to her.

"She is fine. If she was dead, you would have felt the bond break. I can hear her heart still; it is just faint." I tell him. He nods before tucking the blanket under her chin.

"What was that? I could feel it taking you over through the bond." Tobias asks.

I don't know how to explain it. "I'm not sure, whatever magic she possesses is dark and light at the same time. It wouldn't let me go."

"What do you mean, Theo?" He asks, looking at her then, back at me.

"I don't know how to explain it. I have drank from witches before, you can taste their element in their blood, but Imogen is different."

"How?"

"Like, she tastes like all of them combined, like it is too much, overpowering everything. To think I thought she was crazy when she said she wanted to take down the council. But after tasting whatever that is, I have no doubt she could."

Tobias' eyes flick to me, and I can see the fear behind them.

"Whatever it is, whatever she is. It isn't just light but also dark. Like the more she uses her magic, the darker it affects her. It is like teetering on the edge of insanity."

"That would explain her mood swings then," Tobias says, sitting up.

"No, it's more than that, Tobias. It's addictive. The more power she uses, the more she will let it overtake her. Her magic scares me." I tell him, honestly. I don't understand how she is strong enough to not give into it. Can't understand how she isn't crazed by it. The malevolence it brings is something I have never felt before. Twisted, dark and so cold.

I can still feel it running rampant, trying to find a way to take over me. She is a newborn vampire with a power I never felt before and being a vampire it is like it is feeding off of her, like a never-ending battery source, only strengthening it.

Now that it is in me, I can feel it trying to feed off me like a leech. Trying to strengthen and take over, making me want to give into the darkest parts of myself. It scares me, knowing I want to let it. But if I feel like this, I can only imagine how she feels.

"So, what should we do?" Tobias asks, feeling my unease through the bond we share.

"I'm not sure, but we can't let her keep harboring that sort of darkness. She will go insane, Tobias."

"Does it feel like it lessened, though?"

I think for a second. Her magic did change toward the end, felt purer not as tainted and twisted. "Yes, the darkness left her and went into me. I can feel it moving through me."

Tobias looks toward me, concern crossing his features. "Can you handle it, Theo?" He asks, and I can feel what he is asking. I have been controlling the darkest parts of me for so long, yet even I feel it tries to taint me the way it does her.

"I'm not sure, maybe in small doses." I can feel his thoughts running through his head and I know what he wants to ask but doesn't know how to. "I know what you want Tobias; I can do it, but Imogen may not agree. She will feel the effects of it leaving her and I think she might not want to give up the power it offers."

"We will see how she is once she wakes up," he says before walking into the bathroom. I nod, not really liking the idea, but it might be my only choice. I know the sort of power she has will eventually become all-consuming if we don't find a way to control it.

"She won't be happy when she wakes up," I tell him, imagining her anger that will be aimed at us.

Tobias chuckles, nodding his head. "Hopefully, you, taking some of the darkness also took her anger." He sings out from the bathroom and I hear him turn the shower on.

When he leaves the room, my eyes flick to her face, sleeping blissfully unaware of what just happened and the effect her blood has over me. My gums tear open and my fangs protrude just at the sight of her. Getting up, I walk toward the bathroom, not trusting myself around her. Tobias is in the shower, he opens the door, allowing me to hop in, but his scent is overwhelming with the steam heating the room.

"I need to go, Tobias. I need to try to run it out of my system." I tell him.

I feel crazed and manic with hunger. Tobias looks at me and I can feel it worries him. He nods his head before leaning out of the shower. I kiss his lips before darting out of the room, needing to get away from them before I feed on Tobias. I know I won't stop if I do and I won't risk hurting my mates.

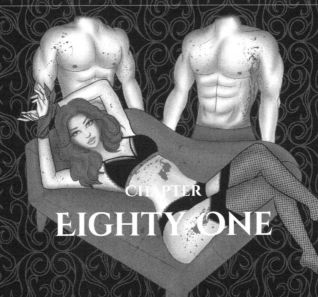

CHAPTER
EIGHTY-ONE

Imogen

Waking up, I stretch my limbs. My body feels stiff like I have been in the same position all night, yet I also feel lighter, and happier than I have in ages. I feel someone move beside me, feeling their warm skin against mine and I know it's Tobias.

That's when everything comes crashing back to me. Sitting upright, I look around the room and realize we are in our bed, Theo is nowhere to be seen. I sniff the air, smelling for his scent, yet I find nothing except the smell of Tobias. My gums tingle as I breathe in his scent. Tobias wakes startled and I realize my growl is louder than I thought. He stares at me and smiles, and I feel anger boil up before spewing over and I'm suddenly on top of him.

Smacking into him as I realize, he just watched while Theo drained me of my blood and effectively knocked me out. My fists raining down on him seemed to have no effect on him at first, until I hit him hard in the face, splitting his lip open.

The smell of his blood fills the room and my senses become over-loaded, and I realize I'm completely ravenous. I watch the blood trickle down his lip and over his chin. Pinning him down, I lean over him before moving closer, completely entranced at the sight of his blood. I run my tongue over his chin to his lip, licking the blood up.

I hear him groan at the sensation of my tongue, running over his warm flesh. Biting on his lip, realization must dawn on him as he tries shoving me off. My nails dig into his arms as bloodlust takes over and I bite into the flesh of his neck. His blood spilling into my mouth makes me moan as it soothes the burning ache in my throat, promising to extinguish the burning throughout my body.

I growl, pulling his head to the side, and I can feel him trying to get me to let go. He grips my hair pulling my head back and I growl at him. I can feel his blood running down my cheek as bloodlust takes over everything and all I can think about his ripping into his carotid artery.

I feel Tobias' worry fleetingly through the bond before he suddenly smashes his lips into mine. The distraction makes me growl before arousal floods me through the bond, making me forget the need to feed.

I kiss him back harder and grind my hips against him, my lips moving to his chest as I taste his salty skin under my tongue. I can feel his hands in my hair as I move lower, pull his pants down and wrap my hand around his hardened length. Lust consumes every part of me. Before I go to take him in my mouth, I'm suddenly ripped back upwards.

"As much as I would love for you to continue," he kisses me softly before pulling away. "I would rather keep my manhood attached to me." He tells me, making me confused.

He chuckles lightly, and I furrow my eyebrows as he moves his hand to my face, his thumb pressing against my fangs, which I realize are still protruding. I sit up, startled at the realization.

"You let him attack me?" I ask him, suddenly remembering the reason I hit him in the first place.

I hear him sigh and sit, draping my legs on either side of his waist. He rubs my bare thighs with his hands, making me shiver. "We didn't have a choice Imogen, you wouldn't sleep." He tells me, observing my face carefully. I try to argue back, but my hunger is out of control. My words slur as I try to speak around my fangs. I eventually give up, knowing he can't understand me, I sound drunk.

"How do you feel, do you feel better?" He asks.

I think for a second. I felt better actually, lighter, like it has lifted a weight off of me. My usual depressing mood isn't weighing me down.

Suddenly, I hear Theo walk in, making my head snap to the door as I wait for him to walk up the stairs. When he steps into the room, he looks different, and I can feel a strange energy rolling off of him. His eyes are darker, and he smells different.

"What happened to you?" I ask.

Tobias is also observing him as he moves closer. He almost seems angry, which I find is true when he walks over, gripping my chin harshly making me look up at him. "Why the fuck didn't you say anything?"

"Theo?" Asks Tobias angrily at Theo's tone.

Theo's eyes turn dark, like raging storm clouds behind their hypnotic green color. "No, Tobias. Shut up. She should have told us how bad it was before it got this out of hand."

I'm confused at what he means and pull my face away from him. He growls, and the sound sends goosebumps over my skin. Standing up, I walk across the bed, heading toward the bathroom.

Stepping off the bed, Theo is suddenly standing in front of me, his eyes blazing with anger. "Why? Fucking answer me, Imogen. Stop trying to walk away."

I shove him backwards and I hear him growl before lunging at me. I get knocked backwards on the bed, Theo towering over the top of me. I feel Tobias jump and try to push him off of me.

"Theo, get off her now," Tobias growls out, grabbing his shoulder trying to pull him off.

"Not until she fucking answers," he bellows, making me flinch at the anger in his words.

"I have no idea what the fuck you're even talking about, Theo." I argue back. He shoves my wrists into the bed so hard if I was human still, I'm sure they would have broken.

"The darkness, you were letting it take over." He screams. Then I realize what he is talking about and I realize why he has had a complete personality change.

"My magic is none of your business, Theo. Now get off me," I yell.

"None of my business? I drained you last night, and now the dark magic that was consuming you is now in me. Tell me how that is not my fucking business?"

"I never told you to drain me. Now get off, it's not my fault you can't handle a bit of magic."

He sits up, and I try to move off the bed when he grabs my wrist. "You should have told us; you shouldn't have been taking this in on your own," he says, making me look at him. He lets go before placing his head in his hands. "It's so cold, it won't let go of me," he whispers, and I see him shake his head.

"You shouldn't have drank from me, what is wrong with you?" I can sense his anger through the bond at my words.

I see his fists clench tightly before he speaks. "You tell me next time as soon as you feel it," he tells me.

I shake my head. "Not if this is how you are going to react, I won't" I tell him getting up.

"It's only this bad because you have let it bottle up, I can feel it getting weaker. It will slowly leave, but make sure you tell me, Imogen. I can help take it away."

"No! I won't let you do that." I tell him.

What I don't say is how comfortably familiar I have become with the feeling. I feel fine now, but the addictive power it offers makes me crave the icy cold sensation running through me.

Suddenly I hear tires on the road outside. Tobias' head snaps to the window, he then turns to Theo.

"Did you ask mom to bring some?" Theo nods his head. I turn to walk downstairs when Tobias' arm snakes around my waist. "Stay here, I will be back in a second."

"I want to see Thaddeus," I tell him.

"You will, but right now you need to feed, so you can't go near him. Mom brought blood bags, just wait till after you have fed," he says, rubbing my cheeks with his thumbs.

"I can feed off Theo," I tell him.

He doesn't answer, but Theo jumps up angrily. "Stay here, Imogen, you're not feeding off me when I have your blood in my system," he says, pulling me against him before sitting on the edge of the bed forcing me to sit on his lap. His arms are strong around my waist; Tobias ducks downstairs. I hear car doors opening and shutting before I hear footsteps on the veranda.

"I didn't mean to get angry at you. I was just scared, knowing you have been letting this consume you for weeks, saying nothing," Theo mumbles against my back.

"I'm fine Theo, I have been fine," I tell him trying to get up, but his grip tightens.

"No, you think you're fine, Imogen. I have had so much time to learn control, so much time to learn how to control the bloodlust. But this, I struggled with. You are to tell me when it gets too much, Imogen, don't let it consume you like you have been letting it. Not when I can help take it away."

"What if I don't want you to take it away?" I tell him and he shifts, pulling me back and looking at me.

I can see the concern on his face. He goes to say something when Tobias walks in, a cooler in his hand. He opens it and my mouth instantly starts watering at the sight of the blood bags. Tobias tosses me one and I bite into it. Tobias hands one to Theo, and he does the same, watching me as his teeth tear through the plastic sleeve. I drain the first bag hungrily before Tobias chucks me another. He holds one out for Theo, but he shakes his head.

Tobias then closes the lid, carrying it back downstairs while I punch a small hole in the bag with my nail this time before drinking it down. Cold blood isn't the same as warm, straight from the vein blood, but does the job. When I finish the blood bag, Theo taps my leg, wanting me to hop up. I stand, shifting out of his way. He takes the empty blood bag from my hand before grabbing my hand and tugging me toward the door.

"Mom has some news about Bianca, but please remain calm when you find out. We don't need any more drama right now."

I growl at the mention of her name but nod my head. I feel a flicker of my magic stir in my veins, Theo must have felt it in the bond as he stops and looks back at me.

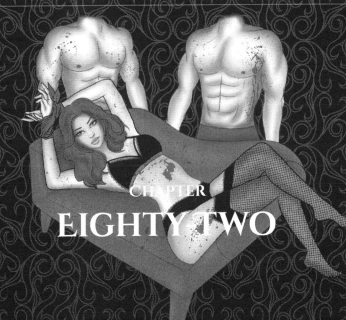

EIGHTY TWO

Walking downstairs, I can instantly sense his presence. The light green essence of my son's aura glows brightly around him as he lays in Caroline's arms; his aura is so pure and innocent as he sleeps peacefully. I walk toward her, only for Tobias to step in my way, taking Thaddeus from his mother. I want nothing more than to hold him, but obviously Tobias and Theo don't trust me. This entire trust thing they have going on with me and my son is really starting to grind my gears.

Josiah looks better today, more life about as his eyes scan the room before landing on me. He smiles, but I can see the worry behind his eyes as he sits on the stool at the island counter. Caroline also smiles sadly at me, taking her seat. I sit across from them and I can tell they aren't happy with the news they are about to share.

"You look well rested, Imogen," Caroline states, making my cheeks heat up. Josiah raises an eyebrow at my blushing cheeks, his eyes going to Tobias, who has a lazy smirk on his face as he feeds our son.

"So, what is this news about Bianca?" I ask, wanting to just rip that metaphorical band aid off. Josiah glances toward Theo and doesn't even try to hide the anger that is directed at him. I can tell whatever happened the blame is being put onto Theo by his father, which only makes me more eager to hear what it is.

"Bianca's hearing has been postponed, the council has called a meeting for some reason and asked us all to attend. Apparently, Bianca is running for a position on the council and Christopher has agreed and wants to have the hearing after she has been sworn in."

Sworn in? If she is sworn in, how will she be reprimanded if she is a part of the council? Who, in their right mind, would give a position of power to a psychotic bitch like Bianca?

"What, but how would the trial be fair if she is a council member? Wouldn't she be able to have a say in her punishment if it has to be decided by all nine members?" Tobias growls at the information and it is clear that he is only just finding out himself right now, like me. I watch as his eyes dart to Theo before he angrily looks away.

"Okay, why is everyone looking at Theo like this is his fault?"

"Because it is his fault. Him and his damn temper, always stirring up trouble that I have to get him out of." His father bellows clearly, not happy about whatever it was his son has done.

Theo just shrugs his shoulders like it is nothing and he can't care less about whatever it is he did. "I pissed off Christopher around a year ago when I fired his son," Theo says blandly, like it isn't a big thing.

"Fired his son? You disfigured him, you fool. The son of one of the highest regarded elders, and you disfigured him!" Josiah yells, making Thaddeus cry.

He quickly sits down and apologizes for his outburst of anger. Tobias gives him a nod and calms Thaddeus.

"Who is his son?" I ask, curious who this person is that Theo injured.

"His name is Max, and he is nothing but a self-entitled idiot," Theo says.

Max? Why have I heard that name before? I know I have heard it somewhere, and I try to rack my brain for where I heard it. Then it hits me, Merida had mentioned Theo almost attacking an employee at work, his name was Max and he left for a rival company.

"Merida said you almost strangled him in a meeting," I say, remembering her words.

"Almost strangled him? He did way worse than that. He took his eye and mutilated his face," Josiah says angrily, making me look at Theo with disgust.

"I thought this Max person was human. Merida said he quit and works for a rival company now." Tobias nods his head.

"He does work for a rival company; he is also human. Similar to you Imogen, his mother was human when she fell pregnant with him. He was changed not long after the incident. Christopher, his father, didn't want to take any chances with Theo being so hotheaded."

"Hey, you can't blame me for this. I did my time over, twelve damn days of constant lashings for one damn eye." Theo retorts, annoyed.

"Be grateful, that's all you got. The boy's eye can't grow back, you're just lucky I still had connections within the council that went to bat for you." Josiah tells him.

"Why did you do it?" I ask, curious as to why he would attack an Elder's son.

"Do you really need to ask? It's the same person we have had constant drama with." Caroline says, frustrated.

"Bianca, always fucking Bianca," I mutter, and Caroline nods, confirming my words.

"Yes, and now that Alaric is gone, she has been getting awfully cozy with Max again, although they have always been cozy. But with Alaric out of the picture, she has sunk her claws into Max. Christopher knows what Bianca did, yet his revenge for his son outweighs that." Josiah announces.

I shake my head and place my head in my hands, trying to think. We just can't catch a break and can't escape Bianca. I zone out, trying to come up with something, anything but I'm not all that familiar with laws of the council. Tobias, placing Thaddeus in my lap, makes me look up. I cradle him in my arms and am shocked he hasn't fallen asleep already.

"If Bianca gets a position on the council, what sort of punishment will she get?" I ask, wanting to prepare myself for the worst-case scenario.

"If she gets a seat at the council, Imogen, she won't be punished." Josiah answers before throwing daggers at his son.

My blood instantly starts boiling at his words. No punishment after what she did at all? It seems impossible, what kind of backwards laws do they have that will allow no punishment for murder and attempted murder? She killed three people for god's sake and kidnapped a baby. How can they not hold her accountable for that?

I don't even realize how angry I am until I feel my surroundings shake violently. The car alarms outside blare loudly, the entire house shakes and the rumbling from the ground sounds like thunder.

"Imogen, get yourself under control," Tobias hisses, running over and ripping my son from me. I try to get a grip of my emotions but enraged isn't even a word to describe the feeling running through me, as I think of all the people she hurt and will get away with. My mother, Claire, my father, me and my son suffered at her hands and they are just going to let her go around like she did nothing.

Electricity starts zapping loudly, the lights flicker, even the fire crackles in the fireplace turns into an inferno, raging up the chimney.

I close my eyes, trying to reign in what little control I have left when I suddenly feel cold hands grip my arms and the rush of air around me. Opening my eyes, I see we are outside in the rose garden. The next thing I see is Theo and I see nothing but red. Red raging fiery anger. This is his fault, she is going to get away with everything because he had some grudge against a council member's son.

"You? You did this. This is your fault!" I scream, taking a step toward him.

His eyes blaze with anger at my words and he takes a step toward me, his hand outstretched, trying to grab me. But I quickly sidestep, I can feel his intention and it is to take the darkness that is spreading throughout me like wildfire.

"Imogen!" He growls when I sidestep again.

I can feel my anger building, igniting my magic, so thick and sweet, addictively cold. Wrapping its thick tendrils around me. I love the feeling of it bleeding into my soul, dangerous, cold and so strong. The day turns to night as the wind picks up, dark clouds filling the sky. Lightning lights up the sky, thunder so loud its crack can be felt as it vibrates through the ground.

Theo lunges at me, and I actually laugh. I predict the move a few seconds before he does it and by the time he reaches my position, I'm ready for him. My hand comes up to the center of his chest, energy bursting from my palm, throwing him backwards with so much force he skids across the grass.

He shakes himself off before standing, I flick my wrist and watch as he screams in agony. I like the sweet sound of his gasps of pain as he drops to the ground. Writhing in pain as I boil the blood in his veins. Standing over him, I look down at him, some small part is nagging at me in the back of my head not to hurt him.

But I want to, and that part is stronger. Kneeling beside him, I watch as his eyes snap to mine. Yet, he doesn't look scared, and I can't smell fear coming from him, but looking in his eyes I can see acceptance of what was about to happen.

And it makes me falter for a second, my mind going blank at the look he is giving me. His eyes glow brighter, burning into me as I feel fog cloud my brain. I try to get rid of the feeling that is trying to take over my senses, dulling the anger but I shake it off, knowing it is Theo's doing.

I hear Tobias yell, making me look at him as he runs out of the house. I notice Caroline's panicked face as she runs out behind him with my son in her arms. Josiah walks out a second after. They start running toward me and I look back down at Theo, turning my head to the side as I watch as he tries to ignore the burning inside of him. His eyes focus on me. I push my fingers into his chest, and can feel his blood coating my hand. I can not only see his pain but feel it searing through my chest as my hand moves inside his chest cavity. I hear Caroline scream loudly, making my attention go back to her.

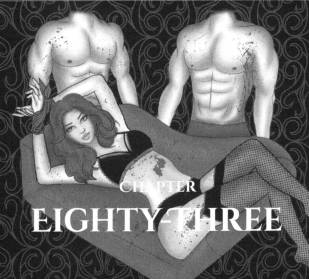

CHAPTER
EIGHTY-THREE

heo's grip on my wrist makes me realize what I'm about to do, giving Tobias enough time to reach me. Tobias grips my wrist, along with Theo, but the darkness is stronger as it surges through me.

Sparks move up my arm from their touch, and I can feel Tobias and Theo lending me their strength through the bond as I fight against the darkness. Encouraging me to fight against it, to fight for them.

"You don't want to do this, Imogen," Tobias says, his grip tight on my arm.

I feel like I'm stuck, not able to move, frozen in time, when I feel the fog rush over me. Only this time I don't shake it off, I let it move over me, letting it relax me and I throw all my focus on the feeling of the fog calming and muting my thoughts that are racing.

I relax and take a deep breath, concentrating on my breathing and I feel my hand release Theo, falling backwards on the grass. Theo pants as he catches his breath, Tobias lays flat on his back, and I know he can feel the pain Theo is in.

Yet, I can still feel the darkness, trying to force its way back, force

484

its control over me as the storm above us rags to magnitude levels. Theo, regaining his strength, sits up and brushes his hand over mine, but I pull mine away. I fear what I could have done to him. I do this, and I finally understand what Theo meant. I'm addicted to the power, addicted to the feeling it gives me. And when I'm like this, I forget who I am, forget what they mean to me.

"I'm okay, Imogen," he says, trying to reassure me.

I shake my head. Guilt eats away at me, I could have killed him, and destroyed Tobias because I let my emotions get the better of me, let the magic have the control it wants. But most of all, I'm losing who I am to something that is going to destroy me and those I love.

I feel Tobias brush his hand down my back as Theo crouches in front of me. I'm torn between what I know I need to do and what I crave. I crave the power that is within me, like a drug. A drug I don't want to admit is a problem.

Yet, my love for them outweighs it. I know if I let the magic have control, if I give in to it, I'm not only going to lose myself. I know I'll lose them too. That isn't a sacrifice I'm willing to make.

Everyone has a breaking point, and I know I reached mine already, and I know they aren't far off from theirs. I know the decision they will make, and it would be the same for me if our roles were reversed. I would turn my back on them for the sake of our son. Thinking of Thaddeus, I feel tears run down my face. I'm angry with myself and what I allow myself to become.

"We are going to work this out, Imogen," Theo says, making me look at him.

Theo is drenched in blood and I did that to him. And he is still here, trying to make me feel better even though I hurt them. He is right, we are going to work this out, but at this moment, I'm a danger to them, a danger to myself. Theo and Tobias must have sensed my guilt as they both try to reach for me, but I shake them off.

"Run," I don't know what makes them move, Theo and Tobias are suddenly gone from my side. I won't risk it taking over, I won't risk losing them when they are all I have left.

Feeling it running over me white hot and angry, the storm reacts to my emotions as I feel it hit me. The pain ripples through me as I feel it strike me down.

Pulling all the energy from the storm, I direct it to where I stand. I scream when I feel it zap through me. The pain isn't like anything I have felt before. The sort of pain where you wish for death just so it would be over with. Every muscle in my body tenses and spasms. Pain shoots down my neck as I feel the power burning up and sizzling, burning hot like lava. The pain cripples me, as I feel the magic leave me, forcing it back into the broken bracelet that sits on my wrist. Now, I know why Witches have talismans.

Sometimes the power is more than we can handle and as much as I want it, I can't control it. My magic isn't worth losing everything, isn't worth losing them. When I feel the last remnants of my magic travel down my arm and creep out my fingertips, I feel this emptiness before I feel my body give in to the pain radiating throughout me. I feel like my soul is being sucked out of my body. My magic has become such a big part of me, and now it is gone. I feel as my fight goes with it. I can live without my magic; I can't live without them.

My body becomes heavy as I can't hang on to consciousness any longer and I don't want to. The pain becomes unbearable. I just hope that when I wake up, it doesn't hurt anymore, and I can't hurt them anymore. The last thing I remember is feeling slight relief as I feel familiar sparks of the bond travel over my body as I'm lifted in someone's arms and I see the darkness of unconsciousness.

Tobias POV

I watch as she loses control, one minute she is fine, the next I can feel the darkness swirling within her. She is a ticking time bomb about to explode. Theo knows firsthand what the darkness is capable of, and I can feel his fear coming through to me as he watches as her eyes blaze. The entire house shakes and the power flickers. It worries me that the entire place is going to come down around us as the house rocks violently.

Theo glances at me and I know what he is going to do, although I'm anxious about him being close to her while she is like this.

Thaddeus screams loudly from the noise, stirring in my arms, Theo reacts quickly as he grabs her, a blur flying past as he runs her outside. Dad and mom look on helplessly, unsure of what is going on. They know she has dark magic but haven't seen the destruction she can cause. Handing Thaddeus off to my mother, I run to help Theo, knowing he will be the first one to cop the brunt of her anger. What I'm not expecting to find as I run out is that Imogen has her hand in his chest, about to rip his heart out. I watch horrified as the two people I love most in this world are on the verge of destroying each other. Imogen glances toward me as we come out, my mother screaming as she witnesses Imogen lose control.

Theo, noticing her distraction, grips her wrist, giving me enough time to reach her. The power surging through her is stronger than both of us put together. I can feel through the bond she is trying to fight against it, it is losing battle. Panic seizes me as I watch her fight herself.

"You don't want to do this, Imogen." I tell her, and I can feel she doesn't want to do it.

I pull against her, but it is like pulling on a brick wall and I don't even think it is her anymore but the magic drawing energy from Theo, feeding into her magic. I can feel her trying not to give in, feel Theo's agony through the bond. When I feel his grip slip slightly, I watch as his eyes glaze over and I watch as he tries to compel her.

She notices the fog and I can feel it breaking down her barriers. Not because he is stronger, but because she is letting it. Imogen doesn't want to hurt him and when I feel her relax, I know he has her. She lets go, and we both fall backwards. I watch her become plagued with guilt, feel it rush over her, and I fear what she would do next as I feel her slip into an overwhelming depression.

We both try to reassure her, try to let her know we can help her. Something shifts inside her, something that scares me. I've never felt her this sad and lost, yet there is also determination in her and I can't understand the intention behind it until it is too late. Theo flicks through her thoughts before realization dawns on him at the same time as she whispers one word. "Run."

I want to stop her, want to help her find another way, but Theo stands up and shoves me back just as the lightning strikes her, pinning her in place. I watch as it wraps itself around her like a lasso, spreading over her skin. Her eyes glow brightly as she screams in agony. Her pain overwhelms me, and I feel Theo drop through the bond. Imogen's pain brings us to our knees as we watch her suffer. The electricity burns her skin and wraps around her before I see the bracelet on her wrist glow angrily and I figure out what she is doing. She is sending it back, letting it go, even though it is destroying her to do so.

I can't catch my breath, feeling her agony through the bond makes it hard to breathe, like she is tearing a piece of herself away. Finally, it fizzles out, the sky clears and the gold in her eyes is gone. She is slipping into unconsciousness and Theo gets to her in time as she collapses. We watch a smile slip onto her face before her eyes flutter shut, only they aren't the gold of her magic anymore but the deep electric blue that we both love.

My parents watch as we bring her inside. No one says anything, we don't have to. We all know what she gave up. We all know how much magic means to a witch. She may not have known what she was for all those years, but we know that losing it will take a huge toll on her. Imogen did it, anyway, knowing full well what she is going to lose. She did it for us, for her son.

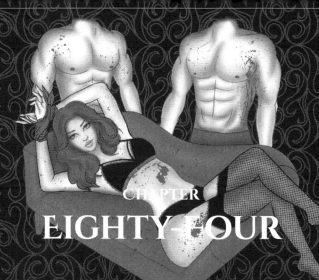

CHAPTER
EIGHTY-FOUR

Imogen

Stretching like a cat, I open my eyes. The light shining through the windows makes me squint at its brightness. I can tell it is morning, and I have slept the entire day and night away. I feel different, but not in a bad way, just strange. Feeling icy fingers run up my spine, sending sparks to my core, I feel my stomach tighten and my walls clench at the feeling. Tobias isn't in bed. Rolling over, I find Theo watching me, his hand moving over my hip with my movement, a book in his other hand.

Sitting up on my elbow, I reach over, running my fingers over his chest. Everything feels different, he feels different, colder than usual. He shivers under my touch.

"What are you reading?" I ask, curious as I haven't seen that book before. It looks different, old, and the paper is thicker than most books, it looks like old parchment. The color of the pages stained yellow in places.

"A book about elemental magic," he says, placing the book down and rolling on his side to face me. Reaching my hand up, I trace my fingertips over his face, loving the feeling of his skin and his reaction to me touching him. Grabbing my hand, he kissed my fingertips.

"I'm sorry" I whisper, feeling bad that I nearly killed him yesterday.

"Don't be, everyone has moments of weakness, Imogen." He tells me, and I can feel through bond he doesn't feel any animosity towards me over what I did.

"I love you," I tell him.

"How much do you love me?" He asks, waggling his eyebrows.

Leaning up, I kiss his lips, and I feel him smile against my lips. I pull back and watch his face drop slightly. "Maybe after I eat, I'm starving."

"I got something you can eat and wrap those pretty lips around," Theo says, not giving up.

"Tempting but..."

"But what?" He asks, moving above me and pressing his erection into my crotch. I moan at the feeling of his hard length, pressing tightly against his boxer shorts.

"We can have a quickie in the shower, before everyone gets here," he whispers next to my ear before sucking on the skin below my neck. His words make me pull back slightly.

"Where is Thaddeus?" Theo holds himself up with his elbows on either side of my face, looking down at me.

"With mom and dad, we weren't sure how you would wake up so thought it's safer if mom had him again for the night." He answers, and I nod my head.

"What about Tobias?" I ask when I realize how silent the house is, I can't hear anything other than us in the house.

"He is downstairs, ironing my shirt."

I snort, trying to picture the big brute with an iron in his hand, doing homemaker duties. Wrapping my legs around his waist, I pull Theo closer. He moves his hips, his lips coming down on mine. I moan into his mouth when I feel his tongue brush mine. Theo groans as I can feel my legs become moist with desire; my panties soaked.

Pulling away, Theo's lips move down to my neck. "Shower, Theo, we still have to get ready to see the council. What time is it anyway?" I ask while his lips venture down. I feel him slide my shirt up, his lips moving to my hip.

"A little after seven, we have plenty of time," he says against my skin.

I feel him slide my panties down, before I feel him suck on my thigh, his teeth nipping at the skin, making goosebumps rise. "Mmm, you smell divine," he says just before I feel his tongue lick my wet folds. I moan and my back arches off the bed at the feeling of his cold tongue, swirling around my clit. He devours me and I feel my skin heat, my body tenses as I pull my thighs further apart, his tongue lapping and sucking sending me crazy. Tobias walks in like it's the most natural thing in the world to walk in on. He hangs Theo's and his shirt on the back of the door. Tobias looks different suddenly, taller and wider, or maybe it's because I just woke up, but everything feels different and looks slightly different.

Theo sucks harder, bringing me back to what it is he is doing. Tobias' lips suddenly land on mine, swallowing my moans. His warm hand goes to my breast as he palms it. I shiver from the contrast of hot and cold before I feel my stomach tighten and my walls clench as I come into Theo's mouth. My body relaxes into the bed as the effects of my orgasm leave me.

"Good morning," Tobias whispers against my lips.

"Very good morning," I mumble. I hear Theo chuckle, as I come down from my high.

Grabbing my hands that are slumped beside me, Theo hauls me to my feet. "Shower time." He announces, pushing his hips into me and I can feel his erection pressing against me. I grab him through his pants, squeezing his shaft softly in my hand. Tobias also steps closer, and I suddenly miss how simple things used to be. I lean my back against Tobias, his hands run up my abdomen to my breasts. His lips go to my neck as Theo steps away, walking toward the bathroom.

Walking in, Theo is already in the shower, I don't even have time to get my shirt off when he pulls me into the shower. My shirt becomes saturated as he pulls me under the stream of water.

Tobias steps in behind me and I feel him tug my wet shirt up before pulling it over my head. I kiss Theo's chest and hear him groan as I kiss my way down before dropping to my knees in front of him. I kiss the knob of his hardened cock before running my tongue along it. I watch as he leans back against the shower wall when I wrap my lips around him and start sucking on him.

I watch as Tobias moves closer, his lips going to Theo's neck and I feel my walls tighten, watching Theo react to both of us touching him. He thrusts into my mouth, making me gag before I relax my throat. Theo's hand goes to my hair as he grabs a handful before thrusting into my mouth.

I place my hands on his thighs when his movements become a little too hard and he slows slightly. Turning, I reach up and grab Tobias's hardened length, running my hand along his shaft; he jerks in my hand. I keep my eyes glued upwards, watching them both as they seem lost in the moment. Theo suddenly pulls his cock from my lips and I turn before taking Tobias in my mouth. He groans and leans into Theo, Theo nips at the skin of his neck as I watch him sinking his fangs into Tobias. Blood runs down his chest before Theo licks it up. Tobias groans and I can tell he is a little dazed from being fed on. I squeeze his balls and he suddenly thrusts into my mouth. I suck harder when I feel Tobias' warm hands under my arms pulling me up.

He grips my hips, and my arms go instantly around his neck before I wrap my legs around his waist. Tobias pushes me against Theo, and I groan when I feel his cock pressing between my cheeks. I lean my head back on Theo's shoulder and he kisses my chin softly feeling Tobias move his hips, thrusting inside me. My walls clench around his cock as he stretches me. I feel my skin heat and I shiver against Theo's cold skin behind me. Theo kisses my neck, and his nails dig into my hips when he thrusts inside of me. It stings a little, but he stops moving while I breathe through the sudden pain. I rarely feel pain like this.

I move my hips against Tobias, relaxing a little, and feel Theo move slowly, one of his hands moving to my nipple as he rolls it between his fingers. Tobias nips at my mark, making my toes curl. The only sounds in the bathroom are our moans and heavy breathing as I get lost in the feeling of them deep inside me. My stomach tightens, and I feel my walls clench tightly around Tobias as my orgasm washes over me. Theo, biting into the soft skin of my neck, makes me moan loudly as he stills inside me. Tobias keeps thrusting a little longer before finding his own release. Theo's fangs pull out of my neck and I feel a little light-headed as my feet touch the ground. I sway slightly and grab Tobias's arm to steady myself.

I feel worry through the bond as I step out of the shower. The steam in the bathroom becomes overwhelming with my already flushed skin. Grabbing my towel, I wrap it around myself before flopping down on my back on the bed.

Theo and Tobias walk out of the bathroom. "Are you feeling okay?" Tobias asks, leaning over me.

Theo comes over and places his hand on my cheek. "You look a little flushed," he says as I lean into the coolness of his hand.

"I'm fine, I just need to eat," I tell them.

Tobias sits on the bed beside me before pulling me onto his lap. I lean against him heavily, putting my head on his shoulder. Tobias runs his nail across the side of his throat, creating a blood trail. I run my tongue along it, but I find it weird when it doesn't entice me like it used to.

"Feed, Imogen," Tobias says, when I don't bite down on him. My belly rumbles loudly and I realize I want real food, not blood. My eyes go to Theo and he is staring at me weirdly.

"What?" I ask, confused at his expression.

"Don't you want blood?" He asks. I shake my head, I want food, actual food, and I realize what he means. I'm no longer craving blood, not that Tobias' blood grosses me out. It still tastes good, but I want food more, for once. Which is a little odd?

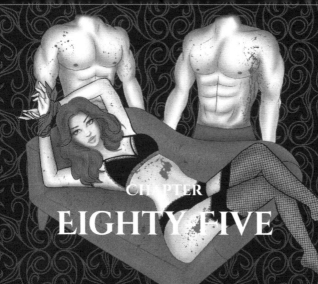

CHAPTER
EIGHTY FIVE

G oing downstairs, I make some toast. Tobias and Theo
watch me, and I can feel their worry through the bond. I
keep seeing them glance in my direction every few
seconds. When I hear a knock at the door, I run to the door and open
it, excited to see my son. Only when I open the door, it is Josiah. I
peer outside toward his car.

"Where is Caroline and Thaddeus?" I ask, a little disappointed.

"They will come after we go and see the council. You okay
Imogen? You seem different?" He asks.

I move to the side, letting him in. "Yep, everything is fine," I tell
him, getting sick of everyone worrying.

I feel normal, more normal than I have in ages. It's a good thing,
so I don't understand why everyone is so worried. Walking back into
the kitchen, I sit at the counter and continue eating my toast and
drinking my coffee. Josiah and Theo are over in the corner, sending
me nervous glances and I know they are talking about me. Tobias
comes over and places his hands on my shoulders, making me look
up at him.

"What are they talking about?" I ask, and he leans down and kisses the side of my mouth.

"Nothing you need to worry about right now." I let it go, figuring they will tell me when they are ready.

Once everyone is dressed, we head to the car. The drive to the abandoned block takes forever and I drift off to sleep. I wake with my head in Theo's lap when he shakes my shoulder to wake me. Sitting up, I yawn and stretch, my back aching from the seat belt clicker digging into it.

Walking through the broken gate, I'm sucked into my new surroundings. It isn't as scary this time since I know what to expect. Percy, a huge grin splitting on to his face, greets us, and Theo tosses him a paper bag which he happily catches before pulling out a stick of red liquorice.

"Do you just carry random paper baggies around with candy?" I ask him.

He smiles and shakes his head. "No, but Percy never leaves the council grounds, so I always make sure I have them when I come here." He tells me.

On the way to the council chambers, we are stopped multiple times by different people. I can tell just by how many people come over to us that Josiah has a pretty enormous influence on the people that live here, and they respect him.

When an elderly lady stops us just outside, I have a strange feeling rush over me. The old woman shakes Josiah's hand, before looking at me. She has the palest gray eyes I have ever seen, her white hair is pulled back in a long ponytail that reaches past her bottom.

I can't help but observe her, and can't seem to pull my gaze from hers. She too watches me like she is shocked at what she is seeing. When she doesn't say anything for a few minutes, Josiah calls her attention away, yet I can't take my eyes off her. Even when Josiah introduces us.

"Imogen, this is Astral," he tells me, and she puts her hand out for me to shake.

I place my hand in hers and her eyes turn completely white. She doesn't scare me though; in fact, I feel really relaxed in her presence, like daydreamy. She grips my hand tightly with both of hers and I see Tobias and Theo step closer, worried. But I brush them off and they remain where they stand. I can't explain it, but I feel a connection to her in some way, like we are sort of the same. I just don't understand why I feel that way.

When her eyes refocus, she smiles. "Been awhile since I found another spirit user. That bracelet won't hold your magic for long, dear. Don't fear it; embrace it. Your mates will keep its darkness away." She says, like it is a normal conversation and she is asking how I like my tea.

"Spirit?" Theo asks, stepping forward.

"Yes, Theo, she is the same as me. For now, she has trapped her magic, but it can't stay that way. The longer she leaves it in that bracelet, the worse it will get and the closer she will get to death."

"What do you mean?" I ask, frightened by her words.

"The magic dear, spirit can drive someone mad. It's the strongest element of magic there is."

I shake my head, not understanding.

"But she is a vampire?" Asks Theo, just as confused as me. I can see Josiah thinking, his hand rubbing his chin like he is deep in thought.

"Of course she is, but the magic will taint her, turn her dark. Spirit isn't an element, more of a life force of every living thing. Imogen technically died, the DNA and her magic brought her back. Because she is unnatural, it taints her magic. To use spirit, it pulls at your life essence, because she is part vampire it pulls on the energy she draws around herself, whatever emotion she feels her magic draws on it, amplifying it to create enough energy. Everything has a balance. Spirit is living while you are dead, there isn't meant to be an inbetween, you can't be both. You need to choose, choose which parts of yourself to give to it or whether to give it up completely." She explains.

"I still don't understand?" I tell her.

"You will dear, but the longer you leave your magic, the closer you get to becoming human, and the fact that you're still partly a vampire, I'm assuming you already died. Humans don't come back to life once they are dead. When you sent your magic into the bracelet, you sent your vampirism with it." She tells me.

"So, I am human?" I ask, becoming more confused.

The woman shakes her head. "Not yet, but the longer you leave it, it will take its toll on you and you will revert to who you once were."

"How do you know all this?"

"I'm an Oracle dear, I saw it when I grabbed your hand. I knew as soon as I saw you that you were a spirit user. Your aura is white, but I can see the darkness that surrounds you, the darkness you trapped in your bracelet."

Tarina walks down the steps toward us, "Time to go, I'm sure I'll see you again Imogen, but for now you must stand up for what is right, for now you have a bigger purpose, and it isn't talking to me." She says, walking away.

Josiah waves his hand to Tarina to let her know we are coming. I try to think of what she means about me coming closer to death. The thought is horrifying, but how do I fix that? I got little time to ponder before we are escorted into what reminds me of a courtroom, except instead of one judge, there are nine seats lined up along the counter.

Only one is empty. Two women and six men sit along the counter as we approach. As we take our seats, they glance at us before resuming their conversation. I can tell they must be elders as they all hold a certain air of authority.

"Let's start, shall we?" A man, around Josiah's age, says, standing up.

He is wearing black robes and has a cruel smile on his face. When his eyes land on Josiah, he smirks, and Josiah growls. I know then, he is Christopher. The two women sitting on either side of him look bored, like they couldn't really care less about what is going on and want to be anywhere other than where they are sitting. The elderly white-haired man on the end looks like he is about to take a nap, as he keeps leaning back in his chair.

The four men all sit staring us down while listening to the man speaking. Theo places his hand on my shoulder as the door at the side opens up and Bianca walks out, taking a seat at the bench next to the man with red hair and freckles.

"As everyone is aware after we lost Alaric, a seat at the council opened up. And since no one stood up for the position, I have appointed Bianca to take her rightful position at the table."

One of the women scoffs at his words, and I can tell she doesn't agree about Bianca's right to the position as she sends her a glare. Bianca rolls her eyes at the dark-haired woman and makes me wonder what Bianca has done that makes an elder all but laugh at Bianca's title?

"Josiah, I know you are here to appeal my decision, so say your piece, and we can get this over with so Bianca can take her rightful place on the council." I can tell by what he says, he won't be changing his mind about giving the spot to her.

Josiah stands up, explaining why she shouldn't be elected, and that she should be held accountable for her crimes and not rewarded. But nothing he says seems to get through to any of the men, yet both women are nodding and agreeing with Josiah.

When he is finished, they call a vote and no surprise all the men on the council vote in favor of Bianca. Everything Josiah explained, I can tell, was a waste of time and in no way did anyone care about her crimes.

When Christopher says his decision remains, the dark-haired woman stands up and glares at him. She is very intimidating when angry, and she looks on the verge of jumping across the counter and attacking the other council members.

Josiah is standing now too, also angry as he shakes his head before saying it is unjust and they should strip her of her new title.

The man next to the woman stands up. His red hair and smattering of freckles make him look younger, around Tobias' age, but age doesn't really matter in this world; chances are he is probably centuries old. He has an Irish accent.

"Nothing can be done, Mara, she has every right to the position. Alaric only held the position because she handed it to him. It is her birthright to take back the position now that Alaric is dead." He tries to tell her.

"She has broken our laws. Laws you helped to write, and you're going to let her take a seat back at the council just because of who her father is?" She screams in anger.

Suddenly, all hell breaks loose, and they are all standing, arguing with each other. I can't help but think if they act like this, how the hell does anything get done? They are all acting like children, screaming at each other and not letting anyone speak. One thing irks me though, and it doesn't click when she says it, but having a few moments to process her words, I realize what she said.

That it is Bianca's birthright because of her father, yet he is also mine. So, doesn't that give me the right to the position as well?

Standing up, I see Theo look up at me. I walk to the front, standing in front of the counter. Theo and Tobias both look at me, wondering what the hell I'm doing. Tobias mouths for me to come back, but I shake my head. I stand there for a few minutes, listening to them argue amongst themselves until the blonde-haired woman notices me standing there and waves her hand, silencing them.

Everyone takes their seats and the blonde haired woman with black eyes cocks her head to the side, examining me before speaking. "Would you like to add something?" I nod my head, wondering how to start. "Imogen, right?"

"Yes, ma'am," I say, politely.

"She isn't part of the council or a community member, she can't add anything." Christopher says, sending a glare my way.

I glared back, holding his gaze, refusing to be intimidated by him. "Well, isn't she the woman the crime was committed against? I would like to know what she has to say," The blonde woman adds.

Christopher shakes his head and goes to speak before the Irish man speaks. "What can it hurt, Christopher? Let her speak, it won't change anything." Christopher sits down, and I turn to face them.

"Well, you said it was Bianca's birthright?" The Irish man nods, and I see Bianca out of the corner of my eye, suddenly looking nervous. She knows where I'm going with this. "So wouldn't it also be my birthright to challenge her for the position?" I ask, turning to Bianca, her face drops and I know I'm right.

"I don't understand, how would it be within your right to challenge her for the position?" The man asks, leaning forward between the pair of us. I realize then that not once did Josiah actually tell them I'm her sister, just stated her crimes and what she did.

"Bianca is my sister, isn't that right Bianca? We have the same father. You remember Bianca, right? The father you killed," I say, turning to her.

"This is nonsense. Cedric only had one child, not two!" Christopher shouts, standing up.

"Not true, I am his daughter, and I'm also the reason she killed my mother. She blames me for destroying her family. When Cedric left her mother for mine, she killed herself," I explain.

It feels strange knowing my father's name, I hadn't bothered to ever ask, and I can tell Caroline doesn't enjoy talking about the events that lead to her life of immortality.

"Have you got proof?" Christopher asks, raising an eyebrow.

"A simple blood test will do if they are sisters," says Mara, with a smile on her lips.

I smile back at her.

"You know nothing about the council. Why would you challenge for a position you know nothing about? You are a newborn vampire and new to this way of life?" Asks the Irish man.

I think for a second. I'm not sure what challenging her means exactly, but I know from what Josiah was talking about earlier that a challenger has to undergo a series of tests before a one-on-one duel against their opponent. Quite a barbaric way if you ask me, and I doubt I will win, but I have to try.

"I don't want the position, but you said she handed the title over to Alaric. So, if I win, I also want to hand over the title." I tell the Irish man.

"To whom, Theo or Tobias?" He chuckles.

"No, Josiah, I have seen how respected he is amongst the community and I know he would make an exemplary member," I say, turning and looking at Josiah, praying it is alright to volunteer him, considering he retired decades ago.

Josiah nods, and a grin breaks out on his face at my words, before he shoots a smirk at Christopher.

"Well, that settles it, we will do the blood test and hold the challenge."

"Unless you object to the blood test, Bianca?" Adds Mara.

"No need. I can confirm we are sisters, no point doing the blood test when I already know what you will find, Mara. Not that it will change anything. Imogen, you must be desperate to challenge me," she says confidently.

"Well, then we shall reconvene in a month for the tests and challenge," Mara announces.

When we step out of the council chambers, Tobias and Theo pull me aside. "Are you nuts? You can't challenge her, she is a lot stronger than you, Imogen. And in case you're forgetting you have no magic. You just signed your death sentence." Theo growls, annoyed, before running his hands through his hair.

"Theo is right, you can't go back on a challenge and we can't help you. Why would you do something like this?" Tobias asks, and I can tell he is angry as he grips my arm tightly.

"Leave her be, she did what she had to. We will figure out a way, even if I have to train her myself," Josiah says, placing a hand on my shoulder and squeezing gently.

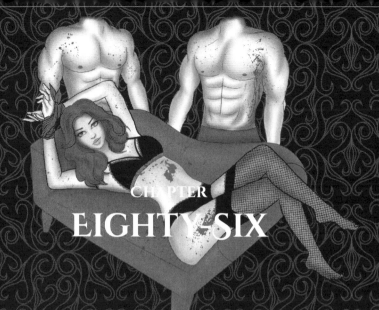

CHAPTER
EIGHTY-SIX

Two weeks pass by quickly. Christopher still demanded the blood test to prove I actually am Bianca's sister and Cedric's daughter. The blood result came back as expected that we are indeed sisters. I also had to sit for a few cognitive tests, and study on community relations and ethics before undergoing the fitness of duty exam, which I passed with flying colors thanks to Josiah and his never-ending knowledge about the council.

It makes me wonder how the hell Bianca has passed, but I doubt she will have to do them anyway with the fact that the council was willing to let a murderer stand on the panel.

Josiah even questioned them about it and believes it was Christopher's way of making things difficult for me. Theo and Tobias have been teaching me combat training, not that it is going to help much against Bianca, and me becoming weaker as time passes. I have asked and begged for them to let me use my magic, but Theo and Tobias keep saying give it time and to let them keep doing research before I make any rash decisions. It worries them that I won't be able to control it like last time.

Caroline and Josiah have all but moved in with us. They are here daily, and I enjoy having their company and never ending help, especially when it comes to Thaddeus.

So, for the last two weeks things have been running smoothly and both Theo and Tobias have been alternating days at work and home. Poor Merida rang me to let me know they have made her their secretary until I can come back to work. She didn't sound impressed, but not much can be done about it. She said it is better than being on the main floor as a receptionist though. Her only dislike, mainly being Theo, demanding coffee every two seconds. I then found out he is deliberately annoying her because he knows she fears him. After a firm word from Tobias, he hasn't been hounding her constantly, and she seems a little more relaxed when he isn't constantly in her presence, she said.

I have just finished training with Tobias, who knocked the wind out of me more times than I can count. My entire body aches, and I want to go shower to get all the sweat off. Walking out of the shed which has been turned into a makeshift training area, I walk toward the house, Tobias is cleaning up and turning all the lights off as I walk up the veranda stairs. Once to the top, I pull my ponytail out, letting my hair fall down my back. Only when I pull my hand back, I notice a handful of hair has fallen out with it. Quickly brushing my fingers through it, more keeps falling out. I stare at the handful of hair in my hand, shocked.

Running inside and up the stairs, I hear Caroline sing out from downstairs. "You okay, Imogen?" She asks, watching me run the stairs.

"Fine, I am..." I don't get to finish when I'm seized by a coughing fit. I can't catch my breath and I feel like I'm choking. Hunched over, I cover my mouth, trying to get control of myself. My coughing is so bad I can't catch a breath and continuously gag.

"Imogen?" Caroline calls, panicked, standing up from her position on the couch.

I catch my breath, but when I look at my hand, it is drenched in blood from my coughing. My heart is pounding so hard in my chest I can hear it thumping loudly in my ears, to the point everything around me is slowly being drowned out by the noise. Clutching the bannister as vertigo sweeps through me, my surroundings move around me, making my stomach turn. I faintly hear Caroline scream for Josiah and Tobias, but I'm too delirious, as I stumble toward the bedroom. When I see the ground rapidly moving toward my face, I know something is majorly wrong. I don't even feel it when I hit the ground. I have no feeling in my limbs at all, just a feeling of dizziness, washing over me and weightlessness. The hallway becomes darker as I feel my body give up and I'm plunged into oblivion.

Opening my eyes, I see the ceiling. My entire body feels like it has been hit by a truck. Cool hands brush my hair out of my face. And then, I feel warmer hands unclasping my bracelet. Looking over to who is fiddling with it, I look into the pale eyes of Astral. She smiles softly before placing my hand on my lap.

"We meet again, Imogen," she says, before lifting my bracelet in her hands and to her lips.

Her eyes glaze over, turning white as she whispers against my bracelet. The pendant glows brightly, a mix of colors appear before it burns bright gold. She suddenly places it in the center of my stomach, making me look down to realize, I only have a bra and boxer shorts on. The pendant glows brighter, becoming hot and burning my skin.

"What did you do?" I ask as it burns, searing my skin.

"Unlocking your Magic, Imogen. Without it you will die," she says, before suddenly my entire body jolts and a cold rush runs over my skin, leaving goosebumps in their wake.

I watch, amazed as the pendant bursts and glows against my skin before sneaking over my skin to the center of my chest where I feel it bleed into me, making my back arch off the bed. It isn't painful but a little unnerving as I feel the rush of magic spread like wildfire through my veins, making everything tingle before I feel myself becoming stronger, making me gasp.

But with it I also feel the unsteady dark magic, cold moving throughout me, freezing cold and like ice in my veins. I look to Astral, who nods to Theo before I feel him bite into my neck, I feel the darkness recede and the coldness leave me. The endorphins in his blood make me feel a little high, but that's not all I feel when I suddenly become aroused, making me moan at his fangs deep in my neck. Theo pulls back and I feel my face heat up, embarrassed that Astral just witnessed that.

"Don't be embarrassed dear, I know how the mate bonds works." She reassures me.

"Now, make sure you let Theo feed off you daily. It will help. It can't be helped." She chuckles.

"But it affects him too," I tell her, worried about what will happen if he consumes too much.

"Don't worry about Theo. He is strong enough, and it leaves his system, eventually. I promise, Imogen, there are other ways to control your magic or get rid of it entirely." She says.

"How do you do it?" I ask, she seems quite sane, but then again, she could just be good at hiding it.

"First of all, I was a pure witch, so it doesn't take so much from me as I'm living. I have found ways to prolong my life. When it gets a bit much, I usually cleanse myself. For you though, Imogen, you aren't quite living or dead. You're in a state of in between that's why your magic has turned dark, tainted by your father's DNA running through you. Letting Theo feed off you will help ease it, but eventually it could become too much." She explains.

"You said she could get rid of it?" Theo asks, his hand rubbing circles on the back of my hand. His eyes are completely black but he looks like he has excellent control over himself.

"Yes, she can, but once it is done, it's done. There is no turning back. She will never be able to feel her connection to her magic again."

The thought saddens me a little. I still ask, needing to know what my options are. "How?"

"By becoming a full vampire, you would need to let Theo or Josiah change you completely, even Tobias, though I don't think you would want to become a Lycan. It is quite painful, I have heard."

The options don't look great. The thought of going bat shit crazy isn't very appealing either.

"We can decide when we have to, Imogen. You don't need to decide right now." Theo reassures me. Is it worth the risk, though? I don't want to be a burden on them or a terrible mother. I also don't want to lose my magic completely, but it doesn't look like I'll have a choice.

I say nothing, instead, just think over my choices and what is best for my son. Then, a thought pops into my head. "What about Thaddeus? Will he turn dark like me?" I ask her.

"I don't have all the answers, your son is one of a kind. I have never met a Tribrid before. I didn't even know two mates could get a female pregnant. Your son is truly one of a kind. I expect great things to come of him, or..." she hesitates.

"Or what?" I ask her, concerned by the look on her face.

"Or terrible things, Imogen. There is a chance he could become the ultimate predator. If his magic is dark, there is no telling what he will become capable of."

Tobias walks in a second later, holding Thaddeus, and I instantly sit up and hold my arms out. Tobias hesitates for a second and looks at Theo. Astral answers his question. "She is fine, Tobias. She won't harm, her aura is white, no darkness present," she tells him, and he walks over, placing him in my arms.

Thaddeus looks up at me and tangles his fingers around my hair. How can anything so pure and innocent become a monster? Looking down at him, I can't picture him all grown. I know one day he will become a man, I just hope we can save him from himself and pray his magic is good.

"He is a cutie," Astral says, rubbing his little cheek. "Well, I better be off. You know where to find me, if you need me," she adds before standing up and walking out the door.

"How long was I out?" I ask, looking up at Tobias.

"Only a day, but you will be fine now," he says, looking toward Theo, who nods his head to verify his words.

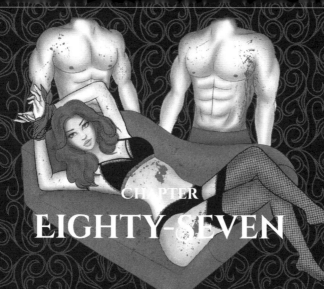

CHAPTER
EIGHTY-SEVEN

That night I suggest that Caroline and Josiah go home so they can have some time to themselves. They have been so busy helping us, I sometimes forget they have their own lives.

Caroline and Josiah bid farewell after dinner, promising to be back bright and early in the morning. One thing I'm most thankful for, is that Caroline has helped get Thaddeus into a more regular sleep routine. He only gets up once or twice during the night now instead of every hour, making night time easier and everyone is getting decent sleep.

Carrying Thaddeus into the kitchen, I make him a bottle. Theo and Tobias keep offering to take him, which is becoming a little annoying. They refuse to leave me alone with him and it is getting on my nerves.

"Here, I can take him, you make the bottle," Theo says, holding out his arms expectantly.

"I'm fine, Theo. I can make a bottle with one hand," I tell him, ignoring him and grabbing the baby formula off the counter. Thaddeus keeps pulling my hair while I make his bottle and I have to keep untangling his little fingers. When I'm done, I settle on the couch and flick on the TV, finding something to watch.

Feeding Thaddeus with his bottle, I can hear Tobias and Theo talking in hushed voices before they turn up in the living room. Tobias sits next to me, rubbing Thaddeus' feet, when he finishes his bottle I stand up to burp him while walking up the stairs to change his bum.

"Did you leave mommy a present?" I ask him, laying him down on our bed. He coos softly while I take him out of his onesie.

"I can change him," Tobias says, stepping into the room.

I reach for the diaper and wipes, ignoring him. Thaddeus sucks on his thumb, slobbering all over it. I pull it from his mouth only for him to pop it straight back in there. Sighing, I quickly change him before tossing the diaper to Tobias to chuck it in the trash. He disappears downstairs, returning before I even have a chance to pick Thaddeus back up.

"Want me to put him down to bed?"

"No, Tobias, I know what I am doing," I tell him, becoming frustrated. Theo steps into the room, watching from the doorway.

"What?" I ask, annoyed that they keep hovering.

"You need to feed, Imogen." Theo says, making me roll my eyes at his tone and his answer. I feel fine, I'm hungry, but I'm not ravenous, and I have control.

"I'm fine, I will after I put Thaddeus to sleep," I tell them, sitting on the edge of the bed.

Rocking back and forth, I watch as Thaddeus' eyes get heavier before they blink back open from the light, beaming down on him. "Can you turn off the light and get out?" I tell them.

Theo flicks off the light, but neither of them leave. I continue to rock Thaddeus and once I think he is asleep, I move and transfer him to his bassinet only for Tobias to wake him as he tries taking him from me.

"What are you doing? You're waking him," I tell him, smacking his hands away.

He holds his hands up in surrender, and I place him in his bed, wrapping him up and tucking him in. Walking to the door, I leave it slightly ajar before walking downstairs. Grabbing his bottle from where it lays on the couch, I walk to the kitchen to sterilize it. Theo and Tobias follow me like a shadow.

"What the hell is your problem?" I ask, turning to them.

"You need to feed, Imogen. It has been hours since Astral brought you back. I know you're hungry, we can feel it," Tobias says.

"I'm fine, Tobias, you don't need to keep trying to take him from me. I won't hurt my son," I growl, pissed off.

"We don't want to risk you hurting him, see how fast you flip," Theo says.

"I'm angry because you are hovering, I'm capable of looking after him."

"We didn't say you weren't, just not while you're like this."

"You made me like this from trying to take over Theo. I was fine until right now," I say, placing the bottle in the sterilizer and turning it on.

Moving to the kettle, I turn it on. Grabbing the mugs, I make coffee as Tobias' arms wrap around my waist. "Don't be upset, we just don't want you to accidentally hurt him."

"The only people who will get hurt around here is you two, if you don't back the fuck off." I tell him, shrugging him off.

I hear him growl before Theo tugs him away. I feel more in control this time, maybe because I can't feel the darkness tainting my magic and I have had my emotions pretty in check considering how annoyed I am. I feel cold hands brush my hair over my shoulder before feeling cold lips on my neck, kissing and sucking on my skin, making my core pulse with arousal. I try to pour the scalding water in the mugs, but his lips are very distracting.

"We are sorry, Imogen. We just don't want a repeat of last time," he says against the crook of my neck. I feel his hands move to my skirt, pushing it up my legs.

"Theo, don't, I'm trying to make coffee, I have things to do."

"Like what?" He mumbles against my skin, before sucking my earlobe into his mouth and biting down. His lips move to my chin as he nips at it. I turn around to shove him away when he grabs my hips, lifting me, forcing my legs around his waist and my arms around his neck to stop from falling and hitting the counter.

Theo walks to the island counter, my ass hitting the cold marble as he fists my panties before ripping them off.

"Theo, seriously I have things to do, I need to put the clothes in the dryer." I tell him, only to see Tobias sit on the stool, watching with hungry eyes.

"It will still be there when I'm done," he says, ignoring me.

Tobias stands up and moves around the island, so he is behind me. I suddenly feel him grip my shoulders, pulling me down, before he plunges his tongue into my mouth. Moaning against his warm lips, I give up. Theo pushes my legs apart and I feel him part my lips with his tongue before sucking on my clit. I moan, my back arching off the counter, only for Tobias to push me back down. His lips attack the mark on my neck, sending pleasure throughout, making my toes curl.

Theo lifts his head slightly, and I grip his hair before shoving him back down. "Don't stop, Theo." I moan.

He chuckles, before I feel his tongue dives back in, before swirling around my clit.

My grip on his hair tightens as I feel my skin heat up. I moan loudly as I'm plunged over the edge, my orgasm rippling through me, and I grind my hips against Theo's face as I ride out my orgasm.

Sitting up, I wiggle my skirt down before hopping off the counter.

"What about us?" Theo pouts, and I stand on my tippy toes and peck his lips.

"Next time don't piss me off," I chuckle, walking back over to retrieve my coffee.

"Oh, no you don't. You're not getting out of it that easily," Tobias says, moving so fast I don't even make it two steps before I'm thrown over his shoulder. He bites the side of my ass through my skirt. Looking up, I see Theo walking behind us with an amused expression on his face. Tobias walks into the spare bedroom dumping me on the bed and I watch as he pulls off his shirt before tearing my skirt up the side.

"Hey, I liked that one!" I tell him as he throws it on the floor.

"I will get you another, now be a good girl and open them legs for me." I shake my head defiantly, a smile tugs on my lips as I cross my legs. He raises an eyebrow before gripping my knees and pulling them apart. "Do you want me to punish you?" He growls.

"Maybe," I smile, and watch his eyes darken as he smiles seductively.

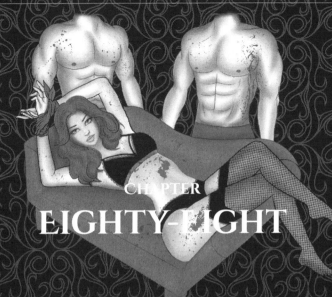

Theo moves onto the bed, making it dip, and Tobias grips my ankles, taking me to the end of the bed before flipping me over, my toes just touching the floor and my ass in the air. I look at Theo, who is watching with an amused expression on his face.

"What's so funny?" I ask, before I hear it. The sound of flesh on flesh as Tobias slaps my ass with his hand. The burning sensation makes me hiss at the sudden pain radiating from my ass, which I'm pretty sure has the full outline of his hand now embedded in my left cheek.

"Son of a, that fucking hurt!" I scream, before trying to scramble up the bed and away from him. Tobias grips my hips, pulling me back down the bed, leaning over me. The warmth of his chest seeps into my back. His hand runs up the outside of my thigh to my hip.

"You should know better than to tease me." He growls into my ear, before leaning back and pulling my hips up.

Thaddeus lets out a noise from the bedroom and I look toward the door before rolling over and trying to get up. "Saved by the baby," I tell him, before going to get up. Theo suddenly darts out of the room, shutting the door behind him. I huff, annoyed, and Tobias smiles triumphantly.

"Looks like you're all mine now," he says, climbing onto the bed while I keep scooting backwards, toward the headboard. His hands grip my thighs before pulling me under him. I feel his hard length against my core as he moves, rubbing his cock between my wet folds to my clit. I wiggle my hips and wrap my legs around his waist, tugging him towards me.

Tobias' lips move to my chin, before going to my neck as he nips and sucks on my soft skin. His hard cock pressed between my lips before sliding inside me. He groans into my neck and I grip his hair, tugging his head back before kissing him.

His tongue fights against mine for dominance, as he deepens the kiss. His hand goes to the headboard, gripping it before I feel him pull out slightly before slamming back in. I move my hips, meeting his brutal thrusts. I feel my walls tighten around his hard length, moaning as he pounds into me faster. I feel myself getting wetter as he slides in and out effortlessly. The wooden bed creaks from the movement, the sound is loud as the wood groans with each thrust.

After a few minutes of his relentless pounding, he slows his pace before pulling out as Theo walks in shutting the door.

"We really need to get a different bed for this room, it makes so much noise," he mutters, tugging his shirt off over his head. Theo climbs on the bed, taking Tobias' position between my legs and I watch as a seductive smile plays on his lips. I feel his cock slide in me before he rolls onto his back and I find myself suddenly straddling him. I move my hips in a circular motion as he grips my hips, loving the feeling of him so deeply inside me. Tobias leans over the side of the bed before opening the drawer and pulling a bottle of lube out.

Theo's grip on my hips tightens as my eyes widen. "Nope, definitely not," I say, remembering the last time I let Tobias fuck my ass. Theo chuckles as I try to get off of him, but he just pushes me back down on his cock. "No, it hurt so bad. You're too big, Tobias," I tell him, trying to get off of Theo's lap.

Tobias moves behind me and I watch horrified as he squirts the clear liquid on his fingers before moving closer behind me. Theo grips my thighs, holding me in place.

"Nope, it is strictly an out hole from now on," I tell them, squirming, trying to get away from Tobias. Theo thrusts his hips up, making me bounce on his cock. My walls tighten at the feeling. I feel Tobias' finger move between my ass cheeks sliding in easily with the lube, making me moan as he twists it in and out.

"Are you sure you don't want me to fuck that tight little ass?" He asks, pulling his finger in and out slowly, making me moan at the feeling. Theo starts lifting his hips, thrusting inside me while Tobias works his finger inside me before pulling out and adding another. His other hand wraps around my throat, squeezing softly before he pulls my head back and forces my lips apart and shoves his tongue in my mouth. I feel Theo lift my hips before slamming me back down on his cock as Tobias moves closer, his cock pressing between my ass cheeks before replacing his fingers.

I tense slightly before I feel Theo twist my nipple between his fingers, distracting me, making me relax. Tobias moves inside me, thrusting into me, making me bounce on Theo before I feel him let my throat go.

I place my hands on Theo's chest and they both start moving inside me, making me moan loudly at the over full sensation. I feel my stomach tighten as arousal floods me. Tobias shoves me back down, pushing my face closer to Theo's and I feel him grip my cheeks, pulling them apart and I hear him groan as he watches himself slip in and out of me. Tobias slams into me harder. Theo moves at his own pace while seizing my lips, kissing me hard before his lips move lower to my chin.

I moan as I feel my stomach tighten and my skin heat. My pussy pulsates as my orgasm washes over me in waves. I feel Tobias still inside me and I know he has found his own release. Theo grips my hips tightly and I feel his seed spill into me. Tobias quickly pulls himself from me and lays next to us, and I slump onto Theo's chest, my breathing fast.

After a few minutes of just laying, listening to everyone's breathing slow down, Tobias pulls my arm and I slide off of Theo before Tobias makes me straddle him. I shake my head.

"No more, I'm too tired," I complain, and he chuckles softly.

"What? No round two?" He asks, thrusting his hips into me. I shake my head before resting my head on Tobias's chest. Even all sweaty, he still smells delicious, and I inhale deeply, loving the manly scent of his skin.

"No, I want you to feed, love, come on," he says, gripping my arms, pulling me higher and I rest my head on his shoulder too exhausted to do anything.

I feel his fingers trail up my spine before I feel him move, running his nail across his neck. Blood runs down to the crook of his neck. His blood is too enticing to ignore as my mouth waters. Lifting my head, I watch it pool in the crook of his neck and feel my face transform, my fangs protruding from gums. I growl softly, hunger taking over before I move to his neck and bite down, my fangs breaking through the skin deeply as I lap at his neck.

Tobias groans next to my ear and I feel his fingers trailing up and down my back. I feel his hands go into my hair and I know he wants me to stop, so I pull my teeth from his neck before licking his wound, watching it close up. Sitting up, Tobias grabs my face with his hands kissing my lips softly.

"Good girl." He mumbles against my lips. Looking around, I see Theo is gone before I hear the shower turn on in our bedroom. I climb off Tobias and make my way to our bedroom.

Thaddeus is still asleep in his bassinet. Walking into the bathroom, Theo is in the shower and I can hear him panting. "What's wrong?" I ask, as he turns to face me. His fangs are protruding and his eyes blazing red instead of green. I slip into the shower and grab his face.

He turns away, trying to regain his composure.

"Tell me what's wrong."

"Nothing, it is just hard seeing you feed, for some reason. I just needed to get out of there."

I kiss his chest softly, letting my lips linger on his skin. Tobias comes in.

"You okay?" I can tell he already knows what is wrong as he steps in the shower. Theo's eyes snap to his neck where I bit into him. Tobias grips Theo's hand, pulling him toward him, leaving me sandwiched between them. I watch as Tobias grabs his face and kisses his lips. My walls throb at the sight and the room fills with the scent of my arousal at seeing them like that.

"Why didn't you just tell me?" Tobias questions before pulling Theo toward his neck. Theo bites into his neck and a guttural growl escapes him as he feeds off Tobias.

I feel Tobias's erection in my back and Theo's pressing against my stomach. Theo pulls away and closes his eyes before opening them and they return to their usual, hypnotic green. Tobias falters for a second and I know he has suffered a fair amount of blood loss as he shakes his head, trying to rid the effects of being fed off twice.

"We need to get more blood bags," he says as he starts to come down from his high.

"Why don't we use them anyway? Seems more practical," I answer, but Theo chuckles softly.

"Tobias enjoys being fed off, but we both can't feed off him. So, we will have to. And I can't just feed off of you," he tells me. I look toward Tobias who has a lazily smile on his face from the endorphins in Theo's bite.

"Yes, he definitely looks like he enjoys it. Maybe he should go to NA," I say before grabbing the soap.

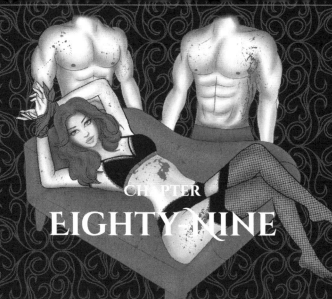

CHAPTER
EIGHTY-NINE

Bianca

I hate this place with a passion, hate every fucking thing about it. Hate having to endure an immortal life.

How naive I was, wanting to become what my father is. The promise of immortality at the time seemed so exciting, so thrilling. Being a part of a secret world, no one knew about. I have always grown up aware of the other world, my father never hid it. Always promising everything would be okay, always promising he would be there for us, and he was. Sure, he would go exploring the world, but he always came back, until one day he didn't.

For years I tried to track him down, and that's how I started working for Tobias and Theo. I met them through Max, and I instantly took a liking to them, and they to me. I kept my father, and the fact that I had ulterior motives, a secret. My father always refused to change me, saying he wanted to find out what effect my blood would have if I died naturally, or some mumbo jumbo, how he reckons dying even without being changed would bring me back. But who wants to be an old wrinkly vampire? Not me, even I will admit I'm vain. No way did I want a life of immortality as an old lady.

My mother didn't even agree, he changed her the moment she had me, yet wanted to hold off with me, saying he wanted to see what would happen.

I couldn't wait, I had them wrapped around my fingers, Max, too. I thought I loved them for years. Yet, Max and I were always closest, not in a romantic way, but he was my best friend, someone I could confide in.

When I met Alaric the first time I stepped foot into the council chambers, he offered me a deal. He knew Cedric was my father, knew I was the rightful heir to his seat on their ancient council. He wanted that seat, and it could only be handed down or challenged for. Since my father was no longer around to challenge, he needed it passed down.

So, at the time I didn't think much of it, I wanted to be a vampire so it seemed like a win-win situation for me. I got what I wanted while he got what he wanted, so I slept with him, which was also part of his plan. I wasn't aware that vampires or werewolves could tell when their lovers had been with another. Alaric gave me his blood and sent me on my merry way, Theo and Tobias promised they would change me one day. But I was sick of waiting, so I took matters into my own hands. They said after we married, they would change me, then it was after they marked me. Always another excuse.

I knew it was Tobias; he wanted to see if he actually had a mate, and I think deep down he knew I wasn't his.

Max and I were fighting in his office. I hurt him when he realized what I had done, that's when I realized his feelings for me weren't just friendly, he wanted more. More than I was willing to give him. Theo and Tobias walked in, and Tobias lost it. He could smell Alaric on my skin, smell Max on my skin when all he did was comfort me, but it didn't look good being found in the arms of another. Tobias lost control and killed me.

Imagine my shock when I woke up back at Max's place.

I never went to see them, instead, I distanced myself from everyone before taking my place beside Alaric, supporting him with the council so no one would find out about our little deal. Max loved me and said I was safest from Tobias and Theo if I remained with Alaric. As much as it pained him to admit. Christopher, Max's father, was livid when he found out about Cedric's heir handing his title over, so then it became a game of who could outsmart the other. He hated Alaric, in fact; I don't think any of the council members truly liked one another; it was always a battle of power, a battle for dominance. They decided out of fear or who had the biggest bargaining chip.

So, when Christopher said he knew where my father was, he knew he had me. He told me he would help me in return for a favor. Christopher hated Theo and Tobias for what Theo did to his son. They worked things out after my ordeal with them, Max remained working for them, but decades of building anger bubbled over the day Max mentioned my name, by accident. Apparently, Theo went berserk and attacked him in a meeting at work.

Christopher helped me find my father. Even after finding out about the new family he created, I was mad, yet I couldn't bring myself to hate him. Forever was a long time, after all. I knew he would come back to my mother after that witch died. She made it very clear she wanted nothing to do with the council or anything to do with immortality; she didn't want that life for her daughter. Then, we became the hidden family, he never told her about the secret he kept hidden from her.

When I found out about her, I confronted my father and he made me promise not to tell my mother. I kept his secret for so long; I didn't want to be the one to break my mother's heart. But when he left and didn't come back, I watched her slowly go into a depression, I knew I needed to tell her. I may have been a daddy's girl, but my mother never abandoned us, she had a right to know.

I told my mother that I knew where dad was when I found him. Found him with that witch; I was heartbroken, he had moved them away from the city and was watching from the shadows. Christopher didn't know about his other daughter, he just knew he had a thing for some witch. I didn't want to hurt my only sibling, I was cruel but not that cruel. After years of watching him watch her; I'd had enough. The witch seemed nice enough, but I needed my father, I needed him to come back and get me out of this mess I created. I needed a parent back in my life since mom was gone.

What I wasn't expecting was finding out my husbands were my sister's mates. That hurt, I loved them, and so my anger towards Imogen grew. If I couldn't have them, why should she? So, I hurt her in the worst way, took from her what she unknowingly took from me, her mother. That brought him back to me, I thought it had worked like Christopher said. My father was unaware of what I had done, I couldn't tell him, it would have ruined everything. I needed him to take his spot back on the council to clean up the mess I made because I wasn't sure how.

Christopher and my father were friends. Christopher wanted him to take his rightful place but when he refused, he became mad. Told me to kill him and he would help get rid of Alaric. I told him I would, too scared to go against him. I moved into my father's home, that he once shared with my mother, at the council.

My father refused to return, and I knew if I didn't act fast Christopher would kill him if he found him. So, I took matters into my own hands. One thing I knew was now that my mother was gone, and I had contact back with my father, he wouldn't deny me anything, so I asked him to visit me. Sneaking him into the council without Percy knowing was difficult, as he is sort of the gatekeeper, but I managed with the help of Christopher.

I told Christopher I wanted revenge, let him believe I wanted to help him get my place back on the council and get rid of Alaric. So, when I got my father home, and had him standing in front of me, I didn't want to kill him. He was my father, despite all his wrongdoings and abandoning us. I was still daddy's little girl, I couldn't risk losing him again.

Leaving the council chambers after the hearing, I make my way into Christopher's office. He sits triumphantly, like he just won the war. "I can't believe she had the balls to challenge you. Why didn't you tell me she was your sister though, Bianca? You made me look like an idiot." He asks, confused.

Walking over, I perch myself on the edge of the desk in front of him before kicking off my heels. He runs his hands up my thighs, it makes my skin crawl having his filthy paws on me.

"Because it didn't matter, I thought she died when I took my nephew. Seems my father was right, though. Vampire DNA does still affect the human body after death." I tell him.

His hands go higher, pushing my skirt up, and I see his eyes light up with arousal as he catches sight of my lace panties. "Are you worried about the challenge?" He asks, looking up at me.

"No, I was at first but then I realized she no longer has her magic." Christopher nods, before tugging me onto his lap, making me straddle him. I can feel his erection pressing against my lace panties through his pants.

"So, she was a witch like her mother then?" He asks against my neck, nipping at my skin.

"Yes, but I can tell she lost her magic. She seems different, almost human," I ponder over my words. Maybe things really are going to work out now.

"And you're sure you can kill her? She is still your flesh and blood." He asks, pulling back slightly.

"If I could kill my father, whom I loved, I can kill a newborn vampire. I have no attachment to her." I lie easily.

I do have an attachment to the girl, a weird one. If we had been a normal family, I may have loved her like a sister. We are very similar, especially in appearance, dads genes are obviously strong. But we are complete opposites: she is everything I used to want to be before I got blindsided by immortality, blindsided with anger.

"Okay, but you need to win. I want them to pay for what they did to my son. And I sure as hell don't want Josiah taking that position. The people love him, and if he does, everything I have built will fall apart, I don't need him challenging me for the head seat," he says, before sucking on my skin.

I nod in agreement. "Well, I need to prepare, and Max will be by soon, I don't think you want your son finding out about our arrangement." I tell him, standing.

"We will tell him after the challenge, it will upset him, but he will come around," he says smiling deviously.

I smile back, hiding the disgust I feel towards the man, before walking out. Heading home, I open the door to my two-story duplex. My favorite place is here where I can relive the memories of my childhood. We didn't live here all the time, we had a house outside the council, but my father would sometimes bring us here and the memories here are only good. Going to the fridge, I feel excitement bubble up as I grab a blood bag before walking to the door in the hall. Opening it, his familiar scent hits me, making all the tension in my body leave.

I walk down the stairs, no matter how many years he has been locked here, he is always happy to see me. I toss him the bag and sit on the seat outside his cell.

"How is my angel today?" He asks.

"Good, daddy."

"When are you going to let me out?" He asks, flicking the TV in the corner of his cell off. He asks every time I come down here, hoping I will release him. My father doesn't understand he is safest here.

"Soon, but I need to tell you something, please understand. It's about Imogen."

His head perks up. I have never mentioned her to him since I trapped him here. The love and excitement that burns brightly in his eyes make me a little jealous. But it is time he knows about what has become of his daughter, time he finds out she gave him an adorable grandson.

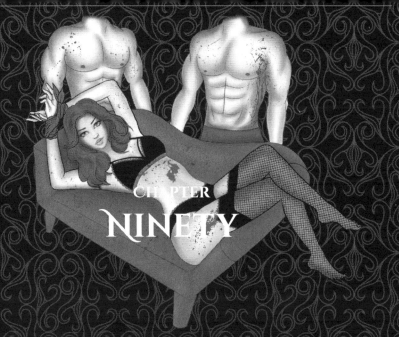

CHAPTER
NINETY

I mogen
The next week passes by quickly, Astral comes by a few times to teach me about my magic. To say it has been a learning experience is an understatement. My magic has no limits and is extremely hard to control once the darkness takes over.

Astral has been teaching me how to regulate my breathing, and self-hypnosis to calm myself. The darkness is there, I can feel it, but it doesn't taint me the way it did before. Astral seems to think it is because I have found my grounding place. Something to hang onto when I feel myself slipping away.

Even with learning control, Theo and Tobias don't give me any rest, constantly watching and hovering, it is starting to get on my nerves. We have been arguing a lot and no matter how much I tell them I'm fine, they don't listen.

They can both feel the darkness inside me, and it scares them. They should feel scared, it is dark and twisted and all-consuming, but with Astral's help I have it managed and under control. If anyone is struggling, it is Theo. The more he feeds off me, the more severe his mood swings have been.

Astral believes Theo might become addicted to my magic, the same way it affected me, changing him to his most primal urges. So, I haven't let him feed off me for two days now, which makes Tobias hover over me every time I have Thaddeus, and eventually I'm going to snap.

I have remained quiet over it, tried to ignore it and even bitten my tongue, but eventually it will become too much. I don't need them mothering me, suffocating me. I just need them to be there when I need them, and right now I feel smothered.

I'm about to go to war with Bianca; I don't want to be fighting them at home.

Astral and I have just come in from training. She has been teaching me how to control the surrounding elements, mainly air. Ways to manipulate it and I'm pretty good with it now, it feels comfortable. Not like the time we worked with fire, which is angrier and when I first started learning, we both nearly lost our eyebrows that first day. I singed Tobias' precious garden and burnt a hole in his perfectly manicured lawn.

Saying goodbye to Astral, I watch as she drives down the driveway before turning and heading inside. The moment I step inside, I can hear Tobias and Theo arguing over something. Thaddeus is upstairs stirring, so I walk upstairs to check on him.

Opening the bedroom door, he is laying in his new crib, watching his mobile go round.

"Hey precious boy," I say, looking down at him. He smiles his big gummy grin and coos back. Leaning in, I pick him up and he instantly looks around the room.

He has become very alert, and being a Tribrid baby he is growing faster than a normal human child. Sitting on the end of the bed, I feel his butt and realize his diaper is quite full. I can still hear Theo and Tobias arguing over something that happened at work.

Apparently, Theo snapped at one of the workers and they quit. Now, the worker has threatened legal action against the company for workplace bullying.

Laying Thaddeus down, I notice his eyes look slightly different, there is something off about him. Pulling his onesie off, I watch closely, and his eyes flicker and I jump back, startled. His green eyes spark before they go completely black like he is possessed.

"Tobias, Theo, come here!" I call out, slightly nervous about our son's behavior.

They don't hear me, too busy arguing; I roll my eyes at them. I change his bum, watching as his eyes go back to normal, deciding I must be seeing things. I shake the thought away.

Maybe I'm more tired than I thought. I quickly dress him and pick him up, when suddenly the entire house is plunged into darkness. Shit, a blackout. As I turn to walk to the door, the lights turn back on and I hear Thaddeus cackle.

"Did you just cackle baby boy?" I coo, looking at him only his eyes are black again.

I watch as he cackles before shoving his hand in his mouth and the power goes out again. My heart rate quickens, and I realized it is Thaddeus doing it.

"Babe, where are you?" I hear Theo sing out.

I roll my eyes and yell back "Upstairs!" Suddenly, the lights turn on again, and I gasp at what I see. All the furniture is floating like in some ghostly horror movie.

"Are you doing that little man?" I ask, noticing his aura glowing around him, fluorescent green. That isn't all I see, the edges are dark, the same darkness that sometimes consumes me, and I gasp.

Thaddeus' eyes snap to mine and the furniture plummets to the ground with a loud crash. Thaddeus starts hysterically screaming, ear piercing screams like he scared himself. "Shh, you're okay. You're okay," I tell him, cuddling him.

Tobias and Theo are up here in an instant, the noise startling them, and I feel panic coursing through them. Tobias rips him from my arms, and I watch horrified as Theo glares at me.

His eyes turn blood red as anger radiates off him. Tobias soothes Thaddeus.

"What did you do, Imogen?" Tobias growls out.

I take a step back, shocked at him. "I did nothing, he scared himself, he-"

I don't get to finish when Theo steps forward like a predator stalking its prey. "What the fuck, you said you were fine!" He snaps, taking a step forward.

"I am, Thaddeus-"

I'm cut off again. "Don't blame him! We felt through the bond your fear, like you did something. Now what did you do?"

"I did nothing, Theo," I say, throwing my hands up.

I know I will get nowhere with them, no matter what, anything I say they aren't going to believe. If they bothered to search through the bond, they could see I'm telling the truth. Giving up, I turn to walk out of the room. They can just find out for themselves.

"Don't just walk away, real mature, Imogen!" Tobias calls out, as I walk down the stairs heading to the kitchen.

Theo follows me and I sigh, going to make a bottle for Thaddeus. I feel him watch me as I grab the formula from the cupboard, placing it on the counter. Tobias comes down a few seconds later. I finish making the bottle and hold my arms out for Thaddeus, who reaches his arms up for me. Tobias snatches the bottle from my hand.

"No, not until you tell me what you did to scare him," he says, before popping the bottle in Thaddeus' mouth who guzzles it down hungrily.

"I did nothing. I just changed him, then-"

"Bullshit, why was he screaming like that?"

"If you will let me finish, Theo, instead of jumping down my fucking throat every god damn second. I can explain!"

Theo growls low in warning.

"You know what? I'm leaving, find out yourselves. I'm going to go buy more diapers." I grab the car keys out of the bowl. Theo moves with blinding speed, standing in front of me. "What? You're both too angry to listen, so move."

"No, you don't just get to walk out," he says, grasping my arm.

"Let go," I scold. I'm so sick of everything I do being judged and criticized by them. They aren't going to listen to me and maybe if I'm gone, they will realize it wasn't me, if he does it again.

"No, explain yourself," he demands.

I shove past him, pushing him out of the way. He jerks me back and I finally snap. Turning around, I shove him back and he staggers, growling. I see Tobias get up, moving away. "Enough," I scream at him, and he goes to step toward me. I flick my wrist and throw him backwards into the pantry door. Tobias is suddenly gone, before coming back without Thaddeus.

He tries to grab me. "It's just the magic, hun, calm down," he says, feeling my anger through the bond. How do they not realize they are the problem, not my magic?

"It's not the fucking magic. It is the two of you. You're driving me insane. You won't hear me out and you are fucking smothering me. Stand down, Tobias, I don't want to hurt you, but I fucking will to get my point across." I say.

Theo steps forward and I flick my wrist again, throwing him back into the pantry. I growl low and stand side on so I can see both of them. Tobias lunges at me, I lift my other hand before slapping it down, and Tobias hits the floor. I hold them both where they are, Tobias on the ground and Theo against the pantry. They struggle against their invisible restraints.

I feel the energy in the room and the lights flicker, my magic drawing on their energy, electricity zapping loudly around me.

I feel the darkness trying to envelope me, feeding off their anger. I close my eyes, breathing and focusing, pushing the darkness back to the edges like Astral showed me. Regaining my composure, I open them.

"Let me up," Tobias says through gritted teeth.

"No, you will listen." He goes silent, I watch his jaw clench and unclench.

"I did nothing, Thaddeus manifested magic, not me. I have control of myself and I'm so sick of both of you hovering. I don't need a mother, I have one of those, well did. So, either step up and act like my mates again or step the fuck out. I won't keep putting up with you treating me like I'm a ticking time bomb. I have control and if I feel off, I will let you know." I tell them.

"This is you, in control?" Theo says, shaking his head.

I huff, annoyed. "Yes, if I wanted to hurt you, I could have, easily might. I have merely restrained you. Now, I'm going to get fucking diapers for our son, understood?" I ask, looking between the pair of them.

They say nothing, but I see Tobias nod. I release them, Theo falls to the floor with a soft thud. His eyes still crimson as he steps toward me, and I hold up my finger.

"Don't. You will see for yourselves I'm not lying. I would never hurt our son and it is about time both of you realize that. I will kill myself long before I will ever harm a hair on that boy's head."

Tobias looks down guiltily, but Theo steps forward again. But this time, Tobias speaks and Theo halts. "Let her go, Theo. I think we all just need to calm down," he says, rubbing his temples. Thaddeus makes a noise and all three of us look up at the ceiling.

"I will go," Tobias says, walking out, heading up the stairs.

I grab my keys again, heading toward the door. Theo sings out as I get to the door. "My wallet is on the hallway stand, can you buy more coffee," he says, coming up behind me.

His eyes, now their usual green and his aura has calmed to a more neutral color. And they think I am the bipolar one. I chuckle at my thought, before grabbing his wallet and going to the car. Hopefully, this will be the end of our arguments now. I have bigger things to worry about with the challenge coming up in four days. I don't need drama at home on top of that. And now, I have another task added to the never-ending list of shit to stress about, that is to find out what is going on with my baby boy.

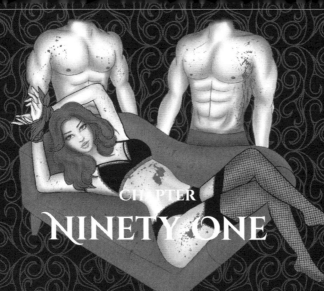

CHAPTER
NINETY-ONE

I know as soon as I drive down toward the house something is wrong; the lights flickering inside the house is a dead giveaway. Pulling up out the front, Theo has hold of Thaddeus, who is looking over Theo's shoulder at the car. Tobias is standing next to the power box, scratching his head, confused. Getting out of the car, I hide my amusement.

"What are you doing?" I ask, hopping out of the car. Theo is watching Tobias, and I can hear him flicking off the switches in the power box.

"Either we have an electrical problem, or the house is haunted," Theo says.

I can see Thaddeus' eyes glowing green, a mischievous grin on his face while he squeals and cackles. His eyes glow with intelligence far beyond his years. When he sees me, he grasps air, holding out his arms, and I smile at him.

"Are you playing tricks on your daddies?" I whisper, taking him from Theo, who still hadn't paid attention to what I said about Thaddeus.

Theo walks over and looks at the power box with Tobias. I shake my head and walk up the porch steps.

"You can't go in there Imogen, stay out here. All the power is off, and the lights are still flickering, a fire could start." Tobias calls out.

I stop, an amused grin on my face as I cock my eyebrow at him. "Typical men aye, in one ear and out the other." I tell Thaddeus, who squeals loudly while eating his hand and slobbering all over it.

"It's a ghost, it is the only explanation. I knew that oracle was conjuring up bad voodoo," Theo says, throwing his hands up in the air.

I can't help it, I burst out laughing. Snort even at how ridiculous they are being. Deciding to play along, I turn to walk inside, carrying Thaddeus and my grocery bag.

"Imogen, did you not hear us? The place is possessed!" Theo calls out.

"Oh, I heard you alright. I can't believe you two are scared of Casper the Friendly Ghost."

"Hey, ghosts are real, I lived in a haunted house once. I'm telling you, Imogen, Astral has brought some bad mumbo jumbo here." Theo calls out to me.

I shake my head. "Did you not pay attention to anything I said earlier?" They both look at me like I have grown two heads. Feeling through the bond, I can tell they have no idea what I'm talking about.

"There is nothing wrong with the house, your son is doing it. You would know, if you bothered to look at him," I point out.

"You expect me to believe a baby is conjuring magic?" Tobias asks.

"Yep, he did it earlier but you two were too busy blaming me for upsetting him and weren't listening." I shrug.

They both come to the porch, looking up at me. "Witches can't manifest magic till they are of age, Imogen. He is two months old."

"Correct, he is two months old, I know when my son was born. But he isn't a normal witch baby, Tobias, he is a tribrid. I also know that he is growing rapidly. What two-month-old is as big as a one-year-old and can sit up and nearly crawl? He is growing faster and beyond his age. The oracle even said she couldn't predict what his future holds. Well now, we just got a glimpse." I try to explain.

They still don't believe me, seriously how thick can one be? As if on cue, Thaddeus starts giggling, and the lights start flickering faster. That's when I realize his powers are manifesting from his emotions. He doesn't even realize what he is doing, just feels the funny feeling of his magic tickling him, well until the darkness around the edges touches him like it did earlier.

I turn him around in my arms, so they can see for themselves. His eyes glow fluorescent green, sparkling, hypnotic eyes peer back at them. Tobias gasps, unable to believe his eyes. Theo is looking from the house to Thaddeus.

"I can't believe not one of you noticed his eyes." I can feel their shock through the bond.

"Well, when shit goes haywire in the house, my first priority is to get him out before the house combusts into flames," Theo retorts.

I turn around, walking inside and going to the kitchen, making a bottle and putting the kettle on. "I think it is time some little boy goes to bed. It is way past your bedtime little man," I tell him, preparing his formula.

"So, what do we do?" asks Theo, grabbing Thaddeus and holding him at arm's length. Thaddeus seems to think it was quite funny.

"You're not scared of him, are you Theo?" I chuckle.

"Of course not, but it is a little creepy."

"Not as creepy as his bloodsucking father," I retort.

"Seriously though, this can't go on, this house is old. The wiring is ancient, I don't think the place will hold if this keeps up." Tobias states. I have been thinking of it when I was driving, trying to come up with a solution.

"Geez, Tobias, I don't know. I didn't exactly get an instruction book for a tribrid baby. They were all out of them at the store. Not that you would read it anyway." I tell him.

"You're enjoying this, aren't you?" He says with a smirk on his face, as he leans back and places his hands behind his head.

"A little, I tried to tell you." Theo walks over and takes the bottle from my hands. Thaddeus drinks his bottle hungrily. It explains why he is constantly hungry. He burns energy constantly and in return, it makes him feed more.

"I'm not sure, I have some idea but not sure how it works exactly or the effect it will have on him. I will have to get Astral's opinion first. See what she thinks."

"What are you thinking?" Tobias asks, leaning forward, and watching Theo rock Thaddeus to sleep, a concerned look on his face.

"Doing what my mother did, putting it in a talisman or amulet." Tobias nods his head.

"Could work, we will speak to Astral tomorrow." Theo walks over to me, and I see Thaddeus is asleep. I kiss his head before Tobias gets up, doing the same. Theo walks upstairs to put him in his crib.

When Theo comes back down, he starts making coffee. "So, we are speaking to Astral then?" He asks.

"Yep, and I'm going to tell her you said her magic is mumbo jumbo." I tell him, chuckling to myself. He turns around, facing me. I prop myself up on the counter and he comes to stand in between my legs.

"I'm sorry about earlier," he says, pecking my lips. When he goes to turn away, I wrap my legs around his waist, tugging him back, before draping my arms over his shoulders. A seductive smile plays on his lips and his eyes darken at my actions.

Theo's lips go to my neck as he sucks and nips at my skin.

"I suppose, I'm making my own coffee then," Tobias says, getting up and walking to the jug.

"He is such a good house husband," mutters Theo, making Tobias scoff before shooting him a look.

"So, are we forgiven?" Theo asks, going back to nipping the skin of my neck. I feel his fingers play with the buttons of my shirt. Watching Tobias over Theo's shoulder, I giggle as I watch him adjust the crotch of his pants. Clearly feeling Theo's arousal through the bond.

"That depends."

"On what?" Tobias asks, turning to face us and watch the scene play out in front of him.

"On what you're willing to do for my forgiveness." I watch Tobias' eyes darken, before he walks over, kissing me over Theo's shoulder. I gasp when Theo's arousal floods into me as Tobias grabs him through his pants. Theo groans loudly at his touch.

I feel Theo's hands suddenly tug on my shirt. "You rip it, Theo, you won't get laid for a week." I warn him, sick of them destroying my clothes. He groans and Tobias snickers, stepping away from him and pouring the hot water in the cups.

"Bed or living room?" Theo asks, thrusting his hips into me. "Never mind, the bedroom's too far away, couch it is," he says, picking me up and tossing me over his shoulder caveman style.

"What about the coffee?" Tobias asks.

"Don't be whining, the coffee can wait. Just hurry up, before she changes her mind," Theo tells him.

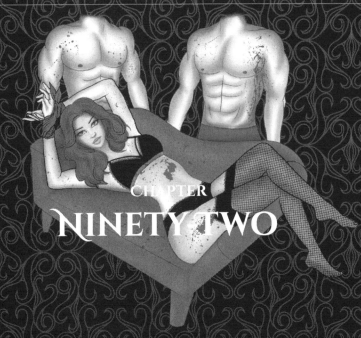

CHAPTER
NINETY TWO

Tobias

  Abandoning my coffee, I follow Theo, his arousal becomes too much for either of us to ignore. I watch as Theo presses himself against her on the wall, only for Imogen to shudder, and a pained gasp leaves her lips.

"What's wrong?" Theo asks, alarmed, wondering if he hurt her.

Imogen leans forward against him before pulling a splintered piece of wood out of her shoulder that has broken off and stabbed into her shoulder. She plucks it out with her fingers, blood trickles down her shoulder blade but she still leans in to kiss Theo hungrily. Only he has gone completely rigid, his grip on her thighs gets stronger, and I watch as his nails dig into her thighs as she hisses, making her pull back and look at him.

The feelings of arousal through the bond are long forgotten, as I'm suddenly flooded with Theo's desire to feed. It isn't the sort of hunger that can be suppressed. This is the sort of hunger that consumes, devouring irrational thinking as it takes over.

Theo's face distorts to the monster he usually keeps well hidden, his fangs protrude and the veins under his eyes ripple under his skin.

Imogen pushes his shoulders, trying to get him to put her down or to lessen his grip. Only it tightens as the terrifying look of a predator takes over. Imogen is stuck between him and the wall, I move towards them and Imogen looks at me in panic. I can feel the adrenaline pumping through her and into me.

Theo seems frozen, the addiction of her blood he craves, and the urge to take it overrides the love he feels for her.

We know he is struggling with the darkness he consumes from her. Theo is the strongest out of us, always the one who seems to have it together when it comes to fighting his urges, yet looking at him now, Theo is gone. The only thing left is the monster he always fought to keep at bay.

He slams her back against the wall, her blood trickles down her shoulder more. He moves his hand to her face, like he is in some trance. His fingers move down her neck, stopping at the vein that is pulsating under her skin.

"Theo! Theo!" She calls, trying to distract him until she realizes he won't be letting her go. "Hun," she speaks softly, moving her hands to his face and tugging his face so he is looking at her. He cocks his head to the side observing her like it is the first time he has seen her.

She kisses him, and he doesn't react, just a blank expression taking over his face. Her proximity becomes too much as I hear him growl. The sort of growl that makes goosebumps rise and sends a shiver down your spine. He is gone, too far gone to come back from. He slams her back, her scream resonates through the house and bounces off the walls as he sinks his teeth into her shoulder.

She fights against him and I move to her. Before I even have time to grab him, he pivots, throwing his arm out and sends me flying into the kitchen door frame. He growls loudly, possessive, and I feel Imogen's magic sizzle through the bond as he sinks his teeth into her arm. Rabid, he doesn't even care where he bites her. He just wants blood, her blood and the darkness coating it.

Thaddeus' screams send the lights flickering and I jump to my feet, trying to get to her only before I have a chance, Imogen smacks him in the face to get him to let go of her arm.

Her blood runs down and drips on the floor before she slaps both hands on the side of his face. Pain radiates through the bond from both of them, as I see white fiery light illuminate her hands so brightly, I can see her veins glowing beneath her skin. A current runs from her chest, up her arms, and into her hands before zapping him. He lets her go, clutching his head. She drops to the floor and I race to her, grabbing her and pulling her to her feet and away from him.

Theo shakes himself off, his hands clench into fists as he spins on his heel and lunges toward us. I shove Imogen away, taking the full brunt of his impact, sending us both flying toward the fireplace. The floor shakes underneath us as we hit the floor.

"Theo, snap out of it!" I growl as he lunges for my throat. I punch him, snapping his head backwards. His nails dig into my shoulders, digging into my flesh, razor sharp. I hear Imogen scream as we fight each other. I try to pin him down, but he can't be subdued long enough for us to make him see sense.

I mogen POV
I watch Tobias try to restrain him, but in this primal and rabid state, Theo is stronger and uncontrollable. I watch as Theo's aura shifts, it has no color as it is consumed by nothing but darkness. I never realized how badly my magic affects him. He is always so good at masking what has been eating him from the inside out.

Theo shoves him off, and Tobias smacks against the stone of the fireplace. The stone cracks up the wall from the force. I watch, horrified, as Theo advances on Tobias like he doesn't recognize the man he has loved his entire life. This is my doing, my magic did this to him.

Theo stalks toward Tobias, and I see Tobias trying to get to his feet, but Theo is quicker, and I waste no time lunging forward as I wrap my legs around Theo's waist, my arm locks around his in a bear hug. My fangs sink into his neck and I taste the darkness as it bleeds out of him and into me.

Theo struggles against me, but I remain focused, trying to hold the magic at bay as it seeps back into me. I can feel my aura shifting, becoming darker, tainted with the madness as it leaves him. That's when I realize I can burn off the energy through my magic. Theo can't, it just lays there dormant, waiting to bust through his barriers and take over.

When I can't handle the darkness and its bitter taste running down my throat, I let his arms go and clamp my hands onto the sides of his face.

I remember what Astral said about my magic being able to heal others, but not myself. I could never harness it properly, most of the plants we tried to heal wilted and died by my fingertips.

But seeing Theo like this tugs at something deep within me, I feel nothing but heartache as my love bleeds into him from me. I feel its energy spreading through me, warm and pure. Focusing on that energy and the love I have for both men, I push it through me and into him. I let it run through him, purifying the darkness that has swallowed him, removing the tainted parts of me from him.

I feel him falter as his knees go weak, dropping him on his knees. He gasps loudly and I can feel through the bond as his mood shifts, the hunger dissipates as he rolls underneath me and I watch as his eyes go back to their familiar, hypnotic green I fell in love with. Slowly, he returns to the man I know he is and not the monster that took him over.

The veins under his eyes disappear, before I feel my magic fizzle. Exhaustion washes over me in waves and I let the magic go, extinguishing the light and leaving me. I'm left panting and out of breath. I close my eyes, the darkness from him and the darkness that comes with using my magic runs rampant through me.

"I'm sorry," Theo breathes, raising his hand, rubbing my face.

I lean into his familiar cool touch, as it cools my now flushed skin. Closing my eyes, I push against the darkness, refusing to let it take over, refusing to give into it.

"Are you okay?" Tobias speaks from behind me.

I nod. I just need to get rid of the icy feeling running through my veins. Thaddeus screaming upstairs is enough for me to pull myself together, remembering my son needs me, remembering my grounding place.

Tobias helps me up, and I lean against him for a second before looking to the stairs.

"I will get him," Tobias says, running up the stairs as Theo pulls me toward him, embracing me. I breathe in his scent and feel the darkness move to the edges before I look up. Theo is watching me, and I can feel his guilt coming through to me from the bond.

"It's not your fault. I'm fine, no harm done." I tell him, before standing on my tippy toes and pecking him on the lips.

"You sure you're okay?" He asks.

I know they can feel the darkness running through me. But I don't fear it anymore, fearing it only amplifies it, when I don't give it that fear, I know I can fight it off. "I'm fine, but starving and can really use that coffee now." I chuckle, before letting him go, walking toward the kitchen in search of the blood bags in the fridge.

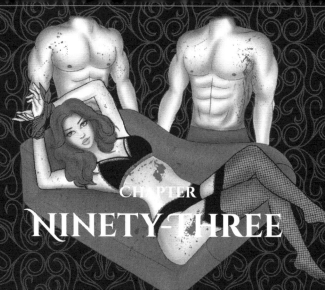

CHAPTER
NINETY-THREE

I mogen
The next day, Astral comes over and we explain everything that happened yesterday. Astral patiently listens before her eyes sparkle brightly as she watches me, and I know she is looking at the aura surrounding me. I know what she will find.

"The darkness is everywhere, yet you're managing to keep it from touching you?" She says quizzically.

"How do you do it?" I ask, looking at hers, which is like looking into a white cloud.

"I channel it into objects or I mask it. Unfortunately, with magic like ours, it can be unpredictable, but still manageable. Yours is different though, because of what you are. Mine doesn't get as dark as yours, doesn't harness as much energy." She tells me, as Tobias brings Thaddeus in.

Astral brought some crystals with her and laid them on the table in front of me.

"What are they for?" I ask. They look like onyx, yet with a red tinge to them.

"These are seer crystals, they pick up energy and magic, here," she says, passing me one. As soon as it touches my hand the stone changes, burning gold with blinding light. "See? Shows that you are the same as me, only stronger. Mine doesn't burn as bright. So, what I want to do is... Tobias put your son on the table for me," she says, patting the table in front of her. Thaddeus sits on the table and instantly starts pulling at the socks on his feet.

Astral then picks up the stones, which glow in her hand the same as they did with me. She whispers under her breath and I watch amazed as she opens her hands, and the five stones rise before moving around my son. Thaddeus watches the stones and suddenly his eyes burn bright green. The stones start glowing and changing as they harness the magic from within him. They burn gold, then silver, then red like lava before becoming a mixture of the three colors swirling within the stones like they trap lightning inside.

Astral gasps loudly and the stones fall from the air and hit the table.

"What happened?" I ask. Astral rummages through her oversized bag, pulling stones and amulets out. I can tell from her aura she is nervous. "Astral, what is it?" I ask again.

"You didn't feel it?" She asks, and I see Theo and Tobias look at me.

"Feel what?"

"Everything," she murmurs, her eyes turning white. "He is everything. The prophecies spoke about this very thing. Someone that could end the world, he has the power to destroy everyone and everything from this realm to the next."

"You're not making sense," I tell her, as she continues to ramble.

"You must save him from it," she mutters before her eyes lock onto my bracelet, and she grabs my wrist, removing my bracelet.

"Save him from what?" I ask, alarmed that something wants to hurt my innocent baby.

"Himself dear, you need to save him from himself. No one should have this much power, no one should be able to harness magic as dark and twisted like that. You need to keep it from him. Take it from him. Magic like that shouldn't exist. It is ancient and old; the sort of magic people write history about after it has ruined the world." She whispers.

I look at my son and can't imagine him becoming a monster. He is an innocent baby for crying out loud, not evil, not a monster.

She places the bracelet back in my hand, and I see my broken charm that held my magic and a new one that Astral placed on it. It looks like a pentagram covered in thorny vines. The sort of charm that looks like black magic or necromancy would hold.

"It's for his own good, dear, he gets a hold of that much power he will destroy us all." She mutters, eyeing my son's angelic face. I know Astral means no harm as she looks at him, but I can sense her fear of him, smell it oozing from her pores.

"So, what do we do?"

"We trap it in there and we hide it for all eternity, no one must ever find it." She whispers pointing to the charm. "Remember when you healed the darkness from Theo? We need to do the same but instead of absorbing it, we need to trap it and we are going to need help." She says pulling out her phone and walking outside, I grab my son from the table.

"Are you sure about this?" Tobias asks, rubbing Thaddeus's arms.

"I don't know, but whatever she sensed in him, scares her. She is the oracle, and if it scares her, it sure as hell scares me." I tell him, and they both agree.

"How will it affect Thaddeus? I mean, taking it?"

I look at Thaddeus in my arms, so pure and innocent as he plays with my hair.

"We never tell him, let him believe he is just a hybrid. If what she says is true, I won't lose my son, I will do what I have to, even if he ends up hating me in the end. We need to do this for him, I won't take a chance, not with him." I tell them.

Astral comes inside. "We need to prepare, the others are on their way. Which is the biggest room in this house?" We point to the living room. Astral shakes her head. "No, we need more room. We might be best off doing it outside, safest that way. And we need salt and lots of it."

"I can go, but are we really not going to question this? Like how someone even has this sort of magic? And he seems fine now." Theo questions her, looking at Thaddeus with concern.

"I'm sorry, but I can't take that chance, we can figure the rest out later. Better to do it now. He won't remember this moment, won't remember the magic. My best bet is that there is something in your ancestry to explain this, then the three of you creating the first Tribrid baby to exist has only enhanced his magic. But I would bet my life on it that your bloodline dates back before there was light and dark magic, when magic was unlimited before we brought forth and found the balance".

"Balance?"

"Yes, between good and evil. Why do you think there are five points to a pentagram? Each one represents a different element; Earth, fire, water, air, and spirit. The section in the middle holds them together. What if we removed it and let them crash, it would create havoc? That's why witches have their own element, the exception being spirit users. They have control over all elements, but predominantly the energy each element brings. What your son has is the darkest parts of all those elements. What he has is something I have never seen before, something new, yet old. His magic is not of this world, it is from the creators of it. I think there was a reason your mother got rid of her magic and a reason she hid yours. I have a feeling she may have seen this. If my guides are correct, she did this to protect, not you, but her grandson. You, awakening your magic, opened the floodgates to something different, something that your ancestors kept buried."

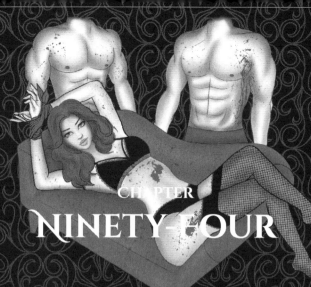

CHAPTER
NINETY-FOUR

Astral and I make a huge pentagram on the grass with salt. Luckily, it is a clear day today, with only a soft breeze. The sky is clear as the sun shines brightly down on us. Tobias watches his perfect lawn with not a blade of grass out of place.

"You know, I only just repaired the grass from the last time you destroyed it, and now, you're mixing salt in it," he whines.

"For someone as dominant and intimidating as you, I never pictured you being a green thumb when I met you," I retort.

"I just like my lawn and gardens looking nice, nothing wrong with wanting nice grass." I shake my head as I hear multiple cars driving down the driveway. Looking up, five cars drive toward the house before stopping out the front.

"Are you sure they won't notify the council?" I ask Astral, worried they might come for my son if they find out.

"Positive, witches stick to themselves, especially when it comes to magic and power, none of us want it falling into the wrong hands." She tells me, as we walk around to greet them.

The car doors open, and women jump out. There are about twelve women who get out, all looking around nervously. Astral introduces everyone and explains what's going on with Thaddeus. Some look skeptical, others scared, and I realize the situation is more dire than I first thought.

I also notice by their auras that there are three air users, three water, three earth and three fire users here, leaving me and the oracle the only spirit users.

"Why so many?" I ask Astral, making her turn to me.

"His magic at the moment is contained inside him and still weak, but once we draw on it. It will awaken and fight against us. It won't be trapped easily. Unfortunately, you and I are the only spirit users alive, so it will take its toll on us the most. Especially you, because your magic is tainted and you're Thaddeus' mother, so it may even try to reach out to you, recognising you as a safe place, but you mustn't give into it."

Suddenly, Josiah and Caroline pull up. Caroline jumps out of the car. "What's this I hear about witches coming and doing stuff to my grandson? I demand answers now!" She says, walking over.

Josiah walks over, calmly placing a hand on Caroline's shoulder making her relax. Tobias and Theo walk out. "Come, we will explain," he says, waving his mother into the house. She eyes us suspiciously before stalking inside. The witches all walk out the back to the pentagram, I watch as each one lines up behind their elemental point.

Astral moves to the center and pulls five small blades from her pocket. She then walks over and hands the first witch at each point a blade, before bringing the last blade and standing on the top point with me. I watch horrified as each one slices their palm before holding it over the point dripping blood into the pentagram. They then move, handing the knife to the next and they do the same. Astral does the same before handing me the blade.

"This doesn't feel very hygienic," I tell her, as I slice my palm and imitate her actions.

Astral chuckles. "You will be fine; you're dead already anyway, what's the worst that could happen?" She laughs. Each witch then circles around the outer ring of the pentagram and Caroline walks out with Thaddeus in her arms.

"I'm telling you witches now, harm even one follicle of hair on that kid's head and I will eat every one of you," she says, flashing her fangs for emphasis before placing him in the center of the Pentagram.

He grabs fistfuls of the grass, making his father groan as he pulls it from the roots. I chuckle before silence falls over everyone as they join hands. I watch the magic go from hand to hand, spreading through each person before finally reaching me. I gasp at its strength as we channel each other's power. When the magic hits Astral, she shudders, and her eyes glaze over before turning an eerie white. Thaddeus must be able to feel the power as he stops and watches for a second before going back to ripping the grass out.

Astral starts muttering under her breath, looking up at the sky before looking straight ahead. She chants in a foreign language and I watch as each witch's eyes glaze over matching Astral's. They chant one by one and when I feel it roll over me. I shudder and become frozen in place, my lips moving yet I don't understand the words leaving them, but I can feel power building to immeasurable levels.

Suddenly, Thaddeus squeals loudly and my eyes snap to him. They burn brightly, flickering between the silver to gold and red, then go black, even his scleras go black. I want to go to him and tell him he is okay, yet I can't move a muscle, locked in place. I see Caroline go to step forward, Josiah pulls her back.

At first, I don't understand why, until I see it. There is a thick mist escaping from my son. He isn't in any pain as it slips out of his fingertips and toes. It pours out of him before forming a cloud above him, growing in size. The clear sky turns to night as strong winds whip around us, the cold of the wind stings my skin. Lightning cracks above us, and I look towards Astral. All the witches look at her in alarm as we watch my son's magic grow bigger. It zaps loudly, angry, and malevolent. The temperature drops massively. I can see our breath in the air and the sky turns dark and angry. The noise is so loud as the winds pick up to hurricane levels.

I think we are going to be blown away, when suddenly, I feel the ground move. Roots shoot from the ground and wrap around everyone's feet, holding us in place.

Everyone has stopped chanting now, I can feel the energy coming from my son's magic and it terrifies me. I thought my magic was dark, but I can't imagine anything more terrifying than the magic that is my son. If my magic were dark, this is a black hole, nothing could escape it as I feel myself being drawn to it.

It starts to absorb everyone's power. Consuming our magic like it is nothing but air. I feel the air become trapped in my lungs as I fight the urge to let go of Astral's hands.

"Hold the circle, don't let it break!" Astral screams. Sweat beads all over my body as I fight against the urge to let go and run. "Keep it centered, push it inside itself!" I try to do as she says, but it is like pushing on a brick wall.

Everyone is straining, trying to hold on when suddenly, I feel it pierce me. The magic hits me in the center of my chest. Stabbing pain radiates throughout my body and I feel every hair on my body stand on end.

"Fight it, Imogen, it can feel your magic. Ground yourself!" Her voice is hypnotic, running through my head.

Suddenly, I see images flashing before my eyes. Like an old black-and-white movie. Images of my childhood, images of my mother. Memories flood into me and memories of my father.

Memories I didn't know existed, suppressed, and hidden away.

He was always there. Then, he would leave, taking the memories with him and each time, taking a piece of my mother who was left to find the only happiness she could, in the bottom of a bottle. Only to return and her light would return, only for it to leave once he would go again, and I recognized that sadness that fell over her. It was the sadness of being without your mate.

Memories of my magic before my mother took it away, memories of her giving hers up for me. The last memory I have of my father is at a park and a woman I instantly recognize as Bianca, arguing with him. I was just a child at the time.

Memories of my mother dying, memories of Tobias and Theo and the months of being together. Every memory we shared, all flashing before my eyes at lightning speed.

I hear Astral scream for me to find my grounding and push the magic out. That's when the picture stills and I find it. My grounding place, my meaning for living. The very person my life is worth fighting for. The one thing that matters most in this world. My son, smiling back at me as he grasps air for me to pick him up. That one image, yet in it I feel nothing but love, nothing but acceptance. The one person I will lay my life down for, repeatedly, just to make sure he can live his.

I feel tears run down my cheeks, and a strength I never knew I had built within me, as I feel light consume me. I scream as I feel it burst from me, shoving the darkness back before wrapping around the darkness, gripping it tightly.

My surroundings become that of the yard and the witches surrounding me. Like an elastic band, everything snaps back into place. I watch as my magic grips the darkness, strangling it and holding it in place, when suddenly Astral breaks the circle but my magic still holds. She then walks to the center of the circle with my bracelet in her hand and I watch amazed as it is sucked into the charm before I feel the ground shake and air rushes past us before everything stills. The clouds up above are clearing and the storm is dissipating.

Astral then walks over and places the bracelet in my hand. "Keep this safe." She says.

I nod before placing it on my wrist. The pendant glows angry but the magic is trapped forever, concealed within the confines of the vines and pentagram.

Silence falls over everyone before they murmur excitedly, and I'm left feeling nothing less than whole. Finally, my life makes sense, as a new sense of clarity washes over me. Bending down, I pick up Thaddeus and he happily tugs on my shirt. I kiss his head and Tobias and Theo come over hugging us.

"I saw him." I whisper.

"Saw who?" Theo asks.

"My father, he was always there. I just didn't know it." I tell them.

Everyone stays for coffee and lunch and by the time everyone leaves, I am exhausted. Crawling in bed, I lay between Theo and Tobias. Thaddeus asleep in his crib.

"What a week?" I mutter, completely drained.

"Hmm, it's nearly over though, one more obstacle then it's done," Tobias says, rolling over and wrapping his arm around my waist. "Are you nervous about tomorrow?"

I shake my head, as barbaric as it is to fight to the death, I'm not nervous. I just want it all to be over with so we can move on with our lives. "No, I can handle Bianca. It's after that I'm nervous about."

"Why is that?" He asks.

"Because we can finally move on with our lives. We have always had distractions, things getting in the way, it will be strange when it's just all of us for eternity." I tell them.

"What do you mean?" Theo asks, rolling over to face me.

"I mean that after it is all said and done, I need to do what my mother did to protect me. I need to give up my magic and become like you."

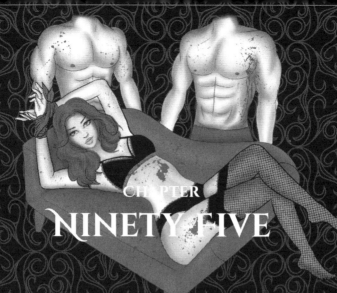

CHAPTER
NINETY-FIVE

Waking up the next morning, I grab Thaddeus from his crib. Tobias is still snoring like a chainsaw and is probably the reason Thaddeus has woken. I seriously don't understand how Theo hasn't smothered him in his sleep. Most of the time I don't notice, but now we have a kid, his snoring is annoying when it wakes the baby.

Grabbing my pillow, I lob it at him, and he darts upright. "What?" He says, looking around the room.

"You woke him again. Seriously Tobias, you might need to sleep outside. It is getting ridiculous," I tell him.

"Doesn't affect my sleep," he says, yawning and stretching.

The smell of bacon wafts through the house and my belly rumbles. Walking down the stairs, I hear the radio playing and can hear Theo rummaging around the kitchen. As soon as I walk in, Theo greets us with a kiss as I sit down on the stool with Thaddeus in my arms. Theo places a steamy cup of liquid gold in front of me and I almost orgasm from the sight of my oversized mug of coffee.

Tobias comes in, sits next to me and pinches Thaddeus's cheeks. Suddenly, Theo turns the radio up and the host is talking about weather change patterns and about a freak hurricane that swept through the city. We all look at each before looking at Thaddeus, who still has his cheeks pinched between Tobias's fingers. I kiss his nose.

"Well, I didn't realize it reached the city."

"Yeah, had some freak talking about conspiracy theories call up the station earlier, claiming the government is behind the severe weather patterns," Theo says. I raised an eyebrow, obviously an eccentric nutter. Theo hands a coffee to Tobias before he pulls out a highchair from the pantry.

"When did you get that?" I ask, as he takes Thaddeus from me.

"This morning, got him this too," he says holding up a porridge packet. We all watch as Thaddeus tries figuring out what to do with his tongue as Theo pops a teaspoon in his mouth. He spits it out. Theo tries again, and this time most of it stays in his mouth as he swallows it down.

"Good, bubba?" Theo asks.

Thaddeus flashes a grin before opening his mouth, wanting more. Theo feeds him his porridge while we help ourselves to the platter of food Theo made. Hearing tires on the driveway, we wait before hearing the front door open.

Caroline and Josiah walk in, Caroline makes herself and Josiah some coffee before joining us for breakfast. I grab them some plates before sitting back down. "Are you ready for today?" Josiah asks, grabbing some bacon.

I chew my food and swallow before answering. "Yeah, just a little nervous about what happens after. Christopher is going to be pissed," I tell him.

"You don't need to worry about him, I can handle Christopher. You just worry about Bianca; you have a son to come home to." He replies, and I nod. Considering how much Josiah hated me when we first met, we have grown pretty close.

"And don't worry about Thaddeus, he will be fine with me." Caroline adds. I know she won't let anything happen to him. It was only yesterday she was threatening to eat an entire coven of witches for him. I chuckle at the memory.

"Well, I better go shower and get dressed, don't think the council will approve of me walking in wearing Winnie the Pooh pajamas." I say, looking down at my clothes.

As I get up, Tobias and Theo watch me leave and I can feel they're nervous for me. Once I reach the stairs, I hear Caroline speaking to them. "Go on, join your mate, she may say she is fine, but I can tell you both aren't."

I hear their chairs screech before I hear their feet on the floorboards. Walking into the bathroom, I strip off and a few seconds later they walk in, doing the same. I step under the stream of the water and start washing myself.

"Quickie?" Asks Theo, a cheeky grin on his face as he tugs me to him.

"Um, no, your parents are downstairs." I tell him. He sulks and I turn my back on him as Tobias steps in.

"You're nervous." He states.

"No, I'm fine. You two are nervous, and I don't know why when I have one thing Bianca doesn't - magic." I say, letting electricity zap between my fingers before zapping him softly.

"Hey electricity and water don't mix," he shrieks.

"I have control, I learned a lot yesterday," I tell them.

Theo pours shampoo on my head before rubbing it in. "That's what worries me. You used a lot of magic yesterday, we can feel the darkness running through you, trying to find a way in," Theo says behind me.

He is right. The darkness is stronger than it has ever been, molding around me, looking for a weakness. After yesterday, though, I have something I didn't have before with my magic, confidence. I know I can control it now, know my limits and know how to use it.

When we finish our showers, I grab my towel before going to the walk-in and grabbing some jeans and a blouse. Putting on my lace bra and panties, I then chuck my jeans on and blouse.

"Are you going to wear that to a fight to the death?" Theo says, shaking his head. "Want heels too?" He asks.

"Yeah, but the black ones, the white ones make my feet ache," I tell him, and he looks at me like I'm insane. "Or I could grab them myself," I tell him, walking past and grabbing them.

"You sure you won't be more comfortable in tennis shoes and sweatpants?" Asks Tobias.

I shake my head before walking past them, heading downstairs. Theo and Tobias came down a few minutes later, Tobias dressed in a suit, while Theo is dressed in casual jeans and a black shirt. Josiah comes into the living room, keys in hand. "Ready?" He asks, and I take a breath.

"Yep, just let me say goodbye to Thaddeus." I quickly kiss his little face, and Theo and Tobias do the same.

Caroline comes over and hugs me tightly before letting go. "Put that wench in her place," she whispers.

Driving to the council takes a few hours. When we pull up at the abandoned school, I don't even hesitate walking straight through the gates to be greeted by Percy.

"Imogen," he says, coming up to wrap me in a hug. He comes up to my waist, so it is a little strange when he hugs my leg. I pat him on the back and Theo steps through the portal, chuckling when he sees Percy hanging off me.

"Percy, get your hands off my woman," he jokes, tossing him his bag of candy.

Walking into the entrance, I notice the court is empty. No stalls, all the shops shut and no people lurking in the streets. I see Bianca, wearing athletic clothes that fit her figure perfectly. She looks like a barbie doll with her pink outfit and blonde hair.

Josiah pulls me towards the court. She doesn't even look in our direction. Instead, I watch her dart over to Percy and bend down to whisper something in his ear, too low for me to hear. I see shock go across his face before he nods his head. Turning around, I follow Josiah who takes me into the council.

Tarina greets us before telling us the challenge will happen in the quad outside, which explains why everything is shut down. Tarina then hands Tobias and Theo some papers with a pen that sparkles. I can feel its magic as they sign the documents, their writing glowing before settling.

"What's that?" I ask Josiah.

"It's a treaty agreement. If you die, it will bind Theo and Tobias not to retaliate. If they do, they will be sentenced to death," he explains. My stomach drops at the thought.

Walking out toward the quad, I find there are seats placed on the side and Christopher and the rest of the council have taken their seats. When we walk out, Tarina follows, handing the documents to Christopher, who glances at it before a smile appears on his face. He claps his hands loudly and Theo squeezes my hand before kissing my temple.

Tobias comes over to me and rubs my arms. "You got this," he says, looking me in the eye before kissing my forehead.

Bianca comes out and stands just at the doors. Tarina walks to the center, motioning for me and Bianca to step forward. We have to shake hands and I feel Bianca grip my hand tightly, trying to hurt me. I squeeze back and she rips her hand from my grip. Tarina then takes a seat and Bianca and I step back from each other.

Bianca smiles cockily, and I return her smile before letting my eyes flash gold. Her smile instantly falls when she realizes I have my magic again. She steps back, frightened.

"What are you waiting for? Start!" Christopher yells to her.

Bianca shakes herself out before lunging forward. I decide to play with her for a bit, sidestepping at the last minute. She spins on her heels before trying to punch me. One thing I'm good at with Theo and Tobias is predicting their moves, Bianca is no different.

As I snap my head back, her hand hits the air as I bring my foot up and kick her in the stomach. Bianca goes flying backwards and I stalk towards her. She gets up and runs at me, but before she can touch me, I lift my hand, palm up before slamming my palm down.

Bianca lifts off the ground and then hits the ground, face first with a loud thud.

I hear Christopher gasp when he realizes I have my magic back. The distraction costs me as Bianca's fist connects with the side of my face.

My head whips to the side before she kicks me in the stomach, sending me hurtling into the brick wall of the lobby. The impact knocks the air out of my lungs and I grunt before pulling myself onto my hands and knees. I don't even have time to get up when I see her running at me. I feel my magic surge through my palms, sickly sweet. I draw on the darkness, taking a little of it before hitting the ground with my palms. The ground lifts in a wave, making her lose her footing. Black vines grow from the earth underneath the stone ground, wrapping like tentacles around her. She struggles against the vines trapping her and holding her in place.

She screams loudly as the thorns pierce her skin, long and sharp, moving over her body like a snake.

"She can't use magic!" Christopher screams angrily when he realizes Bianca is losing. I ignore him, walking toward her.

When he gets to his feet, protesting again, Mara stands, blocking him from the fight. "No one said there were any rules, Christopher. Now sit down, you don't want to anger me," she warns, flashing her fangs.

He sits back down when he realizes the entire council is eyeing him angrily. Mara nods toward me to continue. Bianca squirms in the vine's grip, trying to break free from their restraints. I casually stroll over to her, stopping a few feet off. Now that she is restrained, I feel bad. I hate her, but I won't be any better than her if I kill her. Killing her won't bring my mother back or my life back. Not that I want it back now, anyway. The only thing separating me from her is that I'm not a murderer.

"Finish it!" Screams Christopher, angrily.

I shake my thoughts away, deciding to let the darkness take over. I feel my magic zap and crackle between my fingers. Electricity sparks and I roll my arms, creating an enormous ball of electricity. Bianca watches, horrified, and I look to Theo and Tobias. Both of them turn their heads and I can feel that they don't want to watch me kill my sister, kill their ex-wife.

They don't enjoy seeing me like this, yet if I don't do it, I know I forfeit the challenge. Josiah nods to me and I turn back to Bianca. Her blue eyes are the same as mine, looking back at me pleading. I raise my hands, planning to incinerate her when she screams.

"It was his idea! I didn't want any part of it! I just wanted my father back!" I falter, hearing her pleading.

"Who's idea?" Josiah and Mara say at the same time, getting up from their seats.

Electricity zaps loudly as I feel my magic building still, while I hold it between my hands.

"Christopher's, please, Imogen, you don't want to kill me. I know you don't!" She pleads, looking at me with tears in her eyes. I snap my head in Christopher's direction, but he is suddenly gone.

"Where did he go?" I ask, as everyone looks to Christopher's seat which is now empty.

"Speak?" Mara demands, placing her hands on her hips and glaring at Bianca. Theo places his hand on my shoulder before jumping back, having been electrocuted by my magic running over my skin. I let the magic go, let it fizzle out while we figure out what is going on.

"Christopher didn't want Josiah getting a seat at the table. We made a deal; he would tell me where my father was if I got him to take his seat back at the table. He refused, Christopher said he wouldn't come back because of your mother and that if I got rid of her, he would come back. So, I killed her. I am sorry, Imogen, I can't blame him entirely. I did it and I will admit I enjoyed watching you suffer from it. I was jealous of what you had with Tobias and Theo. Jealous that our father dumped my mother for yours." I feel my anger rise, hearing her confess. "When my father came back, he refused the position, and I gave it to Alaric, which angered Christopher, so he told me to kill dad and he would take care of Alaric, and I could take the position."

"Guards find, Christopher," Mara yells.

Suddenly, men come running out of the empty shops, taking off through the streets.

"Christopher told Alaric information about your wife that he received from me. I was spying on you when you both left. I followed you, then Josiah killed Alaric for Christopher. He knew you would fly off the deep end and kill him and he could also get revenge on you for what Theo did to his son, by getting you punished," she tells Josiah.

"I can't believe you killed your own father for a place on the council" Mara booms, before stepping forward and slapping her across the face.

Bianca spits out blood and coughs from the impact, huge claw marks scratch her face from the blow.

"Find Christopher!" Mara shouts, talking to the rest of the council members, they nod but stop when an unfamiliar voice echoes through the quad. One I haven't heard before.

Spinning around, I hear Tobias growl along with Theo and Josiah. I look in the direction they are looking. "I have him here," says the stranger's voice.

When I lay eyes on him, he isn't a stranger. Percy walks in with another man who has Christopher by the back of his suit. He lays unconscious while Percy and the man get closer, dragging Christopher with them.

He stops in front of me and I look at him in shock. "Hey, Immy," he says, and I can see the emotion he is trying to hide behind his eyes.

"Dad?"

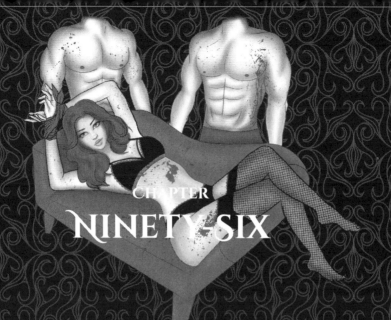

My head is racing, my mind goes into overdrive at the sight of the man I thought was dead, now standing before me.

"Hey sweety, you probably don't remember me," he says.

"You, you fucking killed us and left us!" Josiah bellows, coming face to face with the man that changed them and disappeared off the face of the earth.

"Blame your guard dog there. He chased me away before I could explain," he spits back at Josiah. Tobias growls menacingly at being called a guard dog. Josiah tries to step forward, but Mara gets between them.

"As interesting as this is to watch, we have more pressing matters at hand, and you have some explaining to do as to why you just disappeared for a century." She says, pointing to my father and folding her arms across her chest.

"I was on vacation," he says, eyeing his daughter, making me look at Bianca who has fallen silent behind us, still trapped in the vines. She averts her eyes, and I know there is something my father is hiding for her benefit.

"Guards, take Christopher away!" Mara calls, before turning to Bianca. "Now Cedric, I understand she is your daughter, but we will punish her. I never like these challenges. Such a waste of life," she says, shaking her head before looking at my father.

I can't tear my eyes from him, it is like looking at a ghost. I look like him. I always thought I looked like my mother, but with him in front of me, I'm not so sure. We have the same hair color, the same full lips, he is a bit of a hippy, which I didn't picture, even in the memories I have of him, he was always clean, well shaven and dressed clean. Not in a dyed shirt and board shorts. His feet are bare but his gaze softens as he takes me in and I can tell without a doubt he loves me even if he wasn't there when I needed him or that I could fully remember.

Tarina comes forward, pulling my attention to her. "So, what about the challenge?" She asks and the rest of the council members walk over too, also wondering.

"Will you be taking your position back?" The Irish man asks, looking at my father. My father nods his head, and they look relieved.

"What about Christopher's next in line?" Tobias asks.

"No, I reckon it is time for a change. Let the people vote who gets the head of the table," Percy says, stepping out from behind my father. I forgot he is still here. They all nod in agreement.

"Well, it is decided, Josiah, welcome aboard. I will give you early congratulations as we all know you have the people on your side and after this mess, I don't see anyone stepping up to challenge you for the spot."

Josiah nods his head but adds nothing. Everyone's eyes dart to Bianca, who shrinks under their intense gaze. "Imogen, you can choose what happens to your sister," Josiah says, and everyone looks at me, waiting. My father's eyes dart to hers, worried.

"She can share the same fate Josiah had after he killed Alaric. Then, I don't care what you do with her," I tell them.

Bianca screams and fights against the vines trapping her. Our father walks over to her and rubs her cheek. "You did the crime, now you must accept the punishment," he tells her, and she drops her head, ashamed, before nodding, a sob leaving her lips.

"It's only a month of whipping and having organs pulled, Bianca. You will live, unfortunately. And to add to that, you will become my servant until we can trust you again," Josiah sneers, and I know he will give her hell as his eyes flare.

Bianca pales, and I have to hold in my laugh. I let the vines drop and wobble slightly. Theo grabs my elbow to steady me. I hadn't realized how much energy and power I was burning just by keeping her trapped until I let the magic go. A wave of exhaustion washes over me and darkness pushes against me. Guards haul Bianca away, kicking and screaming.

"We will get out of your hair, go home, Imogen. You did well today. I know this won't be the last time I will see you," Mara says, dismissing everyone before walking off with the rest of the council.

That only leaves Josiah, Tobias, Theo, and my father standing in the quad with me. I look between my father and Josiah, who seem to be having a Mexican standoff. The silence is awkward. What do you say to the man who took your memories of him away?

"Dad, for the sake of Imogen, can you please take it up with Cedric later? As much as I want to skin him alive, he is still her father." Theo says, touching his father's shoulder gently.

Josiah takes a deep breath before sighing. His eyes move to me and he comes over and hugs me tightly. I return his hug. "Take the car. I need to sort some things here. You are lucky your daughter is mates with my sons and the mother of my grandchild," he tells my father, before turning to face his sons. "Your mother is going to have a heart attack when she finds out," he says, looking at Theo and Tobias.

"Bianca said I have an adorable grandson," my father says, looking thoughtful. Tobias growls low and I elbow him. My father smirks at my actions.

"You can meet him, just let me get my head around the fact you are alive first," I tell him.

"Here, put your number in here, I will call you once everything settles down. I really want to meet this grandson of mine and let you get to know me better, Imogen. I never planned for any of this. I loved your mother, still do, and I know Bianca has hurt you, but I promise she isn't all bad. Hopefully, one day you will get to know the better side of her," he says, passing me his phone.

I doubt I will ever feel differently about Bianca, but I type my number into his phone, anyway. Today has been a strange day. Handing his phone back, he touches my shoulder, squeezing softly. "I better head in and I'm sure your father has some choice words he wants to deliver to me," he says, nodding to Tobias and Theo.

"What now?" Asks Theo, watching as my father leaves.

"We go home," I tell him, walking to the portal needing this day to be over with. I just want to go home and see my precious boy.

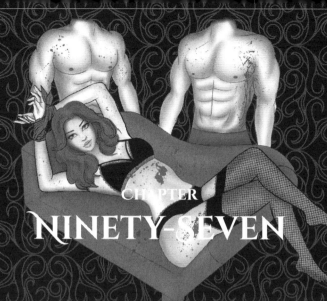

CHAPTER
NINETY-SEVEN

The week after goes by quickly, our life gets some routine about it. I feel like a weight has been lifted, we can finally relax and take a breath. I decide to keep my magic, at least for now, until I know for sure that the drama with Bianca is over. Theo and Tobias agree and say if I give it up, I might regret it, and considering it is the last thing I have left of my mother, I don't want to throw it away without a good reason.

Josiah said Bianca has been suffering for her crimes, and he himself has taken pleasure in torturing her. Caroline has been banned from the council after she snuck in and removed Bianca's fingernails without permission, and tried to gouge out her eyes. I feel nothing towards Bianca, no anger, no hate, no pity. I feel free of her, although I'm not naïve enough to believe I won't have to deal with her again.

My father came over after three days and met Thaddeus.

Things are awkward, but I have hope that we can build a relationship as long as Theo and Tobias can refrain from killing him. Mostly the future looks bright. Tobias and Theo returned back to work full time, and I decided I will work a few odd days when I feel like bringing Thaddeus in with me. Life is looking pretty mundane compared to what it used to be.

Moving on, though everything is a little harder now I have time to think. I often find myself thinking of all the things my mother has missed and all the things I have missed with my father. My moods sometimes plummet, Tobias and Theo are always there to lean on when the darkness would sends into my depression.

They pull me back from the brink and remind me they will always be here for me.

As I walk downstairs, I see Theo is feeding Thaddeus in his high-chair. Thaddeus loves porridge now, it's his new favorite thing to not only eat, but play with. Tobias walks over and kisses me softly while I finish buttoning my blouse. I'm going in with them today, excited to be going back, today is the second day I have returned to work.

The shambles the place was in when I went back the first day had me nearly hyperventilating when I saw the mountain load of paper-work that needed filing. Merida was excited to see she could go back to the tech floor, as one thing she hated was filing paperwork and being Theo's coffee bitch.

Sitting at the island counter, I sip my coffee, watching Theo feed our son. Thaddeus squeals loudly, and I notice my bracelet react to him. His magical pendant glows brightly from his excitement.

My heart skips a beat for a second, and I file it away to worry about another time.

"Mom wants to know if she can take Thaddeus tonight?" Tobias asks me. He wiggles his eyebrows, and I know what he is thinking. Theo looks up and he smiles brightly.

I smile knowingly back at them, "Tell her she can."

Theo punches the air like he just won some victory, and Tobias comes over, wrapping his arms around my shoulders, standing behind me. His stubble brushes my cheek and I cringe at the feeling, he chuckles before rubbing his face in the crook of my neck.

"Stop, you man beast." I tell him, cringing at the feeling. Tobias chuckles before turning me around on the stool and moving between my legs.

He kisses me softly at first before he deepens the kiss and groans into my mouth. He leans into me before I feel his hand move under my blouse and he squeezes my nipple between his fingers.

I moan into his mouth before Theo speaks. "Oi, keep it PG13 a baby is present," he says.

I look back and he has his hand over Thaddeus' eyes. I roll mine at him, it is not like he understands or will remember.

"You don't want to see that, do you, bubba?" Theo asks him.

Thaddeus cackles loudly before holding his arms up in the air. "Mom, mom!" He squeals, and we all freeze.

"Did he just say his first word?"

"I heard nothing," Theo states, and I grin, knowing he heard.

"Mom, mom!" Thaddeus says again, grasping air.

"Traitor, I bring you porridge and you say that witch's name first," Theo tells him. Thaddeus bounces excitedly, holding his hands out for me. I go pick him up, kissing his face.

"What about dadda, say dadda?" Theo tries.

"Mom, mom," Thaddeus says, and Theo throws his arms up in the air.

"This isn't fair. I do the night feeds and the morning stuff and he says mom."

I chuckle at his ranting. "Maybe he thinks you're mom?" Tobias adds in, trying not to laugh.

Theo thinks for a second. "That must be it. We will have to correct that," he says, taking Thaddeus from me and walking from the room, trying to make him say dadda.

I shake my head and Tobias comes over wrapping his arms around me. "Ready?" He asks.

"Yep, lets go," I tell him, and he lets go, grabbing his keys from the bowl and we walk towards the door where Thaddeus and Theo are waiting.

EPILOGUE

One hundred years later
Thaddeus

My name is enough to send most people running, those that don't are fools, for they will feel my wrath. I am the king of darkness. The dark Tribrid they call me, the one that changed the world. I am destruction, and countries have fallen by these hands.

Forgiveness isn't a part of my vocabulary; I don't grant forgiveness or mercy. It is best to stay on my good side. My mother thought she was protecting me, keeping my magic from me. That betrayal hurt the most.

She took a piece of me and I nearly killed her by getting it back. I knew growing up I was different. I saw life differently. Sure, I came from a home filled with love and everything a child could desire. My parents would have moved heaven and hell for me. Yet, that was their downfall. Their betrayal.

From the outside, we were the perfect family. Our lives were great until my sixteenth birthday. I stopped aging at thirty, but the darkness made me feel every bit of the hundred and one years I have lived on this earth. Sucking every part of me away until I become what I am now, I used to fear the darkness, now I embrace it.

The darkness came for me on my sixteenth birthday, and I found the missing piece. The one thing I craved, and that was power. Power to control everything and everyone. My mother tried to save me, tried to even take me down. If she wasn't my mother, the woman who literally gave her life for me, I would have ended her. That wasn't her decision to make. I knew instantly my entire life was a secret; they kept from me.

Astral and the covens came for me once I possessed my power, my mother told them where to find me. I slaughtered them all and have been on my own ever since. For decades, I roamed the earth trying to find meaning, and I stumbled across my mates.

At first, they feared me. Everyone had heard my name by then; not a country left intact as I made my way through each one, trying to figure out my purpose.

I met Ryland first. He was just as evil as me and a werewolf; we continued our reign of terror until we met our other mate. I was hoping for a woman, not that I was uncomfortable with my sexuality. It is what it is, and quite frankly, I would fuck anything with legs to fulfill my needs and those of my mates.

Orion, though, is different, weaker. He doesn't agree with my past and the things we have done; he is much older than both of us and knew of my grandfather. Orion is a vampire and a little old-fashioned, but he is mine, even though he annoys me and frustrates me to no end.

He hated me, but he came to see reason. He has remained by my side, even when he doesn't agree, trying to talk me down, trying to change me. Though now, I think he has given up.

Sitting on the balcony of my penthouse apartment, I look over the city, my eyes scanning as I watch the crowds of people below, unaware of the monster watching them.

I hear movement behind me, and my eyes snap to the glass

sliding doors. She hands me a smoke and I light it breathing in deeply, enjoying the burn in my throat from its harshness.

"When are you going to go home? Haven't you punished them enough? They did it to protect you. It is time you stop this, whatever it is you are doing."

"And what is that?" I ask her, looking back toward the city.

"The destruction, what are you trying to prove? Who are you looking for?" She asks and I sigh. Only she would get away with questioning me like this. I always had a soft spot for her. She listens and doesn't judge, no matter how much I fuck things up.

"I'm not trying to prove anything. I don't need to."

"Then why, Thaddeus, why all this?" She asks.

"Because I can, that is why," I tell her.

She shakes her head. "Your mother said there was still good in you, that we just had to find it, that we could pull you back from the darkness. Now, I'm not sure anymore. I can't watch you destroy yourself, destroy everything you put your hands on. I'm sorry, Thaddeus, but I can't. I'm going home, come and see me when you see sense," she says.

"You're leaving already? You just got here," I tell her, growling at her.

She steps back, frightened. "I'm sorry Thaddeus, but please, just go home, they will forgive you." She says before turning away.

"Tell mom I'm not coming back." I tell her. She smiles sadly before nodding.

She slips inside, closing the door behind her. A few minutes later, the glass door opens again, and Orion comes out before plucking my smoke from my fingers and drawing on it. He leans against the railing, "What did you say to your Aunty Bianca that upset her?" He asks, before passing my smoke back.

"I told her I'm not going back." Orion sighs loudly, looking over the railing. I move behind him, pressing myself against him, reaching around and grabbing his cock through his pants. His dick twitches in my hand responding to my touch. I groan into his ear before I pull at his belt.

"Not tonight Thaddeus," he says, smacking my hand away.

I growl loudly before shoving him away. "Fine," I snap, going inside. Bianca is gone and only her faint lingering scent remains. "Ryland?" I yell. "Hurry up, we are going out," Ryland walks out, a mischievous grin dancing on his lips. He grabs his jacket and follows me to the elevator.

"Where are we going?" He asks.

"I just want out of this house and I need blood." I tell him, he nods. I won't risk feeding on him, my hunger is insatiable and as intoxicating as his scent is, I know I won't stop once I start. Marking him was a nightmare, I nearly killed him, nearly killed my own mate. Orion was different; he is a vampire, so I didn't struggle with him.

Walking outside the breeze makes Ryland shiver slightly. The snow crunches under our feet as we make our way down the street, looking for my next victim. Only when the breeze shifts, I pick up the most mouth-watering, intoxicating scent I have ever smelled before. I follow it before I hear a feminine scream. Something twitches inside me, something I haven't felt in a long time. Fear.

The sound of the woman's voice sends fear racing through my cold veins. Ryland, feeling it too, looks at me and we walk around the corner which is an alleyway. I can see a man standing over someone. The person is thrashing violently as the man tries to pull her pants down.

Her scream sends rage through me, but before I can even move, Ryland is ripping him to pieces with his bare hands. The figure moves and I can't take my eyes off them. Stepping into the alleyway, Ryland is pummeling the man, his face completely unrecognizable as human, his blood seeping into the snow.

The figure, I realize, is actually a woman. She tries pulling her pants up, looking between both Ryland and me and I can smell her fear. She thinks we are here to harm her too.

Ryland stops and looks at her fear-stricken face and reaches his hands out toward her. She slaps his hands away. Her entire body is shaking with fear and adrenaline. The cold is biting at her skin. She is wearing a waitress outfit, not properly dressed for this sort of weather.

The closer I get, the stronger the scent is. She is the addictive mouth-watering scent I got a whiff of. She makes my heart race faster. I didn't think I needed anyone beside my mates, but I want her, need her with every cell in my body. It's calling to her, wanting to taste her. Wanting to see if her skin is as soft as it looks. Kneeling in front of her, she cowers back, her hazel eyes filled with fear, I can tell she knows what we are.

I place my hand out for her to take, but she slaps it away. "Please, I won't tell, just let me go. I saw nothing I promise," she sobs. Her voice is like music to my ears. I could listen to her talk all day. I sweep her light brown hair out of the way so I can see her face, she averts her gaze from my onyx eyes.

"Ours," I gasp.

She shakes her head, and I feel Ryland touch my shoulder, making me look at him. "We are scaring her," he says, and for the first time I can tell he doesn't enjoy the scent of fear, at least not from her. The mate pull is strong, looking back at her, I get up and step back.

"Go," I tell her, and she gets up before running off. Bending down, I pick up her wallet that she left in her haste. Pulling out her ID, I read it - Evelyn Harper. I have never wanted someone as much as I want her, never craved another person more than I do her, she is ours, and yet we can't have her.

She is light while we are dark. Monsters of the night to her. Something made of nightmares. I have to fight with myself to stop from chasing her down and claiming her. I thought I was complete until I met her.

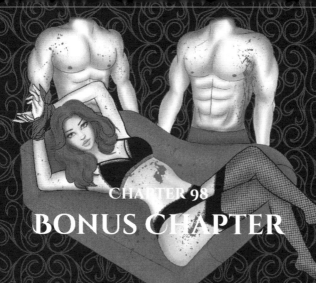

CHAPTER 98
BONUS CHAPTER

1 2 months later

Imogen

The last year has been epic, we are three days out from the wedding. Tobias and Theo are at work and I'm trying to get Thaddeus ready so I can retry my dress. The woman in the shop insisted, which I know is pointless, my body hasn't and can't change, but it isn't like I can tell her that. Just as I'm about to walk out the door, I pick up Thaddeus, only for him to throw up on my dress. My appointment is in forty minutes and it is at least a thirty-minute drive into town.

"Come on, could this day get any worse?" I groan and suddenly, the projectile vomit is all over my hair as well. Why, why did I say that? "You just had to prove it could, didn't you little man? Come on, I need to change you and myself now." I tell him. Walking up the stairs, I place my hand on his head and Thaddeus feels a little warm, making me wonder if he is coming down with something.

Placing him on the bed, I go to the dresser and retrieve him a change of clothes, grabbing a wet cloth from the bathroom to clean his face. Thaddeus watches me from where he sits, his cheeks all red, and his curly black hair covering his eyes.

"Mommy," he cries, making me rush to his side, just in time for him to puke on the comforter.

"What's wrong little man?" I ask, feeling his head, which is beading in sweat. Grabbing my phone from my pocket, I call Tobias and he answers after one ring.

"What's wrong, hun?" He asks.

"Something is wrong with Thaddeus, I think he is sick."

"Sick?"

"Yes, he won't stop spewing and he feels hot."

"Is he teething?"

I run my fingers along his bottom gums, feeling nothing before running my fingers across the top gums and I gasp as I feel the edges of razor sharp fangs, as they cut through the pad of my thumb. I pull my finger back before lifting his top lip to reveal three fangs on either side of his two middle teeth.

"What, babe, say something?" Tobias says alarmed through the phone.

"He.. He has fangs."

"Fangs? Did you say fangs?"

"Yes, Tobias, fucking fangs!" I yell, annoyed from repeating myself.

"We are on our way, I will call Astral and see what she says." Tobias says before hanging up.

Thaddeus wriggles around, trying to get up and I pick him before walking to the bathroom deciding a nice cool shower might bring his temp down. Stripping myself and him off, I turn the shower on so it is only lukewarm before holding his hand and letting him step into the shower. He stands under the water and I hop in with him before grabbing the loofa and soap, washing him.

Thaddeus seems to feel better while the cool water runs over him, as he plays with his truck on the shower floor, while I wash the spew from my hair. Once I am done, I turn the shower off only to hear the front door open. It is too early for them to be back. I only just got off the phone to Tobias a few minutes ago. Grabbing a towel, I wrap it around myself and grab Thaddeus from the shower floor where he is playing.

"Who's that?" I sing out, when suddenly, Theo appears, and I let out the breath I was holding. "Geez, you scared me, did you run here?"

Theo nods before walking over and taking Thaddeus from me. "How's daddy's little man?" He says, kissing his wet little head. "He is quite warm." He states before laying him on the bed and drying him with the towel.

Twenty minutes later we have Thaddeus dressed, and I'm making him a bottle when he starts screaming. Theo tries to calm him, but nothing either of us do makes him settle. Tobias walks in and immediately runs to his side, Thaddeus' face bright red from holding his breath, screaming.

"What's wrong with him, he is never like this?" Tobias says worriedly. Thaddeus quiets down and Tobias seems to have calmed him as he rests his head down on his father's shoulder.

"He is so warm," Tobias mutters, taking the damp cloth from Theo, draping it on Thaddeus' head, trying to cool him down. Thaddeus turns his face and at first, I think he is trying to get away from the cold wet cloth, but then, Tobias suddenly grunts and his eyes glaze over slightly before he shakes his head.

"What?"

"Ouch, geez Thaddeus don't bite." He says, pulling Thaddeus away from him. There are fang marks on his neck and I realize Thaddeus bit him. Theo and I look at each other and I walk over, taking him from Tobias and he immediately starts screaming.

"I wonder?" Theo says before running from the room.

"Did you speak to Astral?" I ask.

"I couldn't get a hold of her," Tobias says.

"Well, what do we do, we can't take him to hospital?"

Theo suddenly reappears, and I can instantly smell blood as it wafts to me. My fangs protrude from the smell. Theo passes Thaddeus a bottle full of blood.

"What are you doing, he is part human? He can't drink that!" I try to protest.

But I'm wrong as Thaddeus snatches the bottle from him, drinking so fast he's choking himself. Theo pulls the bottle from him, "Settle little man, calm down." Thaddeus' mouth opens, trying to get his lips around the bottle again as Theo holds it, forcing him to drink slower. I touch his head and his temperature is going down.

"Problem solved," Theo says, and Tobias runs his hand across his neck. So Thaddeus wasn't biting Tobias, he was trying to feed on him.

"He gotcha good," Theo says, examining the bite on Tobias's neck.

Thaddeus drinks the bottle in its entirety and his temperature goes back to normal.

"Should he be drinking blood at his age?" I ask.

"Well, he settled, didn't he? And I have never met a Trybrid baby so I'm just going to assume it is normal." Theo says and Tobias nods in agreement.

Thaddeus falls asleep in my arms and I watch his little sleeping face, brushing his curls out of his eyes. What the future holds for him makes me wonder... Walking him upstairs, I place him in his crib. When I walk downstairs, Tobias is waiting at the bottom.

He wraps his arms around my waist, pulling me flush against him. His lips move to mine as he kisses me gently before pulling back. "Did you get your dress?" He asks. Shit the fucking dress.

"Shit!" I curse.

"I'll take that as a no? All good, you can walk down the aisle naked." He says, wiggling his eyebrows at me with a smile on his lips.

"Yeah, because I'm sure we can hang those photos on the wall, I think we have tormented the priest enough with him marrying three of us. I don't want to give the old fart a heart attack by showing up naked." I tell him.

"Who's going naked?" Theo says, walking in and sandwiching me between them as his lips go to my shoulder.

"If you're getting naked, can I too." He says, thrusting his hips into me.

"No one is getting naked," I huff at their playfulness.

"You sure?" Theo asks, slipping his hand into my panties, and running his fingers along my slit as his lips trail down my neck leaving open mouth kisses on my skin.

CHAPTER 99

BONUS CHAPTER TWO

I mogen
    I lean back into Theo, his fingers dance over my lips teasingly slowly, his lips nip and suck on my skin. I feel Tobias move closer as he unbuttons my shirt, making my eyes go to his. His warm hands move quickly, opening my blouse before he drops his head, biting my breast that isn't covered by my bra. I moan at the feeling of his teeth biting my skin. Pain and pleasure, the thinnest line to walk, yet so exhilarating.

Theo's fingers finally slip between my now wet lips as he rubs my clit, making me lean into him. I could have gotten lost in the sensation of his fingers, when suddenly, Tobias pulls my pants down, kissing and nipping at my legs, making me shiver, leaving me only in the thin material of my panties.

Theo pulls his hand from my pants and I groan in frustration. I hear Tobias chuckle before he pulls me to him and I wrap my legs around his waist as he lifts me from the ground before slamming me into the wall, his lips hungrily devouring mine as he plunges his tongue into my mouth. I moan into his mouth, grinding myself against his crotch and the growing bulge in his pants.

I feel Tobias tug my panties, trying to get them off, and for once I don't even care when he tears them, feeling the burn as the fabric stings my skin from the sheer force as he yanks them off. I pull at his belt, impatient to get his cock inside me. I can't even remember the last time we had sex, it has been that long. Life becomes busy and with a baby there isn't much time left in the day.

Tobias suddenly moves to the couch, and I grip his shoulders to stop from falling back. He sits on the couch with me on his lap and I lift my weight off him so he can remove his pants.

I feel chilly hands at my back before I feel Theo slide my blouse down my arms and remove my bra, tossing them on the floor. His hands go to my breasts, my nipples harden under his touch. I lean back and look up, Theo grips my neck with one hand before leaning down and kissing my lips, nipping at my chin. I feel Tobias' hands grip my hips before pushing me down on the head of his cock, as I feel his hardened length slide inside, making me moan at the full feeling.

My walls clench around his length. Theo lets go of my neck and I kiss Tobias before biting his neck, making him groan. I lick at the blood trail as he throws his head back, his fingers digging into my hips as I roll them back and forth on his cock. I feel Theo's fingers trail down my spine, making me shiver.

He pulls them back before moving them to my ass, only this time they are wet and I can smell lubricant. He moves his fingers between my cheeks teasingly. I groan in frustration; he knows what I want and yet, he teases me.

He chuckles, seeing me get frustrated as I push my ass against his hand. Tobias sits up more, his lips going to my neck and Theo's to the other side, I feel my stomach tighten with anticipation when Theo moves behind me and his cock slips into me.

I moan loudly at the feeling of him slipping in and out of me, before pushing against him and moving my hips against Tobias. My skin is heating and I know I am close. Sitting on the edge, just waiting to be shoved right over it. Theo speeds up and I sink my fangs into Tobias, his grip tightening on my hips, before he thrusts upwards hard. I feel his hot cum spill into me, sending me over the edge as my orgasm washes over me in waves, making me moan into Tobias' neck. Theo stills a few seconds later, finding his own release.

The air is thick with the scent of our arousal and sex, as I feel Theo's now flaccid cock slip from me and I lift myself from Tobias, who looks a little buzzed still from my bite. Exhausted, we all head upstairs and shower before going to bed.

Waking in the morning I hop in the shower, I really have to make sure I make it in town today to get my dress. Tobias and Theo left early, while it was still dark. I'm in the shower when I hear the front door open.

"Dad, is that you?" I sing out.

"Yeah, kiddo." He calls back. My father said he will help with Thaddeus today, while I do some last-minute things for the wedding. I hear Thaddeus fussing in his crib and jump out, wrapping my towel around myself.

I hear a knock on the bedroom door. "Yeah, I'm still in the bathroom." I call out to him, trying to wrap my hair in the damn towel.

"I will grab him, meet us downstairs," he says.

Us? I wonder who he brought with him. I quickly duck out, find my clothes and get dressed. Walking down the stairs, I can hear my father making Thaddeus a bottle and hear the kettle being turned on.

Walking in, I freeze. "What the fuck are you doing here?" I say, when I see Bianca sitting at my kitchen counter on a stool with my son in her arms.

"Now, now, Imogen, calm down, she is your sister." My father says, looking at me.

"Are you fucking serious? She fucking killed me, you know as in dead." I yell back and Thaddeus cries at my yelling.

"Shh, shh, you're okay, mommy is just mad at aunty." Bianca says, soothing him.

"Give me my son." I say, walking toward her. She passes him to me and I eye her.

"She wants to apologize and make things right. Let her try," My father says.

I glare at him, and suddenly Bianca hops up. "I just want to help, I can help, Imogen. Look, I picked up your dress." She says, grabbing it from the stool beside her.

"How?" I ask.

"I overheard Theo telling dad you were having trouble getting into town, so I went to get it for you. Really, sis, I just want to help and get to know my nephew." She says, waving to Thaddeus with her fingers and smiling at him.

"One chance, I will give you one chance. You fuck with me or my family and I will incinerate your ass got it," I tell her, pointing my finger at her. She nods excitedly.

CHAPTER 100

BONUS CHAPTER THREE

I mogen
Bianca nods her head excitedly, though I still have my doubts about her intentions. Yet, I no longer fear her. I know I can take her down and I can tell she knows I will make good on my word to incinerate her. My father clears his throat, disturbing our little tiff.

"Well, isn't this nice? See? You can get along," he says, making me glare at him.

I know she is his daughter and has an attachment to her, but I don't, so I don't feel an ounce of guilt at threatening her. Growing up, I always wanted a sibling. I suppose this is their way of cursing me with that wish. Bianca holds the dress out to me, and I take it from her. She stands up, making me eye her suspiciously as she glides over to me, ever so graceful with her movements.

"Come, you should try it on." She says, and my father comes over, holding out his arms for Thaddeus. I hand him over and roll my eyes. This is ridiculous, I know already it will fit. My body couldn't have changed any in a couple of months.

Deciding to play nice, I walk up to my room, Bianca's eyes

sparkling when I don't kick her out. She looks around at the photos on the walls of my little family. I place the dress on a hanger before undoing the zip and looking at it. I feel Bianca looking at it behind me.

"It's beautiful." She says, running her fingers over the fabric before slipping the dress off its hanger. I strip my clothes off, leaving me in just my bra and panties.

"God, you have great boobs." She states, making me chuckle as she helps me step into the dress. The fabric feels smooth against my skin, the dress flowing to my feet.

"Can you zip me up?" I ask, looking over my shoulder at her and she nods, stepping closer and I feel her slowly tug the zip up before it catches. She gently tugs on the zipper, but it doesn't budge, and I feel the tightness around my abdomen.

"I can't zip any further. Are you sure you gave her the right measurements?"

"Yes, she even checked them herself," I tell her, and Bianca tries to zip it up once more.

"Argh, it won't go any higher." She curses.

"Shit, what the hell am I going to do? I don't have time to get it altered." I really like that dress too.

"I can fix it," she offers, and I turn to look at her skeptically.

"What? I am being serious. My mother was a seamstress. I can do this. Let me do this for you." She says, looking at me hopefully. Suddenly, the door bursts open and Theo walks in.

Bianca curses, ushering him out of the room and his face matches the same shock I had when I first laid eyes on her in our house. "What are you doing here?" I hear him ask, pushing past her.

"Theo, it's fine." I tell him when I feel he is about to lose his cool through the bond.

"Out, it is bad luck to see her in her dress before the wedding!" Bianca says, pushing him back out the door and closing it. I can feel him waiting outside, ready to jump her.

Bianca helps me out of the dress and helps me place it back in the bag before doing it up.

"Are you sure you can fix it?" I ask her, worried.

"Positive. We will just retake your measurements, and since I don't need sleep I will have plenty of time." She says, draping the bag over her arm.

I nod, but will go and buy a backup just in case, even though I know no other dress will be as nice as that one, but better to have a dress than show up in jeans and shirt. I reluctantly let her take it and Theo knocks on the door, obviously listening in.

"You can come in," I tell him, and he waltzes in but this time with Tobias.

"Why are you home?" I ask, curious about why they left work early.

"Astral is coming over, she wants to make sure the magic is still secure in your bracelet." I nod, Astral comes every couple of months to check the bracelet strength to hold the magic.

Thaddeus' magic isn't like anything we have encountered before, and sometimes I can feel its darkness around us like a dark cloud, trying to get out, though it hasn't actually escaped. We have noticed it reacts to Thaddeus' moods, my bracelet sometimes becomes burning hot against my wrist.

"Well, isn't this a strange thing to come home to, our ex-wife helping our future wife?" Tobias says, shaking his head.

"I don't mean any harm; I just want to make amends," Bianca tells them. Theo and Tobias are unsure as their feelings hit me through the bond.

"Well, Astral is downstairs," Theo says, and we follow him downstairs.

Astral is sitting on the couch and as soon as I step into the room, I watch as her aura glows around her and her eyes turn white, reading the atmosphere and everyone's aura's. She smiles softly before getting up and embracing me. I hug her tightly and Thaddeus runs out, having escaped my father, grabbing her legs. She smiles fondly at him, brushing his hair from his face as he beams his bright smile up at her.

We all sit down, and my father brings out a tray full of coffees, handing each of us our cups. I watch as Thaddeus climbs up on the couch and sits beside Astral, playing with the charms on her bangle.

"You're looking well, excited for the big day or are you getting cold feet?" She says, smiling at the horrified looks on Theo and Tobias's faces.

"Nope, they are toasty warm." I reassure them, and Theo sighs. I know she is having a dig at them. I hand her the bracelet, and Thaddeus instantly tries to reach for it, but she pulls it away; the stones light up at his closeness. She checks it for any cracks, and I watch its aura flicker as it reacts to Thaddeus being so close to it, like it is calling out to him.

She hands it back, frowning. "It is weird. I feel it growing stronger every time I hold it. Do you notice it too?" She asks, and I nod. I haven't told Theo or Tobias. I didn't want them to worry, but I have noticed the darkness sometimes. It makes me feel cold and hollow.

"We might have to put a binding spell on it soon, just to make sure it can't get out, and reinforce the stone." I nod in agreement.

"I see you're doing well, Bianca." Bianca looks at her nervously before smiling, but says nothing.

Bianca has angered many people with what she has done. It will take a while before she earns any trust from anyone, but I suppose to gain it, I have to give it to her.

"Well, I best be off. I will have a meeting with the coven to figure out our next steps." She says, hopping up and drinking the rest of her coffee before placing it on the tray. Tobias and Theo follow me out to say goodbye, and I watch as she hops in the car. She winds down the window as she starts the car.

"Oh, and congratulations!" She yells to us, a devious smile on her lips, making my brows furrow in confusion.

"On what?" I ask.

"You're pregnant, dear. How hadn't you noticed?" I gasp at her words, shocked, and I feel Tobias' and Theo's shock through the bond, before I feel their excitement flood me.

"What? How?" I ask, confused.

"Well, when two or in your case three people have sex..." I cut her off, waving my hand at her, I know how babies are made. She chuckles softly. "You're not a full vampire yet, Imogen. You're still half witch, I can't wait to meet her," she says, before laughing while she winds the window up. I watch as she drives off. I know better than to doubt her, I'm more shocked I didn't pick it up myself. But it does explain how my dress doesn't fit.

Turning around, Theo can't hide his excitement as he jumps up and down, Tobias is side-eyeing him, like he has gone mad. "We're pregnant," I say, letting the words sink in.

SUGGESTED AUTHORS

Authors I suggest.

Jane Knight
Want books with an immersive story that sucks you in until you're left wanting more? Queen of spice Jane has got you covered with her mix of paranormal and contemporary romance stories. She's a master of heat, but not all of her characters are nice. They're dark and controlling and not afraid to take their mates over their knees for a good spanking that will leave you just as shaken as the leading ladies. Or if you'd prefer the daddy-dom type, she writes those too just so they can tell you that you are a good girl before growling in your ear.
Her writing is dark and erotic. Her reverse harems will leave you craving more and the kinks will have you wondering if you'll call the safe word or keep going for that happily ever after.
https://www.facebook.com/JaneKnightWrites

Available on Amazon:
Wild and Blood Thirsty
Wild and Untamed
In his Office
Hers for the Holidays
Mistaken Mates
Her Fae Lovers
Dark Desires

By the Sea
Owned by the Dragons
Her Dominant Dragon
Her Trapped Dragon
Repaying the Debt
Savage Mates
Savage Hunt
Savage Love

Moonlight Muse

Looking for a storyline that will have you on the edge of your seat? The spice levels are high, with a plot that will keep you flipping to the next page and ready for book two. You won't be disappointed with Moonlight Muse.

Her women are sassy, and her men are possessive alpha-holes with high tensions and tons of steam. She'll draw you into her taboo tales, breaking your heart before she gives you the much deserved Happily Ever After.

Dark and twisted, she'll keep you guessing as she pleasurably tortures you with her words, making you ready for the instalment.

Available on Amazon
The Alpha Series
Book 1 - Her Forbidden Alpha
Book 2 - Her Cold-Hearted Alpha
Book 3 - Her Destined Alpha

Magic of Kaeladia Series
Book 1 - My Alpha's Betrayal: Burning in the Flames of his Vengeance
Book 2 - My Alpha's Retribution: Rising from the Ashes of his Vengeance

His Caged Princess

Instagram:
Author.Muse
https://www.instagram.com/author.muse/?utm_medium=copy_link
Facebook
Author Muse
https://m.facebook.com/login.php?next=https%3A%2F%2Fm.

facebook.com%2Fprofile.php%3Fid%3D100068618567349&refsrc=
deprecated&_rdr

Muse Linktree

https://linktr.ee/Author.Muse

ALSO BY JESSICA HALL

Join my Facebook group to connect with me

https://www.facebook.com/jessicahall91

Enjoy all of my series

https://www.amazon.com/Jessica-Hall/e/B09TSM8RZ7

Hybrid Aria Series

Book One: Hyrbid Aria

Book Two: Alpha's Unhinged Mate

Book Three: Fight Between Alphas

Book Four: Alpha King's Mate

Made in the USA
Monee, IL
14 December 2024

73771822R10347